ERROR *of* UNDERSTANDING

Stella McMillan

ERA/ERROR *of* UNDERSTANDING

A Trilogy

ERROR *of* UNDERSTANDING

❧

Book One

Stella McMillan

E

E R A

R

O

R

of

UNDERSTANDING

ERROR of

UNDERSTANDING

Stella McMillan

ERROR of UNDERSTANDING
Copyright © 2007, B J Bree

Publisher B J Bree
Brisbane, Australia
www.stellamcmillan.com.au

ISBN 0957881355
National Library of Australia
ISBN 13: 978-0-9578813-5-8

First edition published 2010

Second edition published 2014

Cataloguing-in-publication data:

    1. Fiction – Romance 2. Past-Life/Reincarnation

The Veil

To "know" the meaning of Life
is to lift the veil of Death.
To lift the etheric film beyond Life
is to peer into the mist beyond Time.
Through the mist is revealed Reality.
In this Realm, ALL ways are seen!

To peer into another Reality
is to look both ways – ALL ways.
To peer forward beyond the NOW
is to look into the Future.
To search backwards before the NOW
is to look into the mist before Time!

To "know" True Reality
is to look every which way.
for that which has gone before
and that which is to go beyond
is all the same – the ONE,
a part of the ALL – Super-Consciousness!

Stella McMillan
15 May, 2007

When one catches a glimpse of a series of events, which occurred possibly in another lifetime, there are two ways that this past-life drama can be viewed.

The person concerned can become involved completely in all that is happening in these regression sessions while feeling all of the love and emotions that were felt by the ones who were interacting with one another in that previous time.

Alternatively, the experiences can be seen in the form of tantalising and successive scenes – as in a movie – while the one involved is but the passive observer and the silent witness to what is occurring in the reality of a time long-past.

So, too, it was with Paula.

Contents

ERROR of UNDERSTANDING

Book One

Prologue

Paula

10 September, 1999

With coffee cup in hand, Paula stood at the window of their suite at the Sheraton Mirage Hotel and she stared out over the wide expanse of blue Pacific Ocean that was shimmering before her eyes. The day was clear and fine. The sky was deep blue and cloudless as she stood mesmerised while watching the surf roll onto the white, sandy beach at the rear of the hotel. She was reminded strongly of her first view of this same setting when she had arrived almost penniless on the Gold Coast, in Australia, ten years earlier. What a topsy-turvy ride life had provided for her since that time.

As she drained the coffee cup, a light plane flew by, obviously on its descent, and she presumed that it was heading for a landing beyond the Broadwater near to the hotel. Her heart pounded a little faster as the memory of her ride in another small plane came to her and it had begun on a beautiful day such as this one while leaving from a small airstrip beyond the Broadwater. What had happened to the years, she pondered.

The sound of the telephone brought her from her reverie and she placed the cup on the table as she lifted the receiver. While she did so, she caressed the petals of the roses that had been delivered from her husband early this morning and she realised that his flight from Melbourne would have landed at Coolangatta Airport by now. He would be en route to their luncheon venue. The lady at the hotel reception informed her that her limousine was waiting. Replacing the receiver, Paula moved to take one last look in the mirror. She needed today to be perfect!

Paula studied her reflection and decided that her figure was not much different from what it had been when she had stayed in this very same suite all those years ago. Looking at herself from every angle, she was pleased with the outcome of her shopping spree, which had resulted in an outfit that was more suited to a garden party than a birthday luncheon. She hoped that she would not be overdressed for the occasion, but where they were going to celebrate today was to remain a mystery. There was a surprise waiting for her, supposedly, and she experienced a tremor of excitement at this thought.

She ran the hair brush through her dark brown, shoulder-length hair yet again; then, before leaving the mirror, she caressed her stomach while gently running her hand over the soft fabric of the pale lilac skirt. This area of her anatomy would be expanding greatly in the months ahead and the thought gave her such a warm feeling of love that it almost took her breath away. She had a surprise of her own to impart on this, her thirty-fifth birthday.

Reaching for her handbag, she left the suite quickly and descended to the hotel lobby. There was a spring in her step as she left the hotel and moved into the black limousine that was waiting for her. The driver confided that he was aware of their destination but, with a wide grin adorning his face, the blonde-haired young man apologised profusely for not being permitted to divulge that information. He was a pleasant man of probably thirty years of age, she estimated, and he seemed to be enjoying his involvement in the plot.

As the vehicle moved slowly away from the hotel, Paula settled back to enjoy the drive on this wonderful day. Her thoughts drifted to her young son who was at their home in California, under the watchful gaze of her mother, his adoring grandmother. How she loved them all. Now, with another child expected, her life was filled to overflowing with so much love – a love that she shared with the most wonderful man it was possible to know.

"You are blessed, Paula . . . truly blessed," she murmured to herself.

The limousine cruised along the highway at a steady speed. The traffic was heavy, with impatient drivers weaving in and out of the stream of vehicles ahead of them. She closed her eyes momentarily as thoughts of home began flooding her mind again. It was then that the sound of screaming brakes and screeching tyres reached her ears, thereby causing her eyes to fly open immediately.

Stones and dust were flying by the windows and erasing her view; then, the rolling motion began. Their limousine was rolling – over and over – and, with it, her own world began turning around and around before her. Fear and panic gripped her as tightly as did the seat belt that was holding her firmly in place. She could hear screaming and she felt that the screams were coming from her own lips, but these few, panic-stricken moments seemed to go on forever. Still, she was not certain from whom those terror-stricken sounds were emanating.

Suddenly, everything stopped. Silence reigned. By any description, it could be explained only as a deathly silence. The vehicle was resting on its side. Paula could not see anything – other than the back of the driver's seat – while the driver she could not see at all. There did not seem to be any movement anywhere. She tried to move her body, but she had difficulty in doing so. She managed to move her left arm slightly before it fell back heavily onto her body. For some strange reason, she could not feel any pain. After what seemed an eternity, there were faces peering into her confined prison cell; then, she saw hands reaching into the vehicle. Relief swept over her as she realised that all would be well and consciousness left her.

Incredibly, it was in this moment that Paula found herself standing beside the wrecked limousine while viewing the carnage in a somewhat detached state. It appeared that she had come out of the disaster unscathed. People were running from one vehicle to another – frantically rushing hither and thither – but, the silence that she had experienced earlier continued now. She saw her young driver sprawled on the roadside and his face and clothing were covered in blood. He was unconscious and she wanted to move to comfort him but, before she could do so, a police officer covered his entire body, including his face, with a sheet.

Paula was shocked. She closed her eyes and remembered his laughing face, with its beautiful smile, when he told her that he could not reveal their destination. Then, she noticed a young woman being placed onto a stretcher on the ground and she saw the paramedics working frantically upon her lifeless body.

Looking around, she noticed many people who were dazed and bleeding, and there were many smashed vehicles, including a coach and a large, articulated vehicle. In a disinterested manner, she looked down at the woman on the stretcher that was being placed hurriedly into the ambulance. She saw the driver running as fast as he could to the front of the ambulance. He jumped into the driver's cabin, started the motor and the vehicle moved towards the road under the direction of a police officer.

Inside the ambulance, two paramedics were working frantically on the woman and when Paula looked more closely at the patient, she realised that she was wearing a pale lilac skirt similar to the one, which she was wearing.

In an instant and without any effort on her part, everything changed. Paula found herself resting on a stretcher in the rear of an ambulance. Looking up into the faces of a young woman and an older man, she saw concern change to relief in an instant.

"She's opening her eyes! Paula? Can you hear me? Paula, squeeze my fingers, if you can."

Paula squeezed the young woman's fingers with all of her might, but there was no reaction from her as she continued to watch Paula closely.

"*Paula*, can you squeeze my fingers?" she asked again.

Annoyed that her first effort was not acknowledged, Paula squeezed again, but more tightly this time. The man reached over at this moment and placed his hand onto her neck, as though feeling for a pulse. Paula, with eyes open, stared up at the woman and continued to squeeze her hand while watching for a response. Suddenly, she looked directly down into Paula's eyes with a smile of triumph.

"We've got her," she stated calmly to her partner.

The man moved his hand from Paula's neck to her forehead and he brushed a strand of hair from her face. He smiled at her then.

"Good girl," he whispered quietly to Paula. "Welcome back."

Paula was wondering about his last words. She wanted to ask him where he thought that she had been, but the mask over her mouth prevented such communication. Without warning, the rear doors flew open and the stretcher – with Paula atop – was whisked out of the ambulance. Everyone was running, except Paula, who remained still and untouched by the commotion that was occurring around her. The doors to the hospital opened to swallow them as the sign bearing the word, EMERGENCY, was emblazoned upon Paula's mind. She lost consciousness again.

Paula awoke to find a man – presumably a nurse – who was wearing a white shirt and white trousers standing beside her bed. At first, he was unaware of her attention on him, because his gaze was fixed firmly on the intravenous sachet that he was adjusting on the stand near her bed. Paula opened her mouth to speak to him. She realised that she was unable to do so. She tried to lift her other hand to reach out to him, but she found that she could not move. After a moment, he glanced down while smiling at her. He appeared to be about forty years of age. He had dark hair and brown eyes that seemed to dance when he smiled. His name-tag bore his identity.

"Hi! I'm Gerard. How're you feeling?"

"As though I've been run down by a lorry," Paula managed to reply, but as panic seized her, she questioned him. "My baby! What's happened to my baby? Please . . . is my baby safe?"

"Your baby's as fine as it's ever been but, I'll tell you this, you're not far wrong about the lorry!" Gerard remarked, with a smile.

"Where's my husband?" Paula asked.

"The police are trying to locate him, but it appears he's not answering his mobile phone and no one seems to know about his movements today. So, do you know where he might be?"

"No," she said, while shaking her head; then, she explained. "I was being taken to a surprise lunch somewhere. The driver knows where that is."

Gerard did not reply, but in a deliberate manner, he focussed his full attention on the intravenous apparatus. Paula was thoughtful for a few moments.

"He's dead, isn't he?" she asked.

She was certain that he was and this was a tragedy, especially for one so young, as well as for his family. Also, she knew that if this were the case, he would be unable to enlighten anyone about their destination now.

"I'm unable to say. There were several deaths in that pile-up and he may have been one of them," Gerard replied guardedly; then, he confided to her. "But, don't worry. The police will find your husband."

"What sort of injuries do I have? Are they serious?" Paula asked.

"The doctor has sent for a specialist and they'll be consulting with you soon, but there're others in worst condition, believe me. At this stage, I can't elaborate on the extent of your injuries, so let's just wait for the doctor's diagnosis. Okay?"

Paula was the only patient in this two-bed hospital room. She studied her immediate surroundings momentarily before glancing through the large glass window to the left side of her bed and she gazed out at the beautiful garden that was bathed in sunlight. There were a few tall trees in the distance while the immediate area was ablaze with an array of rose bushes of various shapes, sizes and colours. It was a peaceful setting.

She saw a movement at the end of her bed and her attention was diverted momentarily. There was a lady standing there and she appeared vaguely familiar. As Paula was watching her, she felt the nurse leave the room and she turned her head to see the door closing behind Gerard. She returned her full attention to the woman, who had dark hair, a slim figure and seemed to be about Paula's age. She was dressed in a long, flowing, white dress that appeared to be almost transparent. She moved gracefully and silently as she came around to the left side of the bed. Upon closer inspection, Paula realised that she was radiating a beautiful light and she seemed almost translucent.

She wished that Gerard had not left so quickly and she thought of reaching for the buzzer to ring for assistance, but her whole body seemed to be immobilised completely. Strangely though, Paula felt not one particle of pain, nor one flicker of fear, because there was a stream of great love flowing from this lady.

"Are you an angel?" Paula asked, in wonder.

"Let us say that I am the angelic version of you," she said with a slight, though enigmatic, smile that held a trace of humour.

It was then Paula realised that the lady had not moved her lips, yet she had heard her words clearly. With a start, she realised, also, that she recognised her. She was a more beautiful and more radiant image of the one that had stared back at Paula, when she had looked upon her own reflection in the mirror before leaving the hotel earlier in the day. What was happening here? Was she hallucinating as a result of the drugs administered by the paramedics?

Panic began to rise. Had she, Paula, died, along with the driver, she wondered. But, she could not have done so, for she remembered the ambulance crew welcoming her back and the rush and bustle as they entered the hospital. Gerard, the nurse, was real. He had been with her just moments ago. Most definitely, he had been here and she had spoken with him. Of that, there was no doubt. Or, was there, she wondered, as the incessant jumble of thoughts kept revolving around in her mind.

"Don't be afraid. I am here to protect you and to surround you in my love. You need to heal now and fear is all that can prevent that. Close your eyes and let me sing a lullaby to you. I feel you will recognise it as soon as you hear the words."

"What is your name?" Paula asked.

"I am called *Selene*. Don't you remember me?"

Paula shook her head slightly and found that she was having difficulty focussing upon Selene who was sitting now on the side of her bed and smiling down at her. Paula felt herself drifting into a deep sleep and she seemed to be unable to prevent this from happening. There were many questions that she wanted to ask Selene, but she could not do so, because a melody was filling her mind and her senses. It was one that her own mother would sing to her often as a child when she was enduring one of her many nightmares. The words of that song, accompanied by her mother's caressing and loving hands, had stilled always those dreadful fears that the nightmares had brought with them.

For Paula, the hospital room and the beautiful Selene ceased to exist. She found herself drifting to another time and another place, guided by and protected by the loving Selene who was stroking her hair and singing to her still. Paula felt that she was floating away, high above a wide river in an area, which was sparsely populated. On the river bank, there were tall green trees, interspersed with thick bush, and beyond this, the district opened up to reveal cleared land with many flocks of sheep grazing on the lush grass. It was an idyllic setting.

All of a sudden, she found herself looking down at a young girl of approximately sixteen years of age. The girl was dressed in clothing associated more with the nineteenth century than this present time. She was alone on the deserted river bank and engrossed in the book that she was reading. Paula concentrated her full attention on the scene before her eyes and she was trying to understand why it all seemed so familiar to her.

The rays of sunlight piercing through the leaves of the trees caught and highlighted the long, auburn curls on the girl's head. Her discarded bonnet had been tossed unceremoniously onto the dusty track and her bare feet peeped from beneath her richly-embroidered long gown.

Paula was but the casual observer of this scene from a long-ago time in history – Australian history, to be exact.

Part One

Victorian Victorians

Chapter One

— Victorian Victorians —

The year was 1867, in the month of September, to be precise. The season was spring, that being a Southern Hemisphere spring. The country was the one known now as Australia, and in the State of Victoria.

Louisa

Coercion and Compromise

A young girl, who was propped against a river red gum tree on the banks of a wide expanse of water that was the Murray River, continued to devour the words that she was reading in the book, which she held in her slender hands. Suddenly, she was distracted from the task in hand by the screeching of a flock of galahs. These noisy, colourful birds chose to perch upon the branches above the girl's head where they continued their vociferous discussion. In disgust, she threw her book onto the grass and, looking up, she shouted.

"You've hundreds of trees to choose from. This one's mine!"

The birds looked down at her momentarily; then, they ignored her completely – but not so the flies. She brushed several flies from her pretty face as she tugged at the fine lace at the neck of her gown.

Beads of perspiration trickled from beneath her long, auburn hair and these ran in uneven lines down her face, thereby highlighting several light brown freckles on her nose and cheeks. She gazed longingly at the sparkling waters of the river. They were cool, inviting and very tempting. The clear water lapped the bank of the river and the lone willow tree bowed down to sample its wares.

The girl glanced furtively towards the homestead verandah where she knew that her father was sleeping on this lazy morning. Standing, she moved farther along the narrow path to where the bush grew thicker and she edged behind the bushes to where she would be out of sight of anyone at the homestead. The only other occupant was Mrs. McBryde, who was the cook and housekeeper to the family. Other than a group of wandering aboriginal people whom she had seen farther upstream earlier, she knew that she was all alone on this beautiful morning.

She removed the heavy clothing that was designed for Melbourne winters and she slid silently into the water, the temperature of which caused her to lose her breath momentarily. This act had been carried out hundreds of times on this river bank in her sixteen years of life, as her mother who was afraid her only child might drown in the river flowing by the front door, had made certain that her child could swim before she could walk.

Moving through the water in a slow, easy style as she had done so many times before, she reached the middle of the river. There, she rolled onto her back and floated on top of the water while allowing her body to drift with the current as the snow-fed waters moved from the mountain to the sea, which was many, many miles away from this isolated, virgin area. The sun shone down on her face from a cloudless, blue sky.

By entering the water, she knew that she was in the State of New South Wales now. How long she floated in this state of bliss, Louisa did not know, but a foreign, alien sound began to penetrate her world and the silence was broken by a dull, throbbing noise. As this reached her ears and brought her slowly out of her reverie, the shrill whistle from a paddle-steamer screamed through the air when the boat rounded the bend upstream and a few hundred yards away from the naked girl. Immediately alert, she swam for the Victorian bank. There was an urgency in those brisk, almost frantic, strokes as she raced for the protection of the bank. Her auburn hair flashed in the sunlight while she streaked through the water. As the paddle-steamer chugged into view, Louisa dived and swam the last few yards underwater. This was not the first time that she had been disturbed in a similar manner. She surfaced, as she had done many times before, beneath a weeping willow tree. This was not the first occasion that its protective leaves had provided her with sanctuary, either. Hidden from the view of the crew on the boat, she gasped for fresh air to fill her empty lungs. She watched the familiar figure of Captain Bill Bartlett as he moved along the deck of the *Charmaine*. She smiled to herself in anticipation of his antics in the kitchen upon his arrival at the homestead, because she knew that they would be staying overnight. She knew, also, that he would attempt, for the hundredth time, to persuade his Brydie to become his bride. As always, his pleas would fall on deaf ears as Mrs. McBryde would laugh and ward off his advances.

"Why would I want another man in my life?" Louisa could almost hear her words again. *"I've enough to do now. I don't need any more socks to darn or clothes to wash, or meals to cook! Be off with you, Bill Bartlett! Allow me to get on with my chores."*

This was a saga that had been repeated so many times that it was a wonder Captain Bill kept calling at all. Except for his great friendship with her father, Bill Bartlett may have been tempted to pass by the homestead without pausing for an overnight stay. Perhaps, his love for his Brydie was so deep that he thought he would win her over in the end. Captain Bill would promise Brydie a life of luxury on board his beloved *Charmaine*. He would feign shock and horror at her refusal of his offer.

The bedraggled girl in the water chuckled to herself. It was then that she noticed the stranger on the deck. He was moving slowly from bow to stern. He appeared to look in her direction and she stiffened while easing herself back further behind the branches as Captain Bill called to him. Then, the man replied. Both men laughed while still looking in her direction. Paddles churning, the steamer moved from view around a slight bend in the river as it headed in the direction of the pontoon in front of her home.

She waited for a few moments; then, she surfaced and ran from the water. She raced to her clothes and grabbed her billowing petticoat in haste before using this article of clothing to quickly and lightly dry her body. She devoted all of her energy to drying her hair, which had a tendency to curl tightly when wet, a tell-tale sign that her father could not help but notice, she knew. She grimaced.

"Why couldn't they have waited another hour?" she moaned to herself.

The flock of galahs had long since abandoned the tree. She dressed hurriedly; then, she reached for her ribbon and tied her hair back in a tight knot. She placed her bonnet on her head while tucking the loose strands of wet hair under it, before tying its ribbons under her chin. The wet petticoat she rolled into a ball and placed behind a log for later retrieval. Barefoot as always – unless necessity dictated otherwise – and clutching her book under her arm, she tripped along the dirt track towards the homestead. George Howard, aroused from his morning slumber, stood holding the verandah rail for support. His frail appearance caused her much concern. A shout from the steamer attracted her attention.

"Hey! Louisa! How's the loveliest lass on my river?" Captain Bill enquired.

Laughing at the cue that he had used for all of her life, she jumped a log and skipped along the narrow dirt track before taking the path that led to the river and, in so doing, avoiding her father's stern countenance for a time, because he could not fail to note her dishevelled appearance. Louisa Howard ran lightly over the grass to the pontoon as Captain Bill jumped onto the grass. He was a tall, well-built man with lightly coloured, unruly hair tucked beneath his old cap. With ease, he grabbed her around the waist and lifted her high into the air. He spun around; then, with a hearty laugh, he dropped her unceremoniously onto the bank by the river's edge. Still laughing, Louisa struggled to keep her balance as her feet landed on the uneven ground.

"Hello, Captain Bill. What brings you back so soon?"

"Change of plans, lassy. Change of plans," he replied.

He left her then as he made his way up the steps towards the sprawling homestead and, giving a quick wave in George Howard's direction, he turned aside, obviously heading toward the sanctuary of Mrs. McBryde's kitchen. Louisa knew her father would be angry, for he approved no longer of these childish games. Since her return from Melbourne and her mother's sudden death, George Howard was a changed man. Grief-stricken, solemn, irritable and with his health causing not-inconsiderable concern, he was difficult to please. What Louisa had considered normal in the past was normal no longer in his eyes. He was watching her behaviour now, of that she had no doubt, but she refrained from glancing in the direction of the verandah. Instead, she lingered by the paddle-wheeler to escape his wrath while Captain Bill went in search of his beloved Brydie. Suddenly, Louisa became aware of the stranger who she had seen earlier on the boat. He was standing at the end of the gangplank and moving onto the pontoon. He had been watching her antics with Captain Bill, also, she assumed.

"Good morning," he called to her as he moved in her direction.

He was a tall man, with dark, wind-swept hair and grey eyes that swept her body, from her head to her feet, in an instant.

"Hello, I'm Louisa Howard. If you've come to see my father, he's on the verandah."

Louisa pointed in the direction of the homestead as George Howard raised his hand in a wave that the stranger acknowledged.

"Thank you, Miss Howard. I am Charles Lyndhurst. Your father has been expecting a visit from me, has he not?"

Louisa looked blankly at him as he scrutinised her countenance. She shrugged her shoulders slightly while showing scant interest in the man who was addressing her.

"Oh! Really. He didn't mention it to me."

Glancing beyond the new arrival, Louisa caught sight of the young deck-hand who had been with the *Charmaine* crew for a short while. Without so much as another thought, she dismissed the visitor from her mind and called to the young man.

"Ben! Do you want to ride? I'll get the horses," Louisa called.

She was pleased to have an excuse to be away from her father's presence for a short time, but the young man who was carrying a bucket and a mop, shook his head sadly. Charles Lyndhurst was watching the exchange between the two of them with much interest. Ben moved along the deck as he called over his shoulder to Louisa.

"Nah! Can't do it now. Captain's given me a dozen chores to do before supper. What about first light tomorrow? That be okay, Lou?"

Disappointed, Louisa nodded in agreement at the arrangement as Ben disappeared from sight. She attempted to hide her disappointment, as she realised that Charles Lyndhurst was standing beside her still. He was watching her closely and she felt the colour rising in her face. Suddenly, she was acutely aware of her appearance. Strands of limp, damp hair had fallen from beneath her bonnet and these were on her forehead now. Her bonnet had fallen back and was resting at the nape of her neck. Unruly auburn curls had crept beneath the lace at her neck, also. She lifted her arm while attempting to tidy her hair and their guest never allowed his eyes to waver from her.

"Perhaps you would be so kind as to escort me to your father?"

Still holding the book, she turned quickly while being unable to find an excuse and reluctant to refuse their guest, thereby incurring more disfavour with her father.

Charles Lyndhurst mounted the steps alongside her. She estimated him to be somewhat younger than Captain Bill, possibly around thirty-five years of age. His attire and demeanour were that of a gentleman; not that of the rough, hard-working, hard-drinking riverboat men whom she had known for all of her life, along with the shearers who came periodically to shear the sheep. George Howard disapproved of her association with these men, Ben included; yet, when her mother was alive, he did not seem to notice whom she befriended. She was at a loss to know why Charles Lyndhurst was visiting with them. That he intended to remain overnight was obvious, as Ben had suggested a dawn ride.

Louisa escorted the visitor to her father on the verandah and George shuffled forward, with his hand outstretched toward the new arrival. He was smiling for the first time in many, many months, Louisa noted, as Charles grasped George's hand firmly in greeting.

"Charles, it's nice of you to come. I didn't expect you so soon."

"Delighted to be here, George. I've not seen you in Melbourne for some time, I think?"

George Howard shook his head without offering any explanation as Charles turned and surveyed the river from their vantage point on the homestead verandah.

"It is a pleasant, peaceful place," Charles commented quietly. "I met with my father in Bendigo and it seemed opportune to visit with you before returning to Melbourne."

"You've met my daughter, Louisa, I see," George said, thus stating the obvious; then, giving her a cursory glance, he snapped an order. "Louisa, you can take Mr. Lyndhurst on a tour of the property after lunch."

Louisa, who had been sidling backwards in the hope of escaping from the encounter between the two men, stopped suddenly and stared at her father. Instantly, fear gripped her to her core. Sir Charles Lyndhurst, who had purchased the adjoining property six months earlier, had visited them recently. This was his son, obviously.

"You're not thinking of selling our home, are you, Papa?" Louisa asked, with her voice betraying the rising panic within her while demanding. "Tell me you're not!"

"Selling? Of course not, child. Don't be absurd!" he replied gruffly.

Surveying Louisa's appearance with obvious disapproval in his eyes, he suggested that she change and join them for lunch. George cast a warning glare at her as he turned to shuffle into the homestead beside Charles Lyndhurst. Her unruly hair, which had managed to curl itself tightly beneath her bonnet, and the dampness of her gown, especially the lace at her throat that was covered in dust now, were all the evidence he needed to draw the conclusion that he had. He had forbidden her to swim in the river. That was one great love of her life. The other was her horse, Hilton.

There was a sinking feeling in the pit of Louisa's stomach as she turned and walked into the house. Instead of walking towards her bedroom, she ran and escaped through a doorway onto the side verandah. She jumped down the two steps, ran across the grass at lightning speed and entered in great haste into the outbuilding, which housed the kitchen. Mrs. McBryde was extracting a tray from the oven. The aroma was tantalising, but Louisa had other important matters on her mind.

"Brydie, why is he here?" Louisa shouted from the kitchen doorway.

Mrs. McBryde turned to survey Louisa and shook her head in mock despair.

"Look at the state of you, young lady! What they taught you at that ladies' establishment in Melbourne, I do not know. But, I do know what your papa will say if he sees you in that state. Go and ready yourself for lunch. It will be on the table in five minutes. Go! Be off with you, for I'm too busy to gossip."

Louisa stood her ground. Her lips formed into a slight pout and an air of defiance was obvious in her stance. Her chin came forward and raised itself into the air in a determined fashion.

"I have to know before lunch. Why is Charles Lyndhurst visiting with us here?" Louisa demanded. "It's not for the improvement of his constitution, I'll warrant."

"I'm not privy to the affairs of your father's friends, child."

Mrs. McBryde was so busy with luncheon preparations that Louisa realised she would not receive a direct answer to her questions at this time. Reluctantly, she turned to leave, but she was stopped in her tracks by Brydie's voice.

"Louisa! Look at your feet!"

Louisa looked down at her bare feet that were covered in dirt, and she realised the state of her appearance more fully than she had before this moment. She remembered the strange look that Charles Lyndhurst had given her at the pontoon, and her father's wrathful gaze on the verandah. She began to giggle. The giggle became a gurgle; then, it turned into an infectious laugh until tears were streaming down her face. As always, when Louisa's laughter filled her kitchen, Brydie softened and, despite her horror at the sight of her charge's appearance, she laughed while looking on Louisa with eyes filled with love.

In an instant, Louisa fled the kitchen and sought sanctuary in her bedroom. She tossed the book onto her bed and walked to the porcelain basin and jug that stood on the table. It was here that she felt she could begin to wash away the sins of the morning although, in her heart, she knew it would take more than a jug of water to erase the first impression that she had given to Mr. Charles Lyndhurst on this fine, September day. Giggling to herself as she surveyed her appearance in the mirror, she began the task of removing the dust-covered clothes from her body, thereby attempting to appear as a lady at the luncheon table. A miracle was needed this day, Louisa felt, in order to accomplish a feat such as that.

It was little short of a miraculous transformation that found Miss Howard seated demurely in the dining room while attempting to show some of the lady-like traits that had been forced upon her at the School for Ladies, where she had been a reluctant and somewhat defiant pupil for the year prior to her mother's death. In the year since then, she had reverted to the Louisa of old, much to her father's horror. This had been her way of dealing with the grief-stricken state, in which she had found herself. Her father, it seemed to her, appeared to find solace in illness.

Later that afternoon, she escorted their guest on a walking tour of the property in the immediate vicinity of the homestead. She agreed to her father's request in this regard, as she was painfully aware of the state of his health and she knew that he would sleep for an hour or more if she relieved him of the responsibility of entertaining Mr. Lyndhurst. The first building that they visited was the stables, which appeared to capture the interest of Charles Lyndhurst greatly and, in particular, her stallion, Hilton. He watched with interest as Hilton nuzzled her hair as she murmured soothing words to him. Her love for this treasured horse was returned ten-fold and Hilton's flesh quivered as her hands stroked his neck. From there, they moved to the shearing sheds.

The last structure to be inspected was the partially completed home on the hill, situated to the right of the present homestead. This inspection was accomplished in a short period of time. Charles Lyndhurst seemed to be more interested in quizzing her, Louisa felt, than in taking much interest in the stables, the sheep paddocks, the shearing sheds or the new homestead. They stood now between the walls of the partly-constructed home, on which all work had ceased on the day Mary Howard died. The sun streamed through the beams of the unfinished roof and vines grew up the frames of the walls. Louisa stood with Charles amongst the foundations where the drawing room had been proposed.

"Papa commissioned a Melbourne architect to design it. Mama was excited about her palace, as she called it. She couldn't wait for it to be completed. Now, I doubt that it ever will be," Louisa confided.

"Your mother died in Echuca recently, I believe?" Charles queried.

Louisa explained a little of their trip from Melbourne and the reason for the family being in Echuca at that time. Louisa had been living in Melbourne and when her year at the school was all but over, her parents had come to collect her. Then, the family had returned by train to Echuca where they were to board a paddle-steamer for the remainder of their journey home on the Murray River, after an overnight stay at an hotel in Echuca.

Louisa remembered vividly the evening of her mother's sudden illness – how they had been with their friends at the vicarage in Echuca for dinner – and with her mother feeling unwell, they had returned hurriedly to the hotel to sleep. Mary Howard became ill suddenly and died in her husband's arms before a doctor could be summoned.

In that instant, Louisa changed the subject and made mention of her father's sister and her husband in Melbourne. It was with thinly veiled contempt that she mentioned, in passing, her time at the School for Ladies.

"You were there against your wishes, I take it?" Charles asked, with a laugh.

Louisa grimaced while nodding slowly. She failed to mention that her parents' unscheduled journey had been necessitated by her letter threatening *'to run away from school'*, which she regarded as a prison, and *'to become a stowaway on board ship'* unless she was brought back to her home and family immediately. This threat her mother had taken seriously, although her father was certain it had been a ruse only.

"I hated the school, *not being with* Aunt Sophie and Uncle Robert… but the whole dreary business of needlework, etiquette and such. It was so tedious and I was homesick. I missed Hilton terribly, also."

Once back home, free from restriction and no longer hampered by convention, her life had returned to one of frantic activity connected with the workings of the property, in which her father had lost interest immediately following the death of his beloved wife. Louisa's days were extremely busy, but the nights were troubled as the grief and the guilt associated with her mother's death possessed her soul. She tortured herself relentlessly over that letter she had written, because she believed firmly that had she not made those threats about absconding then, her mother would not have made the long, tiring journey to Melbourne. Therefore, Mary Howard would be alive still. Louisa did not take into account her mother's heart condition, about which she knew little, and nor did she consider that her mother was not a young woman, having married late in life and conceiving her only child some years later, much to the surprise and delight of her husband, as well as herself.

George Howard's health had deteriorated markedly since that night in Echuca twelve months earlier. He seemed to Louisa to have lost the will to live. Most of this information was imparted to Charles Lyndhurst in an indirect manner. His probing questions and her non-committal replies revealed more than Louisa supposed. With the tour of inspection over, Louisa, with her duty done, deposited Charles Lyndhurst in the drawing room of the homestead while leaving Brydie to serve him refreshments. Louisa sought refuge by her river alone.

In the evening, the peaceful tranquillity of the homestead was disturbed by two outbursts from Louisa. The first was her complaint about the fact that the selection of her attire for the evening had been supervised by Brydie, on her father's instruction. This grievance was aired before their guest joined them for dinner. Her father was unmoved by her loud protestations, which were overheard, in all probability, by their visitor in the adjoining guest room. Louisa's mood was far from accommodating during the consumption of the evening meal. The other objection arose as a result of a request from her father for a rendition on the pianoforte after dinner. This was met with a flat refusal by Louisa and her open display of defiance left George Howard speechless and seething with rage.

"No, Papa, I will not. You cannot expect such a performance, as you know I haven't played since Yvette left. It's impossible. *I will not do so!*"

"Yvette was my daughter's governess, Charles," George explained hurriedly.

He was endeavouring to mask his daughter's open defiance. Louisa remained adamant in her stance while her father's eyes demanded obedience.

"It was remiss of you to forego your practice. It is of the utmost importance to a young lady," George stated.

"Papa! How could you make such a statement when I've aided you every day in the affairs of the property? I don't have time to play at being a lady!" she shouted.

Mrs. McBryde timed her entrance perfectly and the tension was eased slightly. Watching her father, Louisa knew that he was livid, as she was. Glancing at Charles Lyndhurst, she thought that she detected an air of detached amusement at the interchange between father and daughter. Mrs. McBryde's countenance was impassive, as always.

"Nonsense, Louisa. You do exaggerate!" George stated emphatically; then, turning to their guest, he addressed him politely. "Charles, perhaps we could adjourn to the library, as we've much to discuss and we'll not be disturbed there."

George, scowling at Louisa, moved from the table while Charles followed his example. Glancing in Louisa's direction, Charles gave her a quick smile, but her anger had not subsided. She remained rigid in her chair, not responding to his olive branch.

When she was left alone and seated at the dining table, she looked up at Mrs. McBryde who began to clear away the dishes. Louisa was on the verge of attempting another interrogation of the housekeeper when the parlour maid entered the room. Betsy came to the table immediately to assist Mrs. McBryde who kept her gaze averted from Louisa's eyes – deliberately, or otherwise.

Louisa strode to the verandah to calm her anger. She jumped down the step and strolled down to the river bank once again. Her visit to Hilton and her mother's horse, Cadence, comfortably settled in their stable for the night, was the next stop on her journey. Finally, Louisa wandered to the kitchen while hoping to talk with Brydie, only to find her in deep conversation with Bill Bartlett. They were sharing cups of tea at the kitchen table. Betsy was over by the kitchen bench with her arms submerged in a basin of hot water as she washed the dishes from dinner.

Thwarted in her endeavours, Louisa wandered outside the kitchen while listening to the plaintive notes of the harmonica drifting up from the *Charmaine*. She was deeply troubled by the arrival of Charles Lyndhurst, but she could not understand why this would be so. On the morrow, he would be gone, she reasoned with herself. She sat down on the stone steps leading to the pontoon and stared up into the clear night sky, until one persistent mosquito drove her indoors. Louisa wandered alone through the empty homestead. The library door was closed tightly and, as she walked by, she could hear the two occupants deep in discussion, although their words were indistinct. What her father could have in common with their visitor, she knew not.

She remembered the letter that her father had suggested she write to Aunt Sophie and which Charles had offered to deliver to her upon his return to Melbourne. She entered her bedroom and, seated at her bureau, Louisa commenced the letter in the vain hope that her compliance with this directive would placate, in some way, her father's anger over her morning swim and her defiant and angry outburst at dinner.

21st. September, 1867

My Dearest Aunt Sophie,

I write to you in haste as our guest, Mr. Lyndhurst, with whom I believe you are acquainted, has kindly offered to deliver this missive to you. You may recall I mentioned to you that his father, Sir Charles Lyndhurst, had purchased the adjoining property. I am assuming this is a neighbourly visit and hoping it is not anything more than that. Papa's condition appears to have deteriorated. I would be relieved to have a doctor visit him, but he refuses steadfastly such attention. Perhaps you could persuade him, as I fear he dies a little more every day as I watch. His grief is no less now than at the time of Mama's passing, although I fail to understand how grief can cause such a difference in the health of a person of Papa's strong constitution. I would be grateful if you could write soon and advise me in this regard, as the situation cannot continue.

I trust this finds you well and, also, Uncle Robert. We would welcome a visit from you both, although I understand your loathing at the thought of such a long, arduous and dusty train journey. Your kind invitation is appreciated, but returning to Melbourne holds no interest for me. Pray do not take offence, which I know you will not, but I belong here with Papa, my horses and my river. I know your door is always open to me, as you mentioned, and your home is mine, also. This I know and appreciate.

Your kindness to me is a source of great comfort at this sad time. In honesty, attending those endless social activities, which you detailed in your last missive, would excite me not at all, I do assure you. But, I must confess a little curiosity in viewing from a distance our Royal Visitor. Pray write me a detailed account of the Tour, and advise me if Prince Alfred appears any different in the flesh than we lesser mortals do.

My love, as always, to you and to Uncle Robert,

Your loving niece,

Louisa.

Louisa read the letter again. Satisfied with her efforts, she left it on the bureau and extinguishing the lamp, she moved to the windows and opened the drapes. From her vantage point, the *Charmaine* was out of sight, and now there was not a sound coming from the river. The moonlight was shining on the water and Louisa stood for some time, lulled by its soothing rhythm. She was troubled by Charles Lyndhurst's visit and everything within her told her that something was amiss. Perhaps her father had not been completely honest with her regarding the sale of the property, she pondered, as she removed her stockings and shoes. Brydie would know, she was certain.

On a sudden impulse, Louisa left her bedroom and headed in the direction of the outbuilding, which housed the kitchen. Mrs. McBryde may be there still, she thought hopefully. She would ask her advice again. However, Louisa found the kitchen in complete darkness. She was reluctant to disturb Brydie after she had retired to her own quarters and her father had forbidden this – strictly forbidden it, in fact – but perhaps, she would not mind if tonight Louisa called upon her in her private quarters beyond the building that housed the kitchen. After all, the matter was of some urgency. And this, Brydie would appreciate fully, Louisa felt.

In that moment, Louisa noticed the figure of a woman dressed in the long-sleeved, dark grey gown that was the trademark of Mrs. McBryde, coming from the direction of the outhouse further away, toward the bush on the other side of the clearing, and she was carrying a lantern. With the matter decided, Louisa followed the lady at some distance while hoping to reach her private quarters at the same time as Mrs. McBryde did. Her quarters consisted of a bedroom and a separate small sitting room. Mrs. McBryde had entered already by the time she reached the building but, undeterred, Louisa walked quietly along the gravel track, her bare feet soundless as they trod the path.

Despite her father's orders, she had taken this path so many times that the moon, lighting her way, was hardly necessary at all. As she moved beneath the bedroom window while heading towards the front of the compact timber building, Louisa heard a male voice, which she recognised unmistakably as that of Captain Bill Bartlett. She stopped abruptly under the open and well-lit window.

"Come to check on the merchandise for himself, I expect, and he got more than an eye-full today, I'll warrant. I had to order young Ben to swab the deck . . . for a second time . . . to take his mind off the sight. You really should talk to her about that caper, Colleen. She's a sweet kid and I'd hate to see anyone hurt her, but you'd have to agree it's an isolated spot she chooses."

Puzzled by the captain's voice coming from Mrs. McBryde's living quarters, Louisa paid scant attention to his words as she stood on her tiptoes in the hope of seeing where he was. She took a few steps backwards towards a nearby tree. Still, he was obscured from her view, but the matter was urgent. She must speak with Brydie tonight or she would know no peace whatsoever. Glancing up at the tree, she reached for the lowest branch. Despite her long gown and voluminous petticoat, she scaled it with ease before settling herself on the lowest branch, which afforded her a clear view into the bedroom.

This room appeared, at first glance, to be empty, because she did not see him at the outset. It was when he moved to the dressing table and began pouring wine into two glasses that he came into her line of vision. Mrs. McBryde's voice penetrated the stillness as it echoed through the quiet night, obviously emanating from the sitting room, as the woman had not appeared as yet in her bedroom.

"I know! And, it worries me greatly. I've mentioned the matter to George, but I'm not taken seriously at all. I shall try again, although I suspect the die is cast," Mrs. McBryde stated.

Her voice was drifting through from the direction of the darkened sitting room, adjoining the bedroom, from where the conversation with Captain Bill continued.

"I'm so angry with George for allowing himself to be hoodwinked by that evil, old fox who visited him a few weeks ago. I watched them, sitting on the verandah after dinner and talking together as they sipped their brandy. I knew then something was afoot. I could feel an ill-wind blowing. Louisa will be truly horrified, you mark my words!"

Alarm gripped Louisa as icy fingers ran up her spine. She had been correct in her assumption, then. Her father was selling to Sir Charles Lyndhurst and his son would be here to finalise the details, no doubt.

Louisa, perched on the branch, was staring with unseeing eyes through the open window, so close that she could hear very clearly every word that was being spoken. While not paying much attention to what was occurring within, what happened next caused her to gasp audibly. Fortunately, no one heard. The captain had eyes only for his Brydie who had entered the bedroom.

Mrs. McBryde was wearing a dressing gown of the finest lace and of the palest shade of pink – almost white, really. Her brown hair was long and straight. It shimmered in the lamplight as it hung loose, being at least a foot below her waist. She must be able to sit on it, Louisa thought, and she looked so much younger that it was difficult to believe this was the same woman who had arrived at the homestead four years earlier, following the death of her husband in Echuca. She was thirty-six years old then, but never had Louisa seen her as she appeared now. Captain Bartlett placed his glass on the dressing table slowly and deliberately, without taking his eyes away from his companion who moved to him.

To Louisa's astonishment, Mrs. McBryde – cook and house-keeper to the Howard homestead – took a hold of his arms and she manoeuvred him gently towards her bed. There, she began to undress him slowly, until he stood naked in the bedroom and in full view of Louisa's wide, wide eyes.

She wanted to jump down from the tree and run; to run anywhere and to be anywhere else but where she was at this moment. She could not. Firstly, she was too stunned to move and, secondly, she would be heard and caught spying. That she could not bear. It was never her intention to do so. She did not know really how she found herself in this dilemma, but then, rarely did she know how she landed herself in many situations that were not to her liking, she told herself.

Transfixed, she watched as Colleen McBryde spoke softly to him; then, she laughed at his reply, which Louisa did not hear. Mrs. McBryde lifted her right hand and, with arm outstretched, she pushed Bill Bartlett gently, with her hand on his bare chest. He took a step back and fell onto the bed while pulling her with him. Then, while Mrs. McBryde was laying on him, his hands moved to her shoulders and removed the lace dressing gown. To Louisa's amazement, she, also, was naked. They were whispering to each other for a moment or two, before the woman gave a soft giggle and kissed him on the mouth, with her hair cascading around his face and onto his chest.

After that, Brydie moved like a cat and began to engage her mouth upon a part of his anatomy that Louisa had never imagined existed, not having seen a man in a state of undress before this moment.

She wanted to avert her eyes and, afterwards, she castigated herself repeatedly for not having done so. She was mesmerised by the act of love occurring on Mrs. McBryde's bed. Louisa watched for some considerable time, unable to do much else and unable to fathom the scene being played out before her stunned gaze. She held her breath, scarcely daring to blink. Bill Bartlett moaned audibly and reached for his companion while pulling her closer to him and rolling over, thereby taking Brydie with him. And then, Louisa realised, he was laying on top now, with her beneath him. The mosquito diving persistently and noisily towards Louisa's ear was not a sufficient distraction to cause her to lose her deep concentration.

Every move that the couple made was visible to her and emblazoned upon her memory forever. She had not thought that two people, who were so much older than herself, would be capable of such agility of movement as she was witnessing at this point in time.

As the final moment was reached, Louisa was stretching slightly on the branch while positioning herself more securely, when she lost her balance momentarily and almost fell to the ground. It was with great presence of mind that she was able to grasp the trunk, thus preventing her fall and, worse still, bringing attention to herself at this inopportune moment.

Eventually, with activities at an end, the lamp was extinguished and she found herself to be trembling so much that the branch, upon which she was perched began to shake slightly. She had no explanation for this occurrence, or for the sight that she had witnessed. Finally, when all was quiet within the bedroom and she could bring herself to move and stretch her limbs to relieve the numbness therein, she dropped as stealthily and as silently as a cat to the ground.

Collecting her wits finally, Louisa ran as fast as she possibly could away from the building, with all its hidden secrets, and she gained the safety and security of her own darkened bedroom. There, she sat on the bed for at least an hour, trying to comprehend the meaning of the event that she had witnessed. Finally, without arriving at a satisfactory explanation, she undressed and crawled under the covers. Still, it was a long time before sleep came to her that night.

Louisa slept soundly and arose at dawn. She extracted a bundle of clothing from its hiding place behind the wardrobe; then quickly, she slipped into the pair of boy's breeches and an old shirt. These articles of clothing she had procured after much begging and pleading from her friend, James Marshall, at the vicarage in Echuca. They had belonged to one of his younger brothers. Dressing quickly, she rolled the legs of the breeches to just below her knees and tucked the shirt into the breeches while tying them with a length of cord at her slim waist. Hurriedly, she bundled her hair on top of her head. She tied it and tucked it beneath an old straw hat.

Barefoot, Louisa crept to the dining room. She peered into the semi-darkness to be certain the room was unoccupied. As she did so, Mrs. McBryde entered. She was carrying a tray with crockery and cutlery on it. Louisa watched as she placed it on top of the sideboard. She was dressed in her usual heavy grey gown, buttoned to the neck, and she wore a cap on her head, which covered most of her beautiful hair tied beneath it. Louisa, from her vantage point, caught her breath quickly as she recalled the scene that she had witnessed during the previous evening. She shook her head in disbelief and wondering how this could be the same lady who had been on the bed with Captain Bartlett.

When Mrs. McBryde left the room, Louisa slipped in and she left her sealed letter for Aunt Sophie on the table. She hoped that Mr. Lyndhurst would be given the letter and that life would return to normal with his departure on the *Charmaine* later in the morning.

Quietly, she slipped from the house and found Ben waiting for her at the stables. Neither one bothered to saddle the horses. Louisa rode astride her beloved stallion, Hilton, while Ben rode her mother's mare, Cadence. As they had done often on other occasions when the *Charmaine* was on a visit, they set off at a brisk pace. As always, they raced through the paddocks, along the shallow creek bed and jumped the fences with ease while following the track that they took whenever these unexpected adventures presented themselves. With the horses exhausted, the two riders returned to the riverbank.

Louisa knew that Ben loved these times with her and the horses. He would entertain her with stories about his childhood on his family's farm where he was raised. Sprawled side-by-side on the grass while gazing up at the cloudless blue sky, they chatted and joked with each other as they enjoyed the peace and tranquillity of the mighty Murray River. Nearby, the horses grazed beneath the shade of a large eucalyptus tree. While Ben loved his life on the *Charmaine* and the way of life of the riverboat men, Louisa knew that he was homesick at times for his family.

They stayed there talking for some considerable time before mounting and heading back to the homestead for breakfast, after which the paddle-steamer was due to depart on her return journey to Echuca. As the homestead came into sight, they gave their horses free rein. Neck and neck, they raced together across the last paddock; then, as always, they headed for the last fence, which adjoined the stable yard.

Together, they cleared it. Too late, they saw the figure of the man who walked from the stables and straight into the path of the airborne horses. He did not appear to see them until the last moment.

"Look out!" shouted Louisa.

Hurriedly, and somewhat panic-stricken, he turned and jumped clear while rolling sideways as he hit the ground. Then, his body remained motionless. Instantly, Louisa turned her body, with her heart pounding as she peered through the dust disturbed by flying hooves.

Aghast, Louisa and Ben wheeled the horses around and rode back to the man, who was moving extremely slowly and attempting to raise his body from the ground. As Louisa jumped from Hilton's back and ran to him, Charles Lyndhurst eased himself into an upright sitting position on the ground. Finally, he lifted himself very gingerly into a standing position. His face was ashen beneath the brown dust that covered much of it. He adjusted and then dusted his clothing while attempting to maintain a regal air as he did so and his hair tumbled onto his forehead. He lifted his right hand and brushed it back a little before peering at the two culprits who, almost, had caused his demise.

Ben, astride Cadence and holding Hilton's rein, stared apprehensively down at the dust-covered gentleman. Charles Lyndhurst glared up at him before focussing his full attention upon Louisa who stood before him and who was showing obvious concern for his welfare. Charles, shaken and somewhat speechless, extracted a handkerchief from his coat pocket and began to wipe his face and brow.

"Mr. Lyndhurst! Are you hurt? Can you walk? Please . . . speak to me!" Louisa enquired anxiously.

He stared at her in astonishment for a few moments; then, as recognition dawned, his eyes travelled over her, carefully studying the dusty, male attire, which outlined every part of her young body. The auburn hair hung loosely at her neck, still tied behind by the ribbon, but the old straw hat was long gone, while her dusty bare feet were on display for all to see.

"Miss Howard!" he gasped.

Louisa was acutely aware, suddenly, of her appearance and she squirmed a little under his close scrutiny. Her father had forbidden her to wear these raiments. In fact, he had ordered her to destroy them.

"Ben, see to the horses!" Louisa instructed firmly.

Ben, eager to leave the scene of the crime, tugged at Hilton's rein and retreated hastily to the safety of the stables.

"I am so sorry. We didn't expect anyone to be here so early," she said.

Louisa's words were spoken contritely, because she was concerned – genuinely concerned – for his welfare, not to mention her own, should her father hear of her exploits.

"Obviously," came the curt and only reply.

Charles continued to brush his clothing with his hand. His anger was ill-concealed. Then, his ashen countenance took on a different colour tone and one that was more associated with rage.

"You're a danger to yourself, as well as to others!" he exploded.

"I must return before Papa sees . . . that is, before breakfast." Louisa mumbled, while averting her eyes from his constant gaze.

Looking anxiously in the direction of the homestead, Louisa, eager to escape the scene of this near-disaster before her father appeared, became somewhat agitated.

"Does your father approve of this?"

"Of what?" Louisa asked in innocence.

"Oh! Come, Miss Howard, don't play the innocent with me . . . this attire, for instance?" he countered, with a wave of his hand in a motion that encompassed her entire body; then, elaborating further. "And the crazed manner, in which you ride the horses, not to mention the type of company you keep."

"Ben! Do you mean Ben? What's wrong with him?" she asked angrily.

"He's a male . . . that's sufficient! Have the two of you been out all night . . . together?"

"All night? Of course not. Why would we ride at night? That's completely absurd!"

He seemed about to retort; then, he changed his mind as Louisa turned from him and she moved toward the track leading back to the homestead. He followed her as they walked in single-file and in silence, both still seething from the encounter and still reeling from the near-fatal occurrence, which had been averted in but a split-second. As they approached some bushes that opened to a clearing, Louisa stopped to survey the area before daring to cross the open terrain at the rear of the house. Charles stopped beside her. His anger appeared to have abated somewhat during the trek from the stables to the homestead.

"Miss Howard, have you any notion as to the real purpose behind my visit to your home?" he queried quietly, before explaining. "We've not had a chance to speak privately before now."

"I presume to see Papa on business. We are neighbours now, aren't we? That was my understanding," she replied, in a distracted manner.

Louisa was watching anxiously for signs of life on the homestead verandah. Suddenly, her worst fears were realised when the form of George Howard appeared on the side verandah and, worse still, he was pacing. That did not augur well for her first encounter with him this morning.

"Oh! No! He's on the verandah. Would you talk with him, please, Mr. Lyndhurst? Distract Papa for me until I get safely inside. He mustn't see me in this state. He gets upset."

"I don't wonder!" he exclaimed.

Louisa turned two large, green, pleading eyes upon him and his anger appeared to ease a little more while turning instead to slight amusement, although he seemed visibly shaken still by his ordeal. However, his reply was delivered in a stern tone.

"On one condition."

"What's that?"

"You tell me where you've been and what you've been doing. What time did you leave the house?" Charles queried.

"If that's what you wish, though I fail to see how it is relevant."

She answered him with a nonchalant shrug of her shoulders and with her gaze returning to watch her father's every movement on the verandah as he paced back and forth.

"We left at dawn, rode across the paddocks for awhile and, when the horses were spent, we rested them; then, we sat by the river and talked. I can't quite comprehend your interest in this matter, but if that's all you need to know, would you go to him *now, please?*"

"You were swimming, no doubt?" Charles asked.

She blushed involuntarily and looked quickly up at him, with her eyes wide with surprise and alarm.

"Swimming? No, of course not . . . and at this hour of the morning? Besides, Ben couldn't swim to save his life; then, I'd have to rescue him. The whole suggestion is ludicrous."

Two wide, innocent eyes met two very suspicious ones. Finally, Charles grimaced slightly and glanced toward the verandah while watching George Howard as he leaned on the rail and studied the river.

"How old is your friend?" Charles inquired.

"Ben? Almost fifteen. Why?"

Louisa replied in a distracted tone. Then, becoming increasingly concerned at her father's impatience, she looked pleadingly at her father's guest as George Howard stopped pacing and began to drum his fingers on the rail, with his eyes scanning the river bank for his wayward daughter.

"And what precisely is *your age?*"

"Me? I'm much older and much more sensible. After all, *I am almost seventeen!*"

"*You're only sixteen!*" he exclaimed, almost shouting the words.

"Please, Mr. Lyndhurst, can we continue this at a later time, as Papa's becoming impatient and he'll come looking for me soon; then, he'll get upset. That's when his illness appears to worsen. He mustn't see me!"

Charles surveyed her sternly for a moment, and appearing to relent, he sought to alleviate her fears.

"Give me two minutes and then make good your escape, although I don't see why I should assist you, bearing in mind that you almost killed me less than ten minutes ago. However, against my better judgement, I shall endeavour to engage your father in conversation; so rest assured, your secret will be safe with me."

"Oh! Thank you," Louisa muttered, with relief sounding in her voice; then, almost as an afterthought, she added, somewhat sheepishly. "Truly, I'm really sorry about your tumble."

"Tumble! Tumble? Is that what you call my near-miss with death beneath the hooves of two flying horses?" Charles Lyndhurst exclaimed, before asking. "You do realise you parted the hair on my head? That's how close you came to me."

As he moved from her, he gave a slight smile and, under his breath, she heard him mumble the words "*tumble, indeed!*"

Louisa watched him closely as he walked toward the homestead. She had thought him to be quite old but, when he smiled, his face softened and he appeared younger than she had supposed at their first meeting.

"You do appreciate you'll be in my debt forever, Louisa Howard!"

"Hush!" Louisa whispered, quickly and almost frantically.

Louisa waited until her father was deep in conversation with Charles Lyndhurst. Then, as quietly and as swiftly as a cat, she sneaked across the clearing and crept through an open window at the rear of the homestead. Once inside, she ran to the safety of her bedroom.

It was an immaculately and correctly attired Louisa Howard who stared innocently back at Charles Lyndhurst during breakfast. George Howard appeared pleased indeed with his daughter's appearance, politeness and demure manner on this bright spring morning as she engaged Charles Lyndhurst in lively conversation, much to that gentleman's amusement. George Howard had difficulty in hiding his delight at this turn of events after the difficulties of the previous evening. He complimented Louisa on her thoughtfulness in writing to his sister, Sophie Collins, and the letter was duly given to Charles for delivery.

The parlour maid, Betsy, served their breakfast. Of Mrs. McBryde there was no sign. This was a blessing, for Louisa did not know if she would be capable of looking that lady directly in the eye this morning, or any other morning, for that matter.

After breakfast, George remained on the verandah, after having farewelled their guest. He insisted that Louisa accompany Mr. Lyndhurst to the paddle-steamer. As they walked together along the path toward the pontoon, Charles took her arm while stopping close by her on the narrow pathway. Louisa looked up at him in surprise, as he seemed to be struggling to come to a decision.

"Are you totally ignorant of the real reason for my visit, Miss Howard? And, if not, then what is your honest response?"

"I'm not certain I understand you. If Papa is thinking of selling our home to your father, then I'll move heaven and earth to prevent it, I promise you that!"

"That has no bearing on the matter and has never been discussed. He hasn't spoken to you then, obviously. I would suggest to you most strongly that you engage in a lengthy discussion with your father as a matter of urgency. Goodbye."

Hurriedly, he moved by her. Puzzled, Louisa remained on the path while watching the disappearing figure of Charles Lyndhurst as he boarded the steamer. Ben was on deck and he gave Louisa a quick wave before disappearing hurriedly on sighting the figure of Charles Lyndhurst coming towards him.

When Captain Bill appeared by her side, she was startled, as she had not heard him approaching from the direction of the kitchen. She felt the telltale redness on her face as she realised, not without reason that she was blushing beneath his gaze, although fortunately, he was unaware of the cause of her embarrassment

"How's the loveliest lass on my river on this bright, sunny spring morn?" he teased, while tugging on a lock of her hair; then, as he moved by her on the path, he spoke again. "See you next week, Lou. Look after your Papa!"

"Yes," Louisa managed to murmur, while not being able to look directly at him and averting her gaze as she replied. "Yes, of course I will, Captain Bill."

When the *Charmaine* departed a little later, Louisa breathed a sigh of relief. Charles Lyndhurst had left forever while taking her secret with him, as he was true to his word and he did not divulge to her father any details of the morning's near-tragic events that took place in the stable yard. She forgot all about Charles' suggestion with regard to her having a discussion about his visit with her father. He had gone and life returned to normal at the Howard homestead on the banks of the Murray River, north-west of Melbourne.

Chapter Two

– *Victorian Victorians* –

Sylvia

Sylvia Webster walked briskly along the main street of Bendigo and she felt the excitement in the air. The town was a hive of activity on this sunny, spring afternoon, for preparations were underway for the forthcoming Royal Tour. Bendigo was having a much-needed face-lift, she mused to herself, and no expense was being spared.

She entered the front doors of the Shamrock Hotel and mounted the stairs immediately, without looking from right to left and with her mind occupied with other thoughts this day. Absentmindedly, she turned the door handle to enter the room that she was occupying for several nights while fully expecting her maid to greet her. She removed her bonnet and gloves as the door swung open. Before she could toss these onto the bed, as had been her original intention, she noticed a figure laying there. His arms were behind his head and he was fully clothed, except for his shoes, which had been kicked off and were positioned beneath her bed. Her heart did a pronounced leap within her chest, although this occurrence was kept well-hidden from her visitor who grinned at her in greeting. She smiled back at him in return.

"It's about time you appeared! Where've you been . . . and what gives you the right to be here, anyway? How *did you* get in, by the way?" she demanded of him.

"It's nice to see you, too, Sylvia! And, in answer to your last question, it's amazing what a little bribery can do," Charles Lyndhurst replied. "And, where've you been today?"

"To see my uncle, but it's hardly appropriate for me to stay at *that* particular hotel, now is it?" Sylvia answered.

"Umm . . . very wise. It wouldn't do much for your reputation."

"What's left of it, since you came into my life," she murmured.

"Come here . . . now," he requested, with a slight laugh.

He held his hand out to her as he spoke. His request was unnecessary, because she was beside him before the words were out of his mouth. He reached for her, pulled her to him and kissed her. Escaping from him momentarily while perched on the side of the bed, she looked down at him.

"You're not on the hotel register. Where're you staying?" she asked.

He raised an eyebrow in question and, at the sight of his somewhat quizzical expression, she laughed.

"Perhaps, I used a little bribery myself," she admitted ruefully.

"Is that so?" he said, with a soft laugh, before explaining. "I'm not staying in town tonight. I have to go on to Stanton later and, much as I'm loath to leave you, it's unavoidable, I'm afraid."

"So, once again, we have a few hours only," she murmured softly.

"It would seem so. But then, I'm hardly at fault. I'm not the one who's married. Now am I? So, do you plan to waste these few hours in idle chatter, Sylvia?"

Sylvia brought her two hands down and thumped him on the chest. Despite herself, she was laughing. He doubled over, thus feigning an injury.

"One day, Mr. Lyndhurst, you'll push me too far and I won't be responsible for my actions! You'd think after ten years, I'd have come to my senses by now."

His hands were around her, with fingers unbuttoning her gown at the back.

"It's those senses I'm desirous of exploring now. I've missed you, as ten days is a long, long time to be away from you."

His hands continued with their activity behind her as she leaned over him while kissing him on the mouth, with her two hands cupping his face between them.

"It's eleven!" she corrected softly, before resuming her current activity.

Clothes were discarded deftly and quickly, with the love between them diminishing not at all over the intervening years and the passion was as strong as on their first encounter. She loved him so deeply that he was seldom far from her thoughts, no matter where he was in the flesh. And in the flesh, he was with her now and every part of her responded to his every movement with her. What had begun as a furtive affair was an open secret, to which few could object, given the circumstances. No one who knew them could doubt the depth of feeling between them.

Her dark hair lay still on his chest as she lay still in his arms while treasuring every precious moment that they shared.

"You don't doubt my love for you, do you?" he whispered.

Sylvia shook her head imperceptibly. He held her more tightly then, as though she would escape from him if he released her.

"Can you slip away tomorrow around midday, if I send a carriage?"

She lifted her head and stared at him, being somewhat puzzled by the request.

"It's possible. Why?" she queried.

"I thought a picnic would be enjoyable . . . weather permitting, of course."

"A picnic! In the bush? Complete with dust, flies and ants? Are you quite mad?" Sylvia asked, trying to decide if he could be enjoying a joke at her expense.

He nodded solemnly. There was no sign of laughter in his eyes and the expression on his face gave but a small clue to the seriousness, with which he had asked the question. Sylvia frowned while inexplicably feeling vulnerable and sensing something was wrong.

"Is something amiss?" she asked, a little apprehensively.

"Perhaps," he replied. "There's always been complete honestly between us and there needs to be now, more than ever before. But, here is neither the time, nor the place to discuss it. Will you come?"

"If it's important to you, then yes," she said, after due consideration. "But, can you give me some idea as to what this is about, so that I don't stay awake all night wondering?"

"It's to do with my father. That's all. Put it out of your mind now. One way or another, we'll deal with the problem. We've survived worse than this, my darling."

When he clung to her more tightly and kissed her again, with a force that was as demanding as it was comforting, the icy fingers of fear that had begun to creep up her spine, spread quickly then to engulf her entire body, despite the warmth of his body surrounding her own.

Sylvia's night, spent alone in the bed in that hotel room, was given over to fitful sleep and disturbed dreams. The morning dawned bright and clear, so she knew that they would have their picnic this day while every fibre of her being was warning that enjoyable it would not be. She recalled Charles' words: *we've survived worse than this, my darling*. Then, the feeling of dread increased markedly. The tap on the door, followed by the entrance of her maid, Phoebe, brought all deliberations to an end for the moment. Sylvia had other commitments this morning before Charles' carriage arrived, and these included a visit to her two elderly aunts here in Bendigo. She loved them dearly. These two women were the older sisters of her mother who resided still in Castlemaine. Tonight, she would spend at a family dinner in her honour in her uncle's home here in the town. Why it had been arranged, she knew not. On the morrow, she would travel by train to Castlemaine to visit her mother whose relationship with her was decidedly prickly, at the best of times. From there, after an overnight stay in Edwin's family home in that town, she would board the train for Melbourne to return to her home where her husband, Edwin, would be waiting.

Her life, at present, seemed to consist of a series of clearly defined compartments and, as she interacted with others within those separate compartments, she found that she wore a different mask for every occasion. Perhaps this was the secret to her survival. 'We've survived worse than this, my darling,' Charles had stated, but why was it that life must be *survived* and not *lived to the fullest,* she pondered, as she left her room in the Shamrock Hotel after breakfast to visit her aunts who had cared for her from the age of twelve years. Two more loving souls it would be difficult to find anywhere, she knew.

Elizabeth

Within the confines of her greenhouse, Lady Elizabeth Lyndhurst stood peering at the wilting leaves of one of her precious rose bushes, which she had nurtured in its pot for many months. Wistfully, she confessed to herself that she had lost the battle there. Suddenly, a shadow fell across the bench and, expecting it to be her husband, her stomach gave the now-familiar lurch that occurred always when his presence loomed by her. However, turning quickly to confront the oncoming storm head-on, she was surprised and delighted to find her son standing in the doorway. He was watching her.

"Charles!"

"How are you, Mother? You're so preoccupied that I'm reluctant to intrude."

"*This is* a wonderful surprise. I didn't expect you, but you can intrude on me anytime, day or night, and I'd be more than happy to see you. You know that!"

"So, *he* didn't tell you I was coming?" Charles asked her. "Has he mentioned anything to you?"

Elizabeth nodded solemnly; then, placing the secateurs on the bench, she moved closer to him. She kissed him lightly on the cheek, and her old straw hat moved sideways during the encounter.

"I didn't believe him. So, it's true then?"

"Unless I can come up with an alternative . . . and fast . . . then, there's no other option, I'm afraid," he confided.

"And what of Sylvia? Does she know?"

Charles glanced quickly at her while raising an eyebrow slightly.

"You seem remarkably well-informed where my private life is concerned . . . Caroline, no doubt?"

"I may be imprisoned in this soul-destroying mausoleum, but I do still maintain some contact with the outside world. And, no, your sister is not the culprit in this instance; not that it matters. Can you not stand up to him this once? It's a very serious matter. You've seen for yourself the disastrous results of a situation similar to this!"

Charles grimaced slightly and remained leaning on the doorframe of the greenhouse. He was surveying his mother as she removed her gloves and the old battered straw hat that she had been wearing. Her dark hair was streaked with silver and her complexion was as fair as when she arrived in this country as a young mother. She tossed the hat and gloves onto the bench.

"As far as elegance goes, that did little to enhance your charms," he muttered, while eyeing the hat with disdain.

"Do you see dark marks upon my countenance? After all the years in the harsh sun this country provides, it's nothing short of miraculous, even if I do say so myself. If that's what it takes, then so be it. Come and take tea with me. Are you dining with us this evening?"

He nodded in response to both of her questions. Elizabeth placed her hand through his arm and together, they strolled towards the side verandah. She was a tall woman, fine-boned and slim, but her son towered above her. His height and stature had not come from Sir Charles Lyndhurst, who was almost the same height as Elizabeth.

The shade provided by the verandah was a welcome relief from the late afternoon sun, which was burning down on them on this spring day on the sheep property a little to the west of Bendigo. They entered her private sitting room where the butler, Martin Tomms, was waiting. She smiled at him while thanking him with a slight nod of her head for the tea tray provided for them on the table. Then, she watched him as he left the room. Charles seated himself in the armchair opposite her and studied her closely as she poured tea from the silver teapot into the waiting cups.

"How much has he told you?" Charles inquired, while nodding his thanks as he accepted the cup and saucer from his mother's hands.

"Only that you're to marry. I know little else."

"Gloating, was he?"

"What would you expect? He's waited a long time for this, so how else would you expect him to respond? Tell me about the lady-in-question."

Charles began to laugh. He shook his head as though appreciating some secret joke. He bit his lip; then, in a more serious tone, he answered her.

"Lady? I think not. She's a child. I've seen twelve-year-olds who are older, even though she turns seventeen next month. Her name is Louisa Howard. I doubt anyone has ever had much control over her and, before you ask, I doubt she even knows what's afoot here. With a little luck, she'll refuse to have anything to do with the proposal and that'll be an end to it . . . until he finds someone else to dangle beneath my nose. He seems more determined than ever this time. Perhaps, it's because he's never had such a large hold over me before now and he's not likely to again, so he's made his move. But, he's intoxicated by the power, I think," Charles explained, with his contempt thinly veiled.

"Do not make the mistake of under-estimating him, Charles. Leave the country, if necessary. Return to London and go on to Edward. He'd welcome you with open arms. You know that. I may not have seen my brother since the month you were born, but he is still your uncle and he'd be delighted to have you there. Go anywhere. Don't allow *him* to control you to this extent. I can't bear the thought of losing you again, but anything is preferable to this arrangement . . . for both of you. You've seen what comes when duty and obligation are traded for love."

Charles drank the tea in silence. Had he not been seated so close to her, Elizabeth could have been forgiven for thinking that he had not heard her words at all. Undeterred, she tried again.

"Do you doubt the wisdom of my words?"

"Not for an instant. How could I when I've seen what I've seen? My offer to you stands now, and always will, so all that's required of you is to name the day. Then, I'll have you on a ship bound for England before the words are out of your mouth. You know that!"

"Yes," Elizabeth said softly. "The day will come; but not yet, for there're other considerations, mainly my children and grand-children."

Charles placed the cup and saucer on the table that stood between them. He was staring, in a distracted manner, through the open verandah door to the paddocks beyond the greenhouse. Elizabeth watched him and the concern for him grew deeper. He was her first-born child and her only son. She loved him so very deeply and she had endured such a long period of separation from him that the thought of losing him again filled her with dread. However, his happiness was more important than her feelings, for she did not wish him to endure a marriage such as she had been forced to accept.

Her thoughts turned to her husband of almost forty years. She glanced at the clock while knowing that he would be returning shortly to dine with Charles. As though her thoughts had attracted him to her, she heard his carriage on the dirt roadway. As always, her stomach gave a distinct, almost violent, lurch and she closed her eyes momentarily as she fought to control the bile that began to rise within her. She opened her eyes to find Charles watching her. Abruptly, he rose from the armchair while heading for the door. Elizabeth knew that he intended to forestall her husband, thus sparing her the necessity of forcing herself to be pleasant to him, for the sake of her son.

When this involuntary reaction to her husband's presence had begun, she could not remember. That it would never cease while she lived and breathed in this body, she knew without a doubt. At least any woman married to her son would not experience the unexpected and often violent outbursts that had been inflicted upon her over the years. Charles did not possess the same temperament and, for that, she was thankful.

Elizabeth rose slowly while fighting still to control her emotions that were threatening to overwhelm her. She brushed a loose hair from her forehead and moved to the open doorway. Standing on the verandah, she breathed deeply while sucking in the air from the slight breeze that stirred in the nearby eucalyptus trees and drawing it into her lungs. She moved to the rail and leaned heavily upon it. She was fighting more than her reaction to her husband's unwelcome presence in the house. She was struggling to maintain her calmness and her equilibrium in the face of a feeling of foreboding that had been creeping over her for days.

Glancing towards the trees, her gaze fell upon the three white crosses, which marked three small graves and she gave a deep sigh. Turning quickly, as though to erase another set of painful memories, she returned to the sitting room. She would dress for dinner and force herself to sit out the meal with her husband and her son. She would carry off the evening in style, as though Prince Alfred himself were the guest of honour. Her dignity – what little remained – was her only weapon against the man who she had been forced to marry at the age of seventeen years. Not for the first time, she pondered on the cruelty of life. All other options and choices were denied to her – for the present, at least.

One day, she promised herself, she would walk out through that front door and never look back. Where she would go and what she would do, she knew not. She could return to her family home in England and she would be welcomed back by Edward and his wife, Clarissa. They would be thrilled to have her return after all these decades living thousands of miles from them, but there was only so long that she could impose upon their hospitality, she felt.

When she had arrived in this country, she believed that it would be for a short duration and she would return to see her parents again. That did not occur. She must not allow a similar situation to arise where Edward was concerned. After all, she had nieces and nephews whom she had never met, and now, they had children of their own. Where on earth had all those years gone, she pondered. She had lost several old friends in the past years. Return to England, she must, and soon. This was the solemn promise, which she made to herself as she stood before the dressing table in her bedroom. She lifted the miniature from its hiding place amongst her jewellery and studied his facial features closely. Dear George was the last one to depart this world and this was the most recent loss, which she had endured.

Tonight, she would attempt to be a buffer between her husband and her son once again. Tomorrow, she would write to Edward. Tomorrow, she would make her plans carefully. This time, she would follow through with action. She returned the miniature to its age-old hiding place and began to prepare herself for whatever the evening would deliver.

Sylvia

Sylvia Webster acknowledged to herself the feeling of foreboding that was pervading her entire being as she stepped into the carriage that arrived at the front door of the hotel at midday.

"A picnic, be damned, Charles!" Sylvia muttered as the carriage moved along the road out of Bendigo while asking herself the question. "Why, then, do I feel the hangman's noose tightening around my throat?"

The countryside slipped by unnoticed. At a fork in the road, a lone horseman was waiting. Her heart skipped a beat at the sight of him, but the degree of fear within her crept markedly higher at the same moment. Sylvia smiled at him in acknowledgment of his presence as his horse fell into step beside the carriage that turned now down a narrow, little-used track while leaving the world that they knew far, far behind them.

"Whatever this day brings, Sylvia, you'll remember it for all of your life."

She murmured this dire prediction to herself as the carriage came to a halt beneath a massive eucalyptus tree. Sylvia took Charles' extended hand as he assisted her from the carriage. A man appeared from the bushes and climbed onto the seat of the carriage beside the driver. The carriage departed then. Charles hobbled his horse by a creek and escorted Sylvia to a blanket on the grass beneath the shade of another tree near the water's edge. There was a picnic basket beside it. During these proceedings, not one word had been spoken between them. He moved to the creek and removed a bottle of champagne from beneath the cool water.

"You've left no stone unturned in your efforts," Sylvia remarked, when finally able to find her voice as she settled down on the rug.

"Dust, flies and ants notwithstanding," Charles replied.

She smiled at him while preparing herself as best she could for whatever was to come. She watched him pour the liquid into two crystal glasses as she removed her bonnet and gloves before tossing them onto the rug beside her. Handing her a glass, he waited until she had sipped the liquid before sitting beside her, with glass in hand.

"I'm to be married," he stated quietly.

Dumbfounded, she turned to stare at him, with her mouth wide open and with the glass slipping from her grasp as its contents soaked the blanket between them. Neither one moved at all. They remained locked together, frozen in the moment and with eyes fixed firmly on each other. Finally, through a dry, hoarse throat, Sylvia's words escaped from her.

"Married? Why? Who?" she gasped.

"Why? That should be obvious. I've little say in the matter. It's been planned and orchestrated by my father, for his own ends ... why else? Who? It's a young girl that I met a few days ago for the first time. In fact, she almost killed me ... accidentally, presumably ... because I don't think she has any idea of what lies ahead ... for either of us."

"I don't understand," Sylvia murmured, while trying desperately to grasp his words in a mind that was tumbling over itself with questions; then, she asked. "Charles, you're thirty-seven years of age, how is it possible for him to have such a hold over you? You have your own life and your own means. This is not possible ... not happening to us!"

He retrieved her glass and flicked away a couple of ants that had taken possession already on its rim. He reached for the bottle, carefully refilling her glass and handing it to her. He drank slowly and deliberately from his own glass before replying.

"You know of the problems we've encountered with the shipping line. It's been a series of disasters that no one could've predicted, much less prevented. There's an ongoing dispute with the insurance agents, which seems far from being resolved in the immediate future. If I were the only one involved, I could cut my losses and walk away. But, three of my closest friends have invested heavily in the venture and, as you no doubt recall, I was the driving force behind it. They're men with families to consider, and they've exhausted all other avenues, as I have. Through me, we've been thrown a lifeline, but it comes with a very heavy price tag," Charles stated softly. "Sylvia, he wants grandsons ... and ones with the Lyndhurst name.

Before now, he saw no other way of gaining his ends. It's been a gift from heaven, dropped straight into his lap."

Sylvia continued to stare at him. Her heart was pounding furiously and her mind was racing even faster still. She took a large gulp of champagne before she spoke again.

"With me, he won't have that . . . after Edwin, I mean. Is that what you're saying?"

"Precisely! That'd be his thinking, I'd imagine. He's not stupid. You've been married many years, with no issue, and Edwin has children by his first wife, so that speaks for itself. Don't under-estimate him, my love. He's a wily, old fox, with not one redeeming feature. What he wants, he gets . . . one way or another . . . and how is irrelevant."

She was struggling to understand his words. To comprehend, and to accept, the situation was not possible at this stage. Suddenly, Sylvia realised that Charles was continuing his explanation about the shipping company, of which he was a part owner.

"It will be resolved . . . the insurance . . . there's little doubt on that score. But, in the meantime, we're desperately short of cash. In other words, we'll fold. I wouldn't have approached him, except in desperation. Trust me on that. So, these were his terms. Because of your situation, we've never had long-term plans. I don't know what else can be done."

The picnic basket, presumably filled with food, was forgotten. They drank in silence. Sylvia continued to shake her head from time to time, but her thoughts never stopped racing ahead, every one rejected in turn. Unfortunately, a solution did not come to her.

"*There is one way,*" Charles ventured quietly as he explained his plan. "I could sell everything I own and book a passage for the two of us on a ship bound for San Francisco . . . give everything to the company, in the hope it'd survive until the insurance money comes through . . . then walk away penniless, *just the two of us.*

Would you be prepared to do that? I'm certain we wouldn't be the first to arrive in America in such a state and survive. Could you do it, Sylvia?"

"*And leave Edwin* in his hour of need? He'd never do that to me. He may have many faults, with his affairs high on that list. But, he'd have stuck with me to the end. Can I do less for him?"

Charles shrugged while refraining from commenting on her unanswered question and as he refilled his glass. Sylvia drained her glass and held it out to him to be refilled. Her head was beginning to spin. She had not eaten since breakfast, but food would be impossible to swallow at this moment. She found that she was trembling violently, but whether this was with shock, outrage, the effects of the alcohol or a combination of all three, she did not know. Leaving Melbourne with Charles, in a penniless state, was not an issue. That, she would do in an instant, as she was not without means herself. Abandoning her husband, she could not countenance, for he needed her at present. The timing of this situation was staggering, she realised. It played beautifully into Sir Charles Lyndhurst's hands. There must be another way!

"When?" she inquired.

"The banns go up in five days."

"Five days! Oh! For heaven's sake, this can't be happening!"

Sylvia needed time to think. She needed to be alone and to come to terms with what was happening here and now. Charles reached absentmindedly for the basket of food and began to remove small packages from it.

"Don't bother with that on my account. I need to return to the hotel as soon as I can. When will the carriage return?"

"In another hour. When can I have your answer?"

"You're serious then?" she queried, while frowning at him.

"Absolutely . . . never been more so in my life! I'll come to the hotel tonight and stay, if you wish it. We can discuss this some more then. You're in Bendigo again tonight, I take it?"

"Yes, I'm dining with my family, so I could be late. I should be back at the hotel by midnight."

Charles nodded slowly, without looking at her; then, he tossed the food back into the basket and stretched full-length on the blanket. He was staring with unseeing eyes up at the few white clouds that drifted by in the blue sky above them as he placed his hands beneath his head for support. Sylvia watched him for a moment while sipping the champagne, which caused her head to spin even more than previously, and realising it was many hours since she had partaken of a light breakfast.

"Ten years . . . and it's come to this, Charles?" she murmured.

"It would seem so. This is the third time he's interfered in my life, and always with disastrous results . . . the first time, when I was nine; then again, when I was twenty-one. He wins out always. It seems he has once again. An irreversible decision is being forced upon us, whether we're ready for it, or not. What we decide in the next couple of days will have far-reaching implications, my darling. Make no mistake about that!"

Sylvia stretched out on the blanket, with the wet patch in the centre separating their bodies. The day was warm. Her clothes were beginning to cling to her body and the breeze that drifted by in gusts brought the predicted dust with it, while the flies buzzed around her head and several ants began to explore her hands and arms. She sat up suddenly and removed her shoes, as well as her stockings and the garters that held them in place; then, she stood up and walked to the creek. From experience, she knew the result of sleeping in the middle of the afternoon after drinking champagne. She was not prepared to endure the headache that would follow invariably such a deep, deep sleep.

Lifting her skirt, she walked the few steps to the creek and stepped into the cool water that lapped her ankles. She was looking into the water while wrestling with the problem that Charles had presented to her this day when, suddenly, she felt his arms around her as he stood behind her. She spun around and clung to him as he crushed her to his body. Then, his mouth came close to her left ear and his urgent whisper reverberated through her mind, stunned and numb as it was.

"I'm sorry, Sylvia . . . so very sorry it's come to this. We vowed always to be honest with each other and never to make promises we couldn't keep. Truly, I did not see this coming. In hindsight, knowing him as I do, I should've done, but I promise you I did not. When I came here to Stanton to approach him last week, for the second time, he hit me with this proposal, but he'd already set the wheels in motion. I visited the family, at their home on the Murray River, as a courtesy call . . . nothing more. I felt there'd be a way out of it even then, but it seems there isn't. The girl's father took my visit as con-firmation the marriage was to take place. I need you to believe that!"

She clung to him, not acknowledging that she had heard his words. He moved her body away slightly and looked into her face, with his eyes pleading for understanding. Sylvia shook her head slowly and her gaze never wavered from him.

"You may be many things, Charles, but a liar you are not. Please . . . I don't want to talk anymore. Just let it be. I need to go back to the hotel alone and to think this through. My head is spinning and not just from the champagne. But, it's the timing of this that's astounded me."

He gave a harsh laugh and pulled her to him again. Her skirt and petticoat were dangling in the water as it swirled about her ankles. He whispered, through clenched teeth, into her ear again as she felt her hair beginning to come loose from the pins.

"The timing is perfect, because *he* planned it so. I've told you before. He's little short of the devil in human form. Never doubt that!"

Finally, they returned to the blanket. Charles cradled her in his arms while enjoying what little time was left to them before going their separate ways on this lazy, sunny afternoon spent by a creek in the Victorian countryside. When Sylvia attempted to make her appearance sufficiently respectable to enable a return to the hotel, he watched her in silence; then, jumping up, he reached down with his two arms and pulled her to her feet. Her skirt and petticoat were damp as these flicked by her ankles. He reached over to brush a strand of her hair back beneath her bonnet.

"Consider carefully, Sylvia, for how will you feel when this wretched engagement is announced and the gossip-mongers begin their work? It's a serious matter. This marriage will proceed, I promise you that."

"No! No! No!" she screamed at him.

"Yes! Most definitely . . . there is no doubt," he stated quietly.

"You brought me here, to this isolated spot, so I could scream my lungs out without embarrassment to you, didn't you? Sometimes, I think you're as devoid of feelings as your father!"

Sylvia grabbed her reticule from the rug and hurried towards a large tree to wait for the carriage. As she rushed beneath its shady branches, his scathing words reached her.

"If that were the case, would I have bothered to mention the matter to you at all? You'd have heard it first from Isobel Fox!"

Chapter Three

− *Victorian Victorians* −

Elizabeth

Charles had taken his leave of her just before lunch and Elizabeth had no notion of when she would see him again, or what his decision would be. As always, his visits to the family home at Stanton were brief and this one was not an exception. Usually, he did not remain overnight, especially when his father was in residence. Any further discussion had been curtailed during dinner the previous evening, as the subject of the forthcoming Royal Tour occupied much of her husband's thoughts. He had revealed to Charles that it was his intention to travel to Adelaide to be there at the start of Prince Alfred's Tour – the first Royal Tour for this country. It was with great relief that Elizabeth heard those words.

Any talk regarding the forthcoming marriage would have been held behind closed doors in the library after dinner. To this, of course, she was excluded. She knew only that they had talked long into the night and that the discussions had been heated, to say the least. Elizabeth could only pray now that her son would not walk the same disastrous path she had walked herself. Deeply troubled, she returned to her greenhouse where she could be certain that she would not be disturbed. On the morrow, her husband would leave for Adelaide.

"Just be thankful for small mercies," Elizabeth said to herself, as she donned her old straw bonnet and the gloves, which she kept for gardening.

Later that afternoon, Elizabeth began to compose her letter to her brother. She had been delaying this missive for months. Perhaps, Edward knew already of George Carstairs' death in Sydney a few months earlier; still, it was her duty to inform him of the event, she felt. They were close friends from birth and they had grown up together, as close as any brothers could be; then, George moved to Sydney where he had established a thriving retail business. He returned to London some years later and married Edith, whose friendship Elizabeth had cherished throughout their formative years. Edith passed away peacefully two years earlier and now, George was gone. He left two sons and a daughter currently living in Sydney, along with grandchildren, and how many of those there were, Elizabeth did not know.

All of this information was communicated to Edward, although she was certain that he had been in close contact with his friend for many, many years and he was aware already of these details. After that, she broached the subject of a visit in the near future and, of course, she informed Edward that she would be accompanied by Martin Tomms, the butler, whose loyalty and devotion to her knew no bounds. He had accompanied her to this country, all those years ago – at her father's insistence – himself being the son and grandson of previous butlers in her father's employ.

Martin was on Edward's payroll to this day, a fact that kept him by her side constantly, much to her husband's annoyance. He was the one crutch, which her husband had been unable to dislodge, because he was not about to dispense with the services of a valuable employee whose wages were paid annually from another source. Vindictive, he was; but, he was pragmatic, also, and this kept Martin Tomms with her permanently, as her father had intended.

Elizabeth supposed that, in earlier times, reports on her welfare had been forwarded to London from time to time, as a part of that original arrangement. She did not inquire. Martin did not volunteer any information on the subject. Her gratitude at her father's foresight and generosity in this matter was enormous. That her brother had seen fit to continue the arrangement spoke volumes to her of his continuing love for his younger sibling. How she would love to visit them all and to spend precious time with Edward, for they had been apart for such a long, long time. Perhaps, it was time now to bring this horrendous chapter of her life to a close. It would take courage, determination and careful planning to escape from her captivity at Stanton. But, she did have an escape route, through her son, and a destination provided by her brother.

"What more could one ask? Others have much less, so take the opportunity as and when it's presented to you," she told herself firmly.

Elizabeth partook of an early supper alone in her sitting room, thus avoiding any contact with her husband at dinner this evening. He was to depart early on the next morning, so she would not see him again for several weeks, and the relief that this prospect brought was massive. This evening, he was locked in the library while attending to matters relating to his properties and business interests. He had left instructions that he was not to be disturbed.

She read her novel for a while, but was finding difficulty in concentrating. Charles and Sylvia were on her mind. She had never met the lady-in-question, but had known of the relationship for many years. By now, Sylvia would be aware of the plans that were being made, and her heart went out to her. Perhaps, even at this late stage, another solution could be found. The feelings of foreboding returned suddenly as she saw her own history repeating itself before her eyes.

Abruptly, she moved from the chair and tossed the book across the room. It hit the wall with a loud crash and the silent house made the sound seem louder than it was in reality. Making a sudden decision, Elizabeth left the room. She extracted a set of keys from their hiding place and she opened a locked cabinet in the dining room. There was one attribute, which her husband possessed and that she found appealing, for he had a refined taste where fine malt whisky was concerned. She reached into the back of the cabinet and extracted a bottle before rearranging others to cover the space where it had been. He drank so much of the precious liquid that she doubted he would realise this one was missing. At this moment, she did not care, really.

Replacing the keys, she returned to her sitting room and hid the bottle. When Martin had retired for the evening and her personal maid was dismissed, she would open the bottle and, all alone, she would hold a wake for the late George Carstairs. And after that, she would hold a wake for every other one of her departed family members and her friends. If she emptied the bottle before she ran out of names and faces, she had an ample supply ready and waiting for her in that cabinet in the dining room. Perhaps, by the time her husband returned from South Australia, she may have emptied the cabinet completely, although she doubted that Martin Tomms would stand by and allow her to do so. But, tonight, he would not know!

Elizabeth collapsed into bed in the early hours of the morning, after having wept her tears of grief and sorrow and relived, alone in her sitting room, happier times. She drifted very quickly into oblivion.

The first gunshot echoing throughout the silent house caused her merely to stir slightly. Three more shots followed and she awoke with a start while sitting up in bed and staring into the darkened room in a confused state. Suddenly and silently, her bedroom door opened. The windows and drapes in the sitting room were open still, as this was where she had been resting while staring at the moon and delving through her memories on the previous evening. She glimpsed moonlight flooding into her sitting room through those open drapes now as the door to her bedroom opened. Just as quickly, the door closed, thereby shrouding her room in darkness again and leaving her to wonder if she had imagined the whole incident, for she had not seen anyone enter.

Frowning slightly, Elizabeth slid back under the covers, instantly pulling these high over her shoulder and covering her ear, thus drowning out the scurrying footsteps in the passageway and the irate shouts of her husband. Whatever was happening, he would deal with it and it was not going to concern her. She was beginning to drift into sleep again when she heard a slight tap on her bedroom door.

Once again, the door opened and Martin Tomms entered. He was carrying a lamp, which he placed on the bedside table. She opened her eyes and surveyed him in his night attire, with his night-cap slightly askew on his ruffled grey hair.

"What is it?" Elizabeth asked in a bored tone, as she attempted to ignore the headache that was threatening to engulf her. "What's he about now?"

"Sir Charles disturbed an intruder, m'lady. It seems he's been shot, as there's a considerable amount of blood on the stairs. Are you certain you're unharmed?"

"Who's been shot . . . the intruder or my husband?"

"The person attempting to break into the upstairs safe, it'd seem."

"What a shame," she muttered, almost to herself.

Reluctantly, she sat up in the bed and moved the pillows behind her shoulders. She studied Martin Tomms and she smiled at him.

"You do look a sight, Martin. Go back to bed! Allow the poor fellow to make good his escape. I'll help him myself, if I find him. I might even shake his hand first."

"Are you certain you've seen no one? I don't wish to alarm you, but the trail of blood leads through your sitting room. Perhaps, he escaped through there and out onto the verandah."

"Then, he's long gone. Let that be an end to it. Go away now and leave me alone, as I wish to sleep," Elizabeth stated firmly and emphatically.

Martin seemed unconvinced and he was somewhat reluctant to leave. Elizabeth sensed that he was determined to stand guard over her for the remainder of the night.

"Martin, if you do not leave now, I swear I'll not be responsible for my actions. I'm perfectly safe. Go!"

"I'll leave the lamp then," he stated firmly as, reluctantly, he left her.

Elizabeth waited until the door closed behind him before she moved the pillows while intending to extinguish the lamp and settle back to sleep. From the corner of her eye, she caught sight of a slight movement of the drapes covering the window. Turning to study it, she noticed what appeared to be droplets of blood on the highly polished floor and on the rug beside her bed. Her heart began to beat faster and her breathing became restricted as her chest tightened. She opened her mouth to call to Martin, but no sound escaped her lips.

As she stared at the drapes, a man's hand appeared as he pulled them back. There, standing before her was a young man who appeared to be in his early twenties. He had blonde hair, laughing blue eyes and an impish smile, which he bestowed on her now. She caught sight of a large dark stain on the coat sleeve of his left arm. With her mouth and eyes wide open, she peered at him, being unable to move temporarily.

The man lifted his right hand and placed a finger to his lips to ensure her silence; then, he moved to the door that led into the sitting room. He opened it and peered cautiously into the other room. Turning quickly, he winked at her in a brazen manner, smiled, raised his right hand in a salute and disappeared with the door closing quietly behind him.

By the time her mind had processed all that had occurred in the minutes since Martin had arrived with the lamp, Elizabeth had slipped from the bed and moved to the window in her nightgown. She lifted the drapes and peered out into the darkness. The trees were silhouetted in the moonlight while their branches, which were moving imperceptibly in the slight breeze was all the movement that she noted. Dropping the drapes, she frowned while being deep in thought. In the distance, she could hear her husband as he continued to shout orders. These sounds were coming from outside the house now. The house itself was silent.

Elizabeth moved to her dressing table and retrieved the key to her silver jewellery box, which she unlocked. She did not bother to check the contents as her fingers rummaged through the pieces until they located the miniature of George Carstairs. She took it to the lamp and studied it once more. Frowning deeply, she glanced from the face in her hand to the drapes while noting the bloodstains on the edge of the fabric. The resemblance had been uncanny, even to that impish smile – complete with dimple – that she had known so well in years past.

Reaching for her dressing gown and sliding into it as her feet found her discarded slippers, she walked to the sitting room in a troubled state. Without a second thought, she reached for a glass and she was lifting the whisky bottle from the tray when the door opened. Martin re-entered the dimly-lit room, with the only light coming into the sitting room being from the lamp in the bedroom and from the flood of light from the passageway behind him.

"Are you intent on spying on me, Martin Tomms?" she demanded.

"M'lady!" he replied, in a shocked tone.

"Don't scold! Don't even begin to do so. I know what I'm doing."

His eyes stared at the bottle in her hand and his face was shrouded in disapproval. Undeterred, she poured the drink and replaced the bottle on the cabinet. However, she did not reach for the glass.

"It took so long to break the addiction. You suffered so much. Why now?"

"Don't fuss. You know why. *George!* He was here. I saw him . . . just after you left!"

She held up the miniature for Martin to study. He looked at the face of the recently departed man; then, he glanced back at her while frowning. Slowly, he shook his head.

"Are you telling me that you saw an apparition?" he asked, with his voice carrying an incredulous tone.

"Well, no . . . he was flesh and blood. In fact, certainly blood, for it's on the drapes in my bedroom, the floor and the rug. Come and see."

Elizabeth hurried into her bedroom, with Martin following closely at her heels. She held up the drapes for his inspection. Then, he turned his attention to the floor area. He pursed his lips and rearranged the nightcap on his head.

"I'd better inform Sir Charles. He's on the verge of sending someone into Bendigo, as he feels the police should be involved."

"Under no circumstances!" Elizabeth stated firmly.

She sat down slowly on the side of the bed while Martin remained studying the bloodstains, but she was determined that her husband would not be informed of the matter.

"You could've been injured . . . or worse. I should've remained with you," Martin muttered.

"There was no danger, as he seemed perfectly amiable . . . I think," she stated, with a laugh, before questioning him. "So, if it was not George and, obviously, it couldn't have been . . ."

"No, definitely not! George Carstairs died in Sydney months ago. He was sixty years of age at the time of his death. *We both know that much!*" Martin interrupted her, while stating this fact firmly and emphatically, as though trying to make her accept the truth of the situation.

" . . . It must've been one of his sons then, because, I swear to you, this is exactly what he looked like . . . the younger one probably . . . the other one would be much older now," she murmured, mostly to herself.

Martin was staring at her while shaking his head, as though his mind was attempting to accept that this was the most likely explanation.

"It can't be . . . not after all this time. It doesn't seem possible," he murmured.

"There's no other explanation. Someone, as proud as George was, wouldn't go to his death while knowing that there was something in existence, which could destroy his reputation long after he'd gone. No, Martin, no . . . he's told his family, on his deathbed, in all probability. Now, they want to retrieve and destroy it. I need tea . . . bring me a large pot of tea and don't breathe a word of this to anyone. You do understand?" Elizabeth queried.

"Yes, I understand completely, m'lady," he replied, while nodding slowly.

As Martin left the room, Elizabeth sat staring at the miniature in her hand without seeing it. She was in another place at another time. The place was Lyndhurst Park in Melbourne, beneath a tree on the river bank in front of her home there, and the date was the time of Caroline's birth, twenty-eight years ago this year. Sometimes, it seemed so long ago. At other times, such as now, the events of that evening happened only yesterday.

She had relived every moment of that terrible night before Martin – fully dressed now – returned with the tray carrying the tea that she ordered. When he placed it on the side table, she reached for the teapot and poured one cup of black tea for herself. Lifting the silver teapot high in the air, she tipped the hot black liquid onto the rug and the floor. After that, she took the drapes in her other hand and poured the remainder of the contents of the teapot over the offending bloodstains on the fabric.

"Have someone clean it up in the morning. Tell them it was the efforts of an inebriated, old woman," she stated, with bitterness sounding in her voice.

"Certainly not!" Martin stated firmly as he retrieved the teapot and tray. "Goodnight, m'lady."

He left the room quietly, without looking back. Absentmindedly, Elizabeth picked up the teacup and began to sip the hot liquid, which caused a feeling of relief to sweep through her body and began to ease her headache ever so slightly.

She left the bedroom, with cup in hand, and wandered into the sitting room. A lamp had been lit on the small table by her armchair. As always, Martin had anticipated her movements. She glanced at the cabinet. Then, she stopped still, staring at the empty space where the bottle of whisky and the glass had stood. They had both disappeared. Lost in thought, she sipped the tea again.

"Oh! Martin, my protector always," she muttered aloud.

Elizabeth allowed a laugh to escape from her body. It was not a laugh that could ever be associated with feelings of happiness. This was a laugh filled to overflowing with an emotion bordering on despair.

Louisa

Louisa was seated in the library at her father's bureau. The books spread out before her detailed the accounts of the property and the household. Her neat print in the journal and ledger bore testimony to her labour of love. The pen in her hand moved swiftly down the columns of figures. Although not touching the page in front of her, its nib assisted her to focus on the figures that she was calculating. Lost in deep concentration, she did not hear the door open. Her father entered quietly, standing and watching her in silence for a few moments before speaking.

"Can we survive another week, do you think?" he asked softly.

Louisa jumped involuntarily while giving a noticeable start; then, she turned to survey him.

"Papa! Three columns I'd added . . . now, you've made me lose count. Don't sneak up on me like that! I will not stand for it. And, yes, we can comfortably survive another week . . . and fifty-two more beyond that. Everything is fine."

"I'm relieved to hear it. Why I employ a bookkeeper, I'll never know. Between you and your mother, he's not needed to do a day's work in years."

"That's as well. He's always so drunk; we'd have been at the mercy of the banks long ago if Mama hadn't taken charge. Why you keep him around, I'll never know. Friendship is a fine trait, but indolence and insolence are unacceptable ones," she stated firmly, while instantly wrinkling her nose in disgust at the thought of the man of whom they were speaking.

"Oh! The high and mighty standards of youth, eh? He was not always in the grip of the rum, sweetheart. He was a good man and a true friend for many a year . . . to me and to your mother. I can do no less for him now, so a little tolerance and understanding would go a long way."

Louisa gave a grunt in disgust and she was about to return her attention to the journal when George Howard reached over and took his daughter's hand. This being unexpected and out-of-character, Louisa stared up at him in dismay. At the same time, he reached over and pulled a chair beside her while easing his heavy frame into it slowly.

She watched him in sorrow while remembering the healthy and energetic man that he had been not much more than a year previously. A frown creased her forehead as he released her hand. She twirled the pen while she wondered what was to become of him, for she worried about him constantly.

"Please, Papa, you must consult a doctor, for I'm so concerned about your health. Why won't you do so?"

"Don't trouble yourself about me. There's a matter I need to discuss with you and I can delay it no longer. There's no point in beating around the bush . . . you won't thank me for that or for what I'm about to reveal to you . . ."

"You're not going to die! I won't accept it! You're not, Papa. Do you hear me?" Louisa exclaimed.

"We're all going to face that fate sooner or later, child. But, I must be assured of your future before that event occurs. I can't leave you to Sophie and Robert, as that'd not be fair to them . . . or, to you," he stated softly, but with a deep sadness reflecting in his eyes.

"No, Papa . . ." she interjected.

"Hush, now; be still and listen to me. Besides, they could not control you for a minute. You'd run rings around them if you stayed with them for any length of time. You had their measure by the time you were two years of age and Robert was dancing to your tune long before that. No, I must make provision and you . . . you, sweetheart, must abide by my decision, no matter how distasteful it may seem at the outset. You know how much your mother and I loved each other. You know we did, don't you?"

"Of course, but I don't know what you're talking about and if you think, for one moment, you're packing me off to that horrid school again, I shan't go! Not under any circumstances will I do so!"

"Louisa, for once, will you allow me to speak without interruption? You'd try the patience of any saint, Catholic or otherwise!" George exclaimed, in exasperation.

"Sorry, Papa. Do go on . . . I'll try," she said demurely.

Suddenly, in mock anger, George reached over and tapped her on the wrist. Louisa lifted her downcast head and peeped at him through her long, dark lashes as her green eyes filled with laughter.

"Don't try that demure, little miss routine with me, for it won't work. I know you too well. Just hear me out now, please."

Louisa began to giggle. The sound rumbled up from within the depths of her body and it cascaded into an infectious laugh. Despite the seriousness, with which he had begun his discourse with his daughter, George laughed with her as the sound of her laughter filled the room.

"Oh! I'm going to miss you so much when you leave me."

"Leave? Me? I'm not going anywhere . . . Papa? What are you not telling me?" Louisa, immediately suspicious, narrowed her green eyes until they resembled a cat poised to spring on its prey as she demanded an answer.

"It's what I'm trying to tell you, but can't find the words. I've been trying for days now."

"Never mind how long! Tell me now!"

George grimaced and studied her as he waited expectantly for the volcano that he knew would erupt at his next words.

"Charles Lyndhurst . . . you remember he was here a week ago. He's Sir Charles' only son."

"Did you lie to me? You promised you weren't selling. Papa, you promised! Oh! How could you contemplate such an event?"

"No, no, child, it's not that, but Charles asked for your hand in marriage," George revealed hurriedly, as he braced himself as best he could, while he watched his words being absorbed by his daughter.

"Marriage? Marriage! Impossible!" Louisa exclaimed.

She began to laugh. She stopped abruptly while surveying her father; then, she laughed again. She was shaking her head and enjoying the joke that they were sharing together.

"That's a great lark! He thought I was something between a spoilt, wilful hoyden and a street urchin, I think. You're teasing me."

"No. I confess he did think that, in all probability, and you did nothing to dissuade him though, did you? Still, the offer has been made and I've given my permission and my blessing. *So, that's* the end of it!"

Louisa dropped the pen, which she had been twirling between her fingers and stared at him. There was a mixture of disbelief and horror on her face. She shook her head slowly while trying to ascertain if her father was teasing her; but when, finally, the serious nature of his statement sank into her mind and the determination on his face registered completely with her, her facial expression changed to one of anger and open defiance.

"No! No! No!" Louisa shouted at him.

"The banns go up in a few days. There's nothing more to be said on the subject, Louisa. I've never been more determined about anything in my life. Mark my words. This marriage will take place. Nothing can stop it . . . not even if you threaten to run off and stow away on board ship! Charles Lyndhurst is the one person to whom I'd trust my most precious possession, and if you mention James Marshall, I assure you that this will never happen. He's a young boy who's destined for England and the Church. I'll not part with you to become a minister's wife, in a country thousands of miles away. Lord knows what would become of you. He certainly could not restrain you. No, this is how it will be!"

So saying, he stood to leave, obviously anxious to escape his daughter's wrath, for he knew her too well to delude himself into thinking that this was anything more than the first round in the match about to be fought between them on this issue.

"I can't marry either of them. Neither one is of the Catholic faith. I can marry only a Catholic and that's final. Mama said so, and so does Father Frank. Besides, I've no intention of marrying anyone, ever!"

"Your Mama's religion didn't save her when the time came to pray for her health to be restored, did it?" George hissed at her; then, with bitterness and anger sounding in his voice, he advised her strongly. "Forget all the nonsense that your Mama and her brother put into your head. Forget the Church of Rome. In seven weeks, you'll stand beside Charles Lyndhurst and you will become his wife. That is final, Louisa! It's absolute and final. There'll be no further discussion on this matter!"

George Howard stormed out of the room while slamming the door behind him. Louisa sat stock still in the chair, staring in horror and astonishment at the closed door of the library. Many times, she had witnessed her father in his moments of anger, especially during the shearing season when he became frustrated with the shearers who came to do the wool clip. But, this outburst was directed at her. It was directed at her in a way that she had never thought possible. She was convinced now that he held her responsible for her mother's death. Her threat to stow away on board ship had been taken seriously, as she had suspected. She wondered if this was the punishment to be metered out to her for her behaviour at that time.

Her father's anger, coupled with this declaration and its ramifications for her, were beyond her comprehension at the moment. Hilton! She would ride Hilton and perhaps a solution would come to her then. She jumped from the chair and upended it in the process. Louisa ran from the room, crossed the dining room, jumped across the verandah and ran towards the stables as fast as her legs would carry her.

Astride Hilton, she could forget everything. He had been there for her always, since the day when she had watched him come into the world, with Cadence nudging her new-born foal onto his shaky and uncertain legs. Today would be no different. Today, she needed to feel him beneath her more than ever, and to ride until neither one had an ounce of breath left in their bodies.

During dinner in the evening, neither one spoke a word. Mrs. McBryde bustled around and the parlour-maid eyed warily both combatants, seated at either end of the long dining table, while the meal was served. Both were anxious to leave before the expected fireworks began. The air was charged with so much tension that there would be no flint needed for a fire, should one be required. The spring evening was warm, however, and the meal progressed in the silence, in which it had commenced. Finally, when the two women had left the room and the doors were closed, George and Louisa found themselves alone in each other's company. It was George who broke the silence.

"You will kill yourself on that horse one day," he muttered.

"Then, that'll save me having to drown myself in the river before seven weeks elapse," she retorted through clenched teeth; then, in a sarcastic tone of voice, she queried him. "Isn't it necessary for me to sign something . . . a piece of paper . . . a certificate of some description? So, how do you, and your newly-acquired friend, Mr. Lyndhurst, propose to make me do that? Or, is there some skulduggery afoot here? A forgery, perhaps?"

As Louisa asked the question, she was trying desperately to curl her lip into a sneer, but she failed miserably and her father ignored her completely while choosing instead to concentrate all of his efforts on the pudding that he was devouring currently.

"I won't do it. You know that! How old is he anyway? He's got to be fifty!"

"Charles is thirty-seven years of age," George replied quietly, while keeping his eyes glued on the pudding in the dish before him.

"So! Old enough to be my father! I've got one father. I certainly don't need another," she exclaimed; then, when that did not elicit a response, she continued with her tirade. "*One is enough!*"

George Howard threw his spoon onto the table and stared angrily down the table at her. His face was lined with sorrow, coupled with extreme exasperation.

"Stop this right now! It's not going to do you any good! I can't be here to care for you, Louisa. And, he will. Let that be an end to it!" George shouted at her.

"I won't! You can't fob me off like that and think I'll accept your outrageous plan without question. You know me better than that!"

"Indeed, I do," he murmured, while giving a deep sigh.

"If you think you're going to die soon, why won't you consult a physician? Go to Melbourne and consult the best there is. Why won't you do so? Answer me that, Papa!"

"It'd be a waste of time and effort. I know the answer. Now, let it be. What I was trying to tell you this afternoon was that I didn't meet your mother until the day of our wedding. We had a wonderful life together. We corresponded and letters took a long time to come from Ireland. But, she agreed to marry me, and came with her brother on the ship. Your uncle married us the day she set foot in this country."

"I know all that. He's a Catholic priest. And, it was in a Catholic church in Sydney! I won't accept marriage outside of my own Church. Not ever will I accept it. Go to a physician in Melbourne and if he says you're dying, perhaps, I'll consider the matter seriously," Louisa stated quietly, but reluctantly.

George retrieved his spoon and recommenced his assault on the pudding in front of him. He ignored her for some time.

"No, I told you. This matter is not open for discussion."

"Like hell it isn't! This is my life we're discussing. Mama would turn in her grave if she could hear this conversation. I'm not a piece of meat to be sold to the highest bidder. I promise you, I'd make Charles Lyndhurst's life a living hell!"

"I am certain you will, Louisa," George said, while emitting another deep sigh. "At the outset, that is. But then, I think he will have the upper hand. I won't be here to see it either way. Reverend Marshall has agreed to perform the marriage. It will take place out there, on the side verandah, in seven weeks, after which you will leave immediately with your new husband. Your aunt and uncle will arrive a few days beforehand, bringing your wedding gown. It is all arranged."

"Is that so?" Louisa asked, as she studied him with a calmness and a cold stare that did not augur well for his proposed plans.

"Definitely so!" he stated emphatically.

With his demeanour, he was daring her to flout his authority over her. The remainder of the meal was accomplished in silence.

A stony silence permeated the Howard residence for the three days that followed on from George's declaration. Louisa went about her work on those days as she attempted to pretend to herself that all was normal in her world, while her father occupied his time by sitting alone on the verandah in his favourite armchair and ignoring his daughter as much as possible. Mrs. McBryde was a silent witness to all that was occurring, but she did not presume to intervene in the ongoing battle between father and daughter.

On the fourth day after George Howard's announcement regarding his daughter's forthcoming nuptials, Louisa entered the dining room to find him seated at the table already, as he awaited the luncheon to be served. He appeared tired, dejected and somewhat distracted when Louisa entered. She placed a mound of accounts before him, along with a pen and inkwell. She sat the cheque book, as well as a sheet of blotting paper, on top of them and, in a detached manner, he began to sign the cheques, without questioning her or checking the invoices in front of him.

Her father ignored her, almost as though she did not exist. Her concern for him grew markedly, in that moment, as he continued to sign the cheques in a rote manner. She did not want to be parted from him, either through a forced absence in Melbourne; or, through death, as had been the case with her mother. But, at the same time, she was at a loss to know how to handle this current situation with her father.

Louisa had been giving much thought to his proposal regarding her marriage. He was troubled deeply, she knew, and grieving even more deeply still. She did not know how to relieve him of his self-imposed burden, but she sought to try to gain some small concession, if he was determined to force his will on her in this regard. He had been intransigent, when faced with hostile opposition, after he had proposed and arranged Louisa's enrolment at the School for Ladies. When in an obstinate state, such as he was at the present time, nothing would move him from his course of action.

As she sat in her usual place at the table, she noticed a sealed letter waiting for her. On closer inspection, she found it to be a missive from Aunt Sophie, so she opened it immediately. On reading the first paragraph, she gasped in astonishment. She glared at her father.

"This is from Aunt Sophie!" she exclaimed, while waving the letter in the air.

"I received one from her, also. No doubt, it contains much the same advice," he murmured, as he began to consume the food that Betsy placed before him.

Louisa continued to read the letter while Betsy remained in the room. Silently, Louisa absorbed all the words that it contained. As the maid left them momentarily, she confronted him.

"The banns are to be read. They'll be there, in Melbourne, for all to witness! How is this possible, without my consent?" she demanded.

"Presumably, they will go up in Echuca, also, for all to see. The matter is final, Louisa. There's nothing more to discuss. Perhaps, during your last few weeks here with me, you may wish to end your open and futile opposition to this definite decision, which is a fact-of-life for you now. Accept it with good grace and try being a little more pleasant and accommodating, so that we can enjoy each other's company in the short time that is left to us."

Louisa was silent for quite some time. In a disinterested manner, she watched as Betsy returned, carrying a plate of food, which she placed before Louisa. The girl left rather hurriedly. But, her departure went unnoticed by Louisa, also, because she was distracted by the contents of Aunt Sophie's letter and by her father's insistence that she comply with his plan for her to marry Charles Lyndhurst.

She did not wish to marry anyone and it had never been her intention to do so at all, because she had planned always to remain at home to care for her father, following the death of her mother. That not only was he sending her far away, but also, he was pushing her away from him – and this hurt her more than he would know in his lifetime. His reasoning was plain to her. He wanted to die in peace, so that he could be with his late wife, and he was prepared to sacrifice Louisa to do so. That was her interpretation of the situation.

Louisa had given much thought to the matter during the previous days. She was making her decision while accepting that, in all probability, she had no choice in this arrangement at all. Her horror at having to leave her home and to go to Melbourne in the company of a stranger was enormous. But, she would return. Without doubt, she would return.

She may have been forced to remain in Melbourne when she attended that horrible school for those other soul-destroying months, but this time, she would come home of her own volition and at a time of her own choosing. After all, Mr. Lyndhurst could not keep her under lock and key forever. She would escape and come back. But, in the interim, she would have achieved one, great, personal goal. With these thoughts in mind, she broached the subject with her father.

"Then, I will do so," Louisa agreed, in a very quiet tone.

George Howard, immediately suspicious at his daughter's apparent acquiescence, held his spoon, laden with pudding and custard, halfway between the dish and his open mouth. He stared at Louisa over the spoon. He waited for a few moments while knowing that there was another attack on the way.

"If?" George queried.

"If you consult a physician in Melbourne prior to the marriage occurring and he agrees that you are dying."

"Absolutely not!" George countered.

"Then, I will have your solemn promise that you will do so within four weeks of this marriage taking place," Louisa stated.

She was holding her breath and awaiting his reply while believing it was his life that was at stake at this moment. If this was the only weapon, which she possessed to force him to visit a doctor, this was the sacrifice that she was prepared to make, for his sake.

"Done! Now, let that be an end to the matter."

"But, it doesn't count. Don't you see that? It doesn't count . . . not with a minister from the Church of England performing the ceremony . . . and on a verandah, of all places! I'm assuming here that your new friend, Charles Lyndhurst esquire, is not a Catholic. If it's not a sacred sacrament before God . . . *in my own Church* . . . it doesn't count for anything. Mama always said that!"

"In a Court of Law . . . in a civil court . . . it is binding and it is final. Make no mistake about that, Louisa. You will be married legally to Charles Lyndhurst once that ceremony takes place."

"In my heart, I'll know the truth. I will keep my end of this bargain, if you give me your solemn word, with your hand on your heart and you swear before God, that you'll keep your part in it. Do it, Papa, now. Otherwise, there'll be no marriage, I swear. I absolutely promise you."

George placed the spoon in his mouth. Then, slowly, he returned it to the dish, all the while studying his daughter at the end of the table. Louisa had given much thought to this serious matter while sitting under a tree, after one of her many rides on Hilton. There, alone with her beloved horse, she acknowledged to herself that her father's determination was strong, and it had been no different on the only other occasion when he had forced his will upon her.

This had occurred when, against her mother's wishes, he had enrolled Louisa in the School for Ladies in Melbourne. All of her pleas and those of her mother had fallen on deaf ears then; but now, she would extract a promise from him while she had bargaining power still. She would not acquiesce without her father giving some ground. This had been the one decision that she made on this fateful day, just weeks prior to her seventeenth birthday. Eventually, George gave another deep sigh. He raised his right hand and he placed it over his heart.

"I hereby promise to consult a physician in Melbourne within four weeks of my daughter, Louisa Mary Howard, giving herself freely and *with good grace*, in marriage to Charles Lyndhurst."

He removed his hand and moved to retrieve his spoon. Louisa was staring at him in disgust. In mock surprise, he surveyed her.

"What now?" George asked, while feigning innocence.

"You didn't swear before God. You must do so; or, it doesn't count."

In absolute exasperation, he groaned aloud, before placing his hand over his heart again while glancing heavenwards for strength and perseverance as he did so.

"I swear this pledge before God."

Louisa remained silent and concentrated on the dish before her. Her heart was heavy. She felt as though her life was coming to a complete end and this would occur not long after her seventeenth birthday.

"Thank you, Louisa. You cannot know the relief this has afforded me," George stated.

Louisa threw her spoon onto the table and ran from the room while heading in the direction of her bedroom. George Howard continued with his meal alone. He made no attempt to follow her.

Chapter Four

– *Victorian Victorians* –

Sylvia

The front door of the Melbourne residence of the Webster family swung open and Sylvia entered to be greeted by the butler. Before she had removed her bonnet, the door to the dining room flew open.

"Sylvia! It's about time. Luncheon is about to be served. Come join me, for you know I loathe eating alone," Bertie Webster exclaimed. "I was hoping you'd be back today."

She tossed her gloves and bonnet onto a chair in the vestibule; then, she entered the dining room behind him. He sat down at the table and Sylvia sat opposite him while across the table, he grinned at her in greeting. His brown eyes studied her and his unruly light brown hair that tended to curl around his face, gave him a boyish appearance that belied his years. Bertie was not a tall man, being but fractionally taller than she was herself and, unlike his father who was tall, slim and with little hair to speak of, Bertie would be described best as rotund in polite circles. His happy disposition endeared him to his many friends and he did not appear to have an enemy in the world. In this, also, he differed from his father.

"How is your father?" she inquired.

"Oh! So, that's your first inquiry? Not *how're you on this fine day, Bertie?* It's a matter of priorities, I see."

"I'm not in the mood for flippancy today. Answer me!" Sylvia replied, while giving a deep sigh.

"So, that's how it is! Did you miss your assignation with Lyndhurst? Is that it?"

Sylvia cast him a scathing look and he grinned at her in return. The luncheon dishes appeared and were placed before them, so all conversation ceased until the servants left the room. Bertie lifted his wine glass and drank its contents while Sylvia sat awaiting his reply and savouring a cup of hot tea. After today's tiring train journey from Castlemaine, yesterday's heated confrontation with her mother and the sleepless night that she had endured while considering her future, with or without Charles Lyndhurst in her life, the hot beverage was reviving her lagging spirits ever so slightly.

"He's . . . umm . . . restrained," Bertie replied finally.

"Not physically, I hope?"

"I'm afraid so. You know he responds only to your voice. When you're not here, he's impossible to manage. Those women who care for him around the clock deserve a medal. One of them, the older one . . . Martha . . . she's sporting a black eye this morning. No need to inquire how she came by it."

Sylvia closed her eyes and rubbed the centre of her forehead with her fingers. The headache that she had been fighting all morning was becoming a persistent throb.

"Are you unwell?" he asked.

"A slight headache . . . that's all. I've much to discuss with you and I've a major decision to make before this evening; so, really, I need to make you aware of what's afoot. We'll talk after lunch in the small sitting room where we won't be disturbed. Can you spare me an hour of your time, Bertie? But, I must check on your father first."

"Of course, but if Lyndhurst's coming tonight, I'll remove myself early. I need to return home shortly anyway and you won't require my services any more after today, will you?"

Sylvia shook her head. Bertie's home was no more than a few blocks away and on the rare occasions when Sylvia was required to leave home, he would come to stay, so as to be on hand to handle any eventuality that may occur. She was grateful for his attention to his father and to her needs. Sylvia was but five years older than her step-son of sixteen years and, in those years, a close bond had developed between them.

"I saw Paul in Bendigo and he didn't seem very happy. Have the two of you fallen out again?"

Bertie cast a long, warning look at her and continued to eat his lunch while ignoring her question totally. He was devouring the meal as though it were his last for this lifetime.

"I'm hoping to arrange a week-long house-party at Castlemaine before the Royal Tour gets underway here. Do you have any objections?" Bertie inquired.

"No, it's your family home, for goodness sake! You don't need to ask my permission. I stayed there myself last night and it's becoming very shabby indeed. It needs a major refurbishment," Sylvia stated.

"I know, but it's not in my interest to do so, as I wish to buy the place from you in the near future; then, I'll alter it to suit my own needs."

"Bertie! Your father's property is not to be discussed with me while he's living and breathing in the upstairs bedroom," Sylvia said.

"Breathing, yes . . . living? *I think not!*" Bertie countered.

Sylvia studied the food before her; then, she pushed the plate away with the food untouched. Bertie was eyeing her plate with a wistful look as he wiped the remnants of the gravy from his own plate with a slice of bread. She poured more tea and collapsed into silent contemplation. Food was the least of her requirements when she was agitated; and, agitated she was now, although she tried to hide this from him, without much apparent success. Bertie removed his plate and reached across the table to take the one that she had discarded.

"May I?" he asked, as his hand lifted the plate.

"Be my guest. I'd choke on it at the moment."

"Lyndhurst?"

"Yes! *And, my uncle* wishes you to accompany me to Bendigo to dine with them, my mother included, in a few weeks, to coincide with my birthday. I can't fathom the reason and they're all being very secretive . . . my mother and my aunts, as well. What do you think? Will you come?" Sylvia asked.

"I could be persuaded. You attended my thirtieth dinner party, so I owe you that much, although I fail to see what they could want with me, as I barely know them. Speaking of which, I've a function of my own that I'd be grateful if you'd accompany me. Perhaps later, we can clarify dates in our diaries before I leave today. You've no idea as to why they would request my presence?"

Sylvia shook her head absentmindedly, the effort reminding her of the state of her current headache. With her husband incapacitated, Bertie was her constant consort where social engagements and events were concerned and, several years ago, they had come to an arrangement that was suitable to both of them. Neither one had expected Edwin to live as long as he had after his devastating accident while horse riding some three years earlier. She became aware of her surroundings once again and found Bertie's eyes upon her, with a frown creasing his brow.

"It must be serious," he muttered, before commenting softly. "It's not often you're so distracted. Can I help in any way?"

"Only by listening . . . it's my problem, though not of my making, but I'm the one who'll need to live with the consequences, although you will be the one whose inconvenienced the most, depending on which option I choose."

Bertie lifted his glass to his lips and drained its contents; then, he gave a soft laugh.

"If it's a choice between duty and love, then let it be love every time. Does that answer the question for you, Sylvia?" he asked, with a supercilious grin on his face.

"As if I'd listen to a hopeless romantic such as you, Bertie Webster!" Sylvia replied, while feigning exasperation.

Bertie was laughing as she rose to leave him to check on her husband's condition.

Bertie, with his hands clasped behind his back, stood by the window in the small sitting room and stared out into the garden as the late afternoon sun cast its last rays onto the fountain in the centre of the immaculately kept lawns. Finally, he turned to look at Sylvia who was lost in thought while being seated in a comfortable, old armchair.

"Go with him! To hell with everything! It'll sort itself out in time. I'll make certain your interests are protected here. If he's prepared to risk all for you, he must love you. So, grab it with both hands. You've known so little love in your life, Sylvia. In your position, I wouldn't hesitate. Go for broke. That'd be my advice to you. But, I hate the thought of you leaving me. I've no idea how I'll survive without you."

Sylvia eyed him with an expression of slight amusement on her face. She had known all along what his reaction would be and she was amused by the fact Bertie was so predictable that she could read his every mood.

"Everything isn't always black and white. There's Edwin to consider," she murmured.

"He has everything he needs. He always will. I'll see to that. If I don't, I've four sisters who'll tear me to shreds, and no one is indispensable, not even you. I must admit; Charles Lyndhurst has come up a notch or two in my estimation after this, though. I always thought . . . Oh! Never mind what I thought. You've all your jewellery. That's worth a packet on its own and I know you've money. What on earth are you waiting for?"

"I've my family to consider, as well as your family and their reputation . . ."

"Hogwash!" Bertie exclaimed, instantly interrupting her. "Just go! Don't look back. If the roles were reversed, what do you think my erstwhile father would do? *Ask yourself that, Sylvia!*"

"He'd put the family's reputation first," she stated firmly.

"Again, I repeat . . . *hogwash!* You'll rue the day you make a decision other than the one I'm suggesting. I'm right and you know it. I'd throw away everything for a love such as that! Don't come crying on my shoulder in six month's time when your whole world falls apart. Can you bear to go to social events, seeing another woman on his arm?"

Sylvia shook her head slowly. She pursed her lips; then, realising pain was emanating from the area, she ceased abruptly while he stayed by the window surveying her.

"Honestly . . . I do not know what is for the best any more."

"Yes, you do. If he can throw away all for you, why can't you respond in like fashion? Don't you love him . . . is that it?" he asked.

"More than my life!"

"Then, let that be your answer," Bertie stated, with exasperation beginning to sound in his voice as he glanced up at the clock on the mantelpiece. "I've guests arriving for dinner at home this evening, so I need to be away. I'm sorry to leave you in this state, Sylvia, but I'll call around in the morning to see you. Throw caution to the wind and don't look back. A love such as that is rare. If you don't know that, then take it from one who does!"

He walked across to her and his hand reached over. He squeezed her arm as he moved by the armchair, on which she was seated, and she smiled at him in response.

"It's come upon me so suddenly. I've only hours to decide now," Sylvia explained, while glancing up at the clock.

"There's no decision to make. Let that be an end to it," he replied.

Bertie left the room hurriedly, without a backward glance, but Sylvia knew that his swift exit had little to do with the arrangements for this evening's dinner party, which would have been planned perfectly and well in advance. He left nothing to chance where the entertainment of his guests was concerned. Invitations to his functions were highly-prized in certain circles and his guests were disappointed rarely.

In her mind's eye, Sylvia saw a set of scales. On the tray on the right side stood all of her family and her few close friends, prominent amongst these was Bertie, of course. Balancing the other side, on the left-hand tray, Charles Lyndhurst stood alone. She was required this night to choose one tray or the other. A decision needed to be made. There was so little time.

"And, I'll never see you again either, Bertie," she murmured aloud.

Another hour elapsed before Sylvia's consciousness returned to her surroundings and she raised herself ever-so-slowly from the armchair. In the semi-darkness, she walked to the table in the corner of the room and poured a glass of fine malt whisky from the crystal decanter, diluting it a little with just a touch of water. She allowed the amber liquid to swirl slowly around in her mouth before swallowing. With one mouthful, her shoulders relaxed instantly, her spirits lifted considerably as the effects pulsed throughout her entire body, and she allowed a deep sigh to escape from within the depths of her being.

She left the room while taking the glass with her as she ascended the stairs to her bedroom. She would dress for dinner and dine alone. Then, Charles Lyndhurst would arrive. He would expect an answer. There would be no turning back once the decision was made. Sylvia knew that well.

Locked tightly in his arms, Sylvia watched the dawn breaking through the open drapes of the window near to her bed. She did not know how she would do so, but somehow this morning, she needed to impress upon Charles the enormity of his request, and its repercussions should she accept his suggestion of walking away together from everyone and everything that was dear to them in the life, which they enjoyed here in Melbourne.

Slowly, she edged her way from the bed. He stirred slightly, before relaxing into sleep again. She reached for the light dressing gown draped on the end of her bed. She slipped her feet into her slippers and quietly left the bedroom. She hurried along the gallery that led to Edwin's bedroom. Once inside, her eyes adjusted quickly to the sombre surroundings and soft lighting. She discerned the figure of Martha who was dozing in an armchair by the bedside; then, she noted the swelling and slight bruising around her left eye. She was grateful for the patience and devotion of these women who cared for her husband.

"Martha!" Sylvia spoke softly.

Martha's eyes flew open with a start and a look of apprehension, mingled with guilt, crossed her face. Her eyes darted immediately to the bed where her charge was propped up on several pillows and his eyes were on the two women.

"Mrs. Webster! Is something amiss? I'm sorry. I must've dozed for just a moment."

"It's alright. Everything is as it should be. I'll sit with him awhile, if you like. Go and have some tea. Take a twenty minute break."

Sylvia watched as relief swept over the older woman's face.

"That's kind of you, ma'am. Indeed, I shall," Martha replied. "He's been an angel this night, he has."

Sylvia nodded slowly and smiled at her. She gazed across at her husband and, try as she might, she could not conjure up one, single angelic image on that blank countenance. Martha bustled from the room as Sylvia moved to the bedside while noting that the restraints had been removed from his wrists, at Sylvia's insistence.

Absentmindedly, she lifted the hair brush from the table and smoothed what remained of Edwin's short hair. Two vacant brown eyes stared back at her as she rubbed her hand gently down his cheek and whispered softly to him. The words were of no importance in themselves. It was her voice, to which he seemed to respond, for a reason that was beyond her comprehension.

Sylvia lit several lamps so that the room was bathed in light. She opened the drapes to allow the first rays of the morning sun to stream through the panes of glass when these broke through the dark clouds that hung over Melbourne this day. The weather set the mood for the day that was to come, she mused.

Leaving Edwin alone momentarily, she returned to her bedroom. To her surprise, she found Charles standing in the centre of the room and he was partially dressed while struggling into his shirt.

"Good morning, darling," he whispered.

Sylvia walked over and kissed him. Then, she took his hand and led him towards the door. He frowned markedly and she reached up to smooth his brow.

"Come with me. I've something I need you to see."

She led him along the gallery to the next bedroom and entered quickly while dragging him in behind her. This was one room in her home, to which he had never gained admittance before today, and it was the element of surprise that enabled her to bring Charles this far without protest, but his reluctance was obvious.

"Sylvia, no . . . I can't . . ."

He stopped and stared at her husband who was gazing out of the window. As Charles whispered to her, Edwin turned and looked over at them. She felt Charles stiffen as the eyes of the man in the bed peered through them. Sylvia left Charles and she moved to the bedside; then, standing beside Edwin, she stroked his hair with her hand as she rearranged his pillows. All the while, Edwin's eyes followed her movements while never once acknowledging the presence of anyone else in the room.

Sylvia dropped a brief kiss onto his forehead before glancing over at Charles who stood motionless while watching the proceedings as though he had turned to stone. Suddenly, he turned away while spinning around swiftly and leaving the room. Sylvia followed him and entered her own bedroom but two paces behind him.

"What was that charade for?" Charles demanded of her after she closed her bedroom door.

"To show you the full extent of your request and what it entails for me. The repercussions of what you're asking of me are enormous," she informed him.

"Do you think I'm not aware of it? And, what of me? Is it any different for me? It need not be forever. You do realise that? We can be married at a later date and return here then. It's not a permanent arrangement and I do intend to marry you. You know that, don't you? For pity's sake, you don't think I'd desert you, in some far off country, with no means of returning here ever! Tell me you don't believe me capable of that, Sylvia?" he pleaded with her.

"No, I believe you . . . of course, I believe you, but I don't think I can do this right now. Try to understand, please. He'd not do it to me."

Charles gave a harsh laugh and raised his right hand to brush the hair from his forehead. He shook his head as he spoke, with his eyes never drifting from her face.

"Most certainly, he'd have done so long ago, if the roles had been reversed. Mark my words! He'd have had you committed to a lunatic asylum within weeks of the accident occurring and he'd have moved his lover into this house immediately. Who else have you discussed this with? Bertie?"

"Yes, and before you ask, no one else knows at all. Bertie is a clam. He would not mention our affairs to anyone," Sylvia stated.

"Despite the fact that he's inherited his father's nose for intrigue. But, perhaps, you're correct in that assessment," Charles muttered, with a nonchalant shrug of his shoulders. "And his response?"

"Go and don't look back."

Charles nodded slowly and thoughtfully. He moved to the window to stare out as the first drops of rain began to strike at the window panes. A strong wind was beginning to stir the branches and the leaves of the trees. The day would not be a pleasant one at all.

"You must give me your unequivocal answer now. There's *no turning back* from this decision. Do you understand that clearly, Sylvia?"

"Yes," she replied, while nodding her head to reinforce the fact. "Bertie has promised to look after my interests here, if I do choose to go."

"*If?*" Charles queried, while turning abruptly and raising an eyebrow at her. *"Is there a doubt?* Is there really a doubt at all?"

Almost imperceptibly and involuntarily, Sylvia shrugged her shoulders and leaned heavily against the brass bedpost at the end of her bed for support as he watched her closely.

"Don't count on Bertie too much. He'll do what he can, but with four older sisters calling for your hide, he may be unable to do as much as he thinks he can for you. I need you to accept fully that you're walking away from everything to throw in your lot with me. If, by some miracle, Bertie can protect your interests here, that is a bonus. We'll leave together before this week is at an end and you can bring very little with you. Is that understood clearly?"

Sylvia nodded again, more slowly this time. Somehow, she knew that she could not bring herself to do as he was suggesting. It was too hasty a decision. She needed more time to think about the situation. Time was not something that was being offered.

"Come here," Charles whispered, while holding out his hand to her.

Standing by the window, he took her hand as she moved closer to him. He held it against his bare chest. His shirt was hanging loose, with the buttons remaining unfastened.

"What do you feel?"

"Your heart."

"Yes . . . beating very fast, because I'm full of life and desperately in love with you. Look into my eyes . . . what do you see?"

Sylvia looked into his eyes and, without warning, tears began to well in her own eyes. Suddenly, he pulled her to him and held her in a crushing embrace. He murmured into her ear.

"The person in that other room is a breathing corpse . . . no more than that! I'm sorry to be blunt, but at a time such as this, there's no place for niceties, as we haven't that luxury. I've eyes that are full of life and full of love for you. His eyes are that of a dead man. Don't discard all we have for the sake of someone who never loved you; who possessed you simply because you're so beautiful and someone whom he could have on his arm as he walked into a room, knowing all heads would turn in his direction. He was a vain creature, addicted to power and to intrigue, and he cared for no one but himself. Are you going to spurn me in favour of a dead man, Sylvia?"

"I have family to think of, Charles."

"As do I."

Sylvia pulled away from him. She stood by the end of the bed, while frowning deeply as she fought desperately against the tears that were threatening to engulf her. A part of her was refusing to accept that this situation had arisen between them.

"Are we to leave Melbourne together this week, Sylvia?" Charles asked, in a quiet but deliberate tone.

Slowly, Sylvia shook her head as she watched him. His face was impassive. He had known all along what her answer would be, she felt. Still, he persisted.

"Answer me, please. At least do me that courtesy."

"I can't . . . please, try to understand," she murmured.

"Is that your final answer?" Charles queried, in barely a whisper.

She could hear the raindrops splattering against the glass and the wind gusting through the trees. She felt that she could hear her own heart beating at a very fast rate and the blood pulsing throughout her body before a persistent ringing tone reverberated loudly in her ears. Still, he awaited her reply. Charles had not moved a muscle. He just stood there, waiting. Finally, Sylvia found her voice again, albeit a whisper in the semi-darkness of her silent bedroom.

"No, I cannot leave. I'm sorry . . . so sorry. I can't go with you to places unknown. This is my home."

Without a word, he walked quickly by her while brushing her arm as he reached for his coat and waistcoat and lifting them swiftly from the chair. He was tucking his shirt into his trousers as he left the room with his other apparel slung over his arm. Very quietly, he closed the door.

"Charles, no! Don't leave like this . . ." Sylvia called after him.

She found that she was talking to the closed door. Her feet wanted desperately to run after him and to cling to him as she changed her decision completely. But, she did not move. Now, she was the one who had turned to stone.

Once again, she leaned against the bed frame. Her light gown had slipped open and the brass was cold against her bare skin. She did not take any notice of the sensation.

The shock of the encounter with Charles Lyndhurst had left her shaken. There was a coldness and a numbness forming about her, totally submerging her in a soul-destroying grief, the like of which she had not experienced since the death of her young brother when she was twelve years of age. Many years had past since she had known such a deep-seated pain as she felt possessing her entire being at this moment. Sylvia Webster knew, without doubt, that she would remember this day for the remainder of her life. Also, she knew, without doubt, that she would regret this decision for the remainder of her days. But, it was done. It could never be undone.

Slowly and in a rote manner, Sylvia removed the garment while replacing it with a warmer dressing gown that was more suitable for the prevailing weather conditions.

She returned to Edwin's room to keep vigil until Martha's expected return.

Chapter Five

— Victorian Victorians —

Sylvia

Seated at her bureau in the small sitting room, Sylvia was struggling to find suitable words to communicate her feelings to her mother as she twirled the pen in her hands and stared at the blank page before her. There had been a heated exchange between them at their last meeting in Castlemaine when they stood across from each other in the cemetery two days earlier. Between them lay the freshly-sealed grave of Sylvia's late father. In death, the man had achieved sainthood in her mother's eyes, a state denied him while in the flesh – and for many very sound reasons. These reasons were the cause of the argument, as Sylvia had been attempting to reiterate her father's faults to his grieving widow. This had been a mistake, she knew, but her patience had been tried to its limit.

She had spent a sleepless night in Edwin's old home in that town while dwelling on Charles' recent revelations in Bendigo. It was not surprising, given the circumstances, that angry words were spoken. Today seemed to be a day for regrets, she mused to herself. She was roused from her sombre thoughts by a tap at the door, which opened promptly before her words had left her lips.

"Come in, Bertie," Sylvia called, without turning her head. "I'm in a foul temper, so be warned before you cross the threshold."

Sylvia tossed the pen onto the blank page and ink from the nib splattered onto the writing sheet, so she was required then to soak the ink with the blotting paper to hand. It was only at this moment that she swung around in the chair. Standing by the closed door and watching her closely was Charles Lyndhurst.

"Am I the reason for your foul temper?" he inquired.

"A good part of it! What're you doing back here? I thought I'd seen the last of you!"

"Then, you don't know me as well as you thought you did, Mrs. Webster."

"Is that so, Mr. Lyndhurst? *And, have you* done what you set out to do this morning? Have you settled matters legally?"

"The wheels are in motion. There's no way back now."

Charles walked over and picked up a straight-backed chair before placing it beside her at the end of the bureau. He sat down, stretched his legs in front of him, crossed them at the ankles and leaned on the bureau. Sylvia watched him in silence for a few moments.

"To what do I owe the honour of this visit, then?" she inquired.

"To straighten issues between us. I wish to continue our relationship. How do you feel about that?"

Sylvia stared at him while shaking her head in surprise. She opened her mouth to speak; then, she closed it again, unable to find the words to express her emotions, which were a mixture of anger, pain, outrage and shock all mingled together, with a feeling of betrayal lurking there in the background to add to the mix.

"I don't believe I'm hearing this," she muttered finally.

"Why not? It didn't seem to matter when you were the married party, so why should it matter if we're both in the state of ... umm. . . *wedded bliss*, so to speak?"

"You're asking this of me, knowing how I feel about you . . . and you about to marry someone else? I can't comprehend this. Truly, I can't," Sylvia stammered.

"For one, it's not a marriage, as such . . . more a business arrangement. And two, you don't really love me . . . not the way I love you . . . for you chose all of this!" Charles stated, instantly waving his arm in the air to encompass her home. "All of this above me, including a living, breathing corpse, I might add. How do you think that makes me feel, Sylvia?"

"I'll thank you not to speak of Edwin in such manner, or you can leave now! And, what of your fiancée . . . how do you think she'll feel when she discovers the truth of it? In a place like Melbourne, where gossip is the main occupation of many, she'll know in an instant."

Charles raised an eyebrow but remained silent while watching her closely and awaiting her answer to his proposal. When Sylvia remained silent, he reached over and grasped her hand.

"Let's be frank, shall we? You and Edwin parted a long time ago, by mutual consent, and I suspect I know the real reason, though we'll not muddy the waters by delving into that now. We've been together a long time. We can go on for a long time to come. Louisa is a child and she appears to have no interest outside of her horses. The agreement with my father was that I marry her . . . nothing more. If the marriage is never consummated, then I've won and there'll be no grandsons, will there?"

Sylvia gasped audibly and stared at him in amazement. Still, she was having difficulty in finding words to answer him as he waited for her reaction to his words.

"I told you," he continued. "He's intervened in my life three times. This is the last time. I need him this once, but never again! He's won this round. However, the match will be mine, I promise you. *And, we're not playing* by the rules of the Marquess of Queensberry!"

"*It's a game?*" Sylvia queried, while being completely astounded by his attitude.

"A power game . . . with my father, that's what keeps him alive. Perhaps, I'm no better than he is. I see his traits in myself at times and shudder to think I may be a mirror-image of him, but I think there's a little humanity left in me yet, whereas he's devoid of all feeling. He has no morals, no conscience and no principles whatsoever. I don't think I've quite reached that stage yet. I hope not, at least."

"You say she's a child, but children do tend to grow into thinking and feeling adults, Charles. She may look elsewhere."

"And, you think I'd sit back and allow that to happen? Give me credit for possessing a little common sense. I'm not an idiot!"

Sylvia removed her hand from his grasp and stood up. She walked to the window and gazed absentmindedly at the rain as it poured in torrents from the dark grey sky.

"It's devious, dastardly and despicable. What you're proposing is truly terrible. I'm shocked and stunned. And, you're asking me to be a party to this? Do you know what it is I find so awful in this?"

Charles looked at her in a totally disinterested manner while giving her to understand that his mind was set already on the course of action he was planning.

"Enlighten me."

"What it is I find so awful is that you can't see anything wrong with this scheme you're proposing. To me, it has disaster written all over it. No good can come of it, believe me. You can't treat people like chess pieces to be moved around a board at a whim. I have to live in this city still, and move in the same circles as you and your new wife, so I've to look to my own preservation now. I won't always have the umbrella of Edwin's family name to protect me. In fact, I'd be surprised if he lived longer than three months, as there's been a rapid deterioration in him recently," she advised, in a tone that spoke of disillusionment.

Charles Lyndhurst sat looking over at her and appeared completely unmoved by her speech and its implications.

"If that's so, then there's much irony in my father's timing. We'd be discreet, Sylvia. We always were. Perhaps the past year or so, we may have become a little careless, but your welfare and reputation have been my greatest concern always. They'll continue to be so. And, you may not be aware of this, but Sophie Collins is Louisa Howard's aunt . . . her father's sister. I thought, perhaps, I'd better warn you about that fact."

Sylvia spun around and walked over to him. She stood staring down at Charles while he looked up at her with a bemused look on his face. Her anger was rising fast and he was well aware of the fact. That Sophie Collins was undoubtedly the greatest gossip the city had to offer was acknowledged widely.

"That obnoxious woman! I have to face her, knowing her niece is marrying you. What else aren't you telling me?"

"Nothing. But, let me remind you, this choice was your own. It was not mine. Do we continue this relationship?"

Sylvia, knowing she had made one decision that was not to her liking this day, was reluctant to make another error of judgement, even though the temptation to throw his proposal in his face – along with anything else she could find to hand – was extremely strong, at present. In fact, it was more than strong. It was something that she desired greatly and found great difficulty in suppressing. By some miracle, she did so. Instead, she decided, on the spur of the moment, to buy herself some time.

The other issue was, of course, that she did not know how her life could continue without Charles Lyndhurst as a major part of it. The thought of never seeing him again – and never having him to hold and to love again – was not only more than she could bear to contemplate, at this stage; but also, it was something, with which she could not contend at present. This whole terrible business had been sprung on her so suddenly that she was having difficulty accepting it was already a reality.

"Are you invited to the soiree at the home of Mrs. Fox on next Thursday evening?"

"Presumably," he answered, with a disinterested shrug. "What's that to do with anything? I never attend those functions where boredom is the order of the day and music the last sound anyone hears. You know that. It's a gossip-monger's haven, as anything held at the home of Isobel Fox would be. Why do you ask?"

"Because, if you happen to be there, I shall give you my answer then. It will require much thought."

He threw back his head and gave a harsh laugh while standing abruptly as he did so. He moved to her and placed his hands on her waist.

"Who's playing games now? We both know what the answer is. But, if that's your desire, I'll be there. I'll promise you this though . . . I won't be sober. Under no circumstances would I endure such an evening without a little assistance, fortified by a few stiff drinks. Is that to your liking, *my love*?"

"Don't make a spectacle of yourself, *or of me*. That's all I ask!"

He kissed her gently on the lips. Then, he pulled her more tightly to him and kissed her passionately.

Sylvia was still in his arms while gasping for breath when there was a light tap on the door. It opened slowly and they broke apart as Bertie Webster entered the room. He stopped in the doorway while taking in the scene before him momentarily. He was about to withdraw when Sylvia stopped him.

"Come in, Bertie. Mr. Lyndhurst is just leaving."

Charles laughed again and moved a little way from her as Bertie came into the sitting room somewhat reluctantly.

"So I was," he murmured, while nodding to Bertie and saying in a somewhat supercilious tone. "Good-day to you, Mr. Webster . . . Mrs. Webster."

Bertie nodded to him in acknowledgment; then, Charles was gone, with the door closed firmly behind him. Sylvia found herself trembling while staring at the door when Bertie spoke to her. She heard his words as though in some distant place.

"What the hell was that about? Are you staying or leaving, Sylvia?"

"Staying . . . and I need a large, strong drink now, Bertie, if you please."

"Oh! Thank the Lord for that," he said, with a huge sigh of relief. "I couldn't imagine my life without you in it. We'll have many drinks, mostly in celebration, I think."

With her hands trembling and her knees threatening to give away beneath her, Sylvia sank slowly into Edwin's old armchair in the corner. She was lost in her thoughts while Bertie poured the drinks.

She was staring at the closed door and shaking her head in disbelief at the pantomime that had taken place just now when he moved from the drinks cabinet and handed the glass to her. He raised his glass in a toast.

"Just you and me against the world *again*, eh?"

With a soft laugh, which became almost a nervous giggle, she raised her glass slightly in answer to him and studied the immaculately dressed gentleman before her.

"How many crises have we survived together, do you think?" she asked him.

"The first was on the day I met you. That'd have to be the most painful day of my life. He said: *Bertram! This is your new mother!* And, having never met my old mother, what was I to say? There'll be many more crises in the future, I suspect. But, let's drink to true friendship, for without that, none of us would survive very long. You *do know* that?"

Sylvia nodded and continued to drink the burning liquid in silence. He watched her for a time until the curiosity was burning fiercely within him. She smiled as she remembered Charles' words about Bertie inheriting his father's nose for intrigue. Finally, he could contain himself no longer.

"Out with it *now*, madam!" he demanded, with a grin on his face.

Suddenly, he reminded her of the young, fourteen-year-old boy who had come to her, at his father's direction, to beg forgiveness for a perceived wrong-doing that was more of a misunderstanding than any preconceived plot on his part to frighten her. Startle her, he had done. Thrash him, his father had done. The frog – a cherished possession from his extensive collection of reptilian and amphibian creatures at that time – had been boxed, gift-wrapped and handed to her as a wedding gift from her only step-son who wanted desperately to make a good impression.

Later that night, she went to his bedroom and held him, as she had heard him whimpering from the hallway. That was when she made the promise to him – *just you and me against the world, eh?*

Having realised that she had been a great disappointment to her husband on their wedding night, she had needed a friend desperately in the household and a true friend Bertie Webster had become over the past sixteen years, but never more so than now.

"Not one word of what I tell you is to leave this room; promise me that, or I won't tell you anything at all."

"My silence is assured. You *know that!*"

Sylvia nodded solemnly, and took another gulp of the whisky from the glass in her hand; then, she revealed to Bertie Webster all that had transpired since he left the house on the previous afternoon. In stunned silence, he stood still while staring down at her. Finally, he shook his head and moved to the cabinet to refill his glass. Eventually, he settled in the armchair opposite her and studied the amber liquid in deep concentration before giving his considered opinion on the matter under discussion.

"Scandalous," he murmured.

Bertie remained silent again momentarily before he continued with his advice to Sylvia.

"I advised you to accept his first offer. You disregarded my advice, but I advise you strongly now to refuse his second offer, for you are the only one who'll be hurt, and possibly destroyed, by this when it explodes . . . as it will, one way or another. But, you'll disregard my advice a second time, I know. Talk about wanting to have it all! Good luck to him, if he can achieve such a feat, but I doubt it can be done and it can't be without someone being hurt. *I don't want that to be you. And, Mrs. Collins* in there to stir the pot, as well! Oh! This just gets better by the minute!" Bertie exclaimed, before adding somewhat softly. "Her husband's mistress is with child; did you know that, Sylvia?"

The last piece of information was added so quietly that Sylvia could have been forgiven for missing it altogether. Suddenly, she frowned.

"*What?*"

"You heard me," he said, while laughing as he went on with his revelation. "That may be a useful tit-bit for you, should you feel the need to use it sometime."

Despite the trauma of the past forty-eight hours, Sylvia began to laugh. She held out her empty glass to him, obviously requiring a refill. She was laughing when he stood and removed it from her grasp.

"You never cease to amaze me!" she stated; then, with deep feeling, she spoke softly to him. "Thank you for being here for me always, Bertie."

He turned from the cabinet, smiled and winked at her, before returning to the task at hand.

"Despite everything, you can still laugh, Sylvia," Bertie murmured.

"What else is there to do? My hands are tied," Sylvia replied.

Bertie took his leave of her shortly afterwards and Sylvia was left alone.

The racecourse at Flemington was bathed in sunshine and the gardens were at their spring best. Studying the race book in her hand, Sylvia did not know which horse she preferred and a cursory glance at the race horses in the enclosure had done little to sway her from her original choice; so, she decided to stay with the one that Bertie had recommended for this particular race. Suddenly, another booklet appeared over her book and a male arm appeared in front of her face.

"Race four, horse two," he whispered in her ear.

She looked into Charles' eyes and, despite her deep-seated and smouldering anger, she smiled at him.

"Is that so? It can't lose, I suppose?"

"Not a chance . . . I've just had a word with the beast. It's an understanding we've come to," he replied.

Sylvia laughed softly while turning to face him. He smiled at her and from the corner of her eye, Sylvia saw heads turned in their direction. The marriage banns were up for all to see and the news of his forthcoming nuptials was flying around Melbourne. She would play his game, she decided, for the moment anyway, and let the world look on with interest, disgust or otherwise.

"With the horse . . . or with me?"

Charles laughed, without taking his eyes from her. She knew many eyes were upon them – as did he. The race meeting was a social affair and it was well-attended.

"I'd say with both of you. You're not really going to make me wait until Thursday evening . . . don't keep me in suspense any longer?"

"You can wait. You're trying to wriggle out of the soiree evening, for *I know you*. I shall see you there, Mr. Lyndhurst. Now, go away and leave me alone. We're causing no end of interest."

"This is nothing! Wait and see what happens on Thursday at the home of Mrs. Fox. I'll see you there then, if that's how you want to play this," he said, with an exaggerated groan.

Sylvia did not reply, but turned her attention back to the book in her hand and not one word of print did she see. Her mind was racing, and faster than any race horse could travel. Charles sauntered away. He joined a group of his friends by the track as the horses moved toward the barrier for Race Two of today's meet.

Sitting beside Bertie on the uncomfortable, hard, high-backed chairs provided for the guests at Mrs. Fox' musical evening, Sylvia was fighting the urge to wriggle in her seat. She wished that she could turn around and see if Charles had arrived, although her pride would not allow her to do so. The chamber music droned on endlessly and intermission seemed hours away. Finally, the rendition ended to loud applause, although Sylvia suspected the applause was due more to the fact that the audience was relieved the piece was over, rather than because of the musical talent that was on offer and had been endured. Bertie stood slowly and stretched his limbs as he did so. He was surveying the room and its occupants in his usual unobtrusive manner while missing no one. He bent down and whispered in her ear.

"Your friend is here . . . to your right and slightly behind you. He's with his friend, Hugh Travis, and his wife. No, wait! He's just been accosted and claimed as a long-lost friend by Sophie Collins. Oh! Sylvia, I wouldn't have missed tonight for anything. Thank you for dragging me here *and he'll* hate you for forcing him to attend."

Sylvia smiled slightly and she knew immense satisfaction. She did not turn her head, but gave Bertie her full and undivided attention.

"Thank you, Bertie, a glass of wine would be wonderful. As you say, the music was divine. I'm grateful you insisted we attend this evening. Thank you," she stated quite loudly.

Bertie grimaced and sauntered away while smiling to himself and shaking his head slightly. She had been forced almost into bribery in order to persuade him to escort her here to the function.

Within a few minutes, Charles Lyndhurst was beside her, immediately settling himself into Bertie's recently-vacated chair. He reached over, took her hand, placed it to his lips and kissed it while gazing deeply into her eyes as he did so. There was a supercilious expression in those eyes as Sylvia looked at him in some surprise.

"Good evening, Mr. Lyndhurst," she said evenly, removing her hand from his grasp rather hurriedly and hissing at him under her breath. "What the hell do you think you're playing at?"

Charles leaned across until his mouth was so close to her ear that she could feel his breath on the side of her face. He had been drinking heavily, she suspected.

"You *were* warned," he muttered, still gazing into her face.

"Did you enjoy that last piece?" Sylvia asked quite loudly, while knowing that there were few guests who were looking elsewhere.

"Oh! The game continues! Shall I call on you this evening?" he whispered in her ear again.

"Go to hell!"

Charles laughed loudly. Sylvia watched as Sophie Collins swivelled in her chair while studying them closely, and Sylvia knew a moment's triumph. Silence reigned between them for some minutes while Charles made no attempt to move away.

"I could be persuaded to relent, but there's a condition," Sylvia murmured, while moving closer to Charles so that she could not be overheard. "Our relationship ends on the day of your marriage."

She felt him shudder in his chair and he looked at her with an incredulous expression on his face. Finally, he shook his head, definitely rejecting the proposal.

"You jest! That's when I'll need you *more*," he exclaimed, although lowering his voice a trifle before he explained more fully. "I'm deadly serious about how it'll be with this new arrangement. It's a business deal . . . nothing more!"

"That's my *arrangement*, Charles. Take it or leave it," Sylvia stated firmly, but quietly.

Charles reached over, reclaiming her hand; then, he leaned closer to her, looking directly at her face. She knew that they were creating no end of speculation. He brought her hand to within easy reach of his lips again.

"Tonight?" he queried, with one eyebrow raised in query.

"No. But, you may come tomorrow night and dine with me, if you wish."

"When does what *I wish* ever enter the equation? I'll be there . . . *the rest* is up for negotiation, Sylvia," he stated, deliberately moving his face to within inches of her own.

She stared at him, torn between wanting to kiss him passionately and wishing to slap his face instantly, thereby removing the supercilious expression from it. She did neither.

"*The hell it is!*" Sylvia hissed at him, as softly as she could, while attempting to contain her anger at the manner, in which he was compromising her now. "You made the choice you did. You'll have to live with it, as will I. As I stated, that's the condition and under no circumstances is it up for negotiation! *And, I'll thank you not* to use me as a pawn in your game of chess."

"You mistake me . . . *you're my queen*," he replied quietly, although Sylvia could not help but note the sarcasm in his voice.

"A discarded one!" she countered.

He moved close to her ear again, with his breath brushing her cheek, as she turned her face away from him.

"I love you," he whispered softly. "Until tomorrow night then . . . *and, you'll never* be discarded . . . certainly not by me!"

He kissed her lightly on the side of her face, beside the ear, into which he had been whispering. Charles stood abruptly and walked away. She watched him as he moved to rejoin his friends.

Bertie returned to her then and she could see the look of disapproval etched on his face. As Bertie sat beside her, she leaned towards him.

"Don't you start on me, as well, Bertie Webster! I'm not in the mood!"

Bertie nodded his head and, wisely, remained silent as he handed her a glass of wine. Fortunately, the musical programme resumed and all attention was focussed on the players.

Sylvia determined that she would not remain for supper. She was trembling still and a slight headache was pulsing at her temples. In an angry response to her encounter with her lover, she decided then that Charles Lyndhurst could do whatever he chose with his new wife, but she would not be waiting in the wings for him. On this, she would not compromise, because as Bertie had stated so vehemently, she would be the one who would be hurt emotionally and socially, if tonight could be used as any type of gauge.

If a night of musical entertainment was to be endured at the home of Mrs. Fox, her lavish suppers were to be praised to the heavens, so there was not the slightest possibility that Sylvia could expect to drag Bertie away early. When she saw him join a group, comprising several of his closest friends, she realised that she would be leaving alone. Undeterred, she sought out her hostess, thanked her profusely for the enjoyable evening and, feigning a slight headache, she took her leave.

"That's such a shame, Mrs. Webster, but I understand completely. How is your husband this evening? Is he much improved in his health?" Isobel Fox queried, rather pointedly, Sylvia felt.

Sylvia glanced quickly at the older woman who, being some twenty years Sylvia's senior, was beginning to appear very matronly indeed, Sylvia noted, although she did concede that she had been an extremely attractive woman in her earlier years. Sylvia grimaced slightly before replying to her hostess' somewhat sarcastic tone of questioning.

"Mr. Webster is as well as can be expected. Thank you for your concern, Mrs. Fox. Good evening," she said, while heading for the door.

"Good evening. Do take plenty of rest so as not to aggravate your headache, Mrs. Webster."

Sylvia swivelled her head around to look directly at the woman who was Sophie Collins' closest friend and, in reply, she bestowed upon that lady a knowing smile.

Chapter Six

− *Victorian Victorians* −

Louisa

Louisa had ridden Hilton hard this morning. It was to be their last time together and both knew it, for if there was anything troubling Louisa, always Hilton knew so at once. So, it was with great sadness this day, on the morning of her wedding, that she stroked and brushed her beloved horse that quivered and snorted at her touch while his mother, the mare, Cadence, watched the performance from her stall. She, too, was nervous and skittish today.

"So, this is where you are! I thought I'd find you here."

Louisa turned her head at the sound of his voice coming from the direction of the doorway to the stable. She smiled at him. He was tall, with greying hair and lively blue eyes that danced whenever he looked at his favourite and only niece. He was the opposite end of the spectrum to her father in every way. His height, his almost-regal bearing, his handsome countenance that had, no doubt, turned many a head in his time and his gentle manner were in stark contrast to her father who was of solid, stocky build with a brusque, energetic manner that spoke of a no-nonsense approach to life and to those around him.

Whereas George Howard was accustomed to working on the land with the animals, the shearers and the rough farm-hands whom he employed, Robert Collins was more at home in the drawing room or ensconced in his library, which many years ago, he had declared out-of-bounds to all females, his wife included. This was his sanctuary from the world and he spent much of his time there with his precious books. Louisa was the only one for whom an exception was made and she had spent many, many hours sitting quietly in that protected hide-away while reading from his great selection of books. Being a teacher, his guidance in these matters was given to her in a way that was as subtle as it was gentle.

"Good morning, Uncle Robert. What brings you out here so early?"

"My concern for you. What else? How goes it, Louisa? Today has arrived for you finally. I wish that it were otherwise, my lovely one. I wish there were some way I could change this situation, but I'm powerless to do so. You're the only one who can put an end to this charade and I strongly advise you to do so, even at this late hour. Then, we will weather the ensuing scandal together. I'm sorry to be so blunt, but I've not had a chance before now to speak with you while your aunt and your father will do all in their power to prevent me doing so. I'm playing truant at the moment . . . in your best interest, of course."

Louisa dropped the brush and went quickly to him. She put her arms about him and he crushed her in an embrace. A soft, almost inaudible sob escaped her. He lifted her chin and looked into her fathomless green eyes.

"Tell me why you're doing this. I need to understand. You're dearer to me than any daughter could be. You're quite capable of making up your own mind on your future. Why, child?" Robert Collins queried, in an earnest tone.

"Haven't you seen Papa? Haven't you noticed? He wants this so badly, for my sake, and he's dying. I know he's dying, for anyone with eyes can see that. I've lost Mama. I can't bear to lose him, as well. If I'm not here to worry him so much, perhaps, he'll recover from whatever ails him. Did you not see? You must've seen the change in him."

Robert Collins sighed deeply; then, he brushed a strand of loose hair from her face and released her. He walked to Hilton and began stroking the stallion, all the while lost in deep thought.

"So, that's it, is it? Emotional blackmail, eh?" he asked, before he held up his hand and shook his head as Louisa opened her mouth to interrupt him. "Don't interrupt . . . he's not well and anyone can see that. But dying? I doubt it. I've seen what grief can do to a man and I'm certain he'll recover, as many before him have had to do, simply because life's demands require it to be so, eventually. As long as there is nothing wrong with him physically, and this I cannot state categorically, as I am not a physician, but it would be my considered opinion that this state of melancholy, which seems to have possessed his soul, is due more to your Mama's passing than to the prospect of his immediate demise. You *cannot* throw yourself away on the likes of Charles Lyndhurst! Please reconsider, I beg of you."

In an absentminded manner, she studied her uncle before moving back to Hilton's side. She retrieved the brush, thereby resuming her work on the stallion's back as Robert stood watching her.

"You are determined, then?" he asked softly.

"Try to understand. I'd do anything to avoid this situation. Even now, at this late hour, I cannot refer to it as a marriage. But I cannot do so, because I made my decision, for Papa's sake, and for no other reason. I will not break my word. I shall go through with what you term a *charade*, for indeed that's exactly what it is, and we are all well aware of that fact. There's nothing else to be done, at this late stage anyway."

"Louisa, you've only to say the word and I'll put an end to it instantly. Mark my words! Give me your permission and I'll do so now. It would give me the greatest pleasure in this world to send Lyndhurst on his way . . . and I'll not hesitate to do so!"

"No, Uncle Robert, no," Louisa stated, immediately shaking her head for more emphasis, and not looking at him as she concentrated on the brush stokes while pleading with him. "Just let it be, now. Thank you for your concern, but just let it be. I'll survive this. Really, I will."

"I hope so. I truly hope so," Robert said, with feeling; then, he turned abruptly and, without another word, he walked quickly from stables.

Louisa continued to brush Hilton for a long, long time after the departure of Robert Collins from her sanctuary.

Louisa settled herself comfortably into the bath that was filled to the rim with steaming hot water. Her hair was piled high on top of her head, and when she moved, the water lapped her chin as the residue spilled over the side. It was running between the cracks of the floor in the separate bath-house adjacent to the main homestead.

Aunt Sophie had come to her bedroom to inform her of the arrival of her fiancé, so Louisa had escaped promptly to the bath while leaving strict instructions that she was not to be disturbed by anyone under any circumstances. These were her last moments alone and she would treasure every one of them. On that, she was determined. She did not wish to set eyes on Charles Lyndhurst – not today, or on any other day – but sooner or later, she would be required to dress for her wedding.

Her aunt and uncle had arrived on the previous day and her aunt had produced five new gowns, all of which were hideous, as far as Louisa was concerned. The wedding gown was the least repulsive of all but, even so, it seemed to have yards and yards more lace than Louisa felt was necessary. As for the others, the colours were more suited to Sophie Collins' greying blonde locks than to Louisa's vibrant auburn ones. It was as though they had been purchased for a very young Sophie, rather than for Louisa Howard. As soon as she reached her destination, which she presumed to be Melbourne although no one had bothered to inform her directly of this fact, Louisa determined that she would dispatch the new gowns, the wedding one included, to a charity house somewhere. Never would she be seen wearing such obnoxious creations.

Finally, when she could delay the inevitable no longer, Louisa stepped from the bath and began to towel-dry her body. She had, as a last defiant act, spent an hour swimming in the cool waters of the Murray River this morning. Her hair was soft, fresh and clean as a result of that exercise in those clear, clean waters and her body had been tingling when she emerged naked onto the bank. Had anyone been watching, she would not have cared at all today, for this day promised to be one of the worst days of her life, second only to the day when her mother died.

Sophie Collins was bustling around the bedroom when Louisa returned to it. Sophie was a few years younger than her husband and her brother, who were fifty-five and sixty years of age respectively. She would have been a pretty girl in her time. Now, she appeared older than her years. She was short, plump, with large, brown eyes that resembled Louisa's father. If there was one activity that marked her character above any other, it was her ability to bustle, and bustling she was now, much to Louisa's annoyance.

She needed peace and quiet, not the ministrations of a matronly lady who was recalling no doubt her own wedding day and who was, in all probability, assuming incorrectly that her niece was as excited and as triumphant as she had been at landing the most handsome gentleman in Melbourne at that time. This did little to appease Louisa who felt her temper rising alarmingly as she struggled into her under-garments and her silk stockings.

"Where's the other stupid garter?" she demanded.

Instantly, Sophie produced it and handed it to her niece who was perched on the side of the bed. The lady-in-question was standing at the end of the bed. Ominously, she grasped the brass bed-end with both hands, closed her eyes and took a deep breath. Louisa was oblivious to her aunt's discomfort until she spoke in a tone that made Louisa swivel her head to observe her.

"Louisa, I must speak with you. It is my solemn duty to do so, as your dear Mama is no longer here to perform this odious and difficult task."

"What is it, Aunt Sophie? Are you ill?" Louisa queried, with one leg partially encased in a white stocking and waving about in the air while her two hands struggled with the tightly-fitting hosiery.

"No, no, of course not, except ill with discomfort, I expect one could term it. It is to do with tonight . . . your wedding night . . ." Sophie Collins stated, and gripping the bed-end more tightly as she spoke. "It's a terrible ordeal you'll be required to suffer at the hands of your husband. Now, I know you . . . and I know your vile temper even better, having been on the receiving end of it more times than I'd care to remember. You'll be staying at an hotel in the Echuca township, no doubt. So, if you begin to smash windows and the hotel furniture, then you'll cause great embarrassment, not only to yourself, but to Mr. Lyndhurst. Every bride must endure this unspeakable act on her wedding night. It's compulsory, painful and, unfortunately, a fact of life that cannot be delayed or denied."

Louisa stiffened and placed her two feet firmly on the floor. One stocking lost its fight with gravity and slid around her ankle as Louisa twirled the lace-embroidered garter in her hand. She opened her mouth to speak, still trying to fathom the direction of the conversation, when her aunt held up one hand to her. Suitably silenced, Louisa eyed her aunt with suspicion, her green eyes narrowing as a cat about to surprise an unsuspecting mouse.

"Do not interrupt, I beg of you. That is a grave failing you have, child. Pray, allow me to continue. I just called you *child* and, after this night, you'll not be so again . . . not ever . . . for you'll be a woman . . . a married woman. So, do not attempt to prevent your new husband from doing what must be done to consummate this marriage. It is a legal requirement, you see. Take my advice, for it is sound, well-meant and would be what your dear Mama would be saying to you, if she were here now, I promise you," Sophie Collins concluded, seemingly well satisfied with her efforts on her niece's behalf.

"No! Oh! No, she would not, *I promise you*, Aunt Sophie! And, do you know why? Because this idiotic pantomime wouldn't be taking place at all. Mama would see to that. In fact, there's no doubt in my mind that she's not just turning, but she's rolling over and over in her grave, trying to get out to prevent it. Now, I've not the slightest idea of what you're attempting to warn me, but I swear, on my sweet mother's grave, that if that . . . *that* . . . *person* who I'm marrying today, dares to lay a finger on me, or comes near me, I'll . . . I'll . . ." Louisa, angry and frustrated, stopped mid-sentence while shouting at her aunt.

She was twirling a garter on her index finger as she eyed Sophie Collins ominously; then, she allowed the garter to fly across the room before continuing with her tirade.

"I'll happily slit his throat. And, after that, I'll . . . I'll open him up and have his guts for garters!"

"Louisa Howard! Mind your language! What on earth did they teach you at that School for Ladies? Your father is absolutely correct in arranging this marriage. The sooner you are away from here and these rough, uncouth types with whom you are associating, so much the better. Tonight, you will sleep in your husband's bed. The best advice I can give is to be submissive and quiet. In that way, you'll get *the whole, damn, messy business* over and done with before you realise it. If you're fortunate and the union is a successful one, you'll most likely be spared the ordeal again, for at least six to nine months or so. Let us hope for small miracles, shall we?"

Louisa, who was standing in her underwear, lifted her chin in an act of defiance, but she wore a puzzled look on her face. She required more explanation on this matter. Her aunt took her hands from the bed-end and reached for Louisa's white wedding gown; the ordeal for her was over, obviously. For her niece, though, the subject was far from closed.

"No, we shan't hope for anything. You need to tell me what form this attack will take, so I can be prepared. Aunt Sophie?" she demanded.

"That, my girl, is all I'm prepared to say on the matter. Be submissive. Be quiet. Accept what comes, as it is an inevitable consequence of the marriage state. Focus on a point in the room, stare at it and pretend you're somewhere else, if necessary. Do whatever it takes to get through the ordeal, for it must be endured. Demolishing the bridal suite will only make the exercise a more lively and a more entertaining one for the other party, I would wager, so just be smart. That's the end of this conversation. We'll never mention it between us again. Is that understood clearly?"

Louisa stood shaking her head in astonishment. She stared uncomprehendingly at her aunt who did everything in her power to look elsewhere, quickly averting her eyes and avoiding Louisa's glare.

"Aunt Sophie, I have not the faintest idea of what you are speaking."

"By this time tomorrow, unfortunately, you shall."

Sophie Collins turned quickly and promptly left the room, thereby leaving Louisa in a totally perplexed state. She sat on the side of the bed while staring at her reflection in the mirror on the wall. Her reflection stared back and it did not seem to have any answers, either.

"Well, forewarned is forearmed, wouldn't you say?" she queried the young girl in the mirror. "*Then armed* is what I shall be. He'll rue the day he met me!"

Suddenly, she reached for the garter that had flown from her hand earlier and fixed her stocking in place with it. She dragged on her old black leather boots over her white silk stockings. She pulled her old, green muslin gown over her body. With her hair tied up high on her head still, she ran out to the side verandah outside her bedroom, skipped across it and jumped down onto the grass.

Louisa raced as fast as she could to the sanctuary of Mrs. McBryde's kitchen. When she entered, she found Captain Bartlett seated at the kitchen table, with a glass of dark liquid in front of him.

"Hello, Captain Bill, is Brydie here? Oh! Poof! What's that smell? You're drinking rum. That's the foulest smelling drink on earth, I should think. Why are you all dressed up like that? I've never seen you so spruced up. Anyone would think you're getting married and I'd sooner be marrying you, you know."

"Is that so, lassy? I'm spoken for, I'm afraid; otherwise, I'd be proud and honoured to be of service. Now, the reason I'm drinking rum is because I love the stuff . . . nectar of the gods, it is. As to your other question, I'm dressed in my Sunday finest, because I've been asked by your Papa to stand up beside your fiancé at your ceremony this morning, which unless I'm mistaken . . . " he said, while extracting a gold watch from the pocket of his waist coat and flicking it open. " . . . is scheduled to commence in some twenty minutes."

Louisa moved to the kitchen cabinet and opened a drawer, through which she began to rummage furiously. Bill Bartlett remained seated at the table. He was watching her with amusement, and drinking his rum.

"Perhaps, with a little luck, they'll accomplish the whole exercise without me. I'm only needed to sign the piece of paper at the end, anyway," Louisa muttered.

She slammed the drawer of the cabinet closed firmly; then, she opened the second one and began to rummage, with some urgency, through it.

"Isn't it wonderful to see such a radiant bride on her wedding day?" he remarked as he raised the glass to his lips, still surveying her and making a prediction. "Mrs. McBryde will be back shortly and . . . wedding day or no . . . she'll tan your hide for what you're doing to her kitchen cabinet. You know *everything has its place* in here."

Louisa glanced over at him and grimaced while tilting her head to one side.

"*I know* . . . and there's a place for everything! But, I need a knife. I need a sharp knife . . . a really sharp one! And one that I can conceal on my person. These are all too large and too sharp. I'll do an injury to myself more like with one of these."

She was holding a large and very sharp carving knife in her hand as she turned it over and studied it in detail. Bill watched her in some amusement. He cocked his head to one side and the corners of his mouth were twitching ominously. He raised one eyebrow in her direction.

"Now, far be it from me to inquire as to why you'd be needing such an item, but I've a precious one of my own here," he said.

Bill reached into the pocket of his trousers and withdrew a penknife, which with the slight flick of his finger, sprang to life and produced a sharp blade from the depths of its being. Louisa gasped in appreciation. Her eyes danced with delight at the sight of the object; then, dropping the large carving knife on the table, she moved to him and reached for it. He relinquished it to her and watched with a smile on his face as she turned it over in her hands.

"Careful! It's very sharp. Now, if it's a matter of life and death, I may be prepared to give it to you, in appreciation of our sixteen-plus years of friendship, and as a wedding gift."

Louisa gasped audibly. She looked over the knife at him in surprise. Before he realised what was occurring, she planted a kiss firmly on his cheek. She flicked the blade closed and slipped the object into her pocket.

"Thank you, Captain Bill. I'll treasure it always. I'll never receive a gift as precious . . . or as useful . . . as this one, I swear to you."

"There's one other thing you can promise me, lass. Don't ever tell your husband where you got it from," he said, with a somewhat harshly-sounding laugh as he reached for the glass of rum, which he drained.

Louisa threw back her head and laughed as she rushed toward the kitchen door. She stopped and looked back at him while shaking her head slowly.

"I'm going to miss you all so much," she murmured.

"We'll miss you more. This place'll be dead without you. It was last time you left and it'll be so again. You light up every room you enter. Be off with you now, before your father comes after you!" he warned.

"One more thing . . . if you've to sign a paper today, try to mess it up so that the document's not legal, eh?" Louisa quipped, as she disappeared through the doorway.

She could hear his laughter still as she ran across the yard toward the homestead. She saw Mrs. McBryde coming from the verandah, so she changed direction and veered around the back of the house where she ran headlong into Charles Lyndhurst behind the building. She bounced backwards from him as he reached for her arms to prevent her from falling to the ground. She managed, with difficulty, to maintain her balance and she pulled away from him. Her right hand moved involuntarily to her pocket and the feel of the knife gave her back the courage that the sight of him had caused to slip from her momentarily.

"Miss Howard! I apologise. I didn't mean to startle you, but this is indeed fortunate. I've just come from the stables in the hope of seeking you out. I thought, perhaps, you'd be saying your farewells to your horses, seeing as no one in the homestead seemed to be able to locate you," Charles Lyndhurst explained.

"I'm not late yet!" Louisa stated, with a defiant challenge in her eyes.

"No, no, of course not, and what does time matter at this late stage in the proceedings? It's just that I wished to . . . umm . . . assure you, or to ascertain for myself that . . ." Charles murmured; then, he stopped, shrugged his shoulders and looked at her pleadingly.

"What is it, Mr. Lyndhurst? You need not beat around the bush with me. Say what you need to say and be done with it!"

"You're nothing, if not frank, are you? I need to know you're doing this of your own free will. You do not know me at all, nor I you. We've met once only, so tell me honestly. Are you being forced into this marriage? Have you been coerced in any way?" he asked directly, intently studying her face for telltale signs to interpret.

Louisa studied him candidly for a moment before replying to his questioning. The temptation to call an end to this fiasco right now was overwhelming, but finally, shaking her head slowly, she replied.

"I don't wish to marry anyone. I don't know you. I don't like what I've seen of you thus far and that is how it will continue, in all probability. But, I do intend to carry through with my promise, and that's an end to the matter. Excuse me, for I must go now," she said.

Louisa stammered the last of her words to him; then, pushing by him, she raced around the corner of the home, jumped the one step onto the verandah and flew into her bedroom where, despite the heat of the day, she slammed the door, locked it and drew the drapes.

She flopped onto the bed and she found that she was trembling. One more minute with him and she knew she would have accepted gratefully the option that he was giving to her, albeit subtly. It was in that moment Louisa realised that possibly he wanted the marriage even less than she did. How was it possible for any couple to live happily-ever-after – together for a lifetime – after a beginning such as this, she pondered.

Finally, the chiming of the clock in the hallway reminded Louisa that she was late already for her own wedding. She was not even dressed for the occasion. Instantly, her aunt bustled into the room then and took charge of the situation. She was carrying her mother's jewellery case.

"Your Papa asked me to give this to you. There are some exquisite pieces in here, and very expensive. They're all for you, Louisa."

"A salve to his conscience, no doubt," Louisa muttered.

Sophie Collins gave a deep sigh and remained silent, thereby electing to sidestep the call-to-arms from her niece. She could read Louisa's moods and knew, from bitter experience, when the moment for complete silence had arrived. That moment had been reached now.

She assisted Louisa to dress while choosing Mary Howard's small white pearls to adorn Louisa's neck. White satin shoes were substituted for her old walking boots. Sophie insisted that Louisa leave the room with her and outside, George Howard was waiting. His eyes surveyed her and a look of approval followed his look of appraisal, which was tinged with pride and love. He held out his arm to his daughter who placed her hand there. She did not speak to him.

"You are beautiful, Louisa. I am so proud of you," George murmured, not attempting to hide the emotion in his voice.

"My hangman awaits. Escort me there, if you please, Papa."

With her head held high and her demeanour that of a queen heading for the gallows, regal and proud to the end, she walked beside him.

Louisa knew a moment of satisfaction as she felt her father stiffen at her words and he pursed his lips noticeably, but remained silent. Together, they walked to the side verandah where the Reverend Marshall was waiting. In front of him, Charles Lyndhurst stood, with Captain Bill Bartlett beside him. Mrs. McBryde was dressed in a gown of dark blue silk and she looked elegant, Louisa thought. It was only then that she realised Colleen McBryde was her matron-of-honour, so little attention had she paid to the details of this pantomime.

So it was, then, that Louisa Mary Howard was given in marriage to Charles Frederick Lyndhurst, in the month of November, 1867, with the majestic Murray River forming a backdrop for the wedding ceremony.

An intimate wedding breakfast followed, after which Louisa withdrew to her bedroom to change her gown. For her river cruise to Echuca, she chose the oldest and most faded muslin gown that she could find in her wardrobe while leaving all of her other gowns and garments to be packed into trunks by other members of the household. None of these matters were of interest to her. It was then that she sneaked to the kitchen once again to find Brydie in residence in her favourite domain. Brydie, who had changed back into her serviceable grey outfit, turned to look at her as she entered.

"You're wearing that outfit, I assume?" she queried, with eyebrows raised.

"I am!" Louisa stated, instantly awaiting a challenge.

Colleen McBryde laughed and returned her attention to the contents of the pot that she had been stirring on the range when Louisa entered.

"Under the circumstances, I'd do the same. I expected no less of you."

Louisa relaxed and laughed with her. Then, her lip trembled and she fought to control the tears that were threatening to overwhelm her. Colleen dropped the ladle and reached for her while wrapping her tightly in her arms.

"You've not so much as shed a tear for the loss of your Mama, have you?"

Louisa, with her head buried on Brydie's shoulder, shook her head furiously. Brydie moved her away from her body and held her there while looking directly into her face.

"Then, you won't do so this day. Do not give them the satisfaction! But, one day soon, when you're all alone, do it, for until you do, the healing process cannot begin. Promise me now!"

Louisa nodded her head furiously before she buried it back on Brydie's shoulder.

"Write to me. Tell me all about everyone, especially Papa, Hilton and Cadence, as well as all those other matters regarding the property," Louisa pleaded.

"I shall do so. I swear to you, Louisa. Now, go! Hold your head high . . . as high as your Mama would do . . . and don't look back. *Don't look back ever!*"

Louisa ran from the kitchen and across the yard to the homestead. She located her bonnet, her silk reticule that had been a gift from Brydie, her gloves and cloak. As hot as the weather was, she needed to carry the cloak, for a change could occur at any moment. Rain clouds appeared on the horizon during the ceremony, she observed. She walked to the verandah and shook hands with the Reverend Marshall. She gave her aunt a quick hug, with an even quicker one for her father while murmuring forcefully in his ear as she did so.

"Four weeks! That's all you've got. Then, *I will* be back! You mark my words, Papa!"

Louisa pulled from him; then by contrast, she bestowed a generous embrace upon her uncle, who did all in his power to hide a smile. Ignoring Charles Lyndhurst, she left the verandah and headed in the direction of the stone steps that led to the pathway and the pontoon where the *Charmaine* was waiting. It was here that Betsy, the parlourmaid, caught up with her. She handed a small hand-crocheted doily to Louisa and with a shy smile on her face.

"I made it myself . . . just for you," she whispered shyly.

Louisa squeezed her arm and smiled at her. She shared a bitter secret with Betsy, although she was uncertain how much Betsy had witnessed, or what she suspected had happened in a certain event ten months earlier. Louisa knew the truth and she had suffered many a sleepless night in remorse over the incident. When she reached Echuca, she would slip away and visit Mrs. Marshall at the rectory while hoping to glean some further information on the man-in-question.

Betsy left her as Charles approached. He took Louisa's arm firmly. He studied her appearance in detail, quickly taking in the faded gown and the old walking boots that she was wearing. He shook his head in mock despair.

"Oh! Dear me, Louisa, I can see a few battles-of-will looming," he murmured, with a slight chuckle.

Mindful of Mrs. McBryde's advice, she tossed her head to one side away from him, held herself erect and put her chin in the air. She attempted to remove her arm from his grasp but, unless she used her knife, there did not appear to be any way of doing so. The knife was her secret weapon for a later time.

Without a backward glance, Louisa stepped aboard the paddle-steamer bound for Echuca. The paddlewheels at the sides began to churn the water as the steam engine sprang to life. Her trunks were carried on board. She caught sight of Ben who gave her a slight smile before scurrying off to attend to his chores.

Captain Bill was at the wheel with his Sunday finest discarded and his riverboat garments, complete with cap, restored to their usual place on his person.

Louisa did not turn; she did not wave; she did not look back and, most certainly, she did not cry. Louisa Mary Lyndhurst left her family home of seventeen years, without a backward glance, but with a heart that was as heavy as any ship's anchor could be. When she would see her home again, she knew not. To what she was going, she knew not, and she cared even less.

The *Charmaine* chugged around the bend in the river and, slowly, the paddle steamer headed in the direction of the town of Echuca, the rail-head where the bales of wool that floated down the river on barges towed by the river steamers, were loaded onto trains bound for Melbourne.

Presumably, as with a bale of wool, she would be loaded onto a train, also, bound for Melbourne. As though to mirror her mood, the clouds that had been threatening all morning, brought a quick shower of rain.

Chapter Seven

– *Victorian Victorians* –

Louisa

S he remained on deck, with her gloved hands holding her bonnet in place and the wind playing havoc with her cloak, which was whipping about her body as she stood by the rail. Finally, when the rain did not ease, Charles came and reached for her arm as he drew her into the shelter of the cabin where Bill Bartlett stood at the wheel.

"The next bend in the river is mine, Captain Bill," Louisa stated matter-of-factly.

He turned in her direction. Then, she saw Bill cast a glance at her new husband who was standing behind her. Sadly, the captain shook his head.

"No, lassy, not this time, I'm afraid," he muttered, while deliberately not looking directly at her.

"Why not?" she demanded. "This has always been where I take the wheel. For as long as I can remember, this has been my stretch of the river. You know that! You started it!"

Bill Bartlett pursed his lips and remained silent and unmoved – or, so it appeared to Louisa – as he peered directly ahead. Then, he turned to her, with a wink and a grin.

"Unwritten code of the river, Lou. Married ladies can't take the wheel. It's a bad omen. The men would mutiny. I'm dreadfully sorry about that."

Louisa moved swiftly across the wheel-house and she thumped Bill with some force on his right arm. He grinned at her again and this infuriated her even more. With hat in hand, Charles Lyndhurst was leaning back against a large crate while silently observing them, although he appeared unmoved by the playful exchange between these two friends.

"You just invented that rule. I know you did and you can't fool me. I shall write and tell Brydie, if you don't let me do so!" she threatened.

"And in my defence, I'll have to reveal that I wasn't the one who upset her kitchen cabinet. I took the blame for you. You do realise that and my ears are still ringing. And now, this is the thanks I get for my pains."

Charles moved to her, gently reaching for her arm. Louisa stiffened instantly at his touch, a reaction that did not pass unnoticed by either man.

"The rain has ceased. Shall we go out on deck?" he asked softly.

Although it was phrased as a question, it was a directive that would brook no argument, unless she wished to bring matters between them to a head so soon and so publicly at this time and this place. Once again, she lifted her chin, stood erect and strode out while casting Bill Bartlett a scathing look as she departed.

"I'll not forget this, Captain Bill. I've a long, long memory."

Bill Bartlett groaned in mock despair. Then, he winked at her again.

Outside on deck, Louisa resumed her lonely vigil by the rail while watching the bird-life in the trees on the riverbank as the *Charmaine* continued her slow journey. To her chagrin, Charles took up his position beside her. He leaned his back against the rail and surveyed her.

"Do you suppose it's possible to at least be civil to each other? After all, we've a long way to go from here," he queried.

Louisa looked at him with disdain. There appeared to be a slight twitch at the corner of his mouth and his eyes could not hide his amusement that was so obviously at her expense. His right hand came up and brushed his windswept dark brown hair back from his forehead.

"Are you laughing at me?" she inquired coldly, but quietly.

"I confess to some amusement, yes."

"Why?" she inquired even more coldly and quietly.

"For all the world, I never expected to see you, of all people, wearing the mantle of martyrdom. It does not sit well on your shoulders."

Louisa looked at Charles with as much disdain as she could muster. Quickly, she turned her face from him while attempting to hide the giggle that was beginning to erupt within her body. She suspected that this was caused more by her nervousness at her uncertain future and the events of the morning, rather than at his comment. Try as she might, it would not be suppressed. Despite herself, she began to laugh. He laughed with her and the tension between them eased a little.

"May I ask a question?" she queried.

"You may ask anything you like. I can't guarantee you'll like the answer, though. But, ask away!"

"Where are you taking me?" she asked.

"Has no one told you anything?" he asked, in genuine surprise.

Louisa shook her head. He frowned markedly. Then, he turned and placed both his arms on the rail while leaning on it. She glanced down at his face, with a questioning look on her own.

"We're spending tonight in Echuca, at an establishment that tries to masquerade as a first-class hotel. I am very sorry, but at this late stage, that's all that could be arranged. Tomorrow, we go by train to Bendigo and spend the night at another hotel, although a much more comfortable one. Then, on the following day, I'll take you to Stanton, my father's property just a few miles outside of Bendigo and there, I shall introduce you to my mother. Then, we'll spend another night at the same hotel in Bendigo before travelling on to Lyndhurst Park, the family home in Melbourne. Is that to your liking?"

Louisa looked at him and shrugged her shoulders in response, so he continued with his explanation.

"We must be in Melbourne by the time Prince Alfred and his entourage arrive. We've many royal functions to attend, I'm afraid. While these may be to your liking, they're not to mine, but they're compulsory, nevertheless, if one wishes to participate in that fair city's social scene."

"And, you do?" she asked.

"It's necessary," he replied simply.

"Will your father be at Stanton?"

"No, he's in Adelaide, no doubt ingratiating himself with Prince Alfred and his party at present, as I understand it. I wouldn't take you there if he were at home. I wouldn't subject you *to that* . . . not at this stage anyway. Perhaps later, it may be unavoidable."

"He's not a nice man," she commented quietly.

Charles gave a harsh laugh and nodded in approval at her comment.

"That, I'm afraid, is the greatest understatement I've ever heard and you'll get no argument from me on that score, so you're a good judge of character," he stated; then, he added softly. "Do you think, perhaps, we could move beyond civility and try to be friends? After all, we've become inextricably linked this day and it could be we're together for quite some time. Had you thought of that?"

Louisa shook her head. She turned her body while leaning back against the rail. He stood erect beside her and appeared to be awaiting an answer. Finally, Charles was the one to break the silence between them. It was a question that she was not expecting.

"Tell me why you agreed to this farce, as so obviously, it's not to your liking?"

"That's not important now. I suppose we can try to be friends, although I don't see how that can be so, as we're both so different. I must admit I am at a loss to understand your motives, also. But, if it becomes too awful, I could drown myself in the Yarra River," she murmured quietly, almost to herself.

Louisa felt him stiffen. For a moment, she had the distinct impression that he was going to grab her shoulders and shake her. Instead, he controlled himself – although not without some difficulty – and when he spoke, it was through clenched teeth. Had they not been in full view of Captain Bartlett, she suspected that he may have given into the temptation.

"Don't, I beg of you, even jest about something as serious as that. Your father has placed you in my care and that's a responsibility I take very seriously indeed. I shall not allow any harm to come to you, self-inflicted or otherwise. Do you understand me?"

Louisa lifted her chin in the air and flicked her head away; then, she turned back to watch the bank again. He gave another short and rather harsh laugh.

"Well, that was the shortest friendship in history, I expect," he stated.

There was little conversation between them after that. Charles Lyndhurst moved to the wheelhouse and conversed with Bill Bartlett for most of the remainder of the journey, only rejoining Louisa but five minutes before the paddle steamer drew alongside the wharf in Echuca. She had remained by the rail, lost in thought. She had made this journey so many times in her life that she could not remember how often she had stayed at the main hotel in the town. Somehow, she must slip away and visit the Marshalls' home, as well as her mother's grave, before the train departed tomorrow.

Louisa was accustomed to rising around dawn, so she was determined to be out of the hotel long before breakfast on the following morning. Charles Lyndhurst could say whatever he wished. She would not be boarding that train until she had completed what she felt she needed to accomplish for her own peace of mind. On that issue, she would not be deterred, for she knew not how long it would be before she could return here to Echuca, or to her home. But, return she would do, as soon as an escape route could be found. Her deadline of four weeks would be a definite schedule for her unless her father visited her before that time elapsed.

They walked along the dusty roadway. It was a short distance to the two-storey timber structure that was the hotel, which Louisa entered slightly ahead of Charles who was issuing instructions regarding her trunks. As she came through the front door, the lady standing by the desk turned and glanced at her; then, as recognition dawned, her face spread into a wide grin. As Charles crossed the threshold, Mrs. Spencer came forward to greet Louisa.

"Louisa! Oh! Luvie! It's been so long. How's your Papa? Is he with you? It must be over a year since we saw you both here."

"No, Papa is not with me and he's not at all well, Mrs. Spencer, I'm afraid," she replied, while shaking her head sadly.

Mrs. Spencer glanced behind Louisa to Charles and she nodded to him in acknowledgment before she returned her attention to Louisa.

"What brings you to Echuca, child? I was not expecting you and we're completely full . . . right up to the rafters. You weren't seeking accommodation?"

Charles placed his hand on Louisa's arm, thereby taking possession of his newly-acquired property for all to witness and drawing her towards him.

"Mrs. Lyndhurst is with me," he declared quietly.

Mrs. Spencer's wide eyes opened wider and her mouth dropped open as she looked to Louisa for confirmation. Louisa bit her lip and averted her gaze.

"Oh! I see," Mrs. Spencer responded before, almost inaudibly, she murmured. "So, the rumours were true, then."

The older lady flicked her head in the air and began to turn away as Charles manoeuvred Louisa towards the steps leading to the upstairs rooms. Suddenly, Mrs. Spencer spun around again and she directed her attention toward Louisa, with a look of shock and horror on her face.

"Holy Mother of God!" Mrs. Spencer exclaimed. "You're in the room allocated to Mr. Lyndhurst last night! I'm so sorry, Luvie. I'm ever so sorry. I didn't realise. It's not possible to change at this late stage."

The woman stood still, staring up at Louisa who had stopped on the second step with Charles Lyndhurst beside her, as he looked on with interest and an expression of puzzlement on his face. He listened to the exchange between the two women. Louisa bit her lip again. She shook her head slowly and raised her shoulders almost imperceptibly.

"It's of no consequence, Mrs. Spencer. Do not trouble yourself at all, for it'll be alright," Louisa stated.

Louisa wrenched her arm from Charles' grasp and walked quickly up the steps to the floor above. She headed in the direction of the main room that she knew was positioned in the front of the hotel overlooking the Murray River and with a generous view to the surrounding area. That particular room was the best that this establishment could provide, she knew, because her father booked it always, whenever he came through Echuca on his way south, whether that was to Melbourne or simply to stay in Bendigo with friends. She waited by the door as Charles came beside her and fumbled in his pocket while seeking the key.

"What, may I ask, was all that about?" he queried.

"'Tis no matter. It's not important."

He opened the door. Louisa gasped audibly as she surveyed the room, which had been painted since her last visit. The walls were white and there were new heavy brocade drapes on the french doors leading to the verandah. These were burgundy in colour, and the bed was new, too, she noted as she stood transfixed on the threshold. The old timber-framed bed, covered by many coats of heavy varnish, had vanished. In its place stood a new brass bed with its covers matching the drapes.

The room did appear, at first glance, to be different, but the rugs on the floor were the same. The rug, onto which her mother had collapsed as she stepped from the bed in the early hours of that dreadful morning, was on the floor and staring back at her now. Try as she might, Louisa could not bring herself to enter. Her breathing became laboured and there was a restriction around her chest, thereby preventing her lungs from expanding. She closed her eyes momentarily while concentrating on her breathing.

"I won't do anything to hurt you," the male voice beside her spoke very softly before, jokingly, he explained further. "You can enter of your own free will; or, I can carry you across, if that is your preference."

Louisa glanced up at him with a look of horror and loathing on her face. He laughed at her. Then, she brushed by him, ran across the room, opened the doors to the verandah, crossed it and grasped the railing in both hands. The view was obscured by the mist before her eyes. She gasped for breath and allowed her head to fall down onto her chest. How long she stood there, she did not know; but, when she found her breathing returning to normal and the mist clearing somewhat, she turned to find him standing in the doorway to the verandah as he studied her intently.

There was a tap at the main door to the room and, in response to Charles' command, a man entered, followed by another who was carrying the small trunk that Aunt Sophie had packed for her, *especially for your wedding night* she had stated pointedly. Charles spoke with the first man as the second one placed her trunk by the bed. Both men left hurriedly. She was standing by the french doors as he turned back to look at her, with a slight frown on his forehead.

"Come. It's time to dress for dinner. Don't, I beg of you, seek to embarrass me by wearing something as outlandish as that dairy-maid's outfit you have on at present. I'll leave you alone now and return for you in an hour. It seems somewhat incredible that you do not have your own personal maid. However, Joseph has vowed to rectify the matter as soon as we reach Bendigo, for he's afraid he'll be required to tend to your requirements. It's put the fear of the devil into him, I'll tell you," he stated with a laugh.

He removed his gold watch from the fob pocket of his vest and glanced at it, before snapping it closed quickly. He studied her again, thoughtfully choosing his words.

"This situation is somewhat uncomfortable for both of us, Louisa. So, let us try to be as pleasant as possible to each other. Perhaps, we can come to some arrangement that is mutually accept-able when we reach Melbourne. Will you settle for that?"

Louisa bit her lip again; then, she nodded slowly. He gave a slight nod of approval in acknowledgment before spinning on his heel. He left the room while closing the door gently.

Relief swept through her as she found herself alone finally and she collapsed onto the winged armchair that had been re-covered in a burgundy fabric since her last visit. From there, she stared with unseeing eyes at the new bed.

In her mind, the slats of the bed-end of the old bed were still in place and on that bed was the body of her mother where George Howard had placed her. The doctor was bending over Mary on one side while her father stood clutching her mother's hand on the other side of the bed. It was then that the doctor had pronounced her death. He stated that even had he been called sooner, there would have been little that he could have done, as he felt Mary Howard had been dead by the time her body hit the rug on the floor. This was what he confided to her father as Louisa sat numb with shock and disbelief in this same armchair, which had been deep blue in colour at the time.

This fact she remembered very clearly, too, but even after all this time had elapsed and she found herself in this less than tenable situation, she could not cry at all. Her life had ceased that day. She doubted that it would ever start again. She closed her eyes and tried in vain to remove the memory and, when this failed, she brought memories of Hilton to the surface of her mind, concentrating deeply on her beloved horse.

It was a strong male hand upon her shoulder that woke her some time later. A soft voice was whispering in her ear.

"Louisa! Wake up now."

She peered through glazed eyes into Charles Lyndhurst's grey eyes. He dropped to one knee beside her and took her hands in his large hands that dwarfed her own. She opened her mouth, but she had drifted into a very deep sleep and words would not come to her lips. After what appeared to be an eternity but which, in reality, was probably no more than a few seconds, she came to the realisation of her surroundings.

"Did you forget something?" she queried innocently.

He smiled at her before gently raising her to a standing position. Charles released one of her hands and pointed to her trunk while taking her with him in its direction and still holding her hand. It was in this moment that Louisa realised he had changed his clothing.

"Shall we attack it together?" he queried.

"Oh! Have you returned to collect me? I don't know what came over me," Louisa stammered – more to herself than to him – then, she issued a warning. "If you like. But, I warn you, the gowns Aunt Sophie purchased for me in Melbourne, I'd not put on a donkey!"

He threw back his head and laughed. He gave her a look of appreciation before bending down to unlock the trunk. He lifted the lid and began to extract several silk gowns, which he threw onto the bed. After that, he rummaged deeper into the container. He pulled out a heavy nightgown in a dark check design, with pink bows and pink roses attached. The long sleeves of this garment buttoned at the wrist and high at the neck. He opened his mouth and stared at the garment in some astonishment.

"Aunt Sophie?" he queried, with one eyebrow raised.

Louisa smiled at him, despite herself and her depressed mood, and she nodded furiously. He shook his head again. He was staring in wonder at the garment.

"This was meant for your wedding night and in the heat of summer . . . amazing! I take your point; I *do* take your point. As for the gowns, that was no exaggeration either. You'll have a new wardrobe the moment we reach Melbourne. Are the ones in the other larger trunks any better? I'll have them brought up for you in an instant."

Louisa laughed then and shook her head. The other gowns were much older and had been purchased by her mother for her to wear at the school in Melbourne. She had been fifteen then and, although her body had not altered much since that time, the gowns were well worn. She moved to the bed and fingered the creations in disgust. Finally, she decided on the pale green silk; although not to her liking, it would suffice for the evening meal at this hotel.

"Perhaps, in this, I may not present as a maid heading for the milking shed," she questioned, and holding the gown up for her inspection, rather than for his approval.

"Best of a bad lot, I agree. It'll do fine. Do you require my assistance?"

"*No!*" she shouted in horror.

Charles laughed again as he headed in the direction of the door. He turned and surveyed her, with a smile on his face.

"Ten minutes . . . that's it! Then, I'll be back, ready or not, madam."

"I'll be ready," she promised in a definite tone as the door closed behind him.

Dinner in the busy hotel dining room, which was bustling with patrons and activity, was a silent affair for Louisa and Charles. He poured wine into her glass, which she ignored totally. Apart from three gentlemen, immaculately attired, seated at an adjacent table, no one appeared to take any notice of the newly-wed couple.

"You've not touched your wine? Would you prefer something else?"

"No, water is all I require, thank you," she replied, as she placed a food-laden fork into her open mouth.

He drank wine from his glass and glanced casually around the room. One of the gentlemen nearby nodded to him and, with an almost imperceptible movement, Charles returned the greeting before turning his attention back to Louisa. Without knowing how she knew, she realised that no one and nothing in that room had escaped his scrutiny in the brief moment when his eyes had swept the dining room.

"Why?" he asked, in a bored tone.

"Why I don't drink wine? I took a pledge, you see; on my confirmation day, I vowed not to touch alcohol until I reached my majority and, as that is four years away, I've a time to wait."

"And, you take that seriously?" he queried, with amusement appearing to replace his boredom momentarily.

Louisa's two green eyes opened wide as she studied him, never for a moment considering that he may have been teasing her.

"Of course! It was a pledge before God, in church. Father Frank, he's . . ."

"I'm well aware of who *he is*," he stated, in disgust as he grimaced before adding. "Pray continue."

"Oh! Well, that's why, anyway," she concluded with a shrug.

"I was referring to your religion . . . Catholicism, is it not?"

"My faith is my life. It's who I am. Don't try to take that away from me," she stated, with a definite challenge in her voice.

He grimaced slightly and continued to eat his meal in silence. Louisa remained still while watching him intently across the small table before speaking again.

"Apart from the weather, we've little subject matter that could be considered common ground," she commented.

He raised his glass to his lips and smiled at her before drinking the liquid. As she returned her attention to her meal, he replaced the glass on the table, picked up a knife, reached across and tapped her on the wrist with it.

"What was that for?" she demanded.

"For attempting to bait me. You're determined we shan't be friends. I'm equally determined we shall. So, let that be an end to the matter. Horses! We can discuss horses, although I much prefer to watch them running around a race track. Tell me how you came by your precious Hilton?"

Louisa spent the next twenty minutes lost in a one-sided conversation as she related to him the story of Cadence and her mother's reluctance when she discovered her father's intention with regard to her gentle mare. She described the prize stallion that had arrived and her mother's response when she saw him, for he was a large animal. Mary Howard was horrified, as she was very protective of her beautiful and docile Cadence. Then, Louisa mentioned Hilton's birth, on the night when she was summoned from her bed to the stables to assist her father in that duty, because her mother had been taken ill that evening.

Hilton's arrival into her waiting arms was alluded to but briefly while his first faltering steps were given a more detailed description. This was followed by an explanation about the many hours that she had devoted to training him to respond to her every command.

"Louisa, that's a very interesting tale, I'll admit, but apart from this evening, I'd ask you not to relate it at any future dinner party in polite circles. Is that agreed? Good, now my next question is this . . . did your training of Hilton include killing me on sight?"

Louisa began to giggle. Her face lit up as her eyes danced and sparkled. The giggle rolled from deep in the region of her stomach; then, it became a gurgle, before bursting forth from her lips as an infectious laugh. Charles began to laugh with her and many eyes were turned in their direction as her melodious laughter permeated the busy hotel dining room.

"I promise you if I'd known your intent with regard to me, then most assuredly, I'd have spent all night preparing him for that particular morning and its outcome may have been different. As it was, we happened upon you by accident."

Charles poured more wine into his glass. He leaned back in the chair to savour the drink and he surveyed her with a calculating look on his face, but one that was tinged with amusement. Louisa continued to devour the evening meal while attempting to ignore his continued scrutiny upon her. Eventually, with dinner at an end, Charles escorted her upstairs to the bedroom.

"I'll leave you now," he stated, as he deposited her in the bedroom before he issued his stern instructions to her. "Please, don't take it into your head to leave here and go for a midnight stroll, Louisa. I have no interest in scouring Echuca for you in the dead of night. But, rest assured, I'll locate you wherever you happen to be. Do I make myself clear?"

Louisa eyed him in disgust and she remained silent. He stood in the doorway as he awaited her response to his directive.

"I'll have your word on it now, madam," he demanded.

Louisa continued to eye him in disgust – and in silence – but, with the deliberate and defiant tilt of her chin, she was giving more cause for concern than she realised. He took a step back into the room. He left the door open and the sound of voices coming from the hallway drifted into the room.

"I'll not move from this room tonight," she stated finally, and rather quickly, but with definite defiance sounding in her voice.

"See that you don't!" Charles ordered, before walking through the open door and closing it firmly behind him.

Louisa rummaged through the trunk and she found another old nightgown. The heavy and hideous check one was tossed unceremoniously onto the floor. The white lace on her old night-gown was somewhat tattered while the white cotton beneath it was definitely tending to a cream colour now, but it was a comfortable, if well-worn, garment. Comfort, she needed this night. She emptied the contents of her reticule onto the bed as she located the precious pen-knife. This item, she placed safely beneath her pillow for easy retrieval should it be required. Charles had stated that he would not hurt her, but Aunt Sophie's warning was ringing in her ears loudly and clearly.

As for the new gowns and other items of clothing that were scattered across the bed, they met the same fate as the other night-gown. With the floor strewn with garments and female apparel, Louisa moved behind the screen in the far corner of the room to the wash-stand where a jug of clean water stood waiting, being positioned inside the porcelain bowl. A discreet commode chair, cleverly disguised as an ornate chest of drawers, was positioned out-of-view of any other occupants of the room behind the screen and beside the wash-stand. Louisa poured water from the jug into the waiting bowl and commenced her toiletries as she prepared for bed.

Ablutions completed, she threw the pale green silk gown onto the floor with the rest of her apparel, with her shift, pantalets and petticoat meeting the same fate. Beside the metal trunk, from which several other garments were emerging at various angles, she tossed her shoes and stockings while the garters she hung on the corner post of the bed.

Remembering then that she would be required, in all probability, to wear that silk gown, in preference to her old muslin one, on the train journey to Bendigo – her wardrobe being somewhat limited at present – she decided to hang the garment in the only wardrobe. This ornate piece of furniture matched the imitation chest of drawers behind the screen, as well as the chest of drawers by the bed. It was stamped inside, with indelible ink in several places, with the words so often seen on furniture: *made by European labour only*.

Suddenly, as she was reaching inside to hang her gown there, she was stopped in her tracks by the sight of male attire hanging on the racks therein. She had assumed that this room was her own, for her use alone. Charles Lyndhurst's clothes were hanging in her wardrobe.

In slight confusion, she studied the male garments for some moments. Then, she concluded that Charles must have come into the room and changed for dinner while she was sleeping in the winged armchair. When that realisation came upon her, she gasped in horror. She remembered Mrs. Spencer's remarks earlier about this being Mr. Lyndhurst's room and her horror increased markedly. She recalled Aunt Sophie's words again. Slowly, she turned and surveyed the room. There was one bed only.

Louisa moved to the armchair and sat there motionless while staring at the bed intently. She realised her own parents had shared the same bed for all of her life and this was no different when they stayed at this hotel while Louisa had occupied a small room at the end of the corridor always. However, this was a different matter entirely. What was to be done, she wondered.

She glanced around the room. The only other furniture, other than the lamp table by the bedside, was the writing bureau with a chair in front of it. Her mind made up, she jumped up and ran to the chair, which she placed in front of the door. After that, she manoeuvred it into a position whereby its top section was tucked neatly beneath the door handle. Anyone attempting to open it would be prevented from doing so, temporarily at least, and even so, there would be a dreadful racket as it collapsed. She would be awake by then and out of the room through the verandah doors, if necessary. Perhaps, she was mistaken, but regardless, she would take this precaution.

Her only other recourse was to leave and perhaps call on the Marshall family. She knew that the Reverend Marshall intended spending the night at her home with her father before returning to his family on the morrow. She would be welcome there, although with six sons ranging in age from two years to eighteen years, as James was, there would not be any beds available in that home, she supposed. No, there was nothing else to be done. She would retire, with the knife at the ready, and with one eye definitely open. Under no circumstances would she be sharing a bed with Charles Lyndhurst, or anyone else, this night or any other night.

Having slept soundly on the armchair for an hour during the late afternoon and with the sudden realisation that had come upon her in recent moments, Louisa found it difficult to settle in the bed, despite it being a very comfortable piece of furniture. There was continuous, raucous laughter emanating from the public bar beneath her bedroom and this was not conducive to sleep. She had left the drapes on the verandah doors open to allow the moonlight to flood the room so that, in the morning, she would be able to watch the first rays of the morning sun. However, this was before she discovered that she would not be alone this night. Still, the moonlight would enable her to see any intruder more clearly.

She extinguished the lamp and attempted sleep once more. Finally, in the early hours of the morning, she relaxed a little as there was no sign of Charles Lyndhurst; so, perhaps, she had been worrying over nothing and he was safely tucked up in his own bed in another section of the hotel. Eventually, sleep overcame her.

Chapter Eight

— *Victorian Victorians* —

Louisa

L ouisa had not heard a sound. She had been in a very deep sleep. But now, as the first rays of dawn were creeping into the room, it was the movement of the bed that startled her and had her in an upright sitting position before her eyes had opened. There was a body creeping into the bed beside her. It was a male body. It was naked. She was reminded suddenly and forcefully of the many glimpses that she had had recently of Captain Bill's naked form and she was horrified.

"Who are you and what do you think you're doing?" she demanded in a loud, clear voice that belied her trembling body.

"Hush, Louisa, who the hell do you think it is? Go to sleep."

"I was asleep. You go to your own bed," she demanded more forcefully as her courage returned and her feet landed on the rug on the other side the bed.

"This is my bed!"

"Where's mine then?" she demanded.

"This is it. Take it, or leave it. If you don't like this arrangement, you can find yourself somewhere else to sleep, although at this hour, I don't like your chances. How many times have I got to say it? I'm not going to hurt you in any way whatsoever. Get back into bed and go to sleep."

Louisa remained rigid, with her gaze fixed on the shape, which had slid beneath the bedcovers and was snuggling into a more comfortable position in the centre of the bed while appearing to have forgotten her existence completely.

"What about Bendigo and Melbourne? Do I have my own room there?" she demanded, while standing by the bed and looking down at him.

"Yes," he mumbled, before settling comfortably on the pillow and appearing to be fighting exasperation as he added. "You can have whatever you want. Is that it?"

Louisa's nostrils were twitching as an aroma filled the room. The public bar was quiet now. She did not know how long she had slept, but it could not have been many hours, she determined.

"I can smell whisky! Have you been drinking?"

"Excessively," came the curt reply from beneath the covers.

"This whole room reeks," she muttered, in a firm, accusing tone.

"It's doing more than that. It's spinning around and around. You're framed in moonlight, but you keep moving in a clockwise direction."

"I've not moved a muscle."

"Then, that's not a good omen, so I'm not lifting my head from this pillow. I'm not speaking to you, or touching you; nor am I going to argue with you. You can have half of this bed, or you can sleep on that armchair. They're the choices. Make your selection, but do it in silence. Your chances of surviving this night depend on your absolute and total silence from this moment. So, I would advise you to err on the side of caution. Goodnight."

With those words, he pulled the second pillow more closely to his body and his breathing changed distinctly. Louisa stood barefoot, in her old, white, cotton nightgown with the slightly tattered lace, beside the bed. Thoughtfully, she considered all of her present options. At this moment, there did not seem to be many, she concluded. It was then she remembered the knife beneath her pillow that Charles had tucked now against his chest, presumably in the vain hope of preventing the room from spinning, which indeed it was not doing, from her perspective at least. Come what may, she had to retrieve her knife. She may need it later.

Louisa was loath to touch the bed with her new husband ensconced therein, but her weapon needed to be on her person. Gingerly, she leaned a little toward the pillow and slipped her right hand beneath it. His breathing had changed again. She was uncertain if this meant he had slipped into a deeper sleep, but she hoped that this was the case. She hoped most sincerely that it was so.

There was nothing beneath the pillow. Slowly, she moved her hand back and forth. However, she could not locate her precious object. With utmost caution, she lifted one knee and placed it gently onto the side of the bed. She rummaged around, all the while moving closer to his chest with every inch that her fingers covered. Carefully, she began to ease her searching fingers a little lower in the bed while seeking her elusive prize, but to no avail.

Suddenly, without warning, his hand clasped around her wrist in an iron-like grip. Startled, she gasped audibly while struggling to swallow a scream as she moved her knee quickly from the bed.

"What part of my anatomy are you seeking? Tell me and I'll gladly place your hand upon it. Anything for peace and quiet! What do you want, *madam*?"

Charles' eyes were staring up into her face, with his head remaining attached firmly to the pillow. She bit her lip and struggled to free her arm. This was a hopeless endeavour.

"What?" he demanded again.

"My . . . my pillow," she stammered. "I want my pillow. I'm going to sleep on the armchair."

"You're a hopeless liar!" Charles hissed at her.

He flung the pillow in the direction of her body. Louisa caught it and ran to the armchair, instantly flinging herself into it. She did not dare to move and she barely allowed herself to breathe. Finally, she heard him snoring. By now, daylight was beginning to pierce the room and she could see more clearly. She was not inclined to try to reach for her knife. If he was snoring, he was in a deep sleep, so she would not require it at the moment. Later, she would locate it – perhaps after breakfast.

With the first light, she became quite chilled while sitting barefoot in her nightgown in the armchair. Cat-like, she made her move on the bed again. Carefully, she lifted the blankets – an inch at a time – leaving Charles covered only by a sheet. Wrapping herself in a cocoon of blankets, she settled into the armchair and, with the pillow beneath her head, she dozed fitfully until she heard the telltale signs of the first stirrings of the busy hotel downstairs.

Coming to the realisation of her surroundings again, she determined it was time to be about her errands before Charles Lyndhurst awoke; for otherwise, he may try to prevent her. She tossed the blankets and pillow onto the floor. There was little space to walk, she noted, once her eyes adjusted to the daylight, because with blankets, a pillow, silk gowns, a check nightgown and sundry other pieces of apparel littering it, she had to pick her way through the jumble.

Despite his drunken state, Charles' various articles of clothing – by contrast – were folded neatly and spread on the chair at the door. The chair, which was the one that she removed from the bureau, had been returned to its position at the door, with its top section positioned beneath the door handle. It was a deliberate provocation, she knew, because he would have come through that door, as the french doors to the verandah were bolted on the inside. Not only was Louisa not amused by the sight – if that had been his intent – but also, she realised it infuriated her greatly.

She picked her way carefully to the screen while gathering her old muslin gown and other undergarments en route; then, she began her morning toiletries. She dressed quickly before sitting on the arm-chair to slip her feet into her silk stockings. With her old walking boots under her arm, she slipped from the room after dropping his clothes onto the floor for good measure and upending the chair in the middle of the room. Two can play that game, Mr. Lyndhurst, she thought to herself, as she closed the door silently behind her.

On the top step, Louisa stopped and sat down. Here, she placed her feet into her boots and laced them quickly before she skipped down the stairs. As she reached the open front door, Mrs. Spencer walked by her. She was carrying a large tray and heading in the direction of the dining room. Louisa gave a soft whistle and waved to her. She received a beaming smile in reply as she disappeared out onto the dusty street.

Hurrying by the wharf, she noticed the *Charmaine* secured at her mooring. Ben was on deck and she called to him. He dropped the bucket that he was carrying and he gave her a quick wave. Before he could call out, she had broken into a run while heading in the direction of the cemetery, which was deserted at this hour of the morning. She had decided that she would not disturb the Marshall family so early. The rectory was on the other side of the cemetery and she could see smoke pouring from the kitchen chimney, so someone was awake and moving about the house. However, it was far too early to be calling on the family. Her father would be horrified if he learned that she had done so. Echuca was a small, though bustling, township and somehow, she knew that he would hear of it, sooner or later.

Locating her mother's last resting-place was not difficult, because its whereabouts were etched in her memory. She sat down on the large sandstones that surrounded the grave and, as she removed her garters, stockings and boots, she related to her mother all that had occurred in the previous twelve months. It was then that she placed the boots, with stockings and garters atop, onto the grave and she continued her one-way conversation until she heard a sound behind her.

"Louisa! I thought that was you. I couldn't believe my eyes. I had to come to see for myself," James Marshall said, while stammering his words a little as he looked at her.

"James! Thank goodness you're here! I must talk to you on an important matter and I need to see your mother."

"Did you do it? Lou, did you go through with the marriage?" James demanded, while appearing to hold his breath as he awaited her answer.

Louisa looked at him for a moment; then, she nodded her head very slowly. He had a crestfallen look on his face and she thought, for one brief moment, that he would burst into tears. James was staring at the ground. Suddenly, he recovered himself and grabbed her by the arm. He was a rather handsome boy, in his own way, with his sandy coloured hair and deep blue eyes. He was not much taller than she was and she had known him for all of her life.

"I'm s'posed to be milking. Come and help me," he ordered.

"Alright, but tell me you're not mad at me. I had to do it."

"I'm very, very mad at you. You promised to marry me on your eighteenth birthday. You know that. You crossed your heart and promised. I don't know what I'm going to do now," he stated.

"I was nine and you were just ten! It was a long time ago and well, now, you'll go to England and become a clergyman, like your father . . . and you'll not be encumbered by a wife you can't afford to feed. So there! It's all for the best," Louisa concluded, somewhat breathlessly.

They had reached the back fence of the rectory and, together, they climbed through the old timber structure. There were two cows in the milking shed. Louisa smiled to herself as she took up her position on the stool beside one of the cows while recalling Charles' words when he called her muslin gown *a dairymaid's outfit*. Now, here she was proving his words to be correct. With the milking chores completed, they walked side-by-side toward the house and carrying a bucket apiece. It was then Louisa broached the subject that had been on her mind.

"I need another outfit. I need one more pair of breeches and another boy's shirt. Get them for me, James. It's important, as I may not have another chance to see you and you're my only source of supply."

"No, not a chance. Mama's still demanding to know what happened to the others. They were Billy's and she knows every item of clothing we own. They were meant to be handed down to Jack. It's impossible. She'll kill me. She knows I'm responsible for their disappearance and I can't do it, Lou. Just can't, *so don't ask!*"

Louisa looked at him in disgust. He walked beside her and they mounted the steps to the kitchen, at the rear of the main house while depositing the milk buckets inside the separate building. From there, they went to the main house where Mrs. Marshall was busy organising her sons. At the sight of Louisa, she rushed forward and embraced her warmly.

"Oh! Sweet child, you're a sight for sore eyes. I'm so happy to see you. How are you?"

Louisa felt the warm, loving arms around her and she missed her mother more in that moment than she had done previously. Her lip trembled, but no tears were shed. Mrs. Marshall shepherded her into the dining room where all the boys were seated around the table. They were arguing and teasing one another. They stopped momentarily to greet Louisa warmly.

"Look who's joining us for breakfast," Mrs. Marshall stated, without issuing an invitation to Louisa.

An enormous breakfast appeared from the kitchen and Louisa ate her fair share, along with the boys. It resembled old times. It seemed as though only a week had elapsed since she had been sitting here at this table with her parents. The boys took turns at teasing her and arguing with her as though their own long-lost sister had returned to them. With the meal at an end, Louisa was invited to play cricket on the roadway outside their home. She accepted, but before doing so, she sidled along to Mrs. Marshall as she thanked her for her hospitality; then, as casually as she could manage, she queried her about the stockman who had suffered terrible injuries some months earlier.

"Dear me, Louisa, he's not well. Mr. Curtis can hardly move about and cannot work at all. He tends my vegetable patch for me and I feed him in return. We managed to find a spare room for him with one of our parishioners, but he's no money for rent. All his family are in Queensland, too. I did offer to write to them on his behalf, because he doesn't read or write. But, he refused. He said he didn't want to burden them with his troubles. It is all very sad."

Louisa mumbled her regrets and escaped to the dirt roadway where the cricket match was in progress. Her remorse and her guilt over the stockman were great and hearing Mrs. Marshall's tale regarding him did little to ease her troubled conscience. Immediately, she was allocated a fielding position and she took to her role with gusto, thus freeing her mind for the time being of the troubles regarding their former employee, Mr. Curtis.

With numerous balls coming her way, she was kept busy blocking them and returning them to the bowler who, at this precise moment, happened to be Billy.

"Louisa, move back and to your right. James will hit there, so be ready! And don't drop any. Okay?" Billy ordered, as Louisa nodded in acknowledgment of his stern direction.

Billy continued to rearrange his field. Then, he bowled the cricket ball to his older brother who smashed it in her direction. With both feet off the ground and her right hand outstretched, Louisa caught the ball while almost breaking her hand in the process. However, unable to keep her balance as she landed, she skidded onto the ground on her buttocks. With great foresight and determination, she managed to hold her right hand above her head. Billy was beside himself with glee. Louisa was triumphant and elated by her catch.

"How's that? *Out!* James, you're out for five. Great catch, Lou! It was a cracker!" Billy shouted.

Suddenly, Louisa noticed the look of horror that appeared on James' face. Unable to accept that this was generated by his inability to accept the cricket-related decision, she followed his gaze. Sprawled on the dirt roadway while still clutching her prize, Louisa's gaze fell upon a pair of highly-polished – although a little dusty – black shoes, above which were trouser legs belonging, obviously, to a gentleman. Instantly, two male hands reached down and pulled her roughly to her feet. He removed the cricket ball from her hand and, without a word, he tossed it unceremoniously to Billy. Silence reigned. All the boys stood opened-mouthed while staring at Charles Lyndhurst.

Ignoring this new arrival in their midst, Louisa pulled from him and moved to the boys – slowly, one at a time – and hugged them. Lastly, she reached James who was holding the cricket bat still. With his eyes on Charles Lyndhurst, James dropped the bat and his hand shot out. He shook Louisa's hand firmly and wished her well. Then, he turned away and walked toward his home, a very dejected figure.

Without so much as a word being spoken, Charles moved to her and took her by the arm while pulling her back toward the path and leading her into the cemetery where he stopped in front of her mother's grave. Without speaking to her, he reached down and he began to dust her gown. He devoted much more vigorous effort to the back of her skirt than she thought was necessary.

Finally, he pointed to her boots and stockings. Silently, she sat back down on the grave and she began to place her dusty feet into the stockings. He took his watch from the fob pocket in his waistcoat and glanced at it before snapping it shut and replacing it. His right hand moved to his head and he brushed the hair back from his forehead. He appeared to be fighting a great emotional battle within himself.

"I could happily throttle you at this moment, so be warned and don't do anything more to rile me. The train was due to leave ten minutes ago and they wait for no one, I'm informed. Hurry yourself!" he stated, through clenched teeth before elaborating. "If you think I'm spending another night in this place, you're mistaken. Come on!"

He grabbed her hands and pulled her to her feet, thereby propelling her away from the grave. Louisa glanced back and jerked her arm from his grasp, instantly pulling him to a stop. She made the sign of the cross on her person as he waited with eyes narrowed and daring her to flout his instructions.

"Rest in peace, Mama," she said, sincerely and quite loudly.

In absolute exasperation, Charles grabbed her arm once more and rushed her through the cemetery beside him, obviously heading in the direction of the main gate. At the gate, there was a man standing waiting for them. He held Louisa's cloak, reticule, gloves and bonnet, as well as what appeared to be a parcel. He had been in the hotel room the previous evening when her trunk was delivered, she recalled. Leaving Louisa near the gate, Charles went to him and relieved him of her apparel, along with a parcel wrapped in a cloth. The man hurried away and Charles returned to her.

"Who's he?" she queried.

"My valet. His name is Joseph and you're not his favourite person, believe me. He's standing in line to throttle you when I've finished with you, as he was required to pack your clothes this morning after finding the room as though a cyclone had hit it dead-centre. Have you a thought for anyone but yourself?"

Louisa shrugged her shoulders deliberately and she did all in her power to hide the smile that was threatening to surface. She tried to appear remorseful, but the exercise was doomed to failure for, instead, she felt elation.

"Cover yourself with this cloak, for goodness sake, until we get on board. You're not fit to be seen by anyone," Charles ordered.

He placed the bonnet on her head while tucking her hair beneath it and attempting to tie the ribbons until she pushed his hands away and completed the task herself. She slipped her hands into the gloves and put the reticule over her arm. He tossed the parcel to her.

Grabbing her arm once again, he tugged her along beside him on the roadway.

"Your breakfast, madam! It's a long way to Bendigo."

"I've eaten an enormous breakfast, but thank you anyway. And, for your information, we haven't missed the train. Look!" she stated triumphantly.

Louisa pointed in the direction of the station as they rounded the corner. The train was at the platform and passengers were waiting by the open carriage doors. There were four railway employees – all dressed in uniform – on the tracks and they were peering beneath the carriages while obviously discussing a problem with the under-carriage of the train.

"They've a problem. The train's been delayed," she exclaimed, in obvious delight.

Charles appeared unimpressed by the situation and hurried toward the platform, with Louisa in tow. Suddenly, he inclined his head towards her while whispering in her ear.

"I paid them handsomely to have a problem," he hissed at her.

A group of young boys was playing a game of marbles by the roadside and, as they walked by, a marble shot out of the ring and came toward them. Louisa jumped sideways and placed her foot on it, thereby stopping it in its tracks. She grinned down at the young boy who came to retrieve his precious object. She tossed the breakfast parcel to him while Charles fumed impatiently beside her.

"Here, share this with your friends," she said, as she moved her foot, thus releasing his marble.

"Gee! Thanks, miss," the boy replied, with a large grin on his face.

Charles Lyndhurst, with his temper frayed to breaking point, dragged strongly on her arm and rushed her onto the platform. He opened a carriage door and pushed her unceremoniously inside.

"Sit there! Don't move and don't speak," he ordered.

He walked to the carriage door but, before he stepped out onto the platform again, he turned back to her.

"Don't dare to defy me," he warned.

Louisa watched through the carriage window as he moved to speak to three gentlemen on the platform. These were the men whom she had seen at the table adjacent to them in the dining room on the previous evening. They were intent on travelling on the same train to Melbourne, via Bendigo and Castlemaine. That much was obvious to Louisa. Charles turned abruptly and he returned to the carriage. Sitting down beside her and placing his arm through her arm while holding her more tightly than she considered necessary, he spoke sternly to her.

"Now, we need to have a very serious discussion, madam," he whispered in her ear as he drew closer still to her. "I've spoken at some length at breakfast with the lady who runs the hotel . . . Mrs. Spencer, I think? Then, I visited the *Charmaine*, expecting you to be plaguing the life out of Bill Bartlett. But, no . . . I was required to search further. With information from your young friend who was involved in my recent near-demise, I was able to ascertain the direction that you had taken. Are there any other details you wish to reveal regarding your exploits this morning?"

"Well, I don't see how it's any of your business, but I did have a long conversation with Mama at her grave, the contents of which are private. After that, I helped James to milk the cows, followed by breakfast with the Marshall family at the rectory. Mrs. Marshall will vouch for that, if you don't believe me."

"You were suitably dressed for the milking, at least," he muttered, before querying her further. "*And*, the young man with the cricket bat . . . James? Your lost love, is he? Is that it?"

"*Poof! Love!* He'll get over it," Louisa stated with obvious disdain, before asking a question of Charles. "How can a promise made when I was nine count for anything? Besides, it's bad enough that I've married outside of my own faith, let alone contemplate marriage to someone who's headed for the clergy in the Church of England! Mama *would turn* in her grave, then. Why are you looking at me like that? Are you laughing at me again?"

Charles' shoulders were shaking. At the same time, his eyes were watering and the corners of his mouth were twitching ominously. He shook his head and she determined then that his anger at her was short-lived.

"Perish the thought!" he murmured, as he remarked with a voice that was quivering. "It's wonderful to see that you have such great compassion for his unrequited love."

"How did you know anyway?" she demanded. "No one said anything to you."

"I saw the look of despair on his face and it reminded me of an event many years ago. I felt sorry for him, for it's difficult to recover from one's first love, especially at his age. Nineteen, is he?"

"Not yet . . . in a few months," Louisa replied.

The train engine sprang into life. The day was fine, with clear blue skies. Louisa wriggled in the seat, but she was wedged between the armrest at the centre aisle and his body. He appeared to have no intention of releasing her. Charles seemed lost in deep contemplation, and it was quite a while before he spoke again for he, too, was studying the scenery through the open carriage window. There were several other passengers in their compartment, including a family with six children in tow. At the far end of the carriage, she noticed the three gentlemen from the platform. One turned and looked in their direction but, when he met Louisa's gaze, he turned away quickly. Finally, Charles broke the silence as he turned to her with a serious expression on his face.

"Last evening, I enquired about the content of the conversation that you had with Mrs. Spencer. Why on earth did you not tell me? Do you think I'm so devoid of feeling I'd allow you to sleep in the room where your mother died . . . and on your wedding night! Great God in heaven, do you have such a low opinion of me? Have you, by any chance, been the recipient of some of Melbourne's gossip-mongers and their juicy tit-bits of information, most of which is ill-informed and incorrect . . . and one particular lady comes instantly to my mind?" he asked quietly; then, he enquired. "Are you afraid of me, Louisa?"

"Poof! Afraid of you! Don't be absurd."

He moved his hand, instantly flicking his wrist as he did so. Her pen-knife, so recently acquired, flew into the air, did a small somer-sault and it landed on her lap.

"Your dagger, I believe," he stated, with one eyebrow raised in query.

"Ha! I . . . umm . . . forgot. I did intend coming back. Truly, I did."

"Have you any idea the ruckus it would've caused had the chambermaid found that in the bed, instead of me? She'd have taken it to the public bar and the ensuing laughter would've raised the hotel roof. You do own it, I presume?"

Louisa reached for it with her free hand, scooped it up and hid it at her side as she wedged it between the armrest and her body.

"Yes. I thought I'd need it to . . . well, to stop you from . . . from doing . . . umm . . . that *damn, messy, business* that's painful and . . . well, I don't know what else," Louisa stammered, thereby some-what lamely concluding the explanation with a slight shrug of her shoulders.

She bit her lip and stared out of the train window. Charles was looking intently at her as the train gave a massive jerk forward a few feet. Then, it stopped. The engine had a full head of steam and soot came flying in through the open window. His hand reached over and gently touched her chin before turning it so that she was facing him, with their faces but inches apart.

"I told you I wouldn't hurt you. It wouldn't take a genius to deduce how you came by that classic piece of information. Robert Collins has my deepest sympathy and respect," he spoke quietly, but clearly and distinctly, before inquiring further. "What else did she tell you?"

"Aunt Sophie? Nothing, only that it was her duty to inform me, as Mama would've done. And, it was my duty to allow . . . oh! and not to embarrass you by smashing the windows and all the furniture. That's all," she concluded.

"All?" he queried, with one eyebrow raised. "I'd have been heading for the hills alone, and at a very fast pace, had I been in your shoes. We've not gotten off to a good start, have we?"

As he spoke, he removed the glove from her left hand and gently slipped a gold ring on her finger, beside the gold wedding ring that he had placed there the previous day. She held it up while admiring the large green emerald, which was surrounded by diamonds. Rays of sunlight streamed through the window and caught the beauty of the stones.

"How did you know the size?" she queried.

"The same way I knew the size for the wedding band," he retorted dryly.

"Papa?" she enquired.

"How else?"

"It looks very expensive," she stated, while inquiring innocently. "Did it cost more than thirty pieces of silver?"

Louisa felt his body jerk slightly and stiffen considerably beside her as the train engine, with its connected carriages, jerked abruptly once more. But this time, the forward momentum continued as it commenced its southward journey through the Victorian countryside and it headed toward its eventual destination in Melbourne. Charles gave a deep sigh and she knew a moment's satisfaction. She would not allow him to buy her good opinion, she decided.

"Considerably more! In fact, you've no idea the toll that's been exacted over this business! *Now,* you see those three gentlemen at the end of the carriage . . . they're waiting for me. They relieved me of a small fortune at poker last night and I've every intention of retrieving every last h'penny, and then some! While I'm thus engaged, you'll remain here. What you do to amuse yourself is up to you but, for the duration, I'll have one eye on the cards and the other on you. Any questions?"

Louisa looked at the men momentarily and then, she glanced back at Charles. He stood up, removed his coat, which he tossed on the seat beside her, and he was in the process of rolling up his shirt sleeves when she shook her head in answer to his query. He leaned over her so that his mouth was beside her ear.

"Two more pieces of advice for you to ponder. *One* . . . if you remove that ring and throw it out of the window, I shall stop this train and sit beneath a tree until you find it, regardless of how long it takes and whether ten trains or twelve travel by us. Is that understood?"

Louisa bit her lip, more to prevent the laughter that was threatening to flow than to bow to his directive; then, she nodded solemnly. Charles continued.

"*Two* . . . if you should take it into your head to derail this locomotive . . . or part thereof . . . be assured that many innocent people will be hurt or killed. But, when the smoke and dust have settled, there shall I be, rising like a phoenix from the ashes. You shan't be rid of me as easily as that. How do you propose to spend the next few hours, Louisa? Dare I ask?"

"I shall do as I always do on this journey. I'll be sleeping like a baby," she announced; then, as she began to remove her boots again, she stated clearly. "I didn't get much sleep last night, as I recall."

He opened his mouth to speak, thought better of the matter, and remained silent. He stood watching her intently for a moment, as the boots were tossed aside on the carriage floor. She looked up at him in innocence.

"Your friends are waiting," she reminded him.

"They're not my friends. They're business acquaintances. I've very few friends. Those I do have, I'd give my life for them! *And*, it's beginning to seem as though I may have done so already . . . or, if not my life, my sanity, at the very least!"

So saying, he turned on his heel and strode to the end of the carriage before taking up a position where his new bride was in his line-of-sight at all times. Rather than allow him this satisfaction, Louisa settled lengthwise on the seat while making herself as comfortable as possible on the hard bench.

She tossed her bonnet, gloves and reticule onto the opposite seat after having first taken possession of the pen-knife and stored it safely away for future use. She removed her cloak and placed it over her body. This left her without a pillow and her head continued to bump up and down. All that Charles Lyndhurst could see from his vantage point would be her feet. She had considered removing her stockings, also, but as she remembered a certain cricket match and how dirty her feet were as a result, she decided against that move. He may see it as deliberate provocation and, very definitely, she preferred him to remain where he was for the remainder of the journey.

Finally, she reached for his coat, rolled it into a ball and placed it on the seat under the window. With this serving as a comfortable pillow, she allowed herself to be lulled into a deep sleep by the chug-chug of the steam engine and the steady and relentless roll of the carriage.

It was from a very deep sleep indeed that Louisa was awakened. The hours had slipped by without her knowing anything about the long journey and, for this, she was thankful. What she was not thankful for was the fact that two male lips were placed firmly against her own. Her eyes flew open and she found Charles on one knee beside the bench seat with his mouth on her own.

Instinctively, she tried to pull away. Her shoulder was pinned firmly to the seat and he had her other hand in his grasp. He moved his face away slightly, with laughter twinkling in his eyes. She pursed her lips and wrinkled her nose, with definite distaste showing on her face.

"Why did you do that? Poof! You've been drinking whisky! The last man who kissed me had a rum-soaked breath and he was lucky to escape with his life. In fact, I almost set him alight!"

"Then, I'm fortunate indeed," he said, with a laugh, as he explained. "I'm desirous of retrieving my coat, and not wishing to have a dagger plunged into my heart, I thought to wake you gently. We'll reach Bendigo in five minutes. Is it too much to ask that you at least make some attempt to appear respectable?"

Slowly, she lifted her head and he pulled his coat from under it while releasing her as he did so. He stood erect, held up the coat and shook it. Disgust was showing clearly on his face as he surveyed the crushed garment.

"I had hoped that at least one of us would appear in this fair town in sartorial splendour; but alas, it appears it's not likely to be so," he said, as he shook his head slowly.

"Did you win?" she asked, before reaching for her boots.

"Cleaned them all out!" he said triumphantly, while studying the coat as it hung in a crumpled state on his body and he shook his head sadly, before remarking to her. "Louisa, if you stay around much longer, I fear I'll lose my valet. He won't stand for this and there've been many who've tried to poach him from me in the years since I brought him with me from London."

"You weren't born here?" she asked, while securing the second boot.

Standing beside him, she reached for her bonnet, placed it on her head and tucked in the loose strands of unruly hair. He glanced at her, with a look of amusement on his face. She felt that he had consumed much alcohol. She had been around the farm-hands, the shearers and the river-boat men for all of her life and she knew the tell-tale signs well. She observed a silver hip flask in his pocket as Charles moved to join the card game earlier.

"Twenty-four hours into this marriage and, now, you seek to take an interest in my life history?"

He placed her cloak around her shoulders and his arm around her waist. Leading her toward the carriage door, Charles watched as she reached hastily for her reticule and gloves. The rings on her finger caught her eye. She knew a moment's pleasure at the sight and relented grudgingly.

"Thank you for the ring. It is beautiful," she murmured.

"It's my absolute pleasure. *Now, Mrs. Lyndhurst,* let us show a united front to the world!"

Charles stepped from the carriage and reached for her hand. As she stepped onto the platform, he reached beneath her cloak and placed a possessive arm around her waist.

Together, Charles and Louisa walked along the platform beneath the station canopy and out into the sunshine while heading in the direction of the waiting carriage.

Chapter Nine

− *Victorian Victorians* −

Louisa

L ouisa was left alone in her room at the Shamrock Hotel where she had stayed many times with her parents. She extracted the pale green silk gown from her trunk and dressed for dinner; then, Charles arrived. Together, they descended the stairs to the dining room, which was crowded on this Friday evening. When he returned her to her room, he left her outside the door while bidding her goodnight. With utmost relief, she watched him disappear downstairs again and she presumed that he was heading for another card table. Louisa opened the door to her room to find a young, dark-haired girl inside. She was extracting garments from the trunk and arranging them in the wardrobe. Upon seeing Louisa, she turned and smiled shyly.

"Who're you?" Louisa demanded.

"Charlotte, ma'am. I'm your new personal maid . . . that is, I will be if you approve of me. Mr. Lloyd said you mightn't . . ."

"Before you go any further, who's Mr. Lloyd?"

"He's Mr. Lyndhurst's valet. He said so, anyway," Charlotte replied, in an uncertain tone.

Receiving an absentminded nod from Louisa, Charlotte continued with her story. Joseph, Charles' valet, had instructed Charlotte that the position was available, subject to Louisa's approval. Her father was deceased and her mother was raising six children alone now. Charlotte was the eldest of these offspring and her previous employment had ceased, due to the death of the lady-in-question. She needed to find another position as soon as possible, as her mother relied upon Charlotte and her younger sister, Bridget, who was in service, also, for financial support. Charlotte continued her work history while explaining the reason why she had been dismissed from the position, which she had held with her former employer.

"She died in childbirth. It was so sad, there being three older children and the new baby who survived, so they had to find a wet nurse for him. Now, I've been without employment for four weeks and I'd be much obliged if you'd consider me, ma'am. I come with excellent references."

"Where is your home?" Louisa enquired.

"Here, in Sandhurst. That's where Mama lives. I was born here."

Louisa was lost in thought. She knew the locals regarded Bendigo as Sandhurst still. The town had been called that for many years before gold was discovered on the banks of Bendigo Creek, the year after Louisa's birth. After that, the population grew rapidly as gold-seekers from all over the world descended on the town and its sister-city of Ballarat, whose streets were seen to be paved in gold, also, at that time. This had occurred shortly after Victoria had become a separate State, in the fledgling colony, and there were many who believed – to this day – that the gold discoveries had been kept a closely guarded secret until after statehood had been achieved and the ties with the northern State of New South Wales had been severed completely.

The rivalries that existed between both States were legendary. While Victoria had been regarded as little more than an outpost before statehood by those from the first State of the colony, her inhabitants now considered those from New South Wales – and Sydney town in particular – as the poor relations and treated them with disdain, at best. The wealth possessed by the State of Victoria, as well as by her many prosperous and wealthy citizens, was the envy of many. The buildings, parks and gardens of Bendigo left no doubt in the minds of visitors that it had come of age in the years since its fantastic windfall by Bendigo Creek in 1851.

While trying not to appear in complete ignorance, Louisa began to quiz the young girl before her on a totally unrelated subject. She had been somewhat intrigued by the girl's statement.

"What are the exact duties of a wet nurse?" Louisa queried.

"Why, it's to provide nourishment to the new-born child through the breast. A woman was found quickly and one who had her own child at the breast, so she could suckle the new baby. There were several available, so it was a simple matter. The baby didn't suffer; well, not in that regard anyway, although he didn't have a mother anymore," Charlotte stated, while shaking her head sadly. "Do you wish me to remain, ma'am?"

"Yes, I expect so, but it's a terrible chore you're taking on, Charlotte. So, be warned in advance. As for those disgusting items of apparel, when we reach Melbourne, you're to dispose of them immediately. Never will they be worn by me!"

Charlotte studied the gowns while touching the silk with reverence. Then, turning quickly, she looked aghast at Louisa.

"Dispose of them? All of them? But, they've not even been worn."

"And, they're not fit to be! Do what you like with them. I never want to see them again. Now, go and tell Mr. Lloyd you're employed and don't come back tonight," Louisa commanded.

"But, you need me to assist you."

"No, I don't. I'll see you tomorrow," Louisa stated emphatically.

Charlotte pursed her lips as though trying to hide her delight and to suppress a smile. Louisa did not miss the expression on her new maid's face. As Charlotte walked to the door, Louisa thought the girl was attempting to cover her desire to skip and dance, so delighted was she at the prospect of her new position.

"Charlotte! I think we'll do well together, don't you?"

"Yes, ma'am," Charlotte replied as she turned to look at Louisa. Charlotte allowed a grin to appear on her countenance and Louisa laughed as the young girl, who appeared to be no more than two years Louisa's senior, departed.

Having slept soundly, Louisa had completed her toiletries very early and was dressed in her old muslin gown when Charlotte tapped on the door. The girl had no sooner crossed the threshold than Louisa issued her first instruction. Charlotte, after the initial greeting, appeared surprised to see her new mistress ready for the day just after dawn.

"I need my other trunks brought here immediately, as I don't have anything suitable to wear. See Mr. Lloyd at once and arrange it, as I wish to be in the dining room as soon as possible. I need an early breakfast before I go out this morning."

Charlotte disappeared, before returning twenty minutes later to inform Louisa that the trunks had been located and would be delivered to the room shortly. Some ten minutes later, Charlotte supervised their arrival and, immediately, she opened them. Louisa descended on them and, kneeling on the floor with her head buried while concentrating on the task in hand, she began to remove their contents rapidly. She was searching for particular items and, as a consequence, gowns and garments went flying all over the room. Charlotte stood and watched the proceedings in amazement. Finally, Louisa located one gown in the first trunk and another in the second.

"This one, I shall wear now. The other I'll need to have ready for a very important luncheon appointment. So, I'll leave that to you, Charlotte, but I need to dress rather hurriedly now and be out of here quickly," Louisa stated firmly.

She wanted to be finished with breakfast and out of the hotel before Charles Lyndhurst appeared to alter her plans, so she conveyed this urgency to her maid by her hurried movements as she dressed for the outing that she had planned for the morning.

One hour later, Louisa stood in front of the notice board in the vestibule of the Catholic Church, which she had attended always with her mother whenever they happened to be in Bendigo on a Sunday morning. Because of this, she was well aware of the times of holy mass. Her hope today had been the discovery of the time that the priest would be conducting confessions, for there was a matter troubling her conscience greatly and she was desirous of relieving herself of this heavy burden as soon as possible.

Once she arrived in Melbourne, Father Frank, her mother's younger brother, would descend upon her and he would insist on her weekly attendance at holy mass and at confession. This was one misdemeanour that she had no intention of revealing to her own uncle. He would castigate her severely over her marriage, not only because it had taken place outside of her Church, but also, because she had chosen to marry a heathen as he would view the matter. This other trouble she could not reveal. He would know her voice, despite the so-called secrecy of the confessional.

She could not tell anyone whom she knew of the terrible act, which she had committed and that would be with her until the day she died. Even now, all these months on, she could scarcely believe that she was responsible for the dreadful deed. This incident occurred, because of her failure to control her temper, which flared so fiercely, so frighteningly, so violently and so abruptly that she was in fear always of its appearance, which was as unexpected as it was unwelcome. Alas, today she would be unable to unburden her soul, for Saturday confessions were to be held at 2 p.m. She would be dining at Stanton at that time. It was almost a feeling of despair that descended on her as she made her way slowly back to the hotel.

Outside the door to her room, she found Charlotte who informed her that Mr. Lyndhurst was waiting inside. Upon opening the door, she found Charles on one knee while rummaging through her trunks in much the same way as she had done earlier in the morning. He stood as she closed the door.

"What do you think you're doing? Have I no privacy at all?" Louisa demanded angrily.

"None whatsoever, madam! Where're they?"

"What?" she demanded.

"The breeches and shirt . . . the boy's raiments! I know you'll have them with you. I'll take possession of them *now!* Where've you been?"

Louisa stared at him in defiance before another thought struck her forcibly. She knew that she was correct in her assumption and it astounded her. She challenged him.

"You thought I'd gone out in them! You thought I was roaming around Bendigo in them? You are *mad!*"

"Worse!" Charles replied. "I thought you'd have located a local cricket match, thereby honing your fielding skills while wearing those garments."

Louisa stared at him aghast; then, the absurdity of the situation occurred to her and her lip began to tremble as the picture that he painted flooded her mind. She felt the tell-tale sign of the giggle rumbling and, despite her rapidly-subsiding anger, Louisa laughed and the infectious sound permeated the room. He relaxed at the sound.

"I repeat . . . where have you been this morning?" he enquired, in a quiet, though nonetheless menacing tone.

"To church."

"Church? On a Saturday? A likely story . . . why?"

"To establish the times for holy mass tomorrow. I intend attending; so, presumably, you'll not attempt to prevent me from doing so."

"I shall, because you won't be here. We're leaving early for Melbourne. I need to return immediately, as I have business that requires my urgent attention."

Louisa turned and threw her gloves and bonnet onto the bed. She surveyed the trunks, through which he had been searching and she felt her anger rising again. She would not become a prisoner to Charles Lyndhurst, or to anyone else.

"That gown is the most becoming I've seen you wearing," he murmured, in a conciliatory tone.

"That's because I chose it!"

"Let's hope you've another that's as suitable for visiting my mother. We leave within an hour. I'll be back then, so don't go sneaking off anywhere else. *And,* I still require an answer regarding those disgusting clothes. Where are they, pray?"

"They're not with me here," she answered honestly.

"I don't believe you've left them at your father's home. So, be warned. Should I see you wearing them in private, I will remove them instantly. If I should see them in a public setting, upon your person, *I'll not be responsible for my actions.* Do I make myself clear?"

"Oh! Abundantly so, Mr. Lyndhurst," she answered, with as much sarcasm as she could muster.

Charles shook his head and studied her intently. He pursed his lips as though trying to prevent words that he would regret escaping from his lips.

"I'm no saint, Louisa; you'll do well to remember that fact. And, you can push me only so far. Already, you've reached that limit on several occasions and we've been thrust together for all of two days. The likelihood of either of us surviving this experience is not high. I must ask . . . have you set out deliberately to rile me?"

"Well, yes, it had been my intention," she admitted, somewhat ruefully. "At the outset, I thought to do so, but I seem to be able to achieve that end without even trying. When I set out to do so, you will know it. Oh! Most assuredly, you'll know."

"Madam, you'll not win. Take my advice, for it is given in all sincerity. Give up now, before it's too late," he stated.

Louisa looked him directly in the eye and laughed loudly. Then, he continued with his interrupted speech, to which she paid no heed at all.

"Whatever you think to do, know I've done it before you. Wherever you seek to go, know I've been there before you. Whatever mischief you plan, know I've done it already . . . and with greater success than you will ever achieve. So, I'm well ahead of you with every step you take. But, that's the arrogance of youth in every generation, for they think they're the only ones to have engaged in outlandish behaviour . . . that they invented it, without considering for a moment that those who are older may have done so already and been wiser for the experience. Tread carefully from here."

Louisa lifted her chin in a defiant manner and cast him a scathing look. He continued to survey her with the air of one with authority over her.

"You warn *me*? You asked if I know of your reputation; well, I know a little, but it did not come from my aunt who's never told me anything about you. I saw a chart when I was at *that* horrid school in Melbourne. It depicted all of Victoria's most eligible bachelors and your name was on the top of the list. It had a column for positive attributes and one for negative ones. So there!"

"Is that so?" he replied with amusement, which was mingled with much interest written all over his face. "Do tell me more."

"In the positive column was written your father's money, title and connections. That's all."

"I see," he replied, somewhat abashed. "It's not hereditary. You do know that, I take it?"

"What?"

"The title."

"I don't give a fig about that!" she exclaimed hotly.

"I'd hate to think you'd entered into this farce under that misapprehension. And, in the negative column?"

"One word only . . . *Rake!*"

He threw back his head and laughed heartily. He shook his head as he enjoyed his secret joke and laughed some more.

"Is that what's kept all Melbourne's debutantes from my door all these years? I'm eternally grateful to whomsoever compiled that chart. But, let that serve as a warning to you. *Don't* cross me!"

He shook his head and walked towards the door. Louisa stood to attention, clicked her heels as loudly as she could, raised her arm in a salute and spoke loudly and clearly.

"Yes, sir!"

He stopped dead in his tracks and turned to survey her. He shook his head in warning.

"There's a line been drawn in the sand, Louisa," he stated quietly, quite slowly and very deliberately. "For your own sake . . . not mine . . . *don't cross it.*"

Charles Lyndhurst left her room without a backward glance.

Charles gave her a glance of appraisal as he collected her from the room and, as there was not one word of criticism, she assumed that she was suitably attired to meet with Lady Elizabeth Lyndhurst. Together, they descended the stairs. Deliberately, he placed her hand through his arm as they traversed the foyer of the hotel and headed in the direction of the main door to the street where their carriage was waiting. As they crossed the threshold, she felt him stiffen noticeably and he stopped while staring at the couple who walked from another carriage that was stopped by the roadside. The man and woman were moving in the direction of the hotel doorway. They stopped as recognition dawned.

"Aha! Mrs. Webster, I did not expect . . . " Charles spoke haltingly, with surprise registering on his face.

"Mr. Lyndhurst! . . . Ah! . . . Good morning. I wasn't expecting to see you here in Bendigo today. I trust you are well. Bertie, come along. We'll be late."

The lady at whom Louisa was staring in amazement was truly beautiful. Her gown was stylish and her dark hair curled beneath her bonnet. She radiated grace and elegance. In comparison, Louisa felt as though she were the country cousin who had arrived in from the bush. In reality, this was not an unfair description. Mrs. Webster's deep blue eyes swept over Louisa in a swift but detailed glance and she felt that the lady had looked deeply into her soul in this moment.

Charles introduced Louisa to Mrs. Webster although he seemed quite reluctant to do so; then, as Mr. Webster walked beside the lady, he introduced him to her. This later arrival who had paused to exchange pleasantries with an acquaintance on the pavement joined them. He had boyish features, light brown hair that appeared to have a tendency to curl, but not one strand was out of place now. Louisa doubted that any hair – or anything else, for that matter – would be permitted the luxury of being out of place on the immaculately groomed Mr. Webster. They presented as a stylish couple indeed, but his brown eyes were laughing at this moment and he appeared to be enjoying a secret joke although Louisa was uncertain at whose expense. Suddenly and unexpectedly, Mr. Webster offered his arm to Louisa.

"Perhaps, Mrs. Lyndhurst, you would allow me the honour of escorting you to your carriage."

As he spoke, he glanced at Charles who gave one of his imperceptible flicks of his head, thus indicating his approval. Louisa smiled shyly at Bertie Webster and she accepted his arm. As they moved away from the doorway and crossed the pavement, Bertie offered his felicitations on her recent marriage.

"That's very kind of you, I'm sure, Mr. Webster, but it's not necessary, in *my* case. While you and Mrs. Webster may find the marriage state to your liking, I find it tedious . . ."

She inclined her head to one side and surveyed him candidly. Louisa decided to elaborate, much to his delight and further amusement.

". . . No, worse than that. I find it obnoxious and very, very restrictive."

Bertie Webster threw back his head while laughing heartily. He surveyed her with obvious approval.

"I admire your frankness, but if you wish to be accepted in Melbourne society, I'd advise you to temper your remarks a little. But, rest assured, your secret is safe with me. *Now,* shall I tell you one?"

"Oh! Yes, please, I love secrets," Louisa stated, with a laugh.

They were standing by the waiting carriage. He glanced over at Charles and Mrs. Webster, Louisa observed, before he spoke softly to her. He was leaning forward as though this were a part of a conspiracy, in which they were involved at present.

"Mrs. Webster and I are *not married.* I should think I'd find the married state less to my liking than you do, if I wished to be honest. No, Mrs. Webster is my mother," he said, with a grin.

Louisa spun around to look at the couple standing in the doorway. They appeared to be having a very heated exchange of views. Louisa wondered if Charles Lyndhurst was disagreeable to all women. She returned her attention to Bertie.

"Your mother! She can't be . . ."

"I jest. Sylvia is my step-mother. She's married to my father, but forgive my teasing. I couldn't resist that," he confided to her.

"Oh! I see," Louisa said, with a smile. "I suppose I shall need to know these details, especially if there'll be entertaining done at Lyndhurst Park. Do you dine there on occasions, Mr. Webster?"

"No, never. The only person I know who ever dines there is your husband. I've been in Melbourne for most of my life and that's always been the way of it. Are you desirous of changing this state of affairs?" Bertie Webster enquired.

"Me? Goodness, no! That arrangement will be altered over my dead body. Rest assured of that! Please, forget I mentioned it."

Bertie Webster laughed again and nodded his head in agreement. He glanced back at the couple in the doorway. Charles and Sylvia were in a deep discussion. He frowned markedly. He seemed to be glancing at other people who were passing by and Louisa realised that the sparing couple in the doorway was attracting not a little attention. Bertie turned and assisted Louisa into the carriage.

"Forgive me, but we must be on our way this instant. We're late for an engagement with the family. I'm delighted to make your acquaintance and I'm certain we'll meet again. As for all the social gossip, you need look no further than your aunt for information. Mrs. Collins can give you all the details you require, I'm certain."

"Thank you, but I doubt I'll bother. I don't give a fig for any of that stuff-and-nonsense. Goodbye, Mr. Webster."

"Good day to you, Mrs. Lyndhurst. Take care," Bertie Webster murmured as he turned and hurried to Mrs. Webster's side.

Louisa watched from her vantage point in the carriage as Bertie interrupted the conversation between the couple in the doorway. With a flick of her head, Mrs. Webster turned away abruptly and entered the hotel, with Bertie beside her. Charles Lyndhurst strode toward the carriage. He entered quickly while snapping an order as he did so, and the carriage moved immediately. He threw himself onto the seat opposite Louisa and placed his feet on the seat beside her. She glanced down at them in surprise. She was tempted to place her feet on the seat beside him, but the expression on his face was thunderous, so she resisted the temptation. He was staring out of the carriage window at the passing scenery as Bendigo slipped away behind them.

"She's extremely beautiful . . . and so very elegant," Louisa stated eventually, and with a certain amount of awe sounding in her voice.

He brought his attention reluctantly back into the carriage and stared at her. He eyed her suspiciously before speaking while seeming to choose his words carefully.

"To whom do you refer?" he queried.

"Mrs. Webster . . . the lady we just met."

"Mrs. Webster would never be seen on a public thoroughfare, playing cricket with a gang of street urchins, I can assure you."

"Street urchins? They were the Reverend Marshall's sons!" Louisa exclaimed.

"Oh! Is that so? I stand corrected," he muttered.

"Anyway, I don't give a fig for what you say, I took a marvellous catch and there was no doubt James was out."

He seemed to relax a little and he smiled at her before nodding his head in agreement.

"I could not argue with that. It was worthy of the hallowed turf at Lords'. By the way, if you wish to attend church tomorrow, you may. Take the maid with you."

"I thought you said . . ."

"There's been a change of plan. We'll be in Melbourne on Tuesday," he snapped at her.

Louisa opened her mouth to speak.

"Leave it be!" he snapped again, but this time it was irritably.

Charles turned his attention back to the scenery, which had changed to that of the countryside now as his mood had changed back to its original state.

"I wonder if she'll like me. What do you think?" Louisa asked.

He snapped his head around and stared at her. He frowned deeply as he surveyed her.

"Mrs. Webster? What's it to you? What was Bertie Webster saying to you? You seemed to be having a deep conversation with him."

It was Louisa's turn to stare back at him. She, too, was frowning.

"Nothing much. It was a private conversation. *And,* I was speaking of your mother."

He pursed his lips while studying her closely. Then, he appeared to relax again.

"My mother? Oh! I see . . . the subject matter has changed. The attention span is not of a long duration then, is it?" he muttered; then, he replied. "Yes, I expect so. You're kindred spirits!"

"How so?" Louisa queried, quite pleased to be described as such.

"She married the devil himself. You aligned yourself with his son. You've much in common, I should think!"

"Why can't you explain something as simple as that to me? Is it too much to ask that you at least give me some inkling as to what I'm walking into, here?" Louisa asked, with her nervousness at the forthcoming encounter beginning to surface.

He grimaced slightly before replying in a nonchalant manner.

"You'll be fine. She won't eat you, I promise. *Now*, if I were taking you to meet my paternal grandmother, that would be another matter. You'd have good reason to be concerned. She's dead now, but she truly was one callous, cruel, fire-eating dragon who could only have produced the son that she did."

"You really hate him, don't you?" Louisa asked.

Charles returned his attention to the exterior of the carriage and, for a time, she did not think he would reply. Finally, he returned his attention to her.

"Do you want me to kiss you again?" he asked.

"No . . . absolutely not," she replied, immediately recoiling in horror.

"Then stop prattling on and asking so many infernal questions."

"I only wanted to know . . ." Louisa began to say.

Deliberately, he placed his feet on the floor. Then, he moved to her, with his face close to her own. She looked at him aghast, instantly pulling away and with her head pressed against the back of the seat. He placed the index finger of his right hand against her lips.

"Not another word until we reach Stanton. For the duration of our time there, and that should be no more than a couple of hours, would it be possible for us to declare a truce? Could we do that, do you think, Louisa Mary Lyndhurst?"

Louisa pursed her lips – with his finger attached to them still – and, deliberately, she looked him directly in the eye. She shook her head defiantly. He gave a slight smile, settled back on his seat and emitted an exaggerated sigh.

"I thought as much. At least, I've secured a period of silence, if nothing else," he murmured, almost to himself.

Charles Lyndhurst promptly closed his eyes and Louisa felt him dismiss her totally from his presence. The remainder of the journey was accomplished, by necessity, in silence.

The two-storey stone homestead was a considerable distance from the main gate. Louisa peered out of the carriage window in order to snatch a closer look as they approached up the long, dusty track. It was an imposing structure and one that did not look inviting at all. Charles was either asleep, or giving the impression of one who was in deep contemplation. Louisa adjusted her bonnet, brushed the dust from her gown and attempted to tidy her appearance. Charles spoke, without opening his eyes or moving at all.

"Be still. You're worrying about nothing."

Louisa did not answer. The carriage rolled to a standstill outside the front doorway, which was sheltered by a wide verandah. Charles stepped down and reached for Louisa's gloved hand. She alighted and walked with him to the front door, which was opened by an elderly butler who accepted Charles' hat without speaking.

"Morning, Tomms," Charles greeted him before he inquired about his mother's whereabouts. "Where is she? In the greenhouse, as usual?"

Louisa stepped into the house and stopped dead in her tracks. She shuddered visibly before she gazed around with a terrible feeling of dread descending over her.

"What's the matter? You can't be cold on a day as hot as this," Charles said.

Louisa looked up at him, with apprehension shining in her eyes. She looked from Charles, to the butler and back to her husband.

"No. Someone just walked over my grave," she stated emphatically while giving another slight shudder.

"Is that so?" Charles queried with a laugh. "How could it be otherwise? You've just stepped into the devil's laird. Am I not correct, Tomms?"

Martin Tomms glanced around as the lady of the house sailed into the main foyer. Louisa did not know from where she had come, or what she had heard of their conversation. She was tall, with slightly greying hair swept up on top of her head. Her bearing was that of one who would command attention wherever she went. Her features, her colouring and her height were mirrored in her son. Had she been twenty years younger, they could have been twins, Louisa thought. However, her eyes held much pain but, also, much kindness, and Louisa was drawn to her immediately.

"Pay him no heed, Martin. He's baiting you, as usual. Louisa, my dear, come into my sitting room and have some tea. I'm very pleased to meet you at last."

Elizabeth Lyndhurst came to Louisa, swept an arm around her shoulders, planted a quick kiss on her son's cheek as she moved by him, and she ushered Louisa to a room off to the left of the impressive entrance, from which a wide carpeted staircase swept upwards to the upper level of the home. The feeling of dread did not leave Louisa as she was shepherded into a waiting armchair in the small sitting room.

"Charles, sit there and be quiet. Don't interrupt us, as Louisa and I need to become acquainted."

The butler appeared with a tea tray, on which was a silver tea service. He placed this on the small table. Lady Elizabeth Lyndhurst smiled her appreciation at the butler who left the room. Charles sat opposite Louisa. He stretched his legs in front of him and placed them under the table.

"We shall have tea to wash away the dust from your journey. Then, we can have some lunch. How was your trip from home to Bendigo? It is quite a long way," Elizabeth asked politely.

"It was made all the longer due to the necessity to stop for a game of cricket on the way," Charles murmured.

Louisa could contain herself no longer, for her temper had been barely under control since they left Bendigo. She stared across at him defiantly.

"You just never stop!" she flared at him in warning as she advised him. "One day, my temper will fly and you'll end up dead, in all probability. You have been warned."

Louisa, suddenly realising where she was, bit her lip and looked contritely up at Elizabeth whose son Louisa had threatened to kill in his mother's presence.

"That was unforgivable but, you are absolutely correct. He is always baiting someone, Lady Elizabeth, and I won't stand for it."

Elizabeth stared at her new daughter-in-law in surprise and what seemed to Louisa in delight and with approval, although why this would be so, Louisa could not comprehend, because she had threatened to end the life of Elizabeth's only son.

"*Elizabeth!* . . . Please, call me Elizabeth, Louisa. Charles! Leave us this instant. Go! Take your refreshments in your father's library. I'm certain you'd prefer something stronger than tea, anyway. *And,* we need some peace. Be off with you."

Nonchalantly, he rose, grimaced slightly and moved away from the armchair while lifting a biscuit from the tea tray as he went.

"May I be delivered from fierce, fiery females!" he prayed, in a pleading tone and looking heavenwards for assistance as he sauntered from the room at his mother's command.

Stopping momentarily in the doorway, Charles placed the biscuit in his mouth and raised his eyebrows at Louisa before closing the sitting room door while leaving her alone with her new mother-in-law. Upon reflection, Louisa decided that if she were required to choose with whom she would prefer to be left alone, her choice would be with his mother, rather than with the son. This realisation did not augur well for her sense of peace and her state of happiness for the remainder of her natural life.

Chapter Ten

— *Victorian Victorians* —

Elizabeth

Elizabeth studied the young girl who was seated across the small table from her as Louisa Lyndhurst, after having tossed her bonnet and gloves onto the chair vacated recently by her new husband, sipped her tea. She appeared ill at ease in Elizabeth's company and this was to be expected. To ease her discomfort, Elizabeth asked after her father as she proceeded to draw the girl out slowly – a little at a time. In answer to Elizabeth's probing questions, Louisa explained some of the circumstances of her life on her father's property on the banks of the Murray River. Her heart went out to her new daughter-in-law. Elizabeth's ears heard the sounds of loneliness and homesickness that permeated her story, as well as her fears concerning her father's health.

Elizabeth's longing for her home in England had been strong in those early years when first she had arrived, on the arm of her new husband, in this new colony with her young son in her arms. It was a wild, untamed place then, less than fifty years after it was first settled by the soldiers, the convicts and a handful of enterprising early settlers. They had lived in Sydney at first before moving on to Melbourne some time later. Louisa's current feelings, Elizabeth understood well.

Louisa was still talking when she finished her tea. Elizabeth suggested that she may wish to freshen herself before lunch and, when Louisa jumped from her chair, eager for escape, Elizabeth escorted her to the small guest room that doubled as a children's room during Caroline's regular visits. As they walked between the staircase and the library, both women glanced inside. Charles was seated in his father's chair near to the large oak desk and by the window. He had a glass in his hand; his feet were placed on the window sill and he had his back to them as he stared out through the open window into the paddocks. He did not appear to hear them pass by, as he seemed lost in thought.

Elizabeth opened the door to the downstairs guest room at the rear of the house and allowed Louisa to enter. There were three single beds in the room and, in one corner, stood a small, iron-framed cot. A screen stood in the other corner. A wash stand, complete with a porcelain bowl and jug, soap and a towel, were waiting there.

"Take your time," Elizabeth suggested.

"Thank you," Louisa replied as she closed the door.

Elizabeth returned to the library doorway and watched Charles momentarily. He seemed preoccupied still.

"Charles, could you spare me a moment?" she called.

She continued on, immediately returning to her small sitting room. When he entered, with glass in hand, she pointed to several parcels, gift-wrapped, on a chair in the corner.

"They're wedding gifts. Some are from Caroline and the others are from me, so I'll have Martin place them in the carriage. Allow Louisa to open them when you return home."

"There was no need . . ." Charles began to say.

"Nonsense! Caroline visited early this morning. She wouldn't neglect to give you a gift at the time of your marriage. She apologised for not staying, but they were expecting guests themselves."

He nodded, while moving to the window and raising the glass to his lips as he did so. Elizabeth watched him in silence before broaching the subject on her mind at present.

"She called at the milliner's shop to collect a parcel for me on her way through Bendigo and she saw a couple coming from the station, which is opposite the milliner's shop, if you recall."

"It's not something I would know . . . your point being?"

He had turned to look at her now, a challenge in his eyes, and he knew exactly the point that she was endeavouring to make.

"The woman was Sylvia Webster. Tell me you haven't arranged an assignation at *this time*? Surely, you wouldn't do so?"

He gave a short, derisive laugh and returned his attention to the view from her sitting room window. He did not answer.

"Is she staying at the same hotel?" Elizabeth asked.

She was determined that he would not change the subject before she had her answer. Finally, he turned and surveyed her – more in amusement than annoyance.

"Yes . . . and no, it was not arranged. I was as surprised as Sylvia when we met today; but, I'll tell you this . . . I've read an account of the American Indians who send up smoke signals to communicate with one another over long distances. Fortunately, we do not need that form of communication in this country. We have my sister."

Elizabeth ignored the sarcasm and his implied criticism of her daughter. Undeterred, she pressed on with her inquiries.

"And, you intend to continue the relationship *here*, under Louisa's nose, within days of your marriage? Is that so?"

He drained the glass and placed it on top of the bookshelf by the window. He gave her a cursory glance and shrugged his shoulders in a nonchalant manner.

"Let me put it this way. If I'm at a table and I'm dealt a royal flush, do I ask the dealer to take back my cards and deal me something else? No, I don't. I play the hand I'm dealt. That's what I plan to do now. *And, Louisa* can know or not know . . . like or not like!

I really don't care. Speaking of her, where the hell is she now? She cannot be left unguarded for one moment; or else she's into some kind of mischief!"

So saying, he rushed for the door with Elizabeth following him while she explained that his new bride was ensconced safely in the small guest room at the end of the hall. She followed him as he rushed by the open library door. Two steps on, he stopped abruptly and came back, thereby causing Elizabeth to sidestep to avoid colliding with him. He moved to the library door.

"Louisa! What on earth are you doing? Good grief . . . !"

Charles rushed inside as Elizabeth followed two steps behind him. Louisa was balancing on a stool, with one foot on that piece of furniture and the other placed precariously on the shelf higher up the bookcase. She had dislodged several books with her shoe in order to have a foothold and was reaching for a book on the top shelf. She had this in her hand as Charles shouted. Startled, she turned. Momentarily, she lost her balance while teetering a little; then, she steadied herself, only to topple sideways. Charles reached for her as she fell. He crashed to the floor and he fell heavily.

He was sprawled on his back, with his head beneath the window and his feet near the desk. Louisa had fallen onto her back, also, while being draped across his chest. Her skirt was above her knees and the book, which she had been holding landed at Elizabeth's feet in the doorway.

Before she could react, Elizabeth watched in astonishment as Louisa twirled her body around quickly and, on her knees beside him, she began pounding Charles' chest with her fists, both of which were flying rapidly through the air. He was stretched out where he had landed while struggling to regain his breath. Martin Tomms, on hearing the crash and the shouts, came running. He stood stock still in the doorway beside Elizabeth and the butler was gazing in surprise at the scene before him. Finally, Charles reached up with his hands as he grabbed Louisa's wrists and he held her arms in the air.

Still on her knees, she wriggled her body while trying to free herself from his grasp as he attempted to breathe more freely and deeply.

"Enough! Enough," Charles gasped; then, regaining his breath, he murmured aloud. "For someone who was desirous of making a good impression, you've not done too well. In the twenty minutes we've been here, you've threatened to end my life in front of my own mother, and now, you're beating me to death, in full view of witnesses."

"It's no more than you deserve. You'd no right to shout at me. This wouldn't have happened if you hadn't interfered. You always interfere!"

Charles looked beyond Louisa's shoulder as she struggled still to release her wrists from his grasp. The corners of his mouth were twitching as he looked up at Elizabeth in some amusement.

"Mother, have I introduced my new wife to you?" he queried.

Louisa's head twirled on her shoulders. She stared up into Elizabeth's face; then, she glanced briefly at Martin and returned her gaze to Elizabeth. A deep crimson colour appeared on her pretty face, which was slightly suntanned, due no doubt to her outdoor life-style. There were freckles across her nose and her auburn hair had come adrift, with her hair ribbon hanging loose on her shoulders. The green eyes, clear and insightful, peered into Elizabeth's amused ones. Elizabeth drew in a deep breath, for she realised instantly that she was gazing down on the face of pure innocence.

Not for the first time since she met Louisa this morning, Elizabeth wondered if Charles would come to the realisation – before it was too late – of the precious diamond that had been placed into his two hands. She doubted it greatly and knew a moment's sadness.

Registering on Louisa's face was surprise now and she glanced from one to the other as her audience waited expectantly for her next performance. Suddenly, without a word, she sat back on her heels as the absurdity of the situation seemed to register with her;

then, a gurgling noise rumbled within her. This became a giggle, which exploded then into an infectious laugh.

Charles released her wrists and laughed with her. Elizabeth and Martin found themselves drawn under her spell, also. Elizabeth looked down in amazement at her son whom she had not seen laugh in a long, long time. She had witnessed him laugh in a sardonic tone, or in a derisive manner, but not in obvious enjoyment. Truly, it was a rare sight.

Elizabeth felt the old house creak and groan as though there had been a massive energy shift within its walls. Still laughing herself, she turned to Martin who made no attempt to hide the smile on his own face.

"Laughter is a rare treat in this house," she whispered.

"It is indeed an alien sound, m'lady!" Martin replied softly, before raising his voice as he advised clearly. "Luncheon is served."

So saying, he disappeared in the direction of the dining room. Elizabeth reached down and extended a hand to Louisa, who was on her hands and knees reaching for the book that she had mislaid. She accepted Elizabeth's assistance and came to her feet while clutching the book to her chest. She was thin – painfully so – Elizabeth noted. She led her from the library as Charles called from his position on the floor.

"Would anyone care to inquire about the state of my well-being?"

Elizabeth threw him a look of disdain; then, she smiled benignly at him.

"Not really, so deal with the situation as best you can and we'll both be in the dining room, if you care to join us."

Without a word, Charles took up his position at the head of the long dining table and Louisa and Elizabeth sat opposite each other. Louisa placed the book on the table beside her. As she chatted to Elizabeth about her time at the school in Melbourne, Charles reached across and flicked through its pages. He frowned and raised his eyebrows.

"Egypt . . . the Pharaohs? I don't believe it," he commented, while appearing slightly surprised and somewhat amused.

"Why not?" she demanded. "I love ancient history, and most especially Egypt and the Pyramids. Uncle Robert taught me all about it when I was little. As it seems I'm to spend several days caged in a room at the hotel in Bendigo, I need something to occupy my mind. Otherwise, I shall go insane!"

Elizabeth raised her eyebrows and cast a questioning, almost accusing, look at her son. This was met with a warning glance, which gave her to understand very clearly that he would brook no interference in his affairs.

"I assumed you were returning to Melbourne tomorrow," she queried.

"It seems not," Louisa replied, with a grimace while elaborating on their plans. "For it's to be Tuesday now."

Charles ignored the conversation taking place around him and continued to devour his lunch. Elizabeth continued her conversation with Louisa and ignored him.

"Louisa, I've some romantic novels belonging to my daughter on the bookshelf in my sitting room. Perhaps, you'd find those more to your liking at this time. You're more than welcome to them, so if you wish to browse through them before you leave, feel free to do so."

"I've never read a romantic novel," she answered in all innocence.

"Your education's been sadly lacking then," Charles exclaimed, with sarcasm sounding in every syllable, as he continued. "Caroline's a prime example of what one becomes when saturated in such nonsense."

Elizabeth lifted her foot in a reflex action and Charles stiffened noticeably as her shoe struck the flesh of his shin bone. He smiled to himself and reached down while rubbing his leg. He looked heavenwards as though for assistance.

"May I be delivered from fierce, fiery females!" he prayed aloud.

Elizabeth stood on the verandah and waved as their carriage disappeared as it travelled along the dusty track toward the main gate of Stanton. She shook her head sadly as she considered the future of her son and his new wife. Martin Tomms was standing by the door as she turned. She inquired about the conversation between Charles and Louisa when they had entered the house on their arrival. He repeated the episode. Elizabeth was surprised to learn of the feelings of the young girl upon entry to the house. Perhaps, Louisa possessed a psychic knowingness, she mused to herself.

She returned to her own bedroom and rummaged in the wardrobe for her other small jewellery case, which she kept under lock and key. She placed it on the bed after closing the drapes and lighting the two lamps on the bedside tables. She sat on the bed, extracted the contents and unravelled the silk scarf. Her grandmother's tarot deck appeared and she fingered the cards lovingly. She had been taught to read them at an early age, along with the etiquette for doing so. She was about to breach one of those restrictions now and squashed her conscience with the thought that she needed to know Louisa's future. Peering into that, without the young girl's permission or knowledge, was regarded as snooping and spying, at best. Still, she had Louisa's best interest at heart, as well as that of her son, Elizabeth felt.

Elizabeth shuffled the cards, spread out the scarf on the bed and settled herself comfortably on the bed, after having first locked the door to ensure that she would not be interrupted. Several minutes later, she stared down at the spread before her as it lay open on the colourful piece of silk. For this reading, she had chosen the ten-card spread of the Celtic Cross. Studying it closely, she drew in her breath sharply. She did not wish to see any more. She knew that she should not have peeped. She heard her grandmother's voice as it came to her from her childhood while instructing her sternly that the cards are never wrong, although her interpretation of their message could be incorrect or misconstrued, because she wished to believe certain events are – or, perhaps are not – going to occur in her life.

Elizabeth castigated herself once again for not resisting the temptation to delve into that which was not her business to know, or her right to access without permission. She grabbed the cards, swiftly bringing them together without studying the rest of the spread, and she returned the tarot deck to its hiding place. Donning her straw hat and gardening gloves, she hurried to her greenhouse to reflect on the events of this day.

An uneasy feeling crept over her body and it had been present before she touched the cards. These had been merely a confirmation of what she had known from the first moment when Louisa Lyndhurst walked through the front door of her home at Stanton. Charles had his life to live, as did Louisa, and they would make their own choices and their own mistakes, as she had done. Would that she could change some of her decisions! Unfortunately, this was impossible. She could pray for them in their future life together, but she could not walk their paths for them. As difficult as it was, this was a fact of life, which she must accept.

Elizabeth walked to her greenhouse as she considered the situation. She prodded one of her precious plants in her outdoor sanctuary. Lifting the secateurs, she snipped three white roses from a bush and she left the greenhouse. She walked slowly up the slight incline in the direction of the three small graves where three tiny baby boys rested beneath the large eucalyptus tree.

These were but three small mounds of earth – side-by- side – separated from one another by iron bars attached to, and suspended on, sandstone bricks, which served as the cornerstones of the graves. There were no headstones and no names. Their passing was marked by three simple, white crosses, with three different dates, which were fading in the rays of a harsh sun.

She sat under the tree, watching the roses – every one attached to its own, individual cross – waving in the slight breeze that was blowing. Elizabeth was unable to shake the feeling of melancholy that had descended upon her from the moment of Louisa's first greeting. It was a long, long time before she could persuade herself to re-enter the house where she occupied two rooms downstairs while her estranged husband lived on the top floor of the two-storey building, which she had never been able to bring herself to describe as *home*.

Sylvia

Sylvia paced back and forth across the hotel room. Her heated argument with Charles at the front door of the hotel was fresh in her mind. In fact, it haunted her. Her subsequent heated discussion with Bertie troubled her equally, for rarely did they argue. He remained silent during lunch in the hotel dining room but, upon coming upstairs, he left her in no doubt of his anger over the fact that he felt she had made a spectacle of herself in public this morning. Unfortunately, she had to agree with him. She would not do so again. Bertie had left her then while intending to spend the afternoon with his own friends in Bendigo.

She was troubled and she was finding it difficult to settle to anything. She knew that it was too early to begin dressing for the dinner party, which her uncle had insisted on giving in her honour to celebrate her thirty-fifth birthday, this being the reason for their presence in Bendigo on this particular week-end in November. Bertie had accompanied her from Melbourne, under sufferance, and she was at a loss to know why her uncle had insisted on his presence. Other than her uncle and her two elderly maiden aunts, no one else would be present to her knowledge. Her mother had refused to travel from Castlemaine to join them, this much Sylvia did know.

There was a light tap on the door. Expecting her maid to enter, Sylvia waited. When the unlocked door did not open, Sylvia moved to it. Wrenching it open, she found Charles Lyndhurst standing before her. He glanced furtively along the hotel corridor, then back at her, and he was looking a little sheepish, she had to admit.

"May I come in?"

She did not answer, merely opening the door wide for his entry and stepping aside herself. She watched him in silence.

"Happy Birthday for last Tuesday!"

Unmoved, Sylvia nodded in response while waiting for his next comment.

"I need to explain something to you, for we appear to be at cross-purposes."

"How so?" she enquired, while raising an eyebrow and assuring him. "I assumed we understood each other perfectly . . . especially after what occurred this morning! I'd have thought little was left unsaid!"

"I apologise profusely. It was unforgivable, but you took me unawares . . ." he began, before stopping and giving a slight shrug of his shoulders.

Sylvia studied him for a moment; then, very deliberately, she turned away while walking over to the window and staring outside at the street below. She was watching the citizens of Bendigo as they were strolling by on this clear and fine Saturday, with dusk beginning to settle over the buildings. Preparations for the Royal Visit were almost completed and the town's festive air was in stark contrast to the heavy atmosphere in the room.

" . . . That's not an excuse, I know, but I'll *never let you go*, Sylvia."

She spun around, with fury sounding in her voice as he concluded his apology.

"Two days ago, you married someone else! How on earth can you think to have a claim on me now? Answer me that!"

Charles shook his head slowly. He took a step toward her, but she turned her back on him, instead preferring to return her concentration to the street where normal people were going about their normal business affairs. Nothing seemed normal any more in her world. He remained standing by the bed and he seemed undecided on what to do or to say next; then, finally, from the corner of her eye, she saw his hand move to brush the hair from his forehead and this was a sign that she knew well. It happened whenever he was troubled, frustrated or angry. He seemed to come to a decision at this moment.

"There's something you need to know, but it's between the two of us. Don't tell anyone, not even Bertie Webster, I beg you. In fact, I didn't intend sharing it with you, because I didn't want to give you false hope . . . but I've formulated a plan," he confided, almost in a secretive tone.

Sylvia turned from the window while looking at him in a detached way. She seemed to be detached most of the time these days. It was as though everything was happening as in a dream sequence and she had little, if any, control over the events that were affecting her life so disastrously at present. Patiently, she waited for him to continue.

"I'm hoping . . . no, planning . . . to arrange an annulment at the appropriate time . . . as soon as possible, in fact."

"An annulment? You *can't really* be serious? And, *your new bride's* in complete agreement with this proposal?" she queried in an incredulous tone, while being unable to stop the sarcasm from surfacing in her voice.

"I've not mentioned it as yet," he admitted, somewhat reluctantly.

Sylvia knew a brief, almost fleeting, glimmer of hope; then, in an instant, she squashed it. There would not be any annulment, even if Charles Lyndhurst believed it to be so. She could not accept that he was being so naïve as this; or, that he thought her so.

"It will not happen, for *she'll* never agree. Anyway, I'd imagine there'd need to be good reason and there doesn't seem *to me* to be any. But then, I don't claim to be an expert on such matters. Also, I'd be inclined to think your young bride may be required to submit to a compulsory medical examination, so have you considered that? Those are the legal grounds for the granting of an annulment . . . at least, that's my understanding of the matter anyway," Sylvia stated coldly and clinically, with a detachment that surprised her.

"She's a child, placed in my care and I take that duty very seriously indeed. She'll be returned to her father *intact*, believe me, for I'll not take advantage of this unfortunate situation."

"A child! For goodness sake, Charles, your wife is seventeen! Who're you attempting to fool here . . . yourself or me?"

"*He'll not win!* I'm determined on that score. Believe me when I state this! My father will not have the final say in this matter. There'll be no grandchildren, bearing the Lyndhurst name, to come out of this fiasco."

Sylvia shook her head slowly, but she refrained from commenting, because the determination on his face was set and his hatred of his father was very obvious in that moment. What did shock her more than his words was his determination to outwit his father, not only at Sylvia's expense, but also at the expense of his new wife who was to be discarded as easily as Sylvia had been set aside. It was as though she was witnessing a side of Charles Lyndhurst that she had never seen before this day.

Oblivious to her close scrutiny, Charles continued with his explanation, almost as though she did not exist, and he was outlining his plans aloud, merely for his own benefit. Perhaps, in so doing, he could convince himself, as well as Sylvia, that the impossible was possible. After a brief pause, he continued to divulge – to a detached and disbelieving Sylvia – his well-thought-out, though ill-conceived, plan.

"Possibly, there may be some slight disgrace attached to her because of this," he continued very calmly while, obviously, choosing to ignore her interjection. "And one that'd constitute a valid reason. Her behaviour is so outlandish that it's only a matter of time before she does something that is unacceptable socially, if not unforgivable . . . "

"And, you'll come out of the whole affair unscathed while she is an outcast socially?" Sylvia interjected again, and aghast at such callousness.

Charles shook his head and moved closer to her. Sylvia stood her ground while giving him to understand clearly that she did not want him to come near her or to touch her. His eyes pleaded for understanding.

". . . Don't you see? Louisa doesn't care about that and all she wants is to return to her home. You don't know anything at all about her. *She loathes me.* Truly, she does. She cringes if I so much as move to touch her hand while she trots along at my heels and all the time wishing she was anywhere but in my company. So, I know she'll jump at the chance to be rid of me, at any price. I've yet to determine how she was forced into this marriage, but much pressure has been applied, I know."

Sylvia turned to him with a look of disdain, combined with disbelief, registering on her face while he watched her closely.

"It will mean I lose all claim over Lyndhurst Park, as well as everything else he owns, for he'll disown me instantly. On that, you can place all your money but, it's a small price to pay, because we'll be together."

"It won't happen! I can tell you now; you won't succeed with this diabolical plan. Have you had this in mind all along?" Sylvia queried.

Charles nodded slowly and he studied her closely as he awaited her reaction; then, he explained the situation more fully for her benefit.

"Of course. I intend returning her to her father; then I'll leave for London and I'll wait for you there. *For as long as it takes, I will wait.* You can join me as soon as you're free to do so. While that's been my intention all along, I wasn't planning on sharing it with you, or anyone else, for that matter. Now, you've forced my hand, so this must be between us, Sylvia."

"Your secret is safe with me, for I'll not mention it to anyone. It's so far into the realm of fairytales, it beggars belief! Just don't raise your own expectations too high . . . or, your hopes and dreams, for that matter . . . as they're likely to explode in a puff of smoke.

And, Charles Lyndhurst, don't expect me to fall into your arms while sharing your dreams. It is not possible. You made your choice, so live with it!"

Sylvia turned away. She was staring down at the street scene once again. There was a coldness enveloping her and it frightened her a little. It was a similar feeling to that which she had experienced when, just prior to her thirteenth birthday, her father had come to her bed one night. The memory of his rum-soaked breath had seeped deeply into her consciousness and remained with her to this day. Whenever she smelled that particular drink on the breath of any male, she was transported instantly back to her old bedroom. He had broken a sacred trust that night. Perhaps, the breaking of a trust was the basis for her feelings now. However, this was neither the time nor the place to explore such matters. She glanced up at the clock.

"I'm dining with my family tonight. I need to dress. Will there be anything else?" she asked haughtily.

He studied her as though he had never seen her before. Then, he frowned. If he wished for his compliant Sylvia back, he was about to be disappointed. He reached out his hands as though to touch her, but she stepped away, and he allowed his arms to drop back to his sides.

"Presumably not," he muttered, before making a suggestion. "Unless you're prepared to stay over for an extra night and we can spend some time together."

"With your new bride in a room down the corridor? Is that what you are asking of me?" she queried, with more than a tinge of sarcasm.

He shrugged and his hand reached up to brush the hair from his forehead again.

"I returned your birthday gift to your home, by the way . . . *unopened,"* Sylvia stated, very casually.

"Then, I'll bring it back to you personally when I return. This *is not over* between us. Don't think, for one moment, it is. What time will you be back here tonight? It's of no consequence . . . I'll be waiting."

"Don't bother . . . *and* close the door on your way out."

Charles walked to the door and opened it. He looked back at her.

"Till tonight then," he said, before closing the door quietly.

Sylvia remained standing alone by the window and it was some considerable time before her maid, Phoebe, arrived to assist her to dress for her birthday dinner. She had continued her lonely vigil by the window while being frozen in time as darkness descended and night engulfed Bendigo and its citizens.

"*Happy Birthday, Sylvia Webster!*" she whispered to her reflection in the glass of the window pane.

In reply, she received a vacant and disinterested stare as, strangely, the reflection mirrored her mood totally and completely.

Seated at the dinner table while surveying her family, Sylvia could but wonder once again on the reason for tonight's special dinner party and to ponder on what exactly they were celebrating. She had witnessed many birthdays prior to this one and those did not warrant much attention, as she recalled. Bertie, despite his previous reservations, warmed immediately to her Uncle Thomas, Aunt Isabella and Aunt Miriam. These two older women were fussing over him as though Prince Alfred himself had walked through their front door this evening. He was listening attentively to her uncle's story about his arrival in the colony. Sylvia had heard it all so many times in the past.

Thomas McMillan was born in Glasgow and lived in the old family home that he had inherited from his parents, with his three unmarried sisters, Isabella, Miriam and Norma. While he worked as a shipping clerk on the docks, his sisters operated a small, but lucrative, business from the confines of their home. In his capacity as a clerk, he met and became firm friends with a seaman by the name of Michael Doherty, a wild, hard-drinking Irishman from Belfast.

Thomas, being a tee-totalling Scot with a passion for his church, that being Presbyterian, was a most unlikely companion for Michael Doherty, but a strong friendship grew between the two men.

When Michael met the pretty, vivacious youngest sister of Thomas, he proposed almost immediately and Norma accepted on the proviso that he gave up his life on the high seas. Subsequently, with assistance from Thomas, he obtained a position as a barman at the local inn, *The Seaman's Arms*, and the couple married immediately.

Within the first year of marriage, that being 1832, their eldest child and only daughter, Sylvia Isabella Doherty, was born. The family had remained within the household of Thomas McMillan, all living under the same roof, although this was intended to be a temporary arrangement only.

With constant news of the penal colony in New South Wales trickling back to them through their association with returning seamen, Thomas and Michael began to formulate a plan to journey there as free settlers. An uncle and some cousins of the McMillan family had done so already and the two men felt that, with contacts there already, they would not be arriving in a new land as complete strangers.

Formulating the plan was the easy part. Convincing the female members of their family to accede to it was another matter. Finally, under constant pressure, the women relented and it was decided that the men would go alone. If the stories were true and it was *a land of milk and honey* – where, with hard work and enterprise, one could attain a better standard of living than the one they were enduring – then, the ladies would follow at a more suitable time. This would eventuate when their menfolk had established themselves and could provide a home for the rest of the family. If not, the men would return to Glasgow after a year's trial in the fledgling colony. As the ocean voyage to Sydney would take many months each way then, it was understood and accepted that they were likely to be absent from the family for at least two years.

Being dressmakers, Bella, Mim and Norma had many clients who were loyal to them and, with assistance from their brother, they had established a small haberdashery and millinery outlet in the front section of the family home. Consequently, the women were not without means of their own on which they could rely for a time, with all three contributing to the business venture. And so, the matter was decided. Michael was to work his passage while Thomas would travel steerage; but the adventure was postponed temporarily as they awaited the birth of the next offspring, namely Patrick Michael Doherty, in 1834. Within weeks of his birth, the two men were farewelled as they embarked on their journey that would take them to the other side of the globe.

Sylvia was six years old when the women and children arrived in Sydney in 1838 to be greeted by the two men; then, during the following year, Sean Thomas Doherty was born. It was some years after Sean's birth that the family moved south to the new colony that became known as Victoria, and where Thomas McMillan's relatives had secured large tracts of land for themselves in the south-eastern corner.

Thomas and Michael set about establishing themselves there, but they elected to settle in the township of Melbourne where they acquired land. On this, together, they built an inn to meet the needs of a thirsty population, after having seen first-hand for themselves the amount of alcohol consumed in Sydney by the male population who outnumbered greatly the female population in that town. Melbourne, at that time, was not an exception to this rule. Therefore, the two men were convinced of the success of their enterprise.

Thomas built a cottage for his two older sisters and himself while Michael elected to live at the inn with his wife and children. Some years later, Thomas obtained a position as a clerk to a prominent lawyer. Through his travels with his employer, he was in a position to know where good land was available. Then, just prior to statehood being declared in 1851, he managed to secure land at Sandhurst.

Shortly afterwards, Sandhurst was placed on the world map when gold was discovered in large quantities at Bendigo Creek in that same year. Thomas was in an excellent position to be one of the first miners on the goldfield. Michael left Norma in charge of the inn and he joined Thomas at the diggings as the population of Melbourne swelled enormously, almost overnight. It was with great alarm that Thomas' employer accepted his resignation, but not before he attempted to dissuade this careful Scotsman from such a course of action, even enlisting the services of a minister of his church to point out to him the dangers of leading an unstructured and dissolute life. However, the windfall from their endeavours at Bendigo far outweighed the dangers lurking there on the goldfields for the unwary.

In due course, Thomas built a home for his two unmarried sisters and himself in Bendigo and they settled there permanently, with Sylvia staying with them there for a time, just prior to her marriage to Edwin Webster. Sylvia had been placed under the protective wing of her uncle some years earlier when Norma, while citing the unsavoury characters at the hotel as the reason, had taken Sylvia to his home, thereby removing her from the clutches of her alcoholic father completely. Sadly, Sean had drowned in a creek at the age of five years, not long before Sylvia's removal from the inn and following her father's attack on her.

The inn in Melbourne was sold and Thomas and Michael went their separate ways after they left the diggings, with Thomas remaining in Bendigo and Michael building an inn in Castlemaine. Having Michael Doherty in charge of another hotel, at that particular stage of his life when two of his children had been removed from him, was similar to placing a thief in charge of the Royal Mint. He was estranged from his wife who blamed him for the death of her younger son and she could not forgive him for that grave sin, nor for the attack on their daughter.

As for Thomas, his family, his home and his church became his overriding passion and he remained a solid, church-going citizen of Bendigo to the present time, thus proving the assumptions and assertions of his former employer to be false and ill-founded, to say the least. At present, he worked as a bookkeeping clerk at one of the lesser known hotels in the town, but this was more as a means of keeping himself occupied, rather than one of financial necessity.

Now, in this year of 1867, Sylvia's father was dead and, because she refused to attend his funeral, she was estranged from her mother who presided still over the family hotel in Castlemaine. So, it was then that those accusations and the subsequent argument, which ensued during Sylvia's last visit, came to a head. It was when, finally, she had located her mother in the cemetery while placing flowers on the grave of the man who Sylvia had come to loathe, that the issues between the two women exploded, with the freshly-covered grave all that separated them. It was the story of the family's arrival in the colony that was being told now – and for Bertie Webster's benefit this evening.

"Have you heard from Patrick at all, dear?" Aunt Mim enquired.

Sylvia snapped out of her reverie with a start while realising that dinner was at an end and everyone was preparing to adjourn to the parlour.

"No, not at all, Aunt. I wrote to the only address I had for him at a boarding house in Sydney and advised him of *his* father's passing, but there was no reply. He may not even have received it."

After all these years, she could not refer to Michael Doherty as *my* father. Why that fact should surprise her, Sylvia did not know. Bertie was in the process of giving high praise to her uncle over the glass of fine malt whisky, which he was savouring. The appearance of this alcohol, so obviously for Bertie's benefit, surprised her greatly, because her uncle, despite being a long-term employee of a particular hotel in the town, had remained true to his vow to never touch alcohol, as did his three sisters.

As she watched them now, Sylvia was intrigued still by this gathering. There was a sense of expectation, even excitement, in the air. Uncle Thomas appeared to be relishing the role of Father

Christmas as he presided over Christmas dinner while her aunts – his co-conspirators – were his eager and willing helpers. She pondered again over their motives and intentions, but to no avail. Finally, her uncle settled into his favourite armchair and decided it was time to end the suspense, much to Sylvia's relief.

"I . . . that is, we . . . brought you both here this evening for a particular reason, over and above the celebration of Sylvia's birthday. Bertie, did your father ever, by chance, mention ownership of the Royal George to you before his tragic accident? Or to you, Sylvia, for that matter?" Thomas McMillan enquired, and frowning slightly as he did so.

Both Sylvia and Bertie glanced briefly at each other and shook their heads simultaneously. Sylvia gained the distinct impression that her aunts were experiencing great difficulty in containing their glee as Thomas continued.

"I spoke to him just days before his fall. He'd promised to set the wheels in motion. I'm part-owner of that lucrative establishment, you see," he confided quietly.

Sylvia's mouth dropped open in surprise. He had been the book-keeper there for as long as she could remember. It was a rough-and-tumble establishment which she avoided, only visiting there to speak with her uncle on rare occasions. It had had different names over the years, the current one being the Royal George hotel.

"I don't believe it! *And you've allowed* that woman, Mrs. Duncan, to speak to you the way she does!" Sylvia exclaimed.

"Alas! She was unaware, you see. That was a part of the arrangement when I provided the funds to extract the owner from a difficult situation . . . after I'd managed to extract the pistol from his mouth, just prior to it discharging, I might add."

"Good grief! When was this?" Bertie demanded, evidently sensing a good piece of gossip unravelling before him.

"Many years ago now, I'm afraid. However, his gambling habits have resurfaced. He's lost his half-share to someone who is a visitor to our shores. He hails from the east coast of America . . . South Carolina, I understand," Thomas stated.

"After that terrible and brutal civil war, it's a wonder anything's still standing there . . . probably be relieved to be out of the place for a time," Bertie replied.

"Yes, quite," agreed Thomas, before explaining further. "The fact is that the Duncans have parted company, as a result of this awful affair. Mrs. Duncan has packed her family off to Ballarat to her sister's home and Mr. Duncan has departed for places unknown. They're destitute. I own half the hotel and this unknown American owns the other half. *Now,* I wish to retire and spend the remainder of my life in my vegetable garden."

Sylvia and Bertie looked at him in surprise while waiting expectantly for more information, which was forthcoming eventually. He had been planning his retirement three years earlier; then, a week prior to Edwin's accident while he was visiting Bendigo, Thomas had broached the subject of transferring his share of the hotel to Sylvia. Thomas did not need the money from the hotel and his church activities made it an embarrassment to be receiving income from the sale of a product that caused such suffering in so many lives, as had been witnessed first-hand in the lives of his youngest sister and her children.

"Me! To me? What on earth would I do with it? I've seen the work involved with my mother and *that ramshackle place* in Castlemaine. Uncle, that's most generous, but I couldn't accept such a gift. I . . . "

"Hear me out, my dear. This is my gift to you. You're the closest I've had to a daughter and, if the truth be known, you're more my daughter than that of Michael Doherty, God rest his tormented soul! I have a great love for you. Your devotion to your family over the years and now to your ailing husband has been a blessing to us all. So, why should you deny me the pleasure of passing something on to you? You will be as I was . . . a silent partner. That's all."

"... I don't know what to say," Sylvia muttered, thereby conclud-ing her original exclamation as her two aunts hung off their every word before she questioned her uncle further. "What was Edwin's reaction?"

"He was delighted . . . thought it most generous and he prom-ised to handle the details. I've been reluctant to broach this subject with you, considering the delicate state of his health, but this new development has forced my hand as I've no wish to be involved with any newcomer. I'll stay on as bookkeeper only until the new owners have taken over . . . and that means you, Sylvia, and your unknown partner."

Sylvia stared at him in astonishment and in silence. Her aunts were grinning at her with delight registering on their faces while Bertie appeared amused, as well as not a little surprised. *They were planning this surprise for me all along,* Sylvia thought, *while all the while, I was contemplating leaving the country, as well as my invalid husband, to live elsewhere with Charles Lyndhurst. What a dreadful mess I would have left in my wake.* She gave a deep sigh and turned to Bertie for assistance. He was studying the glass of amber liquid in his hand somewhat intently. Finally, he glanced at her, smiled and then looked over at her uncle.

"I'll look into the matter on Monday morning as a matter of urgency, Thomas, if that's your wish. I've no idea if my father did anything about it at the time. I handle all his affairs now, as you know, so I'll give it my immediate attention. Do we know where this mysterious American is hiding?"

Thomas shook his head slowly while his sisters shook their heads in unison.

"The poker game took place in Sydney. That's all I know," Thomas said, before addressing Bertie. "I'll leave this in your capable and trusted hands, Bertie. As soon as the new . . . and currently miss-ing . . . owner contacts me, I'll send him on to you in Melbourne, if that's not too much of an imposition. I've every confidence you'll look after Sylvia's interests admirably."

"You can be assured of that! In fact, you have my word on it," Bertie stated emphatically, while standing and extending his hand to her uncle.

In stunned silence, Sylvia watched the two men shake hands while her aunts smiled in obvious approval. Aunt Bella offered more apple pie. Aunt Mim rushed to the kitchen for more tea. Uncle Thomas refilled Sylvia's wine glass, then he refilled Bertie's glass with whisky, much to that gentleman's delight. Never had Sylvia seen alcohol in his home before this evening and she had lived with them from the age of twelve years until she married Edwin Webster at nineteen years of age.

She visited her family here regularly while her parents in Castlemaine she had visited irregularly, despite Edwin's family home being in that town. The Melbourne residence was the one, which her husband had purchased when they married and he had left his four daughters in their Castlemaine home under the guardianship of his sister. His only son, Bertram, he had brought with them to Melbourne.

Sylvia was attempting now to come to terms with the realisation that she was to be the part owner of the hotel where her uncle had spent many years of his life keeping a scrupulous record of all the details of that establishment's income and expenditure. The books would be in good order. Of that, she was certain.

"I'm sorry, Uncle, if my response to your generous gift has been less than enthusiastic. I am truly stunned and amazed. I had no idea," Sylvia said, before adding softly to him. "Thank you!"

Sylvia moved to him. She placed her arms around him and hugged him briefly. Normally, this would have been shunned, for Thomas McMillan was not accustomed to physical contact with anyone, and especially not with the women in his rather drab and sombre life. Tonight, he accepted her embrace, brief though it was.

As she left them at the front door later that evening, she promised to stay one more night in Bendigo and to return to them at midday on the following day to partake of Sunday dinner with them. With Bertie beside her, she returned to their hotel. He was lost in deep thought, as she was, in the carriage during the short journey. As they entered the hotel, he whispered to her.

"Have you any idea what your sudden departure with Lyndhurst would've done to them?" Bertie queried.

"Don't even mention it to me. It's been haunting me all evening," she responded, with a deep groan. "I've spoken to Charles and I've taken your advice. I'm sorry about this afternoon, Bertie. I should not have spoken to you in the way I did. Forgive me."

Together, they mounted the stairs to the first floor and Bertie walked with her to the door of her hotel room where he paused momentarily.

"There's nothing to forgive. I needed you to see that the only person to be hurt in all this is you. Remember, Sylvia, it's your reputation that is at stake here. When my father dies . . . and it's imminent, I feel . . . then, you'll be the one wishing to pick up the pieces of your life. *And, you've still* to live in Melbourne. *He* can do as he pleases, as he does always. But, you cannot afford that luxury."

Bertie stated his concerns in a very serious tone and not much above a whisper. Sylvia nodded slowly while acknowledging silently the truth in his words. She touched his cheek lightly and smiled. He took her hand and squeezed it.

"Thank you for being there for me tonight. It's been a truly remarkable evening and one I won't forget in a long time," Sylvia stated.

"Think about all of this very carefully before you make your next move. It was an enjoyable evening in the end. They're wonderful people who love you very much. Do you know how rare that is?" he asked. "I'd give my life for it! I'll see you in the morning before I leave and, *before you ask*, I'll go straight to your home and remain there until your return. Sleep tight!"

So saying, and with a wave of his hand, he sauntered off down the hotel corridor toward his room.

"Goodnight, Bertie," she called after him.

Chapter Eleven

– *Victorian Victorians* –

Sylvia

B efore she could open the door to her room, her maid, Phoebe, was beside her. Sylvia glanced at her in some surprise while noting the agitated expression on the girl's face.

"Where've you been?" Sylvia inquired.

"Waiting, ma'am. It's Mr. Lyndhurst. He's inside . . . in your room and you said I was not . . ."

"What! Did you let him in?" Sylvia demanded, with her anger rising.

". . . He tapped on the door and I opened it. He told me to leave, as he said he'd be waiting for you," Phoebe said nervously as she continued her explanation.

"I see," Sylvia muttered, lost in thought; then relenting, she spoke to the maid again. "You did well. Come back in ten minutes."

Relieved, the young girl, who had been with Sylvia for at least four years trotted away down the corridor. Sylvia waited until she disappeared completely before entering her room. She expected to storm in and challenge him. Instead, she found him asleep on her bed. His coat, waistcoat and neck tie were placed neatly on a chair and his shoes were beneath her bed. She stood by the bed while gazing down at his sleeping form and it took the greatest effort on her part not to curl up beside him. She had consumed quite an amount of alcohol and holding him at bay while feeling for him in the way that she did, would be an almost impossible task – if she were sober.

At present, she felt that she was floating on air, but Bertie's words of warning were fresh in her mind. Slowly, she sat on the bed beside him and moved her hand through his hair. He stirred slightly, but did not wake. Finally, she shook his shoulder gently and he opened his eyes. He looked up at her. Deliberately, he raised one hand to brush her cheek lightly.

"I never meant to hurt you," he whispered.

"It doesn't alter the fact that you have," she replied softly.

He moved his hand until it was behind her neck and he lowered her face to his as he kissed her. She relented momentarily. Then swiftly, she pulled away while moving quickly from his grasp and standing erect. He did not move. He focussed his gaze on her completely.

"Please leave now," she said, in a hoarse whisper.

Sylvia was struggling desperately to regain control of her emotions while Charles did not move. He kept watching her intently.

"I mean it, Charles. Do I have to lose my temper?"

He gave an imperceptible shrug of his shoulders. He rose from the bed while deliberately taking his time. He reached for his shoes and slipped his feet into them. Still, he did not speak. Sylvia watched him in silence as he dressed.

"This is *not over* between us," he stated emphatically.

"Why? Because *you've not* ended it? It is finished. *We were* finished the day you left Melbourne to marry. I don't want to see you again."

"You will though. Trust me, *you will.*"

"Go to your child bride and leave me alone!" Sylvia hissed at him.

There was a light, tentative tap on the door, much to Charles' annoyance. At Sylvia's call, the door opened slowly. Her maid appeared. She was standing by the open door and looking as though there were a thousand other places that she would rather be at this moment.

Charles cast an angry glance in Sylvia's direction before addressing her.

"Goodnight, Mrs. Webster."

He collected his discarded clothing and he walked by Phoebe. Charles left the room without a backward glance.

Sylvia retired for the evening while sleeping not at all this night, for she found her mind wandering aimlessly back to her childhood and to the father whom she had adored. He was a larger than life character who attracted people to him with his vibrant personality.

After their arrival in Melbourne, he had moved his family into the residence of the newly-constructed inn there when that city was in its infancy. It was in this establishment that Sylvia was to learn much about life and about the other women who moved through her father's life when his wife's back was turned. Norma worked tirelessly to keep the kitchen and dining rooms operating smoothly for the benefit of the clientele and her family alike.

When Sylvia was twelve years old, Michael Doherty, at Patrick's insistence, had taken his three children, including her five-year-old brother, Sean, on a fishing expedition to a nearby waterhole. There, in a drunken stupor, Michael had fallen into a deep sleep on the bank beneath a shady tree. Shortly afterwards, Sean disappeared. One minute, Sylvia recalled, that he was standing on the bank of the creek; then, when she turned back, she could not find him. Immediately, Patrick began diving for him in the muddy waters while Sylvia had shaken her father relentlessly.

Desperately, she had pleaded with him to wake up and to find Sean for them. Unable to rouse her father, she had run as fast as she could to seek help while Patrick almost drowned himself as he tried frantically to find their young brother. It was two hours before his body was located and Michael Doherty awoke from his slumber to find that he had a tragedy on his hands. Then, he was required to return to the inn to break the terrible news to his wife, Norma. For this, and for his many other sins, he was never forgiven.

Two months later, he committed another offence, for which he was never forgiven by his wife, Sylvia suspected. Once again, this occurred while he was in the grip of the drink that he loved so much and without which he could not live, for his daily intake was substantial. This time, his crime was committed in Sylvia's bedroom. Her screams brought her mother running to her aid as her father's rum-drenched breath reached her nostrils and his slurred words echoed in her ears.

"No man alive will ever get to my beautiful daughter before I do," he hissed.

His slobbering mouth sought her lips to silence her screams while his hands were groping between her legs; then, the cast-iron frying pan collided with his skull while sending a sickening sound reverberating around her bedroom. The fury on her mother's face was visible in the light shining through the open doorway. The anger over the death of her drowned son, the regular beatings that she had endured at his hands and this sexual attack on her only daughter had boiled up inside of her. This exploded in that instant. Michael Doherty never knew what hit him on the night. Sylvia was stunned herself and not a little shaken. Within twenty-four hours, she had been packed up and bundled aboard a coach at first light. From there, she was taken to her uncle's home.

For Sylvia, it all seemed so long ago as she stared now at the ceiling in the hotel in Bendigo on this November evening. She remembered being escorted by her mother and her brother on board the coach and arriving at the door of Uncle Thomas' home. She believed her father to be dead and that her mother would be arrested soon for his murder. It was only later – many days later – when Aunt Bella found her crying in the back garden that she learned Michael

Doherty had merely been rendered unconscious by the blow and was back on his feet again.

Her mother had remained but one night there and how much she revealed to her older sisters, Sylvia never knew, but her uncle was unaware of the real reason, Sylvia was certain. The incident was never, ever mentioned between mother and daughter. Norma Doherty returned immediately to her husband and she had taken full control of the inn.

Some years later, her father made the mistake of showing his violent streak in front of Patrick, who by this time was a tall, sturdy lad for his seventeen years. In that instance, Patrick had stood between his father and his mother and he rendered Michael unconscious on the floor of the public bar. When Michael awoke from that altercation, he found that his son had packed his bags and left for Sydney, never to return.

When Sylvia's father died, at the age of sixty-three years, her mother and a few of her closest friends in Castlemaine were the only mourners at his funeral. Soon, Sylvia may need to travel to Castlemaine to eat a little humble pie while trying to repair the rift between mother and daughter. Dawn was breaking as Sylvia drifted into a light sleep, which was anything but restful.

Later in the morning, Phoebe had no sooner left Sylvia when Bertie arrived and he announced that he was leaving for the train station. Then, there was another tap at her door and Bertie answered it while finding there a young boy who was holding a letter. Sylvia ripped it open. She gave but a cursory glance at the few brief words, which were written in it.

"Lyndhurst?" Bertie inquired.

"No. Uncle Thomas. He's asking after our well-being, as my aunts have come down with heavy colds. He's cancelled our luncheon engagement today, but he's in good health, he assures me. I'll need to go to them. I'll stay in Bendigo until they've recovered. Will you remain at my home with your father until I return? I can't say how long I'll be away."

Bertie agreed while leaving her to return to Melbourne. Sylvia went to visit her aunts.

Louisa

Louisa dined alone early that Sunday morning in Bendigo; then, she headed in the direction of the church. She had seen no sign of Charles Lyndhurst since dinner on the previous evening and this was to her liking. She took Charlotte with her as Charles had directed until she reached the church. Once there, she instructed the girl to visit with her mother for the remainder of the day. After holy mass concluded, Louisa loitered by the front door of the church. She was anxious to gain a moment alone with the priest in the hope that he may spare her a few minutes to hear her confession. She was not hopeful as she watched his regular parishioners gathering around him, all attempting to gain his attention.

"Louisa! Dear child, where did you come from?"

Louisa wheeled around and her eyes lit up with joy as she found herself in the embrace of an elderly couple who had been her parents' dearest friends. They were both aged in their mid-seventies and as happy together as on the day when they were married.

"Uncle Joe! Aunt Mary! What a surprise."

When she escaped from their embraces finally, they took one arm each and marched her to their home, which was a few hundred yards along the road. The weather had turned cold as a strong wind was blowing and rain clouds threatened. The wind whipped her skirts as they hurried along the road. Once inside their sturdy stone cottage, Joe lit the fire in the fireplace and Louisa accompanied Mary to the small kitchen where she put the finishing touches to the dinner, which she had prepared earlier. By the time that the trio sat down to the midday meal, they had extracted all of her news from her.

Her recent marriage was the greatest surprise of all. They insisted that she should bring her new husband to meet them in the evening. In fact, she was ordered to bring him for supper, but Louisa did not reply, for she thought she could send Charlotte around with an apology later, rather than disappoint them now. She helped Mary take the dishes to the kitchen; then, Louisa insisted Mary join her husband while she washed them. This chore took considerable time and when she returned to the parlour, they were in their respective armchairs in front of the cosy fire. Both were sound asleep.

Louisa curled up on the settee and watched the flames dancing in the fireplace. She could stay here a little longer, she thought, until Mary and Joe wake up; or, she could return alone to the hotel room and read the book on Egypt. She decided the fire and the company were preferable.

She was awoken by Mary with a cup of tea placed in her hands. Glancing at the clock, she was astounded to learn it was almost four o'clock. Not wishing to offend, Louisa drank the tea; then, she departed hurriedly. She returned to the hotel room to find a somewhat angry Charles Lyndhurst waiting for her in her room.

"Where the hell have you been this time?" he demanded.

"To church. It's Sunday."

"I'm aware of the day, as I'm aware of the time. Explain yourself."

"I met some old friends and they invited me home to Sunday luncheon. What is that to you?" she enquired, while trying to appear nonchalant in the face of his ill-concealed anger. "How is it your concern?"

"It's very much my concern! Who are they? Where do they reside and what've you been doing with them all day?" he demanded angrily.

"You can come and meet them for yourself, if you wish, as we've both been invited back there for supper this evening. Will you come? They said they'd love to meet you and they're expecting us."

"What? Don't be absurd!" he replied.

Louisa shrugged and tossed her gloves and bonnet on the bed. She flopped onto the bed and stared up at him in all innocence. Charles appeared unable to know how to respond to her. He stood by the window, with his hands behind his back and his pose rigid as he gazed out at the darkening sky.

"It's only a few minutes walk from here. It's more congenial than a stuffy, old hotel room where there's nothing to do."

When he did not answer, she threw her legs onto the bed. The lamps had been lit, so she assumed that Charlotte had returned to the hotel. He seemed lost in thought as he stared through the window. Absentmindedly, she picked up the book that she had brought with her from Stanton and she began flipping through the pages. She stopped at the place where she had marked. She read on, with the Egyptian pyramids coming to life before her eyes. She dismissed him from her mind and attempted to forget about his presence in her room momentarily until she felt his eyes upon her.

"Very well. I'll come with you, just to see for myself what you've been up to today," Charles stated.

He appeared to be watching intently for any telltale signs of subterfuge on her part. At his words, Louisa shot up in the bed and stared at him in complete surprise. He smiled down at her.

"You will!" she exclaimed.

"That's shaken your little world, hasn't it? I'm more than happy to play your games and I call your bluff, madam."

Louisa giggled momentarily. She checked herself while trying desperately to stop herself from laughing and knowing that she would enjoy tonight immensely.

It was sometime later that she knocked on the door of the home of her friends. Charles stood beside her, with an expectant look on his face. It was Uncle Joe who answered the door and he beamed when he saw her.

"Oh! Child, you've come back! And this is your husband. Come in, sir. Joe Johnson!" he said, while extending his hand to Charles as he spoke. "How do you do . . . I'm pleased to meet you, Mr. Lyndhurst."

"Uncle Joe, I said we'd come. This is Charles," she stated in an off-handed manner.

Charles, somewhat stunned, stared at the elderly gentleman before him and shook his hand automatically. Louisa kissed Joe on the cheek and danced on into the parlour to be wrapped in Mary's arms once again. Charles stood by the door, nonplussed, and Louisa was well pleased with her efforts thus far this evening.

"Aunt Mary, this is my husband, Charles Lyndhurst. Is there anything I can do to help?"

"Yes, run along and make the tea, dear. Everything's ready in the kitchen," Mary replied; then, turning to Charles, Mary addressed him with a warm smile. "And please, Mr. Lyndhurst, do come on in. We won't bite you. I'm so very happy to meet you. We'd no idea of your marriage until we found Louisa at mass today, so accept our rather belated congratulations!"

"I'm pleased to make your acquaintance, Mrs. Johnson," he murmured as Louisa left him alone and walked into the kitchen.

Charles was silent for most of the meal, although pleasant to their hosts when pressed on a question. Louisa chatted to them and they laughed as a threesome over past events, the subject of her mother's death being the one topic that was not discussed. It had been covered in great detail during the luncheon visit.

When supper was concluded, Louisa stacked the dishes and removed them to the kitchen. She was filling the large tub with boiling water from the kettle when Charles came to the door.

"What're you doing?" he enquired from the doorway.

"The dishes. What does it look like? Go back to the parlour and don't leave them alone," she directed.

He frowned at her; then, obediently and to her surprise, he turned and walked back into the parlour. She washed and dried the dishes before stacking them neatly into the kitchen cabinet where they belonged. She had completed this task so many times over the past years that she knew where everything belonged. She heard the sound of the pianoforte being played and she remembered many evenings by the fire while listening to Mary play as they all sang along with her music. The poignant memories of her mother's laughing face began to surface, but Louisa squashed them immediately. She could not afford to be sentimental now.

Leaving the kitchen, Louisa returned to the parlour and stopped abruptly in the doorway. Once again, Mary and Joe were dozing in their respective armchairs while Charles, lost in a world of his own, was playing a soft melody on the instrument in the corner of the room. Louisa, somewhat taken aback by this surprising turn of events, slid into a chair and she was lost in the haunting melody when he turned and smiled at her. With one of those imperceptible flicks of his head, he motioned for her to join him.

She moved to the pianoforte and stood there. She watched his hands move effortlessly over the keys while caressing them as the notes filled the room. She glanced around and her gaze rested on the elderly couple. They were dozing in the armchairs and happy with the companionship that they shared together. The fire was glowing and flickering every now and then. It warmed the parlour on this cool evening as his music permeated the room.

Almost as a mist descending, all at once, a peace descended over her for the first time in several years. It was in this moment that Louisa felt the Presence of her mother. The feeling was so very strong that it was undeniable. She felt her stand beside her, with her arm slipping around her waist. The sudden onset of those feelings of peace and love were explained in an instant. She would take this peace away with her tonight and treasure it always.

When the music concluded, Louisa woke the sleeping couple gently and explained that they were leaving to return to their hotel. After being wrapped in Mary's arms again and enjoying a warm embrace from Joe, Louisa, with Charles beside her, left the couple. From Louisa's perspective, it was with much reluctance.

As they walked back to the hotel, Charles took her hand, wrapping it under his arm. The wind was cold and whipped around her ankles, but the rain had ceased for the moment.

"*Vixen!*" he whispered in her ear.

Louisa looked up at him in innocence.

"You set a trap for me tonight and I walked straight into it. I'll be more circumspect next time, believe me."

Louisa giggled beside him as she whispered to him.

"But, you turned the tables. I didn't expect you to play the pianoforte so beautifully. When did you learn?" she enquired.

"As a child, at my grandmother's insistence. She was not one to be refused."

"Is this the fire-eating one?" she asked, with a laugh.

"The one and only! One learns very fast when the teacher . . . in this case, my grandmother . . . is brandishing a large rod above her head. It'd come down with great force onto my knuckles with every incorrect note. At ten years of age, and with no parents for protection, it's advisable to be a fast learner. It's called *self-preservation*."

"Where were your parents?"

"Here! I was sent to London at nine. I came back at nineteen and under sufferance, I might add. I left Melbourne the day after Caroline was born and she was ten years old when I returned. Is it any wonder she's a stranger to me . . . that we hardly know each other? Still, that's the past. This, Louisa, was a very pleasant evening. Seeing you with your sleeves rolled up and your arms in a tub filled with dirty dishes, has made my evening completely," he stated emphatically.

Quite deliberately, he reached over while playfully tugging on a stray strand of her hair that had come loose beneath her bonnet. Charles spoke very softly to her.

"Thank you for tonight, even if its main purpose was to teach me a lesson."

Louisa laughed with him. She glanced up as a carriage slowed by them while, walking together slowly, they approached the front door of the hotel.

"No, truly, it was not really so," she protested laughing, before she confessed to him. "I did want you to come, but when you didn't believe me, I was happy to prove you wrong. Look! Isn't that Mrs. Webster alighting from the carriage? She didn't acknowledge us. Perhaps, she didn't see us."

Without taking his eyes from Louisa's face, he removed his hand from her arm. Deliberately, he placed his arm around her shoulders as he guided her slowly towards the main door of the Shamrock Hotel.

"Presumably not," he replied quietly.

Charles deposited her in her room and he left immediately to return to his own room. Being a Sunday evening, the hotel was deathly quiet. It could not be any other way. The vigilance of the Sunday Observance League would see to that – always.

Louisa Lyndhurst had not the slightest inkling of the residence, to which she was being taken, or of its whereabouts in Melbourne. As she was not interested in the least, she had not asked, so she was not told anything. Therefore, the first sight of the large iron gates of Lyndhurst Park was a surprise, as was the long, wide carriageway, which led to the home in the distance. The carriageway was lined with trees and, to her right, she could see horse paddocks. Closer to the main house, the stables and a carriage shed were visible. When the impressive home came into view more clearly, she was impressed and agreeably so. Viewing it from a distance, it appeared to dwarf the palace, which her father had been constructing for her mother.

On the left of the carriageway as they approached the house, she glimpsed through the trees the sparkling waters of the Yarra River, on which the city of Melbourne was built. Louisa moved closer to the window of the carriage in order to command a better view of the home, which was a white, two-storey building with verandahs surrounding both the top and bottom levels. White wrought-iron railings complemented the verandahs and there was an impressive front entrance.

As Charles stepped from the carriage and assisted Louisa to alight, she noticed a tall gentleman standing on the top step of the home. He hurried forward, with a beaming smile of welcome on his face. Behind him stood the butler. Louisa was introduced to the gentleman first and she assumed immediately that Mr. Travis was Charles' secretary. Upon entering the home, she was greeted by the butler, Benson, who had various staff members waiting in line to greet her. By the time that she had been deposited in the small front drawing room, to the left of the front door, she was a little confused and could not remember any names, except for Mr. Travis and Benson.

Instantly, Charles disappeared and she drank tea, thankful for some time alone to reflect on the strange events of the past two months. These events had changed her life irreversibly and she was not optimistic that the future would improve her lot at all. The event that she was dreading most of all was the Governor's Grand State Ball, to be held during this coming week in honour of His Royal Highness, Prince Alfred.

It was not the fact that the ball would be an unpleasant event. Her aunt had invited her many times to stay with her during the period of the Royal Tour and Louisa declined all invitations, because she felt that she was needed at her own home and she could not spare the time to be engaged in such frivolous activities when there was so much to be accomplished on her father's property.

Now, here she was in Melbourne, with little hope of returning home in the near future, and she was troubled deeply by her father's health problems, not to mention her own predicament at present. She would need to leave here shortly and return home – with or without Charles Lyndhurst's consent – if her father did not appear in the city within the next three to four weeks. Until then, she was determined that she would not correspond with him, so that he would have to come to visit her to ascertain her state of health and well-being. These were her rather vague plans at this precise moment. She was lost in her own world when the door opened abruptly.

Charles was surveying her intently as she began to pour another cup of tea and she noted that he had changed his attire, as he was dressed now for riding. He held a riding crop in his hand as he stood by the doorway. She glanced up at him while taking in his attire with one, intense sweep of her green eyes.

"I've a pressing matter requiring my immediate attention. I'll take you on a tour of inspection when I return home. Till then, stay out of mischief, Louisa, *please.*"

"Am I permitted to breathe during your absence, Mr. Lyndhurst?" Louisa inquired, while adopting as innocent a pose as she could manage.

"Be my guest. You may walk in the garden, if you wish, but for anything else, call on Hugh Travis who is across the foyer in my office. Ring for Benson should you require more refreshments. I shouldn't be gone too long."

"Don't hurry your return on my account, for I am certain I'll have no trouble finding ways to amuse myself," Louisa murmured demurely.

"That's precisely what I fear most!" he responded forcefully, before closing the door and leaving her alone.

Sylvia

Seated at the bureau in the sitting room of her Melbourne home, Sylvia pondered over the words of the long-overdue letter that she had been attempting to write to her mother for weeks. All previous drafts of the missive ended in the waste basket and the one before her now was destined for the same fate, she knew. Still, she persisted. Their relationship was a difficult one, almost from birth, Sylvia suspected, while her brother, Patrick, who disappeared without a word when he was seventeen years of age, was the golden-haired boy in her mother's eyes to this day. From rumours that Sylvia had heard of his wild exploits in Sydney in recent years, it seemed he almost resembled his father of earlier times. But, perhaps, she misjudged him. After all, any rumours Patrick heard of his sister were, in all probability, just as colourful and less than accurate.

Studying the page before her, she did not respond immediately to the light tap at the door. Finally, turning to see who had entered the sitting room – all the while presuming it to be Bertie who she was expecting to join her for lunch – Sylvia's heart skipped one, definite beat on viewing her visitor. Despite this involuntary reaction, she remained frozen in her chair. Charles strolled over to her and, standing beside her, he placed a small parcel on the bureau in front of her. She recognised it immediately.

"Your birthday gift," he murmured.

Sylvia gave a deep sigh and leaned back in the chair to survey him.

"You still believe you've the right to enter here whenever the whim strikes you. You really are impossible," she muttered eventually.

Charles picked up another chair and moved it beside her while seating himself so that he was facing her. Stretching his legs, he folded his arms while he watched her.

"When you look me in the eye and tell me honestly that you don't love me, I will go and never darken your door again."

Slowly, and in a determined manner, Sylvia pushed her chair a short distance away from the bureau. Squarely, she faced him and she stared directly at him.

"I don't love you," she said, as she spoke quietly and deliberately. "I don't want to see you again," she stated emphatically.

He reached over, picked up the gift and dropped it onto her lap. He stood erect while leaning over her.

"Let that be a parting gift then."

He turned abruptly. He was half-way across the room when she called to him.

"Charles . . . wait . . . "

He stopped in the centre of the room and looked inquiringly back at her as she struggled for the words that she needed to speak at this precise moment.

". . . Occasionally, I've been known to lie," Sylvia stated, trembling markedly, as she spoke while attempting to control her emotions.

"Is this one such occasion?" he inquired, almost nonchalantly.

She bit her lip and nodded, without looking directly at him. He was by her side in an instant. He reached for her arms, pulled her to her feet and placed his arms around her waist as she tossed his unopened gift back onto the bureau.

"I'm going to regret this, I know," she whispered. "For, definitely, it goes against my better judgement."

"*No!* You won't have any regrets, for I'll see to that, my darling. You are so very precious to me and I can't live without you in my life. We will be together always . . . everything else is just temporary. Truly, I promise it is so. Trust me for a little longer and I'll bring everything with Louisa to a swift conclusion. I need a little time, that's all," he pleaded softly.

Charles kissed her passionately. Moving his mouth to her left ear, he continued to whisper to her while making promises that she knew were pure fantasy. But, she listened nonetheless.

"My father's as good as lost this time around, you wait and see. His only bargaining chip has been played and the annulment is my next step. That should wipe the smug sneer from his mouth. I've waited so very long to do so!"

"And, where does that leave your precious shipping line?" Sylvia asked, instantly wondering why on earth she was playing along with his ridiculous schemes and dreams.

"Rolling in cash!" he replied, with a derisive laugh. "Because, you see, I doubled the original asking price. After that, I watched him squirm. Louisa won't be harmed by all this. She despises him almost as much as I do and when she's offered an escape route by me, she'll be gone before anyone . . ."

Before he could finish the sentence, Sylvia placed her arms around his neck and pulled him to her. They were locked in a passionate embrace when the door opened and Bertie Webster's head appeared. Just as quickly, it disappeared again and the door closed softly. She moved from Charles momentarily.

"Is that the answer you've been seeking, Charles?" she inquired softly.

He smiled at her before kissing her again.

"Why the change of heart so suddenly?" he murmured in her ear.

"Life's *far too short* and I can't live without you in mine. That's all!" she replied, before remembering that Bertie was waiting for her, so she made her request. "Join us for lunch?"

"No," he muttered, with a grimace. "I'd better be going, I suppose. I've just arrived back home and there're many matters that need to be dealt with, for I feel as though I've been away from Melbourne for months. Can I see you tonight?"

"Was there ever a doubt?" Sylvia queried, with a laugh.

He laughed as he crushed her body to him while kissing her again. He appeared most reluctant to leave her. Whether this fact was due to their reconciliation in this moment, or to his ardent desire to place time and distance between himself and his new wife, Sylvia did not know. Nor did she care, for Charles was back in her arms and the future would need to take care of itself from here, she decided, because tonight, he would be back in her bed.

Louisa

Louisa summonsed the butler and asked for Charlotte to come to her. When the maid appeared in the small, drawing room, Louisa announced her intention of changing her attire before the luncheon was served. So, with assistance from Charlotte, Louisa was shown upstairs to the guest room, which was located to the right of the staircase and which possessed a commanding view of the river. She hoped, rather than believed, that this would be her own room. However, for the moment, it would suffice for her current circumstances, as her new husband had neglected her needs completely this day.

Finally, having changed her gown, she descended the stairs and enquired of the butler the whereabouts of the dining room. To this inquiry, she gleaned the information that all meals were served in the ballroom and she was escorted to that room, which was at the rear of the small drawing room where Charles had left her some time earlier.

Charles Lyndhurst arrived home from wherever he had ridden after their arrival at Lyndhurst Park. He joined Louisa for lunch, which was served at a small table positioned at one end of the massive ballroom, at the far end of which was an impressive mantelpiece above a fireplace, with a pianoforte off to the side by the window. Positioned nearby that musical instrument were two armchairs and a billiard table. Other than that, the entire room was devoid of furniture. It did seem such a waste of space. Lunch was accomplished in silence, for the most part, as each seemed absorbed in thoughtful contemplation of matters concerning their own future welfare.

When lunch was at an end, Charles took Louisa on a quick tour of inspection of the home. After that, he deposited her in the bedroom, which adjoined his own room before explaining – possibly by way of an apology for the state of the room – that the last person to occupy it had been his sister, Caroline. He could not remember exactly when that was, but upon reflection, he thought that it was possibly twenty years earlier. He left her then as he disappeared through the connecting doorway into his own room, which for reasons known only to himself, he did not include in this initial inspection.

Louisa studied her pink bedroom with disgust. The paintwork was faded and the drapes were old, but the room was light and airy, with french doors that opened onto the side verandah on the upper level of the home. There was an internal door that opened into the corridor and another one that opened into Charles' bedroom. To his bedroom door, there was no key, she noted. His bedroom was situated in the front of the house and opened onto the front verandah with wide sweeping views of the river.

Across the corridor was the guest room and behind it was a room stacked with old furniture, trunks and a cot. Charles had described that as the nursery, to which Louisa gave but a cursory glance. At the rear of the upstairs section, there were other bedrooms and a large dormitory. The guest room, she assumed, was kept available for his father on his visits to Melbourne. Whether Elizabeth visited, she knew not.

In the afternoon, she ventured outside and wandered to the croquet court at the side of the house. From there, she descended the stone steps to the river bank and she wandered along the pathway to the small timber jetty near the steps.

Louisa spent the night alone while burying herself in her book on Egypt and retiring early. She knew that Charles had left the house immediately after dinner and he had not returned when she descended into sleep. For this, Louisa was exceedingly grateful.

With a visit from Aunt Sophie on the following morning, Louisa was kept busy while escorting her aunt around the home, into which few had gained admittance in the past. Sophie Collins could not contain her excitement as Louisa took her from the small, front drawing room, to the massive, almost-empty ballroom behind it. Across the hallway from the ballroom, there was a large dining room, which appeared not to have been used for many years.

Downstairs, in the front section of the house, beneath Charles' bedroom, was his private domain, which housed Charles' office currently. This room, he had informed her firmly, was out-of-bounds to everyone, with the exception of Mr. Travis, and he was adamant that this directive included Louisa. She paid scant attention to his sternly-spoken words.

Louisa had been granted a tour of inspection to this impressive, L-shaped room during the previous afternoon. Its door was at the base of the sweeping staircase and off to the left as one descended the stairs. On entry to the office, Louisa had found herself facing a massive bookcase, with its shelves weighed down with volumes of old books that were locked behind glass doors. She decided that she would spend the rest of her life reading every one of them. That should keep the boredom away – to some degree, at least.

In the mid-section of the office was Charles' large desk, with the river in the background and visible through the french doors. At the far end of the room was the desk occupied by Mr. Travis, who was a quietly-spoken gentleman to whom Louisa warmed from the moment when she met him.

The office was light, airy and had several french doors, as well as bay windows, from which the river could be seen. She determined it to be the best room in the house and she felt that it had been the original drawing room when the house was built. Louisa refrained from taking her aunt into Charles' office, much to that lady's annoyance.

Sophie Collins spent two hours with Louisa. During most of that time, she was issuing stern instructions regarding Louisa's attendance at the forthcoming Governor's Grand Ball and the behaviour that was expected of her niece during the evening. To these directives, Louisa heeded not one word.

After her aunt's departure, Louisa summonsed a carriage and, taking Charlotte with her, she visited her mother's dressmaker who lived in two rooms behind a shopfront where she worked. The shop was situated between Lyndhurst Park and the Collins' residence. Having fallen out with the woman many years earlier, Sophie Collins refused to patronise her business. Louisa had known the lady for many years and she hoped that she could be persuaded to perform a miracle, thereby producing a new gown for her to wear to the Governor's Ball, which was but a few days away.

Having heard of Mary Howard's demise and being informed now of Louisa's recent, fortuitous marriage, the dressmaker gave Louisa her undivided attention. Promising to refrain from sleep, if necessary, she vowed to meet Louisa's request and arranged a fitting for the following afternoon at Lyndhurst Park. Well pleased with her first day's activities, Louisa returned to her new home, which she regarded, in her mind, as a temporary arrangement.

After dinner, Charles left the house immediately. Louisa retired to her room alone while, once again, reading for several hours before sleep engulfed her.

By the time that the night of the ball arrived, Louisa felt as though she lived alone in the big, old house, for she had seen Charles Lyndhurst but rarely. He was either ensconced in his office from where he operated his shipping business; or, he was out of the house while visiting his club, she had been informed. The arrangement was one with which she could settle happily, for the time being, because it would make her escape plan easier to formulate and execute when she decided to return to her real home. Never would she be reconciled to the fact that Lyndhurst Park was her home.

On the evening of the Governor's Grand Ball, Charlotte assisted Louisa as she dressed for the event, which was gripping Melbourne in a frenzy of excitement. No one could have been less impressed or less interested than Louisa Lyndhurst. The light cream silk gown, trimmed with fine lace, was a perfect fit as Louisa knew that it would be.

Charlotte was noticeably impressed as she surveyed Louisa. With her shoulders bare and a simple gold and diamond pendant, which had been her mother's treasure, adorning her neck, Louisa was studying her own reflection in the mirror when Charles entered unannounced from his own bedroom. Charlotte, somewhat intimidated by his presence as always, left the bedroom with her eyes lowered at the moment when he entered. He surveyed Louisa critically.

"Simple, but elegant," he stated, with a nod of approval. "You are just skin and bone, aren't you? We shall have to feed you more regularly and with larger portions."

"I'm not a prize pig to be fattened for market!" she exclaimed hotly.

"If only it were as simple as that, eh? My next question, madam, is this . . . *do you dance?*"

"What a ridiculous question!" she stated, with disdain. "I love dancing and I've been doing so for well over ten years. Uncle Robert taught me, with Mama accompanying us on the pianoforte. It was always such fun!"

"Then, let us away, shall we?" he suggested.

So saying, he opened the bedroom door and she sailed out into the corridor, with Charles Lyndhurst in her wake.

The streets of Melbourne were decorated with bunting and all the gas-lights were ablaze, thereby illuminating the major buildings in the city. There were many banners displayed, all welcoming their honoured guest. Charles pointed out the spectacular sight of an electric light, which was affixed to a building and that he described to her as being a new invention. As their carriage wound its way through the city, Louisa noticed that there was a great crowd lining the streets, no doubt in the hope of catching a fleeting glimpse of His Royal Highness, Prince Alfred, Duke of Edinburgh, on the first Royal Tour of these colonies. Everyone was cheering and waving. Louisa could feel the excitement in the air.

The ball was being held in an enormous building, into which Louisa had never entered prior to this night.

The atmosphere inside the building was one of fevered excitement and tremendous expectation on this hot night in late November as they joined the invited guests who were awaiting the arrival of Prince Alfred. The interior was a mass of floral arrangements and greenery, interspersed with water features. It appeared to Louisa that they had entered a cool, colourful, leafy forest area rather than a ballroom. Her head was in a whirl within a few minutes of their arrival as she was introduced to strangers, one after another. Charles appeared to know everyone and everyone seemed to know him. She wondered how they would ever find Robert and Sophie Collins in this large gathering.

Prince Alfred and his entourage had not arrived as yet and Louisa scanned the room while searching for her aunt and uncle, as they were the only familiar faces that she felt she would see this evening. A friendly face was what she needed at present. However, she was whisked onto the dance floor by her new husband and for the next thirty minutes, he did not leave her. At the end of a dance bracket, he deposited her unceremoniously with her recently-located aunt and uncle. He issued stern instructions to Louisa, regarding the behaviour that was expected of her, before disappearing immediately into the throng of revellers.

The entrance of Prince Alfred, accompanied by his extensive entourage of distinguished guests while being flanked by his two, ever-present equerries, brought an immediate halt to all proceedings.

The rolling waves of excitement that rippled around the ballroom were silenced instantly by the playing of the National Anthem. Everyone stood to rigid attention until the final bars of *God Save the Queen* echoed around the assembled guests. Louisa, while standing on tiptoes, managed to catch a brief glimpse of the prince.

Prince Alfred was twenty-three years of age, she knew, and he was the captain of the Royal Navy's steamship, *Galatea*, now at anchor in Port Phillip Bay after having tied up initially at Port Melbourne where the Royal party had left the ship. Prince Alfred had taken up residence at Government House.

Louisa danced with her uncle who returned her to her aunt afterwards as he left them to seek refreshments. Her aunt took possession of Louisa's arm instantly and she was bustling forth – as only Aunt Sophie could bustle – and wheeling her niece from one person to another while making introductions endlessly.

Louisa's boredom was growing by the minute when, suddenly, she glanced up and peered into two, laughing blue eyes that were accompanied by an impish grin, complete with dimples at either side of his mouth. These were adorning a handsome, young face that was surrounded by blonde hair. He offered her his arm, without speaking one word and without taking his eyes from her face. Before her aunt had realised what was occurring, Louisa was in his arms on the dance floor.

"Phillip . . . Phillip Carstairs. And you, lovely lady, are . . .?" her new dance partner queried.

"My name is Louisa. I'm Louisa Howa . . . Lyndhurst," she replied, while wondering why she was trembling all of a sudden.

"Oh! Related to Sir Charles, I presume?" Phillip asked, in a disinterested tone.

Louisa nodded, without elaborating.

Phillip Carstairs danced with her for several dances while seeming most reluctant to leave her side. Her aunt's eyes never wavered from Louisa and her countenance was showing signs of impatience and growing anger. But, Louisa was enjoying herself immensely; so, she ignored her aunt completely. Several times she caught a glimpse of Charles and, every time, he had Sylvia Webster in his arms on the ballroom floor. Somehow, before many dances were through, Phillip had whirled his way into her heart and the feelings that were stirring within her were quite unfamiliar, as well as being most disconcerting. And, she had no explanation for them.

Before Louisa could return to the dance floor with Phillip Carstairs once again, a gruff and arrogant, older man pushed between them while shoving him aside forcefully and unceremoniously. He grabbed Louisa's arm and pulled her onto the ballroom floor with him.

"Stay away from the likes of him! Do you hear me, *madam*?" Sir Charles Lyndhurst snarled at her.

Louisa had met him only on the occasion of his visit to her father's property when, presumably, he had put forward his proposal for this arranged marriage. She did not like him then. She loathed him now.

"I'll do as I please. *And, you* can unhand me!" she demanded, while pushing him in the chest so that she could move from him in order to breathe.

He continued to hold her tightly as they moved around the floor to the music. He was not as tall as his son, but he looked down on Louisa. His eyes were small and brown while his hair was grey, thinning and wispy. His hand slid lower down her back than she thought was fitting. His breath was on her face as he whispered angrily in her ear.

"Carstairs is nothing but trouble. Don't go near him again."

Instantly, Louisa's chin flicked defiantly into the air and her anger began to rise. There was only one way she knew that would ensure her escape from her new father-in-law, without creating a scene on the dance floor. Therefore, she began to stomp heavily onto his feet at every opportunity. The strategy worked as, after a time, he manoeuvred her across the floor and deposited her beside Charles who was standing with Sylvia Webster. They were enjoying glasses of wine together while talking quietly. They turned to stare in some surprise at the new arrivals in their midst.

"Take care of your wife!" he snarled at his son, before continuing angrily with his discourse. "The company she's keeping leaves much to be desired. No Carstairs can be trusted, ever!"

Sir Charles shot a scathing look at Sylvia, another one at Louisa and a menacing glance at his son, before disappearing into the crowd. Louisa looked up at Charles with a defiant look.

"Don't *you* dare to tell me with whom I can dance!" she snapped at him before he could speak; then, on spying her uncle nearby, she called to him. "Uncle Robert! Come and dance with me!"

Robert Collins was standing with a group of male friends while sipping wine and talking quietly with them. He shook his head vigorously at Louisa and continued his conversation. She spun around and walked over to him, instantly taking the glass from his hand as he raised it to his lips.

"Just one dance. That's all I ask! Come along."

Louisa took his arm and, as she was walking by Charles, she thrust her uncle's wine glass unceremoniously into her husband's hand. With his mouth open, Charles stared at her in surprise for a moment; then, taking a step forward, he grabbed her wrist, thereby pulling her to a standstill momentarily.

"Behave yourself. *And, don't* speak to your uncle in that manner," Charles snapped at Louisa.

"What manner? I've been speaking to him like that for all of my life. Don't interfere in my family!" she hissed at him.

Louisa continued to pull her uncle along behind her and Charles released her wrist. Robert Collins, unaware of their exchange, was continuing his conversation with his friends over his shoulder as Louisa dragged him toward the dance floor. From the corner of her eye, she saw a look of astonishment, mingled with amusement, on Mrs. Webster's face. Louisa smiled at the lady, in recognition and acknowledgment. It was in this moment that she overheard Charles' whispered words to Sylvia as he placed the glasses on the tray of a wandering servant.

"Save me from this insanity and dance with me."

Mrs. Webster laughed and placed her arm through his arm in a familiar fashion as they, also, moved onto the dance floor. When Louisa allowed her uncle to leave her side, she waited as far away as possible from her aunt while knowing, without doubt, that Phillip Carstairs would return to her. In a matter of moments, he was by her side and, together, they danced again. He remained by her side for much of the evening until Charles came to claim her to escort her to supper.

Louisa's head was spinning and her thoughts, along with her emotions, were in chaos as she returned with her husband in the carriage to Lyndhurst Park. The Governor's Ball, which she had been dreading, became a memory to be treasured forever. Charles did not speak to her on the homeward journey as he appeared to be lost in deep contemplation himself, although she suspected that he was less than pleased with her. But then, that was not anything unusual, Louisa reminded herself.

Tomorrow, she was to attend the Free Banquet, arranged to feed the poor of Melbourne, in honour of Prince Alfred who was to open the event in the afternoon. This was another of the functions on the Royal Tour calendar and, at her aunt's insistence, Louisa was to aid the Ladies Committee that had been selected by the Organising Committee to assist with the work.

Try as she might, Louisa could not find any way to avoid attending the event. She had resigned herself to the day in order to placate her aunt, who was less than pleased with her niece over her behaviour at the ball, as well as over the fact that she had chosen not to wear the special gown that Sophie Collins had designed and purchased especially for Louisa.

As the carriage rolled to a standstill at the front door of Lyndhurst Park, Charles assisted her from it and he escorted her inside. Then, he turned to leave. The butler stood by the front door, but he turned away as Charles leaned over to whisper in Louisa's ear.

"Tomorrow, we'll speak at great length about tonight's atrocious behaviour," he muttered to her.

Before she could respond to his threatening words, Charles spun around and returned quickly to the waiting carriage, which departed immediately. Benson asked her if she required any refreshments, but she just shook her head and smiled at him.

With disinterest, Louisa had watched Charles leave. To the butler's apparent amusement, she waltzed up the internal staircase with an imaginary Phillip Carstairs in her arms.

She danced into her bedroom where Charlotte was waiting. Louisa threw herself onto the bed and laughed aloud.

"Oh! Charlotte, that was *the most* wonderful and *the most* magical night of my entire life!"

Paula

10 September, 1999 – Gold Coast Hospital

P aula took stock of her immediate surroundings as the saga of the Victoria Victorians began to recede in her consciousness.

She realised that she was standing outside a major hospital. In fact, she was in front of the doors, which were marked as the emergency entrance and she was near to an abandoned ambulance. While contemplating the scene before her, a group of paramedics emerged through the main doorway. The two men and one woman approached the parked vehicle. They were talking quietly together as they came to a standstill beside the ambulance. They did not acknowledge Paula's presence as she watched them while standing in the main driveway.

The time appeared to be late afternoon, because the sun was descending quite quickly towards the western horizon. Puzzled by her surroundings, Paula stood as the silent observer while other staff members and visitors emerged from the hospital.

Glancing towards the front of the building, she read the name that distinguished it as the Gold Coast Hospital. How did she come to be here, she pondered, and why was she here all alone. On studying the outfit, which she was wearing, she noticed that it was a pale lilac skirt, with a matching blouse in a slightly paler shade of lilac.

She did not recall buying these items, so how did she come to be wearing this apparel today?

Recalling the story of Louisa Lyndhurst, she pondered on its meaning and on why she had become absorbed so completely in events that appeared to have occurred in a long-forgotten period of Australian history. The lives of those involved seemed real and the events that happened to them were taken very seriously by the people who were interacting with one another at the time. Would others view this present time-frame in much the same way as Paula was studying those Victorian people, she wondered.

All of a sudden, her immediate attention was drawn to another ambulance that was approaching at a fast rate while the first one, with its crew aboard, moved away from the entrance to the hospital. No one from the first ambulance looked in her direction when they drove by her. The second ambulance, with lights flashing, sped towards Paula who was standing in the centre of the driveway. Obviously, the driver had no intention of slowing the vehicle, or of making any attempt to avoid her.

Somewhat belatedly, she jumped from its path and moved quickly towards a nearby lamp post, which she grasped with her right hand to steady herself. She managed to keep her footing and to remain upright, but with great difficulty and with even greater dexterity. The driver did not appear to notice her, so deep was his concentration as he manoeuvred the vehicle to a screeching halt at the doors to the emergency section of the hospital.

Shaken badly by the experience, Paula released her grip on the lamp post slowly. If the sirens had been sounding, she had not heard the warning at all. She had no idea why she was here in this place and at this time. She puzzled over the incident and wondered why the driver had not seen her. Visibility was clear. At this moment, nurses came rushing from the hospital to assist the paramedics as they removed a patient hurriedly from the rear of the now-stationary ambulance. The concerned group appeared anxious to move the new patient inside as quickly as possible.

Paula glanced to her left as a slight movement caught her eye. The nurse, Gerard, was standing nearby and she walked slowly over to him. He did not speak to her, but in a gentle manner, he took a hold of her arm. He led her to what appeared to be a walkway beside the building. Here, they entered through an iron gate.

On the other side of this fence, there was a beautiful garden that was tended lovingly, obviously. Paula studied the area and it was a very peaceful setting indeed. The sun was shining brightly while birds flitted from tree to tree as they sang their sweet songs. There were many rose bushes and these brightly-coloured roses, as well as the unopened buds, were swaying in the gentle breeze. What a wondrous place, she marvelled.

Gerard led her slowly along a garden path to a ramp, which they ascended before entering the two-bed hospital room where she had been resting previously. Paula glanced around at the now-familiar surroundings before returning to the bed. Once settled comfortably there, she watched as Gerard turned and he headed in the direction of the door, which led to the corridor. He had not spoken a word to her and this puzzled her. Finally, it was Paula who broke the silence. He stopped as he listened politely to her questions..

"Why am I here? And, what is wrong with me? Obviously, this is a hospital, but it does not seem all that familiar. Am I in another country and why am I all alone? Where is my family?"

"You were involved in a car accident while holidaying in Australia. Your family is in the US, as I understand it. I'm not sure if they have been informed of your condition as yet, nor if your husband has been located," Gerard stated in a matter-of-fact tone. "Don't worry about anything now. The police will bring him to you soon, but you may need to be patient for a little longer. The results of all of your tests are not available as yet, so I can't answer your question regarding your current condition."

He turned abruptly as Paula's frown deepened. She had more questions, but these were eluding her at present, because she was becoming very drowsy all of a sudden. The nurse left the room without another word. She stared at the closing door for some moments in a vacant manner. Almost instantly, she dismissed Gerard from her mind as, quite deliberately, she returned her gaze to the beautiful garden outside the hospital window and she studied these peaceful surroundings.

Paula's concentration wavered at this moment. She wondered what had become of the Victorian people who appeared to be very familiar to her when she had followed their life story. As this thought came into her befuddled mind, she left the hospital setting and she returned – in her present consciousness – to the city of Melbourne and in the year of 1867.

Part Two

Victorian Victorians

Chapter Twelve

— *Victorian Victorians* —

Sylvia

Ultimatums and Undertakings

S nuggled beside him in her bed, Sylvia stirred slightly; then, reluctantly, she opened her eyes partially and peered out at the world. Through the edge of the drapes, she saw bright sunlight. She had no idea of the hour. His body was wound around her and a feeling of contentment flooded her being. She moved her body a little, but his grip tightened although he did not stir otherwise, not even to open his eyes.

"Don't even think of it," he whispered in her ear, with his breath brushing the skin on her neck.

"What?"

"Moving from me," he murmured, still without opening his eyes, but with his hand roving to her breast.

"Again?" she queried, with a slight laugh.

"I'm here till midday. Settle back to enjoy . . . this"

Charles whispered as his lips moved to replace his hand. Sylvia relaxed into his embrace while enjoying these precious moments with him. There would be time enough for regrets later. But, for now, they had each other still.

They shared a late breakfast on the verandah, although the heat of the day was fierce, even at this hour. There was a hot northerly wind blowing and this, along with the dust it brought with it, drove them inside the house and they adjourned to Sylvia's sitting room. Charles had surprised her during the previous evening as he danced with her for most of the night at the Governor's Ball. Finally, it was Louisa's behaviour with the young man, Phillip Carstairs, which forced him to abandon her in favour of his new wife, along with the renewed demands from his father to take charge of the situation before he himself intervened. Charles complied eventually, much to his bride's displeasure, which she had not had the good grace to attempt to hide. Louisa would lead him a merry dance before she was through, Sylvia predicted to herself, as they sipped tea together.

Sylvia had barely arrived home herself from the ball and she was in the process of saying farewell to Bertie at the front door when Charles' carriage pulled to a stop. He had bounded up the steps to her then and it was easy to pretend for a time that nothing had changed between them. This pretence could not last forever although, for now, Charles was with her. Little else mattered.

"It'll be a scorching day at the Free Banquet. I'm pleased I declined the invitation to serve on the Ladies Committee. I couldn't think of anything worse . . . heat, dust and flies. How I loathe them!" Sylvia stated emphatically. "What're your plans for today?"

He replaced the empty cup onto the saucer on the small table in front of him and stretched his legs, seemingly well contented with his life at present. He pondered her question for a moment.

"I'm entertaining friends at home," he replied casually.

Sylvia looked over at him in some surprise.

"You? Entertaining at Lyndhurst Park? That's rare," she commented, with a laugh. "Marriage certainly has changed everything for you."

Sylvia felt – rather than saw – him bristle at her flippant words.

"It has nothing to do with *that*! The event is *not* uncommon . . . occasionally, I do hold card evenings, although today it's an afternoon affair, which *is* unusual. That's more to do with men having free time on their hands, due to their wives' involvement in this banquet. I should imagine it'll go well into the night. There's *big* money involved . . . and that is definitely between you and me."

Sylvia knew, before the next words had escaped from her lips, that she should not have asked the question. It was one of those rare moments when she was in a totally relaxed state and, because of this, her guard was down. Therefore, these words bypassed her conscious mind completely.

"Louisa will not intervene then?" she queried softly.

Charles stiffened and pursed his lips. Abruptly, he stood and walked to the window. With his hands behind his back, he stared out into the garden. Finally, he turned to her. He was frowning and he brought his hand up to brush the non-existent strand of hair from his forehead.

"Sylvia, when this relationship first commenced all those years ago, you agreed to see me, but on *one condition*. Do you remember?"

Sylvia frowned and she was biting her lip while wondering to what he was alluding. Slowly, she shook her head as she looked up at him. She returned her cup to the table.

"No . . . no, I cannot. I can't recall placing any conditions on you at all."

"Well, you did! *And*, in case it's slipped your notice, I have abided by it . . . rigidly, if the truth be known," he stated emphatically, before continuing with his explanation. "It was that never would Edwin, or your relationship with him, be spoken of between us. Remember? Now, I respected your request in this regard and I accepted the condition you imposed . . . up until the time of his accident, at the very least. I'd ask for a similar courtesy in return."

In astonishment, she heard the rebuke in his words as she continued to stare up at him. Another wedge was being placed firmly between them. She felt it keenly. Charles came to her and knelt on one knee beside her as he took a hold of both of her hands.

"I'm sorry. I didn't mean that as it sounded . . . not as a rebuke. *But,* you must understand. I'll handle my wife how and as I see fit. She'll be brought to heel. *And,* it'll be in my time. Certainly, it will not be at the direction of my father, or anyone else. Do you understand?" he asked.

Sylvia removed her hands from his firm grip while folding them on her lap as she watched him.

"*Your wife* is a vibrant, headstrong, young girl," Sylvia said, speaking quietly and choosing her words carefully. "She'll not take too kindly to being treated as an animal in need of training and to be bent to your will. Take care, that's all. *This subject* is closed between us, now and forever. Please, understand *me*, Charles. I'm not attempting to interfere in your marriage, but I've been placed in a difficult situation here, so you'd do well to acknowledge it sometimes."

"I do realise it," he replied, instantly rising to his feet, but remaining beside her. "As long as we understand each other. Leave all else to me. It's my problem, of my making, and I'll deal with it. If I have to be heavy-handed, I will, and that'll be because it's long overdue and should've been attended to by others long before now. I'm treading a fine line here, for you know what I'm hoping to achieve; but, by the same token, I'll not stand idly by and be made to look a fool either."

Sylvia stood up slowly, moved to him, placed her arms around his waist and leaned her body against him. He held her tightly.

"It's been a wonderful night, followed by an even more wonderful morning. Let's not end it in this manner," she reminded him.

Charles placed a finger under her chin and lifted it slightly.

"No, let's not do so," he murmured, as he kissed her.

Releasing her, he looked down into her eyes, with his arms holding her about the waist, still. His face was showing a supercilious smirk.

"I'll trade you some information. What do you say?" he inquired of her, with a sly, maddening smile.

"Oh! What's that?" she asked, already suspecting a trap.

"There's someone whom *I suspect* you know. He's but recently arrived here from Sydney . . . with one, Phillip Carstairs esquire. They appear to me to be the best of friends, so find out all you can about that particular gentleman, as well as his habits and haunts, please. *And,* I'll be eternally grateful."

"Who is it I'm supposed to interrogate on your behalf, Mr. Lyndhurst? *And,* more to the point, just how grateful is implied in the word, *eternally*?" Sylvia asked, and laughing as she did so.

"Oh! You'll see," he replied, with a soft laugh before revealing more information. "The man's name is Patrick Doherty. I do believe you've heard of him?"

Astounded, she moved from him slightly. She scrutinised him for several moments to see if he was teasing her.

"Patrick! My brother, Patrick? Here? In Melbourne?" Sylvia shouted, while thumping him on the chest as she did so. "And, you've waited till now to tell me! I could kill you. Really, I could. I think I was twelve years old the last time I saw him and that's over twenty years ago now. I can hardly believe it! Are you certain? Where's he staying? Answer me at once."

Sylvia looked up at him expectantly as Charles drew her back to him.

"With Carstairs, I believe, and there's a strong family likeness, so I can state confidently *I am quite certain*. Does that piece of information please you, or not?" he queried.

Sylvia pondered the question for a moment before answering. Patrick had been ten years old when Sylvia was deposited at her uncle's home and into his care, so she had not lived under the same roof as her brother since then. She did not know him at all, she conceded to herself. She was even more surprised that Patrick had not arrived on her doorstep immediately, and not a little disappointed.

"Yes, it pleases me greatly, but it'll please my mother even more. He's been missing for so long and she prays for him every night. What do people say about parents and their black sheep? I'm certain I never get a mention in her prayers. I'm too safe and dependable."

"I can vouch for that! You wouldn't leave and come away with me when you had the chance to do so," Charles reminded her.

Sylvia squeezed him more tightly and she bit her lip firmly again so that no more unguarded words would slip from her this day.

"I'll make some inquiries," she promised, and she felt him nod his approval in reply to her words.

Louisa

The morning after the ball dawned hot, dry and windy. Louisa left home early and arrived at her aunt's home before the appointed hour. She was hoping that her punctuality might help to ease the tension, which had arisen between them as result of her perceived misbehaviour at the ball.

Upon arrival, Louisa discovered the events of the previous evening were long forgotten and she was bustled upstairs immediately to her old bedroom. She was as much the daughter of Sophie and Robert Collins as she was that of George and the late Mary Howard and her room was as it had been always. Some of her old gowns were hanging in the wardrobe to this day. Spread across the bed now was a white gown and Sophie Collins' maid was waiting to attend to Louisa.

Dressed in the gown, which was plain and serviceable, she descended the stairs to find her uncle in his library. He glanced up from his desk as she entered.

"I see you've been seconded to other duties this day," he commented.

"I don't seem to be very popular in many quarters at present. I'm attempting to make amends."

"And, well you should, but I'll say no more on the subject. No doubt, you're ears are burning already from the scoldings."

"Surprisingly no, not yet," Louisa replied, with a laugh. "But, I suspect my sins are all mounting up on a slate somewhere. I expect they'll catch up with me soon enough. They do have a habit of doing so when I'm least expecting it. I seem to attract problems without really trying, Uncle Robert. Have you noticed that?"

He looked on her with kindly eyes and laughed in response.

"From the day you were born, child, it's been that way."

Before Louisa could reply, her aunt was at the door. She took Louisa by the arm and manoeuvred her out into the hallway where she attached a blue rosette to the bodice of her white gown.

"This is a great honour that's bestowed on you today, as the committee is under the auspices of the Governor's wife who has kindly supplied all our gowns and everything we shall need to feed these *poor unfortunates* this day. It's a great charitable service we're providing, so we can only hope *they* have the good sense to realise all the sacrifices we're making on their behalf," Aunt Sophie stated emphatically, instantly wrinkling her nose at the unpleasant prospect.

From the hallway, Louisa glanced at her uncle over her aunt's shoulder and grimaced. He winked in response as he raised his expressive eyebrows in exasperation as he did so.

Louisa was bundled into a carriage and taken to the riverbank at South Yarra. The hot northerly wind that had been stirring early was at full force when they arrived. There was a long line of trestle tables, which were covered by white linen tablecloths. These tables were stretched along the river bank in the parkland setting and a large marquee had been erected in the vicinity.

A substantial crowd was in attendance already, but the picnic area was roped off at present and accessible only to those who were to work at the Free Banquet. Louisa had read in the newspaper about the banquet that had been proposed to allow the ordinary citizens of Melbourne to participate in the Royal Tour. There had been great controversy regarding its organisation, or indeed the need for such an event to be staged at all. Everything that was required for the day had been donated by the various business houses around the city, at the request of the Governor's wife. Prince Alfred was due to open proceedings mid-afternoon.

Excitement was building in the air as the members of the Ladies Committee gathered and were shepherded through the crowds, ushered beyond the ropes and led to the large tent that was to be their sanctuary for the day. Inside, chairs and tables were set up for the use of the ladies who had donated their time to serve Melbourne's poor on this special day. Sophie Collins sat down immediately on one of the chairs provided and began chatting with friends while sipping champagne. How they could do so, Louisa did not know, as the heat inside the marquee was oppressive and would be worse before the day drew to a close.

Louisa, looking for an escape, moved outside and over to the tables where other ladies were working. She offered her assistance and was assigned the tasks of covering the sandwiches, as well as ones relating to the table settings – and, in particular, the placement and the filling of the water jugs and the glass finger-bowls, which seemed somewhat unusual to her. She glanced up at the sea of people and it appeared to have doubled in number in the short time since their arrival. Studying them from a distance, she doubted that many would have used a finger-bowl in their lives and wondered whose idea it was to provide such items today.

She shrugged slightly and continued with her task as the perspiration rolled down her face and back. The dust that filled the air covered the tables and floated on top of the water in the jugs and bowls as she filled them. The wind was blowing in strong gusts and blown along with it came the bush flies that stuck to her face and eyes. It would be another two hours before Prince Alfred's arrival and she had no idea how the ever-increasing crowd of hot, irritable, thirsty people – baking in the blazing sun, without any shelter – would be kept behind the thin rope barriers until that hour arrived.

She heard a rumour that the temperature had moved already above ninety degrees Fahrenheit before midday and Louisa could well believe this to be correct. She pressed on with her task as men mounted ladders and, using thick ropes, levered large wine casks into position on the branches of every tree in the area. To these sturdy casks, they attached long hoses that ran to the hastily erected wine fountains that were interspersed at intervals amongst the trees. Every need had been met, it seemed. The only eventualities that had not been taken into consideration on this hot day in November were the prevailing weather conditions and the size of the crowd. Of those gathered already, there were many who were becoming somewhat unruly. Louisa had seen only a handful of policemen in attendance.

Undeterred, she continued along the long line of tables while filling the bowls from her water jug before returning to the large water containers set up beside the marquee to refill the jug at regular intervals. Not for the first time, she wondered how she came to be here when there was so much work to be done on her father's property and there was no one there to take charge since her departure.

She gave a deep sigh as she contemplated the situation that she had left behind her there. If her father did not appear in Melbourne within the next week or so, she would escape and make the journey home alone. When Charles had challenged her in Bendigo regarding the boy's clothing she possessed, she did not lie to him, as she did not have them with her. In fact, she had posted them on ahead in a parcel addressed to herself, at her aunt's address, and supposedly posted from her father. Her aunt delivered the parcel to her on her first visit to Lyndhurst Park.

She planned to dress as a boy and make the journey to Echuca alone. There, she would change into a gown and return to her home to confront her father regarding his failure to present himself to a physician in Melbourne within four weeks of her marriage. This was the bargain, which she had made with her father. She would carry out her plan – come what may – and the devil take Charles Lyndhurst and his repulsive father!

Louisa had seen little of her aunt during the day and, as the hours wore on, the number of people grew to such a degree that she could not see how the needs of all could be met from the food available on the tables, despite there being a copious amount set out in readiness. And on the food, the flies were roaming freely and the dust particles were settling rapidly. She looked with distaste upon the prepared banquet and, not for the first time, she brushed the dust from her own eyes.

She watched as several youths sneaked under the barrier rope and they were being chased by officials. The crowd, having tired of waiting and with the fierce sun bearing down on the heads of all assembled there, began laughing and cheering. Spurred on by the involvement of the amused onlookers, the young men ran around while weaving back and forth so as to avoid being apprehended. Finally, they relented and returned behind the barriers, much to the merriment of all.

Louisa was at the far end of the tables and had just sought shelter from the sun beneath a large tree when she heard the enormous roar from the crowd. Someone shouted that Prince Alfred would not be attending. An official had mounted a dais before making this unwelcome announcement. Instantaneously, the sea of people surged forward. As one, it moved toward the tables, the wine fountains and the food.

Louisa pressed herself back against the trunk of the tree and froze. She could watch only in horror and disbelief at the spectacle before her eyes. Men, women and children began grabbing everything within their grasp while those closest to the tables began throwing food back over their shoulders to ones behind them. Men were jumping in the air to catch the missiles of bread and sundry other foodstuff that floated by their heads. Women were drinking the water from the finger-bowls that Louisa had filled and children were screaming in terror as they struggled to keep their feet during the mayhem.

Suddenly, a mince pie hit Louisa on the side of her head while hitting her bonnet. Then, pieces of fruit began to stick, as a syrup-like substance, to the side of her neck. Above her, a young man laughed aloud at the spectacle. He was perched on a branch high above her and he had cut the hose leading from the wine cask with the sharp carving knife that he was holding in his hand.

"Here, Luvie! Wash it off with this!" he shouted to Louisa.

With that, white wine began flowing onto her head and neck, much to the amusement of those who were close by. She felt her gown becoming soaked and she ran from the tree, instantly removing her bonnet and throwing it on the ground. She tried to push her way through the people, but she found herself surrounded. She kicked the man in front of her behind the knees; then, when he staggered as a consequence, she managed to move a little to her left and into a clearing closer to the next tree, which had been commandeered by several young men. They were enjoying themselves immensely as they sprayed the crowd below them with wine from the hose that had been severed there.

Louisa took a deep breath and stood still, trying to fathom her next move. To return to Aunt Sophie and the marquee was impossible. To find higher ground was the best plan, she felt, so that she could ascertain where she was at this precise moment. While contemplating the next step, she felt a thud as something hard hit her chest. She looked down to see her white food-splattered gown soaked in red wine. At her feet was the missile that had struck her forcibly. It was a large loaf of wine-soaked bread. If she had not known better, she would have thought that she had been shot and was bleeding as a result.

She decided to move, rather than to stand still in the one place and risk becoming a target again. She moved to her left, as she suspected that by moving from the area of the river, this would give her a better vantage point. If she could see the marquee, she may have some idea as to where she stood precisely. But avoid the trees she must, because wine was showering down from all of them now and men and women were grabbing whatever containers they could obtain so that they could have their fill of the free-flowing liquid.

It was as she moved closer to the roadway that she caught a glimpse of the tent where she assumed her aunt and the other ladies were sheltering. All of a sudden, a tremendous roar erupted as the ropes of the marquee were severed. The whole structure collapsed on top of those who were sheltering inside while the spectators adjacent to the area laughed uproariously at the sight.

Louisa raised her hand to her mouth in horror. In this heat, the occupants could suffocate easily if they were not rescued quickly. The youths who had caused the commotion and subsequent mayhem were running now from the police whose numbers seemed to have swelled considerably. Many men were working frantically to release those who were entombed inside the tent.

Louisa's first reaction was to rush back there to assist her aunt, but common sense prevailed. Between her and the demolished tent were hundreds of people. Such a feat would be impossible.

She turned and, once more, walked in the direction of the road, although she could not see it from her vantage point. As she moved forward, a mass of people began swarming in the opposite direction to her as it headed toward the area by the river, in search of free food and wine. She pushed against this sea of humanity as a tiny boat would do as it moved out to sea in the face of huge waves. Suddenly, two strong, male hands grabbed her from behind and these grasped her around the waist. She knew a moment of sheer panic.

"*Stop*, for pity's sake, Louisa!"

She turned to look into the face of a breathless and red-faced Phillip Carstairs who appeared almost on the verge of collapse.

"Come with me," he gasped, immediately taking her hand and dragging her with him.

Not having a definite plan of action herself and being jostled in all directions, she allowed him to lead her back toward the river. The faster that they walked, the further they moved away from the tables and the banquet area. The milling crowd began to thin as they hurried along the bank of the Yarra River. Finally, he pulled her toward some bushes not far from the river and he collapsed on the grass as he threw himself onto his back while gasping for breath. There were but a few people in this area. She sank to her knees beside him.

"Thank you," she gasped.

Phillip pulled a silver hip flask from the back pocket of his trousers and, without a word, he pushed it at her. She unscrewed the lid and sipped the contents, all the while expecting it to be alcohol, because she detected the smell of whisky, which had been its most recent contents, obviously. He was studying her in some amusement.

"Water!" she gasped again, this time between gulps of the precious clear liquid.

She passed it back to him and threw herself on her back on the grass beside him. The hot wind whipped around her face and her hair. The dust continued to follow her relentlessly, but she was free of the noisy, unruly crowd, so nothing else mattered at this moment. Phillip rolled over and looked at her. He leaned on his elbow and grinned at her as he studied her appearance. Two deep dimples danced on his cheeks, just above and on either side of the corners of his mouth. Louisa had noticed them first when he smiled at her as they danced together at the Governor's Ball.

"I've never seen such a mess in all my life. Whatever became of my belle of the ball? You're a disgrace!"

"You're not exactly unscathed yourself," she stated, while studying his wine-soaked clothing and his food-splattered face.

Phillip laughed again and rolled onto his back beside her as they both tried to breathe more freely. Finally, he sat up again and looked down at her.

"I've chased you through the crowd since you were hit by that pie. I shouted and shouted, but you just kept on running and thumping everyone who stood in your path," he explained.

"Truly? I didn't hear you. I was trying to reach the road. I thought I'd get home that way, as I can't be far from Lyndhurst Park, I'm certain."

Louisa sat up beside him. Looking into his laughing blue eyes, the feelings that had stirred within her during the previous evening surfaced again. Not understanding them, she squashed them instantly. She looked longingly at the river. Without warning, she jumped to her feet and ran to the water's edge while knowing that he was following her.

She knelt on the bank and cupped her hands in the fast-flowing water. In one sweep, she brought the water up and splashed her face and neck, vainly attempting to remove the remnants of the mince pie from her hair as she did so. The feeling was so wonderful that she repeated it over and over while realising that Phillip was following her lead. Then, she sat back, stretched her legs out in front of her and pulled up her skirt to wipe her face.

He glanced up from the water and he was staring unashamedly at her legs. She flicked her skirt down and placed her hands on the ground behind her, thereby supporting her weight as she gazed across the river. He removed his coat before tossing it on the ground and he moved to her, immediately sitting close beside her. She felt the heat of his body near to her own. Glancing at her gown, she studied it in detail. There was hardly one inch of white showing in the sea of food and wine that soaked the garment.

"What a waste!" she muttered, and thinking of her aunt, she knew a moment's remorse. "I hope Aunt Sophie managed to escape."

"It was every man for himself in that melee," Phillip muttered; then, he questioned himself aloud. "Now, whatever am I to do with you?"

"Show me how to reach Lyndhurst Park," she suggested.

He threw back his head and laughed loudly. He moved to where his face was almost touching her face and he stared at her in surprise.

"That was the last plan I had in mind," he murmured, before grinning at her in a brazen manner.

Louisa moved her body slightly away from him.

"What were you doing here anyway?" she asked.

"I escorted my sister and her friend here, as they were expected to help on the Ladies Committee. When I was assisting them from the carriage, I caught sight of you, with a jug in your hand and intent on some chore. I changed my plans instantly. I'd almost reached you when that announcement was made and, before I knew it, the crowd surged, taking me with them."

"And your sister?" Louisa queried.

"Elizabeth? I've no idea," he admitted, with a nonchalant shrug. "Every man for himself, as I said. As for taking you back to your home, I'm not much help, I'm afraid. I've not been here in Melbourne long myself. Which direction is it?"

Louisa studied the river and the surrounding area. She pointed to her right.

"It's that way, I think. I live on the river, so perhaps, we could find someone with a boat. But not just now . . . in a bit . . . I don't need to go yet. Tell me all about yourself and why you're here in town anyway."

"If that's your desire . . . but, let's go back to the shade of those bushes. It's too hot here."

So saying, he jumped to his feet, grasped her hand firmly and pulled her with him as he grabbed his discarded coat with his other hand. Together, they returned to the shaded area, which was quite secluded and he settled on a place where the grass was thick while pulling her down beside him. Phillip stretched out on the grass, placed his arms back behind his neck and crossed his legs at the ankles. Louisa settled back and she relaxed beside him on the grass. She listened intently to his voice while closing her eyes to block out the glare of the afternoon sun. He began to relate some of his life to her.

Phillip explained that he had been born in Sydney and had lived there until the death of his mother two years earlier; then, he had travelled to England to visit his sister and her husband. When his father became ill in Sydney a year later, he returned with Elizabeth and her family, with the exception of her eldest son who had remained in England. Elizabeth was anxious to return to her son and she would be doing so, after this visit to her friends in Melbourne. His sister had timed their visit to coincide with the Royal Tour here. His father died in Sydney some eight months earlier. He revealed that Elizabeth was anxious for him to accompany her back to England within a few months.

His older brother, George, who lived with his own young family in Sydney, had inherited his father's vast business interests and rural properties in New South Wales. He was demanding that Phillip remain in Sydney to assist him in the operation of his many business ventures.

"Old George is threatening to cut off my annual stipend unless I obey his commands. Elizabeth is standing between us at the moment and she has my interests at heart, I know, but me? I'm between the devil and the deep blue sea, as the saying goes. I haven't made up my mind as yet." he revealed. "Now, your story, if you please, Louisa Lyndhurst. How did you end up married to *him*, of all people? Was it for the money, the social position or were you forced in some way?"

Louisa pursed her lips and grimaced, not wishing to reveal too much about her father and his insistence on the arranged marriage. She explained about her mother's death and her father's subsequent illness, while revealing little about herself and the reasons for the marriage. Suddenly, she jumped to her feet.

"I need to go. Let's walk," she said.

Louisa began heading in the direction of the river and walking away from the banquet area where the participants appeared to be becoming more unruly with every passing moment and every ounce of alcohol consumed. Phillip, with his coat over his arm, caught up with her and walked beside her in silence until they reached a slight bend in the river. As they rounded it, they came upon a collection of rowing boats of various shapes and sizes.

"Which one has *madam* set her heart upon . . . the blue or the red?" he asked, as he swept his arm around in an arc and indicating the boats.

Louisa had walked on by, lost in her thoughts, and she had not noticed them. He took her arm and led her back to where the boats were tied. These were down a small embankment, sitting in mud and tethered to individual poles secured on the bank.

"I'll row you home," he suggested.

She stared at the boats and glanced quickly back at him as she gasped.

"That's stealing!"

"No, we're just borrowing. I'll return it in good time and no one'll be any the wiser. Have you a better suggestion? We could walk for miles and still not be able to reach your home. The river bank looks rather overgrown further along, in case you hadn't noticed."

Louisa bit her lip and studied the terrain, toward which they were walking as she realised that he was correct in his assessment. He took her hand and smiled at her.

"I'll get you home, Louisa . . . I promise, although I can't give any guarantee regarding the hour. Will you accept my offer?"

Suddenly, she threw back her head and laughed. Nodding her head, she pulled her hand from his grasp and jumped down the embankment. She sat on the bank and, lifting the crinoline slightly, she began to remove her shoes, because without them, she would be able to wade through the mud to the small vessel more easily. While he was occupied untying one of the boats, she slid her hands unobtrusively beneath her skirt and removed her garters and stockings while having almost accomplished this task before he turned to her.

Phillip glanced at her bare feet and her slightly-raised skirt. He lifted an eyebrow as he did so, but he made no comment. He removed his waistcoat and neck tie while throwing these items carelessly with his coat onto the seat; then, he moved their new mode of transport through the mud and into the water, with his boots sinking deeply as he did so. Tucking her discarded apparel inside her shoes, Louisa grabbed for his outstretched hand and she waded into the mud while sinking to her ankles, also.

Laughing, she stepped into the rocking boat as it wobbled dangerously in the water, despite the fact that Phillip was attempting to hold it steady for her. She fell heavily onto the coat, which he had placed there and she dropped her shoes onto the floor as she gripped the two sides for support. Phillip pushed off, hurriedly climbing aboard quickly. The mud had seeped into the hem of her skirt, but she did not care, as she decided she could not arrive home looking respectable now, no matter how hard she tried.

Her misdemeanours were mounting on that imaginary slate, she confided to herself, as she watched Phillip man the oars as though he had been rowing boats for all of his life. Once he had manoeuvred the boat away from the bank, he settled into a steady rhythm and moved the oars effortlessly through the water. His white shirt became soaked with perspiration in no time while his broad shoulders and strong arms were accentuated by the material clinging to his skin. Louisa looked ahead as she tried to avoid his gaze, which never left her face. She tried to determine how far away Lyndhurst Park would be, but she could not see any familiar landmarks. Despite being on the river, the hot northerly wind pursued them.

"What kind of reception are you expecting at home?" he queried, as though reading her thoughts.

"Hostile, I'd imagine," she replied, with a slight laugh and a determined toss of her head in a small show of defiance.

"You don't care, do you?" he said, as he laughed with her.

Louisa laughed again and shook her head furiously. Phillip was facing her and she found his constant gaze disconcerting, to say the least. She placed her hand in the water, thus allowing it to drag along with the movement and watching it intently so that she could avoid his scrutiny. Finally, as they rounded a bend in the river, she spied her destination. Lyndhurst Park loomed in the distance. She pointed in its direction and he turned his gaze to follow her outstretched arm.

"That's it! The white home with the wide verandahs. I knew it couldn't be far at all," she exclaimed in triumph.

"I expect it's not, if one is just sitting back and enjoying the view," he stated, with a broad grin on his face.

"Are you tiring?"

"Of course not," he replied, instantly panting and puffing in an exaggerated manner.

Louisa laughed with him; then quickly, she averted her gaze again. She found his presence and his constant scrutiny very troubling, for she did not have any explanation for the feelings that she experienced when their eyes met.

"Do you love him?" he asked suddenly.

"Charles? No, not at all!" Louisa replied, surprised by the unexpected question. "I don't think I even like him really. That's not surprising though, for I hardly know him, as we're practically strangers who are living under the same roof. He thinks I'm spoilt, undisciplined and too outspoken, I'm certain; whereas, I see him as extremely selfish, arrogant and being accustomed to having his own way at all times."

"Why, then, did you tie yourself to him?" he asked the question again.

"I'd rather not talk about it. There were reasons and others to be considered. That's all," she replied, with a slight shrug of her shoulders.

He rowed in silence until the small timber jetty on the bank beneath the large white house came into view; then, he changed direction and moved the boat toward it.

Louisa allowed a deep sigh to escape from her body. The upcoming confrontation was inevitable. Suddenly, she wished that she could ask Phillip to keep on rowing and take her as far away from Lyndhurst Park – and its main occupant – as he could manage. But, the reality was that this was where she was expected to reside at present. Somehow, come what may, she was determined it would not be a permanent arrangement. How it could be changed, she knew not, at this stage. She would find a way to escape permanently, she promised herself.

Chapter Thirteen

– Victorian Victorians –

Louisa

Phillip brought the craft alongside the jetty and Louisa threw her shoes, with her silk stockings and garters attached still, up above her head as the boat rocked beneath her feet. She heard these items land on their target. She grasped the short ladder and climbed the few steps up it while trying desperately to keep the crinoline and skirt as close to her legs as was possible under these trying circumstances. The wind was working against her in this endeavour as Phillip clutched the pylon for support. The pylon itself was large and looked to have been hewn from a huge tree trunk.

Having found her land-legs again, with her mud-stained bare feet firmly planted on the timber decking, Louisa caught the rope that he threw up to her and she was securing it around the post when he jumped up beside her while taking it from her grasp and tightening the knot himself. Dusk was falling as they stood together.

"Can I have that, Louisa . . . as a memento?" he asked, as he smiled at her and with devilment dancing in his impish blue eyes.

"What?"

"The rosette! I shall remember you by it always."

"If you wish," she answered, with a soft laugh.

Louisa removed the blue rosette that her aunt had attached to her bodice and she handed it to Phillip who slipped it into the pocket of his trousers. As she did so, she was looking towards the house, partially hidden from view behind the trees and the thick bushes of the bank while trying to ascertain where Charles might be. Without warning, Phillip slipped his arms around her waist and kissed her passionately while clutching her tightly in the embrace.

Louisa, taken by surprise, found herself pinned tightly against the pylon. She knew that to move in either direction would take them both into the fast-flowing waters of the Yarra River. Her legs felt as though they would not hold her. There were fast-flying butterflies doing loops and turns within the region of her stomach while her heart was pounding rapidly. Without understanding the reason, she relaxed into his embrace and responded to him. Phillip released her momentarily and looked deeply into her eyes.

"I'm falling madly in love with you," he murmured softly in her ear, with his breath on her neck causing a strange sensation to float down her spine.

"What! With me?" she asked, wide-eyed.

"Oh! Louisa," Phillip said, with a soft laugh while murmuring in her ear. "You're such a tease!"

Then, smiling at her, he moved his mouth to her lips and he kissed her again before she realised his intention. Suddenly, coming to her senses, Louisa tried to push him away and to free herself from his arms, but he was too strong for her. With a great effort, she brought her two hands onto his chest to push him from her. However, as she did so, she felt one of his hands reach beneath her skirt. He was lifting the crinoline and caressing her bare leg; then, roving along the leg of her pantalets, it began to snake along her inner thigh. She pulled her face away from him and she gasped.

"What on earth are you doing?" she demanded.

"A married woman? *And, you're asking me?*" he whispered in her ear, instantly laughing as he uttered the words.

Furiously, she struggled with him. Just as she felt herself losing the battle with him as he sought to push her down toward the deck, and with her knees bending beneath the pressure, she heard footsteps on the gravel path, which led along the bank to the jetty. It was then that the smell of cigar smoke reached her nostrils. She knew whoever was heading their way must be a visitor, for she had never seen Charles Lyndhurst with a cigar. Phillip's mouth was on her cheek and moving toward her lips once again. Quickly, she turned her face away from him.

"Release me now!" she demanded loudly and clearly, while hoping that the person would hear her.

Phillip's reply was a loud chuckle. The footsteps came onto the jetty and, as Phillip heard them, he stiffened noticeable. Giving an audible gasp, he released his grip on Louisa as this sudden interruption brought home to him the danger, in which he found himself. Louisa pulled away from him and looked at the gentleman who was immaculately attired and drawing on a large cigar as he surveyed them, with obvious amusement dancing on his countenance. She had never seen this young man before in her life, but at this moment, he was the most welcome sight that she had beheld ever.

"Good evening," he greeted them in a voice that was cultured and decidedly English. "Extremely hot weather we are enduring. Would you not agree?"

Without a thought to her appearance – or, to her apparel discarded on the jetty – Louisa spun around and ran as fast as she could away from the two men. She brushed by the stranger as she rushed from the deck; then, running along the gravel path, with her feet hardly touching the stones beneath them, she reached the stone steps. Breathlessly, she mounted the stairs to the main carriageway.

As she crossed it, she heard a carriage and pounding hooves some distance away while coming from the direction of the main gate. Louisa jumped the two front steps onto the porch, pushed the heavy door open and rushed inside the home.

Benson was leaving the ballroom and he stopped to stare at her in utter astonishment. She collapsed on the bottom step of the internal staircase and sat there as she tried to refill her depleted lungs. The air in the house was hot – stiflingly so – and it was filled with cigar smoke. There were male voices coming from the direction of the ballroom. Quickly and furtively, Benson closed the double doors of the ballroom as though trying to hide some deep secret behind them.

"Water," Louisa gasped as she spoke. "Hurry, Benson, for I'm parched."

He was turning to attend to her direction when the gentleman who had rescued her entered through the front door the house and, at that same moment, the carriage pulled to a halt outside the front door. The man was holding her shoes, with her stockings and garters peeking from the top of them. He walked over and, without a word, placed them beside her on the step. He no longer held the cigar, she noticed, as he smiled down at her, and he had a kindly, boyish face. As her laboured breathing became easier, she nodded to him in acknowledgment for all that he had done for her this evening.

"Thank you," she murmured.

"It's my pleasure," he replied, still appearing amused by the situation; then, indicating the arrival of the carriage with the slightest movement of his head, he advised her. "You have just made it home in time, I should think, Miss Lyndhurst. Irate fathers aren't easy to deal with . . . it is Miss Lyndhurst?"

"Louisa," she mumbled.

"Then, I am very pleased to make your acquaintance, Louisa. Shall I stay and be your protector again?"

Before she could reply, Benson returned with the glass of water on a silver tray as Charles bounded up the steps and came through the open front door. The stranger watched with interest, as did Benson. Louisa reached for the water and brought the glass to her lips while Charles came to an abrupt stop in the foyer. He was staring down at her in astonishment. Ignoring him, she gulped down the water as though it could be the last drink that she would have in her entire life. She did not stop until the glass was empty.

"Good grief, Louisa! Look at the state of you! Are you injured? Is that blood on your bodice?" he demanded.

"No, it's red wine," she replied, instantly shaking her head and endeavouring to explain her appearance to him. "I'm in a dreadful mess, I know, but the whole horrendous day was such a fiasco. I've never seen the like of it, ever!"

Louisa stood up and Charles' gaze swept her whole body while taking in her mud-caked bare feet, her soiled and stained once-white gown and her hair, which was streaked with the remnants of the mince pie and other sundry pieces of foodstuff, not to mention grass and twigs.

"And, I sincerely trust I'll never see the like of this again . . . ever!" he gasped, obviously trying to comprehend her outrageous appearance. "Go upstairs and try to repair the damage at once, for goodness sake."

The smirk on the face of the gentleman by the door was hidden from the gaze of Charles as Louisa looked over Charles' shoulder at him. She averted her eyes to prevent herself from laughing. Louisa looked over at Benson, whose normally blank poker-face was struggling now under the weight of his suppressed emotions. Charles appeared too astounded to speak again. Louisa turned to Benson with ill-suppressed laughter in her eyes.

"Benson, I've not eaten since breakfast and I'm famished. I'll be down in thirty minutes and I'll need a mountain of food and a copious supply of tea . . . hot and strong!"

"Very good, madam," he said.

Suddenly, a deep frown crossed the face of the gentleman by the door as he heard her addressed as such; then, as she placed the empty glass onto the tray that Benson was holding, the man glanced down at the rings on her left hand as the light caught their movement.

Louisa bit her lip as she realised that he had guessed the truth of the situation; then, she bent down, retrieved her shoes and bounded up the steps – two at a time – toward her bedroom. Charles, she knew, was but two steps behind her. She gave a deep sigh while knowing that the confrontation, which she had been dreading was imminent. Glancing back, she saw the young man by the door and he was watching her intently. He was frowning markedly.

"Your maid . . . what's her name?" Charles asked.

" Charlotte, why?"

"*Charlotte!*" he shouted.

"Why do you always have to bellow? She won't be far away," Louisa demanded.

As if by magic, Charlotte appeared at the top of the stairs. She took one look at Louisa and placed her two hands to her face as she gazed in horror at her mistress' appearance. Louisa giggled. Then, she erupted into a laugh and she felt the warmth of several tears as these began to roll down her face when the emotion and the tiredness took its toll. The tears stopped as quickly and as unexpectedly as they had begun.

"Draw a bath for Mrs. Lyndhurst at once," Charles ordered.

Then, taking Louisa's arm, he drew her to her bedroom as Charlotte lowered her eyes instantly and the maid scurried away down the hallway. He closed the door behind them.

"Now, I'll have an explanation. Where've you been? How did you come home? Your aunt hasn't set eyes on you for many hours and they're beside themselves with worry."

"Oh! Aunt Sophie! Is she unhurt?"

"Yes, but badly shaken. Your uncle has taken her home. They've spent hours searching for you . . . *as have I!* I'll send word to them that you're safely home. I'm well aware of what took place, as I've been there and witnessed the aftermath for myself," he stated angrily. "What a debacle! The Organising Committee ought to be taken out and shot, one-by-one. No one would listen to reason. We'll be the laughing stock of the entire country. The Sydney newspapers will crucify us mercilessly over this madness . . . as well they might!"

Charles sat down on her bed and stared up at her. Louisa, for the first time, took in his appearance and she realised that he, too, was splattered in red wine and food particles. He was waiting for her explanation.

"Why?" she gasped.

"Why what?"

"Why did you bother? You don't care a fig about me. Why would you make the effort to come looking for me? I'm nothing but an encumbrance . . . a nuisance . . . to you. I don't understand why you won't just release me and let me go home."

"You are home!" he stated quietly, but firmly. "Now, answer my questions. I've guests downstairs and I've neglected them for many hours on account of you."

Louisa shrugged her shoulders and wandered to the end of the bed. She gripped the bed-end for support and, as she did so, she caught sight of her reflection in the long mirror on the wardrobe. She stood still – totally transfixed – trying to come to terms with the sight that met her astounded eyes.

"Jesus, Mary and Joseph!" she exclaimed aloud, as her hands flew to her face in a manner similar to Charlotte's initial reaction.

Her face was streaked with dirt and grime, with telltale rivulets where the few tears she shed so recently had run down her cheeks. There were pieces of fruit in her hair, remnants of the pie and, as well, particles of wine-soaked bread. She knew that she looked a sight, but she had not been prepared for the extent of the disaster, which met her astonished gaze now. Her muddy feet were below the level of the mirror, so she was spared the finishing touches that these extremities added to the overall image.

"Where did you pick up that language?" he demanded.

"What? Oh! . . . from Mama . . . it's a small prayer she used to say often."

"Refrain from using that expression again. How did you come home, Louisa? I'll have an answer if I've to sit here all night."

"By the river. A gentleman rescued me and he borrowed a boat."

Charles' frown deepened and his eyes narrowed as he surveyed her.

"A gentleman, is it? Pray, who might that be?"

"He knew me," she said, with a shrug. "He was introduced to me last night at the ball. He knows your father."

"And, his name?"

Once again, Louisa shrugged her shoulders and she shook her head in a helpless gesture.

"I was introduced to so many people. I lost track of names after the first five minutes. I can't be expected to remember everyone on my first outing."

He watched her with deep suspicious eyes for some moments, but her gaze did not waver from his face and she did not flinch beneath his constant scrutiny. Finally, he stood and walked to the connecting door.

"Joseph!" he yelled.

"Why can't you ring a bell like everyone else? There's no need to *bellow* all the time," Louisa stated.

He looked back at her with disdain momentarily. He turned and spoke through the open doorway to his valet who had arrived in his bedroom at a fast pace. Charles returned his attention to Louisa as Joseph went to do his bidding.

"This is not finished! Don't think it for a minute, as you've much to answer for. Make yourself respectable and try to keep out of mischief for what's left of today. I need to return to my visitors."

Louisa watched in relief as the connecting door closed behind him. She rushed down the hall to the bathroom and plunged into the tub as soon as the soiled garments had been discarded. She sank beneath the water while immersing her head and hair completely. As she did so, she placed her feet above the end of the tub. The mud ran in dark rivers onto her ankles and shins. She laughed and water rolled into her nose and down the back of her throat. With a start, she sat up quickly, immediately coughing and spluttering; then, she settled back and considered all that had happened this day as she paid special attention to her final encounter with Phillip Carstairs. She was puzzled still by this experience, as well as the strange feelings accompanying it, when she left the bathroom with Charlotte in her wake.

Dressing quickly, she hurried downstairs. She was beginning to feel light-headed from lack of food. She opened the ballroom doors and stopped in her tracks. The small dining table, around which they sat at meal time, had disappeared and this end of the room was in darkness. At the far end of the ballroom were many tables and this section was ablaze with light. The cigar smoke and the noise resembled the smells and the sounds that emanated from the bar at the hotel in Echuca. There were many gentlemen present and most were seated at tables, some with their shirts open down the front. All had discarded their coats, waistcoats and neckties and were engrossed currently in playing cards. They were talking and laughing together while smoking and drinking.

As she was taking in the unusual sight, Louisa glanced up and she saw Charles, with glass in hand, standing at the end of the room. He was leaning on the mantelpiece above the empty fireplace and he had changed his apparel, she noted. At present, he was engaged in deep conversation with the gentleman who had rescued her from Phillip's clutches earlier. Both men looked over at her simultaneously. Quickly, she backed out of the room, swiftly closing the two doors. She found Benson beside her.

"I've taken the liberty of serving refreshments in the drawing room, madam."

Louisa nodded to him in response, her thoughts with Charles and the other gentleman. She was troubled by that particular meeting, and not without good reason.

"Benson, do you know any of these people?" she enquired.

"No, madam," he responded, instantly averting his eyes.

"I don't believe you for a minute," she muttered.

She left Benson standing by the double doors to the ballroom as she moved to locate the food that was waiting for her in the small drawing room at the front of the house.

In a pensive state and troubled deeply by the events of the afternoon, Louisa stayed for several hours while sitting alone in this room where Charles had deposited her on her first day at Lyndhurst Park. She tried to read a newspaper, but found the task impossible today, so she escaped upstairs when she heard the first of the carriages arriving to collect the guests.

Louisa wandered out onto the front verandah and gazed down at the river bathed in moonlight, with thoughts of this afternoon's adventure flooding her mind once again. She pulled the small cane chair over by the railing. She sat down to enjoy the peace and quiet while hoping that her husband would not appear to spoil the moment. She was pondering on Phillip's words about his love for her and she wondered if these were the feelings that were stirring within her. She had never been in love, so she had nothing, against which to compare them, but she could not comprehend how one could fall in love so fast, given that this time yesterday, they had not even met.

"A penny for them," the voice beside her said softly.

Charles Lyndhurst pulled a chair over and sat beside her. He appeared to be drinking whisky and he placed his half-empty glass on the nearby table.

"My thoughts are my own. I allow no one inside my mind," she replied quietly.

"Very wise."

They sat in silence as the hot wind that had been so forceful all day, decreased to a soft warm breeze. The evening was too hot still for sleep and, inside the house, the air was stifling. Charles moved in the chair, placed his feet onto the rail and crossed his legs. He took a hold of her hand.

"You're not an encumbrance, Louisa . . . quite the reverse. You've brought this old mausoleum back to life in the short time you've been here. You remind me of a cyclone that's swept in from the sea, leaving all the debris in your wake; then, while everyone's trying to fathom what's happened, you've moved on to your next disaster. We're all just trying to come to terms with the *advent-of-Louisa!* Bear with us awhile, please . . . and with me, most especially."

Louisa remained silent. They sat together, without speaking a word, for quite some time. Finally, Louisa removed her hand from his grasp and she walked to her bedroom. Charles remained by the rail with his gaze fixed on the river.

The following morning, Louisa arose early, just as the house was beginning to stir. After consuming breakfast alone at the end of the ballroom, which had returned miraculously overnight to its original state, she decided to explore her immediate surroundings. Leaving the house, she descended the stone steps leading to the river. At their base, she turned right, rather than head in the other direction, which led to the jetty.

When she reached a gigantic tree some distance along the bank, she sat down and removed her shoes and stockings. And, as she did so, a tingling feeling began creeping up her spine and she felt a *Presence* descend over her. She shuddered markedly before leaving her discarded footwear on the ground as she jumped to her feet. Hurriedly, she ran away from the awful feeling that had engulfed her so completely and so unexpectedly.

Moving along the path for some distance, she spied a narrow, disused track that branched off to her right and, on impulse, she followed it. This tangle of bush became a small jungle the further that she moved from the river; then, as she was on the verge of turning back, she saw it. There was an old, overgrown cabin peeping through the thick undergrowth. Undeterred, she pushed on as branches hit her face and vines tangled around her free-flowing hair. Finally, she broke through the maze of greenery and stepped inside the open doorway.

There was a dirt floor, on which stood an old hand-made bed with one leg missing completely. At the far end, there was an old bench, which was made of rough timber and it was attached to the wall, with several shelves beneath it. Louisa walked inside, with her bare feet leaving footprints in the dirt, and she wandered over to the side wall where she lifted the piece of timber that was at waist level. She pushed on the rotting timber, which at first refused to give an inch.

Suddenly, with a groan of surrender, the solid timber window-frame moved outwards while being hooked to the wall by two large hinges above her head. From there, all that she could see was bush, bush and more bush. But, a cooling breeze shot through the opening and whisked through her hair as it passed her by while the open doorway behind her created a draught. Turning, she could see the waters of the river and excitement swept through her. She had found a refuge from the oppressive air of the big white house. That oppressive air had little to do with the summer heat, which Melbourne was experiencing at present, and more to do with the increasing feelings of suffocation that engulfed her within its walls. These were closing in on her, she felt, as walls of a prison would do to its inmates.

Skipping back along the path, she stopped in her tracks as she came to the tree where her shoes were awaiting her, but the feeling of foreboding overcame her again, so she hurried on toward the stone steps. Mounting them, she ran upstairs and inside the house as she reached the seclusion of the little-used drawing room. Here, she selected a comfortable armchair and she was about to drag it across the room when Charles entered behind her with his gaze sweeping her appearance, which was somewhat dishevelled as a result of her morning's explorations.

"You look a sight! Where're your shoes? You are mistress of Lyndhurst Park, *madam,* so kindly bear that in mind. Never are you to appear looking as some unkempt street-urchin, *and never* are you to be seen by anyone in bare feet again . . . certainly not in my home! Is that understood?"

"*Yes, sir!*"

"Save your games, for I'm not impressed by them," he muttered, in a bored tone. "Now, I've something to show you later this morning, so don't venture far."

"*No, sir!*"

"You can't help yourself, can you, Louisa? Well, I shan't rise to your hook, no matter how alluring the bait."

So saying, he left the room and Louisa took hold of the armchair again. She dragged it toward the door. She peeped out into the vestibule, but there was no one in sight.

She had managed to manoeuvre it out through the front door and across the carriageway while having almost reached the stone steps when Benson appeared at her side.

"Allow me," he said, immediately taking the chair from her grasp and lifting it into the air before inquiring haughtily of her. "Where does madam require this piece?"

Louisa lifted her arm and pointed in the general direction of the old cabin. Benson, erect and regal, descended the steps with Louisa but two steps behind him.

"There's an old cabin. That's where I want it," Louisa stated.

Benson continued on his way and he was giving the appearance of one who was carrying the crown jewels that belonged to the Queen of England. She glanced back toward the house to see Charles Lyndhurst and Hugh Travis, who were standing side-by-side in their joint office while peering out through the open doorway. Both were laughing unashamedly at her antics.

Having explained to Benson exactly what her plans were for her new refuge and where she intended to place her furnishings as she located them, she sat down in her new surroundings and surveyed her palace. With a nod of his head, which Louisa suspected was hiding a suppressed laugh, Benson left her. It was quite some time before she returned to the tree and gathered up her shoes, garters and stockings; then, carrying them in her hands, she mounted the stone steps once again.

It was at the top of the steps that she heard the sound. It was unmistakable. It was unbelievable. It was undeniable. It was a sound, which she knew so well. It was a familiar whinny.

"Hilton!" she screamed, as her shoes and other apparel flew into the air above her head.

Louisa ran, with her bare feet flying over the pebbles of the carriageway before landing on the turf nearby. She jumped the small, immaculately kept hedge in one leap and bounded down the side pathway toward the stable yard, which was positioned between the sheds that housed the carriages and the stables where all the horses were kept.

He knew that she was there before he saw her. He reared, with his front hooves flailing the air as the two grooms, one either side of him, grappled with his bridle. His black coat gleamed in the morning sunlight as Louisa took in the sight of her large, magnificent stallion responding in heated protest at his confinement by strangers.

"Leave him!" she shouted over the noise and commotion. "Leave him be! At once, do you hear me?"

They turned – as one – to gaze at her in surprise as Hilton's hooves hit the ground and he galloped to her. Louisa climbed the timber fence, a rung at a time; then, she reached eagerly for him and grasped him with her two hands as she did so. The horse threw his head around in a flurry of excitement as her hands touched his flesh. Louisa was trembling with excitement and she could barely contain herself.

Astride the top rail, she slipped onto his bare back with ease. The grooms dived for cover as she hurtled across the yard astride him. Suddenly, she wheeled him around and galloped him toward the fence, over which she had climbed. Then, with one, clear intent, she urged him forward. Charles and Hugh appeared and they were hurrying around the front corner of the house. Together, they stepped onto the side lawn. Looking toward the house, Louisa saw faces at every vantage point and she realised, without the fact actually registering with her, that every eye in the house was upon her at this moment.

Louisa knew that she needed to clear the fence before Charles arrived to prevent her, so she gave Hilton his head. Having been confined for so long on the journey, he needed little prompting from her.

"Louisa! No! Don't . . ." Charles shouted, as Hilton's hooves left the ground and horse and rider became airborne.

Together, they cleared the fence and his hooves tore up the manicured lawn on the other side of the path before she turned his head and headed him toward the paddocks at the rear of the house. Louisa's skirts were flying in the breeze and her bare feet and legs were on display for all to see. As they flew by the back hedge, she heard Charles' call.

"The branch! Look out!" he shouted frantically.

From the corner of her eye, she saw it. Another second and it would have been too late to take evasive action. Instinctively, she pressed herself fully against Hilton's neck and hung on tightly. She felt a few strands of her hair catch on it as she skimmed beneath the offending limb and she breathed a sigh of relief at her miraculous escape from certain death. She sat erect again and glanced back to see Charles, Hugh, the two grooms and several other employees standing on the pathway. They were all staring after her, with their mouths hanging open in disbelief.

She tossed her head in the air and laughed aloud, with open defiance visible in every movement of her slender body as Hilton thundered, his stride unabated, toward the fence of the next paddock.

With her auburn hair flying wildly behind her, Louisa urged him at the obstacle, which he glided over with ease. She had no idea where she was or where the boundaries of the property were, so she allowed Hilton to charge ahead. She clutched the reins tightly as she settled in to enjoy the ride without a thought to the consequences, which would be facing her upon her return to the house – and, no doubt, to one irate husband. Laughing aloud, she shouted to Hilton.

"Go for broke, boy!"

Hilton was happy to oblige.

Louisa stalled her return to the house for as long as was possible, thereby spending much time alone with her beloved animal. Finally, by early afternoon, she started heading toward the stables, for she had ridden away from the river and she could not find any water for her horse. The tall, sturdy, handsome groom, whom she had noticed often about the stable yards, came forward to meet her as she slid from Hilton's back.

The gardeners were removing the offending branch, which had almost claimed her life earlier, and she gave it but a cursory glance. When they walked by, the two men turned to stare at her; then, as Louisa, Hilton and the groom walked slowly along the pathway at the side of the house, Hilton began his old trick of bunting her between the shoulder blades and pushing her forward. Louisa kept stopping to allow him his little game before relinquishing him to the groom who was watching her antics and laughing at the performance of horse and owner. She handed the reins to him and stroked Hilton while whispering in his ear as she did so. The groom watched her, with awe visible all over his face. Hilton's flesh trembled at her touch.

"It's alright," she said, as she addressed the groom in a serious tone. "He'll behave for you now. He has given me his word."

The young man threw back his head and laughed heartily, furiously shaking his head as he looked at her in open admiration.

"C'mon, m'lad. I'll take care of you now," he promised, and giving the horse a look of respectful admiration.

"You be certain you treat him with great care. What's your name?"

"Nathaniel, ma'am. Hilton's as safe as the Bank of England with me," he assured her.

"He'd better be, Nathaniel, or you'll answer to me personally. *And*, it won't be pleasant . . . I'll have your guts for garters!"

He looked at her in shock and astonishment as her words penetrated his consciousness. She turned toward the house and groaned as she saw Charles, with arms akimbo, waiting for her by the front corner of the house. She walked over to him and there was defiance written all over her face.

"That was some display! Come inside . . . *with* your shoes on," he hissed at her.

"Now comes the scolding! That's all adults know how to do," she muttered in reply as she crossed the lawn while heading in the direction of her discarded shoes.

"Adults?" he asked, as he stopped in his stride to stare after her. "And pray, what does that make you?"

Louisa did not reply. She collected her shoes and returned to the front porch. Sitting on the step, she proceeded to encase her feet and legs in respectability before entering his house. Charles held open the door to his office as she crossed the vestibule. Seeing no means of escape, she entered to discover that she was alone with him. Hugh Travis was nowhere to be seen. She was disappointed, for a friendly, sympathetic face would have been welcome now. Louisa walked to the french doors and stood watching the river.

"This promises to be the shortest marriage in history, for you're determined to kill yourself," he said quietly.

"That's one way to gain my freedom," she replied; then, turning to face him, she hurled her direction at him. "Say what you've got to say and be done with it!"

"And, what difference will that make?"

"None whatsoever," Louisa answered honestly.

"Then, it seems, we've reached a stalemate. Do you have a suggestion or a solution as to how we proceed from here?"

Louisa bit her lip and, slowly, she shook her head as he watched her for a moment, and in silence.

"Neither do I," he confessed quietly.

"Who arranged for Hilton to come . . . Papa or you?" Louisa asked.

"It's not only Hilton. Cadence is here, as well. And, it was at my instigation, if that's of interest to you. Why?"

"I'm truly happy about it and I appreciate the thought and the effort. Don't think I don't. I didn't see Cadence. She's Mama's mare. Did you know that?"

Charles nodded, seemingly somewhat distracted. He picked up the newspaper from the desk and fumbled with it in his hands.

"Tomorrow morning, I will ride with you. You're never to go alone again. If I'm unavailable, Nathaniel will go with you . . . always. There's no exception to that rule. You came within a whisker of killing yourself on that branch. Now, I'd be sitting down to write a soul-destroying letter to your father. Did you think about that?" he demanded of her.

"It's of no consequence," she murmured, with a shrug of her shoulders, as she felt him stiffen at her words.

"Here, go and read about that banquet fiasco," Charles ordered, thereby dismissing her and unceremoniously thrusting the folded newspaper into her hands in an exaggerated show of annoyance. "It'll give you something to talk about at the races. That ridiculous debacle is on everyone's lips, believe me."

"If Prince Alfred had arrived as planned, it'd never been so bad. The crowd surged as soon as *that announcement* was made," Louisa stated emphatically.

"No! It was the correct decision, because his safety couldn't be guaranteed. The organisers expected ten thousand *and seventy thousand* was the last estimate! What, with all this Protestant and Irish-Catholic sentiment bubbling away beneath the surface, and with one death attributed to it already, his life could've been in danger had he attended. Still, I intend to discover who brought you home, so don't think for one moment that it's been forgotten. *And, believe me,* I'll not rest till I do so. Do you wish to reveal his identity now?"

Charles walked over to her and placed his two hands firmly on her shoulders. He looked down, with ill-concealed anger obviously bubbling beneath the surface of his otherwise outwardly calm demeanour, as he studied her.

"You'll trifle with me once too often, Louisa. Be warned," he stated, with the words issuing forth from between clenched teeth. "But, I've an appointment at Port Melbourne, as we've a ship that's arrived with important cargo, so I must be there. Otherwise, we'd thrash this out now. When the madness of this Royal Tour is at an end, you and I will come to *an arrangement.* Until then, I'd advise you to tread carefully. Do not cross me again. Is that clear?"

Louisa turned away while flicking her head in the air in yet another show of defiance. His grip on her shoulders tightened as, roughly, he pulled her around to face him again.

"Do I make myself clear?" he shouted. "Answer me at once!"

"I have heard your words," she muttered, very slowly and evenly, through clenched teeth herself.

"*Heed them well then,*" he stated loudly while hurling the words at her. "For your own sake . . . not mine, because I've a temper to equal your own. Don't cause me to lose it. This is your final warning."

Without warning, Charles released her and turned away, immediately moving to his desk that was littered with papers. He picked up what appeared to be a ship's manifest and concentrated his attention on it, apparently losing interest in her as he did so.

"Now, get out of my sight!" he snarled at her, without looking up.

Hurriedly – and without a word – Louisa left the room, only to find that, once outside, she was trembling violently. She heard him walk over and he kicked the door shut with his shoe as the sound reverberated throughout the silent house. For once, Benson was not hovering nearby to attend to her needs. She had not eaten since her early breakfast but, under the circumstances, she decided that it would be prudent to wait until Charles Lyndhurst left the house before making any demands on his servants.

Slowly, and still clutching the folded newspaper in her hands, she mounted the stairs to her bedroom where she found Charlotte attending to her new gowns that had been delivered in her absence. With disinterest, she glanced at them until she realised that the girl was staring at her with a look of awe on her face. It mirrored the one that she had seen on the countenance of the groom, Nathaniel. It was then the full impact of her new life came home to her. What she regarded as normal, the inhabitants of this house, and probably this city, regarded as extreme, to say the least.

Louisa felt that she had arrived on a different continent and never in her entire life had she felt as alone as she did at this moment. Her consolation and saving grace would be Hilton and Cadence, as well as the refuge, which she would make for herself in the cabin that she had discovered this morning. These, she determined, she would make her life, for the remainder of her time here. She promised herself then that her stay would be of a short duration at Lyndhurst Park.

Chapter Fourteen

– Victorian Victorians –

Louisa

Louisa was sitting alone at the top of the stone steps in the moonlight and staring at the river as it meandered by the front door of the house. She heard the carriage coming, but she did not move or turn around, although she felt some annoyance at the interruption to her solitude. Charles alighted; then, the horses and carriage made the circular sweep around the house, following the carriageway that encircled both the house and the adjacent croquet lawn. Instead of entering the house, he came over and sat down beside her. He did not speak at all while he sat looking at the water with her.

"Do you smoke cigars?" she asked finally.

"No, it's not a habit of mine. Why?"

"You reek of cigar-smoke. That's how I know when you've been to your club. What else do you do there?"

"Eat enormous dinners, drink copious amounts of alcohol, play endless games of billiards and enjoy other sundry delights," he explained; then, laughing softly, he commented. "Quite the amateur detective, aren't you?"

Louisa laughed. He leaned over her, with his face almost touching her head and she detected a trace of whisky on his breath as he breathed deeply and in an exaggerated manner.

"Now, *you*, for example, have washed your hair. It smells of lavender. You smell . . . umm . . . delicious. See, two can play that game," Charles stated.

"*Delicious*? I'm not an apple pie, but yes, you are correct on both counts."

He remained silent for a few minutes; then, to her surprise, he placed an arm gently around her shoulders and drew her more closely to him.

"Answer me honestly. Did you see that branch this afternoon before I called out to you?" he queried a little hesitantly, as though reluctant to broach the subject of this day's hostilities.

Slowly and deliberately, she shook her head. He was silent again for quite some time before he spoke again, but his arm remained around her.

"One of these days, I'll throttle you in a fit of rage and then I'll swing for it, even though it'll be all your own fault, because you've done something absolutely outrageous. Yet, today, I saved your life, because you did do something absolutely outrageous and, ironically, that won't count for anything in my defence. Hardly fair, is it, Louisa Mary Lyndhurst?" he queried.

"When you make a ridiculous statement such as that, I know you've been drinking," she muttered, almost under her breath.

"Oh! You've no idea!" he replied, with a laugh. "Come on, inside with you. Tomorrow is a big day and you need your beauty sleep."

So saying, he pulled her to her feet unceremoniously. Louisa was tempted to refuse, but after the events of the day, she decided that it might be wise to comply with his wishes this time. Another confrontation was to be avoided, if at all possible. In a proprietary fashion, he placed his arm about her waist – as one who had the right – and he led her inside the house while climbing the stairs with her. He opened her bedroom door. Instead of going directly to his own room, he followed her inside. Charlotte who hovered nearby, disappeared immediately while scurrying down the hallway as she was wont to do at Charles' appearance.

He walked across to her wardrobe, opened it and began rummaging through her new gowns. He selected three of these and he threw them onto the bed, one at a time, after having given them very close scrutiny.

"I see you took me at my word and bought new ones. You've done well," he commented; then, indicating the gowns he had selected, he added. "Wear one of those tomorrow."

"Silk? To a race meet?"

"It's Flemington and a royal occasion . . . Prince Alfred will be in attendance and nothing less will suffice," he stated, while watching her intently across the bed; then, raising an eyebrow in query, he queried her. "Is there a problem?"

"I expect not," she answered quietly, instantly averting her eyes from his gaze and shrugging her shoulders.

Charles continued to scrutinise her in a way that was disconcerting; so, to mask her confusion, she picked up one of the gowns while moving to return it to the wardrobe. He stepped aside, but remained within close proximity and watching her every move.

"Do you, by any chance, own a riding habit?"

Louisa nodded without looking up at him. As she replaced the gown on its hanger, he lifted his hand and touched her hair lightly.

"It's so soft . . . like silk . . . with such a brilliant sheen to it that it appears to be on fire when the lamplight catches it," he murmured, closely studying the strands of her hair in his hand.

Quickly, he released the hair that he was holding and he seemed to collect himself. Abruptly, he turned from her and, thankfully for Louisa, the somewhat-intimate moment past.

"I'll ride with you in the morning and show you the extent of the property. Then, you'll know where the boundaries are . . . not that I expect it'll make one bit of difference to you. You know no boundaries," he stated curtly.

"Is that an invitation or a directive?" she queried, quite coldly.

"Does it always have to be a confrontation? I can spare you a couple of hours early. That's all. Would you care to ride with me?"

"Yes, thank you."

"I'll bid you goodnight then," he said, as he spun on his heel and left her bedroom through the connecting door.

Louisa breathed a deep sigh of relief; then, she returned the gowns to the wardrobe and wandered aimlessly about the bedroom. She could not fathom Charles Lyndhurst's behaviour and she did not know how to respond to him. He was either shouting at her for some perceived misdemeanour on her part, or he was attempting to befriend her, as was the case tonight. But then, she realised, the difference seemed to be when he had been drinking alcohol. So, she noted that observation for future reference as she wandered out through the french doors onto the verandah while seeking fresh air.

Walking by Charles' bedroom, she noticed Joseph, his valet, busy within the confines of the room when she moved by the side windows. The drapes were partly open. As she watched, Joseph left Charles' room with a coat and a waistcoat in his hands. On rounding the corner to the front section of the verandah, she stopped in her tracks. Charles was standing there and he was holding the verandah post, with both of his hands gripping it tightly while he was leaning his forehead against it. She frowned as she remembered her father in a similar pose after an extremely heated exchange with Louisa. Her mother had sent her to apologise and she had found her father tapping his forehead against the post of the verandah while he was clutching it, so she had assumed that he was venting his anger on the structure. Perhaps, this was the case now. Charles' shirt was open and hanging loose. Without turning, she backed away, with the clear intent of returning hurriedly to her own bedroom. But, he heard her and spun around abruptly while staring at her.

"Come here," he said quietly, as he held out a hand to her.

Tentatively, she walked over to him and he placed an arm around her shoulders while drawing her close to him.

"You have no idea, have you, Louisa?" he murmured, as he kissed her lightly on the top of her head. "You've no idea what this is all about . . . what marriage is all about, or what a shudder you sent through all of us with your madcap antics this day?"

"All I know is that I don't wish to be here any more than you want me here."

"That's just the problem," he whispered, quietly confiding to her. "I can't quite imagine this place without you in it, even after this short space of time."

He turned her body while pressing her against his bare chest and he placed his arms around her, instantly crushing her to him as Phillip had done. He held her tightly for some minutes and she could feel him breathing as his chest expanded and contracted against her. And, she felt the warmth of him. Finally, without warning, he released her, urgently whispering to her.

"Go to bed . . . *now!*"

Louisa spun around and ran to her bedroom, still unable to fathom his strange behaviour.

Louisa awoke to two hands stroking her face and hair. Her green eyes popped open and stared into Charles' face. He was sitting on the side of her bed and he smiled down at her.

"Wake up now. Be downstairs in ten minutes. We had an arrangement for this morning. Remember? And, you are already late."

He stood up, walked to the door, opened it and was almost out of her bedroom before she realised where she was, what was happening and why he was dressed for riding. Scrambling from the bed, she rushed to dress and doing so before Charlotte appeared at her door. Fifteen minutes later, Louisa charged downstairs to find him waiting by the front door. He flung a canvas bag at her.

"Breakfast," he said, while striding through the front door and along the walkway in front of the house.

Clutching the bag of food and drink, Louisa hurried along at his heels as she struggled to keep up with the fast pace that he was walking. Reaching the stable yard, he spun around and confronted her.

"Before there're any arguments, I'm riding Hilton this morning. I've a death wish myself, it'd seem. That's your ride!" he stated firmly, while defying her to challenge his directives.

Louisa stopped in her tracks by the fence. She followed his gaze and stared at the animal-in-question. The mare was being held by the groom, Nathaniel, who she realised was struggling to keep the grin from his face as he watched her. In amazement, she looked at the animal, which appeared to be at least twenty years of age and obviously wishing to be anywhere but saddled and ready for a long ride. Louisa's gaze travelled to the saddle on its back.

"What in the name of all that's holy is that?" she asked, in horror, as she pointed at the offending saddle.

"That?" Charles queried gravely, as Nathaniel averted his eyes, but with his shoulders shaking vigorously.

"That, for your information, madam, is a side-saddle, which is an apparatus for fine ladies to use when riding," Charles explained, in an exaggerated manner.

Louisa looked from the saddle to Nathaniel who was struggling still to contain his laughter; then, she glanced back at her stern-faced husband who was awaiting her response. Louisa collapsed on the ground and she was rocking back and forth while being consumed by laughter. Finally, with tears rolling down her cheeks, she glanced up to see both men laughing with her. She shook her head.

"I'd rather be dead!" she exclaimed loudly.

"You very nearly were yesterday," Charles stated seriously, before nodding to Nathaniel who led the horse away at his silent directive.

Charles came over to her, lifted her to her feet and began to dust her riding habit where dust and grass had attached themselves to her skirt.

"It's no matter," she muttered, as she attempted to move from his grasp. "I trust you've had your joke, so let me have Hilton's rein."

"No, I'm serious. I'll ride him today."

Louisa studied him for a moment, but she was distracted by the arrival of the groom who led Cadence, already saddled, to her. Her mother's mare nuzzled Louisa and she stroked the animal. She was reluctant to cause a scene in front of the groom, as Charles well knew. He was waiting, with a challenge in his eyes.

"You cannot mount Hilton unless I speak to him first. He will not let you ride him without my prior approval."

He smiled and moved his arm in a flourish, thereby indicating for her to come to Hilton whose bridle he was holding and to play her childish games. Louisa, under the scrutiny of both men, whispered her words of comfort and encouragement to her horse. Finally, she turned to Charles with disdain.

"He's agreed to allow you to mount him," she informed him seriously.

"Kindly relay to him that I am indeed honoured."

She thought that she heard a snigger from the groom, but when she glanced in his direction, he stared innocently back at her as Charles positioned himself on Hilton's back. Without another word, she threw the canvas bag up at him and mounted Cadence while refusing Nathaniel's offer of assistance. She rode through the gate; then, as Charles caught up with her, she leaned across and grabbed his arm.

"You've no idea how greatly you are in my power at this precise moment!" she snapped at him.

Louisa urged Cadence forward while leaving Charles and Hilton in her wake. The estate was large by Melbourne standards, but it in no way matched the size of her father's property, or of the landholding at Stanton. Charles rode alongside her as he began explaining about the boundaries and where the road that bounded the property on one side would lead, should she decide to take it, although warning her that she was not to venture there alone, under any circumstances. He knew every inch of the land and painstakingly showed her every acre. They ate breakfast while sitting under a tree and before riding home together.

Upon entering the house, Benson informed that her there was a visitor waiting for her. Louisa's heart jumped momentarily while she hoped that it was her father. Charles had remained at the stables with Nathaniel.

She entered the drawing room to find her uncle, Father Francis Bourke, waiting for her. This was a meeting, which she had been dreading since her arrival in Melbourne, but the priest greeted her warmly.

"Louisa, my dear, it's been so long. You're looking well," he said, instantly taking both of her hands and squeezing them as he spoke.

"Good morning, Father Frank. It's nice to see you."

"How is your father?" he enquired.

"Ill! Very ill and I'm so very worried about him. He's supposed to come to Melbourne to visit doctors, but he's not arrived as yet. Have you heard from him?"

"No, not a word, child. And, your husband?" he inquired.

"He's here," she said nonchalantly, with a slight shrug of her shoulders before indicating her riding habit, and she elaborated. "We've been riding, as you can see."

Benson arrived with a silver tray and he was followed by one of the parlour maids. They served morning tea as the priest sat opposite Louisa in one of the winged armchairs.

"I trust I'll see you at holy mass every Sunday from now onwards," Father Bourke stated, in a tone that was not to be questioned. "You're not in the wilds of the bush now, so you've no excuse for non-attendance at weekly mass."

"Yes, Father," she muttered.

To her immense relief, Charles appeared in the doorway and, at the sight of the priest, he stiffened noticeably and scowled markedly. But, he came forward and extended his hand to Louisa's uncle as she introduced the two men. Benson and the maid left the room immediately and Charles removed his watch from his pocket. He glanced at it rather pointedly.

"I must remind you, Louisa, we've an engagement. We must leave shortly. We can't be late."

"Yes, of course," she agreed demurely.

The priest who was sipping his tea, looked from one to the other.

"This is just a quick visit, as I was almost passing your gate. I'll call again and we can have a long discussion then, Louisa. In the meantime, I'll keep your father in my prayers."

"Thank you, Father."

Charles snapped his watch closed, instantly replacing it in his pocket. He shot Louisa a glance of impatience before farewelling the priest; then, he left them alone.

"We've much to discuss and this is not the right time, obviously. I'll call again in a few days, so you might keep an hour or two free for me. In the meantime, I shall pray earnestly for you," the priest said.

Louisa bit her lip and averted her eyes. Her mother's only surviving sibling was determined to reprimand her severely for her sins but, at least, today would not be the day, so she must be thankful for small mercies, she decided. Finally, after some twenty minutes of explaining about his parish and the duties attached to it, he left her, much to her great relief.

After farewelling the priest at the front door, she bounded up the stairs, two at a time, and raced to her room to dress for the race meeting at Flemington Racecourse. That thought filled her with excitement – on two counts. One, of course, was the race meeting itself and she knew that she would enjoy this thoroughly, while the second reason was her anticipation at the thought of yet another chance meeting with Phillip Carstairs.

Louisa elected not to wear any of the gowns, which her husband had chosen on the previous evening, instead opting for a gown of her own choice. As much as she loathed the stays and crinoline that were required on occasions such as this, she moved impatiently from one foot to the other while trying to be patient as Charlotte laced her into these undergarments. Without the hot and heavy petticoats, there was more freedom of movement beneath the crinoline, so she was not concerned as, finally, Charlotte threw the green and white pin-striped silk gown over the array of undergarments, in which she was encased at this time. Today, the weather was threatening to be as hot as on the day of the Free Banquet, so freedom of movement was important and the petticoats were restrictive.

Finally, with her bonnet in place, she reached for her reticule, gloves and parasol before studying her reflection in the mirror. She grimaced at her reflection as Charlotte watched her in some amusement; then, Louisa left the bedroom, well pleased with the selection of her new wardrobe and grateful to the dressmaker who had worked so tirelessly to provide her with the stylish gowns that she possessed now.

There was not one complaint about her appearance or her fashionable attire from Charles as his eyes swept her body when she met him at the front door at midday and he assisted her into the carriage. Louisa was having difficulty containing her excitement as the carriage moved through the front gates of Lyndhurst Park as it headed in the direction of the racecourse at Flemington.

Sylvia

Sylvia was descending the internal staircase when the butler opened her front door to the visitor. She stared at him in amazement.

"Patrick!" she shouted, quickly running down the remaining steps.

He was very tall, as her father had been. Patrick Doherty was a strikingly handsome man, with broad shoulders and a swagger that spoke of a self-confidence bordering on arrogance. The dark hair and deep blue eyes mirrored her own. She ran to him and he grasped her around the waist, unexpectedly swinging her into the air as he did so. The act happened so swiftly and so unexpectedly that she was taken off-guard. She threw back her head and laughed.

"Put me down this instant," she exclaimed, as the butler watched the proceedings from the front door.

"You're a sight for sore eyes, Sylvee!" Patrick exclaimed, with a hearty laugh. "Wasn't sure of my reception, though I didn't expect this! You're as small as Mama."

"No, I'm not!" she retorted. "It's just that you're peering down at everyone from such a great height. My goodness me, you are tall. You didn't stop growing at all, did you?"

"If you continue to make disparaging remarks, I won't stay with you . . . that is, if your husband will have me. It's just for a few days till I go to Castlemaine. Where's Edwin?" Patrick inquired.

"Oh! Dear me, we do have much to discuss," Sylvia muttered. "Have you eaten breakfast? Come into my sitting room where we won't be disturbed and you can enlighten me on the details regarding last couple of decades of your life."

He had left his large duffle bag by the front door and he was dressed more for shipboard life than for the drawing room. Sylvia took a few moments to arrange his accommodation and to order some food to be prepared for him; then, she settled back to listen to his tales of adventure.

Before doing so though, Sylvia revealed to her brother the state of affairs in her household and, more particularly, the state of Edwin's health at present. She left out much, only giving him the barest of details and concentrating most of her news on matters relating to her mother, as well as her uncle and her aunts in Bendigo. Of her part ownership of the hotel in Bendigo, she did not mention one word. She listened intently then, with great interest and amusement, to the stories he had to tell.

Patrick Doherty had spent much of his life working on ships, sailing the Pacific Ocean, mainly between this continent, New Zealand, Fiji and as far away as Hawaii. He worked for a time on prawn trawlers in the north, but always returning to Sydney where he appeared to be on intimate terms with the lady who owned the boarding house, which was the last known address that Sylvia had had for him. Of late though, he had found a new and seemingly lucrative occupation and this appeared to involve playing billiards in hotels. His talent had earned him quite a nest egg, he revealed to his sister in confidence.

"All those years playing around on the tables in the back room of the family inn have paid off. I've no need to return to the heavy work I was doing," he confided, in an almost secretive tone and leaning closer to her as he whispered to her. "Now, I've a small favour to ask. Would you have a gentleman's outfit of Edwin's that I could borrow? I'm going to the races at Flemington with a good friend today and I'm afraid I'm not equipped with any such attire at present."

Sylvia frowned and scrutinised him. Edwin had been as tall as Patrick, but not as broad across the shoulders. She was uncertain that his clothes would be of much use, but perhaps some quick alterations could be accomplished, even at this late hour.

"It may be possible. Edwin's but a shadow of his former self, so I can't quite remember, but come upstairs with me and we'll see what can be arranged. What's your friend's name?"

"Phillip . . . Phillip Carstairs. Do you know him, by any chance? Probably not, as he's just come down from Sydney with me," he replied, thereby answering his own question.

"I can't say I've met the gentleman at all. You must introduce us and you can come with us to Flemington, if you wish, for Bertie will be calling for me at midday. Come on. Let's see what we can find in the way of an outfit for you."

With her hand linked through her brother's arm, Sylvia led him upstairs to one of the guest rooms before depositing him there while she went to search through the contents of the wardrobe in Edwin's former bedroom. She found herself reliving old memories with every article that she touched and she knew these clothes would never grace Edwin's back again.

They had become good friends in the latter years of their marriage, so it was not surprising that a deep sadness filled her at this thought and many regrets came to her as she fingered the clothing, which had not seen the light of day for several years. Usually, she managed to keep these thoughts at bay, but today, for some reason, they flooded her mind and threatened to drown her – body and soul. This was as unexpected as it was unpleasant. She chided herself while knowing that it was the sight of the brother who she had not seen for all those years – all those wasted years in many ways – that was causing these emotions now. If she allowed them to swamp her, she would not be in any state to attend the race meeting in a few hours.

Finally, she extracted several items of apparel and took them to Patrick's room for his perusal. Even though Charles had warned her of Patrick's presence in Melbourne, his presence in her home was unsettling indeed, she confessed to herself.

Her maid, Phoebe, was her resident seamstress in emergency situations – as this was – so she placed Phoebe in charge of Patrick's apparel.

Sylvia retired to her bedroom to prepare for today's social event on the Royal Tour itinerary at the racecourse at Flemington.

Louisa

Having been deposited with her aunt and Hugh Travis' wife, Margaret, Louisa listened to the incessant chatter, which as Charles had predicted, centred on the recent banquet for the poor and its disastrous aftermath. Bored, Louisa sidled away after having checked first to see where her husband might be lurking. She caught sight of him by the rail at the track and he was in deep conversation with Sylvia Webster. Confident that she could make good her escape, she blended into the crowd and the excitement that filled the air today soaked into Louisa's consciousness. So, with her feet almost skipping along, she made her way to the enclosure where the horses were being paraded in readiness for the running of the fourth race. Without anyone noticing her departure, she arrived at the fence before glancing over it to study the horses and their jockeys gathered together. The sun was as fierce as it had been at Thursday's banquet, but the hot northerly wind had subsided and a gentle breeze was blowing. This was flapping the colourful bunting and the brightly coloured shirts of the jockeys alike. Louisa leaned against the fence as she watched the horses intently.

"I thought you'd never sneak away," the male voice whispered in her ear.

Her heart flipped violently and the butterflies in her stomach commenced their loops once again as she turned to look into the laughing blue eyes of Phillip Carstairs.

"Mr. Carstairs. What a pleasant surprise," she murmured. "I didn't see you. Have you been here long?"

"I've spent thirty minutes gazing in your direction and you've not even glanced over at me," he whispered; then, he directed her. "Now, shake hands with me and take the note I have there for you."

Surprised, Louisa played his game and held his hand briefly in her gloved one. Grasping the piece of paper, she retracted her hand.

"That's in case we're interrupted. Find a place where we can meet . . . alone. Then, send word to me there. Does your husband know anything about last Thursday?"

Louisa was shaking her head in reply when a gentleman appeared at her side. They both looked up at him as he stopped beside them.

"Good afternoon. *So!* We all meet again," he stated quietly.

Phillip Carstairs nodded to him, gave a slight inclination of fare-well to Louisa and sidled off hurriedly into the crowd while disap-pearing instantly from view. The man was the one who was respon-sible for her escape from Phillip at the jetty at Lyndhurst Park after their return from the free banquet. He was frowning down at her.

"That's a dangerous, little game that you play, I think, *Mrs.* Lyndhurst, so *do take care*," he murmured, before he moved on while leaving her alone in a sea of people.

Louisa slipped the note from Phillip inside her glove and she was trembling as she did so. No sooner was it stored safely than Charles appeared at her side and grasped her arm firmly.

"I can't leave you for an instant that you don't disappear. Why didn't you stay with your aunt where I left you? You're impossible!"

"How can I know which horse will win, if I can't get to see them?" she asked.

"Just ask an expert!" he snapped at her.

"When I find one, I will," she replied curtly.

"You never fail to come up with an answer. Now, what am I to do with you? There's Hugh. Come on! We'll join him and you're not to leave my side for the remainder of the day."

Louisa was positioned between Hugh Travis and Charles Lyndhurst as they stood talking to two other gentlemen while Charles' hand remained grasping her arm tightly. Finally, with the third race over, the other two men moved away. As their topic of conversation had centred on ships and their shipping business, Louisa gathered that these two men were somehow involved in the same company as Charles.

"Perhaps, you could place the next bets, Hugh, as I don't seem able to leave here at present? Do you have a preference?" Charles queried of Hugh.

"Horse four, Mr. Travis. That's the only one worth betting on," Louisa stated emphatically as she interjected.

"Is that so, Mrs. Lyndhurst? How did you come by that piece of information?" Hugh queried, with amusement twinkling in his kindly eyes.

"With my own eyes, of course. If it doesn't win, it'll be the fault of the jockey and not the horse!" Louisa explained to Hugh, while ignoring Charles completely; then, turning to her husband, she demanded of him. "Anyway, why can't you go and, for once, allow Mr. Travis the time to enjoy himself? He does your bidding all of the time."

Hugh buried his face in his race book, but the telltale signs of his suppressed laughter were evident. Charles raised his eyebrows; then, he grimaced at her.

"I stand reproved. If you promise not to leave Hugh, I'm happy to oblige," Charles countered.

Louisa tucked her hand through Hugh's arm immediately, much to his continued amusement, and she ignored Charles who turned away, instantly disappearing into the crowd.

"Can we find somewhere to sit, do you think?" she asked.

"Certainly," he replied, while leading her to a section of seats just below the enclosure designated as the Royal Box.

Louisa glanced up and she was studying the son of Queen Victoria, who was seated in the Royal Box, surrounded by his entourage. They were all laughing at some private joke and appeared to be enjoying themselves immensely; then, suddenly, she spied the gentleman who had rescued her at the jetty with them. She was watching him intently when Charles returned, deliberately seating himself on the other side of her and wedging her between Hugh and himself. He handed some tickets to Hugh and pocketed other ones for himself; then, he handed one to Louisa. She looked at it in some surprise.

"Twenty sovereigns! You placed that amount on one horse? Is it just for me?" she stared at the ticket and back at him in some surprise.

"Well, it's not for sharing with anyone else. Of course, it's for you! Horse Four at five to one . . . see?" Charles said, as he pointed at the paper in her hand.

"It's to win . . . not a place bet. Oh! That's too much!" she stated. Charles smiled, but did not respond. Glancing back to the Royal Box, she glimpsed that particular gentleman again and she pointed him out to Charles while asking the man's identity.

"He's Prince Alfred's equerry . . . one of them, that is. The other one is standing beside His Royal Highness now. They are Lord Newry and the Honorable Elliott Yorke. Why the interest?" he asked abstractedly, while studying the race book in his hand.

"He was at your home the other night," Louisa confided, before spinning around again and, wide-eyed, she asked the question. "Oh! Was Prince Alfred there? Is that where he was when he didn't come to open the Free Banquet? Was he playing cards at Lyndhurst Park?"

Charles and Hugh appeared to stiffen instantly and instinctively, both at the same moment while glancing around in a furtive manner. Charles' hand clasped over Louisa's mouth immediately.

"Don't be absurd! *And,* keep your voice down. You can't spread rumours such as that, Louisa. Good grief, have some sense!"

The fourth race commenced, thus bringing the conversation to an abrupt end. As she watched with bated breath, she saw the horses flash by their vantage point. Louisa was triumphant and beside herself with glee as she handed her ticket to Hugh who was leaving to find his wife while promising to collect her winnings for her.

"Congratulations! What will you be doing with them?" Hugh queried.

"I shall buy a new saddle for Hilton," she exclaimed, immediately hiding her face in shame as she told such a large, white lie.

"I'm fairly certain Lyndhurst Park's coffers can stand the strain of such a purchase. Spend it on yourself," Charles stated, in a slow drawl.

Laughing, Hugh left them. Alone, seated beside Charles, Louisa glanced around while taking in the huge crowd and watching the fashionable gowns as the ladies paraded by her. Her mind was in a frenzy and she had not expected such a windfall to come her way. She was planning her escape meticulously and intending to return to her father's property within the next fortnight, so she needed cash for the rail journey, as well as for other expenses en route.

Louisa had been trying to decide which piece of her mother's precious jewellery she would need to sacrifice and wondering where she would be able to sell such a piece, without creating undue interest. But now, thanks to this money, she would not need to do so. If she was careful, her well-advanced plan would be perfect and she would be long gone before Charles Lyndhurst even realised she had vanished. All that was missing from her boy's outfit was a cap to hide her hair. Then, all was in readiness. Even the canvas bag, which Charles placed in her hands and which contained their breakfast for this morning's ride, was hidden in her room as a part of her travelling needs.

She was determined not to involve anyone in her plans, so no one would be blamed, except herself, for the escapade. Eventually, she would have to pay the piper, she knew, but at the moment, her only concern was her father's well-being and the running of the property, which was being neglected. Several letters from Brydie had confirmed those suspicions for her. Soon, she would be away. In the meantime, she must try not to create suspicion of any description, she determined.

"How long has Mr. Travis been your secretary?" she asked.

She was attempting to make polite conversation, but Charles turned to stare at her in surprise. He seemed to be trying to determine her motive for asking a question such as this one.

"Are you trying to bait me again?" he asked, in a very confronting tone.

"No, of course not," Louisa replied, amazed that even such an innocuous question could meet with hostility, so she sought to explain further. "It was merely an attempt at polite conversation. I don't know why I bother to try, for we've absolutely nothing in common."

"You're serious then?" he queried, seemingly quite amazed by her question.

Louisa nodded in response as she glanced around to see if Hugh was returning with her winnings; or, more particularly, she was trying to catch another glimpse of Phillip, but neither gentleman was in view.

"I apologise then. Your assumption is incorrect. Hugh is my best and closest friend. He saved my life once, so you cannot get a much better friend, I wouldn't think. Also, he is one of the partners in our shipping line, the others being the two gentlemen with whom we were conversing earlier. Where on earth would you get such an idea?"

Louisa shrugged and refrained from answering, for to reveal that in her opinion he treated Hugh in a similar manner to the way, in which he handled the servants, would be to incur his wrath again. She would need to keep the peace as much as possible during the next two weeks. If this meant curbing her wayward tongue, then so be it.

"Perhaps, we could leave now," Charles suggested. "Your aunt has requested we arrive early tonight and before the other dinner guests. She assures me there's a valid reason for this."

Louisa looked at him aghast. There had never been any suggestion of a visit to the Collins' residence in the foreseeable future to her knowledge. She had hoped an excursion to Fitzroy Gardens might be arranged, as a pyrotechnics display was planned for the evening in honour of the city's royal visitor. This had been advertised in both the *Age* and the *Argus* newspapers as being an event not to be missed. She grimaced at the thought of the dinner party.

"Whatever are we going there for?" Louisa exclaimed; then, as a sudden thought struck her, she sought clarification. "Papa? Is he here in town?"

Charles looked at her in surprise and shook his head. He was frowning.

"Dinner tonight was a long-standing arrangement and, no, your father is not in Melbourne. To my knowledge, he has no intention of visiting in the near future. That's my understanding, Louisa. Come. Let's go."

Taking her arm, he propelled her away while heading for the main gate and pushing his way through the crowd, which had thinned considerably.

It was a very thoughtful Louisa who returned to Lyndhurst Park late in the afternoon, on this day in late November.

Chapter Fifteen

– Victorian Victorians –

Louisa

C harles and Louisa Lyndhurst arrived early to dine at the home of Robert and Sophie Collins that evening. Louisa's aunt came bustling out of the drawing room while issuing instructions loudly to the servants who were busy with tasks within that room and out of sight of her early arrivals. She greeted Charles warmly while calling instantly to her husband as she did so, and ordering Robert to take Charles to the library. Turning to Louisa, she bestowed a threatening scowl upon her and grasped her arm firmly.

"As for you, young lady! Go up to your room. I'll deal with you directly!"

Releasing Louisa and spinning around, she bustled her way back to the drawing room as she was giving dire warnings with regard to the consequences for anyone who did not follow her directions to the letter. She left her niece – somewhat nonplussed – standing in her wake. Charles, with one eyebrow raised in query, studied Louisa. When Robert joined them, it was a puzzled Louisa who turned on him.

"What've I done now, Uncle Robert?" she asked, while frowning deeply.

"You're asking me? Really, child, don't you know? I've been lectured about this business since daybreak and I'm heartily sick of it. That's why you were summonsed early. So, for goodness sake, get upstairs and accept what is coming with good grace; then, it'll be done with."

"If you say so, but I've no idea what it's all about. I shall fill my ears with cotton wool before she gets there," she confided to him, still frowning at her uncle.

"I've a supply in the library, if you need some," he offered, with a laugh before turning to Charles. "Charles, let's adjourn there before this battle begins. If we hurry, we may make it there in safety."

As the two men walked toward the doorway, three maids – all dressed in black gowns, with white starched aprons and caps – walked swiftly, and in single file, from the drawing room. They were carrying silver trays laden with papers and letters, which all were attempting to keep from flying off their respective trays. Louisa watched in amusement as they walked quickly toward the staircase leading upstairs.

"Quick march . . . one, two, three, four . . . Emily! You're out of step . . . one, two, three . . . " she directed.

"Louisa!" shouted Robert Collins, in his commanding headmaster's voice and querying her as he did so. "Aren't you in enough trouble already?"

The three maids began to giggle and Emily cast a furtive glance at Louisa who gazed innocently back at her uncle while Charles Lyndhurst looked on gravely. Louisa smiled sweetly at her uncle as Sophie Collins charged from the drawing room.

"Emily! Come back here at once! You've left half the correspondence on the bureau. Can't you do anything correctly?" she called.

Emily, immediately avoiding Louisa's gaze, scurried back to the drawing room and disappeared behind Sophie. The other two maids, eager to be away from the mayhem, mounted the stairs. Robert opened the door to his sanctuary, but turned as Louisa called to him.

"Uncle, please, can't you give me some idea . . . ?"

Robert glanced at Charles and he appeared undecided and somewhat reluctant. Then, he seemed to make up his mind, but with reluctance.

"Very well, I shall give it to you in one word . . . *invitations!* Now, run along quickly," he suggested, immediately holding the door open for Charles to enter.

Louisa, looking somewhat concerned, bit her lip and glanced apprehensively at Charles who was frowning at her. She hurried toward the staircase and almost collided with Emily, who was struggling under the weight of a tray covered in sundry books and papers.

On impulse, Louisa jumped in front of the young girl while turning around and placing one hand on the wall and the other on the banister, thereby blocking the maid's path completely.

"What's the password, Emily?" she demanded loudly.

"Don't, please! I'm on my last warning today," the young girl pleaded.

"*Louisa!*" Robert shouted at her again, before directing her firmly. "Let her be. Do you really have such a death-wish yourself?"

Emily brushed by Louisa as she removed her hands quickly, under her uncle's stern gaze, and she followed closely behind the young girl who was giggling again. Charles Lyndhurst was watching her antics, Louisa was aware, but she did not turn around. Instead, she continued to tease the young maid.

"One, two, three, four . . . keep those feet moving . . . one, two, three, four! Where're you going with those anyway?"

As they walked together along the corridor toward Louisa's old bedroom, she kept in step with Emily and walked side-by-side with her.

"To the attic. Mrs. Collins wants half of these in one chest for correspondence and the rest in with the invoices and accounts. We've been clearing out cupboards all morning," Emily explained.

Louisa opened the door to the bedroom while the girl walked on toward the door at the end of the corridor, as this was the entry point to the attic. No sooner had Louisa entered than she heard shrieks of laughter, which were mingled with alarm and coming from that particular area.

Running down to the attic doorway, she stopped to survey the damage. Emily and one of the other maids were on the floor together – having collided with each other – while the third girl was standing on the narrow timber steps leading to the platform above them, with fear registering on her face. There were trays, papers, letters, invoices and account books scattered everywhere – on the steps, as well as beneath them and beneath the girls on the floor.

While she was surveying the scene before her, Louisa heard her aunt mounting the stairs and calling to her. The three maids looked in alarm at Louisa.

"Gather them up quickly and get them into the chests. Hurry!" Louisa stated.

"We've spent hours sorting them. They're all mixed up now," Emily exclaimed in alarm.

"Who's to know?" Louisa queried. "Quickly now, just bundle them all together and throw them into the chests. Then, close the lids and lock them. No one will know. Whoever is going to come up here to check in the next ten years? I'll stall Mrs. Collins. Come downstairs when you're done. Don't stand there! Do it now!"

The maids sprang to their feet and sprang into action as Louisa ran along the corridor, calmly meeting her aunt at the top of the staircase and blocking further ascent. Sophie Collins, breathless and annoyed, stopped on the top step and accosted her.

"What's all the noise and hilarity? I've taken as much as I'm prepared to from everyone today. Answer me at once, Louisa!"

"Aha! It's . . . it's a mouse," Louisa stammered. "The girls were frightened."

"A mouse! A mouse in *my house! And,* with guests arriving! This is too much," Sophie exclaimed, as she began shouting to the butler. "Reddington! Come quickly!"

As the butler appeared at the bottom of the stairs, Sophie called to him again.

"Get Mr. Collins. There's a mouse up here . . . hurry now."

So saying, Sophie hurried back down the stairs as Louisa ran back along the corridor. She rushed to the doorway at the end and came to a sudden halt.

"It was a mouse," she stated, by way of explanation while panting noticeably.

"A mouse? Where?" screamed Emily, instantly jumping quickly onto the second step and glancing around frantically.

"Nowhere. That's our story, so stay with it," Louisa directed.

Louisa hurried along the corridor once again and this time, it was Reddington whom she met at the top of the stairs. She smiled at him, in all innocence, before brushing by him as he stood aside to allow her to descend. It was a demure Louisa who entered the library as Sophie was leaving. Once again, she grasped Louisa's arm.

"I haven't finished with you, young lady! I want to know why you've not replied to one invitation that's been sent to you. You've upset half of the ladies of Melbourne, most of whom *were* my friends before you arrived in town."

Louisa glanced over at Charles and Robert. She was relieved to see that they were deep in conversation and appeared not to have heard her aunt's hushed, though angry, words.

"We'll discuss this at length later. I've guests due in a few moments."

Louisa escaped and threw herself into the armchair beside the window as the two men continued their discussion. Reddington returned and, glancing sideways at Louisa, he addressed Robert Collins.

"The matter of the mouse has been handled speedily, sir. The problem will not arise again, as the culprit has been cornered and neutralised," he stated haughtily.

Louisa felt the tide of laughter rising within her and she slapped her hand onto the armchair, immediately collapsing and holding her sides as the tears of laughter rolled down her face.

"Oh! Reddington, you are too much! You never fail, do you?" she exclaimed, while looking over at him appreciatively and laughing unashamedly.

"One can but try, madam," he replied, with his poker-face showing no more than a slight quiver at the corner of his mouth as he left the room.

Robert and Charles studied at her as she wiped the tears from her eyes while giggling still. Robert eyed her suspiciously.

"I may be a wine merchant now, but I was headmaster at a boys' school long enough to know a mischief-maker when I see one. There was no mouse, I take it?"

Louisa looked at him for a few moments. Then, she laughed again. She tossed her chin in the air and flicked her head away.

"My lips are sealed," she replied.

"One day, Louisa, you'll be the death of me," Robert Collins announced prophetically.

The dinner guest list included Hugh and Margaret Travis and another elderly gentleman with whom Louisa was acquainted, having met him frequently during visits to her aunt and uncle's home. He was the minister at the local church where Sophie Collins attended irregularly. Puzzled at the uneven number of assembled guests, she watched as the last guest appeared at the door to the drawing room. At first, she did not recognise the lady. Then, as the new arrival turned and smiled at Louisa, recognition dawned instantly.

"Yvette!" Louisa shouted, while rushing across the room and flinging herself into the arms of her former governess.

Yvette, laughing at her boisterous greeting, held Louisa at arm's length and surveyed her critically. She frowned and looked across at Charles Lyndhurst.

"Really, Mr. Lyndhurst, you'll need to feed her well and often. Louisa, you're fading away to a shadow. Let me look at you, dear girl. How are you?" she asked, with genuine concern showing on her face.

Louisa executed a swift pirouette; then, she faced Yvette again as she began to study the woman closely. She was thirty years of age when she left the Howard homestead – just before Louisa's fifteenth birthday. Since that time, she seemed to have gained a considerable amount of weight and she appeared somewhat matronly. Louisa remembered the slim, vivacious woman who had stood on the deck of the paddle-steamer that had taken her beloved governess away from the homestead forever.

Abruptly, a halt was called to all discussion, because the sight of the fireworks emanating from Fitzroy Gardens began lighting up the night sky. Enthralled, Louisa watched with all the guests from the side balcony. Charles came beside her and he placed a possessive arm about her waist, but he did not speak to her. Dinner was announced, so further questioning of Yvette was, by necessity, left for a later time.

During dinner, Sophie broached the prospect of a ball being held at Lyndhurst Park. Louisa bristled with anger while knowing that her aunt was placing her in an untenable position – deliberately so. This was her way of placating her friends who were offended over certain invitations that were hidden in Louisa's bedroom – unanswered.

"Under no circumstances! If a ball is held there, I shall leave town for the duration!" Louisa announced firmly.

The assembled guests continued to consume their respective meals while appearing not to have noticed this sudden outburst from Louisa. Sophie, undeterred, began to relate stories of Louisa's childhood.

Along with Sophie's constant worry over the health of her only brother and his continued isolation on the property on the Murray

River, Sophie bemoaned the fact that Louisa had spent much of her life in that wild country, rather than in civilised society in Melbourne. Casting Louisa an evil eye, she addressed her assembled guests again.

"I received a missive from George recently. It appears my wayward niece hasn't contacted her father since leaving home weeks ago. He's worried about you, dear. Perhaps you might find the time in your no doubt busy schedule to drop him a quick note," Aunt Sophie asked politely and pointedly.

"Not under any circumstances! He knows our arrangement and if he continues to ignore his commitment to me, then he's well aware of the consequences of his inaction. He'll know my wrath soon enough, mark my words, Aunt Sophie!"

The assembled guests continued to consume their respective meals while appearing not to have noticed this next sudden outburst from Louisa. Sophie Collins, undeterred, pressed on with her deliberations.

"Nonsense. Whatever arrangement you have with your dear Papa, I'm certain he will honour it, in his own time," Sophie said, and smiling sweetly at Louisa.

"You are mistaken, Aunt. I kept my part of the bargain," she stated firmly, as she casted a scathing scowl at Charles instantly. "Now, I shall see to it that he keeps his word, which he swore to do before Almighty God."

Silence reigned for some minutes and Louisa was relieved to see her aunt turn her attention to the minister who was seated at her right. Louisa continued to keep her eyes on the plate in front of her while studying the food, although eating but little. She was annoyed with herself for revealing too much information and alarmed that she may have created suspicion regarding her proposed journey.

She was extremely angry with her aunt and she was determined that she would not be goaded into making any more unguarded remarks during the remainder of the evening. But, it was Yvette who came to her rescue as the awkwardness created by her untimely outbursts continued. She proposed that Louisa hold a small, intimate dinner party at Lyndhurst Park – as a first step – rather than a large affair, such as a ball. Yvette suggested sending an invitation to Louisa's father while asking George Howard to attend. With assistance from Mrs. Collins, such an event would be achieved easily and would, no doubt, proceed smoothly, thus being a wonderful success. Louisa grimaced at Yvette, but before she could reply, Charles intervened.

"An excellent suggestion, Mrs. Chambers," he agreed, as he raised the wine glass to his lips and glanced across at his outraged wife. "Consider it done!"

Louisa glared across the table at him while he watched her closely and dared her to make a scene. She flicked her chin in the air, but refrained from replying.

Dinner proceeded smoothly from that moment and the rest of the evening passed without incident. Yvette's musical talents were appreciated as she played the pianoforte and sang for the guests. Sophie Collins appeared delighted by the events of the evening while Louisa was less than happy.

It was while listening to the music that Louisa devised her plan. She would play the dutiful hostess and arrange the dinner party – as ordered – sending a carefully worded, formal invitation to her father, without any other missive accompanying it. He would not attend, she knew, so the morning following the gathering, she would slip away and take the train to Echuca. She would be away from Melbourne long before anyone realised that she was missing from Lyndhurst Park.

Her father had been given every opportunity. This was his last chance before she appeared on his doorstep again; then, he would know the rage that was seething inside of her at his betrayal of her trust and their verbal contract. She knew his reasoning. He thought that he would have died by now, thus saving himself the long trek to

Melbourne to consult physicians about his terminal disease, which he believed – genuinely believed – he possessed. When Louisa appeared at his door, he would wish for death more ardently than he did now, she vowed.

She brought her attention back into the room and began studying Yvette as she entertained those assembled in the drawing room. There was a deep sadness pervading this lady's countenance now. From the time of Yvette's departure from the Howard family until now, Louisa's life had been topsy-turvy and, at this point, she acknowledged to herself that everything was deteriorating. Yvette had left them to marry a young man who had received his discharge from the Royal Navy, due to ill health. They had married in Melbourne and lived with his aunt in her home. Six months after the wedding, he died and Yvette was a widow.

This was all the news that Louisa had managed to glean from her father, as Yvette's special friendship with Mary Howard meant that any new information was not forthcoming after the death of her mother. Louisa was at a loss to know why the lady for whom she felt a great affection was visiting tonight, for she was not a close friend of either Sophie or Robert Collins.

Riding home in the carriage with Charles, she was lost in deep concentration while pondering on her plans for the future. Excitement was mounting as she realised that, within a fortnight, she would be back at her own home. The problem with this was, of course, that Hilton and Cadence were at Lyndhurst Park now and this was an unforeseen complication to her plan. However, she was in no doubt that Charles would come to collect her eventually and she would be returned to them. In the meantime, matters at the homestead would be brought under control and her father would be made to face up to his health problems.

Being focussed totally on her own problems, she did not realise that Charles had not spoken to her at all since their arrival at the

Collins' home. His words – unexpected as they were now – shot her out of her reverie.

"Whenever I decide you cannot outdo your last performance, you prove me wrong. Your behaviour this evening was atrocious . . . absolutely atrocious. Do you have anything to say in your defence?"

Louisa gave a toss of her head in a useless show of defiance before replying to his question.

"No."

In the soft lighting that was flickering in from the lamps of the carriage, she watched him as he shook his head slowly. He did not speak again until the gates of Lyndhurst Park were in sight.

"Whatever arrangement you've made with your father, his inability to comply may be due to illness. But, I suppose you'd not consider this aspect of the situation. He doesn't appear to me to enjoy good health and a pleasant missive from you, advising him of your own good health and happiness, along with news of the safe arrival of the horses, may go a long way in assisting his recovery. That's only a suggestion, mind you . . . and definitely not a directive. I'd not presume to interfere between father and daughter."

"I sincerely hope not!" she replied.

When the carriage came to a halt at the front door, he assisted her to alight, but he lingered to speak to the driver as she entered the house. She ran up the stairs and was entering her bedroom when he reached her door. He followed her into the room.

"Where are they?" he demanded.

"What?" she queried innocently, while having forgotten all about the neglected invitations.

"The invitations, to which your aunt was referring. She seems very upset about them, so produce them now, this instant!"

Louisa pointed to the small metal chest on top of her wardrobe and Charles moved to lift it down before placing it on her bed in the centre of the room. The timber on the floor of her bedroom was highly polished, relieved only by a rug at the side of her bed – near to the door – and another rug at the end of the bed.

It was on the one at the end of the bed where she was standing now while he leaned over the chest, instantly flinging open the lid. He gasped in dismay and lifted the envelopes in his hands before allowing them to fall back into the chest. He stared at her momentarily before returning his attention to the correspondence.

"There must be at least thirty of them! *And*, you didn't even bother to open them?" he asked in astonishment.

"Why would I?" Louisa queried.

"Because it's common courtesy. There's no excuse for rudeness . . . not under any circumstances is there an excuse for rudeness."

Charles walked to the door and shouted for Benson. He strode back to her bed, immediately closing and fastening the chest; then, he carried it to the door where he met the panting butler who had hurried up the stairs at his master's call. She heard Charles giving instructions to Benson before returning to her and closing the door behind him. He stood looking at her. He was shaking his head in disbelief.

"Tomorrow, you'll go, with those invitations, to your aunt's home and there, you'll try to repair the damage that's been done, if that's at all possible. Do I make myself clear?"

Louisa shrugged her shoulders nonchalantly and she tried while to appear as disinterested in the matter as it was possible to be. He shook his head again before frowning at her.

"Why?" he gasped, finally able to find words to speak to her.

"It's of no interest to me. I didn't ask to be brought here and I've no intention of being a part of the nonsense that consumes Aunt Sophie night and day. I agreed to one request only! *And, that* was to stand on Papa's side verandah and sign a piece of paper. I did so. Now, he can keep his part of the arrangement. I agreed to nothing more and certainly not to spending hours of my time replying to endless invitations from people I don't know and don't wish to know. What more is there to say?"

Charles sat down on her bed while looking over at her as she stood there. She was separated from him by the brass bed-end. His hand swept the hair from his forehead as he studied her, seemingly as astounded by her reply as by her inability to grasp fully the situation as he perceived it.

"You're beyond belief and your logic is totally flawed. To what arrangement do you refer?" he asked.

"I thought you said you'd not presume to interfere between father and daughter."

"So I did," he agreed, and giving a deep sigh. "What you fail to grasp, deliberately or otherwise, is that in signing the marriage certificate, you became my legal property . . . lock, stock and barrel. Therefore, you'll do as I wish, when and where I wish, so live with that, *madam!*"

Suddenly, Charles glanced over at the small, lead-crystal clock, with the black and white face, that was standing on the chest of drawers positioned between the far wall and Louisa's bed. He grimaced and stood up, still watching her.

"I'm late for an appointment, so I've no time for this nonsense now," he stated, before moving to the connecting door to his bedroom.

"It's eleven-thirty," she murmured, briefly glancing at the clock herself.

"Therefore?" he queried, instantly raising one eyebrow while surveying her, with a definite challenge in his eyes. "Would you prefer I stayed?"

"No!" she exclaimed quickly.

"I thought not," he muttered, with a somewhat harsh laugh.

He strode from her room without a backward glance and closing the door quietly behind him. Louisa heard Charles descend the stairs a short time later. She wandered out through the side doors and walked to the front verandah where she observed him entering the carriage, which was waiting at the front door. With a sigh of relief, Louisa watched as it disappeared down the carriageway in the direction of the main gate. She sat in a cane chair outside of his bedroom while gazing at the river once again.

Sleep did not come easily that night. If Charles Lyndhurst came home at all, she did not hear him, for with Phillip's face before her eyes, sleep overcame her a little before dawn.

Sylvia

Sylvia sat alone in her sitting room as she awaited the arrival of Charles and she was pondering on her brother's revelations at dinner. Bertie, sniffing an intrigue unfolding, cancelled his plans for the evening and joined them after the Flemington race meeting, which had been financially successful for all three, thus adding to the hilarity at the dinner table where the wine flowed freely.

Patrick did not need any prompting to turn attention to his own life story and, as he had been missing from her life for as long as he had, Sylvia was all too eager to listen. On the infrequent occasions when there was a lull in conversation, a quick, pointed question from Bertie or from Sylvia herself, started Patrick on another tack, or on yet another tale of adventure. Ever mindful of Charles' request, Sylvia brought the subject of Phillip Carstairs to the fore eventually. On this, Patrick was not reticent at all, as his admiration for his friend knew no bounds.

Patrick had met him when Phillip, having heard of Patrick's reputation with a billiard cue, appeared at his elbow at the table in the back room of the hotel, which was one of Patrick's favourite haunts when in Sydney. From there, the friendship became stronger until it reached the point where Phillip was sending young gentlemen to Patrick while claiming that he could not be beaten at his chosen game. Then, the pair would split the profits that resulted from the ensuing gambling venture. But, it was Patrick's respect for his friend's conquests where ladies were concerned that caused Sylvia to listen with renewed interest. His tales on that score, whether embellished or not, raised even an eyebrow on Bertie's normally impassive countenance.

In particular, there was one incident, which Sylvia found troubling and she had difficulty in accepting the truth of the matter. Still, she would pass it on to Charles and he could make of it what he would. Thankfully, after dinner, Patrick left the house before Charles' arrival and the clock in the hallway had struck midnight before Charles came to her. Then, Patrick and his tales were forgotten at once. So, it was not until breakfast on the following morning that found Sylvia relating the most interesting parts of Patrick's revelations to Charles.

"A bride? On the eve of her wedding?" he asked, with an eyebrow raised in question and a frown appearing on his face.

"Her father surprised them in the back garden," Sylvia replied, with a slight nod. "And, Patrick swears it's true, because he was a witness, due to the fact that there was a wager between them on the outcome of the encounter."

"Is that so?" Charles murmured, somewhat thoughtfully.

"The matter was suppressed until the couple returned to Sydney some weeks later. It was then the rumours began circulating furiously. So, they were required to leave town again . . . rather hurriedly, it would seem. Also, it appears that Carstairs' older brother threatened to cut off all money from the family coffers if he didn't come to Melbourne with his sister . . . or, so Patrick said," Sylvia confided.

"Oh! George would've, too. He's a hard man, that one!" he commented quietly, grimacing as he did so.

"That's not the worst of it. Carstairs let it be known that he was not the first, if you take my meaning."

Charles' frown was even more pronounced at this revelation. Lost in thought, he nodded his head slowly before speaking again some minutes later.

"Then, I'm obliged to you, as that's the confirmation I needed. Thank you, my darling, and now, I must be away, so I'll see you tomorrow night."

"And, what're you planning to wear to the Fancy Dress Ball? It's our last royal function remember, after Prince Alfred returns from his country tour," Sylvia asked, while watching Charles as he was preparing to leave.

"That's highly secretive information, which I'm not at liberty to share with anyone," Charles replied, with a grin.

Sylvia laughed and she followed him from the side terrace where they had partaken of breakfast, and on through her sitting room.

"You haven't any idea, so be honest now," she challenged.

"Not the slightest," he admitted ruefully. "I don't suppose you'd tell me if I asked what outfit you've chosen."

"Nothing would induce me to divulge that to you, or to anyone else."

"Then, we shall have to wait and see what that evening brings, won't we?" he answered, with a soft laugh as he reached for her and kissed her.

Once again, Sylvia sat alone in her sitting room and in a very pensive mood for quite some time after Charles' departure from her home. The subject of Louisa was never raised between them, but she could not accept that he had such a pretty and vivacious young girl living under his roof, as his legal wife, and that he had not touched her after all these weeks they had been together.

Charles' ridiculous plan regarding an annulment was never mentioned again and she had assumed many weeks ago that he had abandoned any hope in this direction. Sylvia had not placed any credence in his outlandish scheme at any stage, so her expectations were never raised in this regard. That he regarded Louisa as a daughter over whom he assumed guardianship temporarily was inconceivable to Sylvia.

Whether or not Phillip Carstairs had Louisa Lyndhurst in his sights – as the next conquest on his long list – she did not know. But, if there were to be another wager between her brother and his friend on that score, Sylvia was certain Charles that would not stand idly by and allow this to occur.

There was little that happened in the city of Melbourne that escaped the notice of either Charles Lyndhurst or Bertie Webster. Sylvia had the ear of both; therefore, nothing escaped her scrutiny, even if she allowed little to leave her lips in the way of gossip. Her name had been on the tip of too many wagging tongues over the years to participate in that game herself, at someone else's expense.

Gossip that involved Charles Lyndhurst would draw her name to the surface always, regardless of how little she was involved, because she was damned by association. She was certain that, at this stage, Patrick was unaware of her involvement with Charles. His recent arrival in the city was one factor, which would be keeping him in ignorance of the arrangement and, after dinner on the previous evening, Patrick had left her home to meet with Phillip Carstairs. As yet, he had not returned.

The other issue, which was troubling Sylvia was that when her brother returned to Melbourne after his visit to their mother, he would expect to come back to her home and to take up residence here for the duration of his stay in this city. While he was very welcome, it presented a problem for Sylvia. If this were to occur and his friend did have Louisa Lyndhurst marked as his next romantic conquest, Sylvia would find herself in an untenable position, especially in her own home. She would have her brother spying on her – on behalf of Phillip Carstairs – so that they would be aware of the comings and goings of Sylvia's lover, that being the husband of Louisa Lyndhurst.

She gave a deep sigh and wondered how it was possible to be in a situation such as this, without even realising that it was occurring. Tomorrow, Patrick would leave for Castlemaine to visit his mother who had not sighted her only surviving son since he was seventeen years of age. If Patrick thought to take over the running of the hotel from his mother, he was in for an unpleasant surprise, to say the least. Norma Doherty would never release the reins to anyone, no matter how great a regard she had for the person, if they indulged in the drinking of alcohol. As Sylvia's brother seemed to have no intention of reforming overnight, Sylvia felt that he would be back on her doorstep in a very short space of time.

She laughed quietly to herself while knowing that Patrick had no inkling of the situation, into which he was stepping in Castlemaine. *And*, she had no intention of enlightening him on that score, because he may postpone the visit, thus depriving her mother of the long-awaited reunion of mother and son. Sylvia was determined to keep her lips sealed on that subject.

Chapter Sixteen

– *Victorian Victorians* –

Louisa

Louisa rode Hilton while the groom was astride another horse from Charles' large stable. Nathaniel was riding behind her. She spent two hours exploring and, finally, as she was about to return to the house, she spied the perfect meeting place. It was located quite close to the road and very secluded while being out of sight of anyone on the road, or of anyone who happened to be riding on the well-worn path where she was sitting now on Hilton as she surveyed her surroundings. She slid from his back, immediately handing the reins to the groom, and she walked the short distance to the clump of bushes. Beyond these, she found smooth boulders beneath shady trees. Had she designed the area herself, she could not have produced a better assignation point for her proposed meeting with Phillip. Well pleased with her discovery, she returned to the house at a fast gallop and leaving Nathaniel far behind her.

Seeking food before anything else, she changed quickly and descended the stairs to enjoy a late breakfast – hopefully alone – and she was seated at the table when Charles came into the room. She was certain that he had not been at home when she left to go riding, for she opened their connecting door a fraction to peep inside and his bed seemed not to have been disturbed. With a sigh of relief, she had raced to the stables to go riding with Nathaniel, rather than await her husband.

"Good morning!" Charles announced cheerfully as he opened the morning newspaper in his hands. "How're you this fine morning, Louisa?"

With her mouth full of toast, Louisa nodded in answer to his surprisingly cordial greeting. After the previous night's argument, she expected another lecture, but this did not seem to be forthcoming, much to her relief. A visit to her aunt's home was planned for the afternoon in order to placate him and to keep the peace until she could make good her escape to her father's home. Phillip Carstairs was on her mind and she was planning to draw a map of the area, which she located on this morning's ride; then, she would send it to him while suggesting a time for their first rendezvous. That should ease the boredom a little for her, she decided. Charles appeared content to drink tea and did not seem to be interested in eating, so she wondered why he bothered to inflict his presence upon her when he could go to his office to read his paper. His next question surprised her.

"What do you plan to wear to the Fancy Dress Ball?" he enquired.

Louisa was thoughtful for a moment, after having given the matter not one thought at all.

"Umm . . . I thought I'd go as a highwayman. Can you lend me a pistol or two, please?" she asked, thereby feigning innocence.

Charles laughed and, moving the newspaper that was partially covering his face to one side, he began to study her closely. He watched her with suspicious eyes. Then, he laughed again.

"That's an excellent idea! I shall adopt it immediately," he replied.

"Not for you . . . for me!" she stated emphatically.

"Then, you'll have to come up with something more becoming for a lady of your standing in our little community. What's your next suggestion?" he queried, with sarcasm sounding in his voice.

"Then, I shall pull out the oldest muslin gown I can find and go as the dairy maid that you say I resemble."

"That's twice you've answered me, *and both times*, there was a baited hook awaiting me. I shall not be tempted, so try again."

Louisa continued to eat her breakfast, desperately trying to ignore his scrutiny, his questioning and his presence. Finally, he picked up a knife from the table and tapped her on the wrist with this item of cutlery.

"I'll not be ignored. Give me an answer by the end of the day, for I'll not have you making a spectacle of yourself in some outlandish outfit, just to spite me and to bring attention to yourself," he ordered.

Charles returned his attention to the newspaper and he ignored her completely once again as Benson came to the table with a plate of scrambled eggs for Louisa. These she set about devouring with gusto. Benson left and, eventually, Charles rose to leave her.

"I can't quite comprehend how someone can eat as much as you do and yet remain mere skin and bone," he muttered, intently watching her.

Louisa looked up at him and she gave him a contemptuous glance.

"*And,* I can't quite comprehend how someone can be as critical as you are and yet expect to remain friends with me."

"Then, perhaps, the fault lies with the one who continues to flout all rules," he suggested quietly.

"Then, perhaps, it may've been wise for you to *plight thou troth* to a demure, little mouse who'd sit in the corner all day, doing needlework and speaking only when spoken to," Louisa countered. "Unfortunately for you, that's not my style."

Charles placed the newspaper under his arm as he turned to leave the room.

"I live in hope," he murmured, as he strode toward the door.

"*I've only just commenced,*" Louisa muttered, under her breath.

He spun around, immediately frowning and staring at her, but she was undecided as to whether or not he had heard her last comment clearly. He gave her a scathing look before continuing on his way.

And, Louisa knew a moment of triumph.

Later in afternoon, after having spent several hours in her aunt's company while attempting to smooth ruffled feathers in that arena, Louisa decided to wander to her cabin in the bush. She left the house with a book under her arm, crossed the carriageway and sat on the top step leading to the river. Here, she removed her shoes and placed her bare feet onto the stone step. She did not bother to wear stockings for the short trek from her bedroom to the front door. On the step now, she left her shoes there – in full view of anyone who happened to be in Charles' office – and knowing that her provocative act would not go unnoticed.

She descended the steps and tripped along the path beside the river before veering right along the path that was just beyond the tall tree, which left her feeling sad and vulnerable whenever she moved beneath its branches. Today was no different to any other day in this regard.

Louisa entered the cabin and stopped in her tracks, instantly looking around in surprise. On the previous day, she brought a lamp here and this was standing where she had left it, on top of the rough timber bench. Also, she had positioned a parasol beside the armchair in case the roof leaked, because this was a distinct possibility. There were many large cracks and open holes visible from beneath its weathered beams and rusted tin sheeting.

Now, she surveyed the room in astonishment. Beneath the lamp was a white, stiffly-starched cloth. The chair was covered with a small crocheted blanket and, on the dirt floor, was a brightly coloured rug. A small table was placed beside the armchair and another lamp was standing there, with a white lace cloth beneath it.

She walked to the armchair. She sat down and placed her book on the small table as she studied her surroundings in detail. Then, she noticed, almost out of view behind her chair, a small, highly polished trolley and, instinctively, she knew that Benson was the culprit. Before she could comprehend the sight before her eyes, she heard footsteps on the path and, assuming that her husband was coming to disturb her again, a feeling of annoyance crept over her. However, one of the parlour maids entered, followed closely by Benson whose regal bearing belied his surroundings. He had a white cloth over his arm and he was carrying a silver tray with a silver service atop. The maid carried a tray laden with freshly baked cakes, which she placed on the trolley.

"Afternoon tea is served," Benson announced loudly, clearly and haughtily to all assembled, this being Louisa and the maid who was trying desperately not to giggle, and failing miserably.

"*And,* about time, too!" Louisa reprimanded, having not ordered anything at all.

That comment was too much for the maid, Evelyn, who could not refrain from laughing. Benson maintained his regal bearing under the most trying of circumstances while he served tea in these salubrious, if somewhat less than palatial, surroundings.

"Thank you for all of this, Benson. I know you're responsible, so don't even think to deny it. I'm truly grateful," Louisa stated, with a smile.

Finally, in return, she received a slight smile from the butler as he gave a small nod of acknowledgment. As they prepared to leave her alone, a shadow fell across the doorway and Louisa managed, with great difficulty, to stifle a groan. Charles Lyndhurst stood in the doorway. He was leaning against the door jamb and surveying the scene before him while he appeared to be having some difficulty in keeping the laughter from his face. He stood aside as Benson and Evelyn departed, in single file, through the lopsided doorway. He looked around the cabin, obviously taking in everything in that one, imperceptible, but sweeping, glance.

"I'd forgotten this place existed," he commented, before querying Louisa. "Your doll's house, I presume."

"Would you care for some tea, Mr. Lyndhurst?" she inquired haughtily.

"Thank you, no. But, it never ceases to amaze me how I feed, clothe and pay the servants' wages, *yet you*, who has been here but a few weeks, can have them dangling on a string, tumbling over one another to do your bidding. How can that be, Louisa?" he queried.

"I give them something else. It's called *respect*. You'd do well to take a leaf from my book."

"You push it to the endth degree, don't you? I came to see what you're playing at and to inquire about your proposed outfit for the ball. But, at the risk of seeming somewhat naive, may I ask what you propose to do when it rains in here?" he asked.

Without looking at him, she reached for the parasol and opened it. Holding it above her head, she lifted the cup in her other hand and raised the hot tea to her lips.

"I've seen everything now," he muttered, with a groan; then, shaking his head in mock despair, he advised her. "Play your games while you can."

"I've decided to ask Benson to lend me a uniform belonging to one of the maids to wear to the ball," Louisa stated, with a trace of defiance sounding in her voice.

Charles walked over to the plate of cakes, selected one, placed it in his mouth and walked from the cabin, without another word, or a backward glance.

And, Louisa knew another moment of triumph.

Louisa decided, while sitting alone in her new hideaway, that she would need to give some thought to an outfit for the Fancy Dress Ball. It was not a matter that was concerning her greatly. She knew that she would be at her father's homestead by the time the night of the ball arrived. However, if she continued to ignore the event, Charles may become suspicious. Therefore, she would take a visit to the city on the following morning to purchase a cap for her outfit to wear to Echuca and she would dispatch the missive, with a map enclosed, to the address, which Phillip had given to her at the race meeting. Also, she would ride to the secret meeting place, climb a tree and place a scarf around a branch, so there would not be any mistake about the place-in-question.

Well pleased with these plans, she turned her attention to another matter and that was how to handle her uncle, Father Frank, when he arrived next on her doorstep. He would castigate her severely, she knew, over her marriage to Charles Lyndhurst and there was no easy solution to that dilemma. The other matter requiring her attention was the dinner party at Lyndhurst Park. She would speak to Benson on this issue. She had persuaded her aunt to send the invitations, on Louisa's behalf, and these were already on their way to the invited guests. At dawn on the morning following the dinner party, she would be away from here before the house stirred. Nothing would sway her on that decision.

On the following morning, she rode with Nathaniel and, leaving him with the horses beneath a tree that was well out of sight of her secret meeting place, she ventured into the thick bush until she came upon the boulders in the small clearing. Here, she removed a green scarf from her pocket and, climbing a tree, she managed to tie the item around the branch without any difficulty whatsoever. Then, she returned to Nathaniel and they rode back to the house. Louisa was dressed ready for her excursion into the city when visitors were announced. Expecting one of them to be Father Frank, she descended the stairs slowly. To her great surprise and relief, she found not only Yvette Chambers, but also James Marshall, waiting there. Yvette was holding a small child in her arms and Louisa was delighted to see them all.

James explained that he was en route to England to stay with his father's family where he was to become a minister of religion, thereby following in his father's footsteps. Yvette introduced her daughter, Simone, who was the first baby that Louisa had seen at such close proximity. She was undecided what to do with such a creature, especially when the little girl began to cry. Her mother, after having placated her a little, stood her on her shaky legs. The child proceeded to take a few steps, only to fall over immediately, thus bringing on another bout of tears.

The visit lasted for over an hour, after which she farewelled James, never knowing if or when they would meet again. It was a sad parting for two friends who had known each other for all of their lives. During the visit, Yvette explained that Simone was born after the death of Yvette's husband and, although they continued to live with her late husband's aunt in Melbourne, Yvette required a means to provide for her daughter and herself. She was teaching music – specifically, the pianoforte – from their home. Now, since Mr. Lyndhurst had located her for a specific purpose, she would be visiting Louisa three times a week, with this arrangement commencing on the following Monday.

Taken aback, Louisa stared at her former governess in astonishment, much to James' obvious amusement.

"You don't know anything about it, do you, Lou?" he asked.

"No, not at all. What do you mean by *he located you?* And, why would he go to such lengths?" Louisa queried.

"He has your interests at heart, dear girl. It seems you expressed a wish to become proficient at the pianoforte again. So, he obtained my address from your father and he came to visit me. That was when I received an invitation from your aunt to dine with them the other evening. Did you not know anything about all this?" Yvette asked.

"No, I did not," Louisa replied thoughtfully.

The trio departed shortly afterwards while leaving a somewhat stunned Louisa standing by the front door. After lunch, which she enjoyed alone, she was about to order the carriage once again when her uncle arrived. Rather than have him lecturing her endlessly in the house where he could be overheard, she whisked him away and escorted him to the jetty. Standing by the pylon where she struggled so recently with Phillip Carstairs, Louisa listened to the tirade from Father Frank, which ended finally with the words regarding her mother.

"Gracious me, your mother would turn in her grave, Louisa. It's such a tragedy. You'll need to pray every day for forgiveness and for a solution to be given to you. Every day you spend with this man, you are living in mortal sin. In the eyes of Mother Church, you are unwed."

"Yes, Father," she murmured.

Louisa answered contritely with her eyes downcast while looking beneath the jetty and visualising Phillip in the stolen rowing boat that had been secured there.

"You may not come to the altar rails to receive Holy Communion, for it will be my solemn duty to deny the sacrament to you. You do understand and appreciate fully my position in this sad affair, I presume?"

Father Frank's tirade continued unabated while Louisa nodded her head solemnly. Then, as he made his next demand, her brow creased into a frown.

"*And, all of your children* must be brought up in the fear and love of God while being baptised within His Church. There cannot be any exception to that directive, or the fires of hell are all you can look forward to from here! *And, you must* remarry in God's Church. There's no question on that score, so it's to be arranged as soon as you can persuade your husband of its importance and necessity."

"Yes, Father Frank."

Once again, Louisa answered softly and demurely while all the while wondering how she was to obtain said children, in order to have Father Frank baptise them in his church. Pondering on this question, Louisa decided that, perhaps, she would discuss the matter with Yvette in the near future. But, of immediate concern was how to be rid of her irate uncle, so that she could embark on her errands.

Finally, after what seemed an eternity, she steered the conversation back to her father and his health problems as she asked the priest to remember him in his prayers. It was then that she made the excuse of her husband expecting her to accompany him on a fictitious excursion, in order to bring the never-ending meeting to an end. Father Frank left shortly thereafter. Louisa was able to make her way into the city to complete successfully her errands.

She arrived home with a tam-o'-shanter, which she hid with the rest of the outfit for her adventure, the thought of which was causing her great flutters of excitement. Another matter causing her great flutters of excitement was the planned meeting with Phillip. If this was love that she was feeling now, Father Frank had not scratched the surface of her sins; so, if the fires of hell were awaiting her, she had little to lose really, she decided. She was damned already in the eyes of her Church, which had been her life – and her reason for being – for as long as she could remember.

Being Tuesday night, she dined alone. Why this was so, she knew not. But, always on a Tuesday evening, she dined alone. Pondering again on Phillip who seemed to be invading her thoughts more often than not these days, Louisa was struck by a thought. Aunt Sophie had pleaded with Louisa to journey to Melbourne and to spend a few months with them during the time of the Royal Tour. In fact, from the moment that the Tour was announced, although no dates were given, Aunt Sophie's pleading letters had begun to arrive at the homestead.

The thought, which was occupying Louisa now was that had she been more obliging and moved to Melbourne at her aunt's request, she would have been unmarried on the night when she met Phillip and the whole situation would have been entirely different from what it was today. In such a case, there would have been hope; whereas now, there was none.

This thought did little to lift her spirits as she mounted the stairs alone and entered her bedroom. The little crystal clock, with the black and white face, was showing nine o'clock and she was not tired at all. The heat was trapped in her bedroom, so sleep would not come, even if she slipped beneath the sheets. Charlotte was nowhere to be seen and this was unusual, for she was waiting always to attend to Louisa.

On impulse, Louisa descended the stairs again and slipped out through the front door while heading in the direction of the stables. Her shoes made not a sound on the grass as she made her way to visit Hilton. He would keep her company for a short while, she decided.

There was a lamp burning in the carriage shed as she walked by the window. Suddenly, as the scene within registered in her mind, she stopped and retraced her steps and she peered through the open window. There, she spied Charlotte, who was naked to the waist, wrapped in Nathaniel's arms. His mouth was somehow covering one bare breast. Louisa gave an audible gasp, which fortunately, was not heard by the young couple who was otherwise occupied. Memories of Colleen McBryde and Bill Bartlett came flooding back to her and she recalled being positioned on a branch outside that window, unable to move, and watching a spectacle such as this one before her now.

Turning quickly, she ran across the grass, crossed the carriage-way and jumped down the stone steps before reaching the jetty again while not remembering how she arrived there. Wondering about the scene with her maid and the groom, her thoughts turned to Phillip and his comment about her being a married woman when she had asked him what he was attempting to do to her. Then, there was the episode with Captain Bill and Brydie. As well, there was a fact, which she had not considered before now, and this related to Yvette having a baby, an event which followed on from her marriage. Today, Father Frank had mentioned that her children must be baptised in the Catholic Church.

There was a cool breeze whipping around her face and playing havoc with her hair as she sat contemplating these strange matters. The coolness of the breeze by the river was a welcome relief to the heat of the house. However, after sitting alone for some time, she returned slowly to the house and her bedroom to find a tidy and fully-clothed maid waiting to assist her to undress. Louisa glanced at Charlotte and she realised that there were many matters, of which Charlotte was aware and that her mistress – two years her junior – did not know. There was a distinct line dividing them. The questions would remain unasked. Perhaps, she could persuade Yvette to advise her in this regard, although how to broach such a subject, Louisa knew not.

As she extinguished the lamp, Louisa thought of Yvette. She was married to a young man who had been a naval officer. As a result of that marriage, her baby daughter, Simone, had been born after the death of her husband. One day, she would ask Yvette for an explanation to this mystery. Her second last thought, before drifting into a deep sleep, was of James, who was to sail on the morning tide, bound for England. As always, her last thought was reserved for Phillip, with the laughing blue eyes and the deep dimples dancing at the corners of his mouth.

Of Charles Lyndhurst, Louisa thought not at all!

Sylvia

With the events celebrating the arrival of His Royal Highness in the city of Melbourne drawing to a close temporarily, Sylvia found a few days available when she could visit her uncle in Bendigo. Bertie's schedule did not allow for him to accompany her but, true to his word, he had completed all arrangements for the transfer of ownership of Thomas McMillan's share of the Royal George Hotel to Sylvia. The papers were drawn up and were awaiting her uncle's signature. She wrote to advise him of her intention to visit – a fact that delighted him, he advised by return mail.

Taking the train, she decided against a visit to Castlemaine on this journey. The rift between her mother and herself had not been healed as yet and, presumably, Patrick was visiting there at this time. To her knowledge, her brother had not returned to Melbourne. Arriving in Bendigo, Sylvia went immediately to the hotel where she stayed always; then, she visited her family for dinner in the evening while taking her maid, Phoebe, with her. To her annoyance, Sylvia discovered that she was but days ahead of the Royal Party and she had walked into the frantic mayhem and frenzied madness that Melbourne had been experiencing for the past few weeks.

Her aunts were planning on going to view the parade, much to her brother's horror, for as a Scotsman, Thomas possessed a long memory where the English were concerned. However, her aunts would not be deterred and their plans were well advanced for this excursion. With the papers duly signed, Sylvia returned to her hotel. She walked the short distance in the cool air and the soft evening light while being escorted by her uncle and the maid.

On the following morning, an urgent missive arrived from her uncle. This was informing her that Aunt Bella and Aunt Miriam were ill and he would welcome a visit from her. Sylvia left the hotel at once, accompanied once again by Phoebe, and arriving mid-morning, she found both patients in bed. They were suffering symptoms not unlike those brought on by food poisoning. However, the doctor had called earlier and could find no apparent cause for the onset of the problem, from which her uncle did not suffer, at this present time.

Being in the home of her aunts, as they rested between bouts of illness, Sylvia found herself in a strange dilemma. They had been the stalwarts of her life and now, they appeared so frail and so much older than she realised. It was almost as though they had aged a decade in a matter of a day or two.

This fact, Sylvia found disconcerting. Seeing Charles with his new, young wife reinforced for her the fact that she was no longer a part of the younger generation but, with the advent of her thirty-fifth birthday, she must face the inevitable fact that her life was changing before her eyes. When Edwin dies, she pondered, she will be facing a far different future to the one, which she had envisaged always, over the past decade, because Charles will not be a part of that life. For the first time, Sylvia faced the situation confronting her and she found the prospects for her own future daunting, to say the least.

With assistance from the two ladies who appeared daily on the doorstep and who were employed by her uncle – one as cook and the other as housekeeper – Sylvia managed to keep her uncle's household functioning. Her maid, Phoebe, was of great assistance, also, and when each evening came, her uncle spent time with his sisters, thus making it possible for Sylvia to return to her hotel to dine there.

Prince Alfred's arrival in Bendigo was imminent, for according to the local newspaper, the royal visitor had stayed overnight in the town of Castlemaine with his entourage. The event of the parade was causing no end of excitement, in most quarters. However, in the McMillan home, there was great disappointment when her aunts came to accept the inevitable, as they were not recovered sufficiently to leave their respective beds and both were too weak to even consider a brief trip into the centre of the town in order to witness this great event for themselves.

Sylvia was hoping to avoid the crush-and-bustle herself and, with this is mind, she left her aunts resting in their bedrooms while her uncle insisted on reading to them, one at a time. He did suggest escorting Sylvia, but she would not hear of him leaving his older sisters alone. Trying to order a carriage for her on such an evening – with the streets cordoned off for the parade – was an impossibility. So Sylvia, accompanied by her maid, left their home while promising to call on the following morning before returning to her own home and her husband in Melbourne.

The air was still as she stepped onto the footpath and began walking in the direction of her hotel. Every now and then, a warm breeze, slight though it was, brushed her face. With Phoebe walking along beside her, they rounded a corner and discovered that the parade had begun already, while they were wedged firmly in the midst of the crowd that was lining the street. Sylvia glimpsed the earlier floats as these vehicles ambled by and, although the crowd was three and four deep where she stood, she had a clear view of the procession. Children, positioned on their father's shoulders, cheered and waved flags while the colourful bunting was everywhere. It was flying from buildings and other vantage points around the town. No expense had been spared.

She knew that Prince Alfred would be in attendance, but his entourage was nowhere to be seen from her perspective. Sylvia stared in amazement as an exact replica of Prince Alfred's ship, *Galatea*, came into view to loud applause and wild cheering. Upon closer inspection, she realised that the sailors – all dressed in neatly-pressed sailors' suits – were young boys who were standing to attention while brimming with pride. The crush of spectators around her was so strong that Sylvia was having difficulty in breathing freely and the warm evening did not assist the situation in any way. She found it impossible to move in any direction.

Suddenly, as if from nowhere, fireworks exploded. Whether this event was pre-arranged, or an accidental firing, she knew not. However, one wayward missile hit the small replica ship and, by some cruel twist of fate, it landed in a box of fireworks. This container was stored on the deck of the replica of Prince Alfred's ship, which had been built upon a steam-traction engine, especially for the parade.

The box ignited. Instantly, fireworks began hissing and exploding in all directions. The crowd on the street began to scream in fright and horror while no one knew which way to turn or to run. Panic was replaced by terrified screams as, on deck, the sails caught fire. In seconds, on this hot summer's evening in early December, the sails were engulfed in flames.

Before any of the astounded and shocked spectators could react, the blazing sails fell to the deck and these became flaming shrouds while wrapping the tiny bodies of the young sailors completely in their folds. The screams of pain and terror from the struggling and trapped boys filled the air and these horrific sounds mingled instantaneously with the shouts of panic and disbelief from the spectators on the footpath.

The procession came to a complete halt as several men jumped from the crowd and, regardless of their own safety, began their vain attempts to unravel the fiery material from the struggling bodies and to dowse the flames as they did so.

Panic and pandemonium descended on the crowd. Water containers appeared, as if from nowhere, and many hands were reaching onto the float now as tiny, burnt bodies were moved slowly and carefully to the waiting arms of the rescuers on the street. Sylvia, as with most spectators around her, had turned to stone. She could not believe the sight that met her eyes this night, or the scene that she had witnessed.

Glancing sideways, she could see that all of the blood had drained from Phoebe's face and she was ghostly white as she swayed slightly. Grabbing the girl by the arm, Sylvia whispered to her to take deep breaths. Then, she pushed her way through the throngs of stunned bystanders, some of whom were beginning to disperse. She dragged her maid beside her. Bendigo's parade, in honour of Prince Alfred's visit, had ended in disaster and tragedy almost before it had begun.

Finally, on reaching the hotel, she took Phoebe to Sylvia's room initially and, once there, she forced her to sit on the chair by the window, with her head between her knees, until the girl was able to focus more clearly.

Although shaking markedly, Phoebe was able to stand and partake of a glass of water after some ten minutes. Then, Sylvia sent the girl to the servant's quarters to recover fully. Unable to prevent herself from trembling as the events of the evening played over and over in her mind, she rummaged through her personal case until she located a small container of brandy. After several large gulps of the alcohol, she was able to steady herself and to compose a note to her uncle, in which she detailed the shocking events of the evening. She descended the stairs and dispatched the note at the hotel desk. She went to the dining room to partake of a light meal before retiring for the evening.

After a brief visit to her uncle and his sisters early the following morning, Sylvia was assured that her aunts were much recovered and she returned to the carriage bound for the railway station. The journey to Melbourne, which stopped at Castlemaine and Sunbury en route, took over two and a half hours and she was never as happy to see her own home loom before her as she was on this day.

The news of the tragic events that occurred in Bendigo on the previous day had reached Melbourne. Subsequently, Sylvia discovered that several of the boys had died as a result of the horrific event, which she had witnessed, and others were injured seriously. Momentarily, she closed her eyes and she could hear still the terrified screams of those little boys who, minutes earlier, had been so full of pride as they stood to attention on deck. The memory, along with the tragedy of her young brother's drowning, would remain with her forever.

Walking into her home, with its familiar surroundings, filled her with relief as Sylvia sought to bring some semblance of order to this day. She made her way to Edwin's bedroom immediately, only to find him asleep and unaware of her presence. In earlier times – no matter what had occurred – she was able to sit quietly always and to talk through the problem with Edwin. Today, more than ever, she missed his calm and steady guidance.

Returning to her sitting room in a pensive and sombre mood, she was mulling over the events of the previous evening again, when

Bertie arrived while announcing his intention of spending some time with her. Relief swept over her at the sight of his beaming smile and at the prospect of enjoying his cheerful presence. For Sylvia, knowing that she would not be dining alone made this night seem bearable.

Several months ago, had she found herself in a situation such as this one, she could have sent a message to Charles when she was troubled deeply – as she was now – and he would have stopped whatever he was doing and he would have come to her immediately. How life had changed for her in a few short months!

Chapter Seventeen

− *Victorian Victorians* −

Louisa

L ouisa left Nathaniel quite a distance away from her meeting place with Phillip and she walked to the designated area with a book tucked under her arm and swinging a canvas bag by her side. The groom and the horses could not been seen from her vantage point, so as soon as she had ascertained that the coast was clear, she pushed her way through the last of the bushes as her excitement continued to mount. She did not know if Phillip had received her missive and map; or, if he would arrive today. Charging through the final clump of foliage, she received her answer.

He stood waiting, with hat in hand. Phillip came to her and was about to take her in his arms when, to his absolute astonishment and complete surprise, she produced her knife that was the gift from Bill Bartlett, and which she held up before his startled face now. She gave the lever a small flick with her right thumb, instantly causing the blade to spring to life before his amused eyes. He began to laugh.

"Touch me again the way you did last time and I'll not hesitate to use this. That is a promise, Mr. Carstairs!" Louisa greeted him with this warning. "Now, unless I have your word on the matter, I'll be gone and I won't return *ever*."

"Ha! Foolhardy, I'm not, *Mrs. Lyndhurst.* You've *my word.* Are you alone?"

"Don't be silly! Do you think me a complete fool? Of course I'm not, as the groom is with me. *And,* he's bigger than you, just as strong and what's more, he's within earshot. Do we have a deal?"

"We have a deal," he agreed, reluctantly and sitting down on the flat boulder.

Louisa sat on the boulder facing him and started to laugh at her apparent easy victory over him. He watched her in amusement for a few moments as she opened the bag that she was carrying and she produced sandwiches and some water. She handed the flask to him.

"Here, I'm returning the favour. You gave me water last time."

"Whisky's my favourite drop, but water'll do fine for now and I'd kill for one of those," he stated, while pointing to the food.

She handed him a wrapped parcel of sandwiches and began drinking some water herself. The breakfast was prepared for her alone, so only one flask of water was provided and they were required to share it. Having established the ground rules for their regular meetings, Louisa advised him of the days when she rode with the groom. There appeared to be set days when Charles rode with her, but these were subject to change at a moment's notice, so she advised Phillip that she could not promise to be here always.

Although Charles appeared to be a creature of habit and of set schedules, these could be altered at a moment's notice, depending on his shipping business, which by necessity was ruled by the ocean's tides.

"I shall endeavour to be here on the allocated days, if you still wish to meet with me," she informed him.

"I do," he murmured. "I can't seem to get you out of my mind. You're plaguing me and I hear your infectious laugh when I'm least expecting it. Then, I turn around and there's no one there. It must be *love.* I don't know, as I'm new to this experience."

Louisa moved her head to one side and she studied him candidly. He watched her, with a sly grin adorning his face as he sat awaiting her next pronouncement.

"Well, if you don't know, how would I? I've not experienced it either. But, I don't believe you, for I'm certain you must have girls falling over themselves to catch you. You're not without looks and charm," she replied.

"Thanks," he muttered, with a laugh and he confessed to her. "Yes, but their mothers grab, taking them off in the other direction. Even here in Melbourne, I seem to have something of a reputation that's gone before me . . . and it's not undeserved, I suppose, if I wanted to be honest. But, with you, it's different. I just want to be with you always . . . to protect you and to love you. *And,* after such a short acquaintance, I'd be the first to laugh at such an outlandish notion, so feel free to scoff."

"Well, I shan't scoff or laugh, but please don't be offended if I don't believe you. You shall have to prove yourself and your love, before I'll accept your words. Anyway, there's nothing to be done about it, for I'm well and truly married."

This last remark seemed to cause him some annoyance, because with one, quick sweep of his arm, he tossed his hat, which went spinning away on the breeze. They both watched as it landed on a branch. Then, it fell to the ground. They ate breakfast in silence for some minutes, after which Louisa began relating stories of her childhood to him. These were amusing happenings, which had him laughing. He reciprocated while telling tales of his early years when he was growing up in Sydney and, more recently, of his time in the English countryside. This was where his sister lived with her husband, who was a doctor of medicine, he confided to her.

They chatted for quite some time before Louisa realised the lateness of the hour. Hurriedly, she collected the remains of the picnic and rushed off down the slope while waving a quick farewell to him before he realised her intention. When she looked back, he was retrieving his hat and casting a puzzled glance at her as he did so.

Returning to Nathaniel, she found him unconcerned while relaxing on the grass beneath a tree, with a blade of grass in his mouth and staring up at the sky. He would have been working since daybreak, she assumed, so he would welcome this rest time. The horses were grazing nearby and the groom glanced up when he heard Louisa approaching. He sprang to his feet immediately. Nathaniel retrieved the horses. They mounted and returned to the house.

Louisa located Benson on her return and she mentioned her need to discuss the forthcoming dinner with him. Later in the morning, she met with him in the formal dining room, with its extra-long oak table in the centre.

"Benson, this room is hardly presentable, is it? The paintwork is a mess, but I suppose it's too late to do anything about that now. How long is it since it's been used as a dining room?" she queried.

Benson glanced at the faded and flaking paintwork and the tired, old drapes on the bay windows before replying.

"It's not been used at all in my time, madam. But then, I've only been here just over a decade. The family moved out at least twenty years ago, as I understand, when they moved to Stanton."

"A decade you've been here?" Louisa asked. "Why, I was only seven years old then; do you realise that? Not that it matters, because between the two of us, it'll be another decade before it's used again."

"Yes, madam," he murmured in reply to her observations.

Louisa wandered around the room. She had given him the guest list and asked for a place setting for her father, even though she knew that he would not attend. After assuring herself that all was in order, she made her next request of the butler.

"Do you think you could get one of the maids to locate all the recent newspapers on the Royal Tour for me, please? Leave them in here on this big table, for I wish to read certain articles on it," Louisa directed.

She wandered from the room, having lost interest already in the planned dinner party. For the first time, she saw a frown and a slightly puzzled look on his face.

"The maids?" he queried. "I shall attend to it personally and immediately, although I can't promise they'll all be here. Cook may've used some sheets in her kitchen fire."

"Thank you; just find what you can, Benson. I would appreciate it," she replied, with an appreciative smile.

"Very good, madam," Benson stated as Louisa left the dining room.

It was not until she sat down to lunch, with the parlour maid serving the first course, that she recalled the puzzled look, which Benson had directed at her earlier. Then, the realisation dawned that, in all probability, few if any of the maids employed there would be able to read. Therefore, they would be unable to determine which newspapers needed to be collected and deposited in the dining room for her.

There were matters pertaining to the Royal Tour that Charles had mentioned to her and, in particular, a certain shooting and the trouble brewing between the Protestants of Melbourne and their Irish-Catholic rivals. So, Louisa decided that she needed to be aware of these issues. Being uncertain of Charles' religion or beliefs – or, if he had any at all – she wondered again if he was affiliated with any church, group or society, other than the prestigious Melbourne Club for gentlemen only.

Louisa had her suspicions in this regard but, with the pressure being applied by her uncle-priest, she needed to know where he stood on these matters, so that if necessary she could plan certain moves in the future. While the thoughts on this subject were flowing through her mind, Charles Lyndhurst entered and strode to the table.

"Good morning! How was your ride?" he asked, in a pleasant tone.

"Afternoon, it is! And my ride was wonderful, thank you . . . very pleasant. However, the dining room is an awful mess and the invitations to this ridiculous dinner party have been sent out, so little can be done now, I'm afraid," Louisa mentioned, while quickly and deftly steering the conversation away from the subject of her ride.

"I daresay it is, after all these years. Feel free to redecorate the whole house at any time should the whim strike you, but don't dare touch my office or my bedroom. Do what you like otherwise. Now, the ball, *madam* . . . ?"

Louisa wrinkled her nose and filled her mouth with food. Benson placed a plate of food in front of Charles before leaving the room. She did have a proposal, which may or may not meet with Charles' approval, but as she would not be here to attend, she did not care at all.

"A gipsy," she muttered, with her mouth filled with food.

"A what?"

"I said I'll be a gipsy," she repeated.

"Does that mean with, or without, shoes on your feet?" he queried, in all seriousness.

Louisa began to laugh before she choked on the food in her mouth. He eyed her with some amusement as he continued to eat his lunch while her eyes watered from the sudden bout of coughing, which she was endeavouring to bring under control.

"I shall have to see the outfit to consider whether or not I approve."

Louisa, somewhat taken aback by this unforeseen complication, frowned and wrinkled her nose again before replying.

"Well, I don't have it yet. There's no point in having such an outfit designed and made, if you don't approve it. Anyway, I should think I'd need a tambourine to add the finishing touches."

"Whatever for?" he muttered.

"How should I know? The picture in the book had one in the girl's hands, but I've no idea where to find such an item."

"In the nursery . . . should be one there, I expect," Charles replied. "You've no idea the stuff that's stored in that room. The crown jewels could be hidden under the trundle bed, for all I know."

Louisa continued eating for a few minutes in silence as she gave the matter serious thought. Finally, she came to a decision, which she revealed to him.

"Perhaps, one day soon, I'll clear it all out; then, I'll turn it into another guest room. That should keep the boredom at bay a little and, anyway, I can't imagine why it'd need to remain a storage room, do you?"

He was silent for quite some minutes and Louisa considered the matter of the nursery closed when, finally, he commented.

"I don't suppose it'll ever be a nursery again, so do what you like with it," he said, somewhat tentatively.

"A nursery is for a baby and there aren't any of those around here, thank the Lord!" Louisa commented, in all innocence.

"Why would you say that?" he queried sharply, instantly frowning at her remark.

"Because they're such strange creatures . . . Yvette's got one," Louisa stated, while wrinkling her nose and showing her distaste, as though it were a contagious disease to be avoided at all costs.

"Usually, it's a natural consequence of marriage, Louisa."

Louisa stopped eating her food and studied him quite candidly. He glanced at her, obviously awaiting her reaction to his comment as he raised the fork. Then, he filled his mouth with food.

"Yes, I observed that with Yvette, for she didn't have one when she left us. Therefore, I'm determined to ask her how that came about."

Charles coughed. He began to choke on the food in his mouth, as Louisa had done earlier. He looked at her in some astonishment. He tried to speak, but began coughing again and shaking his head at the same time while he continued to stare at her. All the while, he was trying to regain his composure. Charles shook his head in disbelief. He reached for a glass of wine and took a large gulp before responding.

"Good Lord!" he muttered, almost to himself. "May the saints preserve us. I've heard everything now! I beg of you, don't . . . please, don't bring up a subject such as this with your former governess, for in all probability, she would suspect you're with child already. It's not a matter for open discussion, and most especially not with anyone but your husband. Is that understood? Promise me now, for I need your word on this matter."

Louisa frowned at him as she studied him candidly. He watched her closely, obviously attempting to gauge her response to his words. She shook her head, totally perplexed. Finally, she answered him.

"I'm not understanding you. I've no notion what that means, although I've heard the term *with child* spoken of, but I don't know how to get one and nor do I wish for one. They seem to me to spend the whole time either crying, or falling over, before crying some more. Besides, I'll not promise anything I can't deliver."

He opened his mouth to speak; then, he changed his mind and closed his lips firmly as Benson entered the room. The subject was closed between them, for the time being at least. With the meal at an end, Louisa rose from the table. She was about to leave the room when, to her surprise, Charles followed her quickly. He grasped her wrist and spun her around to face him. They were alone and she looked up at him in some surprise.

"Tomorrow evening, when we're alone, you and I will sit together quietly and have a very serious discussion. Keep the time after dinner free for me. Until then, do not mention the subject that's just been discussed between us with anyone at all."

"Alright," she replied, with a nonchalant shrug of her shoulders.

"I stated, in the beginning, that when the madness of this Royal Tour was at an end, we would come to a permanent arrangement.

There's but one more event on the calendar, so before Christmas is upon us, we need to sort this mess out, once and for all!" Charles stated firmly.

So saying, he released her wrist and walked away while leaving her even more puzzled than she had been previously. She would listen to his words, but she would not make any promises. On the following night, there would be the dinner party at Lyndhurst Park, and on the morning following that event, she would be away from here, hopefully not returning in the foreseeable future. Whatever Charles Lyndhurst had to say to her would have little, if any, impact on her future life. On that score, Louisa Lyndhurst was very determined indeed.

After dinner on the following evening, it was with great relief that Louisa saw Charles disappear into his office; so, assuming that his planned discussion was forgotten, she escaped to the dining room where Benson, true to his word, had stacked the newspapers of the past weeks. These were placed in two groups, one being the *Argus* and the other being the *Age*. She opened one, spread it out on the table and sat comfortably on the dining chair with the intention of reading for several hours. She commenced reading about Prince Alfred and the Tour, from its beginning in Adelaide on 30th.October through until the present time.

So engrossed was she in her task that it was sometime before she realised that there was music drifting through the house. When the realisation penetrated her consciousness, Louisa rose from the chair and went in search of the source. On entering the ballroom by the doors at the far end where she had crossed from the dining room, she found the ballroom itself in darkness, except for a lone lamp on a table beside the pianoforte. Charles was seated there and he was lost in the music that he was playing.

She watched him for some minutes before moving to the instrument and standing by it. She studied him as his fingers ran lightly over the keys. He looked up and smiled at her, but continued playing. When he did pause, he reached over and pulled a chair beside the piano stool, on which he was sitting and he positioned it beside the stool.

"Sit by me and play a duet."

Louisa sat down, quickly tucking her hands beneath her skirt as he watched her closely.

"More defiance?" he queried.

"No, shame! I've not touched an instrument since Yvette left us three years ago and, until I become proficient once again, I shan't allow anyone to hear my many mistakes, except Yvette, of course."

"I can appreciate that, but in six months, I will expect a performance."

"I expect you'll get one, but perhaps it won't be on the pianoforte," she muttered, giving a slight chuckle.

"Already, I receive more than one daily as it is, so a performance on the pianoforte . . . from you . . . will be an added bonus, I should think," Charles commented; then, he explained softly to her. "I'm playing this instrument now to coax you from your hiding place, so my ruse worked, did it not? You're attempting to avoid our little talk."

Louisa did not answer him as she kept her eyes focussed on the black and white keys. He reached down and took her hand.

"Come upstairs with me," he said quietly.

This was not a directive, but nor was it a suggestion. He assumed that this was by mutual consent, so she allowed him to lead her upstairs where, at her bedroom, he stopped.

"Go inside and ready yourself for bed, but get rid of . . . what's her name? Your maid?" he queried, with one eyebrow raised.

"Charlotte," Louisa replied softly.

She did not respond to his bait, as she knew that he was teasing her over Charlotte's name. Louisa entered her bedroom as he entered his own room. Charlotte was waiting – as always – and the maid assisted Louisa to undress, but she seemed happy to be released early. Louisa had no doubt that she was going directly to Nathaniel, for there was a definite spring in her step as she escaped hurriedly from the bedroom. Louisa slid into her white lace nightgown and she was propped up in bed and reading her history book when Charles entered through the connecting door. He was dressed in trousers and a white shirt – with braces in place still – while having removed his coat, waistcoat and necktie. He had bare feet, which surprised her greatly. He came to her and taking the book from her hands, he placed it on the table beside her bed.

"It's time for our serious discussion, Louisa Mary Lyndhurst," he stated quietly; then, moving onto the bed beside her, he lifted the sheet covering her body and sliding in beside her, he directed her quietly. "Move over. This could take some time, so we may as well be comfortable."

Louisa moved in the bed while wriggling away as far as was possible from him without falling off the other side of the bed. He adjusted his position, thereby pinning her right arm against his body.

"I don't know what you want of me," she murmured.

"No, I realise that *now*. But, until your unexpected revelations at the luncheon table yesterday, I'd suspected you were somewhat naive about certain facts of life. This was to be expected, I suppose, given your young age, your upbringing and taking into account your mother's untimely death while knowing of your aunt's *great endeavours* in that arena. However, your complete ignorance did shock me, I must confess."

Uncomfortable at being in such close proximity to him, Louisa wriggled again. She was endeavouring to place some distance between their bodies, but as the bed was not wide, she found this a pointless exercise. Charles did not seem to be willing to move from her at all. Somewhat bored, she wondered how long this discussion would last.

"I had thought your education at that school here would've opened your eyes a little," he continued. "Knowing the gossip that would have been circulating there and being well aware of the prime focus and main intent of such maidens of virtue . . . from first-hand knowledge, I might add . . . I expected you would have been slightly better informed. But alas, it seems not. Except for our wedding night . . . when you appeared to be making rather blatant overtures in my direction . . . I felt your reluctance was due to your total loathing of me."

"Wedding night! What overtures?" Louisa asked, in absolute astonishment.

"You were groping beneath the sheets while I was trying to sleep," he stated seriously and in an accusing tone.

"Groping? I was not! I . . . Oh! I see . . . well, yes, I suppose I was, but I was trying to locate my dagger before you found it," she admitted somewhat reluctantly.

Charles began to laugh. He looked at her in some surprise while shaking his head as he laughed some more. Louisa laughed with him, thereby easing the tension between them a little.

"Do you really loathe me so much? Are you afraid of me?" he asked, in a serious tone when his laughter subsided.

"No, and I don't loathe you. It's that I am on a seesaw when you're around. One minute, you're teasing me and trying to be friendly. Then the next, you're scolding me as a father would do. I don't know what to expect in any given moment and *I don't know* if I like you or not. There's not been time. One minute, I'm expected to act as mistress of Lyndhurst Park; then, instantly, you change completely and you treat me as a child."

Charles raised a hand and brushed the non-existent hair from his forehead as he lifted an arm while placing it around her shoulders. Louisa found that there was no room to move from his grasp, but she remained rigid in his casual embrace.

"You're honest anyway and that's probably the truth of the matter. Now, I require another totally honest answer. Do you want this marriage?" he asked.

"No, not at all. I'm here, because I have to be here . . . not because of any free will choice on my part. But, you know that already."

"Would you change the situation, if you could?"

"Yes, in an instant. If I could go home to Papa, I'd be away right now, as long as Hilton and Cadence were free to come, as well. I couldn't leave them here indefinitely," Louisa admitted.

He remained silent for several minutes. He was staring at the ceiling in a thoughtful state. For a time, Louisa thought that he had forgotten her existence.

"What if I told you *I want you* to stay . . . that I wish to have a proper marriage, with children to come into our lives. After all, that's what this was about, in the first place . . . to give my father the grandsons he wants so desperately. That's the only prize he doesn't have, as yet. *And, what Sir Charles Lyndhurst* does not have, he craves endlessly!"

"Your sister's given him three already," Louisa reminded him.

He gave a harsh, though soft, laugh and shifted his position, thereby releasing her while placing his hands behind his head and settling himself more comfortably on her bed – much to Louisa's discomfort and annoyance.

"Not with the Lyndhurst name! That is what he desires most and what I've been determined to deny him, but I've allowed my loathing of him to hurt you, as well as others. This needs to be sorted between us now . . . this night . . . and it can't be done while you're in total ignorance of . . . well, of so much."

With his eyes focussed completely on the ceiling, he revealed much to her, after having first asked her if her parents had slept together in the same bed. When she nodded in the affirmative, he explained that his parents despised each other and that his mother lived in the downstairs section of the homestead at Stanton while his father lived upstairs where his mother would never venture. He suspected that there had been much violence in the marriage, although this was kept well hidden, even from him. Then, he explained how it was that most married couples of his acquaintance slept together in the same bed, for this was what a true marriage was, as long as this was a mutual arrangement. He stated that when two people came together – in such a union – then, the usual result, within the marriage, was that the woman would be *with child* in a short space of time.

"There're three ways it can occur . . . in violence, as I suspect has been the case with my parents over the years. But, *outside* of marriage, that's referred to as *rape*. Also, it can take place with indifference on the part of one or both parties . . . as when the man pays a woman to be with him and to indulge him, shall we say. Or, thirdly, it can be done in love. *And, you have no idea* as to what I'm referring, have you?"

"Not really . . . no," she muttered, desperately wishing for a way of escape from this very constricting and confronting situation as soon as possible.

Charles reached over and lifted her left hand before moving it to the lower region of his body. He placed it between his legs where Louisa, to her surprise, felt movement as though something was stirring there. She gasped and pulled her hand away quickly. Immediately, the liaison between Mrs. McBryde and Captain Bill Bartlett flew into her mind and she recalled viewing him clearly, just prior to Brydie's mouth descending on this particular area of Bill's anatomy. She stared at Charles now – wide-eyed and with her mouth wider still.

Slowly, he moved his hand beneath her nightgown and he began to stroke her bare leg softly while the subsequent goose-bumps that this action caused her to experience surprised her greatly. Shortly thereafter, his hand wandered up the inside of her thigh and touched her gently between her legs, all the while he was explaining, almost in a hushed tone, what would occur in a union between them. He revealed that this was a beautiful and completely natural act, the result of which would be that a seed would be planted. From that seed, a baby would grow within her body.

Louisa was silent. She was absorbing his words and frowning at their meaning. Suddenly, Phillip came to mind and she remembered what had occurred between them on the jetty; then, she wondered if she would have been able to restrain him if, indeed, this union between them had been his intention on the day and assuming that they had not been disturbed by the gentleman who arrived on the scene. Phillip's words came to her: '*a married woman? And you're asking me?*' Then, at the race meeting, the equerry belonging to Prince Alfred's party had advised her that she was playing a dangerous game. Louisa's mind was spinning around in circles as Charles, reclining silently beside her, studied her intently.

"What if . . .?" she asked when, finally, she felt able to speak. "What if there wasn't any marriage certificate? Would the result be the same?"

"Why would you ask that?" he asked, suddenly appearing very suspicious.

Louisa shrugged her shoulders slightly, still frowning at him, while remembering Father Frank's words.

"It was something Father Frank said about my children, that's all," she mumbled, somewhat hurriedly grasping for an explanation.

"Yes, the result would be the same and, unfortunately, it is frequently the case, because a situation such as that can . . . and does . . . cause grave implications for all concerned. It is a natural act of love between two consenting adults, in most cases, and whether or not there's a signature on a piece of paper, prior to the union occurring, matters not where Nature's law is concerned. The signing of papers relates to society's laws, by which we all must abide, except for Louisa who flouts them whenever possible," he stated, playfully taking a few strands of her hair and tugging on them.

Sitting upright suddenly, Louisa stared at him in horror, unable to comprehend his explanation fully, yet instantly feeling completely vulnerable and totally trapped.

"You're talking about the *damn, messy business* Aunt Sophie warned me about, aren't you? Are you suggesting you do this . . . *do this to me now?*" she stammered, with her eyes wide with alarm and horror.

"Your Aunt Sophie is hardly one to give guidance on such delicate matters, I feel," he stated, with a slight laugh. "However, would it be so terrible if I were suggesting this union between us takes place? For our marriage to be legal, such a union should've occurred between us already, and that's why I don't want you discussing our private matters and very personal concerns with anyone at all. You do understand that, I sincerely trust. It's referred to as *consummating the marriage*. It is a necessary next step, but occurs usually on the wedding night."

Louisa continued to stare at him in absolute horror.

"Over my dead body!" Louisa shouted at him.

Charles laughed heartily and shook his head again while never taking his eyes from her face.

"That'd defeat the whole purpose, I should think! *And, just for the record,* I cannot recall ever, in my entire life, receiving such an unflattering rejection," he murmured, still laughing at her. "Do you know what happens when a wife refuses to share her husband's bed? He takes a lover. My father has one in Bendigo, with a second family, and the lady-in-question has given him three sons already. That is how this old world works, my love."

"You have other brothers?" she gasped.

"Absolutely not! I claim no connection whatsoever to those unkempt street-urchins terrorising the good citizens of Bendigo!"

"How many children do you have then?" she asked, in all innocence.

"I *do not* have any children at all," he stated, in a definite tone and very quietly, he elaborated a little on the matter under discussion by them. "But, I could be persuaded. That's all. Now, as for your uncle-priest, don't pay too much heed to him. Remember this: no matter whether he's wearing trousers, a cassock, or parading in his church's finery on the altar, beneath it all, he's a man, still . . . with all the feelings, emotions and needs of a man. So, while he's denouncing you for your perceived sins, he's far from a saint himself. Only a hypocrite would preach one set of rules for his parishioners, while having a different set for himself. That's all I'll say on that particular subject . . . *for now."*

So saying, he swung his legs off her bed, much to Louisa's immense relief, as she was trying to remember where she had left her dagger and she realised that it was quite a way out of her reach at this precise moment. Still sitting on the side of her bed, Charles leaned over toward her as she moved back against the pillows, desperately attempting to place a distance between them. He continued in a soft, intimate tone.

"That's Part One of our discussion . . . we'll continue it at a later date and, perhaps, with a different outcome next time . . . we shall see. But, think well on what I've said. You're a free and wild spirit and, much and all as I'd like to give you your freedom, I don't think I could release you now. You've wriggled your way into all our hearts with your delightful and outlandish ways."

He moved to her while kissing her lips lightly. Looking closely at her, he spoke softly.

"You've brought this old mausoleum back to life, for it died when my mother left here, all those years ago."

He kissed her again – more passionately this time – as Louisa sank back against the pillows. She was unable to move from him while wishing to be anywhere but in his arms. He released her and he continued to speak to her in a whisper.

"There's a connecting door to my room and I use it frequently to come in here, but you can use it to come the other way. It's always open to you, if you feel the need to come to me. If you do come to my bed, know that we have a marriage, in every sense of the word, from that moment. *Now,* I'll make you a prediction and I'll make you a promise."

She opened her mouth to speak, but he placed a finger to her lips to silence her. He continued, still speaking in a soft and intimate manner.

"My prediction is that one day, you'll come to me . . . *of your own volition.* It may not be this week, or even this year, for Christmas is upon us already. But, *you will come* . . . and, I'll be waiting. No matter how long it takes, I'll be waiting," he stated, before continuing in the same, secretive tone. "As for my promise, it's this: if any man *takes you,* with or without your permission, I will kill him."

He rose from her bed and stood perfectly still while looking down at her. She was biting her lip and she found herself trembling at his chilling words, spoken so quietly to her. She was wishing that he would leave immediately, but he lingered there in her room.

"I'm going out . . . *right now*! *Do you* have anything to say to me, Louisa?" he queried, with one eyebrow raised.

Louisa shook her head slowly. He turned to walk toward the connecting door.

"Yes! Actually, I do" she stated.

He stopped and spun around quickly while looking expectantly at her, and again with one eyebrow raised.

"*Do you* have a lover, Charles?" she inquired innocently.

"Goodnight, Louisa!"

Charles left her bedroom without a backward glance. Louisa remained completely still and listening for quite some time. She was waiting to hear his footsteps descending the internal stairs. When, finally, she heard them, she gave a deep sigh of relief; then, when she heard the sound of the carriage driving away while heading toward the main gate, she was able to breathe freely for the first time in over an hour.

Louisa left the bed and wandered out onto the front verandah. Sitting watching the waters of the Yarra River gliding by, with moonlight dancing on the surface, Louisa gripped the sides of the cane chair with both hands to prevent herself from trembling. The persistent thoughts were jumbled in her mind, with all of these tumbling around as would a group of acrobats performing at a circus. She needed to make sense of all that had occurred to her this night, as well as all that Charles Lyndhurst had revealed to her. And, more importantly, she needed to gain an understanding of all that he appeared to be proposing.

She decided that the sooner she left his house, the happier she would be. Unfortunately, judging by his conversation tonight, he would find her wherever she journeyed. At present, it would be only as far as travelling home to her father to deal with overdue matters that needed her urgent attention there.

In the future, she was at a loss to know to where she could escape, in order to have her freedom. In the final analysis, there was one place only where she wished to live and, within a few days, she would be there – come what may!

Chapter Eighteen

– *Victorian Victorians* –

Sylvia

T he evening, for Sylvia, began in a disappointing manner when she received a note from Charles advising that he was unable to join her for dinner. Tuesday night was the one night, which they shared together from late afternoon until early morning. He knew, as did Bertie, how much she loathed dining alone and, on this evening every week, Bertie had a permanent engagement. So, Charles, assuming that he was in Melbourne, dined with her always. That had been their own permanent arrangement and, for the first time in a long time, he had left her to dine alone. She hoped that he would have a good explanation, but he was non-committal on the reason for his late arrival, as the hall clock was striking eleven o'clock when he came to her. From the time that they ascended the stairs to her bedroom until this moment – with dawn lighting the sky – he had seemed distracted.

"A penny for them," she murmured, still cradled in his arms in her bed.

"What?"

"We've so little time together these days, so I'd appreciate it if, when you're with me, you could *stay here*, Charles."

His arms tightened around her body and he kissed her on the neck, with his breath causing spine-tingling sensations immediately. "As perceptive as ever, Sylvia . . . I'm sorry. How can I make amends?" he murmured, with a slight laugh.

"By talking to me. You've been shutting me out of late and it's never been that way . . . with Edwin, yes . . . but with us, no, never! I've not experienced it before now and I find it totally unacceptable."

He moved from her then while reaching for the pillows on the floor and propping them behind his back. Sylvia shifted her position to study him.

"You're a very wise woman, do you know that? For everything you predicted is beginning to come to pass. I couldn't see it, or accept it at the time, but you were absolutely correct."

Sylvia propped herself up on one elbow and she was frowning.

"What are we discussing here?" she queried, somewhat puzzled.

"You told me I couldn't move people around as though they were pieces on a chess board, but I didn't believe you. Alas, you were correct, it'd seem. So, unless I adopt my father's techniques while stooping to his level, which I cannot in all conscience countenance, then someone I love is going to be hurt. Does that make sense to you?"

Sylvia allowed a somewhat harsh laugh to escape her.

"*Going to*? What makes you think it hasn't occurred already?"

Charles was silent for some moments, deliberately ignoring her question.

"I have to play by the same rules as he does to win this game. I can't do it!" he admitted reluctantly.

"I never thought, for one moment, that you could. You possess something your father wouldn't even realise exists. It's called *compassion*. You can be as callous and as ruthless as the next man when you choose. But, after the event, you've your conscience to deal with, whereas your father does not, for he dispensed with his decades ago. That's the matter in a nutshell. So, what's your next move?"

He gave a nonchalant shrug, which was followed by his telltale sign that she knew so well as she watched his hand move to brush the hair from his forehead. His arms moved behind his head and he leaned back on the pillows while he stared pensively at the ceiling. Sylvia remained silent. He had charged into the situation where he found himself now. She did not intend to assist him as he sought a way to extract himself from the dilemma, for he would not appreciate her interference anyway. He had made that fact very clear at the outset. Finally, it was Charles who broke the silence between them.

"You stated months ago that the idea of an annulment was ridiculous . . . or, words to that effect. I feel you were correct in that assessment."

Sylvia sat up quickly, with the sheet slipping from her naked body as she stared in astonishment at him. His eyes wandered from her face to her exposed breasts; then, slowly, he returned his gaze to look directly into her eyes.

"You can't be serious? I thought you'd abandoned that path immediately after your marriage!"

Sylvia jumped from the bed before grabbing her dressing gown and slipping into it. She stood at the end of the bed and shook her head in some astonishment. Despite her efforts to the contrary, she shouted her next words at him.

"You asked me not to interfere in your marriage! I've no intention of being drawn into this unholy mess you've created! Extract yourself from it *now* . . . that's my advice. Patrick is due to return here at any time from Castlemaine. I expect him daily and he'll be staying with me then."

"So?"

"*So*, I don't wish to be placed in a position where my own brother is spying on me . . . and on my lover . . . so that *his friend* can have advanced notice of your movements, in order to make his own moves in a certain direction. If plain-speaking is what you want, is that clear enough for you, Charles Lyndhurst?"

So saying, she strode toward the door. Then, she stopped as a sudden thought struck her. She spun around quickly. She realised that Charles was staring at her while appearing somewhat stunned by her unexpected and angry words.

"Remember I told you that there was a wager between them . . . Patrick and Carstairs . . . in Sydney? Do you want similar gossip spread about you and your new bride . . . *if you haven't . . . and he does?* I *can't believe* we're having this conversation! You're a prize fool! Never will *this subject* be discussed between us again. Sort it . . . *and quickly.* Leave me out of this nightmare situation you've created, for pity's sake!" she hurled the words at him.

Sylvia wrenched open the door of her bedroom and stormed through it. She slammed it loudly behind her. The unexpected sound reverberated through the silent and still household. She ran down the stairs and into her sitting room. She was clothed only in the flimsy dressing gown. She walked to the cabinet in the corner of the room and poured a large whisky from the crystal decanter. She was almost finished the drink when he entered the room.

Charles stood just inside the room. He was leaning back against the closed door while wearing trousers, a shirt with the braces slung loosely on his shoulders and his feet were bare. He was staring at her while apparently trying to fathom how to handle this particular situation. Sylvia turned her back on him, finished the drink and reached for the decanter again.

"Can I join you?" he queried. "Or, is this a private party?"

"Some party!" Sylvia responded, as she reached for another glass.

She poured a drink for him and another for herself. She handed the glass to him as he walked over to join her.

"You don't give any quarter, do you? If I wanted it between the eyes, that's certainly where you aimed," he muttered.

"Would you have any respect for me otherwise? It was a bull's eye, I'd say! You have been asking for it for a long time, so I'm more than happy to oblige. Fools, I don't tolerate and you're not one usually, although you're in danger of treading that path, if you're not careful."

He drank from the glass and stood by the window. He was gazing out as the morning light spread its fine feather-fingers quietly and quickly over the garden.

"You're asking me to choose, aren't you?" he asked.

Sylvia sat down on the old, faded winged armchair that had been Edwin's favourite chair when they spent time together in this room. She watched Charles as he stood framed in the window.

"From the time I married Edwin, I was *the other woman*, Charles, because he had a long-time lover whom he was reluctant to relinquish on account of his new bride. They'd come together shortly after his first wife died. That was before you arrived from London, as you know. I tolerated the situation, because I was so much younger than he was and I didn't know what else to do. I had no one to advise me on such matters. Perhaps, that's why I can see both sides of this situation . . . I've been on both sides myself *now*, as a result of your marriage."

He turned from the window and watched her; then, he lifted the glass to his lips, but he refrained from commenting. So, she continued with her explanation.

"From the day you told me you were marrying someone else, I knew the day would come when we'd be forced apart. Make your decision, but leave me out of all this. I'm here for you, should you need me . . . for the time being, that is . . . *but, under no circumstances, take me for granted. I'll not be used again*; not the way Edwin used me. While there's mutual respect, I'm prepared to tolerate this situation for a little longer. For how long, I can't say."

She drank slowly, with the liquid burning her throat while her empty stomach was protesting at its rude awakening this morning. The amber liquid seeped through her whole being, thus making the task of facing this problem a little easier for the moment. That it was a momentary respite, she acknowledged to herself.

Charles finished his drink and returned the glass to the cabinet. He walked over to her and stroked the top of her head while lost in thought himself. She remained frozen in the armchair, not responding to his touch. He bent down and kissed the top of her head.

"May I be spared from fierce, fiery females!" Charles muttered, almost to himself; then, he left the room without another word.

When Sylvia became aware of the unmistakable sounds of her household stirring, ready for the day's activities, she emerged from her sitting room while tucking her dressing gown around her body in the event of walking into one of the servants. She mounted the stairs in a determined manner, being unwilling to continue the discussion with him and hoping an argument would not ensue when she confronted him now.

She entered her bedroom. Then, glancing around the room as she closed the door gently, she stood perfectly still. Charles was no longer there and the room was devoid of all traces of his presence. It was not what she had been expecting.

"Life goes on, Sylvia," she reprimanded herself firmly once again. *"So, live with the fact!"*

Louisa

After Charles' revelations and overtures of the previous evening, it was a very thoughtful Louisa who met with Phillip in their secret hideaway. She made certain that her dagger was within easy reach, although he appeared to have accepted her guidelines for their meetings. During the breakfast that they shared, the subject of horses – and, more specifically, horse racing – was discussed. The raising of such a topic between them was inevitable, given that they both shared a great and common interest in such animals. Their recent attendance at the Flemington race meeting had brought the subject to the fore, on this bright, sunny morning in December. Finally, it was Louisa – rather than Phillip – who issued the challenge, never realising at the time the repercussions of such a madcap scheme, upon which both were embarking.

"Oh! You've struck a cord now!" he countered, and with a definite challenge in his eyes, he teased her. "You've no idea how much I'll enjoy watching you eat my dust, *madam*!"

Louisa threw back her head and laughed at him with as much delight and devilment dancing in her eyes as she saw reflected back at her from his steady gaze. The impish grin that attracted her on their first meeting was visible on his face, as were the telltale dimples hovering by his mouth.

"Name the time and place; then, I shall be there. Do you require a head start? Would a furlong be sufficient, or do you require two or three, sir?" she queried, unashamedly laughing at him.

"You are on! Meet me here tomorrow and . . ."

"No, not tomorrow! I can't! I shall be unavailable from tomorrow, but make the arrangements and I'll race you after my return, as soon as it's convenient. Please don't press me on this issue."

With those words, Louisa jumped to her feet and ran to the tree, which she scaled it easily, despite her restrictive riding habit as he watched her in surprise. Having removed the green scarf from the branch, she slid down the trunk and faced him, immediately sliding the scarf into her pocket.

"I'll secure the scarf to the branch as soon as I return from the journey I'm taking. It's to do with my father's ill health, so I can't be definite on a date. I'm sorry, Phillip, but race you I shall. Be assured on that score," Louisa promised him.

He shrugged his shoulders in a nonchalant fashion and watched her as she began to collect the remnants of their shared breakfast.

"I must go now. I've stayed way too long this morning. I'll see you soon," Louisa stated, hurriedly shoving the debris from the meal back into the canvas bag.

As she turned to go, she looked over at him and she found him looking at her in the disconcerting manner that upset her so much. He did not make a move toward her.

"I love you, Louisa," he stated simply.

Her own involuntary intake of breath took Louisa by surprise. As his words penetrated her mind, she looked at him in astonishment, not knowing how to reply to this declaration.

"I don't see how it's possible after such a short acquaintance, and my own feelings are . . . are so mixed-up at present, I don't know anything for certain any more."

She turned quickly and ran down the slope, not turning to look back at him.

Upon returning to the house, Louisa almost collided with Hugh Travis as she hurried through the front door.

"Mrs. Lyndhurst, just the person I wish to see. How're you on this fine morning?" Hugh greeted her.

"Mr. Travis! I was wondering where you'd disappeared to. I've not seen you for days," she said, as she smiled up at him.

"You thought I'd absconded with your winnings, I'll wager."

"Never! Not you! Many others might, but you'd not be guilty of such an offence. It'd not be in your nature to do so."

"I'm flattered you've such a high opinion of me. I'll endeavour to live up to your expectations. Here you are . . . one hundred, plus twenty sovereigns from the original bet . . . making a grand total of one hundred-and-twenty sovereigns, which I've placed into this money bag for easier handling for you. I trust you approve," Hugh stated, while placing the bag into her waiting and eager hands; then, he enquired of her. "Will you trust me? Or, do you, perhaps, wish to count it for yourself?"

Louisa laughed with him, immediately bringing her two hands together and clasping her precious windfall that was a vital requirement for her adventure on the following day; then, she shook her head vigorously. Leaving her standing by the stairs, he sauntered into the office with a wave of his hand, a smile on his face and laughter shining in his kindly eyes, with the wonder evident on Louisa's face being the source of his amusement.

She raced upstairs and dragged out the canvas bag, instantly shoving the money bag inside the canvas one. After that, she returned it to its hiding place behind her wardrobe. Looking in the mirror, she saw the telltale signs of the mounting excitement within her registered there, although she was unable to decide if the red blushes on her face were due to her well-advanced plans for her escape from Lyndhurst Park, or from Phillip's declaration of love.

The door from the corridor opened and, expecting it to be Charlotte entering, she turned and found Charles surveying her. She had not seen him since their troubling encounter on her bed on the previous evening.

"Have you seen the state of the dining room?" he queried.

"No, I've just returned from riding," she replied, while glancing furtively at her wardrobe and her hiding place.

"Come and look then," he suggested, as he held the door open.

Without another word, she left the room hurriedly and headed to the dining room with her husband following closely behind her. Upon entering, she stopped and stared at the empty room. The only furniture visible was the small dining table, around which they sat usually for meals in the ballroom and, on this, were the two stacks of newspapers, which she had been studying during the previous day. She opened her mouth to question him while knowing that their guests were coming to dinner in the evening. But, he held up his hand to silence her.

"Now, come with me to the ballroom," he directed, as he took her hand in a possessive manner and he pulled her along with him.

Charles opened the double doors to the ballroom and stood aside for her to enter. She did so; then, she stood still and she surveyed the room that had been transformed in readiness for the dinner. The billiard table was pushed to one side and the pianoforte was at a slightly different angle. Furniture that usually graced the small drawing room was positioned in front of the empty fireplace. The two settees and several armchairs were there, along with other side tables and a large rug on the floor.

The remaining two-thirds of the ballroom had been given over to the furniture from the dining room, including the large oak table and chairs, as well as two sideboards and two small serving tables, which were positioned against the wall. The main table was set with eight place settings and the missing person from the last dinner party at the Collins' residence being the Anglican minister who was Sophie Collins' friend. In his place was a setting for George Howard, from whom a reply to Louisa's invitation had not been received.

"I don't believe it!" she murmured, while turning to face Charles. "How is this possible?"

"With a little ingenuity, anything can be achieved."

"So it would seem," she replied, completely stunned by the transformation.

"Hugh gave you your winnings, I believe. I trust you'll not use your new-found fortune to make good your escape from me?" Charles said.

Shock and astonishment were registering on her face as she stared up at him. She was absolutely speechless that he had guessed at her plan. He had told her once that he would be one step ahead of her always, but she found this to be not only ridiculous, but also, quite uncanny. It was only then she realised that Charles was laughing at her.

"That, Louisa, was a joke! Now, do you approve of my arrangements? Is there something you'd wish to improve upon or change in any way? Benson needs to know immediately."

Louisa turned her attention to the room again and, in a state of sheer amazement, she shook her head slowly.

"Good! Then, if my services are no longer required here, Hugh and I need to be at Port Melbourne immediately. I'll see you at dinner tonight."

Unable to find words to reply to him, she nodded absentmindedly. Without another word, he placed an arm about her shoulders and he kissed her firmly on the mouth. Abruptly, he turned and disappeared through the double doors.

Louisa remained perfectly still as she stood by an armchair, on which she had placed her two hands for support while her mind was reeling and her emotions were in turmoil. With Phillip declaring his love for her this morning, and now, with Charles becoming very attentive towards her, she was dumbfounded and unable to fathom where these events were leading. For the first time, the enormity of her escape plan came home to her and she wondered, not for the first time, how she would survive tonight's planned dinner party. How she longed for it to be over!

Slowly, she brought a trembling hand to her lips and she touched them where Charles had kissed her. Spinning on her heel all of a sudden, she ran from the room while rushing upstairs two at a time, so as to remove her riding habit and to wash away the dust, the grime and the troubling memories from this morning's encounters from both her body and her mind.

Louisa, who was dressed in one of her new gowns, chatted with her aunt and Margaret Travis while the gentlemen who were present this evening stood by the mantelpiece in the ballroom where they were engrossed in conversation. Margaret Travis, Louisa had met on several occasions, and she found her to be a warm, friendly lady whose love for her husband was obvious, as was his devotion to her. They were the parents of two little girls, although Louisa had not met these children as yet. Margaret appeared to be of a similar age to Hugh and Charles.

Louisa's aunt informed her that a carriage had been sent to Yvette Chambers' home to collect her, but not one word was spoken of her father. Louisa felt that there was a wall of silence in this regard, almost as though all were afraid to mention George Howard's name for fear of an outburst from her.

Finally, Yvette arrived and Charles, after greeting her at the door, led her into the ballroom. She looked over and smiled at Louisa who was about to move toward her when she noticed the gentleman who was accompanying her. He was standing in the shadows behind her and he was shaking hands with Charles. It was the stock of white hair that first alerted Louisa to his identity. Astounded, she watched motionless while holding her breath until she was certain of his identity.

"Jesus, Mary and Joseph!" Louisa shouted, with her shrill words causing all conversation in the room to cease immediately.

Hurtling across the room, Louisa almost collided with Benson who, with tray in hand, was required to execute a swift and delicate pirouette to avoid a crash, which possibly would have been followed by an embarrassing fall. She rushed to the new arrival while brushing by Yvette and forgetting her presence instantly. She stared at her father in astonishment. George Howard returned her gaze with one of slight amusement.

"None of the afore-mentioned . . . just your doting father. And, you don't appear to have curbed your behaviour any," he stated, in a slow drawl. "How are you, Louisa?"

"It's about time *you* showed up! *And, how dare you* not let me know you were coming!" she screamed at him. "Papa, I'm so angry with you, I don't know whether to kill you, then hug you . . . or, the other way around!"

"Try the hug first, sweetheart; then, you can work your way around to the other at your leisure and, I've no doubt, you'll get to it soon enough," George Howard suggested softly, with a wry smile on his thin, drawn face.

Louisa hugged him and kissed his cheek while he clung to her for a longer period than she could ever remember him doing in her entire life. She looked him over candidly before announcing for all to hear that he was looking awful and the sooner that she had him visit a doctor, the better it would be. He groaned audibly, to the amusement of all. Finally, she greeted Yvette, immediately whispering her gratitude to her former governess for Yvette's perseverance in arranging to bring her father to her.

"Nonsense, Louisa, I had nothing at all to do with it. Your father very kindly came in your uncle's carriage to collect me. It was your own husband who arranged everything else. Surely, you realise that?"

Dinner was announced and Louisa was unable to pursue the matter with Yvette. The meal proceeded without incident, with those assembled chatting and laughing amongst themselves while Louisa watched with interest and with her emotions in turmoil once again. Her proposed adventure was over before it had begun and this change of plan was due, it would seem, to her husband's intervention in the matter. Seated at the end of the table, she looked over to see her father's gaze upon her. She narrowed her fathomless green eyes as she scrutinised him. He was sitting close by her at the long table.

"You've barely made it here in time. You do realise that? I've given you a few weeks' grace, as it is. But, you were about to know my deep, seething anger and to feel my wrath first-hand, Papa."

Louisa had meant these terse words for her father's ears only. But, their guests' conversation came to an unexpected end at this precise moment and she appeared to have the undivided attention of all those assembled.

"I surmised as much," George muttered softly.

"I would've come for you! Then, you'd have wished for death more than anything in this world."

George Howard smiled at the obviously-irate Louisa while noticing the attention that they were beginning to attract. But, not so his daughter, who tended regularly to walk in where angels fear to tread. George concentrated his full attention on the dish before him on the table. However, it was Louisa's aunt who intervened at this moment while taking the matter one step beyond that which was prudent.

"Nonsense, Louisa, don't make idle threats! I'm certain Mr. Lyndhurst wouldn't take you on a journey such as that one, knowing the reason for it. *And*, even you wouldn't be so foolhardy as to undertake such a trek alone into the wilds of that region. You'd never make it there alive."

Louisa laughed quite loudly at the absurdity of her aunt's words, which perhaps in hindsight, taunted her into more unwise disclosures.

"Idle threats? No, Aunt Sophie, there's nothing idle in my words, believe me. As for going *into the wilds*, it's hardly Africa that we are speaking of. We're talking of a mere train journey to Echuca, followed by a short trip on a paddle-steamer. I could do so, with ease."

"A young lady, alone? You could be accosted … even murdered … for who knows what this world is coming to these days. It's impossible," Aunt Sophie declared forcefully; then, shaking her head slowly, she announced her conclusion. "You do tend to exaggerate, child."

"It could be accomplished easily, with one hundred-and-twenty sovereigns and a dagger in my pocket!" Louisa retorted hotly.

Rather belatedly, Louisa became aware fully of the facial expressions of all of the men at the table. All had their respective spoons poised at different angles above the dishes in front of them while their mouths were wide open and their eyes were staring directly at Louisa. Although Aunt Sophie seemed oblivious to the somewhat startling and, perhaps, injudicious disclosures just made by her niece, the other two women were not. But, they concentrated their full attention on the food before them now. Louisa, who was was somewhat horrified once she realised her error in allowing her aunt to goad her to this degree, decided it may be time to commence eating the dessert before her.

"I would have brought you back here immediately," George stated finally, but emphatically, while eyeing his daughter sternly.

"Then, I'd have achieved my objective, would I not, Papa? But why you'd do so, I know not, for there're so many restrictions here, all I'm permitted to do is *breathe*," Louisa stated, instantly casting an accusing glance at her husband who was seated at the head of the table.

All their assembled guests concentrated on the food before them at this precise moment, including Aunt Sophie, who had become aware – finally – of a certain undercurrent at the dinner table. Charles Lyndhurst had a heavily-starched, white linen serviette pressed to his lips. Whether or not this was in order to prevent hasty words from escaping, Louisa was unable to gauge. Finally, removing this item from his mouth, he spoke clearly and concisely.

"*Even that* is at my discretion. *And,* subject to constant review, I might add," Charles remarked.

He continued to eat his meal while deliberately ignoring his wife. The other guests followed his lead, although Louisa felt that she heard one or two suppressed giggles – or gurgles – as the case may be. Louisa pushed her food around the plate; then, she pushed it back again the other way, and all the time desperately attempting to suppress the giggles that were trying to surface, as bubbles do when released from a bottle of champagne. Eventually, she had to acknowledge to herself that all of her efforts, in this regard, were in vain. She allowed the laughter gurgling beneath the surface within her to escape and her infectious laughter filled the room. This act caused an instant unlocking of the tension stored within her and she found tears rolling down her cheeks at this welcome release. Even Benson, who was standing by the door appeared to be affected, although from his outward demeanour, anyone who did not know him would assume otherwise. The assembled guests broke instantly into laughter and all tension was relieved as Benson left the room somewhat hurriedly.

"It's as well that all of our guests are close friends. Otherwise, your first attempt at entertaining could've been the subject of much gossip in Melbourne by tomorrow, Louisa. However, I feel, your secret is safe within these walls and not a word of your ill-conceived flight-of-fancy will leave this room," Charles stated confidently; then, in a playful tone, he questioned her further. "Pray, enlighten us then; when was this great excursion to take place?"

Louisa, having placed a spoonful of pudding in her mouth, was required to wait some moments before answering her husband's light-hearted question. Swallowing slowly, she stared defiantly at him for a few moments while ignoring all others in the room. There was a definite challenge in her eyes.

"At dawn tomorrow," she replied simply and quietly.

A collective, almost inaudible, gasp seemed to circulate around the dinner table. Charles Lyndhurst stiffened noticeably and he appeared to be struggling to breathe deeply himself, as he sought to regain some vestige of self-control.

"A likely story!" he stated loudly; then, turning to Hugh Travis, he queried him in a loud tone. "How is your sister, Suzanne, these days, Hugh? Is she still enjoying her new life in Geelong?"

As the conversation around the table returned to the general chatter that was normal at such a gathering, Louisa found that both her father and her uncle were looking over at her, in their turn, and shaking their heads in absolute dismay. They may have spoken not one word to her, but she knew them both well enough to realise that their demeanour and their eyes spoke volumes. Both gave her to understand – individually, and in no uncertain terms – their thoughts and their feelings regarding her somewhat unwise and untimely revelations, as well as the foolhardy nature of the excursion, which she had planned to execute alone.

She had *no doubt* that Charles Lyndhurst may have similar feelings, which in the fullness of time, he would *no doubt* reveal to her.

Another sin was added to the growing number on the imaginary slate, which had her name marked clearly on the top of it.

Louisa hoped sincerely that God was a more kindly and a more understanding Being than Father Frank gave her to understand. If not, her lot would not be a happy one in the afterlife!

Together, they farewelled their guests this evening. Stubbornly, her father refused to accept their invitation to stay at Lyndhurst Park, even though Charles was the first to make such an offer. George stated that he had been staying with his sister whenever he visited Melbourne during the past decade or so, and he had no intention of changing the routine now. Yvette, rather wisely, offered to postpone Louisa's music lessons for the duration of her father's visit and Louisa agreed with the proposal while declaring her intention of calling early to visit her father on the following day.

Charles, with his arm around Louisa's shoulders, stood on the gravel path by the front porch as they waved away the last of their guests – while appearing as happily-married newly-weds frequently do. Then, he leaned over and whispered in Louisa's ear.

"You need to get down on your knees and thank God . . . should such a Being exist . . . for the fact you were born in a female body. If you were a male, I'd take you behind the wood shed right now and whip you to within an inch of your life!"

"I haven't done anything," she pleaded, before turning two innocent eyes upon him while elaborating, perhaps a little unwisely. "Other than to breathe, that is."

"It's *the intent* that counts and I'm seething with anger over what you *intended* to do," he hissed at her through clenched teeth as he moved from her while holding his two hands up for her to survey them. "My hands are shaking, just itching to encircle your throat. *So,* stay out of my sight for at least a week; or, suffer the dire consequences!"

Charles walked up the front steps to the front door, after leaving her standing on the gravel path alone. She looked after him with disdain.

"If I can be punished for something I *only thought* to do, I may as well have the pleasure of it first. I'd suffer the consequences afterwards, with good grace, for no one would be able to erase the memory . . . or, the satisfaction . . . such pleasure brought to my mind, no matter how severe the punishment!" she shouted her angry words after him as she ran across the carriageway and down the stone steps to the river.

Thankfully, he did not follow her and she ran to the jetty where she sat down on the timber decking, thereby seeking comfort and solace. Her whole world was turned upside-down again, because with the dawn, she was meant to be creeping away from here and returning to her home. Instead, she was here with one irate husband *again*, with open warfare declared between them once *again*.

If only the river, at which she sat gazing was the Murray, and the home on the slight rise behind her was her old homestead, with her mother inside it now. Brydie had advised her to walk away with her head held high and to not look back. She had managed, with a supreme effort, to do so on that day, but to prevent the memories of her childhood there from creeping into her mind and taking up permanent residence was another matter entirely.

She needed another interest and Phillip came to mind instantly. *I love you, Louisa,* he stated to her this morning. That seemed so long ago now. It was then that she remembered the horse race. This thought thrilled her and filled her with excitement. What a great lark that would be! Then, she was reminded of an old saying, which Captain Bill uttered often, and this was: *I may as well be hanged for a sheep as a lamb.*

"My thoughts precisely, Captain Bill!" Louisa exclaimed aloud.

Before the horse race could be arranged, there was the Fancy Dress Ball, with which to contend, and this was to be the last major event of the Royal Tour of Victoria. As such, it would attract all of Melbourne's social elite and it was creating no end of excitement. Suddenly, Louisa was confronted with the need to produce an outfit to wear and, at such short notice, this may be difficult. She had not bothered to organise a minor detail such as this one, because she had no intention of being in Melbourne at the time.

Phillip would be there, she knew, so she would be able to advise him of her change of circumstances and, simultaneously, to make plans for their race. Charles would know – one way or another – that he could not control her!

When she returned to the house, all was in darkness and, once again, silence reigned at Lyndhurst Park.

Chapter Nineteen

– Victorian Victorians –

Louisa

George Howard was determined to spend as little time as was possible in Melbourne; so, to placate his daughter, he visited the doctor whom his sister recommended. After a thorough examination, he was pronounced as being as healthy as a man of his age could expect to be. It was suggested to him that the malaise, which he was experiencing was due, in no small part, to the death of his wife. This news, when revealed to Louisa, delighted but shocked her when the full implications were realised, for her marriage was as unnecessary as it was unwanted.

It was a somewhat subdued and unusually silent Louisa who sat in her uncle's library, with a book unopened on her lap, as she stared in a distracted manner into the side garden. Her uncle's entry disturbed her.

"It's excellent news, Louisa," Robert stated.

"Yes . . . excellent, as you say," she murmured, in a pensive tone. "Papa is determined to leave tomorrow and he's returning home without me. I should be going with him. You were right . . . that morning in the stables at home. I should've listened to you, for you're always so wise."

Louisa looked up at him with deep sadness in her eyes. She lifted her hand and Robert was on one knee beside her, instantly grasping her hand in his and kissing it gently.

"Wisdom comes with age. With age come many other problems. You're not happy, child. I've been watching you for some time and, if he's hurt you in any way, I swear, I'll take a whip to him and the devil take the consequences of such an action."

Louisa reached up and stroked his hair and face. She was unable to imagine for a moment the gentle uncle who she knew so well, taking a whip to anyone, least of all to Charles Lyndhurst.

"There's no need to be protective of me, for I'm well able to take care of myself where Charles is concerned, and you're incorrect in your assumption. He's never hurt me and I doubt he would so. You see, he looks on me more as a spoilt minx that's arrived uninvited on his doorstep . . . a waif, perhaps," Louisa said, with a slight laugh.

This revelation appeared to ease her uncle's mind a little. Robert reached for a footstool, deftly pulling it to him and seating himself beside her knees, although looking up at her with some concern on his face, still.

"Dear Uncle Robert, you care so much, don't you? I take you all for granted but, I suppose, that's because you've all been here for me always. I need to ask you a question, as you are so wise, but it must be between us . . . a secret, please."

He nodded to her, although the frown on his brow deepened.

"Had I taken your advice that morning and called off the wedding, I could've come to Melbourne to you and Aunt Sophie to attend all those functions of the Royal Tour. I do wish I'd done so. Then, this problem wouldn't have arisen, for I'd not have to consider anyone else and I'd have chosen more wisely, I feel."

"I'm not understanding you . . . to what problem do you refer?" he queried; then, his face underwent a remarkable transformation before he continued. "Are you with child?"

Louisa, with a shocked look on her face, stared at him, all the while shaking her head furiously.

"Oh! No! Uncle, don't even suggest such a terrible event. I should be horrified and it'd compound my problem, because I think I'm in love, but I don't know how to tell for certain."

"With your husband?" he asked quickly.

Louisa shook her head slowly, never taking her eyes from his face. He studied her with his mouth open; then, he closed it while pursing his lips, thereby sealing in any hasty words.

"Then, this is grave indeed, especially for a young woman in your position. For a man, perhaps, it's otherwise sometimes, and can be handled with delicacy . . . but certainly not in your case! Forget this man now, for no good can come of it. Don't even fantasise about there being a positive outcome, for it is not possible. Who is he?"

Louisa bit her lip, mainly to stop it from trembling, and he saw her reaction to his words. He took her two hands in his own and he shook his head slowly, with sadness reflecting in his eyes.

"Louisa, dear child, if you are truly in love, you'll have no need to ask me, or anyone else, for you will know, deep inside, in your own heart. You'll want nothing other than to be with that *one person always* . . . and when you are separated, even if it's for a few hours only, you cannot wait to be reunited. Is that how it is with you?" he asked, while speaking with deep conviction.

Louisa nodded to him, with her eyes never wavering from his face.

"Do you see him often?"

Louisa nodded to him, with her eyes never wavering from his face.

"Well, if he lives and breathes still, I am certain that your husband can be unaware of this liaison . Has it become such, Louisa?"

"I'm not certain I know what you mean, but I won't allow him to touch me, for my dagger is at the ready always."

Robert Collins, with surprise registering on his face, laughed softly but involuntarily. After that, he resumed his headmaster's severe countenance.

"Give me a name, child, for I must know?" Robert ordered, but in a soft, gentle tone.

Louisa bit her lip. She was reluctant to mention Phillip's name, even to her uncle whom she trusted above anyone else in the world.

"Phillip . . . Phillip Carstairs," she confided finally, but in a hushed tone.

He stared at her in horror. Louisa saw the horrified expression on his face and she became defensive all of a sudden.

"Good grief! Run from him as fast as you can. Promise me you'll never see him again. He's not to be trusted and a worse rake than your husband ever was. His exploits in Sydney, with young ladies, are the talk of the town. And now, he has my own niece in his sights? This is unbelievable! There's been a family feud for decades between those two families . . . Carstairs and Lyndhurst. So, if he's singled you out, it's for no other reason than revenge, believe me!"

"It can never be so!" Louisa stated, with her temper flaring instantly at his criticism of the man who she loved.

"Thank the good Lord you'd the sense to seek my counsel," Robert said, as he muttered these words almost to himself.

"But, he loves me, *also* . . . he told me so," Louisa revealed firmly.

Robert stood up and he moved to his desk. He was leaning on the edge of it and staring down at the sorrowful girl before him. He folded his arms, with his headmaster's traits not far below the surface.

"Words, child. . . words! Anyone can utter them, especially those with an ulterior motive," he stated firmly, before witnessing the telltale signs of anger and the defiant flick of Louisa's chin, so he changed tack. "If you truly love him and you value his life, walk away now before it's too late. Otherwise, his lifeless body will be found with its throat slit, in a ditch somewhere; or, perhaps in a back alley, for that would be Sir Charles Lyndhurst's style and trademark, being the coward that he is. And, he'll get away with it, for he always does."

Louisa shook her head while giving Robert to understand that she did not accept the scenario, which he was placing before her. Phillip's laughing face flashed before her eyes and she could not believe that he was deceiving her, with his motives being solely those of revenge. Robert gave a deep sigh as he watched his niece. Then, he continued with his discourse.

"You know, I presume, that your marriage, as with many others, was arranged solely for the purpose of producing heirs. Your father-in-law will act instantly if he suspects, for one moment, a member of *that particular* family is making overtures in your direction. Then, your friend's as good as dead. Trust me on that score, please. I know all too well how *this society* functions, believe me!"

His final statement was made forcefully and with ill-concealed contempt. Suddenly, without warning, the door opened to his library and Sophie Collins charged uninvited into her husband's private sanctuary. He reacted angrily and instantly, before she could open her mouth to speak.

"For goodness sake, woman! Give us some peace. Whatever it is, deal with it yourself, for once in your life!" Robert shouted at his wife.

Stunned, both women stared at him while being unable to believe that such an uncharacteristic outburst could come from the staid and dignified gentleman who was Robert Collins. Sophie glanced from one to the other; then, she withdrew without a word and she closed the door quietly behind her.

"I apologise. That was uncalled for and unnecessary, but your revelations have rocked me to the core," Robert said quietly.

Louisa returned her gaze to the side garden and she was studying the croquet court, with its lawn resembling the surface of a billiard table. Finally looking back at her uncle, she realised that he was staring at her and frowning deeply while appearing very troubled.

"I can't accept what you're saying about Phillip, although I know you have my best interest at heart, Uncle Robert. He makes me laugh and that's not something I've known since Mama died. I cannot live without love and laughter in my life. I will suffocate, so *anything* is better to me than suffocation."

Her words were spoken very quietly and without emotion. Gravely, he studied Louisa.

"Then, I'll handle this matter personally. The Royal Tour moves to Tasmania shortly, before going to Sydney after Christmas. And, so too, will your friend. That'll be the last you will see of him. In the meantime, I want your solemn word that you won't meet with him alone again."

Louisa shook her head slowly.

"I can't give it," she replied simply and honestly. "I confided in you, so do not betray my secret, please."

"I shan't betray you, Louisa; nor will I stand idly by while you destroy yourself. I'd be derelict in my duty to you were I to allow you to walk alone into a blazing building to be consumed by fire. The path, on which you have embarked is far, far worse than that. I'm just relieved and thankful you had the good sense to confide in me."

She looked up at him and she surveyed him in the candid manner, which he found quite disconcerting at times, and no less today.

"Don't place a permanent wedge between us by an act of betrayal, then."

Regally, Louisa stood up and she walked from his library while leaving Robert alone and deeply troubled.

Christmas Eve found Melbourne in a state of frenzied excitement once again when the evening of the fancy dress ball arrived, finally. The gipsy girl entered the well-lit and beautifully-decorated ballroom on the arm of the highwayman, although anyone other than Charles Lyndhurst may not have been permitted to attend this royal function with a replica pistol in his belt. The police were on heightened alert for fear of an assassination attempt on the life of Prince Alfred. However, the couple was not detained, or apprehended, as they made their grand entrance, along with all of the other excited revellers.

The invited and carefully-selected guests were wearing a variety of colourful costumes while in varying states of undress. What would have been considered as shocking, under normal circumstances, in the staid, stodgy, stupefying atmosphere of most of Melbourne's drawing rooms – while being always under the ever-watchful gaze that stared down at them from the ubiquitous portraits of their monarch, Queen Victoria – was permitted for this one night only. This was the night when the city let down the locks of its own hair. Never again would it happen in this country, in this century, in this era. Tonight, anything and everything was permitted while the mood of those assembled reflected this temporarily relaxed change of attitude in the presence of one of their monarch's sons.

Louisa's anxious gaze scanned those assembled in the massive ballroom. She was seeking a glimpse of Phillip, but instead, she found her uncle's deeply troubled eyes staring back at her. Quickly, she glanced away and she watched in astonishment as Bertie Webster – dressed as the devil himself and clutching a pitch-fork in his hand – danced gracefully by her, with an elegant Cleopatra in his arms. The absurdity of the pairing of Lucifer with Cleopatra amused her. Noticing her gaze upon him, Bertie winked at Louisa while grinning as he did so. She laughed at him in acknowledgment after having spoken with him briefly on occasions, as their paths had crossed at various functions since their initial introduction in Bendigo all those weeks ago.

That the lady-in-question was stunningly beautiful was obvious for all to see. It was possible, had she been born in another time and place that she may have caused the real Cleopatra to pale into insignificance beside her, while her revealing outfit this evening left little to the imagination. All eyes turned as Sylvia's *Cleopatra* glided by –

with the male ones devouring and the female ones reflecting envy, even malice in some cases. Louisa glanced up at Charles momentarily and the expression on his face took her breath away. He was staring at the couple with a mixture of awe and astonishment mingling there. Charles moved slightly from her and he commenced a conversation with a man who was standing beside him.

Then, Louisa spied him. The devil-may-care pirate – with a patch over one eye and a dagger in his belt – was sauntering toward her, with a beaming smile on his face. Louisa laughed as she looked over at him and she was anticipating his request for the next dance. She was watching the dimples dancing on his face as his smile broadened the closer that he came to her. When but a few feet from her, he lifted the eye-patch; then, he winked at her in a most brazen manner.

Almost instantly, the smile disappeared and the eye-patch was replaced. Phillip stopped mid-stride and he turned aside. He approached another young lady, from whom he requested a dance. Louisa was not only disappointed, but also, she was puzzled – for but one moment only. It was then that a male hand gripped her arm firmly and she was whisked onto the dance floor by her husband, while she noted an expression of immense relief on Robert's face as he danced with his wife a short distance away.

"Not one dance will you have with him this evening! Is that clear?" Charles Lyndhurst ordered, with his words almost a snarl in her ear.

"Shall I, also, make a list of those with whom you're not permitted to dance?" she queried.

"Don't play me for a fool, Louisa. It's the biggest mistake you'll ever make. Don't have anything to do with Carstairs tonight, or ever again! Can I speak more plainly?"

Louisa gave a defiant flick of her head and she turned her gaze to survey the other couples dancing around them while ignoring her husband as much as was possible – given the present circumstances. Finally, unable to contain her anger, she addressed him.

"Shall I find a chair in a corner somewhere? Would that please you? Why did you bring me here, if only to restrict my enjoyment? Or, do you propose to stand up with me every dance?"

His grip on her tightened as his annoyance began to surface. He pulled her body closer to him in a swift, almost-threatening manner.

"If that's what it takes, consider it done!"

True to his word, Charles did not leave her side for quite some time. Eventually, mid-way through the evening, he deposited her beside her aunt and uncle.

"Don't move from here until I return. That's a direct order. Don't defy me, Louisa!" Charles commanded firmly and clearly, obviously fully intending that Sophie and Robert should hear his stern directive.

He was holding her arm still and his grip tightened as he watched her. He was waiting for the expected show of defiance. Louisa did not disappoint in this regard and the anger on her face was ill-concealed.

"Go to hell!" she countered, instantly hurling the words loudly at him.

Sophie Collins' hand flew to her mouth and she turned her head from side to side, furtively glancing about to see who was observing her niece's disgraceful behaviour. Robert's hand reached over and he grasped Louisa's hand. He looked directly at Charles as he did so.

"She's safe with me, Charles. You'll not move an inch from my side, will you, Louisa?" Robert asked, in a soft, even tone.

Louisa looked at her uncle with her usual defiance and not a little disappointment in her eyes. Sophie appeared to be holding her breath, evidently awaiting the inevitable explosion that occurred always when her niece's will was crossed.

"Is this a conspiracy?" Louisa demanded. "I expected better of you, Uncle Robert."

"And, I of you, child," he stated.

Held beneath her uncle's unwavering gaze, finally, Louisa shrugged her shoulders after a few tense moments, and all three observers breathed a collective sigh of relief. Charles relinquished her arm, but not so her uncle, who held her hand more tightly.

"I obliged to you, Robert," Charles said, as he began to move away. "I'll be but a few moments."

Silence reigned. Louisa's eyes roved around the room. She was searching every face on the dance floor before moving her gaze to those assembled along the walls and within her line of vision. Prince Alfred, she could see in the distance, resplendent in his naval uniform, with his two equerries by his side. They seemed amused by the costumes and they were laughing together, unashamedly indicating various guests as they danced by their vantage point.

Phillip was nowhere to be seen. It was as though he had disappeared completely. She noticed Sylvia Webster moving away from a group of Bertie Webster's friends and she was heading toward one of the side doors. Standing waiting by the doorway, while holding two glasses of wine in his hands, was Charles Lyndhurst. Following her gaze, Robert frowned as Louisa looked up at him. She felt his grip tightening on her hand while Sophie moved to talk with one of her friends.

"Shall we dance?" Robert asked of Louisa.

She nodded in the affirmative and he led her onto the floor. Dancing with her uncle, Louisa – in a pensive state now that her anger had subsided a little – continued to watch for Phillip, but to no avail. Unable to prevent the questions that were in her mind from drifting to her tongue, she challenged her uncle.

"Did you say something to Charles? Did you betray me?"

Robert gave a wry smile and slowly, but with some sadness, he shook his head.

"No, and I'm rather hurt that you should've thought this . . . let alone to have asked it. The day when I side with Lyndhurst against my own beloved niece is the day hell will freeze over. It is but your own guilty conscience that is clutching at straws for someone to blame for the dilemma, in which you find yourself. I've no respect whatsoever for your husband, but I'll do whatever it takes to protect you. That is why I intervened. Nothing could've been achieved from such a public display of hostility between the two of you. Neither one was prepared to give an inch."

Louisa bit her lip once again and she was silent for quite some time. The excitement that she felt when coming to the Fancy Dress Ball tonight had reached a height she had never dreamed was possible. Now, the night was ruined. She had shocked her aunt, antagonised her husband, hurt her uncle and been denied contact of any description with a certain pirate whose company she desired more than anything in the world at this moment. This was certainly a Christmas Eve to remember.

Last Christmas Eve, she had shared alone with her father – their first without her mother. Her father had returned home the previous day to spend Christmas alone – without either his wife or his daughter this year – although the fact that the latter was missing from his life and his home was due to his own stubborn and stupid decision, with which he would have to live. Louisa knew that she would have to live with the equally insane decision, which she had made at that time, the consequences, of which she was beginning to realise only now. Despite Uncle Robert's pleas on her wedding day, she had kept her side of the bargain with her father. And now, George Howard had kept his part in that deal. She squeezed her uncle's hand as the music stopped.

"I'm sorry, Uncle. I never meant to hurt you," Louisa said as they walked back to where her aunt was waiting. "Does Aunt Sophie know about Phillip and me?"

"May the saints preserve us! Don't think such a thought! She'd keel over and die of apoplexy! Of course not . . . and I forgive you totally," Robert stated quietly, before he continued in a soft tone. "You're visiting us for our Christmas luncheon tomorrow, so I want you to promise me you will keep the peace until then. We've had you to ourselves so infrequently at Christmas. Please, don't allow this rift with your husband to spoil our day. Promise me now."

"I'll do my utmost."

Robert stopped still. He held her arm and looked down at her, thereby preventing her from moving from the dance floor, which was almost deserted at this moment. Louisa frowned at him.

"That's not good enough, Louisa. I want more than your best endeavours. I want your solemn promise that you will make peace with Charles before your visit to us tomorrow . . . as a mark of respect to your aunt. I take it you are attending Christmas mass in the morning, so don't go there with anger in your heart, no matter how justified you may think it. Well?"

"You ask too much!"

Louisa walked over to her aunt as Charles rejoined them, and the remainder of the evening was spent in the company of her aunt, her uncle and her husband.

The customary silence between Louisa and her obviously still-angry husband, in the carriage on the way home, was evident. She was pondering on her uncle's advice and his request, while wondering if – or how – it could be implemented, despite the fact she was loath to do so. If it had been any night other than Christmas Eve, she would not have harboured *this repulsive thought* for an instant.

Charles assisted her to alight and he escorted her inside the front door. Then, he turned to leave the house as the carriage awaited his return.

"Are you going out?" she inquired.

"I am."

"May I speak with you first?" she asked, a little tentatively.

He raised an eyebrow in surprise while signalling to the driver to wait. He walked to his office, deliberately holding the door open for her and with a supercilious expression on his face. The room was in darkness and he lit but one lamp only, obviously not intending to stay for long with her and his slight impatience was evident.

"You have my undivided attention," he announced, immediately leaning on his desk and folding his arms as her uncle had done so recently.

Louisa bit her lip and looked at the floor while Charles studied her closely.

"I don't know how to say this," she murmured.

Charles seemed surprised.

"When have you ever been lost for words?" he asked, in a supercilious tone.

Louisa frowned at him and grimaced while feeling her anger beginning to surface. He had the ability to upset her with but one short sentence. With great difficulty, she managed to control herself and her fiery temper, not for Charles' sake, she acknowledged to herself, but only because it was Christmas Eve.

"When I'm attempting to apologise to you," she murmured. "Also, when I'm trying to thank you."

Charles did not speak. He did not move. He did not assist her in her endeavours at all. Louisa gave a deep sigh and she embarked on her long-overdue soliloquy.

"Thank you for bringing my horses to me. Thank you for bringing Papa to me. Knowing that he's not dying has been the best Christmas gift I could've received, and he'd not have come without your efforts on my behalf. I don't know how you did it, but I truly appreciate all that you have done. I shall be grateful for that always . . . and for Cadence and Hilton."

If he was amused by this greatly unexpected turn of events, he hid the fact beautifully while assisting Louisa not at all in her next effort.

"I'm sorry for my dreadful behaviour. I've no excuse for it. We've been together but six weeks and I've treated you unreasonably on occasions, often with hostility. If I wanted to be honest, I'd have to acknowledge that fact, I suppose."

"You suppose? Either you have; or, you have not. You cannot have it both ways, *madam*, with an each-way bet! So, which is it?"

Charles appeared to be enjoying himself, at her expense, as he raised an eyebrow in query. Louisa shrugged her shoulders in a display of helplessness that did absolutely nothing to ease her somewhat awkward situation, or to render assistance from her apparently implacable husband.

"I have done so. I'm sorry and tonight was no exception. I apologise for my outburst at the ball, too."

He surveyed her in silence, with all traces of amusement having left his face. Louisa continued to gaze at the floor, unable to raise her eyes to his face, but conscious of his close scrutiny.

"Thank you," he said finally; then, he replied to her in a soft, but formal, tone. "Your apology is accepted. Perhaps, eighteen-sixty-eight will be a better year for both of us."

Neither one moved. Finally, unable to stand his gaze upon her, she walked over, and feeling herself blushing as she did so, she kissed him lightly on the cheek. She turned quickly to leave his office.

"Happy Christmas," she muttered, immediately noting the surprise on his face.

Without warning, he grabbed her wrist, instantly swinging her around and pinning her against his desk. In this instant, Louisa found herself clutched tightly in his arms. Before she realised what had occurred, his mouth was on her own, with his tongue exploring therein. She froze instantly before moving her face from his in one swift action. With an expression of surprise, mingled with revulsion, registering on her face and being unable to move in any direction until he released his grip a little, she struggled in his arms. She was gasping for breath when he whispered to her.

"Happy Christmas, Louisa," Charles murmured in her ear, before he confided to her in a soft, intimate tone. "I'll stay, if you want me. Come to my bed now?"

Louisa, with her face less than an inch from his, was stunned –
horrified at his proposal. He watched her intently. Then, he kissed
her again and he pressed himself against her body as he did so.
She was wedged firmly between his body and the desk behind her.
Suddenly, she felt an urge to relax into his embrace and to give vent
to the feelings – strange and unexpected though they were – that
were rising within her.

Momentarily, she gave in to the temptation, which surprised
and shocked her greatly. Recovering herself, she pushed her hands
against his chest and, after an initial struggle, he released her – albeit
seemingly with great reluctance – whispering to her as he did so.

"One night, you'll come to me of your own accord," Charles
stated his prediction in a deliberate manner.

Louisa looked directly into his eyes for a brief moment. She
shook her head slowly and deliberately before running from the
room. He made no attempt to prevent her flight. By the time that
she had jumped up the internal stairs and reached her bedroom, she
was gasping for breath again. Needing to be alone as she struggled
with unknown feelings and emotions and, at the same time, fighting
desperately to prevent the deep trembling that had surfaced within
her body, she dismissed Charlotte whom she surprised dozing in the
armchair by the verandah door. As the girl left her room, she heard
Charles' carriage moving off down the carriageway.

By her own choice, Louisa spent Christmas Eve alone while
knowing that her father was doing likewise. The grandfather clock
downstairs chimed two o'clock as she climbed into her bed.

Sylvia

Sylvia was alone in the small sitting room when Charles arrived.
Bertie, in his ridiculous devil's outfit, had shared a drink with her just
prior to leaving. No sooner had he departed than she heard Charles'
carriage at the front door.

Charles walked into the room, took her in his arms and kissed her passionately, without a word being spoken between them. Then, he released her.

"I apologise profusely for tonight. I'd not a chance to have one dance with you. I'm so sorry, Sylvia."

"I did not lack partners, Mr. Lyndhurst . . . don't think that for one moment!" she teased, suddenly realising that the champagne, which she had consumed this night was affecting her more than she wished to admit. "I may forgive you, but not yet. My feet are complaining still, for I danced every dance, and if I'd remained there for another three hours, I couldn't have fulfilled every request."

"I'm well aware of it! But, how many of those were solely for dancing?"

"Wouldn't you like to know!"

"I would . . . very much, for they shall all know my wrath soon enough," he stated; then, holding her body slightly away from him, he looked her over appreciatively as he studied her tightly-fitting costume. "I'm surprised you weren't arrested, for this really does go beyond daring. If Lord Newry were not so closely linked to His Royal Highness, I'd have called him out! And, where I saw hands roving during the course of this evening . . . well, it goes beyond what is considered decent in the public domain."

Sylvia laughed, for she was highly amused at his pretence at outrage, although suspecting that somewhere in the depths of his being, there was a little jealousy lurking.

"I did forego a dance to share a glass of champagne with you. You must admit this fact, although I suspect by tomorrow morning, I'll be wishing that was the only one I'd consumed. Were you jealous?" she asked, while laughing with him.

"Decidedly so! In fact, more so than I'll ever admit. But then, if I were to state otherwise, you'd throw me out on my ear. *And that, Mrs. Webster,* would be a tragedy for both of us, especially on

Christmas Eve. Shall we go up? If you've over-indulged, I'm happy to carry you."

Sylvia thumped him on the arm and laughed again while shaking her head as she did so. Charles laughed with her.

"The night when I can't climb those stairs under my own steam, is the time I give up alcohol forever. But, lead me, you may."

She placed an arm around his waist and he spun her around, as though about to whisk her onto the dance floor. Instead, he propelled her toward the door as Sylvia wondered – not for the first time – if this would be the last Christmas that they would spend in each other's company.

Together, with their arms wrapped tightly around each other, Cleopatra and her highwayman climbed the stairs together.

Chapter Twenty

– *Victorian Victorians* –

Louisa

When Louisa left the house to attend Christmas mass, Charles had not returned from wherever he had gone on the previous evening – after their post-ball conversation and confrontation – the result of which Louisa had banished from her mind, at present.

Her uncle's sermon was longer, louder and laced with more fire-and-brimstone predictions and warnings than was normal, on this Christmas morning. Louisa longed for the ordeal to conclude, because the heat was rising rapidly on this summer morning. Afterwards, she was required to wait until the majority of the parishioners departed before she could greet Father Frank with her Christmas wishes, as her mother would have expected of her. There were more people attending than was normal, as many made Christmas their one and only pilgrimage for the year.

Finally, she was able to approach him. Father Francis Bourke greeted her in a happy frame of mind and in no way did he resemble the scowling priest who had addressed the congregation forty minutes earlier. After some ten minutes, she was able to escape and to return home, as her carriage, as always, was waiting by the front gate of the church. This was the pattern that she established at the beginning when she started attending church every Sunday. The carriage returned to Lyndhurst Park after delivering her to the church; then, it returned some ninety minutes later to collect her. Prior to the commencement of holy mass, her uncle insisted on hearing her confession always. As yet, Louisa had found no way to escape this demand. For the time being, she accepted the requirement as a part of her fate for being born his niece.

Once again, Louisa was seated at the breakfast table when Charles joined her and again, he drank only tea – and in silence – while she consumed her food. Suddenly, he took a small parcel from his pocket and he placed it on the table beside her. With her mouth full of food, she stared at the gift-wrapped package in dismay.

"Happy Christmas, Louisa," he said, softly repeating his words from their previous encounter in his office.

Swallowing quickly and somewhat aghast, she continued to look on the parcel.

"Umm . . . thank you . . . I didn't realise . . . didn't think to get anything for you. It never occurred to me," she stammered, hurriedly admitting this omission somewhat reluctantly to him. " I don't have a gift for you."

"I'm not surprised. You didn't expect to be here, for you'd planned your escape meticulously, I suspect."

"Yes," she admitted frankly. "I did mean to spend Christmas with Papa. That's where I intended to be now."

"Did you intend going alone?" he asked quietly.

"Of course! I wouldn't have involved any of the servants, and especially not Charlotte, for you'd have used it as an excuse to dismiss her."

"You've a rather low opinion of me, especially where the servants are concerned, and it's unjustified. But, be that as it may, I wasn't referring to the servants," Charles said.

Louisa frowned at him in all innocence until, somewhat belatedly, the impact of his words took affect; then, with her mouth wide open, she stared at him and unable to speak momentarily. He watched her, carefully scrutinising her face for any telltale signs of deception. Finally, she was able to respond.

"How could you think that of me?" she asked, quite aghast.

"Easily! I saw what passed between the two of you last night and, while it may have been one brief glance only, it spoke volumes. I'm not without eyes . . . don't think it for a moment."

Charles drained his cup; then, he stood to leave her as he looked down at the food before her.

"We're leaving in an hour to lunch with your aunt and uncle. Do you intend to consume all of that before the Christmas luncheon?" he inquired, as though the previous conversation had not occurred.

Louisa was staring up at him still, unable to find any words to answer him when, finally, he turned and left the room while leaving her alone with the unopened Christmas gift before her.

When the door closed behind him, she reached for the gift and opened it, with her eyes and mouth both wide with surprise as she stared at the emerald and diamond bracelet in her hand. It was delicate. The larger stones were the emeralds and these were surrounded in gold while being interlaced with smaller diamonds. Fingering the piece, she allowed a sigh to escape from her as she acknowledged to herself the difficulty of her current situation. However, time was moving on, so she pushed the plate of food aside and returned to her room to dress for their next engagement.

When she returned downstairs, Charles was nowhere to be seen. She opened his office door tentatively and found him seated at his desk, although his chair was turned around and he was facing the window, presumably gazing at the river. She knew that he had heard her entry, but he did not turn around to look at her.

"Thank you for my gift. It is beautiful," Louisa said tentatively.

He glanced back over his shoulder at her and merely nodded in acknowledgment.

"We've reached a great impasse, it would seem," he commented.

"I assure you I was going *home alone*. What you're suggesting never occurred to me and I'm shocked you'd think that of me," she stated.

"The *home*, to which you refer belonged to Louisa Howard. Louisa Lyndhurst belongs here . . . at Lyndhurst Park . . . with me," he stated firmly; then, swivelling his chair around to face her, he surveyed her thoughtfully. "Perhaps, the only way to reinforce that fact is to legalise this marriage, once and for all."

Louisa shook her head violently, with absolute revulsion registering very clearly on her face. He spoke quietly then, but with conviction.

"It may surprise you to learn that I wanted this marriage even less than you did. *And, I had other plans, also.* But, these have been shelved now, it'd appear. You and I will make a new start . . . with the New Year, and there'll be no going back to what might have been . . . for either of us. Then, we'll have a marriage, in every sense of the word. I had hoped you may have been prepared to come to me, of your own accord. But, obviously not, as your interests lie elsewhere. *That can never be, Louisa!* So, don't even consider it an option for yourself. He's toying with you, because of your current connection to my family and because you're safely married already, thereby making it impossible for you to make any claim on him afterwards."

Louisa watched him for a moment as she felt contempt rising to the surface. His face was impassive as he continued to watch her.

"You are wrong . . . so very, very wrong . . . about everything and everyone. All I can hope is that, by the time I reach your age, I'm nowhere near as cynical, or as suspicious, as you are. If I am, I should hope someone would have the decency to take me out and shoot me. . . to put me out of my misery. I made a move last night to apologise to you, so that peace could reign between us ... for today, at least. But, you're not prepared to meet me even half-way," Louisa said, with ice crackling in every slowly spoken word.

With fingers that were shaking and fumbling with the catch, she removed the bracelet from her wrist with difficulty. She tossed it at him and he caught it deftly in his right hand, but still surveying her with disdain.

"Keep your trinkets! Save them for someone who'd appreciate them," she stated while observing a sudden frown cross his face at those words as she hurled her next words at him. "As for what else you're suggesting, if I'd understood *that act* was a requirement of marriage, I'd never have consented to be in *this state*! If you touch me, it'll be against my will and against my wishes, so don't bother waiting for the connecting door to open, because it will not do so . . . not from my side . . . *not ever!*"

So saying, she spun around and left the room. She sailed through the front door as Benson held it open for her. She was seated in the carriage when Charles entered the vehicle. Without a word, he sat opposite her. Once again, the journey was completed in silence. As the carriage drew to a standstill outside the Collins' residence, he took her gloved hand, deliberately wrapping the bracelet around her wrist. Impassively and with disinterest, she watched as he fastened it.

"If I've misjudged you, I apologise, but I'm not a fool. So, do not think it so. Let us try to be friends for a few hours, shall we? We owe that to your family and to our friends, if only for today."

By the time that the front door opened and they entered the house, Charles had wound Louisa's hand through his arm and they did their utmost to appear the happily-married couple that no one supposed for one moment they were. However, their playing of this game saved embarrassment for all concerned – this being the purpose of the exercise anyway.

Hugh and Margaret Travis joined the gathering and with them were their two little girls who were aged two years and four years respectively. With lunch at an end, the party adjourned to the croquet court, where the small girls were being taught the rudiments of the game by their father who was holding a mallet. As neither one was able to hold the mallet, Hugh and Charles were assisting in this exercise. Margaret and Sophie sat chatting together on the bench seat in the shade. Louisa strolled out of the house to join them, with her uncle by her side. She slid an arm around his waist and he placed an arm around her shoulders.

"Congratulations! I've never seen such a demure, pleasant, co-operative Louisa in all of my life. You excelled in that role. Might we expect more of the same in the future?" he queried, with a slight laugh.

"Don't count on it! Once a year is the most I can manage, I'm afraid, because as you said, Uncle Robert, *it is Christmas.*"

"Then, I thank you sincerely for meeting my request, because it truly is appreciated. All we need to work on now are the other three hundred and sixty-four days, but that may prove a little more . . . umm, challenging, shall we say?"

They were laughing together as they walked towards the lawn court. Then, Robert leaned over and kissed her on the top of her head. As he did so, he clutched his chest with his other hand in one, sudden movement. He doubled over in obvious pain while leaning heavily on Louisa for support. His wife was at his side in an instant, as was Hugh Travis who witnessed the incident. Hugh supported him, with assistance from Louisa, as they helped Robert to a nearby bench seat beneath a tree in the shade. Robert, who was protesting that he was quite well and suffering only a slight shortness of breath, tried to wave everyone away, but the colour had drained from his face and he was deathly white.

Louisa, with alarm bells sounding within her as she witnessed an event that was well-known to her, watched in horror and dropped down on one knee beside him. She was holding Robert's hand. Margaret gathered the children and took them into the house immediately. After a time, Hugh followed her, as did Sophie, who was intent on sending for the doctor.

"Louisa, stop her! There's no need to bring the poor man out today of all days. It's Christmas, for goodness sake!" Robert whispered, while gasping for breath and absentmindedly rubbing his chest as he tried to speak.

"This is not the first time, is it?" Louisa queried softly.

Robert averted his eyes. Then, he shook his head slowly. Charles was standing behind Louisa and watching these current proceedings with interest, as well as having a deep frown on his face.

"I shall not intervene then, as I'm certain Aunt Sophie knows what needs to be done. Please, will you allow us to assist you into the house now, if you're a little improved? It is but a few short steps to your library and you can rest there on the settee until the doctor arrives."

With one arm resting along the back of the garden bench seat, he remained still and he began taking deep breaths as he tried to regain some composure.

"Give me a few moments then," he stammered, with a little colour returning to his somewhat-ashen face.

After a few minutes, and with assistance from Louisa, he struggled to his feet while definitely resisting the offered assistance from Charles. On unsteady legs, he staggered into the house and he was leaning heavily on his niece, with Charles but one step behind and ready to reach for him in an instant. Robert was settled on the settee and propped up on cushions before Sophie returned to the library. She announced that the Travis family had departed while sending their best wishes to all.

Robert closed his eyes and, following prompting from her aunt, Louisa kissed him on the forehead; then, she followed her aunt and her husband from the library. Once outside the room and with the door to the library closed firmly, she turned on her aunt.

"How long, Aunt Sophie? And, why wasn't I told?" she demanded, as Charles stood by her side.

"Some eighteen months, child," her aunt confessed sadly. "It was your uncle's wish that no one should know, so I trust you'll honour his confidence."

"I'm not *just anyone!* I should've been told. I've seen it all so many times before. This is too much!" Louisa stated, with her annoyance obvious.

"That's precisely why he didn't want you to know. We both knew you would make comparisons with your mother's condition. This is not the same," Sophie stated firmly.

Exasperated, Louisa opened her mouth to speak, but Charles' hand pressed firmly on her arm.

"Perhaps, it may be wise to allow your uncle to rest now. Word can be sent to you as soon as the doctor has made an assessment. Wouldn't you think, Louisa? Is that not so, Mrs. Collins?"

With gratitude and relief visible on her face, Sophie smiled at him as she attempted to escape from her niece's anger.

"An excellent suggestion, Mr. Lyndhurst," she declared.

"Then, I shall leave, but on one condition," Louisa stated to her aunt.

"And, what is that, pray tell?" Sophie asked, almost holding her breath for fear of what the demand might be.

"You call a spade a spade! Don't try to placate me by papering over Uncle Robert's condition. I'll know if you do."

With a deep sigh, her aunt agreed and she escorted them to the door as their carriage arrived. Louisa extracted the same promise again from her aunt before she departed while the maid, Emily, remained hovering by the now-open library door as she stood watch over the resting patient from a distance.

It was a very silent Louisa who returned to Lyndhurst Park late that afternoon.

Several hours elapsed, for it was after dinner before the anxiously-awaited missive arrived from her aunt. In it, she declared that her husband was much recovered from his *slight turn* and all would be well after a good night's sleep, which was without question, because the doctor had prescribed a *draught* for him. Louisa, in some annoyance, rolled the note into a ball and she threw it across the room. Charles watched her intently. She strode across the drawing room and slammed her hand down on the back of the armchair.

"She thinks I'm a fool! Either that, or she's not facing the truth of the matter herself. It was like watching Mama all over again. She would pretend that it was nothing . . . *a slight turn* . . . that's what she'd call it, also. Then, she would go on with her life as though nothing had happened and pretending to us all. Now, that's what Aunt Sophie is calling this."

Louisa wandered over to the french doors. She was looking out onto the croquet lawn as Charles continued to study her. Finally, she turned to him, with anguish visible on her face.

"With Mama, *those turns* got progressively worse until she didn't come out of the last one. Papa left me with her in that hotel room while he went to make arrangements; that's what he called it. And, I sat there, just watching her and praying to God while willing her to wake up and expecting any minute that she would. But, she never did. *And,* that's what will happen here . . . with Uncle Robert," she explained, with a shrug that spoke almost of an acceptance of the inevitable. "And, all this time, it's Papa I've been so concerned about and his health is good, by comparison."

Charles remained silent for several minutes. Then, he rose from the chair and walked across the room.

"Follow me," he commanded.

Louisa, puzzled and drained of any resistance, did his bidding. He walked to the ballroom and, at the other end of the long room, he lifted an armchair, which he placed on the floor while positioning it by the pianoforte. He sat at the instrument and opened it, instantly indicating with a sweep of his arm for Louisa to sit beside him in the armchair. She did so without argument.

Without a word, Charles' fingers caressed the keys lightly as he began to play. Louisa listened to the beautiful music. She was drifting away as the wafting notes filled the silent house. It was some time later when he roused her from her light slumber and she realised that the music had ceased.

"Do you wish me to carry you to bed, or can you make it under your own steam?" he whispered, as he shook her shoulder gently to wake her.

"I'll go alone," she stated, somewhat drowsily coming to the realisation of where she was and, more precisely, of who was with her.

Slowly, she rose from the armchair and, as she turned to leave, she glanced over at him as he prepared to play another piece on the pianoforte.

"Thank you for being so understanding," she murmured.

Charles smiled at her as his fingers moved lightly over the keys once again. Hurriedly, Louisa left him.

For the next few days, Charles insisted on riding with Louisa in the mornings and he was so insistent that Louisa was beginning to suspect he suspected her of meeting with Phillip. However, on Sunday morning, she attended church alone. Charles had not returned from whatever function that he had attended on the previous evening.

Later in the day, she visited her family. She was relieved to find her uncle back to his normal routine and his usually pleasant disposition. Now, Louisa felt that she understood the reason why her father had insisted on her marriage and this was because he would have known of Robert's illness. Therefore, he did not wish his sister to be responsible for his daughter, if Sophie were to find herself widowed after the demise of her husband, Robert. Then, with her brother, George, departing this world, as well, Sophie would be unable to cope with Louisa. That would have been her father's thinking, as at the time, he believed himself to be dying. But, none of these revelations did anything to alter her situation at all in this present moment, she reminded herself.

So, Monday dawned. Finally, Louisa was able to ride with the groom, Nathaniel, and she made good her escape from the house early; then, leaving the groom with the horses in the usual place, she ventured through the bushes to the meeting place. She found that she was holding her breath as she pushed through the last clump of bushes. Phillip was waiting and he greeted her with a welcoming smile. She stared at him in horror.

"What's happened? You're injured . . . show me," she demanded.

"I'm recovered. You should've seen me after the ball. I'm sorry I've not been able to come before today, for I was somewhat incapacitated. Your signal isn't in place, but I waited in the hope you would come."

His face was bruised and his eyes had been blackened, with a yellowish tinge surrounding the bruised area as though the healing had begun. Louisa moved to him and she touched him on the face, but inadvertently brushing against his chest as she did so. He winced in pain at her touch, in both areas.

"Where else are you hurt?" she queried.

Slowly and gingerly, he removed his coat and waistcoat before lifting his shirt for her to survey his chest area. She gasped in horror, gently fingering the bruising near his waist, around his ribs, and noticing an old wound there as she studied his extensive injuries.

"How? How did it happen?" she asked.

"Compliments of your father-in-law . . . I was apprehended at the ball, and very early in the night, by two troopers on the pretext that the weapon I was carrying was a danger to Prince Alfred. I thought they were joking at first, as it was a replica knife in my belt and made of wood. They marched me outside and held me on the ground while the *devil himself* appeared from nowhere and he kicked me senseless with his boots."

"Sir Charles Lyndhurst?" Louisa gasped.

"None other."

"On account of me?" Louisa gasped again.

"None other, but well worth it . . . I'd suffer burning flames on account of you, Louisa . . . willingly, and with a smile on my face."

"Oh! This is too much! I knew he was evil, but I hadn't expected this. Phillip, I'm so sorry . . . so very sorry. I was disappointed when I couldn't dance with you, but I was on the tightest rein possible myself. If it had been otherwise, I'd have come looking for you. What is the other wound? It doesn't look all that old, either."

"Compliments of your father-in-law, also, from a previous encounter. It's a bullet wound. *This is not finished!* I swear, on my father's grave, it is not! He has something belonging to my father and I suspect I know where it's kept. I'll have it, or I'll die in the attempt of retrieving it."

Allowing his shirt to fall, he placed an arm around her shoulders and drew her to him. She did not respond by placing her arms around him, partly for fear of hurting him and partly due to shyness, which for Louisa was a new experience.

"I need to return to Sydney next Monday," he whispered.

Louisa looked up at him in surprise.

"Forever?"

"No, I'll be back, and I'm taking you away with me . . . away from all this . . . away from the Lyndhurst lair, the vicious wolf and from his compliant cub."

"Oh! You're mistaken. Charles wouldn't have been involved in this . . . not knowingly, I'm certain."

"You're as naive as you are sweet and loyal, but you're wrong. Why were you kept on such a tight rein all night then? Ask yourself that."

Louisa remained silent as she explored all of the possibilities in her mind while Phillip eased himself onto the nearest boulder and gently pulled her down beside him. He recounted his story of a night several months earlier when his friend, Patrick, had helped him to break into the homestead at Stanton. Once inside, they had located a wall safe, which was hidden behind a large painting in an upstairs bedroom. He was attempting to open the safe when its owner appeared from nowhere and he was brandishing a pistol, which he began firing at random.

Phillip explained that he had managed to escape through a downstairs sitting room, but he was almost killed when one particular shot struck him quite close to his heart and hitting him on his left side, as well grazing his left arm. He vowed that next time, he would return with an expert who was capable of opening the safe. Once he retrieved his father's property, he would need to leave the country before the troopers caught up with him, as Sir Charles would claim that he had stolen many items and no one would be able to prove otherwise.

He planned to travel to San Francisco with Patrick and he was returning to Sydney during the next week to sell everything that he owned. This included his precious horse that he loved and it was in order to have the means to start afresh in a new country.

"My goodness, you have it all planned out, but it seems such a drastic measure, Phillip. Are you certain the property is worth all this?"

"Most assuredly, for I promised my father on the day he died that I'd retrieve it for him. Besides, how else can I take you away from all this?" he asked, in a serious tone.

"Me? You're taking me? To San Francisco? Oh! I can't see how! Such an idea is not to be considered. I've my family to think of . . . *and, Charles* will find me wherever I go; then, he'll kill you, for he's told me so," Louisa, stunned, stammered in response, with his earlier words registering in her over-active mind all of a sudden.

"He'll not find us, I promise you, so pay him no heed. But, if you love me as I love you, you'll come . . . at a minute's notice . . . and never look back to what might've been here. For you must understand fully that you can never return . . . not ever! It's for the rest of your life, Louisa. Dear God, I love you so. That hurts more than all these injuries and they'll heal in time. My feelings for you are for always."

Louisa found herself trembling and many thoughts were running around and around in her mind. She needed to think clearly. She needed to be alone. She could not comprehend all that he was suggesting.

"When?" she queried, finally able to respond.

"In two to three months! Allow the dust to settle and let the old goat think he's won. It'll take me as long as that to make arrangements and to put everything in order, for I'll be severing ties with my family, also. And, my brother will make certain I don't receive a ha'penny from that day onwards. Rest assured on that!"

Louisa was silent again. What Phillip was suggesting was so preposterous that she could not take the proposition seriously at this stage. Perhaps, in time, she may be able to consider the suggestion, but acting on it was another matter. To spend the rest of her life with him would be the most wonderful dream come to fruition, but there were others to consider and she loved them more than she loved herself, Hilton included. His plan was beyond her comprehension at this time.

"I need to ask you something. The first night when we met at the State Ball; did we meet by chance? Or, did you single me out, because of the Lyndhurst connection?"

"The latter, I must confess. The chances of us meeting by chance in that crush of bodies was nigh impossible," he admitted, with his arm tightening around her shoulders. "Then, I became ensnared. Now, I resemble a dingo caught in the squatter's trap, awaiting my ultimate fate. I'm pleading for a stay of execution . . . for at least fifty years. I'll be your devoted husband and servant for all of that time. I give you my solemn promise on that score."

His hand sought her chin while turning her face toward his own; then, looking directly at her, he searched for the answer that he was seeking.

"You're without fear. You dive in without thought where others dread to go, so I know if you love me, you'll come. Do you love me?" he questioned earnestly.

"If you were asking me to go to Adelaide, or to Tasmania, I'd leave in an instant with you, but to the other side of the earth and never to return, for the remainder of my life? It cannot be possible. Forget Sir Charles, for he wins always. Leave whatever is in the safe where it is and, I beg of you, please, consider other options, Phillip. This is happening too fast . . . too soon. We hardly know each other."

He shrugged his shoulders and shook his head slowly.

"What's there to know?" he murmured, gently moving his head towards her and kissing her lightly on the lips.

Louisa rested her head against his shoulder as she considered all that they had discussed while comprehending none of it. What he was proposing was impossible.

"I'm not asking for an answer now. I'll return in a few months but, at this stage, I can't give an exact date. I'll find you wherever you are."

Louisa moved from the protection of his arm slowly. Then, pulling the green scarf from her pocket, she climbed over the boulders and reached the tree while scaling it immediately. She tied the scarf to the branch again. Sliding down with ease, she returned to him as he watched her with a look of amusement on his face.

"If it's not in place when you return, then I'll be elsewhere. If it's here, then know I'm *in residence*," she explained with a laugh.

Phillip nodded in agreement. Giving a chuckle, he grinned at her in a challenging manner.

"Now, about our horse race! I've found the ideal location, *if you dare*."

"The race? Oh! I'd forgotten all about that. Alright . . . where?" she asked, while laughing softly as the tension eased a little within her.

"The racecourse at Flemington," he replied simply.

"Flemington!" Louisa, absolutely aghast, stammered while staring at him; then, throwing her head back, she began to laugh loudly. "Oh! That is daring!"

"Next Sunday . . . that's the one day when no one will be around. The Sunday Observance League will see to that. *And, I've searched* the whole place. I've found a side gate that can be forced. It is in a secluded place and wide enough for a horse to enter. Can you get away on that day?" Phillip asked, as he grinned at her in a maddening and challenging manner.

"It may be possible," she said, as she pondered on the possibility while her thoughts raced on frantically. "I go to my uncle's church every Sunday morning and it's quite near there, although I'd only have a ninety-minute window of opportunity, at the most. But, yes, it could be done. Yes, it just may be possible."

Louisa scrutinised him for a moment, after which she threw back her head and she tossed it to one side as her auburn hair came loose slightly from beneath her bonnet. The laughter bubbled up from within the deeper region of her person and she shook her head – partly in anticipation and partly in glee – as she surveyed Phillip.

"Oh! This is too much! Let me plan it out and meet me here tomorrow. Then, we can finalise all of this, just in case Charles decides to ride with me later in the week and we can't meet again. This is unbelievable. Certainly, life is never dull when you're around."

He was laughing with her and watching her closely as her eyes danced with excitement. Her infectious laughter permeated the area.

"You'd better be quiet, or your groom may come snooping. Come alone, Louisa, on Sunday, for it'll be our last day together for some months. We don't need any interruptions when we say goodbye."

Louisa shrugged her shoulders. He leaned over and kissed her again, this time finding the response, which he was seeking. Suddenly, she pulled away from him and she jumped to her feet.

"I must go, for I've stayed too long. Till tomorrow then, when we can plan this together. It'll be such fun!" she stated.

Phillip was sitting on the boulder. He was watching her and laughing as she danced down the slope to the bushes that hid their meeting place.

"Bye, Louisa," he called after her.

With a wave of her hand, she dived through the foliage and he was lost to her vision.

Nathaniel was standing by the tree where she had left him. He was holding the horses and frowning at her, seemingly troubled and, possibly, a little suspicious. Louisa mounted, instantly riding in the direction of the house. As it came in sight, she turned to him, but she was choosing her words carefully.

"Do you have special duties to perform on Sunday, Nathaniel?"

"Just the usual, ma'am," he replied casually.

"I may have need of your services mid-morning. Is that possible?"

Nathaniel, brought his horse level with Hilton and he was walking his horse beside her. He glanced over at her, with a trace of suspicion in his eyes.

"If *you* need me, I'll make m'self ready for whatever it is," he promised.

"Thank you. I appreciate that and I'll let you know well in advance."

On reaching the stable yard, she dismounted and walked from Nathaniel without another word.

Leaving the groom at the stables, Louisa returned to the house with much to consider, not the least being her feelings for Phillip Carstairs, which were thrilling her and frightening her, all at the same time.

His plans for their future together were so far-fetched as to belong in the realm of children's fairytales, so she gave them no more than a fleeting flicker of interest and scant consideration. There would be time in the future to consider his proposal, as he would not return from Sydney for several months. All that mattered now was the race and, for that, her secret weapon was Hilton.

Phillip had arrived in Sydney by ship, so his own horse was at his home there. Therefore, he would be relying on a borrowed animal while she possessed a magnificent, black stallion that could not be matched by any horse that Mr. Carstairs was likely to obtain in the foreseeable future.

After next Monday, life at Lyndhurst Park would become very dull indeed. This race would be a wonderful way to bring to a close these chaotic weeks that saw, firstly, her marriage to Charles Lyndhurst; then, secondly, the commencement of the Melbourne and Victorian part of the Royal Tour, with all its excitement and frivolity. She was aware that Prince Alfred and his party were planning to leave sometime during the first week of the New Year, bound for Sydney via Hobart where the Tasmanian leg of the Tour would commence.

For Louisa, the first Sunday of the incoming New Year of eighteen hundred and sixty-eight would be locked in her memory forever.

Chapter Twenty-One

– *Victorian Victorians* –

Louisa

Meticulously, Louisa planned the day. She dismissed Charlotte as she declared her intention of dressing herself in readiness for holy mass. If Charlotte was surprised, she did not give any indication. Then, when she was alone, Louisa changed into the old, collarless shirt and the boy's breeches that belonged formerly to one of the Marshall boys. She decided to wear a tight-fitting cotton and lace camisole beneath the shirt, because even though her breasts were small, she did not wish to draw any suspicious glances from curious bystanders on the journey between the rear of her uncle's church and the side entrance to the racecourse at Flemington.

As Charles rarely arrived home before lunch on a Sunday, she was confident that he would not cause a problem today, because he knew that she left for church early every Sunday morning. After depositing Louisa at the church gate, the carriage would drive on to collect him from wherever he happened to be and it would return him to Lyndhurst Park. It was then that the carriage would be sent back to the church to collect Louisa at the appointed hour. All of these long-standing arrangements were taken into consideration when she made her plans.

When Charlotte was leaving her room, Louisa directed her to go to Nathaniel immediately and to deliver to him a tapestry carry-bag, which contained her riding boots and other sundry items that she would require this day. She advised her maid that she would not be requiring her services again this morning. Louisa's faded, old muslin gown, which she had retrieved from her old bedroom at the Collins' home, was from her schooldays and was not as tight-fitting as her current gowns. It buttoned in the front and reached high at her neck. She slipped this over her outfit while knowing that she needed a gown, which she could pull over the boy's clothes and fasten herself when the race was over and she needed to return to the church to await the carriage. She had hidden the tam-o'-shanter in with the riding boots while laughing at the fact that, finally, she was able to wear this particular item, which was purchased for another adventure. Instead, it would be useful for this one today.

When she arrived at the church, she was early, thus avoiding a chance meeting with her uncle. This was one factor, which she could not control, so she breathed a sigh of relief when that eventuality did not occur. She walked quickly along the pathway alongside the church; then, she skirted the timber building at the rear, which was used for storage for the most part. After that, she walked briskly to a park area by the roadway and situated behind the buildings.

There, to her immense relief, Nathaniel was waiting with the horses. He glanced at her as she walked toward him. She retrieved the tapestry bag that he was carrying for her and she ordered him to await her return.

Hurriedly, Louisa returned to the storage shed and pushed the door open a little way to allow entry. Here, she removed her bonnet, gloves, reticule, shoes, gown and petticoat, after having dispensed with the crinoline, stays and stockings for today's activities. Then, she tied a piece of rope around her waist as a precautionary measure – although this was not necessary, she felt – because the breeches were quite tight on her hips and at her waist. She threw her shoes into the tapestry bag with the rest of her apparel and pulled on the riding boots. Lastly, she tightened the bow on her hair at the back and wound it above her head before fixing the tam-o'-shanter there to add the finishing touches to her disguise.

Satisfied that all was in readiness, Louisa walked boldly outside while carrying the bag. As she approached Nathaniel, he looked beyond her in the direction of the church yard. He was paying scant attention to the approaching figure of the young boy until she flung the tapestry bag into his arms, thereby startling him momentarily. He swung around, with fists at the ready and intent on attacking his assailant; then, he stopped still and he was staring at her face. His eyes travelled down her body to her feet and returned slowly back up to her face again. He shook his head in disbelief. Before he could speak, Louisa issued an order.

"Fix this to your saddle, Nathaniel, and let's be away!" Louisa directed, as she reached for Hilton's bridle.

"Ma'am!" he exclaimed, as he continued to stare at her.

"We're short on time. Hurry, and stay beside me until we reach the side gate of the racecourse."

Too stunned to argue, the groom brought his horse alongside Hilton and they kept a steady pace – not wanting to draw attention to themselves – although there were few carriages on the roadway and fewer people on the footpath on this Sunday morning.

Arriving at the side fence, Louisa found the entry point with ease and the gate was unlatched as it was swinging freely in the slight breeze. From this, she assumed that Phillip was already inside. Louisa dismounted and led Hilton through the opening, with Nathaniel coming in her wake and having not spoken a word to her at all.

Once inside, they found their way to the race track where, in the distance, she could see Phillip waiting. He was mounted already and speaking to someone who stood beside him on the grass. She slowed in her step momentarily before she re-mounted, but she was frowning as she did so. She was troubled at the sight of the man who was

Phillip's companion. She was worried by the stranger who Phillip seemed to have brought with him as she remembered his instruction to her to come alone. However, undaunted, she urged her horse forward while the groom followed closely behind her.

As they approached the rail surrounding the track, she gave Hilton a command and he sprang forward, galloped to the fence and cleared it with ease. Then, she allowed him to canter along the race track in the direction of her opponent on this day. Her headwear was dislodged with the jump and her long auburn hair was flying behind her as she pulled to a halt beside Phillip. Laughing, she looked over at him and she was amused to find him staring at her in amazement. His eyes took in her wild, flying hair, heightened colouring, dancing green eyes, the boy's apparel and, lastly, he concentrated his gaze on the horse that she was riding. Louisa was laughing at his apparent astonishment.

"Well, Mr. Carstairs, do you think you've met your match this day?"

"I've never seen the like of it in all my life!" he exclaimed, still shaking his head and laughing as he did so. "I can scarcely believe it! Louisa, you look such a sight. How're you?"

Louisa had not explained to Nathaniel the purpose of the excursion, but she supposed that by now he would have surmised the reason for their visit to Flemington Racecourse today. She looked over to where he waited and she realised that the groom had retrieved her headwear from the grass track. He was standing by the rail and holding his horse's reins in one hand and Louisa's tam-o'-shanter in the other. He was looking deeply troubled. She glanced down at the man standing beside Phillip's horse. Instantly, she knew that she did not particularly like him, or the way that his eyes were roving over her body. There was a supercilious grin on his face as he studied her brazenly.

"I'm wonderful, Phillip, and I trust you're fully recovered, so that you cannot use your recent injuries as an excuse for your loss today. Who is your friend?"

"This is Patrick who is here to act as starter and to declare the winner," he said; then, looking over toward the fence, he studied Nathaniel intently. "Is that your groom?"

"Yes, he's here to protect my interests," she stated, with a challenge in her eyes. "Where do we start and where is the finishing line?"

With an arm raised to avoid the sunlight shining in his eyes and squinting a little as he did so, Phillip studied their immediate surroundings; then, he moved his hand as he pointed to various points on the race track. After much discussion, they decided the finer points of the competition between them. Then, without further ado, they rode slowly and side-by-side toward the starting marker that had been chosen.

They were both laughing as they reached it while Patrick walked slowly along the track behind them, obviously heading in the same direction. Nathaniel kept pace with them across the track, but on the other side of the rail. Louisa studied the horse that Phillip was riding and she knew already the result of their race – for this was never in question in her mind – but the confirmation, which she needed was the sight of the small bay mare that he was riding.

"Is that your husband's horse?" Phillip queried as he studied Hilton.

"Of course not; I've raised him since birth. He's all mine!"

"Then, let us see what he can do, shall we, Louisa? Or, should I address you as *Louis* today?"

Laughing appreciatively, Louisa threw her head back and the infectious sound travelled far. She looked down on her fellow competitor with disdain.

"You shan't call me anything. Your mouth will be so full as you choke on my dust, it'll be impossible for you to do so," she stated emphatically and still laughing.

Patrick stood against the inside rail and he raised his right arm in the air while he held a white handkerchief above his head. Nathaniel positioned himself against the outside rail, directly opposite Patrick, while he watched both men suspiciously and warily. Phillip was studying Louisa, with a look of amusement registering on his face. Louisa, without a thought for her own safety – or, to the precarious position, in which she had placed herself so willingly this day – settled down to ride the race of her life.

Hilton, feverish with excitement already, seemed very conscious of his mistress' heightened state at this time. Both horses, as with their riders, awaited – in eager anticipation – the fall of the starter's arm.

Sylvia

Sylvia awoke from a troubled sleep and found that she was wrapped tightly in Charles' arms. He had arrived late on the previous evening, after having dined first at his club; then, after a few drinks together in the sitting room, they came to bed. Not wishing to spoil their precious time together, she did not mention the disturbing information that she had managed to glean, during dinner earlier in the evening, from her brother. Patrick had returned from Castlemaine some days earlier, after having argued with his mother, as Sylvia had predicted that he would.

What did surprise her was that he had stayed there as long as he had. However, he had been reticent about his friendship with Phillip Carstairs since his return, but the wine that he consumed during dinner on the previous evening, loosened his tongue a little, especially with regard to Sir Charles Lyndhurst's violent attack on his close friend. He made several dire predictions on the fate of that particular coward when Patrick came face-to-face with him.

After this tirade, he began to laugh quite loudly while he detailed plans of a certain horse race that was about to take place, and which would be certain to wipe the smug sneer from Sir Charles' face, after the scandal became public knowledge. When Patrick changed the subject, Sylvia refilled his glass quickly; then, she brought the topic back to the race and she discovered finally – and with much prodding and prompting – its location and scheduled date.

Sylvia allowed Patrick to ramble on about his visit to Castlemaine and his mother's intransigence over his proposal to take control of the hotel for her. Subtly, she brought the subject back to the horse race, but she was unable to glean the names of the proposed participants in the event. She felt that she knew. If she was correct in her assumption, as outlandish as it was, should she intervene, she questioned herself. If she was incorrect, Charles would not take too kindly to her perceived interference and the false accusations, which she was making about his wife. But, could she risk not advising him of her suspicions, she pondered gravely to herself, especially when her own brother was involved in the scheme.

"You're damned either way, Sylvia," she murmured to herself.

"What's that?" Charles asked, somewhat drowsily.

Quickly, she slipped from the bed and she was reaching for her dressing gown before replying.

"I'm going down to arrange breakfast on the terrace. I wish you to join me, so can you stay for an extra hour?"

He raised his head, studied her, frowned deeply and allowed his head to flop heavily back onto the pillow. She watched him for a moment. He placed a hand to his head and gave a loud, mock groan of pain.

"Yes, I can stay an hour. I've hardly been home this past week, so what's another hour or two? Am I correct in supposing we drank more wine after I arrived here last night? My head is telling me that, most assuredly, I did! Anyway, you can't go downstairs like that at this hour. You're not decent. Come back to bed now!"

Without replying, Sylvia opened the adjoining door leading into the bedroom that Edwin had occupied once and which doubled now as her dressing room. It was some time before she returned – fully dressed and ready for the day's activities – to her own bedroom, only to find Charles in a deep sleep once again. She sat on the bed and shook him none-too-gently as she endeavoured to rouse him to consciousness.

"Wake up, Charles. I must speak with you."

He opened one eye, groaned loudly and promptly closed it again.

"Go away, Sylvia. If you're not going to join me, then leave me be for another hour or two. Have a heart, please."

"No. This is urgent and cannot wait. I'm not even certain I should reveal the information to you, but if it's as I suspect, you won't thank me for withholding it. Come downstairs now."

Sylvia left the room immediately and she was seated in her sitting room when he entered some time later. He was partially dressed, she noted. She moved to the terrace to partake of the early breakfast that she had ordered while knowing he would follow her. She did not want their conversation to be overheard and being out-of-doors was the safest way to ensure that this would not occur.

Charles sat down on the chair opposite her and he eyed the food with much distaste. His shirt was unfastened at the top and was minus the necktie – although he had managed to wriggle into his waistcoat, which was unbuttoned, also – while his general appearance was one of dishevelment. He scowled at her.

"I'd never taken you to be a cruel woman . . . well, not before today. There'd better be a good explanation for this rude awakening."

Sylvia sipped the hot tea in silence as she acknowledged to herself that she was suffering somewhat as a result of the alcohol, which she had consumed during the previous evening and she would have much preferred to remain in bed with Charles for another few hours. However, her conscience had demanded otherwise. His eyes were awaiting her explanation, but she simply raised an eyebrow in query.

"I informed you last night that my brother returned from Castlemaine a few days ago. Do you remember?"

"As unbelievable as this may sound, I can honestly state to you that it's not uppermost in my mind, at present. But, if you say you told me so, I accept that. Is it important?" he queried, while reaching for a cup of hot, black tea as he spoke.

"Possibly."

Sylvia sat quietly as she drank the hot beverage intermittently while frowning markedly. She was at a loss to know how to begin this troubling discourse, but finally, she decided that all she could do was to outline – word-for-word – the plans, which Patrick had made for today, with his friend, Phillip Carstairs. Then, she would allow Charles to fill in the missing gaps for himself and to arrive at his own conclusions.

Patrick had been very drunk by the end of the night and, in all probability, he did not realise this morning that he had revealed as much as he had to his sister. He staggered up to bed long before Charles' arrival and, when Sylvia checked his room before descending the stairs now, she realised that he had left already for his excursion to Flemington.

"Patrick left my house early this morning to go to the race track at Flemington where he proposes to break in through a side gate and assist his friend . . . a young gentleman of your slight acquaintance . . . who, it would seem, has challenged an unidentified, young lady to race her horse against his own. I was wondering if you'd heard anything of such a wager; or, if you're aware of the identity of the lady-in-question?"

Charles spilled the tea on his trousers as he jumped instantly to his feet. He was brushing the hot liquid from his leg with his right hand while placing the cup on a lopsided angle onto the saucer with his left hand. Then, he turned to stare at her. Unruffled, she returned his stunned gaze, before continuing with her explanation.

"If I didn't mention this to you and the lady turned out to be someone of your close acquaintance, you wouldn't be very happy with me. But, perhaps, you knew already and you were willing to let events take their own course, thereby giving you an excuse for your proposed annulment? If I speak out-of-turn here, feel free to say so . . . *as I've no doubt you will*," Sylvia stated calmly.

"Sylvia! You can't be serious!" he stammered, with astonishment that was bordering on outrage registering on his face. "Louisa attends church every Sunday, if that's who you're alluding to. Her uncle is the parish priest and she wouldn't dare to cross him by not attending mass. My carriage would have left her there . . . well, about now, in all probability. Then, it will come on here to collect me. No, *even she* wouldn't dare . . . I don't believe it!"

"I apologise then. I shouldn't have mentioned the matter, Charles. Forgive me for doubting your wife."

He was silent, obviously lost deep in thought and deeply troubled, if the frown on his brow was any indication of his emotional state. His hand moved to sweep back the hair from his forehead as he continued to stand by the chair and he was watching her, but with eyes that were not seeing Sylvia. She surveyed him in silence. Suddenly, he moved swiftly.

"Lend me a carriage *now, Sylvia! And, do not* mention this information to anyone. Send mine immediately back to the church when it arrives here. Direct them to wait by the front gate until they hear from me. Quickly!"

He was crossing the sitting room already and, by the time she reached the vestibule, he was running up the internal stairs. Sylvia issued the instructions and was by the front door when Charles, with his coat and other sundry apparel over his arm – while adjusting his watch and chain in the fob pocket of his waistcoat – came rushing down the stairs and out through the front door. She walked over to stand beside him as they awaited the arrival of her carriage.

"You're going, just in case it is so?" Sylvia queried softly.

"The church I mentioned is but a stone's throw from the race track. That's my concern. I must be wrong," Charles murmured, without much conviction. "If not, then this truly is beyond the pale!"

As her carriage slowed by the front door, he ran forward while wrenching open the door himself and shouting instructions as he jumped inside, and not looking around to acknowledge Sylvia's presence at all. His face was white with rage as he left her, she noticed, and the disbelief, which he had expressed to her on the terrace, appeared to have changed to a dread of what he would discover at the racecourse. As well, registering there was a firm determination to redress the situation.

It was a pensive Sylvia who walked slowly into the house and she was castigating herself severely for revealing the information. She was wondering if, perhaps, it may have been wiser to err on the side of caution, thus staying well away from the whole affair. However, whatever affected Charles Lyndhurst had a nasty habit of striking at Sylvia as well, and she did not need any more nasty surprises this day – or, any other day – in the foreseeable future.

For Sylvia, her day that had started so badly became much worse by mid-morning when one of the nurses who was caring for Edwin, summonsed her to his bedroom. She revealed that her patient appeared to have slipped into a deep sleep during the night and she was unable to rouse him. His breathing was laboured and there was a definite rattle in his chest.

She knew that sound all too well, as did the nurse, although neither one acknowledged the fact to the other. It was an unspoken acceptance that descended upon the two women as they waited by his bedside for the arrival of the doctor. Before doing so, Sylvia had sent a messenger around to Bertie's home. In the missive, she requested his immediate presence. If he was at home when the message arrived, he would come instantly, she knew. There was nothing more to be done other than to wait patiently and to make certain that the patient was as comfortable as possible.

Sylvia felt a numbness creeping over her and this sensation was mingled with a sense of foreboding. Whether these feelings were on account of her husband and his current condition, her lover and his current dilemma or, it was a sense that, once again, she was a silent player in this game that fate played in her life – and, in the lives of those whom she loved. She twisted the wedding band around and around on her finger as the silence around the two women became deathly.

The doctor and Bertie arrived simultaneously. They were escorted to Edwin Webster's bedside, there to await an outcome that appeared all too obvious to all concerned, on this first Sunday of the New Year.

Chapter Twenty-Two

– Victorian Victorians –

Louisa

W ith thundering hooves and flying manes, the two horses raced neck-and-neck around the race track while keeping level with each other for two-thirds of the distance. It was at this moment that Louisa looked over at her rival and she bestowed upon him a mischievous grin. Leaning slightly forward in the saddle, she gave to Hilton the signal, for which he had been waiting, thereby giving him his head totally.

From then onwards, there was no contest – or race either, for that matter – because Phillip's horse, along with its somewhat rueful rider, was left so far in their wake that they appeared to be standing still on some distant horizon while being but casual observers to the rapid progress of the large, black stallion and the girl with the long, auburn hair flying behind her.

Jubilant, Louisa continued on her way until well beyond the finishing line. There, she brought Hilton to a canter and she turned him before retracing his steps as Phillip came up beside her. She threw back her head as she laughed in triumph and she hid none of the delight that she felt at being the victor this day. He came to her, with a grin on his face.

"We won! We won!" Louisa shouted, carelessly throwing her head back and laughing once again as her hair, in a dishevelled state, fell about her shoulders, with the ribbon but loosely tied.

"I concede," he admitted ruefully. "Although on an animal such as that, only a fool could lose. I knew I'd lost the minute I set eyes on him."

They were both somewhat breathless following the ride, so they rode side-by-side in silence, with the horses proceeding at a gentle canter back toward the starting line where the other two men should have been waiting. Patrick, however, was hurrying away from them. He was heading at what seemed to be a fast pace toward his horse, which was tethered some distance away near the grandstand, while Nathaniel remained at the place where he was standing when the race commenced. He was concentrating his attention on them and he did not appear to have noticed the figure of a man standing some distance behind him. The new arrival stood with arms akimbo while watching intently the two carefree riders on the track.

The appearance of the new arrival was dishevelled, with his white shirt open at the neck, his hair unruly, his waistcoat unbuttoned and he was devoid of coat and hat. Never had Louisa seen the usually immaculately-clad Charles Lyndhurst in a public place in a state such as this. The last time that Louisa had witnessed him in this particular stance was on the day when she had ridden back to the house after her first wild ride on Hilton at Lyndhurst Park. On that occasion, he had stood on the lawn by the front corner of the house – with arms akimbo, also – and with anger showing on his countenance. Whether or not there was anger on his countenance now, Louisa could not tell, because the distance between them was great at this moment. But, there was no doubt from his stance that rage was not far beneath the surface of his being. Phillip's eyes followed Louisa's stunned gaze and he gave an audible gasp as he stiffened noticeably.

"How the hell did he know?" he asked, with a definite gasp.

"I don't know," she murmured slowly; then, she concluded with a prediction. "But, I do not think I'm going to enjoy the next few hours. Leave now, Phillip, while you can. There'll be no reasoning with him, believe me!"

Phillip looked from Louisa to her irate husband and back again while frowning deeply. He was shaking his head slowly and deliberately.

"It'll only make it worse for me, if you stay. Go right now!" Louisa stated, with pleading in her tone.

"I don't want to leave you in his clutches. Come with me now. We can leave here together. I'll take you to Sydney with me tomorrow and hide you there, until we can make good our escape. Please, Louisa, come now. We can be away before he realises what is occurring," he asked, with his hand on her arm as he begged her to agree to his hastily though ill-conceived plan.

Louisa looked at him and shook her head slowly. His face was a mixture of disappointment and relief all rolled in together. They had stopped the horses in the middle of the track now. Louisa reached down and she was stroking Hilton's neck as she watched Charles striding toward the rail at a fast pace. In that moment, Nathaniel turned his head to see what was holding their undivided attention behind him. In this moment, he stared at his employer in some astonishment, which was mixed with not-a-little trepidation, Louisa observed.

"I'm no coward and I'll not run from him, nor from what's coming. Go now!" Louisa commanded.

"Very well," Phillip replied.

He appeared to be reassessing the situation, in which he found himself; then, deciding, perhaps, that retreat was the better part of valour, he agreed to her request.

"Since it's important to you, I'll do so. But, with great reluctance, do I *leave you* to *him* . . . remember that! *And, be ready* for me, because I'll be back for you in a few months."

"Should I live as long as that!" Louisa stated, with a soft groan; then, grabbing Phillip's arm, she implored him. "Kiss me now, before you go."

Phillip glanced over at Charles who ignored Nathaniel completely as he jumped the rail in one stride – as though it were not there at all – and who was descending on them now, at a rapid rate. Phillip looked at her in surprise. Then, he grinned as he leaned over to do her bidding. He gave a soft laugh.

"You don't half like living life dangerously, Louisa!"

"In for a penny, in for a pound," she muttered, with her lips reaching for his not-so-reluctant ones.

He kissed her – albeit briefly – before he urged his horse away from her while riding quickly in the direction of his waiting and anxious side-kick, Patrick. Louisa, with defiance showing in every movement of her slender body that was clothed in boy's raiment, sat waiting for her husband to reach her while Hilton, sensing danger, moved with some restlessness beneath her. She held him firmly and he settled a little. As Charles reached horse and rider, Phillip reached his friend. Then, with one, quick, backward glance and a slight wave of his hand, he rode away beside Patrick. They were out of sight before Charles' hand grasped Hilton's rein.

"Get down!" he ordered.

"And, if I don't?"

Charles did not reply. He turned his head abruptly. Looking directly across at Nathaniel and with one of those imperceptible flicks of his head that his servants knew well, he gave a silent order. The groom responded instantly while running across the track to them.

"Where are Mrs. Lyndhurst's belongings?" he demanded.

Nathaniel, without looking up at Louisa, explained the whereabouts of the apparel, of which he was inquiring. Charles commanded the bag to be left by the rail while ordering the groom to go immediately to the side gate and to send the carriage that was waiting there back to its owner. After that, he was to ride over to the front gate of the church and, once there, he was to await the arrival of Charles' own carriage. He was to lead it back here to the side gate. Then, Nathaniel was to return immediately to Lyndhurst Park with Hilton and he was to tell no one of this day's exploits.

These directives were delivered in such a harsh, demanding tone that to disobey or to question such instructions would have seemed to be taking one's life in one's hands. Nathaniel left them hurriedly, without daring to look back at them.

Charles remained perfectly still and he held Hilton firmly. Louisa sat astride her horse, defiant in defeat. He waited until the groom had carried out his instructions and disappeared from sight before he strode toward the rail. He was leading the horse with its reluctant rider atop. He tethered Hilton to the rail before he looked up at her.

"Do I drag you down?" he queried.

Louisa shrugged her shoulders nonchalantly and, in complete acceptance of her fate, she slid from the saddle. She stepped onto the rail where she balanced deliberately for a moment; then, she jumped down onto the grass on the other side. Charles climbed over the barrier fence in one, swift movement and he landed beside the bag containing her clothing. Louisa, in a disinterested manner, watched as he pulled the garments from the carry-bag. He began to throw them unceremoniously over her body. Firstly, the voluminous petticoat came over her head and it settled into place about her waist, followed closely by the old muslin gown, which, after turning her roughly, he began to fasten at the front. She pushed his hands away and buttoned the gown herself. Secondly, he placed the bonnet on her head, after securely tying her hair with the ribbon and attempting to tidy it beneath the straw and lace headpiece, which was somewhat askew at present. Thirdly, he produced her gloves and reticule, which he tossed at her.

"Now, the boots, *madam!*"

Louisa promptly sank to the ground and she pulled off her riding boots as he reached into the tapestry bag. He threw her shoes at her. These items landed beside her on the grass and she slid her bare feet into them. Two hands reached down and, grasping her waist, stood her unceremoniously onto her feet. While she may not have appeared as fashionably attired as on other occasions, she was at least almost respectable in her husband's cold and angry eyes. One hand came down behind her and, somewhat roughly, dusted the grass and dirt from the back of her skirt. Still, Louisa did not speak to him. Charles threw her boots into the bag and moved to attach it to Hilton's saddle while Louisa stroked her horse as she spoke softly to him.

"He can't be left here like this, without water in the hot sun . . . not after that ride," she stated loudly and harshly.

"You should've thought of that," he replied; then, with a voice dripping with sarcasm, he hissed his next words at her. "After all, you thought of everything else!"

He stepped over the fence again, untethered Hilton and began walking along the track while leading the horse away from her.

"Wait there and don't move one inch!" he commanded.

Louisa watched as he walked to the area on the other side of the grandstand. Then, both of them disappeared from her sight. Not having any intention of following his last directive, Louisa moved to a shaded area by a bush where she threw herself down onto the grass and she was reclining on her back in the shade while looking up at the sky when Charles returned to her some ten minutes later.

She was considering her current position from all angles and she was of the opinion that she possessed little bargain power under these circumstances. She sat up and looked at him with disdain. His rage, thinly concealed, had subsided little, she observed, as he stood above her, surveying her. Nathaniel's return interrupted any verbal exchange that was threatening between them and Charles left her to speak to him.

She watched as Charles pointed in the direction where she had seen him lead Hilton and the groom, with downcast eyes, went immediately to retrieve her horse. Louisa, not wishing to be hauled to her feet again, stood and began walking alone toward the side gate. Then, Charles was beside her in an instant, with his hand fastening around her arm in an extremely tight grip. He pulled her along at his pace until they reached the gate where, without letting go of her arm, he pushed her through and he followed instantly. The footman was holding the door open as they approached the carriage and Charles assisted her inside before flinging himself in beside her on the seat. The carriage moved off, obviously heading for his home at Lyndhurst Park. Not one word was spoken between them on the return journey.

Louisa's feet barely scuffed the surface of the carpeted internal stairs as she was propelled upstairs at a fast pace. Charles flung open her bedroom door, almost flinging her inside with the same movement. She wrenched her arm from him and she moved to the end of the bed where she positioned herself behind the frame of the brass bed-end. He slammed the door shut and he stared at her. He was shaking his head at her, with a look of disbelief and amazement all rolled into the one glance that spoke almost of despair.

"Give them to me," he ordered, as he hurled the words at her.

"What?" she demanded.

"Don't play coy with me! The boy's breeches and shirt . . . now, *Madam!*"

Louisa did not move. He watched her, with his eyes daring her to defy him. When she did not obey his directive immediately, he took a step forward, with menacing intent, and obviously deciding to remove them himself.

"Alright," she muttered, while beginning to unfasten the gown slowly – very slowly indeed – for there were many buttons.

With growing impatience, he watched her performance that no stage actress could have bettered. With a defiant flick of her chin and her head held high, she allowed the gown to fall to the floor before stepping deftly aside and out of the garment. Standing on one leg, she removed one shoe; then, very slowly moving to the other leg, she discarded the other shoe. Moving closer to the wardrobe in order to place more distance between herself and her husband, she discarded the petticoat. Louisa sidled to the other side of the bed and removed the shirt before throwing it onto the bed.

Charles stepped quickly from his position by the closed door towards her bed where he pounced on it; then, before her somewhat startled gaze, he began shredding the garment while his eyes continued to watch her across the bed. Her fingers fumbled with the rope belt at her waist as she stood there while wearing only the breeches and the cotton camisole. She allowed the rope to drop to the floor at her feet as she pondered her next problem. All of her undergarments were knee-length and these were made of cotton and flounced with many layers of lace. These did not fit well beneath the boy's breeches, so she had not bothered to wear them on the occasion of the race while feeling as she did that there would be no need for such items beneath her apparel this day. She studied Charles and considered her current position extremely carefully and very thoughtfully.

With the shirt shredded completely, he turned his attention back to her and he noted her hesitancy.

"Shall I do the rest?" he queried.

"No!"

"Then?" he queried.

"I . . . umm . . . I don't have anything underneath," she muttered, almost inaudibly.

Thoughtfully, he surveyed her, with his next move being considered very carefully indeed. Finally, with great forbearance, he appeared to come to a decision. Slowly and deliberately, he turned toward the door to the corridor.

"I'll be in my office. Have them on my desk in under five minutes . . . *or, else!*" he hurled the angry words at her as he turned to leave.

"Or else what?" Louisa demanded, instantly feeling that she had won this round of the fight.

He looked back at her with dislike and disgust registering on his face. Louisa, defiance obvious in her every move, challenged him openly with every movement of her body. Charles turned his head quickly to study her.

"I'll shoot your horse," he promised, while speaking very quietly and clearly.

Louisa gave an audible gasp. But, afterwards, she was unable to recall how the lead-crystal clock with the black and white face had managed, of its own accord, to jump into her hands. However, this seemed to be how it occurred. This heavy object, somehow being in her hands, then hurled itself across the room and in the direction of the opposite wall. It was never her intention to actually strike anyone, although Charles' head was but inches from her intended target.

He glanced sideways at this precise moment – perhaps sensing the sudden movement to his right – and he took evasive action. Unfortunately for him, he moved in the wrong direction and the flying missile caught him a glancing blow on the forehead as it headed for the wall. Rage overtook him. This was an instant reaction. Shards of crystal flew through the air as the light, which was filtering through the open verandah doors, caught their movement; then, these splintered when hitting the floor while several errant pieces landed on the top of the quilt on Louisa's bed.

A flash of lightning has never flown faster than Charles Lyndhurst did on this day. His hand moved and, with a flick of his wrist, he turned the key in the lock of the door to the corridor. Instantly, he was at the end of the bed, with his arms reaching for her and seemingly before the remnants of the clock had settled on the highly polished timber floor by the door to the corridor, although his shoes were crunching on lead-crystal pieces as he rushed towards Louisa.

Belatedly coming to her senses, Louisa jumped back, quickly avoiding his outstretched hands and observing, as she did so, the blood that was streaming down his cheek from the open wound on his forehead.

She dived to the floor and she was sliding under the bed before he realised her intention. With bare feet, she was prepared to brave the crystal shards on the floor, rather than to allow herself to be in the clutches of a husband filled with rage and intent on revenge. Allowing triumph to surface momentarily, she was almost out the other side when she felt an iron-like grip on her ankle. Her body shuddered to an abrupt halt beneath her bed. *Vulnerable* did not really describe the position, in which Louisa found herself at this precise moment.

Immediately, Charles' head appeared under the bed and she felt herself being flipped over on her back, as deftly as an egg was flipped in a frying pan. His hands dragged her body towards him and out the other side of the bed. She felt them grasp the camisole, which was ripped from top to bottom; then, it was removed in an instant. With his body pressing against her own, she was pinned and unable to move from him while her head remained partially beneath the bed.

"No!" she screamed at him.

In an instant, the breeches were gone and his body was on top of her. Louisa struggled beneath him as she wriggled her body help-lessly and knowing that she was trapped completely.

"No ... don't do this! Not in anger!" she pleaded.

"You're not in a position to bargain."

Immediately, Louisa fixed her gaze on the curled wire of the mattress frame above her head. Beyond that, she noted, was the underside of the kapok mattress. What she did not look at was the partially-clothed male who was struggling with her and attempting to remove his own clothing while trying to prevent her escape, which was impossible at this stage anyway. Had his shirt not been covering his shoulder still, she would have sunk her teeth into this part of his body, but her mouth was nowhere near his bare skin. Suddenly, he moved her legs apart with one, rough movement and he positioned himself between her thighs. Involuntarily, a stifled scream escaped her as he entered her with a force that would have sent her head through the wall had she been close to it. In her ear, his violently-muttered words reverberated through her mind.

"*So! I am* the first!"

Louisa studied the kapok mattress in minute detail as the movement of his body, fierce and forceful, continued to gyrate above her and within her. She did not respond to him, she felt, for she was too detached to do so. She had moved beyond fear, beyond stunned, and she had reached a state of total detachment while she wondered if he realised whose body it was beneath him, so great was his rage.

At this precise moment, a quite amazing event occurred. Louisa found that she moved beyond her physical body. She was standing by the bed while watching in a quite disinterested manner, the couple on the floor. How long she remained in this trance-like state, she knew not really; but, it was then, with his rage placated and his energy-force spent, he collapsed on top of her. It was his words, which were spoken with at least a touch of venom that brought her back to her current reality and to her physical body with a distinct shudder.

"Consider this marriage consummated!" he hissed in her ear.

Still, some minutes seemed to pass before he removed himself from her and he moved beside her. Louisa did not speak. She did not move. She did not cry. She did not tremble. She remained perfectly still. She stared at the wire mattress base as she traced the curling rolls of twirled wire with vacant eyes, as though this were the most important occupation, in which she needed to be engaged at present.

Slowly, he raised himself from the floor by her bed. He stood up and, from her vantage point with her head still under the bed, she observed the movement of his two legs as he sought to reclaim and readjust his clothing. Finally, he reached for his shoes and these, he placed onto his feet as he leaned on her bed. Still, Louisa did not move and she did not speak. She was frozen and without feeling or emotion of any description.

Louisa saw Charles' hand move as he flung back the covers on her bed. Pieces of the lead-crystal clock hit the floor, quietly tingling as they did so. His two hands reached down, one taking a hold of her arm and the other one reaching for her leg as he dragged her naked body from its hiding place. He lifted her in his arms and he tossed her onto the bed, as deftly as a merchant at the markets would toss a sack of potatoes; then, he reached for the bedcovers and threw them back over her body. Reaching for the boy's breeches and the remnants of the tattered shirt, he picked up these items and he walked resolutely toward the door to his own bedroom. He disappeared through the connecting door and he closed it quietly behind him.

Louisa remained still, exactly where she had landed. How long she remained in that position, as far as time was concerned, was debatable. But, it was when the trembling began in earnest that she came to the realisation of the enormity of the attack, which she had endured. That the trembling became progressively more pronounced was obvious, and she wrapped the bedding around her body more tightly as she endeavoured to seek warmth while she curled herself into the foetal position to seek solace.

It was some time before she could move from the bed. When she did so, she studied the blood on her inner thigh and she frowned at the sight. As she moved by the mirror, she noticed blood on her face. It was then she came to the conclusion that the blood on her thigh must have been her own, and that on her face would have seeped from the face, which belonged to her attacker.

In a completely detached state, Louisa went behind the screen and commenced toiletries of a minor nature before slipping into her dressing gown and reaching for the bell-pull to summon Charlotte. She slid her feet into her slippers, as protection from the remains of the clock, and she gave the room a cursory glance before ringing for her maid. Other than the damage to the clock, there were few visible signs of the recent violence that occurred within these walls. Unlocking the door, Louisa reached down and picked up the body of the clock, and in particular, its black and white face. The hands were frozen at ten minutes past the hour of midday. That was a moment to remember, Louisa concluded.

When Charlotte appeared, Louisa ordered her to draw a bath. Had she been in a more stable frame-of-mind herself, she may have noticed the strange expression on the girl's face. However, this day, Louisa was not as observant as usual, so her maid's problems went unnoticed as Charlotte headed in the direction of the bathroom. Louisa soaked in the bath for some time before returning to her room to dress.

Charlotte was waiting and the room was swept clean of all reminders of the violence of an hour earlier. The bed was re-made and the floor was spotlessly clean. As Charlotte attended to Louisa's hair, Louisa glanced at her through the mirror and she noticed tears streaming down her face. How was it possible to cry, she pondered, for this was not something that Louisa could remember experiencing in a long, long time. Suddenly, aware of the girl's obvious distress, she came to her senses and inquired about the cause.

"It's Nathaniel, ma'am. He's been dismissed without references. *And, he won't tell me why,* or anyone else, what's happened. I can't believe I won't see him again, for he's got thirty minutes to leave the property and he has nowhere to go," the girl completed the explanation with a loud sob.

Louisa spun around and she stared at her while surveying her distressed maid until her words penetrated her consciousness fully.

After that, she jumped up from the stool in front of the mirror while upending the seat completely and almost pushing Charlotte over in her haste to redress this terrible situation, which was of her making.

"Nathaniel! Dismissed? The devil he is! It'll be over my dead body!" Louisa shouted at Charlotte.

So shouting, she rushed from the room, descended the stairs at a frantic pace and she burst into Charles' office. She flung the door open as he had done to her bedroom door an hour earlier. Hugh Travis was not at his desk and Charles was alone. He was standing by the french doors and leaning against the door jamb. He turned slowly to survey her in a mildly-surprised manner as she slammed the door forcefully behind her. He was immaculately attired – as usual – but, with the wound above his eye obvious.

"What the hell have you done to Nathaniel?"

"That is none of your business," he replied slowly, calmly and very deliberately.

"It most certainly is. You reinstate him now! And, to his former position . . . "

"Or, you'll what?" he inquired, with a maddening calmness in his tone.

Louisa looked beyond the open doors to the river beyond the trees. She had no idea what she could do, but she uttered the first words that shot into her mind as she moved to his desk. She placed her two hands on it for support while she felt her anger turning to rage – a cold, white rage that frightened her when it appeared suddenly, as if from nowhere.

". . . *Or*, I shall drown myself in that river!" Louisa finished the sentence with this threat.

"Don't be absurd," he stated, with obvious disinterest sounding in his voice at what he saw as her idle threat.

"What? Do you think I'd not do so? Do you honestly think that, after what has just occurred, I wouldn't find drowning a more palatable prospect than life with you?" she shouted at him.

He reacted more violently than she expected, for she did not think that he would take her seriously. He turned abruptly and placed his two hands on the desk. They faced each other across that item of furniture. Anger was visible on his face. There was a mask covering Louisa's face. Had he known her better, he would have recognised this sign as a very dangerous signal. Her seething rage from the violent attack was beginning to surface and he was in her line-of-sight.

"I call your bluff now! You couldn't drown if you wanted to, for you can swim like a fish. I've seen you. The first time I set eyes on you, you were in the water . . . and stark naked!" he challenged her.

"That's a lie!"

"Oh! Is it? On the Murray River . . . one morning in September. *And, I was not* the only one viewing you. Evidently, your fame had spread. I doubt there's a riverboat man plying those waters between Echuca and Swan Hill who hasn't seen you in that state," he shouted at her across the desk.

"You're a bare-faced liar! It is never so!"

"*The mermaid!* That's what they called you. Did you know that?" Charles exclaimed; then, he remarked. "How you remained untouched till now is nothing short of miraculous."

"The riverboat men have more decency than you!" she exclaimed.

"Or, perhaps, more common sense than to try to grab a tiger by the tail," he muttered, slowly shaking his head at his own folly.

"Then," she asked, through clenched teeth. "Why did you marry me and bring me to this prison?"

"For thirty pieces of silver . . . and it was the worst deal I ever made!"

Louisa eyed him coldly. Finally, she lifted one foot onto his desk and she removed the shoe, before replacing her foot back onto the floor. Calmly, she lifted the other foot and she removed that shoe, also; then, she placed the shoes side-by-side in the centre of his desk while standing in her stockinged feet. With growing suspicion, he watched her.

"Then, you can take my lifeless body back to whomsoever made the payment to you. I'll show you how easy it is to drown myself, Mr. Lyndhurst, for when I'm going down for the third time, I'll see your face and recall what you did to me this day. Then, nothing on earth would make me want to resurface!"

In stockinged feet, she moved toward the open double doors. His arms reached for her once again, but she was ready for him, quickly ducking away and deftly slipping beneath his grasping hands.

"Do it then, and I'll come in after you. You can watch me drown with you."

Louisa gave a somewhat harsh laugh as she reached the railing alongside the covered walkway in front of the house. He was beside her in an instant and he grasped both of her wrists. He pulled her back into the office with him.

"Oh! More violence? Is that it? You can't keep me here forever against my will. One day, I'll be gone and you'll never find me," Louisa shouted at him.

"Wherever you go with Carstairs, I'll find you and bring you back. He'll discard you the first chance he gets. I trust you realise that? Everything is just a wager to him."

Louisa pulled her hands from his grasp; then, as he moved his hand to brush the hair from his forehead, she took the opportunity to remove herself from his reach and to position herself on the other side of his desk. He gave a deep sigh while watching her closely as he attempted to ascertain her next move.

"You've no idea the danger you placed yourself in today when you put yourself into *his clutches*, and those of Patrick Doherty."

"He'd have done worse than you? Is that what you're saying? I doubt that very much. It wouldn't have been accompanied by violence. This much I do know," she stated emphatically.

He looked down at her and grimaced, with one eyebrow raised and a supercilious expression on his face.

"Is this because you'd have given yourself to him freely?" he asked quietly, but with a tinge of sarcasm sounding in his voice.

'I'd give myself freely to no man. He knew there was a dagger waiting for him, if he so much as tried! He has never once made a move towards me while that remained between us . . . *and, it was there always!* If there was a wager, it would've been on the race, which I won, by the way."

"You've been hard pressed not to on Hilton," he muttered.

"Who you were going to shoot!"

"I could no more put a gun to the head of that magnificent creature than I could to my own," he admitted softly.

Suddenly, Charles walked across the room and he brushed by her as he did so. He opened the door of his office. He shouted for Benson, who materialised at a moment's notice.

"Tell Nathaniel he's reinstated. I want him here, in my office, at eight o'clock sharp tomorrow morning!"

So saying, Charles closed the door.

"Will that avert a drowning for the moment, Louisa?" he asked quietly.

She looked over at him with distaste, dislike and disgust. She did not deign to answer his question.

"This is just a cat-and-mouse game to you. You don't want me here, but it is good sport to tease me and taunt me. I'll not play the part of the mouse for any man," Louisa stated angrily.

He stood between Louisa and the door. He was looking closely at her, as if he were undecided on what to say or to do next. Finally, he shook his head slowly, as though coming to a decision.

"When you charged in here, resembling a wounded bull on the rampage, I was on the verge of re-instating the groom, having given him time to reflect on where his duty lies. Then, I was planning on crawling up those stairs to apologise to you."

Stunned, she stared at him, for the last words, which she expected to hear coming from Charles Lyndhurst's lips were those of a sincere apology. His face spoke of remorse and sincerity.

"There's nothing at all you can say to me that I haven't said to myself already," Charles stated matter-of-factly.

He raised his hand to his forehead again. He was brushing away the hair that was resting there and pursing his lips as he did so, before continuing with his explanation. The wound on his forehead opened further at his slight touch.

"What I did to you was beyond forgiveness. That this marriage needed to be consummated goes without saying. But, the manner, in which this was accomplished, I find staggering. I can do no more now than apologise most profusely to you and hope that, in the fullness of time, you may find it in your heart to forgive me. I warned you I'd a temper to match your own. So, perhaps now, you may have a healthy respect for it, but be assured I use that, in no way, as a part of my defence. I'm sorry . . . so very sorry . . . *and, you are* wanted here, Louisa . . . more than you'll ever, ever know."

She studied him in silence momentarily. Then, she picked up her shoes from his desk and she cast him another look of disdain, which was mingled with contempt.

"*Sorry* is a very easy word to say. Repairing the damage done is not so easy. How do I know you won't attack me again; then, apologise once more while believing everything is fine between us, because of your stated remorse?" she queried, with sarcasm obvious in her tone.

He was standing between the door and her body, thus baring her escape. Reluctant to move closer to him, Louisa stood her ground. She was staring up at him while studying him candidly.

"I will never touch you again without your express permission. *I give you my word.* My word is my bond, Louisa."

"Then, you shall never have it! Kindly allow me to leave now."

With what appeared to be great reluctance, Charles stepped to one side. Louisa, with her head held high and attempting to convey the most regal bearing possible under the current circumstances, was about to leave when the sound of thundering hooves reached her ears. Instantly, they both turned to see who was approaching at such a break-neck speed. As horse and rider pulled to an abrupt halt at the main door, Charles was out through the french doors, with Louisa following closely behind him and with her shoes in her hand, still. As Charles reached the messenger who was dismounting hurriedly, Benson opened the front door.

"It's Uncle Robert; I just know it!" Louisa shouted.

Charles grabbed the missive from the rider, who announced that he was to await a reply. As Charles walked back by Louisa, he was opening the letter as he re-entered his office.

"It's not your uncle. I know this messenger and where he has come from."

She followed him back into the office. He stared, in stunned silence, at the words on the paper in his hand. In this moment, his arm came down onto his desk and – with one sweep of his right arm and one, loud shout of despair – he removed everything from the desk onto the floor, including the unlit glass lamp. This item smashed instantly as oil began to spill over the rug and all the papers and files alike. Louisa, in shock, watched Charles. She was unable to comprehend what could have occurred to bring on such a display of anger and anguish.

"How can there be a God in heaven? It's all a load of hogwash! Do you hear me?" he shouted at her.

Charles crumpled the note in his hand and he flung it across the room. He walked to the door and shouted for Benson before demanding that his horse be brought around immediately and directing the butler to inform the messenger that he would deliver his reply in person.

Leaving Louisa alone in the office, almost as though he had forgotten her existence, he rushed upstairs, obviously intending to change into his riding outfit for the journey to wherever he was bound on this Sunday afternoon.

As soon as Louisa heard him reach the top of the stairs, and knowing that he was heading for his bedroom, she rummaged through the papers on the floor until she located the missive. As her fingers curled around the letter, she heard the messenger and his mount departing down the carriageway. Gingerly, she opened the letter and she studied what appeared to be hastily-scribbled words, which read:

Charles,

    Edwin passed away peacefully today, just before noon. I would appreciate your presence at this time.

S.

The signature was merely a long flourish, which Louisa felt could have been in the shape of the letter, S. Of this, she could not be certain. She read the words again and again, but these did not mean anything to her. So, she returned the note to where she had found it.

She left the office through the french doors and she crossed the carriageway in her stockinged feet. Leaving her shoes at the top of the stone steps, she descended and ran along the pathway by the river as she headed for her cabin and its sanctuary. The *Presence* beneath the big tree remained there, she noted, as she moved beneath its branches with a distinct shiver.

Louisa had much to ponder as she sat alone in her hide-away this afternoon, on the first Sunday of the New Year. She doubted that the year of eighteen-sixty-eight could have begun in a worse manner than it had for her. Unfortunately, she did not feel, in her heart, that it could improve any from here. The small seed of hopelessness that prior to her mother's death had been unknown to her, began to grow a little in size deep within her being. Her father's words about God came back to her. She remembered how he stated vehemently that He had failed to answer her mother's prayers, with regard to the health problems that, finally, claimed her life.

Suddenly, Louisa shook herself out of her despair while acknowledging that her present melancholy was more a result of the horrific events of this day, than from any deep-seated doubt about her religion and her God. In this frame of mind, she returned to the house as she assumed that her husband would have left already. She went alone to her bedroom where she prayed for guidance, for help and for the ability to forgive, which at the moment was beyond her capabilities. This, she acknowledged freely to herself.

Louisa dined alone this evening at Lyndhurst Park.

Chapter Twenty-Three

– Victorian Victorians –

Louisa

Having dispensed with her maid's services early and needing to be alone this night, Louisa was reading her book as she reclined in the armchair by the open french doors in her bedroom. She felt that, perhaps, she dozed a little – drifting into a light sleep briefly – but of this, she could not be certain. She had heard not a sound from Charles' bedroom, so she assumed that he had not returned from wherever he went on his urgent afternoon ride. Therefore, she was somewhat startled at the sharp but distinct sound by the open verandah door. She looked up to find him observing her from that doorway. She frowned at him, but she did not speak.

"I wish to speak with you," he stated.

"And, I've no desire to speak with you . . . now, or ever."

"Shall we do so here, or do you wish to join me on the front verandah where it's cool . . . and on neutral ground?" he queried.

"Nowhere in *your house* is neutral territory for me," Louisa replied, without moving from the armchair.

Charles walked into the room and he sat on the side of her bed as he continued to survey her.

"You're mistaken. This house and all you see around you belongs solely and totally to my father. I own the horses, the carriages and the clothes I wear. The servants are employed by me and I pay them handsomely; that is why they all stay, regardless of how I treat them, although I doubt they've as many complaints on that score as you have. In addition, *I own you*. That's the sum total of it, Louisa."

Louisa watched him for a few moments; then, deciding that he was not about to vacate her bedroom unless she did, she stood up and walked from the room. On the front section of the verandah, there was a single cane chair facing the river. Beside it was a table, on which stood a lead-crystal whisky decanter that was almost empty, with an empty glass positioned beside it. There was another single cane chair some distance along the verandah and positioned beside the door leading into the house and main hallway.

Charles walked by her and, picking up the chair by the door, he placed it beside the other one, but with its back to the railing so that she would be facing him. He sat on the chair, which obviously, he had been occupying previously and he proceeded to empty the whisky from the decanter into the glass as Louisa stood watching him. He glanced up at her.

"Be a good girl and ring for more whisky," he requested.

Louisa flounced over to the chair and she threw herself into it. She eyed him with disgust.

"Do it yourself! I'm not your servant!"

"You never fail to flare, do you?" he stated, with a soft laugh.

He jumped to his feet and strode to the main door, loudly shouting his orders to Benson; then, he came back and sat on the chair while placing his feet on the verandah rail and reaching for the glass. He was dressed for riding, although he had discarded his coat and waist coat, and Louisa studied his riding boots as these rested on the rail by her head. Nathaniel, she thought, would need to work for at least a year to earn the money to purchase a pair such as those expensive items. Charles Lyndhurst spared no expense where his attire was concerned. Benson arrived. He delivered another decanter filled with whisky and the butler removed the empty one. He inquired if Louisa was requiring anything, but she merely smiled at him and shook her head in reply.

When the butler left, Charles finished his drink and reached to refill his glass. The gash above his right eye was somewhat swollen and dried blood was visible on his forehead, just above the eyebrow. She was staring at the wound when he spoke.

"Tonight, I intend to get very drunk. So, before that moment arrives, I've decided it's time for plain-speaking between us. But firstly, I wish to advise you of a few facts regarding your new friend, Carstairs, who you've been meeting somewhere . . . somehow . . . behind my back, and that piece of information I gleaned solely from what you, yourself, let slip in my office this afternoon. Am I correct in this assumption?"

"It's none of your business," Louisa countered.

"I'll take that as a *yes*, shall I?" he queried, before stating quietly to her. "We've reached a point of no return, Louisa. Had I acted differently toward you at the outset and commenced this marriage in the way it should've begun, right from that first night in Echuca, we'd never have come to this point."

Charles lifted the glass to his lips as he appeared to be surveying the river. Louisa wriggled in the chair and she was wishing to be anywhere but in his presence while being forced to listen to what seemed to be another lecture about her behaviour.

"That I was seeking to outwit my father is my only defence. Why I couldn't accept from the beginning that he'd won, I don't know, for it seems I've learned nothing in the past thirty years. He wins every time, as he has now."

Louisa's anger began to rise again at the mention of Sir Charles Lyndhurst's name, so she interjected at this point.

"*You knew* he'd beaten Phillip senseless on the night of the Fancy Dress Ball, didn't you? In fact, you were probably there, applauding as the two troopers held him down on the grass," Louisa challenged him.

Charles frowned, as turning to face her and staring uncomprehendingly at her, he lifted the glass to his lips again.

"Say that again."

"Your father kicked him savagely. He was hiding in the shadows outside the ballroom and I saw you leaving the ballroom with two glasses of wine in your hands. So presumably, those were refreshments for your father to sustain him during the attack, which was violent, for I saw the aftermath. Violence is a family trait, obviously!" she stated, with deep conviction.

"And, you think me capable of that?" he asked, absolutely aghast.

"After today, I'd say you were capable of anything."

Charles was staring at her and shaking his head slowly in some astonishment. He seemed unable to find the words to speak to her. He picked up the glass and, absentmindedly, placed it to his lips once again. He drank in silence for some minutes. Finally, he offered an explanation.

"I saw my father briefly that night, at a distance, as we were leaving. He was hanging off Prince Alfred's shirt-tails, as usual. Before that, I did not know he was there. If he did what you infer, your friend got off lightly in the encounter, only because of our royal visitor though, as he wouldn't want the scandal of a murder at a function in honour of His Royal Highness. That will be all that saved his life, be assured of that fact," Charles stated, in a matter-of-fact tone. "My father possesses no conscience, no morals and no principles whatsoever. Don't make an enemy of him, but please accept I'm not tarred with the same brush. Do me that courtesy, at least. As for the unfortunate incident that happened between us this day, I'll accept eighty per cent of the blame. But, you were the one who threw the missile, thus sparking it all."

Louisa lifted her chin and flicked her head away in defiance, as she had no intention of accepting any blame for the *unfortunate incident*, as he chose to label the attack.

He reached for the decanter and refilled his glass. She watched, with some concern, at the amount of alcohol that he was drinking while knowing from her experiences when watching the riverboat men just how unpredictable drunken men could be, especially if roused to anger.

"I didn't aim at you," Louisa explained finally.

"Then, you'd be a poor shot with a gun."

"I'm a crack shot. Papa taught me and I've been shooting for years. You moved in the wrong direction and walked into it!"

"One does tend to react quickly when under attack. Be that as it may, today has been a *momentous one* for all of us!"

"Who's *all?*" she queried.

"Never mind that now. It's Carstairs I wish to speak of, for you need to be aware of what you've been dealing with. At least, you'd the good sense to take Nathaniel with you . . . not that he'd have been a match for Patrick Doherty! You're not playing cricket in a country lane with a few boys who were your childhood friends now . . . *and, their mother* was watching through the window on that occasion."

Louisa moved her position in the chair. She was attempting to avoid his close scrutiny, but his gaze did not waver from her face as he continued his revelations in a quiet tone.

"Here, today, you were playing around with two men who're without conscience either, so if I'd not arrived when I did, the gossip would've been all over town by now. He'd have attacked you, found you to be an untouched maiden, after almost two months of marriage to me . . . *and, that* would've been the biggest joke of all! Where would that have *left us* then? I'll tell you . . . in a far worse position than now, believe me, for neither one of us would've been able to hold our heads up in this gossip-laden town again. Shall I tell you of his reputation?"

Louisa stood up and she turned her chair slightly away from him before resuming her seat. But, as she did so, his hand reached over to grasp her arm to restrain her. With a shake of her arm, she flicked his hand away and he released her as his explanation continued.

"Yes, because you need to know, even though you won't see hide-nor-hair of Carstairs again, as he's sailing for Sydney with his sister and her family early tomorrow. I know, because I've checked it out fully."

Charles began a lengthy explanation of Phillip Carstairs and Patrick Doherty's alleged crimes and exploits in Sydney and he concluded with the tale of his liaison with a young woman who was to be married on the following day.

"There was a wager on that encounter, Louisa. Doherty was waiting in the shadows at the time and watching to determine who the winner of the rather large bet was. That's what today's race at Flemington with you was about . . . a wager! And, it was not on the horse race either. Trust me on this."

"I don't believe you and, besides, I wouldn't have allowed it to occur!" Louisa stated defiantly, contemptuously hurling the words at him and not believing for an instant all that he was revealing about Phillip.

"You couldn't have stopped him, any more than you could me!"

Louisa's mind flicked back suddenly to her encounter with Phillip after their return to Lyndhurst Park, following the debacle of the Free Banquet in November at the commencement of Prince Alfred's Victorian tour. She recalled the situation, in which she had found herself on the jetty when they were disturbed by the arrival of one of Prince Alfred's equerries. She had been struggling with Phillip and she was experiencing difficulty in moving from his grasp as he was levering her down onto the timber deck. And, she admitted to herself, he acknowledged freely to her that he had singled her out at the State Ball, the first main event on the Tour calendar, because of her connection with the Lyndhurst family.

Suddenly, a small doubt entered her mind for the first time and she remained silent for some time as she considered the events of the past seven weeks. Perhaps, she had been foolish to be as trusting as she had been. However, this did not alter the fact that she was in a marriage situation that was untenable and from which there was no escape, unless she availed herself of Phillip's offer. Then, she asked herself whether the devil she knew may not be better than the one she knew not well at all. To this question, she did not have an answer. All she wanted in life was to return to her home where she was needed desperately, because the letters coming from Mrs. McBryde were giving her much cause for concern. As for Charles Lyndhurst, she wanted nothing more than to be anywhere but close to him, now or at any time in the future.

"Do you believe me?" Charles queried, thereby bringing her from her intense contemplation.

"No," she replied, immediately standing and walking toward her bedroom door.

Charles made no attempt to restrain her. He waited until she was about to enter her bedroom before he stopped her in her tracks with his softly spoken words.

"I've a proposition for you."

Louisa stayed in the doorway. She was looking back at him. He had his back to her and he was surveying the river while awaiting her response and, obviously, knowing what her reaction would be. She did not disappoint him. Louisa returned slowly and sat down again in the cane chair as she awaited his explanation.

"We start again . . . as though the past two months have not occurred."

"How is that possible?" she asked, aghast. "Today happened! It can't just be swept away as though it did not."

She watched as he poured another drink from the decanter. He seemed to take forever to reply to her query. His wound from today's altercation was patently obvious, whereas her own wounds were buried more deeply than that one.

"I'm handing you a peace offering, if you like. I'm giving you the chance to go to your father's home for a couple of months. Then, when I come for you . . . *and, I will come* . . . we start again . . . start this marriage from scratch. *And, I mean* a proper marriage, in every sense of the word. *Do not* misunderstand me here."

"*Go home? Now?*" Louisa asked, with a gasp, unable to believe what she was hearing.

"This is your home, as it is mine. You belong with me, whether I choose to reside here, or in London. You and I are together for the rest of our lives. It's a daunting thought, is it not? Perhaps, it could be as long as thirty or forty years. That's a long time to live under the same roof while despising each other, although I'm certain others have done so before us. I'm toying with the idea of returning to London. Would you enjoy that, do you think?" Charles asked, with an air of smugness about him and a supercilious grin on his face as the alcohol began to take affect more fully.

"You could force me to go, but you'd be a widower before your ship reaches Cape Town!"

"Oh! Another drowning episode? Perhaps that's the answer then," he replied, before expanding further. "But, you do realise sharks follow the ships . . . and in great numbers. That'd not be a pleasant way to go."

Louisa jumped from the chair and strode to her bedroom, as she left him to his whisky and his plans. She needed to be alone to consider all that he was offering with regard to her return to her home. Mrs. McBryde's regular letters were advising there had not been any changes since her father arrived back home and the bookkeeper was drunk all the time still, so the accounts were not being paid. She had left cheques post-dated with Brydie to pay the wages and these were left on the breakfast table for her father to sign on the due date. Other than that, everything was as it had been when she left her home.

Louisa needed to go there desperately, regardless of the cost. She did not think Charles intended to go to London. She felt that he was baiting her, so she was determined to ignore his bait and accept his offer, despite the fact that the price was so very high, from her perspective.

Slowly and resolutely, she returned to the front verandah. Sitting down on the chair again, she studied him closely before committing herself. She needed to establish that he was not too drunk to remember tomorrow all that he promised this night. He appeared to be expecting her immediate return to him.

"I need to know exactly what you're proposing. I'll leave early tomorrow and I want sixteen weeks in total," she stated.

"Twelve only!" he countered.

"Fifteen!" she replied.

"I could come back with thirteen, but as I'm feeling generous this night, shall we settle on fourteen? I'll take you to your father tomorrow and we'll leave mid-morning, for I need time to consult with Hugh first."

Louisa watched him in disgust. He seemed quite amused by the turn of events. He raised his glass in the air.

"A toast!" he murmured, with a grin. "To better times!"

"You planned this from the beginning. You'd worked it all out before I came out here tonight!"

Louisa was annoyed with herself for falling into his trap so easily, but Charles laughed loudly at her as he raised the glass to his mouth again.

"Damn you, Charles Lyndhurst! This is just another of your cat-and-mouse games!"

"The only surprise this evening was that you began the bargaining at sixteen weeks. I was expecting twenty, at the very least!"

"I despise you!" Louisa stated vehemently, as she stood to leave him to his whisky.

As she did so, Charles's arm reached over, instantly grabbing a hold of her right wrist and gripping it extremely tightly.

"You do understand fully what you've agreed to, I hope. From that day onwards, you will *indulge me* whenever I seek your *company*, shall we say, and with good grace. Agreed?"

"Don't expect active participation!" she snarled at him.

"I'm not so naive. I'll be on your father's doorstep promptly fourteen weeks from tomorrow. *And, that* will be our wedding night. We'll put all this turmoil behind us then and start afresh," he stated quietly and with conviction.

Louisa stared down at her hand and, in particular, the wrist that he was holding in his vice-like grip. He made no move to release her.

"Do we have an iron-clad agreement, *Mrs. Lyndhurst?*"

"How do I know you won't break that agreement? You gave your word this afternoon you wouldn't touch me without my express permission and, at this moment, you are doing so!"

Instantly, he released her, as though she had shot him through the heart. His fingers sprang apart as would a dingo trap when prised open. He brushed the non-existent hair from his forehead and reached for the whisky glass again. As his hand brushed by his eyebrow, the wound opened a little and a small amount of blood oozed from it.

"If you'd been more compliant from the beginning, none of this charade would be necessary. You're the first bride I've known of who'd take a dagger to her marriage bed," he muttered.

"*And, I'd have used it*, even though I didn't understand what form the attack would take. I'd have used it today had I been able to reach it in time."

"I don't doubt it. Knowing you, Louisa, I don't doubt it for a minute. Do we have an iron-clad agreement?" he asked again.

"Yes!" she exclaimed, while spinning around and marching in a determined manner to her room where, despite the summer heat, she closed the doors firmly.

Louisa heard him laugh loudly as she did so. It was then she recalled the crumpled note that she read in his office this afternoon and she wondered again who had sent the missive. She was puzzling over the identity of the man called Edwin. Perhaps, he was a close friend and this bout of drinking was, in fact, a silent and solitary wake for the recently departed man.

There was one matter, of which Louisa was certain. Charles Lyndhurst would be suffering markedly tomorrow as a result of tonight's excessive consumption of whisky. And, in the morning, she would make certain that he was awake early and on the road before mid-morning. Her husband would not enjoy tomorrow at all, Louisa determined, as she removed her clothing and dropped the garments on the floor where she stepped from them.

She slipped into her nightgown before slipping into the bed and, despite her efforts to the contrary, she recalled the horrendous events of this day. Charles was correct. It had been a momentous day – for her, at least. This Sunday began with the excitement of the race, followed by the devastation of the rape and culminated in the promise of a temporary escape. Louisa nodded off to sleep, hardly able to contain the excitement that was mounting within her, for within two days, she would be sleeping in her own bed once more. Her father would know her feelings when she arrived unannounced on his doorstep, just as her husband would know her feelings when she arrived unannounced in his bedroom in the morning. That was a spectacle, which she was anticipating with relish. Despite the events of the day, Louisa drifted into a deep sleep with a smile on her face.

Dawn was breaking on this fine Monday morning, the first one in January, as Louisa began her day. This was long before the household began to stir and before her maid appeared in her room. She opened the french doors to the verandah; then, she moved behind the screen in the corner and there, she began her toiletries before dressing for the day. She had plans for today and she intended to be about them early, so her first port-of-call was her husband's bedroom.

She opened the internal door and crept into the darkened room, which reeked of stale alcohol. If the sound emanating from the large bed in the centre of the room was any indication of its occupant's state, it spoke of someone enveloped in a deep, deep sleep. This knowledge gave Louisa great pleasure as she moved behind the screen in the corner and she picked up the large porcelain jug filled to the brim with cold water, which was awaiting Charles' morning ablutions. Perhaps, he may have these a little earlier than expected, Louisa thought, with a suppressed giggle.

She moved to the bed and positioned herself by his head, the outline of which she could just define in the half-light of dawn. As she did so, the door from the corridor opened and Joseph, Charles' valet, entered. Without glancing around, he walked immediately to the front windows and began to open the drapes. Louisa watched him with interest as he turned and, with a start, he acknowledged her presence in his master's bedroom, as well as the water jug held over Charles' sleeping head. He opened his mouth in dismay at her obvious intention. As he did so, Louisa allowed a small amount of water to trickle onto her husband's head, which she could see more clearly now, thanks to Joseph's intervention with the drapes.

Charles' head moved slightly as he stirred; then, he settled back into a deep slumber. She lifted the jug higher, with her intentions obvious, and Joseph, solicitous of his employer's welfare, took a step toward the bed.

Louisa glanced over at him with disdain, for she did not like the man at all. The rest of the servants disliked him intensely, she knew, and there was open warfare between Benson and Joseph at present. Charlotte had revealed to Louisa that he was referred to as *Creepin'*

Joe by everyone and Louisa felt that this was an apt description of the man-in-question. He did not endear himself to her at all in this present moment.

"Madam! No! I beg of you ..."

Louisa looked at him with a mixture of dislike and disdain on her face as she spoke quite harshly to him.

"Get out!" Louisa snapped at him.

As the words left her lips, she upended the jug while tipping the entire contents, with great satisfaction, onto the head of the soundly-sleeping Charles Lyndhurst. Joseph fled the room in an instant as Louisa moved quickly around to the other side of the bed to make good her rather hurried escape. Charles sat up with a start. He was flicking water around the room as his head moved from side to side.

He flung back the bedclothes and sat on the side of the bed near to her escape route. He stared at her with eyes that were uncomprehending. There was a trickle of blood running down his face from the wound that he had re-opened now and this was intermixed with the water trickling from his drenched hair. Louisa looked at him and she laughed aloud as she flung the empty jug into his hands. He sat there, while reeling in shock and completely naked, on the side of his bed, still clutching the jug and trying to fathom what had happened to him at dawn on this fine summer morning. Louisa was laughing uncontrollably as she stood by the connecting door, with one hand on the door handle, and ready to make good her escape. She was surveying, with great delight and amusement, the aftermath of her handiwork this morning.

"I'm going to visit Aunt Sophie and Uncle Robert now. When I come back, make certain you are ready. We have a deal. Keep to your part in it!" she shouted at him, before closing the door somewhat quickly.

When she entered her bedroom, Charlotte was coming into her room from the corridor.

"Charlotte, good morning! I'm going to breakfast with my aunt and uncle now. When I come back, I'll have a quick bath. Then, we'll be away. Pack everything while I'm out, because we're leaving mid-morning for Bendigo, Echuca and *HOME!*" she exclaimed, with excitement sounding in her voice.

"Today?" Charlotte inquired, while appearing surprised. "How long for, ma'am?"

"Fourteen weeks!" shouted Louisa in jubilation.

"Fourteen weeks?" queried Charlotte in horror.

"Yes," Louisa confirmed; then, a little unnecessarily, she made a suggestion. "Perhaps, you may wish to farewell a certain gentleman of your acquaintance. If so, do it now."

With those words, she left her bedroom hurriedly and before the occupant of the other bedroom came to seek revenge for his rude awakening.

Chapter Twenty-Four

– Victorian Victorians –

Sylvia

For Sylvia, the numbness crept over her and she could not shake the feeling, no matter what she did. She paced around her sitting room alone. The emotional turmoil that she was experiencing was real, with her feelings being mixed – extremely so. She was attempting to fathom her relationship with Edwin, which during the past decade had become more that of siblings who shared a firm friendship, mingled with a deep and mutual respect being the essence of it.

During his life, Edwin Webster was involved in two deep and loving relationships – neither one with his second wife, Sylvia – and, in both cases, with women of his own age or older. Coming to the acceptance of this situation was difficult for Sylvia at the outset, but upon learning the rules of the game, by which he played, she adjusted to the situation uneasily at first. Then, with the advent of Charles Lyndhurst in her life, she found that she could be as devious as could her husband when the need arose.

Charles' visit on the previous day was timely, as well as being appreciated deeply. He had ridden over immediately upon receiving her missive and he was most attentive to her needs during his brief time with her. Bertie had been here with Sylvia during the ordeal of Edwin's passing, as had the doctor and the nurse. After that, Bertie had left her to inform his sisters of the death of their father. The whole family descended on her afterwards, but in the interim, Charles had arrived and his comforting arms, along with his consoling words, did much to ease her pain.

She was pacing still while considering the events of the past twenty-four hours when the door opened and Charles entered – unannounced as usual. He came to her and took her in his arms immediately. She kissed him lightly on the lips.

"Goodness, you're here early. Have you eaten?" Sylvia queried, as she studied his immaculate appearance while fingering the wound above his right eye. "What on earth happened? I noticed this yesterday, but I was too pre-occupied to ask."

"Pay no mind to it. And, yes, I've partaken of breakfast. I've a busy schedule, so I thought I'd call early and I was hoping you were awake. If not, I'd have awoken you. Is it convenient?"

"Yes, of course. I'm alone. Edwin's family arrived just after you left yesterday, so you were spared all that drama," Sylvia stated.

"It was hardly appropriate that I should've been here at all yesterday, but I couldn't ignore your plea, no matter how irrational the request."

Sylvia moved from him and walked to her bureau before glancing back at him.

"I've so many details to consider. Bertie is coming this morning to help me with the arrangements. The funeral will be either Wednesday or Thursday, I expect."

"I won't be attending," Charles stated firmly. "In fact, I've come to tell you I'll be out of town for a week. I'm taking Louisa to her father."

Sylvia spun around and stared at him in dismay.

"Not attending Edwin's funeral?" she asked, with a slight gasp.

"It's hardly appropriate, given the circumstances, Sylvia."

"You'll be just as conspicuous by your absence. Is that why you're running away?"

He walked over to her and took her hands in his own; then, with his face close to her face, he whispered softly to her.

"I didn't come to argue with you. You were correct in your assumption about that race at Flemington and I thank you most sincerely, from the bottom of my heart, for what you revealed to me. Most women in your position wouldn't have done so, especially after I had warned you not to interfere in my marriage."

Sylvia frowned at him. She did not need his problems, which concerned his wife, to swamp her today, as her own emotional state was anything but stable. Nevertheless, she was surprised by his revelations and not a little curious as to the outcome of that particular encounter at Flemington yesterday.

"Oh! I see," she replied. "And, was your arrival there timely?"

In reply to her query, he nodded solemnly before continuing with his disclosures.

"Now, what I'm about to reveal is between us . . . *completely between us*. I'm taking Louisa to her father and, as far as the world is concerned, this is due to his illness," Charles stated, in a hoarse whisper. "But, in truth, the rift between us is so huge that I don't know what else to do. I've no choice now, so forgive me if I seem to be abandoning you in your hour of need. However, that's the way of it."

Sylvia extracted her hands and moved away from him. She sat down on the chair at her bureau to consider his statement. Charles pulled another chair over as he sat near to her, and obviously awaiting her reaction to his disclosures.

"Then, this is grave indeed."

He merely nodded his head in response as she continued to frown at him.

"Yes, and it's of my own making. I can blame no other, unfortunately. I'll return by week's end and we can discuss it all then. We'll have several months to spend together."

"Months?" Sylvia queried, somewhat astounded.

"Yes, and as I've no doubt you'll be observing a period of mourning, I'll be here to keep you company, if that's your desire, of course."

Sylvia shook her head while trying to absorb all that was occurring. Everything seemed to be happening so fast that she was having difficulty in accepting that these events were real. Suddenly, she realised that he was awaiting an answer.

"Yes, of course," she murmured abstractedly. "A period of mourning had not even occurred to me but, of course, you're correct. I'm not comprehending much at present, so forgive me if I seem distracted."

"That's to be expected," he replied. "What of your brother? Is he still here?"

"No, I've not seen him since dinner on Saturday night. His belongings have gone from the guest room, so I presume he has left us . . . and, once again without a word of goodbye. But, with Patrick, that is to be expected. He'll probably arrive on my doorstep in another twenty years, should I live as long as that!"

Charles grimaced noticeably. He was frowning deeply as he did so, but he did not elaborate on the subject of Patrick, to Sylvia's obvious relief. He squeezed her hand firmly before getting to his feet.

"I'll leave you now. Lean on Bertie during this terrible week and I'll return as soon as I can. I've much to discuss with you. Hold your head high, my darling, throughout the service for your husband, because you have handled yourself with great strength and decorum throughout these long and difficult years."

Charles stood beside her. Suddenly, he reached down and retrieved both of her hands. He was holding her hands in his tight grip when Sylvia looked up at him. She was unable to speak and she surveyed him with tears welling in her eyes. Then, he continued to speak softly to her.

"Had you had more consideration for yourself and your needs, rather than placing Edwin's perceived needs above your own, then your life, as well as mine own, would have been very different from this time onwards. You've sacrificed much, so don't forget this fact. Please, do not undersell yourself, for there's much, of which you can be proud. Take your place with dignity while knowing that you've earned the respect you deserve . . . and will receive, I trust sincerely . . . during this trying week. I am sorry I cannot be by your side through the trauma of it all."

Charles leaned down and he kissed her lightly on the lips. As he released her hands and turned to move from her, she grasped his wrist firmly. He stopped and looked down at her while he appeared to be struggling with his own emotional state at this time.

"Is it . . .?" she asked tentatively. "Is it too late for us?"

Sylvia was holding her breath as she awaited his reply to her whispered question.

"Yes," he whispered, with emotion seemingly threatening to overwhelm him as he nodded his head slowly in confirmation. "Unfortunately, it is so."

With those words, he turned quickly and he strode from the room. He closed the door gently behind him. Sylvia remained motionless at the bureau and she was staring down at her hands, but seeing nothing but the tears that were beginning to drop down one-by-one onto them.

Whether those tears were for Edwin, for herself, or for a love now lost, she knew not. But, she did not attempt to stem the flow.

She was in this position still when Bertie arrived some time later. He placed an arm around her shoulders, a glass of brandy in her hand and a light kiss on the top of her head.

But, not one word did he speak.

Louisa

Louisa breezed by the butler at the front door of the Collins' residence. If he was surprised to see her at this early hour, he did not give any indication of the fact.

"Good morning, Reddington. I'm famished, so I'll need breakfast at once. Are Mr. and Mrs. Collins in the breakfast room?"

Without waiting for a reply, Louisa breezed on into the sunroom where she knew that she would find them, despite the early hour. They were seated at the table and Sophie was studying a proposed dinner menu while Robert was engrossed in his morning newspaper. Startled, they looked up at Louisa simultaneously.

"Child, whatever is the matter? Not your Papa?" Sophie inquired hurriedly.

"Nothing's wrong. Everything is wonderful! I'm going home! *And, you'll never guess for how long* . . . it's for fourteen weeks!" Louisa exclaimed gleefully.

Sophie Collins frowned at her in alarm while Robert gave her a puzzled glance. It was Sophie who interrupted first.

"But, you've only been married less than eight weeks!"

Reddington entered the room, so Louisa settled herself at the table, without waiting for an invitation, and she proceeded to help herself to the toast on the rack.

"When do you leave?" Robert asked tentatively.

"Now . . . on this morning's train. Do you have any messages for Papa?" she inquired as the butler left the room.

Sophie Collins appeared deeply troubled. Robert was watching Louisa with suspicious eyes, as obviously he was trying to fathom the reason for such a long visit home after her short marriage.

"Your husband's in agreement, I take it? You're not absconding . . . with a dagger and one hundred and twenty sovereigns in your pocket?" he inquired, in all seriousness.

Louisa threw back her head and she laughed aloud as Reddington returned. The butler placed a plate of eggs and toast in front of her.

"He suggested it," she replied simply, as she began to devour her breakfast as though it were her last one for this life.

Sophie's frown deepened. She glanced across at her husband before she returned her gaze to Louisa, who was ignoring them both as she attacked her breakfast.

"You do know, I presume, that Mr. Webster died yesterday?" Sophie queried tentatively after the butler left the room again.

"Who is he?" Louisa inquired.

"Bertie Webster's father," Robert replied hurriedly, thereby silencing his wife momentarily with one swift and very pointed glance of disapproval.

"Oh! Bertie? I know him. He's quite funny, with a wicked sense of humour," Louisa stated, as she placed more food into her mouth before commenting further. "That is very sad for his family."

Sophie nodded her head slowly as Louisa continued to eat her breakfast. Sophie was glancing over at her niece every now and then while Robert returned his full attention to his newspaper.

Louisa reached for the teapot and she poured a cup of tea for herself, quite oblivious to her aunt's concern. But, had she not been so excited over her proposed journey home, she may have made the correlation between the missive, which Charles had received on the previous day and the death of Bertie Webster's father. However, at this time, she did not do so, because she had other matters occupying her mind at present. Finally, Sophie could remain silent no longer.

"Louisa, do you think it wise to leave town at this time . . . leaving your husband all alone, I mean?"

"He was alone before I came. Alone, he can remain, as far as I am concerned, Aunt Sophie. And, if I never see him again for the rest of my life, then I shall be very happy indeed," Louisa declared forcefully.

"How can you say such . . .?" Sophie began to query, before she was interrupted by her husband's terse words.

"*Mrs. Collins!* Leave it be! Charles knows what he's doing, as I'm certain Louisa does. It is not for us to interfere," Robert stated firmly, with his definite rebuke obvious to both women.

Breakfast proceeded quietly from this point onwards, with Louisa outlining all that she intended to do when she returned to her home and explaining how surprised her father would be when she arrived back so soon after leaving.

With the meal at an end, Robert walked outside to the croquet court, with Louisa and Sophie following closely behind him. This was a ritual that Louisa enjoyed often when she stayed with them. Sophie watched from the bench seat as Louisa and Robert, with mallets in hand, commenced a game, although there was more talking taking place than any serious competition. It was mid-way through the second game that Robert moved closer to Louisa. Obviously, he was intent on talking privately to her.

"By the way, young lady, I have a serious matter to discuss with you."

Louisa glanced over at her aunt who appeared to have lost interest in the game and its two players. Louisa stiffened noticeably, as she waited for her uncle's pronouncement while expecting it to relate to Phillip Carstairs. She was holding her breath without realising that she was doing so.

"Actually, there are two . . . one has to do with a certain gentleman whom we discussed recently. Does your sudden departure from Melbourne have anything to do with him?"

Louisa bit her lip and decided to concentrate on the game more intently. Robert was not about to be ignored. He reached over and took a hold of her arm.

"I'm terribly worried about you and now, you're going away for some months. Has Charles discovered your little secret?" he asked.

"The matter has come to a head between us and we've reached an understanding, let's say. So, there's no need for you to worry about me. I'll be back soon enough; you'll see. As for Phillip, he was leaving for Sydney this morning, so presumably, he's gone from me. Does this answer your question? What is the other matter?"

Robert was nodding thoughtfully, as he appeared to accept Louisa's assurances on this subject and he released her arm.

"I've a set of precious books that no one would dare to touch and one is missing. You're the most likely culprit who comes to mind. Your fascination for Egypt makes you the prime suspect. I would like it returned now, if you don't mind."

Louisa laughed and she tossed the mallet aside onto the grass. She stood on her tiptoes and kissed him on the cheek. Robert laughed at her.

"That won't save you, *madam!*" he stated, while reproving her sternly.

"It's upstairs in my bedroom. I'll fetch it for you now; then, I can leave here with a clear conscience," she replied.

Still laughing at her uncle, Louisa skipped across the lawn court and entered the house where she ran upstairs, two at a time. She rushed into her old bedroom. Nostalgia filled her always when she came into this room, for she had spent many happy times here – despite her dislike for the School for Ladies in later years – and she enjoyed being in this home with her aunt and uncle.

With little difficulty, she located the errant book; then, tucking it under her arm, she walked by the bedroom window. On glancing down at the croquet court situated beneath the window, she stopped still while staring at the man who was standing there and talking with Robert and Sophie. Simultaneously, Robert pointed up to where

Louisa was watching by the window. As one, they all turned to look up at her.

For Louisa, it was a moment that remained frozen in time as she surveyed her husband from the second-floor window. Charles Lyndhurst's face scrutinised her with a look that took her breath away momentarily, for the expression was one that she could not fathom. It seemed to be a mixture of pleading for understanding and begging for forgiveness as they stood locked together in this one, brief moment. It was so far removed from the expression of smugness of the previous night that she could not quite comprehend its meaning.

Deliberately, she tilted her chin and she tossed her head in the air, thereby breaking the momentary connection. Instantly, she turned quickly and she left the window as she hurried downstairs to replace the book in her uncle's library. As she walked into the library, the three of them were walking into the room from the terrace. Robert glanced at the book in her hand and he nodded solemnly.

"You've just saved your own hide, madam. Return it to the top shelf where it belongs, immediately."

Louisa gave Charles a cursory glance as she reached for a stool, on which to stand in order to follow her uncle's directive.

"What are you doing here?" she demanded of Charles.

"I came for you. We've a train to catch shortly."

She moved the stool to the bookshelf. Charles reached for her, obviously intent on taking the book from her hands, while Sophie and Robert were watching the interaction between Louisa and Charles with much interest.

"Here! Give that to me! You know what happened the last time you tried your balancing tricks on a stool at a bookshelf," Charles stated firmly.

"No! Leave me alone! If you hadn't interfered then, there wouldn't have been an accident. All you ever do is interfere! I'll do it myself."

Holding the book in front of her body and slightly out of his reach, she climbed onto the stool. Charles stepped forward and he took a firm hold of her waist with both hands as she perched on the stool while attempting to return the book safely to its home.

"Let go of me, Charles, or I'll drop this book onto your head!"

"Oh! No, you don't," called Robert, instantly interjecting. "That book is irreplaceable. Find something else, with which to crown your husband, Louisa, if you are intent on violence this morning."

Sophie was shaking her head in despair at the antics of her niece and she was giving the impression of one who had given up entirely on the task of making a lady of Louisa. Charles removed his hands from her waist somewhat reluctantly, although watching closely for any sign of an imminent mishap.

"If it's not a book, Robert, it will be a jug of cold water at best, or a dagger at worst. Peace shall reign at Lyndhurst Park for a few weeks, I trust."

They left shortly thereafter, with Louisa farewelling her aunt and uncle fondly as they stood at the front door while Charles waited impatiently by the carriage. He was dressed for riding and his horse was tethered to the rear of the carriage. Evidently, his intention was to accompany Louisa in the carriage on the journey home. Louisa grimaced as this realisation dawned on her.

Waving from the window of the carriage, Louisa watched her aunt and uncle walk inside the house before turning to her husband.

"There was no need for you to come. I can visit my family without you becoming my shadow," she stated, in some annoyance.

Charles did not reply, but he seemed intent on watching the scenery and ignoring her completely. They were almost at their home when, finally, he broke the silence between them while Louisa was happy to ignore him completely.

"Do you know, Louisa, there is but one woman alive who could get away with what you did to me this morning and still live to talk about it. *And, that* is my mother!"

"It's no more than you deserve! I had thought of boiling the water first, but that would've delayed my return home. Besides, it's nothing by comparison with what you did to me yesterday!" she retorted, with utter disgust evident in her voice.

"Am I never to be forgiven?" he queried softly.

"Not while I breathe air!"

"So much for Christian charity, then."

Louisa allowed a deep sigh to escape from her body and she studied him for a few moments before replying. Finally, surveying him critically, she answered him.

"I am a Catholic. I do not pretend to be perfect. However, at least I do try to live by Christian standards, even if I always appear to be doing what others consider to be *sinful* . . . by their standards, that is. But, I don't set out to hurt others deliberately. Perhaps sometimes, others may be injured in the crossfire, inadvertently."

He was staring out of the window of the carriage as they entered the gates of Lyndhurst Park. He appeared to have forgotten her existence. Suddenly, he turned to her while reaching for her gloved hands, which he held tightly in his firm grip.

"Stay with me . . . I don't want you to go. Reconsider, Louisa, please. We can work this out between us . . . here . . . now, with a small amount of compromise and a little compassion and understanding."

Charles was scrutinising her with an intense expression that resembled the one, which she had seen on his face when she was looking down at him from the window at her aunt and uncle's home not thirty minutes earlier. Startled, she pulled back from him while not comprehending his earnestly-spoken request. Then, she looked at him with disdain as she pulled her hands away quickly.

"Under no circumstances. We have an agreement."

Seemingly crestfallen, he shrugged his shoulders slightly in resignation at her reply and he leaned back in the seat. He did not speak to her again as they returned to their home.

Elizabeth

The sound of her husband's carriage arriving at the front door did little to start Elizabeth's day well. His appearance in her sitting room began the day badly indeed for her. How she loathed the sight of him and how short of breath she found herself when he came close to her as he surveyed her with disinterest at this moment. It was either with disinterest or with hostility, she acknowledged to herself. Of these, she preferred the former, for who knows where the latter could lead.

Elizabeth had not set eyes on him in months, not since before Charles and Louisa's first and only visit, but she knew that he would have been following the circuit of the Royal Tour while ingratiating himself with all and sundry as he went his way. Without so much as a greeting, he began his tirade.

"That wife of Charles . . . have you met her?" Sir Charles demanded tersely.

"I have indeed."

"If he doesn't take a hand shortly, I'll be forced to intervene. Wilful, headstrong, *little madam*, if ever I saw one . . . reminds me of you."

"Is that so?" Elizabeth responded, as she fought desperately to keep her emotions and her tongue under firm control before inquiring softly. "Remind me again who it was that arranged the marriage neither one of them wanted."

"I know what's best for my family!"

"You know what's best for the whole world."

Elizabeth walked to the armchair and sat down before reaching for her knitting. Without any prompting from her, he came over and sat opposite her.

"I want them to come here, along with Caroline and Douglas and their family, to partake of dinner one night soon. Arrange it!" he ordered.

"Arrange it yourself. You're forever telling me it's your household."

"So I am! I'm informing you in advance then, as I'll do with Caroline. Also, I want you to come to Sydney with me."

Elizabeth dropped the knitting onto her lap and a ball of wool skipped onto the floor, quickly rolling away from her. Her eyes followed it momentarily; then, she returned her gaze to her husband.

"What?" she asked, with an audible gasp.

"You heard me. In fact, I insist on it! No, demand it!"

"You can go to the devil!" she responded forcefully. "When I leave Stanton, it will be in a box; or, to embark on a voyage to England. Nothing else will induce me to leave. You built this prison and locked me in it, so here I'll stay until I decide to rejoin the outside world, or *that other world*, depending on which comes first!"

Sir Charles Lyndhurst was not one to accept defeat easily. He leaned back in the chair and, slowly, he stretched his legs in front of him.

"You've got friends there still and I know you correspond with them regularly. You can meet up with them again," he suggested, while attempting to tempt her with this ploy.

"I trust you have not been intercepting my mail . . . again."

"It's well within my right to do so," he reminded her. "Prince Alfred is heading there and I want you with me to attend some of the planned functions, to which we have been invited."

Elizabeth stared at him in astonishment. Even after all these horrible, soul-destroying years, he could surprise her – and, this fact surprised her even more. She watched him momentarily; then, she bent to retrieve the ball of wool from the floor. He watched her while not offering to assist in its recapture.

"I am not some painted doll you keep in a closet, to be brought out every quarter-of-a-century and paraded for all to see, just because you need a wife on your arm to attend certain functions that are desirable to you . . . or advantageous, as the case may be," Elizabeth exclaimed.

"It's been a long time since you could be described as such!" he countered, with a sneer.

"Get out! Get out of here now! The answer is . . . *No! No! No!* Could I speak more plainly than that, Charles?"

He rose to his feet with a laugh, well pleased with his efforts in stirring her to anger within the first twenty minutes of his return to his home. Elizabeth ignored him as she fought to control the urge to find a weapon, with which to strike him – not that she had ever done so – but the thought gave her great pleasure at moments such as these ones. He continued to look down at her as she studied her knitting. She did not dare to try to handle the knitting needles while his scrutiny was upon her, as she knew that her hands would be shaking furiously and the sight of the trembling would give him added pleasure.

This emotional response from Elizabeth was not caused by fear. She had moved beyond fear of him long, long ago. The cause was buried more deeply within her and it would never re-surface within this lifetime. However, it was due to her own pride that she would not allow her husband to view the trembling, which was brought on by an anger that was bordering on rage. He would view such a reaction to his presence as weakness, thereby increasing his power over her – in his mind.

"I'll speak to Caroline about the dinner here. Perhaps, she may be able to use her influence to bring Charles' new wife into line. And, you can ask Caroline to arrange for new gowns to be made for you . . . ones suitable for such *royal events* as we will attend in Sydney. You'll be capable of carrying this off with style, even now, if you had a mind to do so. We'll leave for there by early next week," he stated.

Elizabeth continued to count the stitches on the needle, because her mother had advised always to count to ten before exploding. She had reached the tally of thirty-nine stitches when he exploded.

She did not see it coming. His hand flew across to the lamp that was unlit – fortunately – and which was sitting beside her on the small table. He caught it underneath the shade and his action sent the missile flying across the room where it hit the wall. The glass base smashed into fragments, large and small, with these flying all over the room in a shower of light particles as a result. Oil began to pour onto the floor immediately.

The sound of breaking glass was resonating around the room still when the door opened suddenly and without warning. Martin Tomms stood in the doorway, for Elizabeth knew that he would have been hovering outside in the hallway from the moment of her husband's return. She gasped in surprise at the appearance of the butler.

"Is there nothing I can rely on you to do for me, woman!" her husband shouted at her, before turning to see who had entered the room.

Martin Tomms looked a sight. Instead of his usually immaculate attire, he was dressed as Elizabeth had never seen him before this day. She gasped again in astonishment while Sir Charles Lyndhurst stared at the butler. He was frowning at the new arrival as he studied his appearance. Martin, frozen in the doorway, was dressed in his usual dark suit, but he wore a white, blood-splattered apron over it. He did not wear any gloves on his hands, which were covered in blood, also, and he held a large carving knife, with several small pieces of raw, red flesh attached to the rather ominous-looking weapon. Ignoring

Sir Charles, he glanced across to Elizabeth, with his eyes asking more questions than his lips when he addressed her.

"Can I be of service, m'lady?" he inquired quietly, while making an almost imperceptible movement with the knife in his hand.

Elizabeth held her breath. If the situation were not so serious, she would have laughed to see the sixty-year-old butler of tall, wiry build, and with greying hair, offering to assist her in this situation. Her husband, by comparison, was thick-set and of stocky build, although several years older than Martin. The two men faced each other across the room as Elizabeth attempted an explanation.

"There's been a slight accident. It has caused something of a mess, for glass has travelled in all directions and there is oil seeping onto the floor. Have one of the maids attend to it at once," Elizabeth directed, in an even tone.

Martin did not move or flinch, nor did he allow his gaze to flicker as he stared at her husband, with ill-concealed hatred in his eyes. Whatever had passed between these two men, Elizabeth knew not, but something had occurred, because it was many years since her husband had struck her and he had come home drunk on numerous occasions in recent times.

Without another word, Sir Charles strode toward the door as Martin stepped aside, thereby allowing him to leave the sitting room unscathed. He left without a backward glance at his wife. Elizabeth breathed deeply, without having been aware that she was holding her breath during the encounter. Martin closed the door and looked inquiringly at her.

"Are you injured in any way?" he asked her, with deep concern registering on his face and without realising that he had dropped the butler's mask as he did so.

Elizabeth shook her head slowly. She was studying him closely. She smiled at him and her relief was obvious, she knew, as she spoke in a hoarse whisper.

"Thank you, Martin," she said, with a deep sigh. "No, I'm unharmed. Your arrival was timely, as I knew it would be. Why on earth are you in that blood-splattered state?"

"Cook has injured her wrist. I was assisting with the dissection of a recently-killed beast when I heard the carriage. I came at once. I'll have this cleaned up immediately. Is there anything else you need?"

Elizabeth shook her head slowly. Abruptly, she stood on shaky legs and walked toward the verandah door. She was astounded that the man, to whom she was married, could have such an effect on her to this day. She turned her head slightly to see Martin watching her closely, with deep concern registering on his face.

"Fresh air . . . that's all I need. I'll go and talk to my plants. They make more sense than some others around here!" she remarked.

Elizabeth hurried across the verandah; then, she crossed the side yard to her greenhouse, all the while taking deep breaths and reaching for her straw hat and gardening gloves as she entered the structure. Here, Elizabeth began a serious discussion with herself and her roses.

"So, Louisa's the next one in his line-of-sight? We will have to watch that situation closely as it develops from here, won't we, my pretty one?" she asked the white rosebud that was beginning to open to its surroundings in this new world.

It was in this moment that the trembling began in earnest. It came upon her so suddenly that it took her unawares initially. She walked slowly to the rough timber bench that was attached to the side wall as her knees threatened to give away beneath her. With great relief, she sank onto the seat. She placed her head on her hands for support and she concentrated on breathing for several minutes.

When she looked up – as a slight movement alerted her to a visitor – she focussed her somewhat-vacant gaze on Martin Tomms, who stood in the doorway with a tray in his hands. On this, there stood a glass of lemonade. Gratefully, and with a nod of her head acknowledging her gratitude, she took the glass. Without a word, Martin walked away. He disappeared within the walls of the homestead as, in a totally-detached manner, she watched his progress through the open doorway of the greenhouse.

Elizabeth sipped the liquid and pondered this latest development within her family. Her son would need to be warned. Elizabeth knew her husband too well to ignore the warning that she had been given within the past minutes. She would write to Charles and she would give the missive to Martin for dispatch, so as to ensure it reached its destination safely. What Charles did with the information was up to him, but if he were to be forewarned, he would be on his guard, especially if this proposed dinner party were to take place.

Elizabeth hoped sincerely and fervently that it would not eventuate. Caroline must be warned, also, for perhaps, she could use her influence to dissuade her father. If she could not do so, no one would be capable of averting the event, which could end only in disaster.

The feeling of foreboding that Elizabeth knew so well overtook her. It was an old friend – and one not to be ignored.

Chapter Twenty-Five

– *Victorian Victorians* –

Louisa

Two days after leaving Melbourne, Louisa was waiting to step aboard the smaller paddle-steamer, *Mary-Ann*, with her husband by her side. The tension between them had in no way decreased and the only words spoken by either one were those of necessity for two travellers bound for the same destination.

Louisa recognised the gentleman on the wharf in Echuca and she moved to speak with him, with Charles following her at a close distance. He was the stock and station agent for the area and Louisa had known him for all of her life.

"Mr. Bridges! Good morning. How're you today?" she inquired.

"Louisa! Dear girl, you're a sight for sore eyes. I'm well, and if I were not so, who'd want to listen to my complaints anyway? How is your father? I've not set eyes on him in ages?"

"Oh? I was hoping you had. He promised to call on you when he came through Echuca just before Christmas. Obviously, he didn't do so. I'll speak to him as soon as I reach home; then, I'll contact you, as we are in need of two new hands, at the very least. It's a matter of some urgency."

Charles moved forward and introduced himself to the gentleman, as it was obvious that Louisa had no intention of introducing the two men. Mr. Bridges was frowning slightly as he turned again to Louisa.

"Are there problems there? I'll do all I can to help, but you do seem to have lost a few men of late. That is unlike your father to let good men go. And, I only provide the best for him. You know that."

She glanced furtively at Charles before replying to the agent, who was awaiting an explanation.

"Papa hadn't been well, but he's recovered fully now, so everything will be back to normal when I arrive home. I'll send word to you then. We must go aboard now. It was nice to see you again. Give my kind regards to Mrs. Bridges."

With those hasty words, Louisa escaped and boarded the paddle-steamer quickly where she was greeted warmly by the captain and crew, all of whom she knew well. Charles, with a deepening frown on his face, followed behind her. She was disappointed on reaching Echuca to find that the *Charmaine* had left for Swan Hill on the previous day and the paddle-steamer would not be returning for a week.

Louisa and Charles had spent one night in Bendigo en route and, on the previous night, they stayed at the same hotel as on their wedding night. But, on this occasion, it was in separate rooms, at Louisa's insistence. Charlotte was accompanying them to Louisa's home, but the valet, Joseph, was left in Echuca to await Charles' return. Louisa would have preferred to travel the last leg of her journey alone, but her husband would not countenance the thought for a moment.

She had made that suggestion during dinner on the previous evening, but he reminded her of her proposed escapade in December and of her father's threat to return her to Melbourne and to her husband if she arrived alone. She then suggested that he write a missive to her father while explaining that she was travelling with his permission, but he merely laughed at the suggestion. He declared his intention of taking her to the homestead in person and of remaining overnight to discuss matters with her father. So, this morning, it was a troubled Louisa who stood on the deck and she was staring into the waters of the Murray River. She was eager to arrive, but she was all too well aware of what was awaiting her on arrival and she did not want her husband to know her father's business affairs.

"What was that all about?" Charles inquired, suddenly coming beside her.

"What?"

"The man on the wharf . . . who is he and what's wrong at your father's property? I'm not stupid, Louisa. Tell me now."

"Mr. Bridges is the stock and station agent."

"Yes," Charles replied, with some impatience, before probing further. "I gathered as much. Are there problems at the property? A simple *yes* or *no* will suffice?"

Louisa turned away. She was surveying the opposite bank and watching the bird life. The birds scattered and took flight in all directions at the sound and sight of the approaching paddle-steamer that was disturbing the peaceful habitat. Charles moved closer to her, in a deliberate manner, as he awaited an answer to his question.

"It's not your concern. My family's business remains exactly that. Please do not interfere. But, I don't want you to tell Papa how long I'm staying. If he's not handling everything the way it should be done and if he thinks I'm here for a few months, he'll not take up the reins again as he needs to do. Do you understand?"

"No, not at all; because what concerns you, does concern me and will do so always, even if you haven't accepted that fact as yet."

"Keep out of it!" Louisa stated hastily, between clenched teeth.

He grimaced slightly and turned away while walking to the stern and speaking with one of the crewmen who was working there. Louisa was left alone to her thoughts.

It was mid-afternoon when they arrived. Louisa jumped onto the pontoon from the gangplank almost before the boat had come to a complete standstill and she ran up the stone steps to the homestead, with excitement mounting with every step. To be home again was her greatest joy and she ran to the side verandah, eager to see her father. As expected, he was dozing in his favourite chair and she sat in the chair opposite him. Taking his hands in her own, she began stroking them.

Slowly, George opened his eyes. He stared at her blankly. He did not appear to recognise her initially. He did not smile or greet her, much to her disappointment, as she was expecting surprise, mingled with excitement. In fact, recognition was very slow in coming and Charles was approaching behind her before George Howard realised the identity of his two visitors. He smiled slowly; then, he rose to his feet even more slowly and he hugged her, briefly. After he released her, he greeted Charles as he extended his hand and shook Charles' outstretched one.

Louisa was deeply troubled. She was expecting a joyous reunion, but her father seemed somewhat stunned to see her and not a little detached – almost as though there were some barrier between them. This had never been the case in her entire life and she was at a loss to explain the problem to herself, because it was the result of a feeling only and not in any way connected with his warm, if somewhat astonished and belated, welcome.

George Howard, with an arm around his daughter, led them into the house and Mrs. McBryde and Betsy were waiting with welcoming smiles, also. However, the feeling of unease did not leave Louisa as they enjoyed afternoon tea in the drawing room.

Leaving the two men there, she escaped to her father's library, which doubled as an office and she went immediately to the desk, which was littered in papers. Most of these were invoices, which she knew were unpaid and several were marked with the word, *Reminder*.

She had been handling the books, at her mother's insistence and with her mother's assistance, since she was fourteen years of age and never before had an invoice, indelibly marked *Reminder*, crossed this desk since her mother's intervention in the financial affairs of the property many years earlier. Louisa was horrified by the sight and the implications.

Quickly, she removed the ribbon from around her neck and she extracted the key from the bodice of her gown as she did so. She moved to the highly-polished timber cupboard behind the door and she extracted her account books. Glancing through them quickly, she breathed a deep sigh of relief as she realised that none of these had been touched by anyone else. Her greatest fear had been that Jenkins, the bookkeeper, had somehow managed to prise open the locked cupboard where he knew that she kept the books hidden and he had tampered with them. Hurriedly, she returned them to their hiding place and locked them away again. She found the second set of books belonging to the man whom she despised so much and she flicked through the pages.

In a disgusted manner, she lifted them up in her two hands and she flung them across the room; then, with her foot, she kicked them over into the corner before placing a chair over them. That they had not been touched in months was obvious. Therefore, she was of the opinion that he had not been in this room of late and another sigh of relief escaped her with this realisation. She sifted through some of the invoices, statements and correspondence, most of which remained unopened and she was reminded of the unopened invitations that Charles had discovered in her own room at Lyndhurst Park.

"Like father, like daughter," she moaned to herself audibly.

Her father was as disinterested in the business side of the property as Louisa was in the social side of Melbourne's society. But, as far as the smooth running of his working sheep property was concerned, there was no one who could match him for expertise, knowledge and diligence. He would do the work of two men, despite being past his sixtieth year now. She longed for the day when he would do so again.

George Howard disliked paperwork intensely and he would never touch it. Therefore, anything that was opened on the desk, Brydie would have done so, at Louisa's request, and she acknowledged to herself that her return was timely indeed. She would work all night, if necessary, to have these overdue accounts paid and, with reluctance, she would give them to her husband to dispatch in Echuca on his return journey tomorrow.

With these plans, she left the library and went to her old bedroom. She would sleep in here tonight and if her father made any comment, she would have strong words for him. Charles Lyndhurst would be deposited in the guest room at the front of the homestead. On that, there would be no compromise whatsoever. He was on her territory now and he would abide by her rules.

Louisa opened the wardrobe to find some of her old muslin gowns hanging there, and even her old hairbrush was on the dressing-table, with strands of her auburn hair attached to it. It was as though she had never left her home at all.

There was a light tap at the door and Betsy, the parlour-maid, stood there, with Charlotte beside her. The two young women were of a similar age and, leaving Charlotte in Betsy's care, Louisa returned to the drawing room. Charles Lyndhurst was alone. He was sitting in the chair where she had left him thirty minutes earlier and his hat was beside him on the chair.

"Where's Papa?" she inquired.

Charles looked up at her and he raised his expressive eyebrows at her question. She grimaced and bit her lip, immediately looking in the direction of the verandah and presuming that George had returned to his old armchair there while leaving Charles alone. This was something that her father would never have done in years past.

"What's wrong here, Louisa?" Charles asked quietly.

"Nothing I can't handle," she replied, with conviction.

"Do you wish me to stay longer?"

"No!" she exclaimed loudly and quickly.

"I'm happy to do so, if you need me."

"Would that not be a wise move, Louisa?" Mrs. McBryde's voice queried.

Louisa spun around to find Mrs. McBryde standing by the sideboard in the dining room with a tray in her hand. She was looking through the archway at Louisa. Then, she turned quickly and left the room. Louisa turned back to Charles and she was shaking her head in a definite manner.

"Under no circumstances," she muttered, before asking the next question. "Would you like me to show you to the guest room now?"

"If that's *all I am* then, perhaps, you'd better do so."

Louisa entered the guest room and she moved to open the windows and the drapes. He stood in the doorway and he was watching her intently.

"We were not expected, you see," she stated, by way of explanation.

"I'll not leave here tomorrow until I get some answers. What do you plan to do now . . . disappear on me again?" Charles asked.

Louisa spun around to stare at him as she was unable to accept that he would wish to stay any longer than he needed to do. She wanted him to leave as quickly as was possible. The paddle-steamer had left already and it was heading downstream to the town of Swan Hill, but it was to call at the homestead mid-morning tomorrow to collect Charles on its return journey to Echuca.

Before she could reply, Trevor, the overseer, appeared. He was carrying the portmanteau belonging to Charles. He nodded a greeting to Charles; then, he cast a quick, furtive glance at Louisa, which her husband noticed instantly, she knew.

"Nice to see you back, Lou," Trevor stated, with relief sounding in his voice.

"Thanks, Trevor. I'll be down to see you shortly," she said, while hoping fervently that he would leave immediately and as he placed the luggage on the floor.

He turned to do so as he nodded at her in agreement. Then, much to Louisa's horror, he stopped in the hallway and he returned to her. He was rummaging through his pockets as he did so. He pulled out some crumpled papers and, brushing by Charles, who had stepped fully into the room and out of his path, Trevor handed these items to her.

"I've checked off that lot. They just came on the *Mary-Ann* and I'll give yer the rest when yer come down to the yards. A couple of drums of turpentine didn't arrive. Yer did order 'em, didn't yer?"

Louisa grabbed the invoices, which he handed to her and she slipped these behind her back.

"I believe so. I'll discuss it with you later," she muttered.

He nodded to her, as though lost in thought, still. Then, realising he was standing in the centre of their bedroom, he coloured slightly and left hurriedly. Charles moved quickly and he stood by the doorway, thus deliberately preventing Louisa's exit. He tossed the hat that he was holding onto the bed and he began to remove his coat. Without looking at her, he threw the coat over the bed-end.

"*I will stay here* for as long as it takes to get to the bottom of what's going on! I thought your obsession with returning to your father's home was due to your hatred of me. But, perhaps, there's more to it. Am I correct in this assumption?" he asked.

"I don't hate you . . . I don't hate anybody . . . except Jenkins, perhaps; but he's drinking himself into an early grave, so why should I be worried about him? No, that's all. I need to take care of some paperwork until a new bookkeeper can be employed to replace him."

"And, what of the other men who've left recently?" Charles asked.

Louisa shrugged her shoulders in a nonchalant fashion. She was looking away from him and out of the window, because she did not tell lies very well, she acknowledged to herself.

"They must've had other priorities, presumably."

"Presumably," Charles murmured, suddenly stepping toward the bed and sitting on the side of it while addressing her in a very sarcastic tone. "I'll not be detaining you any longer, as it is all too obvious that *you* have other priorities, also. Shall I see you at dinner? Or, am I to dine alone?"

"Papa likes to eat early, so be in the dining room in two hours," she murmured, as she headed at a rapid pace toward the door.

"And, how would you suggest I spend that time?" he inquired.

"Do as you please." Louisa replied, in an off-hand manner. "I seem to recall that you left me cooling my heels alone for several hours on my first day at Lyndhurst Park. I'm certain you'll find some amusement for yourself."

Louisa hurried from the guest room and she went in search of Brydie, as there were many matters to be discussed. She located her in the kitchen with Betsy, but Mrs. McBryde would not speak with her. Their cook and housekeeper declared firmly to Louisa that there was much to be done before dinner and she had no time to devote to other matters at present. Perhaps, in the morning, they could speak at length, Mrs. McBryde suggested. Louisa knew her too well to argue. The matter was decided, much to Louisa's annoyance.

Instead, she left the kitchen and went in search of the overseer, Trevor. The one place where she would not venture was to the cabin that was occupied by the bookkeeper, Jenkins. When she left Trevor, she was in a deeply troubled state. She returned to the homestead while vowing to herself to bring her father to task as soon as possible over the state of the property. She locked herself in the library, so as not to be disturbed, and she began to sift through the mountain of invoices and general correspondence awaiting her there. Absorbed in her work, she was disturbed by a tap at the door some considerable time later. Mrs. McBryde stood outside the door when Louisa unlocked it.

"Dinner will be served in ten minutes, child. Ready yourself now, for your husband's been pacing about for an hour or more. So, don't be late."

"Thanks, Brydie. I didn't realise it was so late. Everything is in such a mess!"

"You're *telling me?*" Mrs. McBryde queried, as she hurried away.

Louisa tidied the desk and she returned the journal to its hiding place in the cupboard, before hurrying to her bedroom to dress for dinner. When she arrived in the dining room, Charles and her father were seated already at the table. Her father smiled at her. Her husband scowled at her. Louisa sat in her usual seat, without a word to anyone, as Mrs. McBryde and Betsy served the meal.

"And, is this a short visit?" George asked of his daughter.

"Why? Don't you want me here?" Louisa challenged.

"Of course I do. You're welcome always. I wondered, that's all. I saw you a few weeks ago and you made no mention of a visit . . . well, not a sanctioned one, at any rate," he muttered, with a soft laugh.

"Charles leaves in the morning and I'll stay for a week or two," Louisa explained, while ignoring Brydie's sharp glance as she made this statement.

Louisa knew that Charlotte would have advised Mrs. McBryde and Betsy of her stated intention of remaining for fourteen weeks. So, the reaction from the housekeeper was not surprising, but her father seemed to accept her explanation and that was a great relief to her. Charles remained silent for most of the meal while the conversation between her father and herself was strained, as Louisa found it difficult to gain a response from him when she questioned him on anything to do with the household or the property. She was having difficulty controlling her temper, for nothing seemed to hold his interest for very long. Finally, as dinner was concluding, she slammed her hand down onto the table. Both men, somewhat startled, stared at her.

"Papa! Why won't you talk to me? I need some answers, now! Why won't you take an interest in anything? You're not unwell; or, so the doctor said. Therefore, there's no excuse for this indolence!"

"Everything is fine here, child. We're all going about our work, as usual," George stated in a slow, even tone.

Exasperated at his calm demeanour and his slowly-spoken words, Louisa stood up and she moved closer to him as he sat at the head of the table. Charles was eyeing her with some concern, as there were obvious signs of her temper rising. It was at this moment that Mrs. McBryde re-entered the room.

"*Nothing's fine!* Jenkins has left everything in a mess, as I knew he would. Why can't you see what's happening before your eyes? Never have the books been in such a state, with accounts unpaid. Not that I expected any different, because I've had the cheque book with me in Melbourne, but no one bothered to write to ask where it was. Not one account has been paid since I left! How do you explain that?" Louisa demanded, almost shouting the words at her father.

George continued eating his meal and he ignored her completely. Mrs. McBryde came and stood beside her. She whispered in Louisa's ear.

"That's enough. Let it be for now. This is your first night back. There's plenty of time for this later."

George Howard suffered from selective hearing loss, but on this occasion, Mrs. McBryde's whispered words were heard clearly by him.

"Pay her no heed, Mrs. McBryde. She's never listened to me, so don't expect her to listen to your advice. Sit down, Louisa, and finish your meal," George stated.

"No! I won't! Don't try to fob me off! Why can't you ride out with Trevor tomorrow and inspect the property? How many head do we have left? How many fences are down? Answer me that!"

George Howard continued to eat his meal in silence. Mrs. McBryde returned to the sideboard, with a look of deep concern on her face, while Charles Lyndhurst watched with not a little interest in the proceedings. Louisa leaned over her father until he stopped eating and he looked up at her.

"Do I have to put a gun to your head to force you?" she demanded angrily, as his silence enraged her still more.

George threw his spoon across the table, jumped to his feet, upending his chair in the process, and he stormed out onto the side verandah. Mrs. McBryde came to her.

"You give no quarter, do you, Louisa? Tonight was not the night. I told you that! You charge in and you don't have all the facts."

"How can I have, Brydie, if no one will talk to me?"

"Tomorrow was soon enough," Mrs. McBryde stated firmly.

"He has had two months of *yesterdays*! Nothing's waiting until tomorrow. *And*, you may as well know I'm here for three months, but don't tell him that!"

"I'm aware of it. Give him more time, child. How can it hurt?" Mrs. McBryde pleaded.

"I've only just begun! He's had all the time he's going to get!" Louisa shouted, as she uttered the prediction in anger while staring at the open verandah doorway.

"God help us all then . . . that's all I can say," Colleen McBryde stated.

Mrs. McBryde turned quickly and she left the room immediately. Louisa looked down at her husband, who remained seated at the dining table and he was wiping his mouth with a white linen serviette.

"*And, don't you* say a word!" she shouted at him.

"Would I dare?" he murmured. "I'm just relieved I'm not the one on the receiving end for once."

Louisa walked over and flounced back into her chair. She reached for a glass of water and she found her hand was trembling so much that she was required to return the glass to the table before it reached her lips. Charles reached for a wine glass and he filled it with white wine. He handed it to her as Louisa began to shake her head firmly in protest.

"Have a few sips. It will help. Trust me."

She took a few sips; then, she followed those with a few gulps, after which she emptied the glass completely while her husband looked on in some amazement and not-a-little amusement. She held up her hands, which were trembling no longer.

"Well, that fixed that!" Louisa stated, immediately reaching for the decanter of wine and refilling her glass. "The other problem is a little more difficult."

"And, which problem would that be?" he inquired quietly.

"One that neither you, nor the wine, can help me to fix! I really am such an awful person . . . when will I ever learn?" she asked, while biting her lip again before placing the wine glass to her mouth.

Charles remained silent as Louisa continued to drink the wine. She was glancing over every now and then at the verandah door.

"How much will I need to drink, do you think, before I can walk out through that door and apologise? Why on earth did God give me such a foul, vile temper, with which to contend?" she queried.

"I've asked that question of myself a thousand times over the years, and still, I have no answer. My worst fear is for our children . . . one must wonder what they will inherit," Charles stated quietly.

Louisa stared at him in horror. Then, this turned to disgust immediately. He was watching her reaction to his words with some amusement in his eyes, although his expression appeared quite serious.

"Don't speak to me of such nonsense! We won't be having any of those!"

"Is that so?" he asked. "As I seem to be the only friend you have in this household at present, is it wise to antagonise me, also, do you think?"

"I'll take my chances," Louisa replied, as she slammed the empty glass onto the table with a thud.

With great reluctance, she rose to her feet. She frowned, as her head seemed to swim and to sway a little at this abrupt movement. Eventually, she took charge of her somewhat relaxed body as Charles smiled at her.

"That's the first alcohol I've seen you drink."

"Yes . . . and I've just broken my confirmation pledge. Oh! My sins keep on mounting and mounting. Father Frank will give up on me shortly if I don't reform and repent."

She had reached the door when she heard his laughter. She turned to look at him with some disdain.

"If only your father and your husband could exercise as much influence and control as that renegade priest!" he stated, through his laughter.

Louisa flounced through the doorway, with her head held high, and she located her father who was leaning against the verandah post, with his forehead resting on it. She walked over to him, placed an arm around his waist and kissed him on the cheek.

"I'm sorry, Papa. Forgive me."

He kissed the top of her head as he placed an arm around her shoulder.

"There's nothing to forgive. Your mother always said we were like two pieces of flint sparking off each other and she was never wrong . . . in this, or in anything else . . . for that matter," he murmured in her ear. "We'd better return to Charles. What must he think of us!"

Louisa felt a retort rising instantly to her lips. With great restraint, she suppressed it as she managed to swallow it completely. Then, she allowed her father to lead her back into the drawing room.

"Forgive us, Charles. We're a pair of hotheads together. My daughter inherited her good looks, her candour and her *sometimes-sweet* disposition from her mother. From me, she got nothing more than a vile temper."

"Which I've experienced, also, George. I'm rather pleased not to be in the firing line for once."

Louisa walked to the table, picked up the remnants of a loaf of bread and threw it at him. Charles caught it in both hands as he laughed at her, but her anger was not far beneath the surface. She spun around and left the room hurriedly.

She went immediately to the library and retrieved her books from the locked cabinet; then, she began to study the invoices as she placed the most urgent ones on top of the pile. With both lamps on the desk alight, she was poring intently over the figures in the ledger. Suddenly, the door opened and Charles and her father entered.

"What are you doing in here at this hour, Louisa?" George inquired.

"The accounts, Papa! What did you expect? I must do them tonight, so if you've come to partake of port or brandy in here, you'll have to pretend I'm not here, for I must be about my work."

"I employ a bookkeeper to do those," George stated firmly.

"There! Over in the corner! Have a glance at *his handiwork*. It looks as though the hens have scratched over the pages . . . *and, they'd* have done a better job with the calculations than he has. We'd be bankrupt if you went by that ledger. The accountant would throw them out of the window, if you had the nerve to send them there!"

"Nonsense, child. You've allowed your dislike of him to cloud your judgement. He's an excellent bookkeeper."

"So you say! Twenty years ago, that may have been the case. Now, he's nothing more than a rum-soaked . . . well, there're no words in the English language to describe what *he's become* . . . none that I'm permitted to use, anyway!"

George Howard surveyed his daughter with ill-concealed annoyance. Abruptly, he turned to Charles as he ignored Louisa completely.

"Perhaps, Charles, we could adjourn to the drawing room. We'll have no peace in here this evening."

George Howard stormed from the room while her husband lingered momentarily as he surveyed the books, in which she was writing. Finally, Louisa glanced up and she glared at him. In return, he smiled at her, in a supercilious manner. Charles turned and left the room without a word.

Louisa breathed a deep sigh of relief and she continued with her calculations as she made the necessary entries in the ledger. She must have everything completed in time for Charles' departure on the paddle-steamer in the morning.

There was much work to be done this night.

Paula

Without one thought to her own predicament, Paula stood watching Louisa Lyndhurst from her vantage point by the window in the library. Paula's current consciousness had moved from her own situation where she had been admitted to a hospital to this other reality, as though it were a dream sequence, which she was experiencing.

At present, Paula was unaware that her husband had not been located – as yet – and that her own condition was listed as critical. These external happenings were not allowed to invade her mind now, because in an extremely detached manner, she was observing Louisa while the young girl continued with her work at the desk in the library. Paula's concentration on Louisa was as intense as was Louisa's concentration on the ledger before her.

Paula had been a silent witness to all that had occurred in the girl's life recently. She was troubled deeply by the experience, but she could find no reason why this should be so. After all, she had a life of her own back in Los Angeles where her young son was waiting for her, along with her mother, Liz. Her sister, Carla, who was living with her husband on a dude ranch outside of Tucson, in Arizona, was due to give birth to another baby at any time. This should have been a happy period within her family unit.

So, all-in-all, Paula's main focus should have been on her own life and on the lives of her immediate family members who, no doubt, would be in deep shock when the extent of Paula's injuries was revealed to them. They would be in a very distraught state over Paula's condition, because they were a close-knit family.

Yet, here she stood, unmoved by her own problems, while she watched by this library window – in a long-ago time-frame – as she studied Louisa Lyndhurst, who was unaware of Paula's presence in the room.

In reality, however, it was the sound of harshly-spoken words that brought Paula back to her present whereabouts with a start. The voice was definitely male and one that spoke of an authority-figure whose orders were never to be questioned.

"I want this patient in theatre . . . *now!* Where are her x-rays?"

Paula could not see anything in this secluded world, for sound was all that there was. Following on from this directive, there came the sound of a screen being wrenched backwards and Paula felt a slight draught of air on her face. Her conscious mind began to question again, but no answers came when she tried to recall where she was and how she came to be here, in this place and at this moment-in-time. Suddenly, her wayward thoughts were interrupted by another voice. This one was soft and female, but tinged with annoyance.

"He's such an arrogant pig! Who does he think he is, anyway?"

"He's the best surgeon around," replied her male companion, who felt – to Paula – as though he could be standing beside her right ear. "And, if you were in this lady's condition, he'd be the only one you'd want to see heading in your direction, believe me. Am I right, Lucy?"

"Huh! I don't care what you say. He's rude and arrogant. Besides, a little civility is not too much to ask. Thank goodness I'm not married to him . . . that's all I know," Lucy answered him. "Let's move her."

"Have they located her husband yet?" the man queried.

If Lucy replied to this question, Paula was unaware of her answer. Almost immediately, Paula felt movement. Her body did not move of its own accord, yet the bed, on which it was resting began to roll as though being propelled by its own momentum. Having no explanation for the events that were happening around her – while feeling, perhaps, that this was but a dream-sequence, which she was experiencing during sleep – Paula's detachment increased.

It was then that she started to wonder about the young girl, Louisa Lyndhurst, and what had become of her. With this shift in focus, Paula's current reality began to recede in her consciousness and she found herself back in the library inside the homestead on the banks of the Murray River.

Paula stood watching Louisa, who was gazing out of the window and looking into the distance as though studying closely an activity that was occurring in the back paddock. However, it was not a present event that the girl was observing, but a past happening. She was reliving a time when Louisa's horse, Hilton, had soared over the head of Charles Lyndhurst and, in that instant, the man had come within a whisker of physical death. Louisa was playing this scene over in her mind and she was castigating herself severely for not having noticed the events, which had been overtaking her at the time. If only other decisions had been made back then, her life would not be as intolerable as it was for her at present. This was the conclusion, at which Louisa arrived as the dawn light flooded the room.

Louisa rubbed the back of her neck several times; then, involuntarily, she gave a deep sigh. It had been a long, long night. Turning slowly, she returned to the chair and seated herself comfortably at the desk. Once again, she reached for the ledger. She sat fingering its pages while attempting to bring her attention back onto the figures displayed neatly on its pages.

Paula's heart went out to the young girl and somewhere, in the depths of her own being, a memory stirred and a deep-seated pain revealed itself. The familiarity of this whole scene puzzled her greatly as she watched the forlorn figure of Louisa Lyndhurst slumped over the desk while staring at the blank wall and the empty fireplace.

That she was dreading the day when Charles Lyndhurst would return to collect her, was obvious. His violent, sexual attack on her was as vivid in her mind now as it was on the day when it occurred. She shuddered involuntarily – with revulsion – every time that she relived this particular sequence of events. That she would be required to submit herself voluntarily to him was not a thought that she could entertain at present.

For a short time, she could play the role of Louisa Howard while resuming her former life, but she knew that the day would dawn when the piper would need to be paid. In her customary manner, she consigned this horrific thought to a small compartment deep within her mind and she sealed it completely. Perhaps, it would never occur; or, Charles would forget that she existed and he would not return at all. Perchance, her knight-in-shining-armour would appear and whisk her away. This thought brought Phillip Carstairs to mind, so she found another compartment, in which to seal his memory, because she accepted unequivocally that he was gone from her life forever.

Wistfully, Louisa tilted her head to one side; then, with great determination, she brought her attention back to her present situation. She reached for the pen and dipped its nib into the ink in the inkwell. With another deep sigh, she resumed her work, as there was much to be done before breakfast. She needed to have all of this correspondence ready for Charles to take with him this morning.

For Paula, the jolt that she experienced as the bed rolled through the doors and into the hospital elevator, caused her to return instantly to her own body and to this physical life.

She realised with distinct clarity that she had no control over what was occurring with her at present – just as she had no way whatsoever of intervening in these events. Remarkably, for someone who had been in control of her own destiny for most of her adult life, Paula felt a wave of relief sweep through her entire being, as inexplicably, a feeling of total acceptance overtook and engulfed her completely.

From somewhere deep within the recesses of her mind, the words came clearly to her:

"Let go and let God."

With her eyes closed and her mind turning over slowly, Paula listened to the sounds swirling around her. The faint noise of the elevator's mechanism hummed below the sound of voices that belonged to those who were huddled together in this enclosed capsule for their short journey. To Paula, the elevator appeared to be ascending while, to her barely-conscious mind, the drone of voices surrounding her began to overlay the persistent hum of the elevator.

The nurse, Lucy, was outlining her plans for the coming weekend on the Gold Coast. These were to involve a man whose name seemed to be Brad and a nightclub excursion, followed by their attendance at an early morning surfing competition. The nurse, Sam, was resigned to the fact that he was working for the entire weekend and he would miss these frivolities completely. Another female voice interjected then and Paula listened as they chatted together while discussing other staff members who were absent from this ascending cupboard, in which all were travelling currently.

Paula had no knowledge of where she was being taken; or, why she was being moved. Momentarily, she wondered about the nurse, Gerard, who had attended to her needs earlier while she was resting in the hospital bed in the two-bed room, although he was not mentioned during the course of the conversation that was taking place at present.

As the elevator came to a distinct halt and the doors slithered open, the bed, on which Paula was resting began to move. The other occupants laughed and joked together; then, the front wheels of Paula's bed bounced over the threshold once again. The drone of voices subsided.

The current reality, in which Paula resided, drifted away. Suddenly, the hospital bed and its surrounding corridor, with its bustle of activity and its constant noise, did not exist in Paula's present world.

Paula's present world became a library at the rear of a homestead on the banks of the Murray River in *Victorian Victoria*. The only other occupant of this room was Louisa Lyndhurst. The young girl was slumped over the desk while seemingly in a deep sleep. Rolling, as in slow motion, Louisa's head moved sideways. It bumped against the ink well and the girl stirred. Lazily, two green eyes opened. Blearily, she peered at her surroundings while Paula watched from her vantage point just inside the room as she stood by the window of the home.

Louisa lifted two arms above her head as she sat upright in the chair once again. As a feline would, she stretched her limbs slowly and gracefully. A yawn escaped from her; then, she placed one hand behind her head at the nape of the neck and she began to rub the area slowly.

As dawn was replaced by the new day, the realisation of where she was dawned on the drowsy girl. She moved her head from side-to-side, thus bringing herself to an awakened state and she rose slowly from the chair. She walked to the side window and gazed out across the paddock. Finally, she turned and moved to the rear window that opened onto the back verandah and, brushing by the silent and unseen Paula, she slithered through the opening and she stood erect on the verandah. From there, Paula watched as Louisa walked to the outhouse, which was some distance away from the rear of the home.

Presently, Louisa returned to the house and she entered her bedroom from the side verandah. There, she began her ablutions at the marble and oak table, on which stood a porcelain jug and basin awaiting her morning needs.

From there, Paula followed Louisa as the girl walked purposefully towards the dining room, which was empty at present. She quickened her step as she headed in the direction of the sideboard, on which stood a large teapot and some crockery. Reaching for a cup and saucer, she poured the steaming beverage into the cup.

In eager anticipation of her first sip of the day, Louisa lifted the fine English bone china cup to her waiting lips. While Paula was watching by the archway, as a silent sentinel would – thus seeing, but not participating, in this scene from a long-ago time – another person joined Louisa. She glanced around as the new arrival, Mrs. McBryde, entered the dining room. Louisa smiled at the lady, of whom she was fond and her smile was reciprocated instantly.

Paula continued to watch them. She felt that she knew Mrs. McBryde extremely well herself, but she could not recall the time and the place where they had met previously. But then, of course, this was simply a dream-sequence that she was experiencing and one that was brought on by the drugs, which were administered to her this day in a hospital on the Gold Coast, in the country known as Australia. *What else could it be*, Paula pondered.

However, the necessity to return to that other world was not a pressing requirement, at this stage. In reality, she could return there at any time of her own choosing. But for now, the dream after all was more interesting than the horror of what was occurring with her physical body in the other world. So, she would remain with the dream, Paula determined.

In dreams, it is true that nothing is predictable. But, at least she was safe here – safe from trauma, safe from pain and safe from decision-making, with regard to her own, personal welfare, as well as from having to live with the aftermath of any decisions that she made. Therefore, the choice to remain with Louisa Lyndhurst for a time – rather than having to face her own world of today – was an easy one to make.

From Paula's perspective, this whole scenario was all make-believe anyway!

Chapter Twenty-Six

– Victorian Victorians –

Louisa

The remainder of the night went by without her noticing. Dawn had broken before she came to the realisation that there was a dull ache throbbing at the back of her neck. Louisa rubbed the area. She stood up and stretched her arms above her head.

Some twenty minutes later, she walked into the dining room where a large teapot, filled with hot tea, sat waiting there. She poured a cup and was taking the first sip while standing by the cabinet when Mrs. McBryde entered the room.

"Good morning, Brydie. Thank you for this tea. I'm parched."

"G'morning, Louisa. Has your temper improved any this morning?"

"I expect not, although I've not been challenged by anyone as yet, so I can't really say," Louisa replied, and she laughed as she did so.

"Then don't cast your eyes in my direction. I'm too busy for such nonsense."

Louisa continued to stand there and she was feeling stiff from being in a crouched position over the desk all night. She was watching as Mrs. McBryde began to place cutlery on the dining table. She was dressed in her heavy grey gown.

Louisa cast her mind back to the night when she had witnessed Brydie with Bill Bartlett on her bed. Knowing what she knew now, that episode made a little more sense to her but, even so, she could not equate this prim-and-proper cook-housekeeper with the woman who had slithered naked on top of Captain Bill and, cat-like, had begun to devour him. In particular, she recalled how she settled her mouth over a certain part of Captain Bill's anatomy and Louisa found this image a rather difficult one to dislodge from her mind. Looking at Mrs. McBryde now, she shook her head while attempting to accept that this was the same lady.

"Brydie, I need to talk to you about Betsy."

"*Oh? Only Betsy?* Is that all you wish to speak of?" Colleen McBryde asked, with not a little tinge of sarcasm.

"No, you're right. There's much to discuss."

"*And, I was* expecting this today . . . although not at the crack of dawn, mind you. I've decided I'll not discuss anything with you without your husband being present. And, you're absolutely correct. Betsy must be settled today!" Colleen McBryde stated emphatically.

"Husband? What's it to do *with him*?" she asked, in astonishment.

"Everything, because he's married to you. He's come up a notch or two in my estimation and he needs to know what's going on here. *And*, it has to be now, as he's leaving this morning. Your father will be up and about soon. Then, it'll be too late. So, what's it to be, Louisa?"

Louisa stood still, sipping the tea and watching Brydie as she bustled about her work. Slowly, Louisa shook her head as she fixed Mrs. McBryde with a scowl.

"No, I can't. It's intolerable. I will not do so."

"Then, there's absolutely nothing more to be said!" Colleen McBryde stated, once again emphatically.

She walked away while speaking and she moved as though she intended to leave the dining room. Louisa replaced the cup on the sideboard and turned to her.

"Why has Betsy to be settled today?" Louisa demanded.

"Ask her . . . not me. If you want my input, then bring your husband out here now!"

Louisa was left alone while standing in the silent dining room. She paced to the window and heard a kookaburra laughing raucously. She wondered at what the bird could find to laugh on this particular morning. She could find nothing at all. She paced back to the sideboard and began to pour another cup of tea for herself. Then, she changed her mind and poured a cup of black tea instead. If Brydie had made up her mind on this score, nothing would change it. Without Bridie's input, Louisa was at a loss to know what to do about the state of affairs of the property and, also, about her father, for something was wrong there. Louisa felt that Mrs. McBryde may know how to deal with the whole situation.

Finally, with heavy feet, she trudged into the guest room. She placed the tea on the bedside table and reached over to shake Charles awake. With great reluctance, which was bordering on revulsion, she took a hold of his shoulder. He stirred a little before he settled back into a deep sleep.

"Charles, wake up!" she demanded, firmly shaking his shoulder again.

He opened his eyes. He looked at her very suspiciously. Then, he glanced around the darkened room. She moved to the drapes and opened them, instantly allowing the early morning light to enter. He rubbed his eyes as he studied her.

"Where's the water jug?" he queried.

"Over there . . . you're safe!" she replied.

"What? No dagger? What did you bring to attack me?"

"Nothing, just a cup of tea for you," Louisa admitted.

He looked intently at the cup of tea before turning back to survey her and he shook his head slowly. Gingerly, he picked up the cup and smelled its contents.

"It's laced with something! You've found the turpentine. Is that it?"

She laughed, despite herself and her current feelings of misgivings. Louisa stood at the end of the bed while holding onto the bed-end. She bit her lip momentarily before speaking.

"I've a problem here, as you seem to have gathered," Louisa admitted.

"Oh! Really! A genius may've realised it before me, but it's hardly a surprise, although I do seem to recall it being none of my business."

"I don't feel it is," Louisa stated, before elaborating somewhat reluctantly. "However, Brydie won't discuss anything with me unless you are present. I need her to do so."

"I see," he murmured, while sitting up in the bed and drinking the tea. "How long have we been married?"

"Two intolerable months! Why?"

"I take two spoons of sugar in my tea. I thought you would have known that by now."

He replaced the cup onto the table and made a movement as though he was about to leave the bed. As, quite obviously, he was naked, Louisa headed for the door somewhat hurriedly.

"Stay there! I'll get it."

Charles laughed and remained in the bed as he reached for the pillows and, propping himself up on these, he awaited her return and seemingly enjoying himself at her expense. Louisa came back into the guest room with a sugar bowl in her hands and she added the required sugar to the cup.

"Would you stir it? Then, *taste* it . . . just in case," he requested, while awaiting her response and when she did not reply, he addressed her in a supercilious tone. "Isn't it amazing how pleasant you can be and how solicitous of my welfare when you want something? You're quite amazing!"

Charles looked over at her and laughed. Louisa pursed her lips as she stood at the bedside while attempting to stem the tide of angry words from flooding into her mind at present. He studied her in some amusement.

"You would dearly love to throw that tea over me and yet, you dare not. Not that you fear me, but you need my services suddenly, so you control your fiery temper. Is there to be a trade-off? You always have a bargaining chip up your sleeve somewhere," Charles stated very calmly.

He lifted the tea cup and sipped the tea while watching her over the rim of the cup. Louisa was struggling within herself while attempting to control her temper, which was rising dangerously. But, it was her pride that was being dented markedly, because he was a stranger – as far as she was concerned – and she did not want him to know her father's business.

Charles was observing the battle that was ranging within her and, obviously, he was amused by the sight. Louisa returned to the end of the bed and she glared at him for a few more moments before addressing him sharply.

"Are you coming to the dining room with me now? Or, are you not?"

"A *please* may've been appropriate although I doubt that this word is a part of your vocabulary. *But, yes,* I'll accompany you . . . only because, as Mrs. McBryde said, I need to know. At least, there seems to be one person around here with a modicum of common sense."

Charles placed the cup firmly on the bedside table and he reached for the bed covers. He glanced at Louisa as he did so.

"Now, I'm obliged to leave this bed, so an unveiling will take place. Do you wish to be a witness?"

Louisa fled the room to the sound of his soft laughter. She returned to the dining room and poured another cup of tea before settling herself on a chair to await the arrival of the other two participants in this round-table discussion at the long, rectangular dining table. It was with mounting concern and great trepidation that she waited, because this situation appeared to be moving beyond her control. She was involving Charles Lyndhurst, not only because Brydie had given her no choice, but also, because she was at a loss to know what should be done in order to avoid the disaster that was looming on her horizon.

Charles arrived shortly thereafter and prior to the return of Mrs. McBryde. He was standing at the sideboard and pouring more tea for himself. He was dressed for riding, with breeches, riding boots and a white shirt, which was open at the neck. Louisa was surveying him in some surprise while trying to fathom why he would dress in this manner, as he was leaving the property in a few hours, when he came and sat down at the end of the table. He sat close by Louisa while placing the cup and saucer on the table in front of him.

"While we're alone, I need you to promise me something," Louisa said, in a soft, secretive tone.

He raised an expressive eyebrow while glancing suspiciously at her as he did so, and raising the cup to his mouth.

"You must not allow anyone, including yourself, to ride Hilton while I'm not there. It is imperative that you agree to this!" Louisa stated emphatically. "*Please*, Charles . . . you must promise me now."

Returning the cup to its resting place on the saucer, he watched her for some moments before responding as she twisted the rings on her finger and the frown on her brow increased markedly.

"There would need to be a good reason before I'd agree to such a request, although the thought hadn't occurred to me to do so . . . before now. Is this another of your secrets?"

Louisa reached for her cup of tea and drank slowly. Finally, moving the cup back to its saucer, she moved her shoulders almost imperceptibly in a slight shrug and she was about to reply when Mrs. McBryde entered the dining room. She glanced over at them before placing a tray stacked with dishes onto the sideboard.

"I've done as you requested, Brydie," Louisa stated, with a pronounced grimace.

"And, about time, too!" Brydie responded emphatically. "Good morning, Mr. Lyndhurst. I'm sorry you needed to be awoken at this ungodly hour, but I'm afraid there're certain matters that must be brought into the open, here and now."

Mrs. McBryde came to the table and she sat down opposite Louisa, but it was to Charles who was seated at the head of the table that she gave her full attention.

"Then, I'm obliged to you, Mrs. McBryde, for having the foresight and the courage to do what should have been done months ago. There's been an undercurrent in this homestead since the first day I entered it, but I've been unable to put my finger on the underlying cause. Please, do me the courtesy of speaking freely about everything," Charles replied. "The time for deception, pride and misplaced loyalties comes to an end this day. You've my undivided attention, but don't give me merely a *part* of the story."

Mrs. McBryde reached across the table and, taking a hold of Louisa's two hands, she spoke to Charles, but her eyes did not waver from Louisa's face. There was much love shining in those eyes as she studied her and it was reciprocated equally.

"I'd no intention of so doing," Mrs. McBryde said. "I notice much, but I say very little, unless and until I feel something needs to be spoken about. Then, I level both barrels. So, with me, you'll have both barrels between the eyes, if that's your preference . . . or, you'll have nothing at all."

Charles nodded in agreement as he sipped his tea. Louisa bit her lip and held her breath as she awaited the inevitable outcome of the disclosures that she knew were coming.

"Now, to begin with, there's Betsy to be considered."

Mrs. McBryde explained about Betsy's position at present. She had been employed there as a parlour-maid for the past five years, from the age of fourteen years. She was needed urgently at her home in Adelaide where her mother was gravely ill. Her father worked long hours as a farrier and there were several younger children who needed care and attention, so he had been pleading with Betsy to come home for many months. However, the girl was refusing to do so, because of her loyalty to and her fondness for the Howard family – and most especially Louisa.

On the previous day, the *Mary-Ann* had delivered mail and Betsy received another letter from her father. It was begging for her immediate return and the girl was distressed deeply by his news. Mrs. McBryde stated that there was another girl in Echuca who was pleading for the opportunity to take the position, so a replacement was not a problem. That could be achieved in a matter of days.

Charles responded to this disclosure immediately.

"So, we've a case of misplaced loyalties here. Perhaps, Louisa, you could release her today and she can make arrangements to go as soon as it is convenient to all. If the situation were reversed, would you not go to *your* mother?" Charles inquired.

"Of course," Louisa agreed, while nodding her head in agreement as she did so; then, forcefully, she explained the problem from her perspective. "But, that's not the end of it! Trevor will follow her. Then, I've lost *my overseer!* As well as that, there are those other two men who left recently . . . not to mention Mr. Curtis! I can't run the property then, can I?"

Charles stared at her in astonishment that was bordering on disbelief. Mrs. McBryde looked on with some satisfaction before intervening.

"*There,* you have the matter in a nutshell, Mr. Lyndhurst! This is a ghost-ship, and everyone is deserting like rats on a sinking vessel, which cannot be run solely and totally by a young girl who has been handling everything since she turned sixteen. *And then,* for the past two months, this property has been run by an extremely resource-ful seventeen-year-old lass *by correspondence* from Melbourne. It can't continue . . . and nor should it! This is too much responsibility to place upon the shoulders of one so young!"

Louisa looked down at her hands, which were encased firmly in Mrs. McBryde's hands, and she bit her lip while avoiding Charles' gaze.

"Is this the truth?" he asked quietly as he studied Louisa thoughtfully.

Without looking up, she nodded her head. She heard his quick intake of breath, but whether or not this denoted anger, she knew not.

"You do the books, as well?" he queried.

Louisa nodded her head once again and without looking up, as Mrs. McBryde squeezed her hands tightly in reassurance before elaborating.

"Not to mention the arranging of the last muster. Also, she organised the arrival of the shearers and the sale of the wool-clip, which by some miracle, was dispatched on barges bound for Echuca but days before your marriage. How she did it, I've no idea, but we all watched in astonishment and amazement," Mrs. McBryde stated, before explaining enthusiastically. "She is truly one remark-able young lady!"

"Everybody jumped in and played their part. I didn't work alone, Brydie. You know that!" Louisa interjected.

Mrs. McBryde squeezed her hands again, before releasing her. Brydie laughed softly, as Charles continued to frown markedly while lost in deep contemplation.

"Oh! Dear girl, it was our absolute pleasure to do so, but the time has come to hand over the reins, for you've other duties and obligations to keep you busy now."

"To whom!" Louisa exploded, as she queried Mrs. McBryde. "To whom do I hand them? To Papa? How can I do so? I can't seem to reach him. He has receded so far within himself, it is impossible!"

"*And,* I don't exist? Is that it?" Charles asked, before turning to Colleen McBryde and, without waiting for a reply from his wife, he requested more information. "Tell me about the overseer . . . this Trevor."

Trevor was a diligent overseer who had worked with sheep for most of his life and who was employed by George Howard many years earlier. He worked extremely well under supervision, but possessed little skill where literacy was concerned. Therefore, he could not make decisions for himself and he lacked the means of communicating directly with Louisa when she moved to Melbourne with Charles. When George was in charge, he followed directions to the letter, but after Louisa's marriage, he was required to correspond with her, through Mrs. McBryde, and this was adding considerably to that lady's workload.

Trevor was desperately in love with Betsy and it would take a miracle to keep him at the property once the girl departed for Adelaide. His loyalty to Louisa was beyond question, as he had watched her grow from a child – always dressed in breeches and an old shirt – while following her father, as his shadow would, wherever George went and doing whatever he did when she was capable of doing so. When she lacked the strength to do a particular job, she would watch others while learning exactly how the task was accomplished to the best advantage.

All this information, Mrs. McBryde conveyed to Charles while patiently explaining that, until she reached the age of fourteen years, George treated Louisa as his son, although she was required always to wear gowns in the homestead. This was a ruling demanded of her by both her mother, Mary, and her governess, Yvette. It was on the day when Yvette announced she was leaving to be married that George seemed to realise suddenly he had a daughter on his hands. He had demanded that Louisa be sent immediately to Melbourne to become a lady overnight.

"Perhaps, your father waited a little too long to achieve success in this arena, Lou," Brydie said, with a soft laugh.

"Rest assured, the matter is in hand. It'll be accomplished one day; or, I'll die in the attempt," Charles interjected.

"I wish you every success, then," Mrs. McBryde stated, while laughing again in an attempt to lighten the tension with laughter, for Louisa's benefit; then, she continued with her discourse. "The other matters concern Jenkins and Bill Curtis. Firstly, that gentleman should've known better. Curtis is a stockman, born and bred, and he had worked in Queensland for all of his life. His accident was in no way your fault, Louisa, even though I know I'll never convince you of that."

Louisa removed her hands from Brydie's tight grasp and she reached for the tea cup. She brought it to her lips, thus in so doing, she was preventing herself from making any rash statements or admissions of guilt.

"At his age, he must bear full responsibility, for he's a grown man... with not much common sense, granted... but he made the choice to ride Hilton without your permission. He knew the risks, because he'd been warned many times, but the temptation was too great for him and his egotistical nature. Betsy told me you ran as fast as you could when she told you what was occurring in the yards, but to no avail. So, perhaps, you can lay that ghost to rest! As for Jenkins, answer me honestly now, in front of Mr. Lyndhurst... did he attack you?"

Louisa bit her lip to hold back the tears that were threatening to flow and she turned her face quickly away from them. Mrs. McBryde reached for her hands again and she gripped them tightly.

"It's no disgrace to cry, especially when you've not shed a tear in years, not even for your dear mother and I know you adored her. Something happened with Jenkins. I know that. I'm sure he watched you often when you were swimming in the river. I'm aware your husband knows you did so, or I wouldn't mention this."

"Then, perhaps I should've sold tickets, for it seems every man and his dog saw me . . . *and, we're miles from anywhere!*"

"*And, how many times* did your parents forbid it?" Mrs. McBryde queried. "I watched you drag out the armchair from the library, followed by the old rug, and you set them alight. No one does that without reason . . . and you were deeply distressed for days. We're not *all* without eyes, you know. If I'd caught him, his days in this world would've been numbered."

Charles sat back in his chair as he watched the interaction between the two women at the table. Finally, he intervened while speaking to Mrs. McBryde directly.

"Perhaps later, I can delve further into that episode. The question, which hasn't been addressed as yet, is that of Mr. Howard. Is his problem stemming solely from grief?"

Colleen McBryde grimaced before answering; then, she explained that it had taken her some time to come to the understanding of what was occurring with George Howard. However, she discovered his secret too late to act upon it before now, as the matter did not resolve itself until his return from his recent trip to Melbourne. It would seem, she revealed, that George had begun self-administering his late wife's medicinal draughts shortly after her death and it appeared that he was unable to function without such medication.

Upon his return from Melbourne, Colleen McBryde discovered a great quantity – obviously newly-acquired – hidden in his room when she was cleaning there and she began to monitor his intake from then onwards. She was aware that he was spending most of his days in his favourite armchair on the verandah. On closer scrutiny on several occasions, she witnessed what she believed was his communication with someone seated in the other vacant chair nearby and she concluded that he believed he was speaking with his late wife.

Mrs. McBryde had kept this a closely-guarded secret, as she was not certain of this fact, but trying to wean him from the medicine was her goal at present. However, when she challenged him, she realised that he believed he needed same. He had declared firmly to her that he required these draughts for medicinal purposes after having spoken with several doctors in Melbourne.

Louisa's sudden return to the homestead on the previous day had thrown him into immediate consternation, as he did not know how to hide his often-confused state from her. As well, George had confided to Mrs. McBryde that he did not recall making a promise to visit Melbourne within four weeks of their marriage, so Charles' letter had come as a complete surprise to him, along with Louisa's invitation to the dinner party. He had been distressed that he had not heard a word from Louisa after she departed on her wedding day.

Charles' timely letter and the invitation had thrown some light on that mystery for him. This was one reason why he had forced himself to take the long trip, which he was dreading. The other reason was his obvious need for a new supply of the medicine. Because of his detached state, he found difficulty in being in company and especially when being around those whom he loved for fear that they would discover his secret.

"How can this be?" Louisa asked, appalled and aghast, as she demanded further explanation. "And, what on earth is he taking?"

"Laudanum," Mrs. McBryde answered.

Charles pursed his lips and shook his head slowly as a horrified Louisa looked to him for an explanation while Mrs. McBryde sat awaiting their reaction.

"It's derived from opium . . . highly addictive, as I understand it, and not to be taken in large quantities or over a long period of time," Charles responded. "Certainly, it should not be self-administered. This would explain his trance-like state I've observed since I came here."

"You mean to tell me he's in much the same state as Jenkins . . . incoherent and unable to function?" Louisa asked, unable to grasp the full implications of these revelations.

Mrs. McBryde assured her that the differences were great, and while she held high hopes of George being willing and able to rise above his current situation, because of his iron will and strong constitution, she held little hope for Jenkins who, she believed, did not have long to live. She stated that she sent Frank Jenkins broth only for his meals and she believed that, one day soon, she would arrive at the door of his quarters to find him dead, either due to a fall rendering him unconscious or from a part of his anatomy giving up its fight for life. Alternatively, there was a possibility that he could choke on his own vomit, hence her decision to send only soup for his meals – a fact that he had not noticed yet anyway.

George Howard, she felt, would take control of himself, his own life and his property only when she convinced him that he had a problem. When that day arrived, he would be mortified if he thought that anyone else knew of his addiction and most especially his daughter and her husband. Mrs. McBryde begged them to leave the problem in her safe hands, for she was certain that she could deal with him. But, it would take time on her part and trust on his side to achieve this goal. Any perceived interference from others would compound the problem. She looked from one to the other to ascertain their opinions on the matter.

"I tend to agree, Mrs. McBryde, and you've certainly given us both much food for thought today. I'll not be returning to Melbourne for a few days. So perhaps, Louisa, you and I can ride out and inspect those fences today. Would that be in order do you think?" Charles inquired of his wife.

Louisa was sitting transfixed while staring at Mrs. McBryde who squeezed her hands once again. Louisa blinked once before turning to look at Charles. Then, she shook her head in disbelief.

"Does this mean that I can rant, rave, jump up and down and it won't make one iota of difference to him . . . to get him motivated . . . all I'd do would be to upset and antagonise Papa?" she asked, in a shocked tone.

"Yes, it is so. But, I'd go further. You would place an immovable wedge between the two of you. So, please, leave your father in my hands for the time you are here and you attend to whatever you feel, between the two of you, needs to be done," Mrs. McBryde confided softly to Louisa. "You see, child, there's a time to be independent and to do everything yourself. Then, there comes a time to request much needed help. It is a wise person who knows the difference."

With one last squeeze of Louisa's hands, Brydie rose from the table. She reached for the empty tea cups in front of them and she collected these soiled items as she began to leave.

"I'll have a picnic lunch ready when you leave for your property inspection and I'll inform the *Mary-Ann* of your decision to stay on, Mr. Lyndhurst. Breakfast'll be in half-an-hour, so bear with me, but I must away now. Mr. Howard will be here shortly and expecting breakfast to be on the table. Is there anything else you need?"

Louisa continued to stare into the open space before her eyes as Charles answered Mrs. McBryde.

"Thank you most sincerely, Mrs. McBryde, for your frankness, your honesty and your concern. It *truly is* most appreciated and especially the fact you'd the good sense to bring matters to a head this morning. It's long overdue and, please, be assured of our strictest confidence in the matters raised," Charles stated softly, sincerely and with conviction. "There is something you can do for me. An employee of mine is at an hotel in Echuca and expecting my arrival today. I'll leave a note for him. Would you see that it's dispatched on the paddle-steamer this morning, please?"

"Gladly. Leave it on the sideboard where I'll leave your luncheon basket."

With those words, Colleen McBryde departed hastily from the dining room while leaving a stony silence in her wake. Charles reached over and placed his hand on Louisa's arm.

"Will you ride with me immediately after breakfast, Louisa?" he asked.

Louisa nodded her head in agreement.

"Is there truth in all that Mrs. McBryde has revealed to us?"

Once again, Louisa nodded her head in agreement.

"Perhaps then, we could forego breakfast and leave before your father appears here, thereby giving us all time to adjust to this sad situation. Do you agree?"

Louisa turned two, wide green eyes on him, with gratitude expressed therein. Once more, she nodded her head in agreement before ceasing this action suddenly when another problem came to the fore.

"What of Betsy?" she asked. "I must deal with this situation."

"Speak with her, if you must, but make it brief, for she's not likely to leave today and another few hours will not alter anything drastically. I'll send instructions to Joseph in Echuca, for Hugh must be informed of my change of plans immediately," Charles stated, before issuing a directive to her. "Go after Mrs. McBryde now and inform her of our change of plan. After that, meet me at the stables. I've a couple of letters to write, so may I use the library?"

Louisa, somewhat stunned after this morning's developments, remained frozen at the table while resembling a plaster statue. Charles rose to his feet to leave her. Before doing so, he walked behind her, placed his two hands around her waist and lifted her to her feet. He walked her toward the doorway and whispered in her ear as he did so.

"Go! Go now, before your father arrives."

Louisa followed his directives. After changing into her riding habit, she was waiting at the stables, with two stock horses saddled when he appeared. He was carrying two canvas bags and two water containers.

Charles came to her and, in a very serious tone, he addressed her, with a grave expression on his face.

"Louisa, do you want my assistance in these matters? *If so*, ask now."

"*Yes!*" she replied quickly and firmly. "Yes, most assuredly I do. I'd appreciate your input, for Brydie is correct. I can't handle this alone . . . *please, Charles.*"

With an almost imperceptible nod of acceptance and agreement, he mounted the horse. Charles, rigid and erect in the saddle, rode away while leaving Louisa to follow behind him. She mounted and cantered the horse along the well-worn track that led away from the stable yards and the homestead. Louisa made no attempt to come alongside Charles. She was in a shocked state and she was content to follow in his wake while allowing the thoughts to flow freely in her over-active mind as she attempted to come to terms with the disturbing events of the morning.

To be involving her new husband in matters, which she considered to be family affairs, was intolerable. From Louisa's perspective, Charles Lyndhurst was a stranger who had no connection with her family. As far as she was concerned, this was the way it would remain. His current involvement was a temporary necessity and that was how everything would remain.

Chapter Twenty-Seven

– *Victorian Victorians* –

Louisa

They rode along the eastern boundary and found that, for the most part, the fences enclosing the sheep paddocks were in order. In places, there were one or two posts that required minor repairs and to these, Charles gave his immediate attention. Others that required a more major adjustment, he took note for future reference. They had entered the bottom paddock on the southern boundary before they located a section of fencing that could have resulted in the loss of sheep. Whether or not this had occurred, they had no way of knowing without another head-count of the sheep on the entire property.

Further along, they came to the shallow creek where sheep were grazing by its banks. It was at Louisa's suggestion that they stopped for an early lunch and both were relieved to stretch out on the grass beneath a large ghost-gum tree positioned not far from the water's edge. Having decided to miss breakfast, lunch was a welcome sight as Louisa opened the food parcels and they began devouring the wares that Mrs. McBryde had packed for them.

Louisa had been unable to speak with Betsy before leaving the homestead as she was busy with her chores, so she advised Charles of this fact now.

"There's no doubt she'll go, and little chance Trevor won't follow her, so let's assume these are the facts of the matter. The next question is how long can *his departure* be delayed. If he plans to marry her in Adelaide, he may be open to an inducement to keep him here until I return and a new overseer can be found to take over. It costs money to marry and set-up house."

"You mean a bribe?" Louisa asked, in a somewhat shocked tone.

"Every man has his price. I assume the return from the wool-clip is in, so the coffers should be in a healthy state, assuming the return was a reasonable one. Am I correct in that assumption?"

Louisa nodded her head slowly, but she was frowning deeply at his suggestion nonetheless.

"Don't give me that look of disapproval. Money is power, Louisa! If you want something badly enough, you must be prepared to pay for it. You want him to stay on, so make it worth his while to do so, and if it eases your conscience any, don't see it in terms of a bribe; call it a *bonus*, in appreciation of services rendered. Make the money work to your advantage. Was the wool sold washed or unwashed?"

Louisa cast him a scathing look, thereby giving him to understand that she was offended by a question such as this one, because the English textile mills were anxious to secure as much fine merino wool as they could locate at present. However, they paid only half the price for unwashed wool. Louisa had ordered that all the sheep were to be washed thoroughly in the creek before the shearers arrived to shear them. This task had been heavy, but necessary work, as well as being extremely time-consuming.

"Do you think me a complete simpleton? Of course, it was washed! *I have acquired* some knowledge in my seventeen years, Charles!"

"Oh! *My mistake* . . . forgive me for inquiring," he replied, with a supercilious smile on his face and with sarcasm dripping from every word he uttered.

Louisa continued to devour the food in front of her while remaining silent as she gave serious consideration to his suggestions.

"You don't agree with my proposal regarding Trevor?" he asked.

"Yes, perhaps," she murmured tentatively. "But, I don't see how I can do so and then not give something extra to Brydie, who has held everything together for the past two months. What she's done has gone beyond the call of duty, also."

"Then, so be it. I've no problem with that. But, *you will* have a problem with my next suggestion. I'll return from Melbourne in ten weeks, instead of fourteen."

Louisa, in complete shock, turned to stare at him. Charles began to laugh as the look of horror on her face changed to an expression of extreme outrage.

"*You did* ask for my help . . . remember?" he reminded her.

"No! This isn't necessary at all! I can handle everything myself, if I do as you suggest."

"Turn around and take a good, long look at those sheep. Some of them are fly-struck. *And*, there'll need to be another muster and head-count shortly, as well as fence repairs. Do you propose to do all that yourself, also?"

"How do you know so much about all this? You're never out of Melbourne, or away from your precious ships," she muttered, still irate at his horrific proposal.

He relaxed on the grass while placing his hands behind his head and staring up into the treetop as Louisa drank water from the canteen.

"I operated Stanton for two years and it's a working sheep run on a much larger scale that this. Shall I tell you about it? Yes, perhaps it is time."

Charles peered over at her. Then, he crossed his legs at the ankles and began to relate to her the details of his time at his father's property outside of Bendigo; then, he revealed much in his discourse and commencing with his time in London.

Charles was studying at Cambridge University, after having left his ten-year confinement at his grandmother's home and her influence well behind him. He received an invitation to stay with his mother's brother, Edward, whom he had met but once before that time, unbeknownst to his grandmother, as contact with his mother's family had been forbidden – strictly so – by his grandmother, during the years that he was living under her roof. At his uncle's home, he was introduced to a neighbouring family and he met a young girl, with whom he fell deeply in love. This, he revealed in an off-hand manner, as though it were no more than a passing fancy for him, although his tone changed markedly when he spoke of her. Louisa surmised that the affair went deeper than he was prepared to reveal. She recalled his comment to her in Echuca, the day after their marriage, when he met James Marshall briefly and he had revealed to her about the depths of feeling a *first love* can evoke, especially so when it is unrequited.

Charles had been quite content with his life at that time until his father arrived on his doorstep – unannounced and having just stepped off the ship from Melbourne – and Sir Charles had demanded that Charles return home to take charge of Stanton, because he claimed that Charles' grandmother had taken ill and his father needed to be by her bedside. As his father controlled the purse-strings tightly, Charles was obliged to obey, after many protests. His first-love, whose name he failed to mention – deliberately or otherwise – accompanied by his father, had come to the ship to farewell him. She had promised to wait for his return, no matter how long that was to take.

Charles had arrived at Stanton and refused to stay at the homestead, or to have any dealings with his mother whatsoever, for there had not been any contact between them for the ten years that he had been away. He slept in a cabin near the overseer's quarters and he learned everything from the man who was employed there as the overseer then and who was at least thirty years his senior. Other than the few years, which he had spent at Lyndhurst Park prior to his hurried departure for London at the age of nine years, he had not experienced life in the Australian bush before that time.

Charles had been born in England and felt more at home in London than in a bush shack on the outskirts of Sandhurst, as the town was known then. He was required, by necessity, to learn fast in order to survive, as well as to assimilate to this new way of life and to interact with the other men with whom he was working daily. So, he assured Louisa, he was quite capable of dealing with any problems that were likely to arise on her father's property in the foreseeable future.

"Why were you estranged from your mother? I find that difficult to accept, after seeing the two of you together. She seems to love you very much."

He was chewing on a blade of green grass and looking, almost with unseeing eyes, at the creek in his direct line of vision. Louisa was beginning to wonder if he had forgotten her existence completely when he shrugged his shoulders and replied to her.

"It was my sister, Caroline, who brought matters to a head between us . . . finally. You haven't had the pleasure of meeting her yet and you're in for quite a shock there, for she's a mirror-image of my father. They are so alike, it's uncanny. Caroline found my mother crying one night and being the nosey-parker she is, she wouldn't rest until she located the source of her mother's unhappy state. When she did, she came hunting for me. I don't know how I came out of the encounter alive . . . *and, she* was all of ten-years-old. She's her father's daughter true enough!" he stated.

"What had you done?" Louisa queried, while trying to imagine what crime he had committed to evoke his sister's fury at that time.

"My crime, Louisa, was to believe all the lies that my grandmother had fed to me from the age of nine," Charles muttered, with a harsh laugh; then, somewhat unnecessarily and very quietly, he revealed more information. *"And, she* was not a nice person to know."

Caroline, then aged ten years, had visited Charles and, in front of the men with whom he was working, demanded that he come to the homestead to talk to her mother. He did not know his sister at all, after having met her briefly once on his arrival when she came up to him in the paddock and introduced herself. He had seen her at a distance, but had made no effort to make her acquaintance. This, she had taken exception to while leaving him in no doubt of her opinion of him within the first week of his arrival.

Later that evening, while he was sitting quietly and drinking with all the men who had gathered in the overseer's cabin, the young girl arrived unexpectedly and she was dragging an old tin trunk behind her. With barely-suppressed anger, she had placed it in front of him and flicked open the lid. Inside, there were bundles of unopened letters. Caroline lifted some of them and threw them at his feet while shouting at him that these were some of the letters his mother had written to him for the first fifteen months after he was sent away from her and which had been returned to her – unopened and neatly packaged – in time for Christmas the second year after Charles' departure from Melbourne. Horrified, he had stared at them while his companions looked on in curiosity.

Immediately, while conscious of their audience, Charles returned the mail to the chest, closed it and he moved it to the bunk where he slept while sliding it beneath it before ordering Caroline to return to her bedroom at the homestead. When she refused, he had picked her up, with her struggling and screaming in his arms, and he had carried her across the paddock and up the hill. Once there, he had deposited her unceremoniously on the verandah outside his mother's sitting room. He returned to the drinking session with the men and the matter was never raised again.

Two days later, he had taken the bundles of letters in a sack, along with his bed roll and two bottles of fine Scotch whisky, and he *went bush* alone. There, in a secluded valley, he had opened the disturbing letters and read every word of every one several times. It was then that he came to the understanding of the great deception that had been perpetrated by his grandmother, but instigated by his father. The proof was undeniable, for he held those letters – sealed, dated and postmarked, in his hands.

Charles had been sent to England when his mother was gravely ill in the days following Caroline's birth. She did not know of his departure until a week after his ship sailed from Port Melbourne. In desperation, she had written many letters. All her feelings for him were expressed in those letters of love, which recorded clearly her regret, her sorrow and her desperation, caused by their forced separation.

Elizabeth had written one letter a week, some of which were asking if he had received the gifts, which she had sent to him. From Charles, there had never been a reply, because his grandmother convinced him that he had been replaced in his mother's affection by his newly-arrived sister and that his mother wanted him no longer in her life. Those letters, he had never sighted before that time.

"That's an unbelievable story!" Louisa exclaimed, in a shocked tone.

"Perhaps, for some, it may be so," he murmured, with a slight shrug. "But, if you know the father . . . and you had known his mother . . . it's not quite so."

"What did you do?"

"I bundled everything up, climbed onto my horse, which knew the way, thankfully, because it was the middle of the second night and I was very, very drunk. Somehow, I arrived in my mother's bedroom, dragged her from a deep sleep and threw the letters onto the bed. After she ignited the lamp to see what was occurring, a realisation dawned on her, because she didn't know that Caroline had taken the letters. We sobbed in each other's arms until dawn."

"Dear God in heaven!" Louisa exclaimed, in genuine amazement. "Do not, ever again, tell me there's no God, for who else could arrange such a wonderful outcome after all those years?"

"If *your God* arranged the outcome, why did He not prevent the original sin?" he queried, in a sarcastic tone.

"You're such a cynic!"

"Am I indeed!" he muttered. "*Now*, Louisa Mary Lyndhurst, it's your turn. Tell me about your parents."

"We won't be home before nightfall at this rate."

"It's no matter. This is important. Perhaps, today is not only a day for plain-speaking and revelation, but one for soul-searching and getting to know each other a little better. Do you not agree?"

Louisa grimaced and bit her lip. Leaning over and snapping off a blade of grass, she began scrutinising it carefully and meticulously, as Charles continued to watch for her reaction. Finally, she relented and decided to oblige him.

"Papa was born in England . . . in the north, he said, and . . . well, Mama came from Dublin. He arrived in Sydney-town when he was thirty-five years, having worked his passage and with money in his pocket to buy land. That was his one-and-only goal. Mama was almost forty when she arrived some years later."

It was through Frank Jenkins, the bookkeeper, and his wife that her parents had met. George Howard had purchased this property, before buying a few hundred sheep; then, he hired a bookkeeper whose wife, Josephine, became cook and housekeeper. Everything was very rough in the beginning, but over time, the cabins were built and then the homestead. It was not until his forty-second year that George Howard decided that the time had come to seek a wife.

Mary Bourke was a childhood friend of Josephine Jenkins and the two women were corresponding several times a year. It was at the suggestion of Frank Jenkins that the correspondence between George and Mary began. Mary was caring for her aged parents at the family home in Dublin at that time. Her older sister had married and immigrated with her new husband to Canada. The couple was never heard from again, as the ship failed to arrive at its destination. Mary's brother, Francis, who was much younger, was in Rome where he was studying for the priesthood within the Catholic Church.

When her parents died within months of each other, Mary accepted George's offer of marriage and, accompanied by her recently-ordained brother, she arrived in Sydney where she was met by Frank and Josephine Jenkins and George Howard. The marriage took place immediately and George brought her here to the homestead where, in 1850, Louisa was born and she was their only child.

"Mama always called me *her little miracle*," Louisa confided, with a shy laugh. "They may not have met before their marriage, but at least they were both in agreement with the arrangement, which is more than can be said for us."

"Too true," he agreed.

"That's why Jenkins can't do anything wrong in Papa's eyes."

"Now, tell me what happened between the two of you," he requested, while sitting up to watch her more closely.

"In hindsight, it was nothing really, but back then, I was very upset, as Brydie said. At the time, I didn't understand what he was about . . . but, I suppose, *I do now!*"

Charles did not respond to this deliberate observation on Louisa's part.

On the day of the incident, Louisa had been swimming in the river in the morning. Then, after lunch and with her father dozing on the verandah, she had entered the library to work on her books.

Some years earlier, Mary Howard had discovered the discrepancies in Jenkins' ledger. Without confiding in her husband, she began another set of books while leaving Jenkins, who had lost his wife, Josephine, a little earlier and who had taken to the rum in earnest, to play with the ones, which he thought were accurate. Finally, some months later, Mary was obliged to tell George and they agreed to let the situation ride until Jenkins came to terms with his grief. When that did not occur and Mary's health became a concern, she turned to Louisa. She taught her daughter the rudimentary skills where the keeping of the books was concerned, just in case the time came when Mary was ill and Louisa's assistance may have been needed for a short time.

It had never been her intention that such a responsibility should fall on her daughter's shoulders permanently, as it had never been her intention to die suddenly, thereby leaving her husband and daughter to cope on their own.

On the day-in-question, Louisa had gone to the library, as usual. As often occurred, the drunken man was dozing in one of the arm-chairs there. Ignoring him, she set about her work until, suddenly, he rose from the chair and approached the desk.

At first, she thought that he had tripped, due to his inebriated state; then, he grabbed her from behind, wrenched her back in the chair and he had his rum-soaked mouth upon her lips before she knew what was occurring. As his tongue entered her mouth, he tore open the bodice of her gown with one hand while holding her about the throat with the other one. This hand proceeded to snake around her exposed breast.

Everything happened so quickly that Louisa was taken by sur-prise. At the time, she felt that he possessed at least six hands, for she was pinned between the desk and the chair, which dislodged subsequently. They fell to the floor together. In his drunken state, he was no match for the fleet-footed Louisa who jumped away from him as he lay spread-eagled on the floor and she escaped through the open window at the rear of the house.

She ran around the verandah and entered her bedroom from there, quickly slamming the french doors behind her. She locked them instantly. She positioned a chest of drawers in front of the lock. Then, she ran to the internal door and repeated the exercise there. When she felt reasonably safe, she tore off her gown and threw herself – gasping for breath – on the bed. It was some considerable time before she could bring herself to dress and leave the room. She went to the safety of Brydie's kitchen and requested tea. Brydie, realising that she was extremely upset, tried to establish the cause, but Louisa had sealed already the incident in a deep compartment in her mind, perhaps for later retrieval; or, then again, perhaps not.

"Did he try it again?" Charles queried.

"No," Louisa stated, while shaking her head slowly. "He came near me a couple of times, trying to apologise, because he was afraid I'd tell Papa. But, I didn't, of course, as he'd not have believed me anyway, for Frank Jenkins can do no wrong. In his eyes, he's the saint who brought Mama to him. Anyway, I don't need others to fight my battles for me and I knew exactly how I'd wreak my revenge . . . to prevent another attack, you see."

"Of course," Charles murmured. "There could be no other motive at all, I'm certain."

Louisa ignored his remark and proceeded to explain further. She had waited for three days and, in the afternoon, when she knew that Jenkins would be in the armchair sleeping, as was his usual habit, she crept into the library and took one of his unopened bottles of rum. Then, she soaked his clothes thoroughly while pouring the entire contents of the bottle over his shirt and trousers. He was using a walking cane at the time, as he suffered from gout, so she took that item and began prodding him. She dribbled the contents of his glass from the side table over his face until he was awake. She had left the window to the back verandah open so as to make good her escape and she had a lighted candle beside her on the desk.

When the bookkeeper opened his eyes finally and stared up blearily at her, she asked him if he wished to make peace with his Maker before she set him alight. It was then that she took a hold of the candle and held it above him. He did not speak, although he did open his mouth to do so, but no sound came out of that orifice. He tried to rise from the armchair, but his legs seemed to give away beneath his body and he appeared to be in a somewhat confused state. But, it was his eyes she remembered vividly. To this day, she could bring them to mind instantly, for his eyes did plead for mercy, she revealed to Charles who was staring at her in some amazement and astonishment.

"Did you do so?" he asked, in a stunned voice.

"Of course not! It was overproof rum, so I imagine it may've caused some damage, had I been so tempted, but by then, I was not in a temper, you see. Three days earlier, I cannot guarantee I'd not have done so, but not then, because this was premeditated and planned to perfection, even if I do say so myself."

"What happened? I'm almost afraid to ask," he inquired.

"Nothing really. He didn't move, except . . . well, let's just say he embarrassed himself, so later, I was obliged to burn the chair and rug. That's all," Louisa stated simply, with a shrug of her shoulders.

"All!" Charles exclaimed, with a definite gasp.

"So, you see, Mr. Lyndhurst, you got off lightly with nothing more than a jug of cold water, but I can't guarantee that's all you'd have received if you'd not proposed this . . . umm . . . cooling off period, shall we say," Louisa revealed; then, she continued her story. "After that, every time he saw me coming, he'd turn tail and run in the opposite direction. So, there you have the story of Mr. Frank Jenkins. Oh! How I loathe him and how I've loathed the smell of rum from that day forth!"

He was staring at her and shaking his head in some astonishment. He appeared lost for words for a time.

"Is there anything else you wish to know, for I'd like to go home now?" she asked, in all innocence.

"Well, yes," he muttered, in obvious awe, as he surveyed her. "I've many more questions, but two spring to mind immediately. The first concerns Hilton. Why can't anyone ride him, if you're not there?"

"Oh! That?" she queried.

"Yes, that!" he countered.

"It's another long story. Are you certain you want to hear it, for I'd much prefer you should take my word that no one's to ride him?"

Charles positioned himself back against the trunk of the tree, folded his arms deliberately and looked over at her while awaiting her explanation. She grimaced at him and shrugged her shoulders as she noted the determined set of his jaw, with his intent being clear.

"You have my undivided attention," he informed her.

"Very well, but I must go back to the night he was born to Cadence. So, bear with me, please," Louisa stated.

"We've all day . . . and all night, if necessary."

She cast him another scathing look, but she did not deign to respond to his barb. On the night in question, she revealed that her mother was ill and could not assist in the birth. Mary Howard had fought her husband over his stated intention of having a neighbour's stallion service Cadence. She was a small, sweet-natured animal and Mary did not want that *brute of a thing*, as she called it, near her *precious baby*, but George persisted and the event took place. Therefore, when there was a problem with the birth, George was frantic with worry for fear of losing both mare and foal, so he roused Louisa from her bed while begging for her assistance. He promised the foal was for her, if it survived.

Louisa, with the small arms and hands of a fourteen-year-old female, was needed to slide her hands inside Cadence and to turn the trapped foal slightly to enable the birth to proceed safely. It had taken over an hour and they nearly lost Cadence during the ordeal. Louisa could work only between contractions and she, herself, was becoming desperate until, finally, the beautiful creature slithered into her waiting arms.

"You delivered him yourself?" Charles exclaimed.

"At fourteen!" he exclaimed again. "When other girls of your age were learning embroidery?"

"I was not alone . . . Papa was there, with several other men, but when Papa saw him, I think he was sorry he'd made such a rash promise to me. But then, without me, they'd have lost both of them and Mama would never have forgiven him. So, he honoured his promise and he's been mine ever since."

"*And now*, the rest of it, if you don't mind."

Louisa grimaced again. She had witnessed the looks of envy on the faces of all the men who had worked at the property back then and who studied her adored pony with admiration. So, she began to train him. With the persistent fear that someone would try to steal him when he was a more mature animal, she decided to teach him to respond to her commands only, with regard to not allowing anyone but herself to ride him. She had confided this idea to her parents, but her father advised her that it would not possible for her to do so and had scoffed at her suggestion. This was all the added incentive that the young Louisa needed to continue with her plan.

Some months later, she proved him wrong, for not only had she trained the animal to allow only those for whom she had given a previous command to ride him, but also, she had a command that would cause him to dislodge anyone from his back at a signal from her. Her parents were astounded when she showed them the proof, although her father refused to allow her to give the second command while he was astride Hilton – for obvious reasons. He had elected to take her word on that score.

"So, on that first day when I rode Hilton and you told me I was in your power, you weren't joking?" he queried, frowning.

Louisa, with a smug smile on her face, shook her head slowly and his frown deepened.

"Who else knows these commands?"

"Mama and Papa . . . that was for safety reasons when I was away for a year in Melbourne," she admitted to him.

"Your mother is no longer with us and your father wouldn't remember, in all probability. You've turned that animal into a lethal weapon and that's no different to holding a fully-loaded, double-barrel shotgun in your hands! *And*, with your out-of-control temper, that's a dangerous combination."

"*And, your foul temper isn't out-of-control, I suppose!* Anyway, he's mine. No one else is to ride him. If they do, then they do so without my permission and that's tantamount to theft. The theft of a horse is a very serious offence in the eyes of the law," Louisa stated defiantly.

"So, too, is murder. There's a fine line here. What happened with this Curtis chap when he attempted to ride your stallion? Did you get there in time, as Mrs. McBryde suggested?"

Louisa bit her lip again and turned away. With deepening concern, it appeared to her, Charles awaited her reply, which was slow in coming.

"Honestly . . . I don't know," she murmured, very softly and very reluctantly.

"*You must know!*" he demanded, in an exasperated tone. "Either you did . . . or, you did not?"

Louisa recalled the day vividly. It was a few months before Charles arrived for the first time in September and Curtis had not been with them long. Trevor sent a message of warning to Betsy who came running in search of Louisa in the library. Together, the two young girls ran to the yards where Curtis had mounted Hilton already and he was having difficulty controlling him, for the horse was awaiting Louisa's command as his training had taught him.

Curtis, somewhat under the influence of alcohol – although not really drunk himself – had made a wager that he could ride Hilton to the large tree in the far paddock and back again while the other men held a clock on them, thereby timing the race. A book had been opened and the bets were in place, as Louisa had discovered later when she demanded angrily their explanation for the series of events that had taken place that afternoon in late winter.

When she arrived in the paddock, breathless and with Betsy by her side, she saw Curtis raise a riding crop above his head and he was about to bring it down on Hilton's back. Louisa was stunned by the sight and she stood transfixed momentarily, with her eyes focussed on the whip. Knowing that Hilton had never been hit in his life, she wondered, just for a split second, if her commands would be effective. Had she not been distracted and delayed for that brief second, she did not know if she could have averted the accident. Hilton was aware of her presence, even though the men had not seen her behind the shed as she approached from the homestead.

The crop came down. The rider was airborne instantly before her startled eyes and before she could react in any way. That was the truth of the matter. Had she not been distracted by the sight of the weapon, which Curtis was holding above his head, she would have given the command for Hilton to allow the ride. Of this, there was no doubt. Immediately afterwards, she would have dismissed the man instantly.

It was during the long sleepless hours, between midnight and dawn, that she agonised over the question and she doubted herself. Then, her belief that she had played a large part in her own mother's death surfaced again and she relived that scenario over and over again. By dawn, on many mornings, she was convinced that she was the most evil person who was born ever. Once again, she begged her God for forgiveness.

On that particular day, when Curtis hit the ground, she ran over and retrieved the crop while rushing to him with her fiery temper barely in check. She knew that she would have struck him on the face with it, her anger was so great by this time. But when she looked down and saw his legs twisted at such a grotesque angle, she dropped the crop and reached for the distressed horse to prevent him from trampling the injured rider.

Trevor and some of the other men made a makeshift trundle bed and, as luck would have it, the *Charmaine* had stayed overnight and was preparing to leave at that time. It was for the benefit of some of the crew of the *Charmaine* that Bill Curtis had staged his display of horsemanship and Louisa thanked God on that Sunday for Bill Bartlett's reluctance to leave his Brydie early.

Curtis was transported to Echuca immediately and Louisa wrote a quick note of explanation to the Reverend and Mrs. Marshall, thereby advising of the accident and asking them to assist the man. Later, she had sent his wages, along with a note inquiring about his state of health, to Mrs. Marshall. The reply that she received stated, in an ambiguous and unhelpful phrase, from Louisa's perspective, the words: *as well as could be expected, given the circumstances.*

Louisa, somewhat sheepishly, looked over at Charles as he sat in silent contemplation while reaching for the water canteen, which he placed then to his lips. When he made no comment still, she elaborated a little.

"When we arrived in Echuca a couple of days ago, I went to visit Mama's grave and, after that, I visited the Marshalls' home. They had all gone to Swan Hill to visit a sick relative, so I spoke to their cook, but she said there had been no improvement in Mr. Curtis' condition. I saw him in the vegetable garden as he was working there . . . he does so for his keep, you see. He was struggling along on makeshift crutches that someone had made for him. I couldn't bring myself to speak to him. I did try, but I could not. One day, I'll have the courage to do so, I hope."

"Perhaps, this is a matter best kept between ourselves, but you'll come clean about those commands before I leave here, or I'll not leave. Is that understood?"

Louisa lifted her chin and flicked her head away, but he ignored her provocative mannerisms.

"Does Nathaniel know?" Charles demanded tersely.

"He suspects. He doesn't know for certain, but I was most insistent he allow no one, not even you, to ride Hilton. He's not stupid and he's been around horses for all his life. So, I suppose, in a way, he does."

"I employ him, Louisa. If I wished to ride the horse, he wouldn't stop me. *So, were you* going to tell me at all?"

"Yes," she said, while reminding him. "I tried to do so this morning. Remember?"

"Then, that's just saved your hide!" Charles muttered, through clenched teeth.

His silence continued for some considerable time. Louisa began to fidget; then, she started to gather the remnants of the luncheon together and to return the debris to the canvas bags. Finally, he spoke to her.

"It's time he earned his keep. I've had several offers for . . ."

"No! You'll not sell him! I'll shoot him first!" Louisa shouted at Charles.

"I seem to recall a time when I was the worse villain in existence for having made a threat such as that," he stated, with maddening calmness. "And, *as I was saying* before being interrupted rudely, I've had offers for his services with several mares belonging to my friends. I'd be able to name my own price in that area. However, Hugh is the first one on that long list. Should I allow it, do you think?"

Louisa sat back on the grass and studied him closely. Finally, she nodded slowly.

"For Mr. Travis, I'd allow anything. He's a wonderful gentleman," she stated, with conviction.

"What he's done to secure your favour, when I've not been able to do so, I know not. He'll be thrilled to hear this."

"But not Cadence . . . never will I allow her to be in foal again. She's too old, so she must be kept away from your other horses."

"That's a trifle extreme . . . seeing as they're all geldings," he murmured, with a soft chuckle.

"Can we go home now?" she demanded.

"No, there's another matter. It concerns Carstairs."

Louisa froze as she reached for the canteen. Controlling her emotions, she uncorked the container and placed it to her lips while attempting to hide the trembling that the mention of Phillip's name caused her to experience.

"You stated emphatically that there was a dagger between the two of you at all times and he knew never to touch you. But, he kissed you . . . that day, on the race track. *And, you allowed it!* I saw that with my own eyes! How many other lies have you told?"

"None! And, I didn't allow! *I pleaded earnestly* with him to do so while knowing you were watching. He obliged. That's all. I wanted to rile you," she admitted, with some satisfaction, as she replaced the cork on the canteen.

"*Then, madam,* we both know it had the desired effect, don't we?" he remarked, while rising to his feet slowly and stretching his limbs before confiding to her. "Well, this seems to have been a very productive day all around, wouldn't you agree?"

With that last comment, he moved to the grazing horses, led them from the water's edge and returned them to the area beneath a nearby tree where he saddled them as Louisa watched him.

Finally, Louisa walked over with the luncheon bags and the canteens, which she attached to the saddles. Moving to her, Charles reached for her two hands and he held them firmly as he spoke softly to her.

"Are you going to continue to fight me every step of the way?"

"Without a doubt in this world!" she exclaimed forcefully.

"Come to me tonight," he requested, in a soft tone.

"No! Our agreement stands, even if you do come back early. We agreed on fourteen weeks. Even then, it'll be with great reluctance and due only to an obligation on my part. Never will it be anything else, believe me!" Louisa hurled the words at him while pulling her hands away.

"'Tis no matter. I am happy to accept that . . . *for the moment.*"

"It'll never be any other way, Charles Lyndhurst. Trust me on that score!" she shouted at him.

"I'm not one for predictions, under normal circumstances," Charles stated. "But, I will make you one now."

Charles paused momentarily while watching Louisa closely before continuing with his prediction.

"*You will come to me,* of your own free will, before the first anniversary of our marriage. That's November. We're in January now."

Louisa mounted the waiting horse and she turned its head swiftly as she flicked her head away deliberately. He watched her with some amusement. She flung her head in the air as a spirited filly would do and she screamed at him.

"Hell will freeze over before that day occurs!"

Charles threw back his head and laughed heartily at her fiery response before mounting his horse and riding after her as Louisa raced the horse across the paddock toward the boundary fence on the western side of her father's property.

Chapter Twenty-Eight

– *Victorian Victorians* –

Louisa

Louisa opened sleepy eyes while knowing intuitively that something was different. Instantly, her two, green eyes peered blearily into two rather bemused grey ones – wide and inquiring – that were gazing back at her. These were awaiting her response to her current surroundings and unusual position. She was stretched out beside him, with the upper part of her body draped across his bare chest. She gave an audible gasp as this starting realisation dawned on her.

"Good morning" Charles said, as he smiled at her.

Immediately, she jumped back while sitting on her knees in the middle of the bed and shaking her head in horror. Looking down at her body, she found that she was dressed in her underwear, this being a cotton chemise and knee-length cotton pantalets, both trimmed with lace, while her feet were bare. She studied her attire momentarily and stared back at him.

"How?" she asked, with a gasp. "Who brought me in here?"

"I did."

"Who undressed me?" she inquired, in an astonished tone; then, with the trace of an accusation, she continued. "Removed my gown . . . unpinned my hair?"

"I did."

Louisa stared at him as she awaited further explanation. Finally, he reached for another pillow from the floor and placed it on top of the other one beneath his head.

"You passed out on the settee while your father and I were in the library after dinner. You resembled one dead . . . I couldn't rouse you, so I carried you in here. What else was I to do, with Mrs. McBryde and your father standing at either elbow? We're supposed to be married. *In fact, we are!* So, I couldn't very well take you to your little girl's bed; now, could I?"

Louisa's mind flicked back to the dinner table when she was struggling to stay awake while Charles was trying to engage her father in polite conversation, especially with the regard to the running of the property. This was to no avail, for George's replies were all non-committal, but Louisa was unable to assist, due to her lack of sleep on the previous night and because of the long day spent in the saddle while inspecting the fences with Charles. Then, foolishly, she drank a glass of wine at dinner. She did not recall settling herself onto the settee, nor being carried to bed. She eyed him now with deep suspicion.

"And then what?" she asked.

"And then, I went to sleep; or, I tried to do so. It's the worst night I can recall, for I was allocated one inch of mattress. Then, this clinging vine began creeping and crawling all over my body. Next time, stay on your own side of the bed!"

"*Me?* It could never be so!"

"Well, there were only the two of us here, believe me. Mrs. McBryde told me you didn't go to bed at all on the previous night and that you worked on the books all night. You're not accustomed to alcohol, so it's no wonder you sank into the depths of unconsciousness."

Louisa, who remained sitting on her knees in the centre of the bed, was contemplating her current situation when he moved from the bed. Immediately, she closed her eyes tightly as his naked body emerged from beneath the sheet while he continued with his discourse.

"You brought me a cup of tea yesterday, so I'll return the favour, as long as you promise not to leave this bed, for there's a matter I need to discuss with you before I ride out with Trevor early to repair those fences."

Louisa continued to keep her eyes closed tightly and she did not respond to his words, for she planned to make good her escape at the moment that he was out-of-sight.

"And, don't try to escape from me, for I'll find you wherever you hide and bring you back. That should cause a slight ruckus at this ungodly hour of the morning in the silent house, wouldn't you think?"

Charles's body landed on the bed in front of her as he knelt with his face close to her; then, he kissed her and her eyes flew open. He had dragged on his trousers, but he was without a shirt.

"Stop this prudish nonsense instantly! It's idiotic," he ordered. "We're married, for goodness sake!"

"*We wouldn't be,* if I'd known about this bedroom nonsense!"

"Too late! Too late! Accept it!" he said, with his face close to her own.

He remained stationary while staring at her as the early morning light filtered through the open window of the guest room, because the drapes had not been closed on the previous evening. Louisa felt vulnerable and uncomfortable under his close scrutiny all of a sudden as he whispered to her.

"With your soft green eyes and your red locks tumbling about your shoulders in the morning light, *I could devour you now*," he stated, very softly; then, in a calm, even tone, he asked his next question. "White, with one sugar?"

Without awaiting a reply, he jumped from the bed, grabbing his shirt and sliding into it as he was leaving the room and before the shocked Louisa could conjure up a reply to his last statement, or to his last question. She moved to the pillows on her side of the bed and, propping herself against the bed-head, she pulled the sheet over her body and up under her chin. She was somewhat stunned to discover that she was trembling not a little.

When he returned, he placed a cup and saucer on her table and he walked to the other side of the bed as he placed his beverage on the table there. He moved onto the bed and propped himself up on the pillows and reached for the hot tea as he did so. Louisa did not move or speak. She awaited his next move with some trepidation.

"I did try to offer you a way out on the morning of our wedding. You do recall that?" he queried.

"As did Uncle Robert," she stated, while nodding in answer to his question.

"Did he indeed!"

Charles sipped in silence for some minutes while Louisa made no move to pick up the cup. She realised that she was shaking markedly and she had no explanation for this occurrence. Today was Friday. It was only on the previous Sunday when she had raced Phillip at Flemington, after which Charles had attacked her. So, that had occurred but five days earlier, yet it seemed so long ago at times. Then, in other moments – such as now – it felt as though it had occurred within the past five minutes.

"I've treated you abominably, Louisa . . . right from the very beginning. I'm trying as best I can to make amends, but I need you to meet me half-way, if there's to be any future for us. I plan to return here in ten weeks to assist with the muster, as the overseer thinks that's urgent and I tend to agree with him."

Louisa moved her body as far away from him as she could, given the size of the bed, in which they were both ensconced presently; then, she reached for the tea cup and began to sip the hot liquid as she tried to ignore her husband as much as possible while he continued with his discourse.

"I'll stick to our original agreement . . . unless you desire otherwise . . . then, we'll come to know each other intimately. In the meantime, let us pretend we are an engaged couple who are getting to know each other prior to our wedding night. Would that be easier for you? Let's pretend that these past few months haven't happened."

Louisa jerked her head around to look at him while being astounded as much by the words that she was hearing coming from his lips as she was by the arrogance, which he was displaying. She slammed the cup back onto its saucer and she shouted at him as the liquid swayed dangerously in the cup.

"Only a male could make a statement such as that! *They did happen!* Until five days ago, I'd never been touched in that way by a man. You knew that, *yet you raped me!* How do you expect me to forget that horrendous experience?"

Louisa, in her study of history, had come across the words, *rape and pillage*, often and she had known the meaning of one of those words previously. But now, she knew the meaning of the other one – from terrible and bitter experience. Also, Charles had made mention of such an occurrence during his lengthy explanation to Louisa some time earlier.

"*Within marriage,* an act of rape cannot occur! You belong to me! *And,* as surprising as this may seem, *I did not know that.* Had you not been offering yourself so freely to someone else, it wouldn't have happened. I regret it bitterly . . . as you regret what occurred with Bill Curtis and Hilton. Unfortunately, once set in motion, these events take their own course," he stated, quite calmly and by way of explanation.

"*An act of violence is exactly that!* I find it quite amazing how you can twist this situation as you try to make me the guilty party," she snapped at him, before explaining her position further. "*Therefore, I can't pretend;* I can't forget; and, try as I might, I can't forgive! That's the way of it, Charles. I'll honour my part in our repulsive deal, but it'll be with immense reluctance and under great sufferance. You'd be a fool to expect anything else. If *I can manage* to bring everything under control here *at my home* within that time-frame, perhaps this mighty sacrifice on my part may have been worth it."

"You really do have a way with words!" he snapped at her, while twisting his head to glance at her. "Why did you marry me? I'm not leaving here until I know the answer to that question."

Louisa lifted her cup and she drank in silence, instantly looking out of the window as the rays of the summer sun broke through a somewhat overcast sky on this January morning. She was fighting to control her emotions and her hands were trembling while the hot liquid within the cup moved to their rhythm. If she could turn back the calendar and the clock by four months, she would change everything. Unfortunately, that was beyond her control now. She cast her mind back to the day when Charles Lyndhurst had stepped, for the first time, from the *Charmaine* onto the pontoon here at their home and she recalled how he had been studying her candidly. He claimed to have seen her swimming in the river, even before they had met. How naive, foolish and childish she was back then, she concluded. Finally, she decided to respond with honesty.

"I thought Papa was very ill and I was such a troublesome burden to him that he might get well if I weren't around to worry him. Aunt Sophie was pleading with me to come to them, but Papa wouldn't allow it, for he claimed he needed me here. But, in hindsight, I suppose he knew of Uncle Robert's illness even then, as Aunt Sophie would have confided in him, I'm certain."

Louisa moved the cup to her lips again and she allowed her mind to drift back to a time seemingly long past and she relived those months vividly. She was silent for some minutes before continuing with her explanation.

"If I'd realised your horrid father had coerced him and Papa made this demand of me in a drug-induced state, I'd have refused totally . . . as, initially, I did. I had never intended to marry anyone. I'd planned to stay here with Papa forever . . . after Mama died. Is that what you want to hear?"

Charles continued to drink in silence and he appeared not to have heard her words, although Louisa knew that every one of those had reached his ears. Whether or not these disclosures were to his liking was of no concern to her, for he was not at all to her liking, if the truth were known.

"Thank you. Finally, I'm getting to the truth of the matter."

He replaced his empty cup on the bedside table and placed his hands behind his head against the pillows; then, he stared up at the ceiling, apparently lost in thought.

"It appears I'm surrounded by self-sacrificing females," he said finally.

"Who else is there?" she inquired, in a somewhat disinterested tone.

"My mother, for one . . . now, *I shall tell you something!* I fought very strongly against this union. When I did cave into the considerable pressure being applied . . . and you can guess the source . . . I hoped you'd the good sense to refuse, even in that last, final hour. But, you did not do so. I was planning to marry someone else, you may be surprised to learn . . . *or, perhaps not?*" he muttered, with an eyebrow raised in query as he glanced over at her.

"Who?" she asked, somewhat surprised.

"It's of no consequence now," he stated.

"Do you love her? Does she love you?"

"Yes, Louisa . . . on both counts."

Stunned by his words, spoken in such a quiet, matter-of-fact manner, Louisa slammed the cup onto the bedside table, jumped from the bed and reached for her petticoat. She slipped into it while he appeared to watch in a somewhat detached and disinterested way. She reached for her gown and threw the garment over her head. She was attempting to fasten the buttons at the back, with trembling fingers, when Charles came to her and, calmly, he began to assist.

When she was dressed, she walked by him. She retrieved her shoes, stockings and garters from the floor as she was leaving the room. There was not another word spoken by either of them and, with her bare feet making not one sound, she padded through the silent house.

The next time that Louisa saw Charles, she was seated at the dinner table with her father in the evening. Her husband came into the dining room and took his place at the table without a word to her, but he apologised to George for the lateness of his arrival. George did not appear to notice his uncustomary unpunctuality, nor did he query the reason, which troubled Louisa greatly, because her father would have known everything that went on in his household and on his property once.

Louisa ignored Charles as he poured wine into her glass before pouring a glass for himself.

"Trevor informed me he repaired the boundary fences today," Charles spoke to George, while ignoring Louisa before elaborating on the subject to George. "That's on the eastern and southern areas, but he's planning on working on the one on the western side tomorrow morning. It's in a bad way, evidently."

"Is that so?" George replied. "I thought we'd done that quite recently. They don't last as long as they did once. Materials aren't up to scratch these days . . . not like they used to be. Nice of you to take an interest, Charles. Don't you agree, Louisa?"

Louisa choked on the food in her mouth. She swallowed hurriedly, reached for the wine and nodded her head in response to her father's question as she lifted the glass to her lips. Silence reigned for quite some time when, finally, Charles opened another topic.

"Mrs. McBryde tells me the *Charmaine* is due here tomorrow evening. It'll stay overnight and head for Echuca on the following day, so I'll need to be leaving then. Louisa will stay on until I can return for her. Is that satisfactory, George?" Charles asked of his father-in-law.

Louisa replaced the glass onto the table with a dull thud while her temper was rising significantly with every word that her husband uttered as she watched her father nodding his head in agreement with this proposal.

"I'm not a piece of meat sitting on this table! I'm a flesh-and-blood person and you don't need to talk about me as though I don't exist," she exploded.

Charles looked across at her in a disdainful manner and continued eating his meal without responding to her angry words. Her father looked blankly at her and frowned at her outburst. Then, he continued to eat his meal.

"What seems to be the problem now, child? You flare at nothing. No slight was intended by either of us. It's time you grew up," her father stated calmly, while brushing the serviette to his lips as he concluded his lecture to his daughter.

Fortunately for all concerned, Mrs. McBryde entered at this precise moment and she began to remove the dishes from the table while Betsy followed behind her. All conversation came to an end. Betsy would be leaving on board the *Charmaine*, also, so Louisa held her temper in check, not wishing the young girl to take away memories that were unpleasant at the end of her long stay with them.

Louisa escaped as soon as possible at the conclusion of the meal and headed for the river where she walked the river bank alone. The night was sultry and the slight breeze was a welcome relief from the heat of the day. Charles, she had noticed, was sunburnt on his face and neck and she knew that he did not arrive back from the day's work in the paddocks until very late, hence his late appearance at dinner.

If his intention was to work with Trevor again tomorrow, he would retire early tonight and, hopefully, he would leave immediately after breakfast on the following morning. So, he would be away soon enough and if she could keep the peace between them until he departed, for her father's sake, that would be so much the better for all concerned. She made a promise to herself to keep her temper in check for the remainder of his stay, regardless of the provocation.

Fervently, she hoped that she would be capable of accomplishing this almost-impossible feat.

The homestead was quiet when she returned and, instead of going to the library to work, she decided to leave the books until the following day when she was certain that she would not be disturbed. She assumed Charles and her father to be in the library at present anyway, so she went to her old bedroom and prepared for bed. After doing so, she dismissed Charlotte; then, acting on a decision that did not give her any pleasure at all, she walked through the silent house and entered the guest room. To her surprise, Charles was in bed, with only the lamp on his bedside table alight, and he was reading a book. He glanced up in surprise as she entered, with a frown appearing on his forehead.

"To what do I owe this honour?" he inquired, in a supercilious tone that had a tendency to rile Louisa at any time.

She ignored him and removed her dressing gown, thereby allowing it to fall onto the floor, this being her usual habit with her discarded clothing.

"It's for Papa's benefit, as you suggested . . . nothing more!"

She slammed her dagger onto the bedside table, pulled back the sheet and climbed into bed beside him. He returned his gaze to his book. He began to chuckle softly to himself and she assumed that this was caused by the words he was reading, but as she made herself comfortable, his soft laughter continued. Finally, he threw the book aside.

"You are priceless! I suspect I'll be a widower by morning," he exclaimed, still laughing at her. "You'll expire from the heat in that outfit. For goodness sake, have some sense! You've miles of material wrapped around you . . . from neck, to wrist to ankle. By the time I'd unwound your voluminous burial sheets and dislodged the dagger from your grasp, I'd be exhausted and would've lost interest anyway. You are safe here and now. I gave you my word on that!"

Louisa settled herself on the pillow, deliberately pulling the sheet up around her neck and ignoring him totally. He jumped from the bed, drew back the drapes, opened the windows wider and turned to survey her in his naked state. Instantly, she closed her eyes, thereby obscuring his form from her view successfully. Exasperated by her reaction, he returned to the bed while Louisa kept her eyes closed tightly. As he settled onto the pillows, she moved onto her side and turned her back on him completely.

"Goodnight, *Mr. Lyndhurst!*"

"Goodnight, *Mrs. Lyndhurst!*" he replied, while turning his back on her and extinguishing the lamp with the same, swift movement.

Chapter Twenty-Nine

— *Victorian Victorians* —

Louisa

L ate in the afternoon, Louisa entered Brydie's kitchen to find Bill Bartlett seated at the table alone. He greeted her warmly. She had worked in the library all day as she was tidying up the accounts, writing cheques for her father's signature, writing a letter to Mr. Bridges, the stock and station agent, and making certain that she had all of the correspondence ready for Charles' departure on the following morning while hoping that he would agree to dispatch same for her. Therefore, she did not know of the *Charmaine's* arrival until walking into the kitchen and seeing the welcome sight of Captain Bill sipping his tea. She reached for a cup and the teapot while helping herself to some tea and sitting down to join him.

"How goes it, lassie?" Bill asked. "I hear everyone about these parts is singing your husband's praises. He's surprised them all, myself included, I must admit. I didn't think him capable of functioning on the outside of those fancy drawing rooms of Melbourne. You may've got yourself a good man there, praise the Lord."

"He's a long way to go before he's held in that kind of esteem by me. I'm just thankful for the wedding gift you gave to me!" Louisa stated.

Bill spluttered noticeably on the tea that he was drinking and he turned to her with a look of complete surprise, which was mingled with mock alarm, registering on his face.

"Snakes alive! Give it back to me now; or, he'll nail my hide to the shed wall!"

Louisa laughed loudly and she was doing so when Mrs. McBryde returned with Betsy to the safety and security of her favourite domain. Immediately, Betsy related to Louisa that Charles had offered to escort her to Bendigo where she was to meet with her brother, who was one year her junior and who was employed by a baker in that city. Together, they would accompany Mr. Lyndhurst to Melbourne where he would accommodate them until he could secure a passage for them on a ship bound for Adelaide. Louisa, frowning markedly, was puzzling over these revelations when Betsy intervened again, thus interrupting her thoughts.

"I'm ever so grateful to you and Mr. Lyndhurst, Lou. I didn't know how to get there from here, 'cause I've little money saved. He won't hear of me paying for anything. *And, not only that,* he's made the same offer to Trevor, as long as he stays on here for three months longer. So, that's a small price to pay, under the circumstances, wouldn't you think? I do, that's for certain, and so does Mrs. McBryde. I'll never be able to repay such kindness, not that it was ever asked of us. Thanks so much!"

"No, Betsy, that's not so," Louisa, somewhat abashed, replied. "You've repaid it a thousand times over, with your loyalty, your devotion to Mama and me, and not to mention your work, especially where Papa's welfare is concerned. It's I who owe you a deep debt of gratitude . . . and *'tis I thanking you* . . . so very, very much."

"Oh!" said Betsy, while blushing deeply and opening her mouth to reply.

However, she could not do so. Instead, she reached into her pocket for a handkerchief, placed it to her eyes and dabbed them individually; then, overcome with emotion, she rushed from the room. Louisa rose abruptly from the chair while intending to run after her, but Mrs. McBryde grabbed her arm.

"Let her be now. Say your farewells later. She's very distressed over leaving us all, but most especially her Trevor, for she loves him deeply. She'll need a letter of reference to take with her, so you'll arrange that, won't you?"

Absentmindedly, Louisa nodded in agreement. She sat down at the table again to finish her tea as Mrs. McBryde moved to the range to stoke the fire under the pot of broth that was steaming there.

"Don't think you'd better be using that weapon around here, lassie," Bill Bartlett said, as he glanced slyly over at Louisa and, with a hearty laugh, he confided softly and conspiratorially to her. "Not unless you want to be lynched, that is."

"What's that?" Mrs. McBryde inquired.

"Nothin'. Nothin' at all . . . just a bit of a joke, eh?" he stated, as he reached over to pull on a loose strand of Louisa's hair.

Louisa grimaced noticeably as Mrs. McBryde shook her head and returned her attention in the direction of the steaming pot as she attended to the preparations for the evening meal. Louisa left them shortly afterwards while knowing that they wished for some time alone.

As she left the kitchen, she noticed her husband nearby with the overseer as the two men inspected the old storage shed near the rear of the homestead. Louisa walked over to them to determine their intention with regard to the old building. They were so engrossed in conversation that they took little notice of her presence until Trevor, with a swift nod to her, departed in the direction of the kitchen, no doubt going in search of Betsy to spend some final hours with her. Charles, she observed, was covered in dirt and dust as a result of his day in the saddle, because they had been working on the last section of fencing that needed repair. The exposed areas of his skin were showing a reddish tinge from over-exposure to the hot summer sun.

"What're you doing?" Louisa asked of Charles.

He was surveying the building from the outside of it. With seeming reluctance, he turned his head and glanced at her; then, he returned his attention to the structure. She continued to watch him while knowing, without doubt, that he was ignoring her deliberately.

"Charles, what were you doing here with Trevor?" she demanded.

"Oh? Were you addressing me? I've not set eyes on you today, yet you cannot prefix your question with a civil greeting of some description. So be it!" Charles stated. "*Good afternoon, Louisa!* In answer to your query, I've been discussing with the overseer the need for some accommodation for a bookkeeper's assistant. I have raised the matter with your father and you will be relieved to know I've managed to persuade him that Jenkins is unwell, so he requires an assistant who'll need somewhere to live. This shed is disused now and it wouldn't take much to convert it into quite comfortable living quarters, for it's a solid structure."

Louisa felt the second part of this dialogue was more a monologue as he came to terms with the idea in his mind. She watched him in silence for some minutes. He entered the building while adjusting the door, which was hanging on one hinge; then, he returned to the exterior and was looking up at the roof.

"You've covered everything, it would seem. My opinions and ideas would be superfluous anyway," she muttered, instantly spinning away and leaving him.

On entering the homestead, Louisa went to the library and she wrote a reference for Betsy to take with her when she left them in the morning. Sometime later, still engrossed in the correspondence that was awaiting her attention, she was disturbed by Charles' entry.

"May I speak with you?"

"Certainly," Louisa replied, with accentuated politeness.

Charles' attire was very different. Obviously, he had bathed and was dressed in his normal attire, which she had become accustomed to seeing him wear in Melbourne. He glanced at the desk.

"What are you doing?" he inquired.

"I am catching up on the correspondence. Would you be so kind as to take all of this with you tomorrow and dispatch it for me? There's a letter here for Mr. Bridges, with a request for two more men to replace the ones we lost recently."

He picked up the letter and gave it a cursory glance before replacing it on the desk; then, he explained that Trevor had given a guarantee to remain for another three months and he would leave at the conclusion of the muster, which would take place within the fortnight following Charles' return to the property. Charles was hoping to arrange for a replacement overseer and he planned to call on the stock and station agent himself before leaving Echuca in two days' time. He promised to hand-deliver her letter to the man-in-question.

"You've thought of everything then," she murmured, somewhat tersely.

"I trust that is so . . . and you did ask for my help, I seem to recall."

Louisa bit her lip and nodded slowly. There was nothing at all, with which she could find fault since Charles' arrival at her home, but she was annoyed with him all the same and she did not have a valid reason – or, none that related to the property anyway. She remembered her pledge to herself to keep the peace at all costs until his departure.

"Yes, you're quite correct and I thank you sincerely for all you've done. I'm certain there were many matters in Melbourne that required your attention and I'm grateful you stayed on here to assist us. It's most appreciated and I thank you especially for all you've done for Betsy. She's quite overwhelmed by it all."

Charles nodded in acknowledgment. Then, he moved the papers and sat on the desk while looking down at her as she reclined back on the chair. She was wondering what was coming next.

"There's another matter. I absolutely forbid you to bring forward the date of the muster. Is that understood?" he queried.

"I'd no intention of doing so," she replied, in all innocence.

"Perhaps not, at this precise moment, but who's to say what you'll do once my back is turned? It came to my knowledge, during innocent conversation with Trevor today, that you were a part of the last muster."

Louisa looked up at him in some surprise. Slowly, she nodded her head, quite unable to fathom where this conversation was heading. He seemed to be fighting to control his emotions and anger appeared to be not far beneath the surface.

"I've been a part of every one we've done for as long as I can recall."

"But, your father was a part of all the others, I assume. Was he on this one?" Charles asked.

"No," she replied, while frowning and unable to understand his questioning.

"And, this was after our marriage banns were up and you were betrothed to me? Am I correct in this assumption?"

Louisa shrugged her shoulders hopelessly and tried to recall the time, to which he was referring. Finally, she concluded that, in all probability, it was within those weeks just prior to the marriage taking place.

"Yes, I expect it was. Why?" she asked.

"You slept out in the paddocks overnight . . . alone with the men?"

Louisa nodded, while frowning deeply once again in response to his question.

"Three nights, actually."

"When you were engaged to be married to me!"

Louisa nodded her head slowly as, finally, she realised where this line of questioning was heading.

"*And*, you do not feel there's cause for concern on my part?" he asked.

There was anger registering not far beneath the surface of his being, but Charles seemed to be fighting valiantly to control himself. Louisa, exasperated suddenly, slammed her hands down on the desk.

"I've no idea what this nonsense is about. Yes, I slept outdoors. Yes, there were men there, including Trevor who would've given his life to protect me. And, yes, I did have a gun beneath my bedroll. But, that was for vermin . . . not to use on the men. I needed to look closer to home for *the snake in the grass*!"

With those words, she flung back the chair, which overturned behind her as it had done when Jenkins attacked her in this room. Angrily, she strode toward the door while moving hurriedly to the other side of the desk so as to avoid him if he tried to reach for her. He did not do so.

"It's impossible to be civil to you, no matter how hard I try. You're determined to rile me," she stated.

"As you attempt to do with me!" he retorted. "Louisa, *wait!*"

She spun around to face him as he jumped from the desk and walked over to her. His words were spoken quietly and precisely, but this was a directive nonetheless.

"What's happened in the past can't be changed. In future, you do not do anything, under any circumstances, without receiving my permission in advance. Is that understood clearly?"

"Go to hell!" she hissed at him.

She spun around and left the room. Charles made no attempt to follow her. When she glanced back, he was settling himself at her desk, after having restored the chair to its original position. He appeared to be making himself very comfortable in her domain. Angrily, she stormed to her bedroom to dress for dinner.

Dinner was another almost-silent affair and she was happy to escape the claustrophobic atmosphere that had permeated her home for the first time in her lifetime. Having difficulty breathing under these conditions, which had little to do with the summer heat, she escaped to the river bank and sat on the old log by her favourite swimming hole. How long she sat there, she knew not, but it was longer than an hour. Finally, with the cooling breeze rustling through the trees and through her hair alike, she retraced her steps as she heard the plaintive sounds of the harmonica drifting up from the paddle-steamer attached to the pontoon.

Louisa discovered her father and Bill Bartlett seated on the chairs on the verandah and they were in deep conversation, so much so that they did not hear her approaching until she skipped up the one step from the path. They looked up in surprise as she appeared beside them.

"It's a beautiful night now that the breeze has come to life, Lou," Bill said.

"Yes, it is indeed so. Papa, you're looking very tired this evening. Are you quite well?" she asked, with concern sounding in her voice.

Before George could reply, the sound of the pianoforte began to emanate from the drawing room. Suddenly, as the notes reached Louisa's ears, she remembered Yvette and those proposed lessons in Melbourne.

"Jesus, Mary and Joseph! Yvette! What must she think of me?" Louisa shouted.

"Yvette?" he father asked, with a sudden frown appearing on his brow before querying her further. "What's the concern with her?"

But, Louisa did not hear the question. She darted into the drawing room, followed closely by George and Bill, with both appearing somewhat surprised by this turn of events and being puzzled by her behaviour. Charles was seated at the instrument and lost in his music. He was unaware of her approach at a very fast rate until she shouted to him so that her voice rose above the music.

"Charles!" she exclaimed.

He stopped playing abruptly and, turning to her with a look of surprise on his face, he raised an eyebrow in query as the other two men looked on with interest.

"Yvette! I forgot. She was to come to Lyndhurst Park to give me lessons on the pianoforte. Will you contact her for me when you go there, please?" she asked, in a contrite tone. "It was remiss of me, I know. Apologise, on my behalf, and I'll write to her shortly."

He looked at her and shook his head in mild disgust.

"The matter was attended to prior to our departure," he stated quietly, while giving a nonchalant shrug of his shoulders. "But, I'm certain a missive from you would be appreciated, despite it being long overdue."

Dismissing her from his presence with a flick of his head and another unmistakable look of disdain, he returned his attention to the instrument as Louisa, somewhat abashed, watched him while her father and Bill Bartlett retreated from the drawing room quietly and somewhat quickly as they returned to the side verandah together.

Louisa went to the library and collected all of the mail for Charles to take with him on the next morning and she removed it to the dining room. She placed it on the dining table for him. With Charles' music drifting through the silent homestead, she moved quickly and silently to her own bedroom and, with assistance from Charlotte, prepared for bed.

Louisa sat on her bed after Charlotte left her room and she picked up a book to read. When she knew that the house was in darkness and Charles' music had long since ceased to penetrate her consciousness, she slipped into her dressing gown and went to the guest room. The lamp had been extinguished, but there was moonlight filtering through the open windows when she entered the room while closing the door softly behind her.

Walking to the bedside, she touched Charles' shoulder and he turned abruptly. He stared up at her through the semi-darkness, as though she had dragged him from the early stages of sleep.

"I've something for you," she stated quietly.

He sat up and fumbled on the table by the bed. Eventually, he lit the lamp. Louisa handed him a sheet of paper, which he opened and held up to the light to read.

"It's the commands I taught Hilton. You requested them."

He continued to study the page; then, he looked inquiringly at her.

"How do I know these are in the right order? If I give them out of sequence, we both know what will happen to me."

Louisa smiled, despite her depressed mood.

"I don't dislike you as much as that," she replied softly.

"I'm relieved to hear it, despite behaviour that gives a contrary impression."

He placed the paper on the table by the bed and patted the side of the bed in a silent invitation for her to sit down beside him. She obliged him, for the sake of peace.

"Thank you for that," he said, before making his next request. "Is it remotely possible that we could at least try to part as friends tomorrow?"

Louisa grimaced noticeably and she gave a slight shrug while Charles watched her closely.

"It's only about twelve hours away. Our previous attempts at friendship have rarely lasted as long as that," she replied, as she admitted this fact to him with a wry smile. "But, *I suppose*, we could try again."

Charles laughed quietly; then, taking her hand, he began stroking it slowly and softly.

"Nine weeks ago today, we stood out there on the side verandah, uttered some vows neither one wished to make and we signed a piece of paper. Now, we are going to be separated for longer than we've been wed. Does that not seem strange to you, Louisa? I'm certain it does to many others and I doubt there could've been a worse start to a marriage."

Louisa studied her hand and arm where his hand continued to stroke it. He appeared to be awaiting her response, but she did not have one. To her, there did not seem to be anything left to be spoken of between them. Finally, she placed her hand firmly over his and the stoking ceased immediately.

"Do you see her still? The girl you love?" she asked.

"Yes."

"Does she hate me?" she queried.

"It's not in her nature to hate anyone," he replied quietly.

Louisa bit her lip and fought back the tears that were threatening to engulf her. Finally, she did control her emotions, but she could not recall a time, other than immediately after her mother's death, when such a dark cloud of hopelessness enveloped her.

"How can it be permitted for you, but not for me?" she queried.

"That's the way of the world!"

"If I'd been born in a male body, life would've been so much different now. I would've been *expected* to take over the running of this property, which I'm quite capable of doing. It's only in a mess, because I had to leave with you and there was no one here to handle the day-to-day problems that arise quite naturally and are expected on any property of this size. I've proven to myself and to everyone else that I could do it. Everything is so unfair in this world and, *with us*, everything just seems so totally hopeless. I have really lost interest in trying."

Charles squeezed her hand and held it tightly.

"Don't give up on us yet. Phoenix could rise still from the ashes, even at this late stage," he whispered.

She gazed down at him in astonishment and shook her head vigorously.

"It's not possible," she murmured.

"Has everyone retired for the night?" he asked softly.

Louisa nodded in response to his whispered question.

"Then, so too, should you. It's not wise for you to be with me here tonight."

Lifting her hand, he raised it to his lips and kissed it.

"After all, it's not seemly for an engaged couple to be in the same bedroom, is it?" he queried, in a whisper again and with an eyebrow raised while her hand remained close to his lips.

"Oh? We're playing that game now?"

"If you slip into this bed tonight, I'm afraid it's a quite different game we'll be playing," he murmured. *"I don't want to leave you here tomorrow."*

Louisa jumped hurriedly from the bed, instantly withdrawing her hand from his grasp. He made no move to prevent her from leaving, but Charles continued to watch her intently.

"I can't do so . . . it's too soon after . . . *after that!"* she muttered, while biting her lip and turning quickly to escape toward the door.

"Louisa . . . wait . . .!"

She stopped in the doorway and she was looking inquiringly at him.

"It's not a sin to cry. *You do know that?* In fact, sometimes, it can help to clear away the pain," he stated.

"The hell it can! I'll not give into such weakness!"

Louisa left the guest room hurriedly and without a backward glance.

There was a firm hand on her shoulder and she felt it shaking her entire body. Through the haze of sleep, Louisa glanced up at Charles who was standing beside the bed in her old bedroom. He raised a finger and pointed to the table beside her bed.

"I've brought you a cup of tea," he said.

"With or without turpentine?" she mumbled the query.

He laughed softly; then, without waiting for an invitation, he sat down on the side of her bed as he settled himself comfortably there. Louisa grimaced, unable to escape his looming presence, but she remained with her head fixed to the pillow. Charles reached across to the armchair and retrieved two pillows. He held these items aloft while waiting for her to move her head from the pillow.

"Come on, sleepy-head. I need to talk to you before I leave this morning and I require your full attention while I do so," he stated.

With a groan of annoyance, she sat up in the bed as she grasped the pillows and began propping herself up on them. Louisa reached for the cup of tea, because sustenance was required before facing another round of arguments with him at this early hour of the morning. She scrutinised his attire. He was dressed immaculately and ready for his journey.

"There's no point, really. It can end only in an argument," she commented.

Charles ignored her provocative remark and launched into his next statement.

"I need to be assured that you understand completely what is happening with us. I'll return here in ten weeks, as agreed with this change of plan regarding the proposed muster. I'm reiterating this fact, because I don't want you to get it into your silly, little head that I won't come for you. That's the first point."

Louisa sipped the tea and stared at the blank wall before her, thus preventing hasty words from slipping unguarded from her lips. Charles continued, seemingly pleased that his third statement had not produced an angry retort.

"Next, I forbid you to leave here unless, of course, you are accompanied by your father. That is in the case of an emergency situation arising. Is that understood?" he demanded.

Louisa continued to sip the tea – hot though it was – and to focus her complete attention on the bedroom wall opposite her bed. Undeterred by her silence, Charles continued with his monologue.

"Now, should you take it into your head to contact your friend in Sydney by mail and to advise him of your current whereabouts, then you would be very foolish indeed. Should he come for you and you leave with him, I'll locate you, rest assured of that. Wherever you go in this world, I *will find you*. If I find you with him . . . or with anyone else, for that matter . . . I shall kill him on sight and ask questions after the event. You belong to me and with me, you will stay. Is that understood clearly?"

Louisa continued to sip the tea – hot though it was – and to focus her complete attention on the bedroom wall. Undeterred by her silence – or, perhaps, because of it – Charles resumed his discourse.

"Do you wish to acknowledge, or to question, any or all of these directives?"

Louisa filled her mouth completely with hot liquid to prevent any words from escaping although, with her temper rising to a frightening degree, she was uncertain whether or not the liquid would remain there for long. She had a vision of it adorning Charles' immaculately-clad body in the immediate future. However, he appeared to be unaware of the danger, in which he had placed himself by standing in such close proximity to her body. With an exaggerated gulp, she swallowed hurriedly and the hot liquid burned her throat; then, she returned her gaze to the blank wall.

"Presumably not," he muttered finally. "That said, I wish to reveal something to you before I depart and you may wish to reflect on the matter at some length while you're here alone. When we were married, I had other plans in mind for your future, as well as my own. I felt that if I gave you sufficient rope, you would hang yourself . . . metaphorically speaking, of course . . . in a short space of time. That you proved me correct, in a matter of eight short weeks, is quite remarkable and shows a great understanding of the human spirit on my part, I should think. *Then*, Louisa Mary Lyndhurst, I intended returning you to your father, after your atrocious behaviour was revealed to the world. I would have annulled this marriage contract between us, because the union had not been consummated, at that point. How do you feel about this revelation?"

Stunned by his disclosure, Louisa filled her mouth with more tea, in order to buy herself some time, in which to contemplate his confession. Every word that he had spoken was uttered in a soft tone, almost as though the walls had ears, with which to hear him. He appeared mildly surprised that she had not chosen to respond to his revelation. When she continued to ignore him and to concentrate on the wall while drinking the refreshments that he had provided so thoughtfully for her this morning, he rose from her bed. Looking down at her, he smiled while murmuring softly as he did so.

"Well, it seems that this has given you some food for thought, just as I expected it would do. So, *madam*, had you not seen fit to throw that missile at me on the first Sunday of the New Year, everything would be very different for both of us now. I would have left already, bound for London, and you'd be back at your father's home permanently, albeit in disgrace. Whether or not your special friend would've come after you then, is a matter of conjecture. My own feeling is that he would not have bothered. His intent was revenge . . . on my family . . . and you were nothing more than his preferred weapon-of-choice. That's all."

Charles continued to study Louisa. Louisa continued to study the wall. Had he but known it, she was trying to recall where she had left her own preferred weapon-of-choice. *And,* she knew exactly where she wished to plunge same weapon. However, it was out of her reach at present, unfortunately.

"Is there to be no response? Well, that's certainly an amazing turn-of-events!" Charles stated, while appearing surprised; then, elaborating a little, he continued. "Now that we've come to this understanding, I can leave you in peace for a couple of months. During that time, you can amuse yourself by playing at being *Miss Howard* once again. When I return . . . *and return I will*, be assured of that fact . . . you will resume the role of *Mrs. Lyndhurst* . . . and, permanently."

With those words, Charles turned and strode purposefully in the direction of the door to the corridor. Undoubtedly, his mission was accomplished and with marked success evidently, from his perspective.

From his wife's viewpoint, it was far from the case. As he opened the bedroom door, the tea cup sailed by his right ear and hit the wall. The liquid and the tea leaves stained the wall immediately while the fine English bone china cup hit the floor noisily as this item shattered instantly into small pieces.

Louisa did not speak one word to her husband. In surprise and not a little amusement, he surveyed the stains on the wall. Then, quite deliberately, he allowed his gaze to follow the direction of the cup, which was scattered in pieces on the floor. He made a slight movement as he turned to survey Louisa who was propped up still on the pillows in her small bed. Simmering anger shone from her green eyes while a look of petulance was evident in her facial expression. That the smouldering anger and the accentuated petulance were accompanied by a look of intense dislike was obvious to Charles. He laughed aloud, well pleased with himself at being able to extract a response such as this one from his wife on their last morning together.

Slowly, he shook his head in slight surprise as, in some amusement, he queried her.

"You never learn, do you, *my love?*" he asked quietly, with his words laced liberally with much sarcasm as he reached for the door handle and opened the door.

He left the room while closing the door behind him ever-so-gently – and deliberately so. Louisa was left alone with her thoughts and her rapidly-rising anger.

In this last moment, she had witnessed, in Charles' behaviour and mannerisms, an uncanny resemblance to his father, Sir Charles Lyndhurst. She shuddered at the unwelcome thought, which she dismissed instantly.

Suddenly, the door opened again and Charles' head appeared around it as he surveyed her critically.

"Remember, Louisa, I hold the trump card."

"What's that supposed to mean?" she demanded, thereby speaking to him finally as she sat bolt upright in the bed.

"Hilton!"

He closed the door swiftly as she reached for the saucer on the bedside table. Louisa could hear the sound of Charles' laughter coming from the direction of the corridor outside her door. This was over-and-above the sound of the smashing crockery as the saucer and the tea cup were reunited – as a complete pair – being shattered together on the bedroom floor.

Louisa was left alone with her seething anger and her vengeful thoughts, of which Father Francis Bourke would not approve at all. Perhaps these, she would not reveal in the sanctity and seclusion of the confessional, for they were too terrible to confess, even to God.

Later in the morning, Louisa went to the kitchen to farewell Betsy and to give her the reference that she had written for her. She had endured a silent breakfast with her father and her husband, with barely a word being spoken at all.

After breakfast, everyone who worked there was heading in the direction of the pontoon and Trevor, a lanky, sorrowful and forlorn figure, was making his way to Betsy's quarters to assist with her luggage. Louisa gave Betsy a quick hug and thanked her again; then, the girl, with tears in her eyes, ran to her quarters where Trevor was waiting for her.

Louisa did not intend to be on the pontoon as the *Charmaine* pulled away. Instead, she would wait on the verandah with her father, after having farewelled Betsy and with little to say to her husband. However, on returning to the homestead, she found that Charles had left already, so she joined her father who was frowning and looking very concerned.

"Go after him, Louisa. Something's not right here!" her father stated.

Had she not been so distracted with the events of the morning, she may have been pleased to note her father's sudden interest in something that was happening around him. However, his intervention went unnoticed by her and she moved inside the homestead. There, on the dining table, she spied all of the correspondence that she had left for Charles on the previous evening and about which she had duly reminded him after breakfast. Hurriedly, she gathered it together and she ran across the verandah before skipping down the stairs to catch up to him. She was anxious to reach him prior to Charles boarding the paddle-steamer.

"Charles, wait!" she called.

He stopped and turned around while glancing in her direction. He did not come back, instead waiting deliberately by the pontoon for her to come to him. She handed the bundle of correspondence to him.

"You forgot these," she stated, somewhat breathlessly after her unexpected exertion.

"Did I indeed?" he murmured.

Louisa looked up at him and she was angered instantly by the smug smile on his face.

"You did that deliberately," she flared, while flinging her accusation at him.

In response, he smiled at her again, in a maddeningly-calm manner; then, he raised an arm in a farewell gesture to her father. With anger scarcely held in check, she shook her head at him while being reluctant to make a scene at the moment of Betsy's sad departure – a fact, of which he was perfectly well aware and that he knew would be the case. Louisa was angry with herself for falling so easily into his well-planned and perfectly-executed trap.

"You're playing your cat-and-mouse games still, I see," she challenged.

"How else could I achieve a result such as this . . . a fond farewell from my bride of nine weeks? Are you going to kiss me, now that you've run in a breathless state to my side as the moment of my departure approaches rapidly?" he queried, as he teased her softly and mercilessly.

"See! I knew it wasn't possible for us to be friends for long! You never stop the teasing, nor with trying to bait me."

Charles laughed at her, thus causing her ill-concealed anger to rise even higher, with her face taking on a reddish tinge to match his own sunburnt one, although her heightened colouring was not due to over-exposure to sunlight in any way whatsoever.

"*And, you* never fail to rise to it! Some events never change; nor do some people, for that matter. They're as predictable as the rising sun in the east in the morning. *And you, Louisa Mary Lyndhurst,* are one of them!"

Charles gripped her arm firmly and kissed her on the cheek before she could move away. Then, turning away abruptly, he stepped aboard the *Charmaine* while leaving her near to the stone steps again, as he had done in the previous September when he had advised her strongly to speak with her father about a certain situation, of which she was unaware at the time.

Louisa looked down at the pontoon and she was reminded immediately of another timber jetty on another bank of another river. Then, Phillip came strongly into her mind. If only other decisions had been made – and most especially by herself – last September, how different her life could have been now. She bit her lip again. With a despondent, albeit an ever-so-slight, shrug of her shoulders, she trudged slowly, but in a very determined manner, up the stone steps to the homestead.

On the top step, she stopped and looked back at the paddle-wheeler as it moved out into the river. Charles was standing at the stern. He was watching her closely. He did not wave or acknowledge her – as she did not wave or acknowledge him.

Louisa studied him for a few more moments. Then, she went alone into the homestead. There was work to be done. She went immediately to the library.

The year was 1868, in the month of January, to be precise. The season was summer, that being a Southern Hemisphere summer. The country was the one known now as Australia, and in the State of Victoria.

But that is another story for another time.

Epilogue

Paula

10 September, 1999 – Gold Coast Hospital

With a disinterested gaze, Paula studied the male nurse who was standing at the end of her bed. His name was Gerard and she recalled speaking with him earlier in this hospital room. However, she could not remember how long ago that was. His concentration was focussed totally on the chart in his hand and he was writing furiously there.

"Where's my husband?" she asked.

Gerard stopped his writing exercise momentarily as he glanced at her in the bed. She was relaxing on several pillows and there was another pillow beneath her arm. This one was supporting the limb, which had an intravenous connection attached.

"Haven't we had this conversation recently?" he questioned, with a grin appearing on his boyish face, which belied his age.

"If we did, I can't recall it and it wasn't today anyway."

"It couldn't have been yesterday, because it is my understanding that you've been in this country for less than twenty-four hours," he stated calmly. "You have been with us for less than an hour."

"That's not possible! Where am I?" Paula asked, as confusion took charge of her wayward mind.

"You're in the Gold Coast Hospital and that is in Australia. You're visiting here from Los Angeles, as I understand it. Your husband is waiting for you somewhere close by and in a restaurant, presumably. There was to be a surprise lunch for you, because today is your thirty-fifth birthday. He will be located shortly, if not already, and he'll be brought here immediately. Can you tell me your name?"

"It's Paula," she answered.

"Is that it?"

Paula was silent for a short time before replying to his query.

"Umm . . . let me think on it for a minute," she said, with a deep frown on her forehead.

Her mind was completely blank and she could not recall her name. This fact frightened her immensely. In fact, she was overwhelmed by a feeling of helplessness, which preceded the more frightening one of sheer panic that overtook her in this moment. Obviously noticing her reaction, Gerard spoke reassuringly to her.

"Don't worry about anything now. It'll all come back to you. The painkillers have kicked in and everything is probably a bit fuzzy at present. It'll clear later. Is there anything that you need?"

"My husband . . . find him, please," she requested. "I was in an accident . . . is that right? Was he driving the car?"

"No, that was someone else. Put it all out of your mind now and try to sleep. He'll be here when you wake up, as will the doctor," the nurse stated in a quiet tone. "I'll see you later and, by the way, Happy Birthday!"

So saying, he walked quickly in the direction of the door that led to the hospital corridor. He left her so abruptly that she was unable to think of another question to ask him. She required more information. She needed to know about her life. She knew that her name was Paula; she lived in another country; she had a husband whose name she could not recall and possibly she had children, also. She knew that today was her birthday. If she had been alive for thirty-five years as the nurse had stated, there must be more to her life than those few details, she queried in her befuddled mind. And, who were those other people?

They were known as Charles, Sylvia, Elizabeth and, of course, the spirited Louisa. What had become of them, she wondered.

Glancing out of the window beside her bed, she studied the scenery. There were tall green trees, which appeared to have a purple hue overshadowing them. These were surrounded by manicured lawns and a profusion of roses that were tended lovingly, obviously. The sky was an azure blue and cloudless while the sun's rays streamed down as these bathed the entire area in a brilliant golden light. What a perfect world!

Paula's present consciousness receded slowly and she returned to that earlier time when life moved at a slower pace than today's world. She was standing by a bush on a riverbank and she was surrounded by tall trees in a secluded bush setting. There, in front of her and sitting on an old log was a young girl of perhaps seventeen years of age. She was dressed in attire that belonged in a different period of history. Paula could see her as clearly as she had seen the nurse, Gerard, a few minutes earlier.

The girl's bonnet was thrown on the dusty track and her bare feet were peeping from beneath her richly-embroidered long gown. She was engrossed in the book that she was holding in her slender hands. She moved one hand to brush the flies from her face and to remove the dust that had appeared there.

In this moment, she was joined by a flock of vociferous and colourful native birds and these feathered creatures settled in the tree above her head. Glancing up, she shouted at the birds and she threw her book onto the ground.

"You've hundreds of trees to choose from. This one is mine!"

The birds looked down at her momentarily; then, they ignored her completely – but not so the flies. She looked longingly at the river whose waters were cool and inviting. Standing suddenly, she cast a furtive glance in the direction of the homestead some distance away.

The only occupants this day were her father and Mrs. McBryde. On seeing no sign of life and making a sudden decision, she removed her heavy clothing quickly while discarding these items of apparel onto the log. She tied her long, auburn hair loosely with a ribbon at the nape of her neck. She entered the water and its cool temperature took her breath away momentarily.

With slow, even strokes, she swam to the middle section of the wide river. There, she rolled onto her back and floated with the current as the sun shone down onto her naked body. She drifted for a time and Paula was, once again, the silent observer.

Paula watched from afar. In deep reverie, Louisa Lyndhurst relived the past four months of her young life. The scenes resembled a dream sequence to her and these, she felt, would be better described as a nightmare experience. The next few months would pass very quickly. After that, Charles would return and claim her as his personal property once again. She remembered, vividly and with clarity, his vicious attack on her, as well as their numerous altercations. These thoughts brought feelings of revulsion to the pit of her stomach. She recalled all of her secret liaisons with Phillip and these memories brought feelings of unexplained joy to the area of her solar plexus as her heart beat a little faster when he came into her mind.

How could her life have spiralled out-of-control to this extent in the period of a mere four months, she queried herself.

The silence was broken by a dull, throbbing sound and the unmistakable whistle of a paddle-steamer pierced the air. Immediately alert, Louisa swam with brisk, almost-frantic strokes towards the Victorian bank of the Murray River. She dived and swam the remainder of the way underwater while surfacing beneath the thick foliage of the weeping willow tree. Many times, these branches had hidden her from view. The paddle-steamer chugged on by her as Louisa took deep breaths to refill her depleted lungs.

Paula studied Louisa from her own silent world. Life goes on, regardless of the reality, in which one finds oneself at any given moment in time, she mused. Perhaps, it was time to return to the reality of her current lifetime as the last days of the twentieth century draw to a close there. With a last, lingering glance at the naked, young girl who was emerging from her hiding place onto the deserted river bank, Paula brought her attention back to the reality of the silent and deserted hospital room.

From there, she gazed out at the sun-drenched garden and she allowed the peace and tranquillity of the scenery to flow over her. In the fullness of time, she would know where she was and she would understand why she was here – in this place and at this time.

Paula closed her eyes. Without any effort on her part, she descended into the depths of sleep once again.

Author's Note

By Way of Explanation

There was a time several decades ago when society's mores dictated that books, plays, television dramas and films, which were portraying scenes of a sexual nature must be scrutinised by a censor. In movies of that era, it was not permitted for two characters to be in a marital bed together, even though the film script referred to them as a married couple. The actors who were playing those roles were required to be in two separate, single beds, if a bedroom scene was a necessary part of the storyline. This was in the period before the advent of the contraceptive pill that allowed women more freedom sexually. Also, in this period, young girls could have their babies confiscated at birth by the authority-figures of the day, simply because they did not possess a marriage certificate prior to giving birth.

In the time-frame, to which I refer most fiction novels written then were mainly love stories that ended usually with the two main characters standing at the altar. The assumption was that they would live happily-ever-after once this binding piece of paper was signed by both parties. It was because of this firmly-held belief-system within society then that I decided to write a novel where two people were forced to live together – in supposed marital bliss – when not only were they complete strangers, but also, they were opposed completely to the union from the outset.

Stella McMillan

With regard to the story, **Victorian Victorians**, that is incorporated within the trilogy, **ERA/ERROR of UNDERSTANDING**, I have to concede that I did not intend consciously to write this particular love story. The tale about Louisa Howard and Charles Lyndhurst came about when I moved to Melbourne in Australia. I fell in love with that city and, almost immediately, I began to explore my new surroundings. While wandering within the walls of an historic mansion, known as *Como House* in South Yarra, I found myself in a trance-like state. Before I could escape from this enchanting place, I had characters running around inside my head and a good part of this story was sealed within my mind before I walked out through the front doors on that day.

Quite simply, they had come to life before my eyes and where they came from, I have no idea. I could speculate, but I will not do so. However, the only way that I could erase them from my consciousness – so that I could function in daily life – was to put these characters and their antics onto paper immediately. And, this I did. So, the first draft was written at that time and over a nine-month period.

The sixth and final draft did not make its way onto paper until July, 2006, and the first print edition was published finally in 2010, which was four decades after my initial visit to the mansion. Consequently, I can assume only that they were determined to have their story released, despite the fact that, for me, life *got-in-the-way*.

In those intervening years, the world has changed markedly and society's customs and conventions have altered greatly. When this novel began, there were two taboos where storytelling was concerned. One was the subject of sex, as I mentioned previously, while the other was death. Since then, it would seem that sex has been *done to death*, one might say, yet peering behind the thin, etheric veil that is physical death has not been accomplished to any great extent. In the writing these two trilogies, I was attempting to do so as the character, Paula, slips from one reality to another; then, she moves back again.

Simultaneously, I have endeavoured to explore the ongoing relationship between two people who were bound to each other for life and who were completely different in age, ideas, upbringing and beliefs while being total strangers when they were forced together in 1867. In the rigidly-controlled Victorian era, an individual who defied convention would have been crushed under the weight of public censure – and this was especially so if this person happened to be a female who was a free and wild spirit.

ERROR *of* UNDERSTANDING covers the first few months after the initial meeting of Charles and Louisa and follows on from their forced marriage. The next book of the first trilogy reveals all that occurred to them during the rest of that first year of 1868, in Victorian Victoria. At the same time, Paula continues to drift from one reality to another while not understanding what is occurring with her – within the time-frame of 1999 and but a few months prior to the commencement of the new twenty-first century.

In 2014, the seventh book of the *Stella McMillan* Series was published. All seven books are available now in both print editions and on eBooks. The first trilogy covers the story of these **Victorian Victorians** who have appeared within its pages. Also, in the first trilogy, the thread of Paula's story is interwoven with that of the Victorian saga.

The second trilogy continues Paula's life story while revealing all that happened to her both before and after the accident, which was life-changing for her. At the same time, she forges a closer relationship with the nurse, Gerard. His words of wisdom resonate with her as she faces the new challenges in her current twenty-first century life, and most especially so when she begins to explore the theory of reincarnation more fully. Having been the silent observer during this first and involuntary past-life regression session while delving into life in nineteenth century Australia, she explores voluntarily another lifetime in eighteenth century Scotland.

Paula is intrigued and excited by the concept and her quest for understanding and enlightenment commences in earnest in the later books of the second trilogy, ***ERA/ERROR of DISCERNMENT.***

The title of the second book of the first trilogy is: ***ERROR PERPETUATED.***

Further information on the *Stella McMillan* Series: www.stellamcmillan.com.au

Stella McMillan Series

Stella McMillan website:
www.stellamcmillan.com.au

Books/eBooks by *Stella McMillan*
First Trilogy:
ERA/ERROR of UNDERSTANDING
Book One:
ERROR of UNDERSTANDING
Book Two:
ERROR PERPETUATED
Book Three:
ERA of UNDERSTANDING

Second Trilogy:
ERA/ERROR of DISCERNMENT
Book One:
AWAKENING TO AWARENESS
Book Two:
ERROR PROFOUND
Book Three:
ERA of DISCERNMENT
Companion Book to the *Stella McMillan* Trilogies:
SUSPENSION – Between Two Realms –
Published 2014

Earlier Books by *Stella McMillan*:
UNDERCOVER STARSEEDS
Published 2000
THE REAL BOOK, REAL BEGINNING
Published 1999

Stella McMillan

The Tenets of the Law of One
Published 2002

Books by Beverly Bree
Published 1992:
THE GOLDEN AGE
(ISBN 0 646 11179 8)
FAMILY OF MAN
(ISBN 0 646 11800 8)
National Library of Australia, Canberra ACT
www.stellamcmillan.com.au

www.ingramcontent.com/pod-product-compliance
Lightning Source LLC
Chambersburg PA
CBHW051634050726
47502CB00011B/52